# Fear

Anatoli Rybakov, who spent his own childhood at 51 Arbat Street, now makes his permanent home just outside Moscow. One of Russia's most successful writers, he is the author of numerous books, among them *Heavy Sand*, a novel about Soviet Jews living in a Nazi-occupied Ukrainian village. An engineering student in the 1930s, Rybakov was arrested and exiled to Siberia but was later 'rehabilitated' when he became a highly decorated tank commander in World War II. He is currently visiting the United States as an adjunct professor at Columbia University in New York City.

Antonina W. Bouis, the English translator, is director of the Soros Foundation–Soviet Union and is the editor and translator of Yevgeny Yevtushenko's *Fatal Half Measures*.

By the same author

*Heavy Sand*
*Children of the Arbat*

# Fear

Anatoli Rybakov

*Translated by Antonina W. Bouis*

ARROW

Published by Arrow Books in 1994

1 3 5 7 9 10 8 6 4 2

© Anatoli Rybakov 1993

English Language Translation Copyright
© 1993 by Antonina W. Bouis

The right of Anatoli Rybakov to be identified as the author
of this work has been asserted by him in accordance
with the Copyright, Designs and Patents Act, 1988

First published in the UK by Hutchinson in 1993

Arrow Books Limited
Random House, 20 Vauxhall Bridge Road, London SW1V 2SA

Random House Australia (Pty) Limited
20 Alfred Street, Milsons Point, Sydney,
New South Wales 2061, Australia

Random House New Zealand Limited
18 Poland Road, Glenfield
Auckland 10, New Zealand

Random House South Africa (Pty) Limited
PO Box 337, Bergvlei, South Africa

Random House UK Limited Reg. No. 954009

A CIP catalogue record for this book
is available from the British Library

ISBN 0 09 930182 2

Printed and bound in Great Britain by
Cox & Wyman Ltd, Reading, Berkshire

*Fear* continues the story begun in *Children of the Arbat*, about the first generation to grow up under the Soviet regime — the children of the Stalin era. The Arbat is the quintessential Moscow neighborhood, the heart of the city, and the young residents there exemplify the different ways Russians lived through the disillusionment with communism that came with Stalin's terror. The two key figures are Sasha Pankratov, a twenty-two-year-old student, and the country's dictator, Josef Stalin.

The story begins in 1934, when an innocent joke — a flippant issue of the school wall newspaper — leads to Sasha's arrest and exile to a remote village in Siberia.

Back in Moscow, Sasha's friends and mother go on with their lives. The diverging lives of his classmates form the core of the plot. Yuri Sharok, a working-class boy, resents his wealthier friends. When tapped by the NKVD (KGB), Yuri decides to work for the secret police. Yuri has an affair with Lena Budyagina, the daughter of a Soviet diplomat. Lena almost dies from her illegal abortion.

Yuri entraps Vika, another friend of Sasha's, the daughter of a famous professor. Vika, who becomes an informer for Yuri, is totally apolitical. She belongs to Moscow's café society, spending her time drinking and dancing and having affairs. She eventually marries a very important architect. Her brother, Vadim, becomes a toadying literary and theater critic. Eventually, he will be ensnared by the KGB, too.

Another young man from their set is Maxim Kostin, who is doing his army service in the Far East. He is in love with Nina Ivanova.

Serious and idealistic, Nina has become a schoolteacher. Her kid sister, Varya, has rejected Nina's Young Communist League ideals. She wants independence. She has been very attracted to Sasha, his courage and integrity — but she is younger and not really part of his crowd. Varya, however, is the only one to support Sasha's mother, Sofya Alexandrovna, after his arrest. She helps Sofya Alexandrovna track Sasha down when he is arrested, standing in the long lines at the prison to deliver parcels to him.

After Sasha's exile to Siberia, Varya takes up with a fast crowd for a while and gets involved with a mysterious gambler. She quickly tires of that life, divorces the gambler, and takes a job as a draftsman for the construction of a hotel, one of Stalin's pet projects. Adding her own notes to Sofya Alexandrovna's correspondence with Sasha, Varya dreams of being reunited with him. By the end of *Children of the Arbat,* the two young people realize that they are meant for each other, although neither has openly expressed this love.

The lives of these young people are intertwined with the historical events transformed by Stalin and his policies. Stalin organizes the murder of Leningrad's Party leader Kirov in December 1934, and then uses that killing as an excuse to unleash mass terror in the country, which is orchestrated by the NKVD (KGB), headed first by Yagoda and then by Yezhov, Russia's bloodiest executioner.

*Fear* takes place against the background of the ruthless terror, unparalleled in history, in the years 1935–1937. Characters from *Children of the Arbat* encounter new ones, and their struggle against the evil of dictatorship shows that people can remain human beings — live and love, experience passion and joy — even in a morally deformed society.

# Part 1

The mail didn't come that day. It didn't come a week later, either. Yet the sleigh from Kezhma did deliver something to Fedya the storekeeper.

Sasha dropped by the store. Fedya let people in through the back door, through the storeroom.

"Did you get supplies?"

"A few things."

"Why not the mail, do you know?"

"Who knows? You need something on credit, maybe?"

"I don't need anything, thanks."

Sasha went to see Vsevolod Sergeyevich. He was in bed covered by the landlord's *barchatka,* a long sheepskin coat gathered at the waist.

"Sick?"

"Well."

"Why are you in bed, then?"

"What else is there to do?"

"Why isn't the mail coming?"

"The mail? You want mail? You'll get fine mail nowadays."

"I don't understand."

"You don't. . . . Do you understand what's going on? The enemies of the working class have murdered Comrade Kirov, and you want them to get the mail delivered punctually. What's the matter with you, Sasha? The authorities have to prepare their response. A blow that will make Russia shudder. So that people don't kill leaders of the working class, so that the enemies of the working class, now being discovered, will not dare send killers, who are also being found out now. And you want letters, newspapers. Why should enemies of the working class get letters? So that they can conspire how to escape revenge for the murder? Newspapers? So that they can figure out what's going on and be able to maneuver? No, no, dear fellow, you won't have that chance. Just be thankful that they're not getting you, forcing you to walk to Krasnoyarsk in this cold."

"All right," Sasha said with a laugh. "Don't try to scare me, and don't scare yourself, above all."

Vsevolod Sergeyevich sat up in bed and fixed his gaze on Sasha. "I'm trying to scare you? When's the last time you saw Kayurov?"

"I ran into him on the street a few days ago."

"You won't be running into him anymore."

Sasha looked at him.

"Yes, yes. They took him away last night, tossed his stuff into a cart and took him away."

"No one saw anything," Sasha said in bewilderment.

"Of course not. The dogs didn't even bark. Everyone was asleep. So there. And remember Volodya Kvachadze, who traveled here with you?"

"Of course."

"Well, guards took him to Krasnoyarsk. And all his like-minded friends from the Angara and the Chuna rivers. And Marya Fedorovna, the former Socialist Revolutionary, and Anatoly Georgyevich, the former anarchists, and that fine beauty...Freda. They're picking up everyone. Our turn is coming. Did you ever meet Anna Petrovna Samsonova? She's an exile in Kezhma."

"Yes, I know her."

"Well they took her away too, and she's seventy-two."

Sasha shrugged. "I don't see the point. The young ones — Volodya, Freda, me, even you — we're worth sending off to the camps; we're free labor. But an old woman like that — she won't make it to Krasnoyarsk, she'll die along the way."

"So what? Who cares? Honestly, you surprise me, Sasha. There is a new order — exiles arrested under such-and-such articles and with such-and-such sentences are to be sent immediately to Krasnoyarsk. You think a local administrator is going to think: 'She's old and sick, I feel sorry for her'?...He'll get shot for disobeying orders. This way, he sends her, he did his job. If she dies along the way, it's not his problem. And if they get her to Krasnoyarsk alive, they'll add to her sentence — five more years in the camps — and send her back. And if they get her here, fine; and if they don't, then they'll write her off. As long as the body count adds up. If you're on the list, it doesn't matter if you're there alive or dead, as long as you're there. If you die, we'll put a mark next to your name and subtract. Actually, I'm not sure about you, Sasha, you're a short-timer, but as for me and Mikhail Mikhailovich, repeat offenders as far as they're concerned, we're doomed."

"Well," Sasha said calmly, "then we'll wait."

And so they lived in their Mozgova, on the edge of the world, cut off from the world, but feeling that something horrible was happening that would soon involve them, too.

Sasha rarely saw Zida anymore. Two teachers had been fired in Kezhma: one's husband was an exile, the other had been an exile herself. And even though this had been known about them earlier, now, when the country was being cleansed of "dubious elements," the teachers were fired and replaced by Zida. She taught in Mozgova from seven to ten in the morning, and then a sleigh took her to Kezhma, from which she didn't return until late in the evening. Nevertheless, when Sasha ran into her on the street, he stopped and said hello and asked gently how things were going. She looked away and said that things were fine, only that she was very busy.

"Zida," Sasha said. "I was wrong then, I hurt you, and I'm very sorry. If you can, forgive me."

She looked up at him.

"All right, Sasha, it's over."

"I know that it's over. But I want us to be friends."

"Of course," Zida said and smiled. "What else?"

The conversation ended.

They didn't meet again. Zida was in Mozgova and Kezhma, and Sasha found a job.

\* \* \*

The cold was fierce in January 1931. Old-time residents on the Angara couldn't remember such a bad winter.

Ivan Parfenovich, chairman of the kolkhoz, worried. Finding a home for two hundred cows in a village where there had recently been two thousand was not a problem — the cattle shed remained, as did enough women in the kolkhoz who hadn't yet lost the habit of tending animals.

But keeping an eye on a herd spread out over a dozen households was not easy. Most of the cows were with calf, and they had to be fed carefully and at least three times a day given water that wasn't cold, which had to be hauled from a hole in the ice of the Angara. They needed fresh clean straw under them, and to be walked two or three hours a day, and to be kept from having things fall on them or bumping into things, and to be brought to a special birthing section when the time came — those were the instructions. There were ten times fewer cows but ten times as many instructions.

The kolkhoz had been building a dairy farm — or more accurately, a big two-row cow shed — for the last two years, but the construction was not moving along.

They had begun by putting together a report on the construction of dairy farms in the region but it turned out that none were being built. People were making do with private cattle farms. The authorities panicked — sending a report like that to the capital of the region meant arrest for sabotaging the development of the cattle industry and could even get you shot. And so the order was given that, come what may, the farms had to be completed by spring, for the mass calving.

Ivan Parfenovich formed a team and put Savva Lukich, Sasha's landlord, in charge.

"Maybe you could help out," Savva Lukich told Sasha. "They'll issue me work orders and I'll give you the money."

"What about Ivan Parfenovich?"

"It's his idea," Savva Lukich replied honestly.

So Sasha became a carpenter.

There were six on the team — Savva Lukich, Sasha, and four others. They prepared logs. They put them on a sawhorse, ran a rope blackened with a piece of charcoal over them to leave a mark, and cut. When they'd done two sides, they would turn the log over, do the other two sides, then the corners, and the log was ready.

Savva Lukich checked the work, walking along the length of the board.

The men sawed, working merrily, without irritation; even if someone pulled the wrong way and spoiled the cut, they moved on calmly, without grumbling. If someone missed hitting a nail, they joked, "I'll bet you don't miss when it's your wife you're aiming at."

Sasha went to bed early now and got up with the old man at dawn. The old woman had breakfast ready for them.

Infrequently, Vsevolod Sergeyevich came by in the evenings. He looked peaked, but tried to appear jaunty.

One day he appeared at their work site in the daytime.

"For you, Sasha." Vsevolod Sergeyevich waved a parcel. "The mail's in! I brought your newspapers and letters."

"Vsevolod Sergeyevich, thank you, dear man!"

Sasha took the letters, pulled off the *kokoldy*, the deerskin work mittens, and then his woolen mittens, tore open the envelope, looked at the date, and then turned the page. Varya's postscripts were always at the end. This letter had nothing from her. He opened the second — nothing again.

And then, the third. At last!

He was overjoyed the instant he saw her handwriting.

Varya wrote briefly — "Nothing new with me. I live, work, miss you. . . . We're waiting for you."

And what else could she write openly to him? Nothing . . . Just as he couldn't write freely to her. But those few words were enough. The important thing was that she was waiting, and that he had less than two years left in damned Mozgova. That's what was important! And after that, whether they allowed him to live in Moscow or not, they would see each other!

Smiling, he put the letters in his pockets. The ones without Varya's postscripts in his right pocket, the one with, into his left.

"Vsevolod Sergeyevich, go to my place and read the papers, we'll be back soon."

Savva Lukich, a kind soul, rolled a cigarette. "Why'd you hide your letters away? Go ahead and read them."

"I'll look at them later," Sasha replied.

It was getting dark, so they finished up work and put away their tools, hiding them among the logs.

At home, Vsevolod Sergeyevich handed Sasha a newspaper and said, "Read this!"

The resolution of the Central Executive Committee of the U.S.S.R. on terrorism, published right after Kirov's murder, said:

> To introduce the following changes in the active criminal and procedural codes of the Union republics on investigating cases involving terrorist organizations and terrorist acts against workers of Soviet power:
>
> 1. The investigations in these cases will be completed in no more than ten days.
> 2. The charges will be handed to the defendants twenty-four hours before the trial.
> 3. The cases will be heard without lawyers.
> 4. Appeals of sentences as well as appeals for clemency will not be allowed.
> 5. Sentence to the highest measure of punishment will be executed immediately upon sentencing.

"Yes," Sasha said thoughtfully. "That's really something."

"That's martial law," Vsevolod Sergeyevich said. "But I don't believe we're at war. In fact, this resolution is worse than martial law, because it's not aimed at a specific crime, but at terrorism in general, and *terrorism* is a very flexible term, dear Sasha. You can call almost anything terrorism and a worker of Soviet power can be anyone at all — from Stalin to the kolkhoz bookkeeper threatened by a laborer who was shortchanged on his overtime. This is a resolution bent on the destruction of innocent and defenseless people."

He shook his head. "Do you remember what Pushkin said to Gogol after reading the first chapters of *Dead Souls*? 'God, how sad our Russia is.' What can you say after this revolution? 'Poor Russia'? And note how quickly it was done. Kirov was killed on December first — and the new law was ready and published. How do you like that, eh?"

"I never told you about my investigator, did I, Vsevolod Sergeyevich. His name was Dyakov. A dried-up fellow in glasses, an exceptional bastard, who tried to trump up charges against me. If this resolution had come out a year and a half ago, he could have charged me with terrorism, too. The logic is simple: 'Why didn't you mention Comrade Stalin in the holiday issue of your wall newspaper? Because you are against Comrade Stalin. You don't want him to lead the country and the Party. And how can you get rid of him? Only by killing him, by killing Comrade Stalin, our father and teacher, our leader. Oh, so you never said that? Of course not, who would? But you thought about it and if the circumstances were right, you'd have done it. You are a potential terrorist, your friends are potential terrorists, and together with them you are a terrorist organization.' That means a trial without a defense attorney, a sentence without right of appeal, and the firing squad an hour after the trial."

"In that sense you were lucky," Vsevolod Sergeyevich agreed.

Sasha chuckled. "I'm fortune's child. Shall we drink to that?"

"Why not? By the way, let me tell you why you really are fortune's child. . . ."

Sasha had some straight alcohol and the landlady put out some smoked fish.

Sasha reread his letters, and Vsevolod Sergeyevich looked through the newspapers.

"Look what's going on, Sasha. . . . Trials, mass executions, a thousand nobles, former bourgeoisie, children of former nobles, and children of former bourgeoisie were sent out of Leningrad — why them? And what about the people? Are the people silently sitting by? Not at all. They're not silent! Just look, read this: The people are demanding revenge. Rallies all over the country, from Vladivostok to Odessa — expose, destroy, execute! And the Party isn't silent, either. At Party meetings they seek out 'hidden' spies; Communists repent, beat their chests, admit their errors. They weren't vigilant enough, they hadn't suspected. But that doesn't help. Those confessions are considered inadequate and insincere."

The landlady took out a cast-iron pan of potatoes. Sasha called Vsevolod Sergeyevich to the table. They sat down, had a shot glass of alcohol, ate some food, and poured a second.

"Then why am I fortune's child?" Sasha asked.

"Because you're in Mozgova," Vsevolod Sergeyevich replied. "You're living in a sterile environment. If you were outside, you'd have to participate in these rallies, demanding exposure, execution, and destruction."

"I wouldn't have to."

"You'd never escape attending these rallies if you were working in Moscow. I'm not saying you'd necessarily speak out against people. No! But you'd vote along with everyone else for execution, raising your hand, because if you didn't, it would mean you were an enemy, too, and they'd arrest you right there."

"And what would you do?"

"Me? I'm not in danger. As long as the Soviets are in power, there's only one thing for me: exile, camp, prison, more camp, more prison. And I hope they're not going to hold meetings like this in the camps and prisons. No one would vote for it there."

"Well, let's say, theoretically, your sentence is over and you're let out. You're living in some little town, and working, and there's a rally at work, condemning the enemies, demanding they be shot, and everyone votes for it — what would you do?"

Silently, Vsevolod Sergeyevich pulled the skin off the fish.

"Well?"

"I don't know, Sasha, honest, I don't. At these rallies there are people who sincerely believe what's pounded into their heads. And there are those who may not believe it but they remember their little children."

"You don't have children."

"No. And I'll tell you, I probably would raise my hand. Why? Because my lone vote wouldn't change a thing. Because if I go to the block alone, nothing will change, they'll be shot anyway, and me along with them. And they're confessing, repenting — why should I die for such weak people? They're the ones who organized all this in the first place, they're Communists and Komsomols, they sent people to their deaths, and now that they're being sent, why should I defend them?"

"But you said that they were exiling former members of the nobility and the bourgeoisie and their children. The children didn't send anyone to die. They have to be defended."

Vsevolod Sergeyevich finished cleaning his piece of fish and took a bite.

"This is good fish, marvelous fish. You've raised a serious question, Sasha. A very serious and timely question. But it's timely for you, Sasha, and not for me — this dilemma is one I'll never face; I'm in a different orbit. But you, Sasha, you're in their orbit and you can't pull away from it, and this is a problem you'll have to face."

"Well, then," Sasha said, "when it faces me, I'll deal with it. But your solution doesn't suit me."

"Then I renounce my solution as unconsidered. I was speaking about how the ordinary reasonable person would behave — he would raise his hand, he would act like everyone else. That is the tragedy of Russia, the tragedy of the Russian people . . . people are human."

"And what about the 'destiny of the nation,' and its 'special mission'? What about this 'Christian, orthodox principle'?"

"Sasha, are you trying with those primitive questions to disprove our — or, let's say, my — philosophy?"

"I'm no philosopher," Sasha countered, "but I'm coming to the conclusion that no nation has a messianic role or messianic significance. There are no supernations, there are people — good people and bad. And we must create a society in which nothing can force them to be bad."

"Any idea of a perfect society is an illusion, Sasha."

"I doubt that there can be a perfect society. But a society that strives for perfection is already a marvelous society," Sasha replied.

"I don't see our society striving for that. Society is people, and we're turning them into nonhumans." Vsevolod Sergeyevich stood. "I'm off. I can sleep all day long if I want, but you have to work. See, they even trust you with carpentry, but I'm not allowed that."

Sasha laughed. "I have a protector." He pointed to his landlord. "Savva Lukich helped."

"Why not?" Savva Lukich said. "We have to finish the work. Orders."

"Why don't you take me?"

"You're an intellectual," Savva Lukich said. "You wouldn't like our work."

Vsevolod Sergeyevich left.

✦   ✦   ✦

Sasha reread his mother's letters and looked at Varya's postscripts again — brief, restrained, but he found a hidden meaning in them. *I live, work, miss you. . . . We're waiting for you.*

He wrote to her just as briefly, mulling over each word. "Dear Varya, when I get the mail, the first thing I look for is something from you." Maybe she would see something behind his words, too.

That was all he dared to do. He hadn't expressed his particular interest in her back in Moscow, and now that interest might seem to be no more than a longing for freedom, for old acquaintances, simply for a woman. Sasha did not want to be misunderstood.

Maybe before, when she had written, "How I'd like to know what you're doing now," she was being more daring, more determined, or maybe it was just his imagination. She was simply trying to give him moral support, a kind girl with a kind heart.

*I live, work, miss you. We're waiting for you.* There had to be something there. . . . Varya's firm belief in the future encouraged him.

His mother's letters were quiet in tone, but something in them made him wary. In one letter she wrote about his Aunt Vera: "Vera moved from the dacha, even though it's quite livable in winter. She doesn't want to bother with the wood and the stove." There wasn't anything strange in that. But in the next letter, she wrote again, "Vera has shut up the dacha for winter." What did it mean? Why mention it twice in a row? Absentmindedness? Or maybe something had happened to Aunt Vera, or her husband, or the children, his cousins. He wrote to his mother, "How's Aunt Vera, Uncle Volodya, Svetlana, and Valera? Where are they, how are they doing?"

He had to reassure his mother. In that letter he also asked her to look through his desk for his college certificate and his driver's license, and to keep them safe until his return. He wrote that to reassure her that he was planning to come back soon. He himself didn't believe in it much. He also asked her to send a few of his books on the French Revolution. He had studied it at school, and after school, too, and had collected books, which he missed now and wanted to read again. He also wrote that he was working on the construction of a dairy farm, that the work was pleasant, the pay good, and he had enough for food and lodging, so she didn't have to send money.

He worked on the letter for a long time. Even the old woman said, "Why tire your eyes? Go to bed."

"The post goes out tomorrow," Sasha replied. "I have to finish."

He went to sleep late, and when he woke, Savva Lukich was already eating breakfast.

"I'll be ready in an instant!"

Sasha dressed, washed, and quickly tackled the eggs waiting for him on the table.

The old man went outside.

"Go on ahead," Sasha called after him. "I'll catch up."

Savva Lukich came right back in. "The police."

"Coming here?"

"Who knows?"

He wasn't packed, he wasn't ready. Sasha looked at the letters; he didn't want a stranger touching them, but he wouldn't have time to hide them. All right, let them come, they'll have to wait while he packed.

So that was it. The end of his life on the Angara. Where would it continue, in what camp? He'd probably never see his mother, his father, or Varya again.

He took out a cigarette and lit up. He looked out the window, but it was covered with hoarfrost and he couldn't see. He listened. He couldn't hear the sleigh.

The gate slammed. The door opened and Savva Lukich came back in. "They're gone, Sasha, thank God," he said, and crossed himself.

"Where'd they go?"

"Around the corner."

Who were they after? Maslov, probably.

"Listen, I'll just run over there, and then come to work, all right?"

"Go ahead," the old man said. "Don't rush, we'll manage."

The sleigh was at the house where Maslov lived. Vsevolod Sergeyevich and Peter Kuzmych were there, too.

As Sasha arrived, Mikhail Mikhailovich Maslov appeared in the door with a suitcase in his hands and a pack on his back. When did he pack? Did he live with his suitcase always ready?

A policeman walked in front of Maslov carrying a rifle, and there was another policeman with a rifle behind, a tall, straight fellow with a scornful look.

Maslov put his suitcase in the sleigh, took off the backpack, and put it in too.

Then he turned to Vsevolod Sergeyevich. They embraced and kissed. And then he embraced and kissed Peter Kuzmych. He offered his hand to Sasha. Sasha shook it and looked into Mikhail Mikhailovich's eyes. Then he asked, "Mikhail Mikhailovich! Would you like me to tell Olga Stepanovna anything?"

"Vsevolod Sergeyevich has the address, he'll write." After a moment, he added, "Thank you for thinking of her."

# ❧ 2 ❧

**S**asha went to the site. The men were framing in logs every two meters, to make partitions for the stalls. Planks were used as siding to make walls.

The work was beautiful and neat. Sasha was astonished that it was done with such simple tools — ax, saw, awl, plane, scraper, plumb weight, and a level.

"Did you see your comrade off?" Savva Lukich asked.

"Yes."

"Where did they send him?" asked Stepan Timofeyevich, a hook-nosed, sinewy man.

"Who knows?" Sasha replied.

"Maybe he finished his term," Savva Lukich said.

"Setting him free, you mean?" Stepan Timofeyevich snorted. "They don't send police to set you free."

"The men in Kezhma are saying that some big boss was killed," said another man, "and that he was killed by a Trotskyite, one of that bunch — that wants to get rid of these collective farms."

"And how are they going to do that, now?" Stepan Timofeyevich laughed. "What's there to give back to the farmers? Everything's been destroyed...."

"Enough now," Savva Lukich said, looking around cautiously. "Just remember, it's all from God. The way God arranges things is how it happens."

"God, God — you keep blaming God for everything," Stepan Timofeyevich said bitterly. "Where is your church? God's not going to do anything for you. Do you think He'll build this cow shed for you? *We're* killing the cows, and *we're* building the sheds."

"Don't, if you don't want to," a third man said.

"Where can we go?" Stepan Timofeyevich said angrily. "This one" — and he pointed at Sasha — "will finish his term and go where he wants. But we peasants have to stay. We don't have passports. They're keeping us rooted to this spot. You call that freedom?"

"Do you know what will happen if anyone hears you going on like that?" Savva Lukich said.

"I do," Stepan Timofeyevich said. "That's why we're all going to ruin, because no one says anything."

"Our business is to work. You've talked the whole morning away."

A week or two later, Peter Kazmych was called into Kezhma. . . . The police didn't come for him, but sent a message through the village soviet.

"Maybe they're letting me out, what do you think, boys?" He looked at Sasha and Vsevolod Sergeyevich, hoping to see encouragement and support. "My sentence was up in November."

"Why were you just sitting here, if it ended?" Sasha asked. "You should have reminded them."

"It's dangerous reminding them; you remind them and they'll add a new sentence. . . . They didn't take me away, the way they did Mikhail Mikhailovich. And I wasn't charged under a political article."

"Not political!" Vsevolod Sergeyevich snorted. "Economic counterrevolution. . . ."

"But that's economic, not political," Peter Kuzmych countered.

"All right," Vsevolod Sergeyevich interrupted. "Go to Kezhma and find out and then tell us about it."

Peter Kuzmych returned that evening, happy and excited. He was released! He showed them the paper. "For serving his sentence . . . falls under Point Two of the Resolution of the Council of People's Commissars on the passport system." That was a minus — he couldn't reside in big cities.

"What do I need with big cities?" Peter Kuzmych said excitedly. "I was born and grew up in Stary Oskol, my wife, daughter, and family are there. That's where I'll live."

"Do you have money for the trip?" Sasha asked.

"I'll get there. . . . I'll go with the mail as far as Kezhma, I'll have to give him a tenner to carry my things. A ticket to Stary Oskol can't be more than twenty-five or thirty rubles. I'll manage on fifty, I'm sure. And I have that much."

"What about food and drink?"

Peter Kuzmych waved that off. "I won't starve to death. My landlady will make me crackers for the road, and some dried fish and eggs, and you can get boiling water for free at the train stations. . . . Don't worry, I'll get there."

The next day Peter Kuzmych left for Kezhma on a kolkhoz sleigh. He sobbed as he bid Sasha and Vsevolod Sergeyevich farewell, embarrassed by his own good luck.

"God willing, you'll get out of here too."

"God willing," Vsevolod Sergeyevich said, gently mocking. "Have a peaceful life, don't open a store!"

"Vsevolod Sergeycvich, of course you can't have a store nowadays," the old man said, recoiling in fear. "I'll be happy if I can work as a clerk."

"Better get a job as a night watchman," Vsevolod Sergeyevich counseled. "It's safer. When you're a clerk, you're responsible for the goods in a store; if there's a problem, they'll blame you. If you're a night watchman, you just sit around in a fur coat and keep warm."

"How can you say that, Vsevolod Sergeyevich? I've known my trade since childhood, I can still be of use." He spoke these last words from the sleigh. . . . The driver jerked the reins and the horses set off.

"The man hasn't learned a thing," Vsevolod Sergeyevich said grimly.

Peter Kuzmych's release lifted Sasha's spirits. And then came the news that Father Vasily in the village Zimka had been released because his sentence was over. They were releasing people selectively.

However, a week later a girl — the daughter of Vsevolod Sergeyevich's landlady — came to the cow shed and told Sasha, "Vsevolod Sergeyevich wants you." He was being sent to the camps. Sasha found him energetic and busily packing. He had been miserable in the uncertainty and anticipation, but now it was decided. Now he knew what awaited him, and what awaited him demanded strength and readiness.

"You've been ordered to show up?" Sasha asked.

"They'll come for me from Kezhma. There's a small group of convicts there, apparently, the last one headed for Krasnoyarsk. You're not part of it, that inspires hope, Sasha. Of course, there'll be plenty of others, so be prepared for anything.... Remember, they didn't take Lidya Grigoryevna Zvyaguro in a group either. There is much ahead. And this is for you," said Vsevolod Sergeyevich, pointing to a pile of books. "I know you're not a great admirer of philosophy, but there are some fine books here, and I can't take them with me.... They'd confiscate them anyway.... If you're taken away, leave them with someone, or, if worse comes to worst, throw them away."

"Thank you," Sasha said. "What do you need for the trip?"

"I seem to have everything."

"You don't have anything," Sasha said. "Do you have warm underwear?"

"I'm not used to warm underwear, I just wear the ordinary type. And the winter's coming to an end."

"I don't have knit, but I have flannel underwear, two pairs. And woolen socks, and a spare sweater — take them."

"Sasha, I don't need all that.... The criminals in the camp will take it all anyway."

"Not before you reach Krasnoyarsk.... I've seen your gloves — they're for strolling on Nevsky Prospect in Leningrad."

"No, my gloves are still good...."

"I'll give you nice warm gloves, wear them over yours. Footwear?"

"Perfect. I have insulated felt boots. That's plenty, Sasha, I have all I need. Except money. But now the state is going to take care of me."

"How do you know that they'll come for you?"

"I know," Vsevolod Sergeyevich said curtly. He trusted Sasha, but he didn't name his source. That's the way life was here — never give names.

Vsevolod Sergeyevich didn't have many things — they fit into one tightly stuffed backpack. "I'm done." He sat down. "Here's what I want to say to you, Sasha, in parting. I'm sorry to leave you; truly, I've come to love you. Even though we're on different sides of the barricades, as they say now, I like and respect you, because you haven't rejected your faith. Your faith is not like the faith of the others — there is something human about it, there is no class or Party limitation. You may not realize it, but your faith is derived from the same source that creates all human ideals.

"But don't turn into an idealist. Be closer to real life. Otherwise, life will destroy you, or even worse, break you, and then. . . . Forgive my directness. Idealists sometimes become saints, but more frequently, tyrants and guards of tyranny. So much evil in the world is done under the guise of high ideals, and so many vile deeds are justified by them. You won't take offense?"

Sasha laughed. "Don't be silly, Vsevolod Sergeyevich! How can anyone take offense at another's thoughts? I don't intend to argue with your theory. And I can't vouch for my future. I will say this. I live on earth, I am an earthy man. That is why I am not an idealist in your sense of the word. I do believe that man must profess ideas, but humane, just ideas. And I came to that conclusion during this year of prison, convict transport, and exile. There is nothing in the world that is dearer or holier than human life and human dignity. Anyone who takes a life is a criminal, and anyone who humiliates the human in a man is also a criminal."

"But criminals must be tried," Vsevolod Sergeyevich said.

"Yes."

"There's the weakness in your thought. Who are the judges?"

"Let's not get too involved in the question. I repeat that the most valuable things on earth are human life and dignity. If that principle were recognized as the fundamental ideal, then with time people would develop answers to the smaller questions."

Vsevolod Sergeyevich harkened to something outside. A sleigh pulled up.

"That's for me."

"Hold them, I'll be right back," Sasha said.

He ran out of the house and saw a sleigh with a driver and policeman in it.

Sasha ran home, grabbed a pair of flannel underwear, the

sweater, the gloves, added two shirts, and came back to Vsevolod Sergeyevich.

"Why are you doing this?" Vsevolod Sergeyevich said. "Look, my bag is full."

"Don't worry, we'll squeeze them in. Open up!"

"Oh, yes," Vsevolod Sergeyevich said. "Here's the address of Olga Stepanovna, in Kalinin. I wrote her a letter, which I hope to send from Krasnoyarsk. But they may send us straight to prison. So please write to her — one of the letters is bound to reach her."

Sasha put her address in his pocket.

The policeman and the driver had finished their tea and went outside.

Vsevolod Sergeyevich put on his coat, picked up his bag, and put it down again.

"Well, let's say good-bye, Sasha."

They embraced and kissed.

Vsevolod Sergeyevich went to the kitchen, said good-bye to his landlords, went outside, and put his bag in the sleigh. The daughter of the house, a jacket thrown over her shoulders, stood in the doorway.

"Well, one more time!"

Vsevolod Sergeyevich and Sasha kissed.

Vsevolod Sergeyevich got in the sleigh, covered his legs, and said cheerfully, "Well, shall we go?"

Sasha watched them disappear around the corner.

And the girl stood in the doorway and watched.

That left only two exiles in Mozgova — Sasha and Lidya Grigoryevna Zvyaguro.

## ❧ 3 ❧

Life on the Arbat continued as usual — as if there were no exiles, no prisons, no camps, no prisoners.

Friends of the prisoners, and friends of the friends, lived as they always had. The newspapers wrote about them, the radio broadcast stories about them, speakers at meetings talked about them: the rank-and-file workers and their glorious work.

They also wrote, broadcast, and talked about people like Sasha Pankratov, but as enemies who had to be destroyed. And those who supported them and sympathized with such people also had to be destroyed. And since no one wanted to be destroyed, no one expressed any doubts that people who had had no trials and whose guilt they had learned about only from brief newspaper articles had to be destroyed.

It was safer not to talk about them at all. Talk about something else. About the valorous pilots who had rescued the crew of the *Cheluskin,* after it sank in the Arctic Ocean. And if anyone thought that rescuing innocent people from prison was as important as rescuing the Cheluskiners, they didn't say it out loud.

Yuri Denisovich Sharok now bore a title — Senior Operations Plenipotentiary — and was subordinated directly to the chief of the First Section, Alexander Fyodorovich Vutkovsky, and his deputy, Shtein. He was also subordinate to Dyakov, but only in Dyakov's role as assistant of the chief of the section.

Vutkovsky and Shtein valued Sharok. He was a serious, diligent, and hardworking man. With a future. Here, a man with a future was someone who could not only "break" a suspect, not only force him to admit his own guilt, but, more important, bring in others and create a group case. The members of the group, in their turn, would lead the investigation to new people, guaranteeing the uninterrupted functioning of the punitive organs.

Sharok had mastered that technique well and early, and he had learned other truths — in particular, not to hold on to anyone's coattails. Berezin was well disposed to him, but Sharok kept his distance. And rightly so. Berezin ended up in the Far East. In an important post, of course, and he had kept his title. But still, he had been removed from Moscow. And his people were spread out all over the place.

Among the truths Sharok had mastered was never to forget that you're walking on the edge of a knife. You save yourself here only with the greatest caution. Let the fool Dyakov be impressed by his own position, being allowed to do whatever he wanted, without punishment, working in the hottest place. Things could change.

Of course, their section was the hottest. The Second Section dealt with Mensheviks, Bundovites, Anarchists; the Third with national movements like the Musavatists, the Dashnaks, and so on; the Fourth, with Socialist Revolutionaries; and the Fifth, with the Church. Quiet sections: who cared about Mensheviks or SRs now ... ?

Sharok would have happily transferred there. Once he had an opportunity to transfer to the Fifth Section on Church affairs, but after some hesitation he refused. He didn't want to hassle with God Himself.

Sharok didn't believe in God. But he was tolerant of his mother's piety — that was her business. And who the hell knew! Educated people believed in God, for instance, Academician Pavlov. A world-famous scientist, and yet he had a chapel in Koltushi, and he bowed and prayed. And still the government was nice to him; Comrade Stalin himself treated him with respect.

Whether it was God or not, something inexplicable had happened. Fate, maybe. ... He had been so upset back in October 1934 when his shitty appendicitis kept him from going to

Leningrad, to see Zaporozhets.* But if he had gone, he'd be in a camp today.

Yuri had come back from work one morning, as usual, and around seven he doubled over. The pain was unbearable, his body seemed to be breaking in half. He couldn't breathe in or out. He tried lying on one side, then the other. He pulled his knee up to his chest, but nothing helped. He couldn't keep back the groans.

His mother paced the room. "Do you want a hot water bottle?" Thank God his father hadn't left for work and knew what the problem was. He did not allow her to use the hot water bottle and said, "We'll call for an ambulance."

Yuri refused. The ambulance would take him to the hospital and he was supposed to be on the *Red Arrow Express* to Leningrad that night to see Zaporozhets. They might not let him out of the hospital, and his trip would collapse, and he'd have to keep working for Dyakov.

"Give me the phone number," his father insisted.

"Don't call, it'll pass in a minute."

"If you don't give me your ambulance service number, I'll call the city one."

Yuri tried to sit up, fell back on the pillow, and realized that he needed help. The ambulance doctor would give him a shot for the pain. He told his father where his phone book was.

A half hour later the ambulance came, and they carried Yuri out on a stretcher. At the Varsonofyevsky Hospital, the NKVD hospital, they put him right on the operating table. His stitches would come out in ten days or so. That's it! End of the Leningrad trip! He was so bitter and upset then, but it turned out that his appendicitis saved him. So how could you not believe in fate after that?

"You're lucky they brought you in time; another two or three hours and you'd have had peritonitis," the surgeon, Professor

---

* In *Children of the Arbat,* Zaporozhets is the NKVD agent who arranges the murder of Kirov, Party chief of Leningrad and possible rival of Stalin. After Kirov's death, Zaporozhets and his colleagues were murdered, purged, or "made to disappear."

Tsitronblat, said. Their best surgeon, and, interestingly, he had a wooden leg.

Two days after the operation a package of fruit — oranges, tangerines, and apples — and a note arrived. "Yurochka, how do you feel? If you need anything, write to me. Lena."

Yuri put down the note. Lena had come! She came after all! Exhausted, in pain, he became sentimental and felt a lump in his throat. So she loved him, she forgave him and wasn't jealous anymore.

Of course, he also had a brief unpleasant thought: What if this was one of their intelligentsia tricks? ... No, no matter what had happened in the past, you have to be kind, help in a moment of need, show sympathy. That's the way decent people behave, and they were decent people after all.... No one else had tried to see him, but she had.

Vutkovsky had called, asked about his health, but as boss, he was supposed to show concern for his staff. His mother came, but that didn't count. She baked pies, the fool, without having asked the doctor what he was allowed to have. And he didn't need anything anyway, the food was good, they knew how to feed people in the central NKVD hospital. ... Lena had behaved like an intellectual — tangerines and oranges weren't real food, not pies made with buckwheat groats, but a sign of attention. So, then, it wasn't just decency that brought her! She couldn't have forgotten him. People like her don't forget. And they don't forget people like him. He was a real man.

On the back of Lena's note Yuri wrote, "Lenochka, thanks for the fruit. I don't need anything, I have all I need, don't worry. I'd like to see you, but you're not allowed in the ward. I'll be up in two days. Come back then." After some thought, he added, "I kiss you."

Two days later, he and Lena were sitting in the small lounge not far from Yuri's room. Lena had a white coat carelessly draped over her blue suit and white blouse. She had tall boots enveloping her plump, strong legs. He could never look at her legs calmly, and her perfume excited him. ... She was beautiful, healthy, glowing and he was in an ugly flannel robe, nothing but underwear under it, he had slippers on his bare feet, and he hadn't shaved.

"You recognized me," Sharok joked. "I must look like a corpse."

"Don't exaggerate," Lena said with a smile. "You're a bit pale, that's to be expected in a hospital. How long will you be here?"

"Two or three weeks."

"Don't be blue, I'll come visit."

What a good woman! A strange one, but a good one. Kind, gentle, she loved him, he could see that. She was ready to do anything for his sake, and yet there was something that drove them apart, that repelled one from the other — that was the scientific term, he thought.

It was her kindness, gentleness, decency, and tact — everything that was so nice about her. He couldn't be frank with her, he couldn't be himself.

With Vika — a semiwhore, a snitch — he could be honest. If she had been his wife and not an informer, he could have talked to her, revealed himself, and she would have understood and given him good advice.

He couldn't do that with Lena. He had to adjust to her concepts of morality and ethics. How could there be any morality or ethics in his work, if they existed at all?

What morality and ethics did her father have, the respected Ivan Grigoryevich Budyagin? How many people did he shoot as chairman of the provincial Cheka? What morality and ethics did he use when he sent people off to the other world? The interests of the proletariat? And who determined those interests? The Party? Lenin?

Sharok also followed the interests of the proletariat, with the sole difference that now they were determined by the current leader — Comrade Stalin. But there was no point in explaining all that to Lena. He had to talk about people, the way she did, respectfully, and about the persecuted, again the way she did, with compassion. He once said something otherwise, and she did not argue but gave him a frightened look, which spoiled his mood.

In bed she was passionate and docile, she attracted him and he couldn't get away. But he still needed someone to talk to. . . . What was the point of her coming to see him in the hospital every day?

He'd like to be able to tell her what was worrying him, so that they could grieve together over losing Leningrad and they could try to guess who would take the spot on Zaporozhets' team. Instead, they talked nonsense, which didn't interest him. He couldn't say what he thought. He was constantly on guard so as not to say the wrong thing, to see her frightened eyes, which humiliated him. But he didn't want to break up with her, either.

When Sharok was released from the hospital, their meetings started up again, but Yuri worked nights, Lena worked days.

They went to Lena's dacha in Silver Wood a few times. It was heated, so people went out there on weekends, and Lena's brother, Vladlen, spent his school vacation there skiing.

Once Yuri called her from work in the evening. She was happy to hear from him and asked how things were.

"I'm exhausted, I've been working over a son-of-a-bitch."

She immediately shut up. He had used the wrong word, a word that was too strong for her. He was worn to a frazzle, he couldn't weigh every word.

"All right, don't worry about me. Tell me about you."

"Nothing new."

"I just called," Sharok said. "I haven't heard your voice in a long time. How are we going to spend the May holidays?"

"How many days will you have?"

"Two."

Those were two heady days. A special bus took them to a resort reserved for scientific workers outside Moscow.

"How did you get reservations?" Yuri asked.

Lena replied with an evasive, "What's the difference?"

But Yuri saw the reservation was made out in the name of Budyagin. Of course, her father....

The house was luxurious, but he didn't recognize a single person while Lena was saying hello right and left. She pointed out a few people: scientists, academicians even, who were here with the wives and children to celebrate the May Day holiday.

They were given a small room facing a birch grove. The branches were still bare but had a barely visible pale green haze, indicating the leaves were just about to burst out of the buds.

"Birches have trunks this white only in the spring," Lena said, looking at Yuri. "Have you noticed?"

No, he hadn't. "I don't even remember the last time I was outside the city," he said.

Young grass was pushing up between the trees, the weather was wonderful, sunny and warm, but the woods were still damp, water slurped underfoot, and the paths were slippery. No one wore a coat, and the women rolled up their sleeves. Beautiful, sleek, pedigreed women.

They played volleyball and croquet. Sharok had never seen croquet before, an old-fashioned game, and it was funny watching respectable academicians and their well-fed ladies arguing furiously over rules Yuri didn't understand — touched the ball, didn't touch it, went through the wicket, didn't. The ones watching the game also joined the arguments, and the players politely but firmly, even sarcastically, asked them not to interfere.

Actually, it was amusing on the croquet field. Yuri watched Lena play, and smiled at her when their eyes met. She didn't look athletic, being big and slow, but as Yuri learned in Silver Wood, she was an excellent swimmer, and here she was good at croquet and volleyball. Good for her. She was merry, calm, her eyes shone, and she was attentive to Yuri.

They were to leave on the second evening. That day they went to bed after lunch. . . . And when it was time to get up, she asked him, lying in his arms, "It was good here, wasn't it?"

"Yes, it was fine," he said sleepily.

"Well, we're parting, Yuri," she said calmly. Yuri thought she even smiled.

Sharok didn't understand right away.

"I don't get it."

"I said that we're parting, Yuri, and this time forever."

"What brought this on?"

"Nothing. It's not something I decided today. But I wanted to part on a pleasant note, a happy one."

"Is that why you brought me here?"

"Yes."

"Well, it's a beautiful, elegant gesture. The queen getting rid of her consort. But I'd like to know why."

"Why?" She leaned away, rolled onto her back with her hands

behind her head. "Do I need to give a reason? You and I aren't children, we're not young lovers. These meetings arranged by phone.... Don't think that I'm leading up to marriage."

"Why not? Maybe I want to marry you."

She laughed. "Maybe you do. But maybe I don't."

Although he had no intention of marrying her, his pride was hurt. "And how don't I suit you? I'd like to know."

"You suit me and I seem to suit you. But that's here or on some other bed. But bed isn't all of life."

"Are you being jealous about Vika again?"

"How do you know that I knew about your affair with Vika? I never said anything."

"You didn't, but I knew anyway. I'm supposed to know everything." Sharok liked using that phrase, whether it was appropriate or not.

"Well, you're right: I did know. I also knew why and in what capacity Vika went to that special apartment you use."

He raised himself on his elbow. Something was wrong here. She knew that Vika was an informer? How had she found out? Had Vika confessed? Now he had a problem.

"And in what capacity did she come to me?"

"I do not wish to discuss it."

He heard the iron firmness of the Budyagins in her voice.

"I'm not interested in that. And it certainly won't go any further. Don't worry, I will never do you any harm. You know that perfectly well. When I saw Vika I was outraged and broke off with you. But later I realized my mistake. So that incident has nothing to do with this. Why are we parting? I didn't want to tell you, but if you insist, I will. I'm pregnant again. I'm going to have a baby. And as you may suspect, I'm not going to have another abortion. I'm going to have a son or daughter. I'm not holding you to anything. Or asking for child support. And I won't register you as the father — I know you don't want that."

Fine news!

But what astonished him even more was her new, calm, imperious voice.

"Why —" Sharok began, but she interrupted: "Don't argue! What we're talking about is too serious."

She hadn't raised her voice, but she meant it.

"Neither of us needs that marriage, and you need it even less than I, so why argue?"

Sharok got up and went to the window, where he stood for a long time.

She was right. She didn't need him, and he didn't need her. He couldn't enter a strange family, live constantly with that inner tension, thinking about every word.

But he was astonished by Lena's insight. He clearly had underestimated her.

"We're strangers, Yuri. We have differing views, values. We barely understand each other. I can see you trying to adjust to me, not saying what you think. It's hard; at any rate, it's a burden."

"What do you mean?"

"I mean your story about Sasha, that you got him three years of exile instead of the camps, and that his arrest was a threat to you. Nonsense! You just want me to think well of you, and I persuaded myself that it was true."

Sharok said nothing.

"And with Vika. It really wasn't appropriate . . . to mix her into our lives."

He sat down next to Lena on the bed, took her hand, and smiled. "Then why did you visit me in the hospital?"

"How could I not . . . I was worried about you. Nina told me you were carried out on a stretcher to the ambulance. And I felt sorry for you. It's very lonely in the hospital when no one visits."

"I see . . . you just pitied me. . . . I had hoped that you loved me."

"Me?" She pondered. "I don't know. I doubt it. . . . But I want us to part amicably, I want us to part on a sunny holiday in May, so that we can remember it just this way."

He shouldn't have brought up the hospital, it gave her an opportunity to humiliate him, to show her superiority. He hadn't visited her in the hospital, when she was dying, dying because of the abortion he had urged her to have, but she came to see him after a simple operation. She was better and nobler.

Now, pregnant, she was taking everything on herself, freeing him of worry, responsibility, financial cares. They must have discussed it in the family, probably her father, Ivan Grigoryevich, himself, had said, "We'll manage without that scoundrel of yours. Have the baby!" Showing once again that they were aristocrats and he was the plebeian, a nobody.

There was nothing he could say. But he had to do something, he had to get out of this with dignity.

"We had a wonderful time," Yuri said. "Let's not spoil it with this discussion. Once we're back in Moscow and you've calmed down, we can talk about it again."

She shook her head. "We'll never talk about it again. We'll never see each other again, Yuri — it's over."

She reached for her watch on the night table, got up, and started to dress. As if nothing had happened, she said, "There are two buses today, at seven and at eight. I signed us up for seven, I want to get home early. Dinner is a half hour early so that we can make the seven o'clock bus. So, hurry up, dear Yuri!"

## ❧ 4 ❧

**V**arya started studying at the Construction Institute. Not the day classes, as Nina had suggested, but in the evening. The stipend was small, Varya claimed, and she didn't want to be a burden on Nina.

Nina was not convinced. Millions of students managed on their stipends. Of course, she would have had to live modestly, but everyone lived modestly nowadays. The country was making every effort to create a mighty socialist state. And you had to give your all for that great goal. Overcoming incredible deprivations, Varya's peers were freezing in earth huts and barracks, building factories and hydroelectric stations. Students were crowded into dormitories with six to a room and eating in cheap student canteens. Yet Varya had a room on the Arbat, so she could certainly take the day shift.

In principle, Nina had nothing against the evening classes. But why lie? Nina knew her sister well. . . . Taking night courses freed Varya from the basic political duties at work, and work freed her from those duties at the institute. She herself had admitted, "Thank God, now I won't have to go to these meetings. Let the others raise their hands and praise their 'genius and wise man,' the sheep!"

She said that to Nina, a Party member! Arguing with Varya was useless, but such bitterness and intransigence at her age was astonishing!

She had hung a picture of Sasha Pankratov over her bed. Nina had the same picture in her album, one of ordinary size, but this was an enlargement, framed, under glass. In a prominent spot. Nina kept a portrait of Comrade Stalin over her desk, while Varya had

Sasha Pankratov, exiled to Siberia under Article 58 —
"Counterrevolutionary Agitation and Propaganda." When people
came to see Nina, they recognized Sasha. What was she supposed to
do, not let people into their room?

"Why did you hang up Sasha's photo?" Nina asked.

"What's it to you?"

"We share this room. We have to consider each other."

"Did you ask me before hanging our best train engineer?" She
pointed to Stalin.

"Why train engineer?"

"The railroad workers call him 'our best train engineer, Stalin.' "

"How dare you! I hung up a portrait of Comrade Stalin when
you weren't here, when you were living with your billiard-hustling
husband. I respect Comrade Stalin."

"And I respect Comrade Pankratov," Varya replied calmly.

"Go ahead and admire him, but keep it to yourself. There's no
need to advertise! Who is he to you? Husband? You had a different
one. Fiancé? Then why didn't you wait for him, instead of
marrying that hustler? You didn't even know him in school. He's
no one to you. No one! Why do you hang up his picture then? For
effect? What do you think it's going to lead to? I'm warning you.
If you don't take it down, I will."

"If you touch Sasha's picture, I'll take down your mustached one,
take it out into the hallway, and tear it up in front of everyone. And
don't doubt for a second that I won't do it."

Nina exploded in anger. A psychopath, that's what Varya was!
She's turned Sasha into an idol — she was a new Magdalene, and he
was the new Christ. A fanatic! She could get five years for just
one-hundredth of what she was babbling. And Nina would have to
answer for her behavior. What could she say? That she didn't know
what her own sister was thinking? The one she shared a room
with?

"I forbid you to talk to me like that! I forbid it!"

"Should I just stay silent?"

"Yes, shut up if you have nothing else to talk about. I'm a
Communist and I won't listen to anti-Soviet lies!"

"Anti-Soviet? Am I saying anything against Soviet power? I'm
for Soviet power, I just can't stand your father and teacher!"

"Don't you dare speak like that about Comrade Stalin! Comrade Stalin and Soviet power are one and the same."

"For you!"

"Not just for me, for the whole Party, for all the people."

"Don't speak for all the people. You're tricking them all with your lies!"

Footsteps in the hall stopped at their door. Just what they needed. Because of Sasha's photo, that bitch next door, Vera Stanislavovna, would start eavesdropping on them.

"I repeat," Nina whispered, "I forbid you to talk to me like that, understand?" Her face was red and she was chopping the air with her hands. "I forbid it! And I forbid you to talk like that not only to me but to anyone else."

"I don't have to talk to you," Varya said, her voice lower, too, "but what I do with others is my own business. And stop waving your arms about!"

"Don't you realize how you're going to end up?"

"No way. I talk only with decent people."

"It's your business. But if you talk like that in front of me again, somebody will leave this apartment forever."

"I'm not stopping you." Varya narrowed her eyes. "Of course . . . you can always send me off to Butyrki prison."

"If you don't start thinking about what you're doing, I may have to."

"Well, it would be very natural and logical for you. But then you'll have to bring me parcels." Varya sang:

> "Don't walk on ice,
> The ice will break.
> Don't love a thief
> He'll be arrested.
> He'll be arrested
> He'll be in jail,
> And you won't like
> Bringing him parcels."

"Stop playing the fool!" Nina shouted.

"Of course, you wouldn't bring me parcels — after all, I'm

anti-Soviet. Others will. All right," she said, standing, "don't worry, we won't talk about that anymore."

Their conversations on that topic and all others stopped. What did they have to talk about? Each led her own life.

But that didn't suit Nina either. These were harsh times. The country, surrounded by external enemies, was struggling with internal enemies too. The slightest doubt in Stalin meant doubt in the Party, disbelief in the work of socialism. Only unlimited, unconditional faith could rouse millions of people to the construction of a new society. Only unlimited, unconditional faith could guarantee success. In combat you don't think twice — you can't, you obey orders, not discuss them. Her sister not only had doubts, she didn't believe. She rejected everything that was dear and holy for Nina and for millions of Soviet people. First it was boys, dances, restaurants, then that billiard-playing husband, a thief and a crook, now it was anti-Sovietism. Where would it all lead? How would Varya end up? And what was in store for Nina? It wasn't a question of fear, it was a question of her Party honesty. In covering up for Varya, she was condoning anti-Soviet conversation, which meant she was condoning anti-Soviet agitation. Thereby she was committing a crime before the Party; she was a collaborator.

What could she do? Go to Varya's boss and talk to him? Inform the Party organization? Denounce her own sister? That would be horrible! They would put Varya away and everyone would know that her own sister had done it. But she couldn't keep silent, either.

Should she talk with the school director, Alevtina Fyodorovna? Nina was her favorite, a Komsomol, an activist — Alevtina Fyodorovna liked that. When Nina graduated from the Pedagogical Institute, she took her into the school to teach history. She didn't let them send her to work in the boondocks. And when Nina wanted to circulate a petition at the time of Sasha Pankratov's arrest, Alevtina Fyodorovna read it and tore it up. "This document never existed."

And a month later she gave Nina a recommendation to help her join the Party.

Nina trusted Alevtina Fyodorovna unequivocally. The short, plump woman with straight limp hair, pince-nez on her round

Moravian face, a participant in the Civil War and Party member since 1919, embodied the Party conscience for Nina and was a role model for her.

And yet, telling her about Varya meant shifting the burden of responsibility onto her. She would know about them, and knowing in these times was being responsible. Nina hesitated, unable to decide what to do. Chance helped her. Alevtina Fyodorovna called her in for a confidential talk.

Alevtina Fyodorovna had been sent from the People's Commissariat of Education to shape up the school, which was notorious for its elitist student body, its reactionary teaching staff, and the unextinguished spirit of the old days.

Alevtina Fyodorovna destroyed that spirit. Young teachers came, among them Nina. Pioneer and Komsomol organizations appeared, and the old obstructionist Parents' Council was replaced by a new, loyal one.

The school stopped being a closed caste institution, as it had been before the Revolution. Now it was an ordinary regional middle school.

But Alevtina Fyodorovna turned into the director of an ordinary middle school. And she had once held a responsible post in the Commissariat and other responsible posts before that. She had been sent to the school temporarily but then been forgotten. For years she waited for a new posting that hadn't come. In effect, she had been demoted.

The aura of lofty significance with which she came to the school dimmed. Her militancy became unnecessary, inappropriate, even silly. Her demanding nature turned to pickiness, her severity to irritability. And then, having had a classical pedagogical training, she gradually came to an understanding with the old teachers, those who demanded knowledge from students, who did not give higher grades to activists, and who rejected pedological experiments. Having discovered that the eighth-graders knew the social genesis of *Hamlet* but not where to put commas, she fired the young language and literature teacher and brought back the old one who had taught the children syntax and punctuation.

Her old friends passed on to her the new resolution of the

Education Commissariat and the Central Committee. It said that history teaching was too abstract, that what students needed was to have historic figures and chronology in their memories.

The teachers had gotten used to the formula — the history of mankind is the history of class struggle, and historical figures were merely manifestations of their interests. Now were they supposed to return to concepts that interpreted history as the actions of great men?

Alevtina Fyodorovna reacted calmly to the new resolution. As a representative of high Party policies, she was never surprised by any changes in that policy. She did not feel any piety for the higher echelons; she had seen the state leaders from close up, could have been one herself.

She knew that the assertion of the individual's role in history meant heightening the role of Stalin. But didn't the individual play an important role? Could the October Revolution have happened without Lenin? Stalin was getting more attention in his lifetime than Lenin ever did. But they were not comparable. Lenin did not need proof of his prestige, and that's what made him Lenin, while Stalin needed it, for he was merely Stalin. But Stalin's authority was the authority of the Party and its cadres, to whom Stalin owed everything.

The new history textbooks weren't yet written, but they could no longer use the old ones. That was why Alevtina Fyodorovna had called in Nina. They were organizing an All-Union summer seminar of historians. The best teachers were being sent, ones who could then lead city and regional seminars for teachers. Alevtina Fyodorovna was proposing Nina.

"Thank you, Alevtina Fyodorovna, I'll try to be equal to it."

"You are," Alevtina Fyodorovna said. "The decision will be made tomorrow, so go to the committee the day after and get the official invitation. You'll have to take good notes so that you can use them for lecture material later."

"I'll remember everything and write down everything."

She wondered whether or not to bring up Varya.

Alevtina Fyodorovna looked at her closely. "What's worrying you?"

Nina laughed and said, "Nothing much."

"Tell me!" ordered Alevtina Fyodorovna.

"My sister, Varya, do you remember her?"

"Of course I do, a beauty. What's happening to her?"

"She married some billiard-player, wanted the good life, then she divorced him and now she's upset, in a bad mood, and so on."

Alevtina Fyodorovna regarded her intently.

Nina stopped, unable to say "anti-Soviet talk." She understood that she shouldn't be talking about it. Alevtina Fyodorovna would take it very seriously, without sentimentality, and the consequences could be unexpected and severe.

"Well?" Alevtina Fyodorovna asked.

"Nothing. You asked what was worrying me, and I told you." She smiled, as if in apology for her momentary weakness.

"The seminar is planned for Leningrad, but it may take place in Moscow, in the Red Professors Institute."

Leningrad would be better. She'd be out of Moscow and away from Varya for two months. Living with her was getting very hard.

# ❧ 5 ❧

Varya was happy that she had taken the evening courses. Now no one at work could drag her to meetings, because she would just say, "But what about the institute?" Besides which, she was allowed extra days off, for exam preparation, and the evening division had almost no extracurricular courses like political economy and she could skip boring lectures by blaming her job.

And most important, the evening division was easy. Among her classmates, simple construction workers, foremen, and such, she was head of the class with her good education and talent for math. She never studied at home, and there wasn't much homework anyway. She was free by nine, which left her time to visit Sofya Alexandrovna or go to the movies.

One day, coming back from the library, Varya ran into Vika.

Vika embraced Varya, kissed her, then took out her hankie, scented with Coty, and wiped the lipstick from Varya's cheek. Beautiful and well dressed, in a light beige coat and beige beret, animated, she attracted attention and people turned to look at her.

"Varya, dear, I'm so happy to see you."

Was Varya happy? It was hard to tell. A stranger, really. But she recalled New Year's Eve, when Sasha was there, the restaurant where Varya had gone for the first time and met Levochka's crowd. And she smiled at Vika.

"Where are you going?" Vika asked.

"Home."

"Would you like to drop by my place?" Vika offered.

"No, I'm expected at home."

Vika walked next to Varya, looking at her, smiling merrily, and it seemed that she really was glad they met. As before, when they knew each other, Vika emanated another life, insouciant, the life of successful happy people who could do whatever they wanted. Varya knew that it wasn't so, that there were no people who could do whatever they wanted. But there was that aura. The life no longer attracted her, but she remembered how once it had.

"I heard you've divorced Kostya," Vika said.

"Yes," Varya replied, not wanting to talk about it.

"Forgive me, but I never approved of your marriage, I knew how it would end. I'm sorry you didn't ask me, talk to me first. After all, Varya, I always wanted nothing but good for you, and I still do — I always liked you. But you broke off our friendship so abruptly, without any reason. Did I hurt you in some way?"

"It just happened," Varya said with restraint.

"I see." Vika nodded sympathetically. "We are all slaves of our passions. You've probably heard whom I've married?"

"I have."

"He's a wonderful man, the most decent, and the rest I don't need to discuss — he's a talent. He loves me. But I never see him. He leaves early in the morning and comes back late at night, and sometimes he sleeps in his studio. But what can I do? He's possessed, like all geniuses. . . . And I have to put up with it. But it's a bit boring."

"You should get a job."

"Get up at six? Get jostled in the trolley across town? I have to deal with the house, and take care of my husband, my father, and Vadim. I've told you how my husband works. My father is no better. He's at the institute, and the clinic, and at the Kremlin hospital. When he's called in at night, I have to see him off, feed him. In effect, I'm a housewife. Vadim has become a famous critic, with a powerful column. Journalists also have crazy lives. They stay at the editorial office until morning. Three such personalities demand care, and I serve them." She squinted at Varya and added, "My men won't even hear of my getting a job."

Varya chuckled to herself. She had mentioned everything except Fenya, the maid, who served Vika coffee in bed.

"Doesn't Fenya work for you anymore?" she asked naïvely.

"She does. But Fenya is Fenya. We have guests who are not ordinary people. They must be received properly, and only I can do that. I'm not complaining. I'm simply telling you about my life. I don't go out anymore. And no one comes to see me. Varya, you should drop in sometime."

"When? I work during the day and am at the institute at night."

"Really? Good for you! Which one?"

"Construction."

"Marvelous! I have lots of friends who are architects, construction engineers. Do you need some help?"

"No," Varya said, "I don't need any help."

"Well, just keep it in mind. I'm not talking about my husband alone. I mean my own friends . . . people with reputations. . . . Just one word from them and you'll have what you want."

"I don't need anything," Varya said angrily.

"Fine — if you don't, then you don't."

Vika stopped. "You haven't lost my number?"

"No."

"Good. Then call me, come over, we'll have a nice chat. . . ."

## 6

The mail started coming regularly in mid-February. Sasha got the newspaper for December and January; the February ones arrived in March.

After Kirov's murder by Nikolaev, the newspapers were filled almost daily with long lists of terrorists who had been smuggled in from abroad and then caught and executed in Moscow, Leningrad, Kiev, and Minsk. The impression created was that they were ones who had killed Kirov.

However, in late December 1934 the newspapers announced that Kirov's murder had been organized by the Zinovievites, former leaders of the Leningrad Komsomol, who had also wanted to kill Stalin and other Party and state leaders.

All the defendants were immediately shot.

And in January 1935, Zinoviev, Kamenev, Evdokimov, Bakayev, and other major Party figures of the past, twenty people in all, were on trial. Their direct participation in Kirov's murder was not proved, and yet Zinoviev got ten years and the others eight, six, or five.

The trial was instantaneous, without defense counsel, but the theory that the Zinovievites had participated in the murder seemed convincing. Who else could have done it? After all, Nikolaev had been a Zinovievite, according to the papers, and all his comrades were Zinovievites, and of course Zinoviev and Kamenev bore the moral responsibility for them. Sasha doubted that they had deserved such harsh punishment, but still, Kirov had been killed! Not by Zinoviev or Kamenev, but by their cohorts.

Back in 1917 Zinoviev and Kamenev had revealed the uprising to the Provisional Government. And in 1926 they had united with Trotsky, who had been declared the most vicious foe of the Party a year earlier. How could the Party relax now, facing the Fascist threat, when Hitler had created an infantry of a half-million men and a powerful air force, and was threatening war? The Party had to respond blow for blow, even though this led to unfortunate mistakes and the death of the innocent.

As Sasha read the papers closely, he tried to find in the hysteria and hatred a vestige of what he held dear, what the country was living for, what he had lived for all his life.

Sometimes Sasha dropped in to see Lidya Grigoryevna Zvyaguro, who still lived at Lariska's, sewing on the machine and by hand, working hard, especially for Kezhma customers. Lariska treated her respectfully and helpfully, because now women came to her house, the house of a divorcée, to discuss what to sew and how, and she participated in this, and her role in the village became respectable. She was in on all the events not only here, but in Kezhma itself. And maybe, she simply feared Lidya Grigoryevna — an imperious woman who knew how to instill respect.

Her son, Tarasik, usually sat on a bench, a quiet boy, playing with a small piece of wood. Lidya Grigoryevna wasn't talkative either — she looked old, was unattractive, and had buck teeth.

Sasha brought her the newspapers, and a few days later she would return them, rarely commenting. But she did say about the Zinoviev-Kamenev trial, "The show's beginning."

"They did kill Kirov," Sasha countered.

"You can write whatever you want in the newspapers," Zvyaguro said acidly. "Zinoviev and Kamenev would never do that, and they didn't need to do it. Kirov's death benefited only one man."

Sasha knew which man she meant.

"But the Party, the people —"

"We don't have a Party," Zvyaguro interrupted. "We have cadres who obediently carry out his policies. He hates the Party and is destroying it and he hates the people and he's destroying them, too."

Sasha ran his eyes over the newspaper pages. "Here's what Stalin says about the people: 'People have to be nurtured attentively, the way a gardener nurtures a beloved fruit tree.' "

Lidya Grigoryevna interrupted him again. " 'Gardener,' 'tree.' How many millions of those 'trees' has he already chopped down in the villages? How many millions have died of hunger?"

"And about the countryside," Sasha persisted, "this is what he said: 'The kolkhoz should have its own private plots, small, but private. . . . There are families, children, personal needs and personal tastes, and that has to be taken into account.' "

" 'Personal tastes,' " mocked Lidya Grigoryevna. "And you believe that nonsense? Of course, he knows that the peasants have to eat something or they'll all die out — and then whom will he rule? You don't know him, but I do. I saw him for many years as closely as I see you now. People, lives — they mean nothing to him. He's worse than a criminal, and he'll not stop at murder if he needs something. He's an actor; he can play any role. Now he's talking about the people, flattering the people. All tyrants do that. The smart tyrant always flatters the people with words, while with deeds he destroys them. Don't you ever think that?"

Yes, Sasha had had such thoughts, and how could he not? But reading Stalin's speeches, he tried to understand the man in his own way, not the way that Lidya Grigoryevna presented him.

"Nothing to say?"

She looked at Sasha mockingly and then her eyes rested on his trouser cuffs.

"Why do you go around so ragged?"

Sasha blushed. This was his only pair of trousers, the suit his uncle Mark had given him.

"I trim the frayed edges with scissors."

"Clever. . . . Sit behind the curtain and I'll repair your pants properly."

Sasha went behind the curtain, took the newspaper with him, and went on reading:

We have in a number of cases facts of cruelly bureaucratic and completely outrageous behavior toward workers. Often people are thrown around like pawns. We must learn to value people, value cadres, value every worker who can be of benefit to our common work. We must understand, at last, that of all the valuable capital in the world the most valuable and most decisive capital is people, the cadres.

That was about him, about Sasha, about people like Sasha. That's what he should have read to Lidya Grigoryevna.

But it felt stupid to talk without his trousers from behind a curtain.

Then Lidya Grigoryevna handed him his trousers. "Get dressed!"

Sasha was planning to leave right away, but Lidya Grigoryevna detained him. "You forgot your newspapers. There are photos of your Stalin everywhere. It turns out that he even led the proletarian regiments in the storming of the Winter Palace."

And there really was a picture of Comrade Stalin in every issue, sometimes even two or three — Stalin alone, Stalin and Lenin, Stalin and Voroshilov, Stalin and Molotov, Stalin and kolkhoz workers, Stalin and soldiers, Stalin and laborers, drawings of Stalin, sculptures of Stalin.

There were victories in the Civil War. The defense of Tsaritsyn, the taking of Rostov, Perm, the Eastern front, smashing Denikin's army — all Stalin.

In October 1917, according to the historian I. I. Mints, "Stalin, performing Lenin's role, led the Bolshevik regiments against the bourgeois government." Ah, this is what Lidya Grigoryevna was so sarcastic about. And it truly was a lie! All the achievements were attributed to Stalin. Everywhere it was Stalin who won victories.

Back in the institute, Sasha had been offended by praise of Stalin, his books, articles, speeches, and works — they seemed primitive to Sasha. The endless repetition, the slowness — "First of all," "secondly," "thirdly," that confining schematicism, the ban on the slightest doubt about any of his thoughts, any of his words — that had a chilling effect.

But it didn't offend others. It delighted them. Could they all be wrong and the ones like him right?

He must not have understood that Stalin had to talk that way, so that the people could understand him, believe him, follow him. These people had lived through centuries of serfdom and backwardness. You had to know how to talk to them, their level had to be raised, but that level had to be taken into account. Sasha was part of the people. He couldn't live without what he had grown up with, his faith in the country and the Party. He had to be with the Party and the country. No matter how he personally felt about Stalin, Stalin now personified them.

For some reason, Sasha kept thinking about writing to Stalin. Everyone was writing to Stalin now. Stalin couldn't possibly read a thousandth of those letters and he wouldn't read Sasha's. It wouldn't even reach him. But still, in appealing to Stalin, he would do his duty. No matter what happened to him, however his life went, he could tell himself, "I had appealed to Stalin."

Two years ago, at the institute, when his sorrowful epic began, he did not feel he had the right to appeal to Stalin, to impose on his time. He thought he could defend himself. Now he couldn't, and only Stalin could help him, otherwise he'd have a new sentence, maybe even the camps — and his life would be over. He would appeal to Stalin because he, Sasha Pankratov, was that "little man" Stalin talked about, the one who would work honestly, diligently doing his work, doing his duty.

Sasha thought about his letter for a long time, weighing every word.

Respected Comrade Stalin!

Forgive me for daring to address you. By the resolution of the Special Meeting of the OGPU on May 20, 1934, I was sentenced under Article 58 to three years of exile in Siberia with time off for my time in prison. I have served over half my term. But I do not know what I was convicted of. I am not guilty of anything. I studied in a Soviet school, a Soviet college. I was a Pioneer, a Komsomol. I worked in a factory. I want to be useful to the country, but I am doomed to inactivity. It is impossible to live this way. I am requesting a review of my case.

With deep respect,
A. Pankratov

He wrote the letter, but he didn't send it, he didn't dare.

Was he being honest? No matter what he thought, what conclusions he reached, in his heart he did not change toward Stalin.

On the contrary, after all he had seen and heard, his doubts about Stalin had increased. And now he was appealing to him. He was persuading himself that he wanted to work, to serve the country and the Party, but wasn't he simply trying to save himself, his life, to change his fate?

And wasn't it naïve to write such a letter? Would it get there or not? Would it be read or not? Would his case be reviewed or not? Of course it wouldn't get there, wouldn't be read, and his case wouldn't be reviewed. Why start the whole thing, why give it to the NKVD to be read? For that's where it would end up.

And yet, and yet . . .

## ❧ 7 ❧

On May 14, 1935, Stalin came to the Hall of Columns at the House of Unions for a special meeting dedicated to the start of the Moscow Metropolitan subway service.

Looking at the young people in the audience — the builders of the metro — at their joyful, happy faces turned only to *him*, waiting only for *his* words, he thought that the young people were for *him*, that the young people who grew up in *his* era were *his*. *He* gave them an education, the opportunity to do their duty and participate in the great transformation of the country. Their age, the most romantic, would always be tied in their memories with *him*, their youth would be forever illuminated by *his* name, and they would carry their loyalty to *him* throughout their lives. *He* must open the way to power for them, because they would be in *his* debt and only *his*.

Bulganin interrupted his thoughts. "Comrade Stalin has the floor."

Stalin walked to the tribune.

The audience rose. . . .

The ovation lasted forever. . . .

Stalin raised his hand, asking for quiet, but the audience would not stop. They applauded in rhythm. It was like the beat of a huge drum, and every blow was accompanied by the thundering chant of just one word — "Stalin! Stalin!"

Stalin was accustomed to ovations. But today's were special. He was being hailed not by clerks, not by Komsomol bureaucrats, but by simple workers — concrete workers, electricians, welders — the builders of the first subway system in the land. This was the people, the best of the people, the future of the people.

The applause shook the room. The young men and women jumped up on their seats shouting, "Long live Comrade Stalin! A Komsomol hurrah for the great leader Comrade Stalin!"

Stalin took out his watch, picked it up, and showed the audience that it was time to stop. They responded with even more noise.

Stalin showed the watch to the Presidium. They smiled, thrilled to be part of the touching simple communion of the leader with the people. And, in deference to Stalin's demand, so democratically put, the members of the Presidium started sitting down.

The audience sat down too, but continued clapping.

"Comrades," Stalin said with a smile, "don't be too quick to applaud; you don't know what I'm going to say."

The audience responded with laughter and more applause.

"I have two corrections," Stalin went on. "The Party and the state have rewarded you for the successful construction of the Moscow Metropolitan, some with the Order of Lenin, others with the Order of the Red Star, still others with the Order of the Red Banner of Labor, and yet others with a certificate of the Central Executive Committee. But here's the question — what about the rest? How about those comrades who put in their labor, their knowledge, their efforts as well? Some of you are happy and others are not sure. What should be done? There's the question."

He paused as silence filled the room.

"So," Stalin said, "we want to correct this mistake of the Party and state before the entire world."

The audience erupted in laughter and applause.

Raising his hand, Stalin called for silence and went on. "I do not like to give long speeches, so please let me read the corrections."

He took out a piece of paper, folded in four, from his breast pocket, and opened it.

"The first correction — to proclaim the gratitude of the Central Executive Committee and the Council of People's Commissars of the U.S.S.R. for successful work on the construction of the Moscow Metropolitan to the shock-workers and the whole collective of engineers, technicians, and laborers."

More thunderous applause.

Everyone rose, and so did the Presidium. There were shouts. Stalin, smiling, stood on the tribune, no longer trying to quiet them down — the ovations were not only for him, but for the government that had expressed its thanks to the subway workers and for the workers who had earned that high gratitude.

When the audience quieted at last, Stalin said, "The correction on thanking all the workers will be made today." With a wave of his hand he stopped the new wave of applause. "Don't applaud me, it is the decision of all the comrades. And the second correction," Stalin looked at the piece of paper in front of him, "I will read — 'for special merit in mobilizing the valiant Komsomols for the successful construction of the Moscow Metropolitan, the Moscow organization of the Komsomol is awarded the Order of Lenin.'"

Another squall of applause. This time Stalin applauded, too, honoring the Moscow Komsomol.

And when he stopped applauding, so did the audience.

"This correction must also be entered today and published tomorrow.... Perhaps that is not enough, comrades, but we couldn't come up with anything more. If there is anything else we can do, let us know."

With a wave, Stalin headed for the Presidium.

The ovation was even greater. "Three cheers for our beloved Stalin!" and the audience roared, "Hurrah! Hurrah! Hurrah!" A girl leaped up onto a chair and shouted, "Three Komsomol cheers for Comrade Stalin!" And once again the rows all cheered, "Hurrah! Hurrah! Hurrah!"

The ovations lasted about ten minutes. Standing and cheering. Stalin stood with the Presidium silently and looked out into the audience. No, these were not the ones who had applauded him a year and a half ago at the Seventeenth Congress; they had applauded insincerely. These people were *his*.

Of course, by its very nature, youth is unstable. Young people grow old, and new ones come along, and room has to be made for them — a constant and painful process.

But renewing cadres is an inevitable process. The important thing was to have the new people be *his* cadres. The new ones don't think about the fact that their predecessors are being destroyed — in taking power they are convinced of its unshakability. And when the time comes for them to go, they will not blame Comrade Stalin, they will blame their rivals. Comrade Stalin will always be the one who raised them to power.

This is what Stalin thought as he looked at the agitated, joyous audience, wild with delight.

Yes, they were sincerely loyal to *him*, with unlimited loyalty, to the end. *He* had to say something else, something simple, human, that would reach everyone's heart, win them over not only with *his* majesty, but with *his* simplicity.

When the applause died down at last, he asked softly, but so that everyone could hear, "What do you think, was that enough corrections?"

A storm of applause broke out with new force.

Everyone stood up.

The Presidium applauded, standing too. Stalin, Molotov, Kaganovich, Voroshilov, Ordzhonikidze, Chubar, Mikoyan, Yezhov, and Mezhlauk applauded. This went on forever. People couldn't move, couldn't leave, couldn't part with Stalin. This was their day, maybe the only day in their lives when they would see Stalin. They wanted to make it last, they wanted to hear from Stalin.

But Stalin had already spoken, he wouldn't speak again, and then someone cried, "Kaganovich now!"

And the audience picked up the cry, "Kaganovich! Kaganovich!"

Kaganovich looked at Stalin in bewilderment. Should he speak after him?

But Stalin said, "Well, Lazar, the people are waiting — talk to the people."

Kaganovich got up on the tribune.

## § 8

After the meeting in the Hall of Columns, Stalin went to Kuntsevo without stopping at the Kremlin, to his new dacha, built last year — a light one-story building in the middle of a garden and the woods. A solarium as wide as the roof. He didn't use the solarium, but let it be. If he didn't like it, they'd build a second story. A covered passage connected the dacha to the service section.

This was the first time Stalin was coming to a house that was ready and waiting for him.

At last *he* was done with Zubalovo, with that chicken coop, where *his* so-called relatives were settled. The old Alliluyevs, who never forgave *him* the death of Nadya, their son Pavel — the one who had given Nadya the revolver with which she shot herself — Nadya's sister, a fat, slovenly fool, in love with her husband, Redens, a handsome man who slept with whomever he could, a coarse, haughty, and offensive Pole.

*He* couldn't stand the Svanidze family either — the relatives of *his* first wife, Ekaterina. *He* had never loved her — a taciturn, docile, but limited, religious woman, alien to *him* in every way. She had hoped that *he* would give up the Revolution and become a priest, she didn't understand a thing. And her sister was bringing up Yasha, his son, the same way — a taciturn teenager who was a stranger to *him*. And now *his* first wife's brother, Alyosha Svanidze, was bringing Yasha, whom *he* basically did not know and never saw, to Moscow.

To study, he said! As if there were no colleges in Tiflis? No, that's not why. He brought the boy to stress that *he* was not interested in the fate of *his* son, and that his uncle, Alyosha Svanidze, has to take care of his education.

*He* had a new family. Why bring in a stepson? A stranger, unloved, who barely spoke Russian? This was nothing other than an attempt to break up *his* family. Nadya had been tactful. If Yasha were sent back, people would think that she had not accepted him, and for her the important thing was what people said.

This was the surprise *his* dear brother-in-law Alyosha Svanidze had given *him*. And that wasn't the only one. He called his own son Johnreed. What kind of a name was that! In 1929! Georgian? Russian? No, neither Russian nor Georgian. It was the name of that John Reed who wrote the lying book perverting the history of the October uprising, a book hailing Trotsky and not mentioning *him*, Stalin, even once. That book had been taken out of the libraries; people got five years in the camps for owning it. And *his* own brother-in-law, Alyosha Svanidze, gave his own son that name. He didn't know who John Reed was? He certainly did. He was an intellectual. Educated. He had studied not at the Tiflis seminary but in Germany, in Jena. He knew European languages, so he understood very well and had named his son that just to annoy *him*.

He married an opera singer, Maria Anisimovna (obviously not a very good singer if she was willing to leave the opera to live with her husband in Berlin at the trade representation). She brought Nadya all kinds of crap from abroad, inculcating a taste for foreign fashion in *his* wife, corrupting her morally and politically. They had done it on purpose — evil, envious people. But they're afraid of *him*. When they play billiards, Alyosha always loses to *him* and then explains to friends, "If I win he'll chop somebody else's head off for it."

That's what dear Alyosha Svanidze says behind *his* back, that's how he mocks *him* publicly!

And why is there this tender friendship between the Alliluyevs and the Svanidzes? You'd think they would hate one another — the relatives of the first wife and the relatives of the second. Could the Alliluyevs like Yasha? Or the Svanidzes like Vashya and Svetlana? They were united by their hatred of *him*. That's what united them.

But this was it! *His* foot would never step in Zubalovo again. Let them live there without *him*, let them be at one another's throats. Stalin wandered in the garden under the warm May sun, enjoying the flowers. Some were still in bud, the others were blooming. Land should not only give fruit, it should gladden the eye. Stalin liked the tended garden, the clean paths, the neat gazebos, and the open decks, with a table and chaise longue.

It was quiet and peaceful, not like Zubalovo with its bustle, gossip, and arguments. Especially *his* mother-in-law, Olga Yevgenyevna, a nasty old woman, always arguing with the servants, accusing them of wasting state funds, practically accusing them of theft. And this when *he* was there, when people might think that *he* approved of treating the service staff that way. The staff didn't like her, and called her "the crazy woman" behind her back; worst of all, she was constantly, unbearably making noise.

Her father was half Ukrainian and half Georgian and her mother was a German, Magdalene Eichgolz, from the German colonists. She spoke with a Georgian accent, and then she'd add a German phrase: "Mein Gott!" Shaking her fists at the sky, "Mein Gott!" That "Mein Gott!" annoyed *him,* drove *him* up a wall.

Old man Alliluyev, Sergei Yakovlevich, was an idiot! He set up a carpenter's bench, tools, pieces of metal, and he cut and soldered and filed, repairing locks at home and at neighboring dachas. A real proletarian, with "laborer's hands."

*He* comes to the dacha, and then some girl shows up asking Sergei Yakovlevich to come fix their lock.

Eh? How does that look?

*He*'ll be sitting on the veranda, and the neighbor's girl comes asking, "Where's Sergei Yakovlevich?"

"What do you need with him?"

"To fix our lock." *His* dacha was turned into a locksmith's shop! And there was no changing the old man's mind. Physical labor, you see, is ennobling. He was an idealist Marxist. From the society of Old Bolsheviks. He met with them and talked too much, just like them. He was writing his memoirs. He spent half the day fixing other people's locks and half the day writing his memoirs.

What was the society of Old Bolsheviks? A charity home! During the January trial of Zinoviev and Kamenev, they were incensed, even tried to pass some resolutions. Vanya Budyagin made a lot of trouble. You can't try Old Bolsheviks. And why not? Why didn't dear Vanya worry when they exiled Trotsky abroad, when they arrested the other Trotskyites? When they exiled Zinoviev and Kamenev? But he protested the Kirov case. Why? Since he had been a personal friend of Kirov, you'd think that he would have been merciless, yet he was against trying Kirov's murderers and those who instigated the crime. Did he know something? Guess? He tried to get others to protest, write letters, and pass resolutions. But they were too afraid.

A wasp nest! What use were they? Why were they separating from the Party? They wanted to create a special position for so-called Old Bolsheviks, they wanted to be seen as the sole representatives of the Bolshevik tradition, the keepers of Lenin's legacy, the highest Party judges, the "conscience" of the Party. The protectors of its unity. Protecting it from whom? They're not protecting the Party, they're protecting themselves — three-quarters of them were former Trotskyites, Zinovievites, Bukharinites, deviationists and oppositionists of all sorts.

The so-called Old Bolsheviks were convinced that their strength was in unity, monolithic action. They were wrong — that was their weakness. Their ties — working, Party, and friendly — were going to be criminal ties: The evidence of one would be enough to put many under suspicion, the evidence of many would be enough to make the rest guilty.

They were quiet now.

But silence was also a form of protest.

What were they publishing? The anthology, *Old Bolshevik,* and newsletters. What did they write there? They were creating their own history. Not the history needed by the Party but the history they needed, in which there is no place for Comrade Stalin — their own personal recollections, memoirs.

What else were the so-called Old Bolsheviks doing?

Arguing among themselves, comparing achievements, accusing each other of collaborating with the tsarist secret police and thereby compromising the title of Old Bolshevik. Their squabbles had to be refereed, and the Party was doing nothing else. Did Comrade Emelyan Yaroslavsky have any other work?

Incidentally, Comrade Emelyan was chairman of the Old Bolsheviks and also head of the Society of Former Political Convicts and Exiles. Of course, that too was an honor, especially since Emelyan was born in Chita, in a family of political exiles. But Comrade Emelyan should think again about whom the society serves. Another charity, but for Mensheviks, SRs, anarchists, and former criminals who pretend to be political. They publish the journal *Hard Labor and Exile*. Whose names do they mention? They have almost fifty branches all over the Union — who are the people there? What is the purpose of that organization? Alienated people, potential enemies of Soviet power.

Let Comrade Emelyan think about this himself, let him propose to the Central Committee that they liquidate the two societies. Then who could say that Comrade Stalin was getting rid of the Old Bolsheviks? No one....

Yaroslavsky was a smart man, and he knew how to do things. A fine man! In July of 1928 he put Krupskaya in her place at the Plenum of the Central Committee. "She came to the ailing Lenin with complaints about being insulted by Stalin. Shame! You can't mix your personal relations with politics on such big issues."

Well said. Not only did he put down Krupskaya, but he clarified that entire unfortunate episode, showed the real culprit, surpassed *his* nobility, for apologizing, taking the blame so as to spare the ailing Lenin. Fine man!

Emelyan had authority in the Party but never tried to rise to the top positions. He had never fled abroad, he was a real Russian, a practical Bolshevik. Individuals like that had to be preserved in the Party. He never finished school or university, but he was educated, like any self-taught revolutionary. He wrote essays on Party history, knew how to illustrate the role of the true leader, although not completely, as he had to be corrected in 1931, politely. "Unfortunately, Comrade Emelyan is no exception here, his books on the history of the CPSU, despite their merits, contain a number of errors of a fundamental and historical nature." He didn't take offense. He understood. And he'll understand about those charity societies too. The Society of Old Bolsheviks would be liquidated, but the Old Bolshevik Emelyan would remain.

It got cool and Stalin went inside.

He had the large room at the back furnished so that it could serve as study and bedroom, even as a dining room when there were no guests. Only people with nothing to do like wandering from room to room; a busy man must have everything close at hand.

By the couch on which he slept was a table with telephones, against the opposite wall a buffet with dishes and, in one of its drawers, medicines. Stalin did not want a desk. It would have made the place look too much like an office, which was inappropriate in a private house. He could work at a big table, with papers, newspapers, magazines, and on one end they could lay a tablecloth when they brought breakfast, lunch, or dinner.

And now, when he came in, Valechka, the housekeeper from Zubalovo, a cheerful and pretty young woman, was setting the table.

"Hello, Josef Vissarionovich, I've brought your dinner."

She looked at him with adoration and fidelity.

"Thank you," he replied.

Yet he had told Vlasik not to bring a single person from the Zubalovo staff to Kuntsevo.

Valechka covered everything with a cloth.

"Clear in half an hour," Stalin said.

"Fine! It'll be done."

Valechka left.

Stalin ate. He pinched off a piece of bread, put a little butter on it, had a shot glass of dry wine, and a half cup of weak tea. He looked through the newspapers.

In exactly half an hour Valechka returned. "Have you eaten, Josef Vissarionovich?"

Valechka cleared the table, put everything on the tray, smiled at Stalin, went to the door with the tray on one arm.

"Have Vlasik come in!" Stalin ordered.

Stalin finished the newspaper, got up, and paced the room.

There was a carpet on the floor and another rug hung over the couch. The two rugs and the fireplace were all the luxury that he allowed himself.

The door opened and Vlasik stood there at attention, like an ordinary soldier.

Stalin looked at him in the way only Stalin knew how.

Vlasik stood there in terror.

Stalin paced the room again, came back, and stopped in front of Vlasik.

"I gave you an order not to bring a single person from the Zubalovo staff here."

"Yes sir, Comrade Stalin, you did."

"Then why did you disobey?"

"No one was transferred, Comrade Stalin, except for Comrade Valentina Vasilyevna Istomina."

"Why was that done without my permission?"

"You just happened to be away, Comrade Stalin. We had a meeting, discussed it, and decided to transfer only Comrade Istomina, since she, that is, Comrade Istomina, knows how to serve and clear. A tested person."

"With whom did you meet, discuss, and decide?"

"With Comrade Pauker."

Stalin turned away, walked to the glass door leading to the terrace and looked at the garden.

"A big meeting.... And did you discuss it long?"

"Why, ..." Vlasik stopped.

Stalin moved away from the door and shifted the inkwell on his table.

"I asked how long you discussed it — one hour, two, three?"

"An hour," Vlasik whispered, forgetting to add "Comrade Stalin."

Now Stalin was staring at Vlasik.

"So, you're the good man, transferring Istomina here, and I'm the bad one who's going to fire her?"

Vlasik said nothing.

"I'm supposed to fire her?" Stalin repeated.

"Oh, no," Vlasik muttered, "Comrade Stalin, we'll do it instantly."

"Instantly?" Stalin blew up. "Idiot! I'm supposed to fire a person because of an idiot!? I'd rather fire you, you fool.... Met, discussed, and decided.... You idiots!"

Stalin walked back to the glass terrace door and, without turning, said, "Go!"

That night Nikolai Sidorovich Vlasik, a coarse ignoramus, complained of his heart for the first time in his life. And Valechka, suspecting nothing, worked in Kuntsevo to the day Stalin died.

\* \* \*

The western terrace, which adjoined the room, had an entrance into the garden. The last rays of the setting sun broke through the lilacs. Stalin tossed his greatcoat over his shoulders and went back out onto the terrace and sat on a chair.

He should have left Zubalovo a long time ago.

He had changed his Moscow apartment after Nadya's death, but he had held up moving to the dacha, wrongly — while this close one was being built, he could have gone to any of the more distant ones. Just not to Zubalovo.

Before, when she was alive, he put up with the relatives, but after her death everything there reminded him of her. And they reminded him of her. He felt reproach in the eyes of the old people.

Why had she done it?

They said *he* was hard to get along with. And which of the great men was easy? Great men with easy personalities did not exist. A real personality, real character, is always difficult.

Nadya saw the titanic struggle *he* was waging, she saw how *he* was attacked, slandered, intrigued against, or did she not understand the state *he* had inherited and the kind of state *he* had to create? She didn't want to understand! She remained a Petersburg Gymnasium girl from a bourgeois family.

A true aristocrat would not have done it. There was a reason why kings always married women of royal blood, who imbibed with their mother's milk an understanding that the interests of the dynasty come first. Even the daughters of bankrupt German barons understood that. They forgave their ruler husbands everything — infidelities, cruelty — because they knew what ruling meant. Catherine I, Peter the Great's widow, had been a simple servant — she was no tsaritsa. Menshikov could do whatever he wanted with her. But Catherine II the Great, even though she came from a minor princely family, ruled everything herself.

To commit suicide! What king's wife would do that? That had never happened anywhere, ever. They understood what ruling meant! They didn't dare cast a shadow on their reigning spouse. Even incarcerated in a convent, they didn't commit suicide.

She didn't understand *his* significance; she considered *him* only one of the leaders, and she was used to seeing "leaders" in the Kremlin; she didn't understand *his* role, didn't understand her role.

And then she heard all sorts of nonsense in her academy — what did she need with that academy anyway, studying artificial fibers! Hah! It was the scoundrel Abel who persuaded her. She heard all those opposed to *him* there. How did she dare listen to them! She shouldn't have listened! She should have made them stop! She should have behaved in such a way that they wouldn't dare speak of *him*.

And she had listened.

Vain, willful, she wanted to rule everything, and it turned out that she couldn't rule *him*. *He* had to rule. She resisted *him*. *He* could see it — she said nothing but she was against *his* every word. Female! If you don't know how to be a wife, then be a mother. All right, Vasily is a boy, he'll grow up, but Svetlana ... the girl's just six years old, who's going to take care of her? She dumped her on *his* shoulders.

The teachers had complained about Vasily — he was doing badly, misbehaving. *He himself* had gone to the school, *himself* had let people know that *he* does *his* parental duties, like an ordinary Soviet person. But these are the duties of the mother. She had left her duties, deserted, got her revenge on *him* — but for what reason? Because *he* wouldn't go to the theater with her? *He* was busy, so *he* didn't go.

But he had loved her. He remembered the day he saw her when she was just three years old. After his escape from Ufa he came to the Alliluyevs and didn't pay any attention to her, but he remembered that day in Tiflis ... he remembered.

He noticed her in 1912, when he went to the Alliluyevs' house in Petersburg. He saw a beautiful eleven-year-old girl, who looked about thirteen. By Georgian standards, a bride. Serious, reserved, taciturn, as opposed to her sister, Anya.

He began frequenting the Alliluyev house, sometimes spending the night in the small room beyond the kitchen, sleeping on the narrow iron bed.

In February, during Mardi Gras, they went for sleigh rides on low-slung Finnish sleighs, *veikai,* ornamented with multicolored ribbons and bells, pulled by sturdy horses with braided manes. Anya, a big young woman by then, squealed when they bounced over snowbanks and played at being girlish, while Nadya sat quietly, without chatting, a lovely young girl in a round fur hat and fur coat.

And at last, March 1917, spring. He arrived in Petrograd, but the Alliluyevs had moved. They were living near the Toritonovskaya Factory, and he had to get there by train. He found only Anya at home. Nadya was at a music lesson.

When Alliluyev came home, they went to the kitchen and sat around the samovar, and then Nadya appeared in the kitchen door, now a tall slender sixteen-year-old beauty. She resembled her father, Sergei Yakovlevich, whose grandmother was a Gypsy, and Nadya had big black eyes, dusky skin, and white teeth.

She took off her coat, and in her school uniform helped set the table, casting looks at *him* from lowered eyes. And when they sat around the table, she listened silently, attentively, and seriously, listened to *him* talk. And that's why *he* did not keep up Sergei Yakovlevich's political chatter, but talked about *his* exile, about Siberia, about fishing, about how he used to try to go for the mail even when it wasn't *his* turn, just to get out of the housework. *He* was funny.

*He* was given the couch in the dining room that night while Alliluyev slept on another couch. Olga Yevgenyevna and Anya and Nadya slept on the other side of a thin partition. *He* could hear their laughter and muffled voices. Then old man Alliluyev banged his fist on the wall. "Shut up! . . . It's bedtime!"

*He* remembered saying, "Leave them, Sergei, they're young, let them laugh."

*He* had said "young" on purpose. *He* behaved as if *he* were older, their father's friend, but *he* was thirteen years younger than Alliluyev, *he* was only thirty-eight then. He wanted Nadya to notice that difference herself, the wrongness of behaving as if *he* and her father were peers, to think, "You're not old! You're young!" Not say it, but think it.

*He* could see that she was interested in *him*. Not the usual interest in an underground revolutionary who had been in prisons and exile — all young people showed that interest. Her interest was special.

In the morning they all had tea in the dining room. Nadya was very familiar and comfortable by then, she came in from the street with the morning papers and put them on the table, as if for everyone, but *he* felt that it was special attention for *him*.

The Alliluyevs were planning to move closer to the center of town and they decided to have a room for *him*. *He* reminded them, laughing, "Don't forget me.... Get a room for me, too.... Don't forget," *he* repeated as *he* left, and shook *his* finger at them.

When *he* shook *his* finger, Nadya smiled for the first time. *He* remembered that well. That was the first time she smiled not at a joke of *his,* but at *him*.

They rented an apartment on Tenth Rozhdestvenskaya, in building number 17a, a good apartment on the sixth floor — a roomy entry, a large room that was the dining room, and two bedrooms ... and at the end of the corridor, a special room for *him*.

In effect, *he* became a family member. *He* saw Nadya every day — *he* was attracted to that girl, beautiful, silent, mysterious. And she was attracted to *him* — *he* saw that and understood.... But *he* was busy with the Revolution, for the first time *he* was openly and legally busy with the Revolution — it was happening before *his* eyes, *he* was part of it. *He* worked at *Pravda,* and often spent the night there; it was a life on the run. It was a struggle, and *his* fate and the fate of their movement was not clear. How could *he* tie that girl to *his* life, so stormy and changeable?

*He* was twenty-two years older than she. In the Caucasus that wasn't a problem, men older than that married young girls. And girls her age were often interested in older men.

She was a revolutionary idealist like her father; did she regard *him* through rose-colored glasses? But family life wasn't romance, far from it. *He* had tried it once. *He* had a son in Tiflis, whom *he* had rarely seen. *He* used to have a wife — and she was a stranger to *him* too. A family for a revolutionary was a burden ... the Revolution was no time for a wedding. All *his* comrades were already married, but their wives were their comrades in the Party.

Nadya was no mate for *him*. First, *he* had to assert *his* place in the Party. On the very first day back in Petrograd, on March 12 (three had returned together, *he,* Kamenev, and Muranov), it was decided in the Russian Bureau of the Central Committee that Muranov be made a member, but *he,* Stalin, was given only an advisory note "in view of some of his personal traits," and Kamenev was "made one of the workers of *Pravda*," to publish his articles but unsigned, because of his unworthy behavior at the trial in 1914.

The next day *he* made them change the decision. *He* was made a bureau member with a deciding vote and a member of the editorial board of *Pravda* with Olminsky, Eremyev, Kalinin, and Maria Ilyinichna Ulyanova. With that staff, *he* became boss at *Pravda*, and three days later, on March 15, he announced the new makeup of the editorial board — Stalin, Kamenev, and Muranov....

Of course, poor Olminsky protested. But what was the point of these protests? Having arrived in Petrograd on March 12, by March 15 *he* had showed them who the real leader was.

Whether or not the position of *Pravda* had been correct then, whether or not *his* position then had been correct in relation to other socialist parties, to Lenin's April Theses, to Zinoviev and Kamenev's strike-breaking — now it had no meaning, but then it did. In the struggle for the leading role of the Party, *he* maneuvered; it was inevitable in those conditions and it yielded results — during the October Revolution *he* became one of the leaders of the Party, a member of the Politburo of the Central Committee, and a member of the first Soviet government.

But then there was the struggle, the newspaper, the maneuvering. *He* didn't run around to rallies, like the others, *he* worked. *He* went to the end with Lenin, and no one could reproach *him* now of anything.

In those days *he* had no time for personal affairs.

*He* saw Nadya rarely, and although the girl excited him, *he* had no time for it. *He* didn't even have the time to think about it.

She did the thinking for *him*.

That memorable June day. *He* was sitting in the small room of the editorial board, writing. People were coming and going and *he* was irritated by the constant banging of the door. *He* had always hated that sound. But *he* had to put up with it.

And *he* had looked up only once when the door opened.

Nadya was in the door. *He* saw her. Then *he* saw Anya.

They had an empty conversation. Why hadn't he been around for so long? His room was waiting for him. It was all empty. The main thing was that she had come to *him*, that she wanted to see *him*.

Anya said, "You haven't been over in a long time. We're worried about you."

Why worry? They got the papers every morning, read *his* articles, knew that *he* was alive and well.

Nadya had come to see *him*.... She missed *him*. That was important, that was the main thing.

And then, when *he* saw her standing in the door, tall, slender, beautiful, *he* decided that she would be *his* wife.

From that day *he* was home more on Rozhdestvenskaya.

The Alliluyevs took care of *him*, fed *him*, even bought *him* a suit. Anya fussed the most, but the real lady of the house was Nadya, the youngest.

Olga Yevgenyevna and Anya bustled, noisily talking and calling across the apartment, annoying *him* with their shouts. But Nadya, in her apron, diligently swept the apartment, put everything back, she loved order and cleanliness — and she did it all quietly, without fuss or shouting. A real housewife!

In the evening she played the piano, for herself, and when *he* came, she would stop.

"Why did you stop?" *he* would ask.

"Rest," she replied. "I won't bother you."

She was still in school, where she was considered a Bolshevik and mocked as "sweet Kerensky" in class. But *he* heard all this from Olga Yevgenyevna, not from Nadya.

Sometimes they were all at the table together in the evenings. *He* would ask Nadya to play the piano, but she would refuse. Then *he* would ask her to read Chekhov; *he* loved Chekhov and she read well.

Sometimes her girlfriends came to see her. *He* could hear their young, girlish voices.... Then they would switch to French.... *He* was angry that they spoke French to hide something from *him* and would leave in a foul mood. But the fact that Nadya knew French, played the piano, and was serious and reserved attracted *him*.

A year later, in 1918, *he* married her. And took her away to Tsaritsyn. But *he* came back to Moscow and never took her with *him* again.

When did their problems start? ... *He* couldn't say exactly when. It must have been right after Svetlana was born.... Nadya suddenly took Vasya and the infant Svetlana to her parents in Leningrad and announced that she would never return. She called *him* crude, a boor. *He* would have never forgiven anyone else saying that, but *he* forgave her. The woman had just given birth and the hysteria that *he* thought inherent in them comes to the fore.

*He* forgave her, called her in Leningrad and asked her to return, *he* even volunteered to come get her. She replied sarcastically, "Your absence would be too detrimental to the state." And she came back by herself.

What had she meant by those words? *He* thought that it was her usual mockery, the usual female sarcasm. But now *he* knew what it really meant. *His* trip to Leningrad a few months after the Fourteenth Congress, after the destruction of the Zinoviev opposition, after the replacement of the Leningrad leadership, could have been misinterpreted.

Kirov had persuaded her to come back. It was Kirov who did not want *his* presence in Leningrad, even then. That's where their tender friendship had begun.

Just before her death she told *him* that as soon as she finished with the academy, she would go to her sister and brother-in-law, the Redenses, in Kharkov and would work there.

Her talk with the nanny was reported to *him*. "I'm sick of everything, it's all empty, nothing makes me happy," she said to the nanny. What did "nothing" mean? What about the children?

She did everything to spite *him*.

She knew that *he* hated perfume and felt that a woman should smell only of freshness and cleanliness. But she wore perfume, on purpose, and she used foreign perfume that her brother Pavel brought her, and she wore foreign dresses, on purpose, that Pavel and the dear sweet Svanidzes brought her. There she was in the academy among simple Soviet people, smelling of foreign perfume. *His* wife ... Eh?!

And why did Pavel give her a gun? What does a woman need with a gun? Who would ever think of giving a woman a gun? Was he preparing her to murder *him*? After what happened, *he* had Pavel's pass to the Kremlin taken away. That wasn't enough! *He* thought of Pavel with hatred. He had to be punished severely. Let him know!

Now *he* would not marry again.

The people would understand. He had lost his beloved wife and did not want another — that's how the people would see it: a good father, *he* didn't want a stepmother for *his* children. And *he* really didn't want a stepmother for *his* children — new complications, new squabbles, new relations, and what would they be like, the new relatives? Loneliness added to *his* simplicity, which so impressed and pleased the people. There was nobody to take care of *him*.

And there was no gossip about *him*, the security organs weren't fooling *him* about that, *he* was very strict about it, *he* checked closely. *He* gave no cause for gossip.

*He* rarely appeared in public, did not go to factories and plants, did not hold rallies; *he* spoke only on exceptional occasions — congresses, plenums and brief remarks in the press. Each of *his* appearances must be an event, every word must have weight. Pushkin was right —

> *Be taciturn; the tsar's voice*
> *Must not be lost for nothing in the air.*
> *Like sacred bells, it must impart*
> *Great mourning or great joy.*

How well said!

*He* had to watch, check, how the preparations were going for the hundredth anniversary of Pushkin's death. Of course, there was much in Pushkin that was unacceptable, but that had to be directed against Tsar Nicholas I and his court. And they had to use what was necessary and beneficial for us. Too bad that there was no poet of Pushkin's greatness in *his* era.

But it actually made sense that there were no great poets under the reigns of great leaders. What great poets existed under Alexander the Great, Genghis Khan, Napoleon, Ivan the Terrible, or Peter the Great? Or, take the contrary — Homer, Goethe, Pushkin, Tolstoy — who were the rulers for them? Who remembers them now? A great poet can have the role of spiritual head of a nation. A great ruler is the spiritual head of a nation, and next to him there can be no other spiritual head.

\*　　\*　　\*

The Old Bolshevik Alexander Semyonovich (Alyosha) Svanidze, the brother of Stalin's first wife, Ekaterina Semyonovna Svanidze, was arrested in 1937 and shot five years later in 1942.

Before the execution he was told that if he begged forgiveness from Comrade Stalin, he would be spared.

"What am I supposed to ask forgiveness for? I haven't committed any crime," Svanidze replied.

When this was reported to Comrade Stalin, he said, "Look how proud he was; he died but didn't ask for forgiveness."

And at the same time, in 1942, Alyosha's wife, Maria Anisimovna, died in a camp in Kazakhstan.

Their son, Dzhonik (Ivan Alexandrovich), or Johnreed, was imprisoned with criminals and was released only in 1956.

Mariko, the sister of Stalin's first wife, was arrested in 1937 and died very quickly in prison.

Anna Sergeyevna Alliluyeva, the sister of Stalin's second wife, Nadezhda (Nadya) Sergeyevna Alliluyeva, was arrested in 1948 and sentenced to ten years in prison. She was in a solitary cell in Vladimirskaya Prison and was released after Stalin's death. Her husband, Stanislav Frantsevich Redens, was shot in 1938.

Pavel Alliluyev, the brother of Stalin's wife Nadya, worked in the armored tank department and tried to defend his unjustly repressed colleagues, after which Stalin stopped receiving him. In 1938 Pavel died unexpectedly at the age of forty-four.

Pavel's wife, Yevgenia Alexandrovna Alliluyeva, was arrested on December 10, 1947, and sentenced to ten years in prison. When Yevgenia Alexandrovna was released on April 2, 1954, and came home in Moscow, she told her son, Sergei, "But our relative did get us out." She didn't know that Stalin had been dead a year by then.

Kira Pavlovna Alliluyeva, the daughter of Pavel and Yevgenia, was arrested in 1948 and released after Stalin's death.

Yakov (Yasha), Stalin's son by his first wife, was captured by the Nazis in the summer of 1941, behaved courageously, and died under unexplained circumstances in 1943.

Yakov's wife, Yulia, was arrested in Moscow in the fall of 1941 and released soon after Yakov died.

## 9

The first one to notice Lena's pregnancy was her mother, Ashkhen Stepanovna.

After dinner, she kept Lena in the dining room. "Stay, I'd like to talk to you."

They sat down opposite each other.

"Tell me, Lena, I'm not mistaken . . . you are pregnant?"

"Yes."

"Does that mean you have a husband?"

"I don't have a husband."

"Forgive me. . . . Then, in that case, who's the father? I'd like to know."

"I don't want to give his name."

Ashkhen Stepanovna shrugged.

Lena added, "And please tell Papa not to ask who the father is either."

Ivan Grigoryevich heard out his wife, and after some thought, said, "It must be that son-of-a-bitch."

"But she broke off with him then."

"They've met after that. Tell her to come see me."

"She's afraid of talking with you. Ivan, she asked me to tell you not to ask her any questions."

"I won't ask her about anything, tell her to come to me."

"Be gentle. Promise?"

"I promise."

Ashkhen Stepanovna went to Lena's room. "Lena, your father wants to see you."

"I've told you everything. I'm not going to say anything else."

"He won't ask anything. He promised. Go see him."

Lena set her book aside, stood up, and headed with determination for Ivan Grigoryevich's study.

Her father was sitting on the couch. He patted the seat next to him.

Ivan Grigoryevich looked at her for a long time and then smiled.

"So, you want to make me a grandfather?"

"If I can."

"You will. Last year's business must not be repeated. I'm not reproaching you, I'm just afraid it may affect the birth. So please see a doctor and remain under his care. Tell Mama, or do you want me to?"

"I'll tell her," Lena replied, "I'll go to the doctor."

"Now for the hard part. Naturally, I'm interested in who the father is. You can understand that. Not because I want to force him to marry you or to get child support. We'll bring up the child without him. But who is it? That classmate of yours . . . Yuri, I think?"

Lena hesitated.

Ivan Grigoryevich watched and waited.

"Yes," Lena said at last.

"Does he know about this?"

"Yes."

"Do you want to marry?"

"Not in the least."

"Will he make any claims on the child?"

"Never."

"Does anyone else know?"

"No one."

"Then everything is all right," Ivan Grigoryevich said. "A child is a child; he'll live with us. But you must be firm — break off with that man forever."

"I already have."

She wasn't lying to her father. After the May vacation, Yuri showed up again. That surprised her. She had been sure that they had had their last conversation, that he would vanish, that his promise to call had been just an empty promise.

In the bus coming back from the resort to Moscow, Sharok had brought up Vika again. "Who told you that about her?"

Lena had heard that Vika was an informer from Nina, who had gotten it from Varya. Varya was married to a billiard-playing hustler and through him she had met Vika.

"Somebody," Lena said curtly.

A few days later Yuri called her at work and asked if she had changed her mind. She didn't know what he had in mind — the abortion or their breakup — but she didn't ask. She said, "No, and I won't change it."

"Then good-bye."

"Good-bye, Yuri," Lena said and hung up.

That's how things were now.

"It's true, Papa," she repeated. "I've already done that."

Ivan Grigoryevich wanted to ask if she was sure of her decision, but he looked into her eyes and the way Lena returned his gaze comforted him and made him happy. They said she was infantile and passive. . . . No! She was his daughter, his blood, his character!

He put his arm around her shoulders, pulled her to him, and she put her head on his shoulder, the way she used to when she was little.

Ivan Grigoryevich's study, always rather dimly lit, had grown completely dark. But they sat on the couch in silence, leaning against each other, father and grown daughter.

The doorbell rang in the hall.

Ivan Grigoryevich kissed Lena on the forehead and caressed her cheek tenderly. "That's it, daughter, that's for me."

He got up, put on the light, and went to the door.

Mark Alexandrovich Ryazanov was in the entry.

He had come to Moscow for the June Plenum of the Central Committee. He hadn't dropped in on Ivan Grigoryevich, but instead had called to ask permission to come by that evening, because their relations were strained: formally, because Ryazanov had not interceded with Stalin on his nephew Sasha's behalf, and Ivan Grigoryevich had expressed his surprise; but in fact, because their differing attitudes toward Stalin had become clear.

Budyagin knew that Ryazanov was having difficulties, that he was being reassigned from his position as head of the country's largest metallurgy plant and transferred to Kemerovo, to a construction complex. It was a strange appointment. Mark Alexandrovich was a metallurgist, not a chemist or a construction specialist. Ordzhonikidze, his boss, must have told him about the new job, but not the real reason behind it. That was what he was here for, of course, to find out from Budyagin what was going on. But Ivan Grigoryevich couldn't help, for he didn't know himself.

They went into the study. Mark Alexandrovich asked permission to remove his jacket. A short, balding fat man with a short apoplectic-looking neck, he was out of breath, and his eyes were restless and wary.

"Well, Mark Alexandrovich, I hear you're off to Kemerovo?" Budyagin asked. By using Ryazanov's given name, he hoped to stress his friendly feeling for him. He knew that Ryazanov needed it.

"I am. I'd like to know the reason for the transfer. But Grigory Konstantinovich didn't tell me."

"It's the will of the Party, to shape up the Kuznetsky Basin. We've given you a medal, that means we value you."

In March, *Pravda* had published a long list of leaders of heavy industry who received the Order of Lenin. Ryazanov was among them. Ordzhonikidze himself led the list.

"I can't understand it. Could it be because of Lominadze? Lominadze committed suicide, but we weren't close, we had never argued, and I'm not the cause of his suicide. He had been called in by Ryndin, the secretary of the Oblast committee, who spoke very harshly to him."

"How do you know that?"

"Everybody knows everything in a plant, Ivan Grigoryevich. Lominadze didn't tell me himself, but they say that he had been shown evidence against him that he headed a conspiracy in the Comintern. And when he was called in one more time to see Ryndin, he shot himself while riding in the car. The bullet did not hit his heart. They came back, he was hospitalized, operated on, but died under the chloroform."

Ivan Grigoryevich listened closely, even though he knew everything Ryazanov was telling him, and even more — the driver's false evidence and the bastards who had been sent to take care of Lominadze on Stalin's direct orders.

"Grigory Konstantinovich liked Lominadze; I know that he was upset by his death. But I had nothing to do with it. . . . I admit I found it hard working with Lominadze at first. He was a major political figure and I was a simple engineer, but I was the head of the construction project. But despite that, I repeat, we had no conflicts. I also knew how Comrade Stalin felt about Lominadze, but I didn't fall into that trap. And then! I was sure that Lominadze would be buried in his homeland, the way Georgians usually are, but the orders were to bury him in the city cemetery, which was done. The Georgians who work at the plant erected a monument. They had collected money by subscription — not a big monument, but a decent headstone — how could I forbid that? Maybe Comrade Stalin is displeased by that?"

"Where is the list of subscribers?" Budyagin asked.

"At the accounting office. It was a voluntary collection, and with that money the plant purchased material, a trifle, but it was all legal."

Budyagin said nothing. He was put off by Ryazanov: Mark Alexandrovich was covering his rear . . . he was afraid. He was keeping the subscription list in his office. Didn't he realize that everyone on that list, all those miserable Georgians, would be exterminated in time? Stalin didn't forgive that kind of charity.

"Ivan Grigoryevich," Ryazanov said uncertainly, "I would like your advice. . . . Of course, I realize that my transfer is not random. But the reasons are not clear to me. There are no work-related reasons. The construction is on schedule, the metal is of high quality, the city is improving, they started the trolley service in January, they're eradicating illiteracy, last year the middle and higher schools had thirty-two thousand students, of whom ten thousand continued working on the production lines. The city is becoming a cultural center, Sobinov and Obukhov, Katayev, and Gladkov came there, even Louis Aragon came. It was all created with our own hands, out of nothing. Why fire me from there suddenly?"

"But you're not being fired," Ivan Grigoryevich countered. "You're being transferred to another, no less responsible, job.

You've done it here, good for you; now do it there. That's our way."

"Yes, of course," Mark Alexandrovich agreed. "I'm prepared to work wherever the Party sends me. But do you remember the story last year with the Pyatakov commission?"

"The one you stopped?" Budyagin laughed.

"I didn't stop it, Ivan Grigoryevich, I just didn't want them coming to the plant before I talked with Ordzhonikidze, and they got insulted and left.... Yes, we had built one movie theater, one club, one Pioneer camp, one kindergarten, and one clinic near a sulfur spring. And not with state funds — people had worked nights and on their days off; they worked with enthusiasm, for themselves, for their children. The plant can't develop without housing and other amenities. The case was examined by Comrade Stalin, and Ordzhonikidze, Voroshilov, and I think Yezhov were there. Comrade Stalin found our actions correct, he approved the construction fully. And he found that Pyatakov had made a mistake, a great mistake, in sending the commission. But a week ago I was called into the Oblast committee, and they demanded a written explanation of the incident. They demanded an admission that the construction had been outside the plan and, consequently, illegal, and that I had in fact interfered with a commission sent by the center. I explained about the meeting at Comrade Stalin's office and said that Comrade Stalin had approved my actions. They replied, 'We're not asking you about the actions of Comrade Stalin, we're asking about your actions. Don't hide behind Comrade Stalin's name; have the courage to answer for your own actions.' I said, 'The workers volunteered their labor in their spare time.' And one old creep said, 'You forced them, so they worked.' And when I tried to explain that the construction was necessary for the plant and for the workers, Ryndin, the secretary, interrupted me and said, 'The workers didn't need it, you needed it personally to create a cheap popularity for yourself.'"

"And what did they decide?"

"To have the Party commission look into it. So I'm leaving with a personal mark in my file — and that's all the reward I get for my work."

"Why don't you talk to Stalin about it?"

Ryazanov lowered his head. "He wouldn't see me."

"But you're a candidate member of the Central Committee, you were at the Plenum."

"I couldn't come up to him at the Plenum. It was a difficult Plenum. You must know the decision?"

Ivan Grigoryevich looked over at the *Pravda* of June 8 with the Resolution of the Plenum of the Central Committee of the All-Union Communist Party (Bolshevik), which Stalin headed.

Stalin had dealt with his best friend, Abel Enukidze, the godson of his late wife, the favorite of his children Svetlana and Vasya, who had called him "Uncle Abel."

And for what reason?

Because in his book about the early days of the Revolution, Enukidze had written the *truth* about Lenin's underground "Nina" press in Baku — which meant he hadn't mentioned Stalin, who hadn't even known the press had existed, an odd situation for one who was supposedly Lenin's closest confidant.

And Stalin had dealt with him.

In just two weeks they created a "Kremlin conspiracy," arrested seventy-eight people, taking them away one by one — workers in the Secretariat of the Central Executive Committee U.S.S.R., workers in the state library and the armory of the Kremlin, and many of the cleaning women and maintenance men in the Government House. They arrested friends of these cleaning women, watchmen, librarians, and superintendents, and friends of those friends; the majority of the "conspirators" had never met. They beat confessions out of them: that they had talked about the deaths of Kirov and Stalin's wife, Nadya Alliluyeva, which qualified as counterrevolutionary slander, discrediting Comrade Stalin and other leaders, and that they had created the "Kremlin conspiracy."

And Abel Enukidze was trampled at the Plenum for that. He allegedly allowed extreme personnel impropriety in the service staff of the Secretariat of Central Executive Committee U.S.S.R, into which the dreaded class enemies had penetrated. He had protected hostile class elements who used him for their vile aims, and his ties to people from an alien world became dearer to him than ties to his own Party. He found himself to be a rotten bourgeois, full of himself, fattened, who had lost the face of a Communist, to become a Menshevik lord.

Budyagin looked at Ryazanov closely.

This had all been said at the Plenum — Ryazanov had heard it with his own ears — but he wasn't telling Budyagin about it.

Why was he so careful? Was he ashamed for participating in the revenge against the Old Bolshevik Abel Enukidze, against simple, defenseless, illiterate people?

No, Ryazanov wasn't ashamed. He was used to it. He didn't want to recount the details, because then he would have to express his attitude about it. He was afraid now, the way he was afraid a year ago to defend Sasha, his own nephew, a good fellow, as innocent of wrongdoing as these seventy-eight people were innocent. In order to deal with one Abel Enukidze, Stalin needed another seventy-eight lives. If he were to condemn Abel alone, it would be clear he was paying him back for the slight in his book; but to condemn a big bunch — that was a conspiracy, and the Baku business had nothing to do with it.

Enukidze was responsible for the Kremlin, there were enemies in the Kremlin, and so Enukidze had to pay for that. And if seventy-eight innocent people had to die — well, so what? ... Many others would suffer, the circles would spread farther, so that everyone who attacked Stalin's version of history should know: He could destroy not seventy-eight people but seventy-eight thousand people. History is more valuable than people.

By Ryazanov wasn't thinking about what had happened at the Plenum. He was worrying about his fate, in which he had sensed a turn; he had been advancing so well, rising so swiftly, and suddenly ...

A transfer to the Kuznetsky Basin was in the order of things. But not without an explanation, not with a mark in his personal record, not with Stalin refusing to see him ... Ryazanov did not foresee a complete crash yet, but the fear had come. And the fear was justified.

Stalin would not look for an assassin like Nikolaev — the way he did for Kirov — in order to get rid of Ordzhonikidze. He would first destroy those of whom Sergo Ordzhonikidze was most proud — the managers Sergo had found, advanced, and brought up, these people Stalin would destroy as enemies, saboteurs, and wreckers and force Sergo either to participate in their destruction or share their responsibility for the sabotage.

Of course, Ordzhonikidze's authority was great, but had the authority of Trotsky, Zinoviev, Kamenev, Bukharin, Rykov, or Tomsky been less? And Ryazanov's case was probably one of the links in his plan — Stalin began plotting far ahead and started his moves far in advance. Ryazanov was apparently a good move for Stalin — Ryazanov believed in Stalin as if in a god, and Ryazanov would break immediately.

And so Budyagin did not share any of his thoughts or his information with Ryazanov. He merely asked, "And, what do you want from me?"

Ryazanov shrugged. "My conversation with Grigory Konstantinovich gave me nothing. I did tell him that I had been called in to the Oblast committee and that they had started a case against me for the extra construction we had done at the plant, but he laughed: 'See what exceeding your authority can turn into?' Even then, in Stalin's office, he did not support me. I'm asking you to find out and tell me the real reason for my transfer, the real reason for starting a personal case against me."

"All right," Budyagin said, "I'll try to talk with Grigory Konstantinovich."

He rose. Ryazanov stood up too.

"I'm not sure that he will tell me any more than he did you. But if the opportunity arises, I'll talk to him," Ivan Grigoryevich assured him.

Then he added, "How's your nephew?"

Mark Alexandrovich sighed. "In exile."

"Where?"

"In Siberia."

"Siberia is big."

"On the Angara somewhere," Mark Alexandrovich said.

"On the Angara somewhere," Ivan Grigoryevich repeated, either thoughtfully or mockingly. "All right! If I find out something, I'll let you know, if I don't, don't hold it against me...."

"Fine, thank you, Ivan Grigoryevich."

## 10

Vika hadn't told Varya the whole truth. The Architect did work a lot, she really did see little of him, but she could have adjusted to that. When your husband is busy all day and you're free all day, you can still arrange a happy life. But, you need money, lots of money, and the Architect gave half his paycheck to his former wife and her children, who were old enough, incidentally, to earn their own keep. And he had this stupid conversation with Vika, telling her that she should do something — get a job or go back to school; it wasn't too late, he said. Just what she needed! She had an official position — *wife*, and according to their official vulgar status, *housewife* — and had the right not to work. . . . It was just that he didn't worry about her or try to protect her. All his interest was in his work and his former family. . . . He not only gave them money, he visited his wife and children, went to their family parties. He even divided up the New Year's celebration — with Vika until midnight, and with them afterward. "I'll go visit the children, I promised." He has a family there, then what does he have here?

He didn't even move his things; he showed up with a little suitcase, and inside there were a couple of shirts, a couple of pairs of long underwear, and suspenders. There's a genius for you! He had not only evenly divided up their "jointly earned property," he left everything at his former home, including his library, which he needed for his work. His real home was there and he would return to it, Vika had no doubts about that. Instead of a party, this life was a drag.

Vika did not argue with him. She knew that their relationship hung by a thread and if they argued the thread would break. It couldn't be broken. She had to create a new life while she was still the Architect's wife. She shouldn't simply be picked up by another man. On the contrary, she would sacrifice her high position and happy home life for the sake of another man. What one does for love! ... And then her new marriage would become an event, especially for her new chosen spouse.

Marrying a pilot was in her thoughts. But where would she find one? That was just a fantasy. Besides which, Vika almost never went out. She was at home all the time.

The Marasevich house was filled with people as usual, lively and hospitable. Moscow celebrities were there all the time. A composer? An artist? No, their positions were too unstable.

Her brother, Vadim, was attacking them all, writing about music, theater, art, and literature. The writer Panferov took a bite out of Gorky in *Pravda*. Vadim said he did the right thing — Gorky was criticizing Communist writers. However, on the same page they printed an unpublished letter of Gorky to Chekhov, and Vadim said sarcastically that was to "sugarcoat the pill." Vadim now was part of the circle of writers and poets, famous writers, famous poets, and many of them came to the Marasevich house.

Vika was the hostess, but it was hard for her to take part in the conversations — to tell the truth, she read nothing. It was all so boring: shock-workers, enthusiasts, factories and plants, cast iron and steel. But she knew how to use her ignorance — she made a point of listening to her guests attentively, delighting in what they said, letting them know that she appreciated their intelligence and education, always flattering them.

One was a young, skinny, small, and fluttering thirty-year-old, who had just published a novel that everyone was reading and praising, which even Vika had read. His brilliant debut had turned his head so that he couldn't hear anyone but himself, and he didn't even appreciate the attention Vika paid him. He didn't want a silent partner, he wanted her to talk about him, about his novel, and since she didn't do that, he told her how others praised his novel.

Perhaps Vika could have entranced him, but he vanished quickly; Vadim said he was off writing a new novel about the Trotskyite underground — he had to follow up on his success.

Another writer appeared, older, probably pushing forty, a Petersburg intellectual, with horn-rimmed glasses, who had lived abroad and wrote something exotic about Asia, but he soon vanished, too, even though Vika thought she had been doing well. She yessed him, and oohed and aahed, but it didn't work. He went off, somewhere in the East, to write a new novel. Vika never did capture any of the guests in their house.

She had stopped seeing her old friends. They used to meet in restaurants, but Vika no longer went — the Architect was too busy, and going without him meant ruining the image she had created for herself of a high-society lady.

She talked on the phone with Noemi, with Nina Sheremetyeva, but the only house she frequented was that of Nelli Vladimirova, who had married a wealthy French businessman, Georges.

Vika didn't like him — he was short and had thick lips, looked at women with his oily eyes, and he didn't speak much Russian, or pretended not to.

But their apartment was terrific, with carpet, antique furniture, and porcelain; they had a car, foreign clothes, lots of clothes. Georges must have been very rich, though no one knew exactly what he did and Nelli was always vague about it.

Nelli was lucky. Why? She was a horse! Healthy, bony, yet men adored her. She landed Georges, who was six inches shorter than she. "Aren't you afraid of smothering him in bed?" Vika joked. "Don't worry," Nelli replied. "He's inventive, we find the right positions."

The household was European in style — Nelli had been to Paris twice and had picked up pointers. They served aperitifs and tiny sandwiches. Nelli drove a car herself. In general she was more than Europeanized, she was Americanized: quick, sharp, a bit loud, but hardworking. She had time to read, she still painted, her easel stood in the corner. . . . And she had her little vices. She went to the races, she bet on the totalizer and always won, she knew how to make money, she sold off her things, not speculating, but just selling the clothes that didn't suit her to her girlfriends — this one was the wrong length, that one the wrong color. She started her "Wednesdays" — her "at homes" for friends.

But the important thing was that she always had guests, lots of guests, and mostly foreigners. This gave Vika a chance. Nelli told her the background of each — age, interests, possibilities, sometimes adding spicy gossip.

Many paid attention to Vika, but they were all the wrong ones. And almost all of them were married. Vika behaved simply, with reserve, with a friendliness that held out no promises, as befit a lady of her status, tactfully deflecting attempts to court her, but not cutting them off completely until she had them pegged.

It was at Nelli's that Vika met Charles.

Tall, blond, with a wineglass in his hand, he was talking to Georges. Vika was struck by his noble face, aquiline nose, and his elegant, simple suit. An aristocrat? And from the way he had stared at her a few times, Vika saw that there was a spark. She could always distinguish between a male's wandering gaze and the real thing.

The next day, when she was going over the party with Nelli, Vika said, "You don't often meet a blond Frenchman."

"All the French aristocrats as a rule are blond. As are all the French from the north, especially the northeast, where they have Teutonic blood," Nelli explained.

Having married a Frenchman, she considered herself an authority on France.

"Is he an aristocrat?"

"You bet. He's a viscount; his name is written with a 'de.'"

"Interesting." Vika laughed. "And what is the viscount doing in Moscow?"

"Charles is a correspondent." Nelli named a famous French newspaper. "His family, one of the richest families in France, owns it. And Charles's fiancée is the daughter of a financier, not Rothschild, but someone like him, I can't remember the name now."

So, Charles was handsome, rich, and a bachelor. This was an important consideration, since Catholics were not allowed to divorce.

At home, Vika considered everything carefully. She could not allow this opportunity to slip away. There was nothing for her in this country. Rudeness, envy, frightening anonymity, slogans and marches, constant fear. Today she was walking around Moscow, tomorrow she could have a phone call — "Citizen Marasevich, this is the NKVD...."

She had to get to Paris! Eternal, majestic Paris. At school she had studied French. Of course, she had forgotten some, but she'd take it up again.... How did that little poem go? ... *"Bonjour, Madame Sans-Souci, combien coutent ces saucisses?"*

She had to get out of there. The Architect would leave any day now, her father would die sooner or later — probably sooner — and then what would she do? She couldn't stand being at the same table with Vadim even now, she couldn't stand his lip-smacking, his disgusting greedy appetite, and the way he talked with his mouth full.

Perhaps something serious would come of it this time. She remembered Charles's eyes and his silence — all those Frenchmen are chatty, but Charles said nothing around her, significantly silent. That's what inspired hope in Vika.

Should she involve Nelli in this or not? That's what she was thinking about.

No, not yet. One wrong move, an approving look, a conspiratorial smile, could spoil everything. It would be another thing if Charles didn't show up at Nelli's anymore. Well, wait until next Wednesday. If Charles came, that would mean the spark was real. And then she wouldn't need Nelli.

The next Wednesday Charles came to Nelli's house.

Of course, Vika was there too. She came, as usual, a bit later than the others.

## ❧ 11 ❧

On June 7, 1935, Stalin chaired the Plenum of the Constitutional Commission.

The commission had thirty members and Stalin was the thirty-first. Everyone was there except Abel Enukidze, who had been expelled from the Party and removed from all his posts, even though formally he remained a member of the Constitutional Commission — an oversight.

The main speakers were Bukharin and Radek, drafters of the new constitution. But, of course, the others would also speak. How else! They would enter history as "Fathers of the Constitution."

The first to speak was Bukharin, who said, "The whole country is centered on the Leninist Party, which is led with an iron hand by the marvelous leader of the workers, the commander of millions, whose name — symbol of the great five-year plans, gigantic victories and gigantic struggles — is Stalin."

And exactly a week later *Pravda* published Radek's article, which even surpassed Bukharin's speech in its praise.

Was this a repetition of the story with Zinoviev and Kamenev? They also had praised *him*, and look how they ended up.

Bukharin said the constitution had to guarantee all kinds of freedoms, the greatest rights in the whole world, full equality of citizens, the most democratic electoral system in the world, the most just legal system in the world. . . .

Even *he* had not expected this much from them. They had surpassed the most democratic constitutions in the world. Naïve men. They had hoped to protect themselves with this constitution, to guarantee themselves a peaceful existence at first and then a "constitutional" change of rulers later. Idiots!

*He* needed that constitution, *he* was the one. It would be a powerful political cover for the coming revolution in the cadres. When power was in one set of hands, when that power is inviolable, when the people support that power, any constitution will do.

And the people were with *him*. Despite the hunger and poverty, despite the millions of victims, the people were for *him*. They feared *him*. And they loved *him*. The main condition for solitary rule was in place. Throughout history, people blamed their sufferings on everyone and anyone except God. You don't criticize God, you thank Him.

Thinking along those lines, Stalin listened to Bukharin attentively. Of course, everyone listened attentively, especially the ethnic minorities. Melting with delight — they were listening to "the Party's best theoretician," "the Party's favorite" — they stared with burning eyes when Bukharin started talking about the sovereignty of the Union Republics. For them, Bukharin was still a leader. They obviously hoped that in assigning him to prepare the new constitution, Stalin was returning Bukharin to power. They wanted that badly. They were jealous of their independence, their irreplaceability, local princelings!

*He* had replaced the murdered Kirov and Kuibyeshev, who had died in January, with Chubar and Mikoyan in the Politburo.

Mikoyan was a clever liar, but he was *his* clever liar and a good worker. And the circumstances of his survival in Baku in 1918 were not clear. All the Baku commissars had been shot, but Comrade Mikoyan was alive. Strange, wasn't it? That man would serve *him* faithfully.

Chubar was a mystery. But *he* had to choose between Chubar and Petrovsky, both candidate members of the Politburo since 1926. Chubar was mysterious, but Petrovsky was clear — an alien, an idealist Marxist, like *his* own dear father-in-law Alliluyev.

And not all of the Russians here were clear to *him*.

Akulov, for instance . . . he had been procurator general, and he got in Vyshinsky's way, so he had to be made secretary of the Central Executive Committee in Enukidze's place and Vyshinsky became the procurator, to untie his hands. Vyshinsky was a scoundrel, but a necessary scoundrel. There he was, frowning, pretending that he was not delighted by Bukharin's report, he was pretending for *him*. He understood everything, the bastard with the neat hair, the gray, neatly trimmed mustache, the expensive suit, the shirt with starched collar, and tie — trying to look like a European intellectual when he was just a criminal at heart.

Sometimes *he* smiled politely at Krylenko, whom he hated and would gladly eat, without salt or pepper.

Krylenko was an enemy, without a doubt. How had he behaved on the matter of criminal responsibility of children? Like an enemy.

Theft of state property continued, especially in transportation. The greatest thieves were children. Yagoda, head of the NKVD, had stressed that in his last report, confirmed by Kaganovich, head of the railroads since February.

But children legally couldn't be tried.

A boy of twelve knows very well that he shouldn't steal, he knows that theft is a crime. But that boy also knows that he can't be tried.

The Criminal Code had to be amended. All criminal responsibility, right up to the highest measure of punishment, applies to all citizens starting at the age of twelve. Then they'd stop stealing, hauling away the national treasure, stop robbing and killing. And that would be a good warning to parents. They would know what was in store for their children.

Yet People's Commissar of Justice Krylenko resisted promulgating such a decree. Krylenko insisted that this law was unprecedented, that it had no analog in world practice, that allegedly no country in the world executed twelve-year-old children, that children could become the victims of a false accusation or a misunderstanding, and that passing such a law in the eighteenth year of Soviet rule would create a horrible impression abroad and undermine the prestige of the Soviet state.

When did Comrade Krylenko become so humane, when did he start worrying about bourgeois public opinion? ... Before, when he was the prosecutor in the trial of the Promparty, the Mensheviks, he didn't worry about it.

Until recently Comrade Krylenko had maintained that "demanding absolute objectivity from a judge is pure utopianism." He insisted that the rights of the defense be limited, since, as he so correctly then said, the Soviet court itself defends the defendant. He had practically suggested doing away with the procedural code, calling it a "copy of bourgeois law."

And now this one-hundred-eighty-degree turn. It was bad enough that he had publicly rejected *his* own views, publishing a book in which he argued for revolutionary legality, absolute objectivity of evidence, and a strict observance of all procedural norms.... All that had been directed against Vyshinsky, who correctly understood the aims of the court and the procuracy at this stage. It was directed against the Party's struggle with its enemies.

Right after the trial of the Mensheviks, Krylenko asked to be people's commissar of justice. Krylenko did not want to appear in court anymore, since he saw which way things were going. He fought against enemies outside the Party, but he did not want to fight enemies inside the Party. He was trying to compromise Vyshinsky.

But Vyshinsky was needed. Vyshinsky had no ties with the Bolshevik faction; consequently, he was better suited for the struggle against enemies within the Party. He knew his place, he still trembled with fear, and he was prepared to fulfill any order.

At the Seventeenth Congress, Krylenko was not elected to the Central Committee or the Commission of Party Control. That had been a warning to him. He was offended, but didn't draw any conclusions. Today was his fiftieth birthday. Let him read congratulations in *Pravda*. The Central Committee wasn't planning to congratulate him. That was a warning, too. The last one. Let's see if he draws the right conclusion now or if he continues putting spanners in Vyshinsky's works. When people don't get along, usually that's good. They compete to show their loyalty to *him*. But that wasn't true in the Krylenko-Vyshinsky case. Vyshinsky was loyal to *him* — loyal out of fear, but still loyal. Krylenko wasn't loyal. He didn't belong to any of the oppositions, not the Trotskyite or the Bukharinite. But he didn't speak out against them, either. An undependable man. An alien man. And that man would perish in the fire of the cadre revolution.

There were many alien men, many undependable men. Here

were thirty men sitting with *him* now. How many of them could *he* trust, more or less? Voroshilov, Zhdanov, Kaganovich, Meshlis, Mikoyan, Molotov. How many was that? Six out of twenty-nine. And the bastard Vyshinsky made seven. Seven out of twenty-nine, not even one-fourth.

Who was more or less neutral? The old mummies with Party service — Krasikov, Stava, Kalinin, Litvinov, Petrovsky.... Actually, Petrovsky didn't belong there, a lot of trouble might still come from him.

And so, there were four neutrals, along with the dependables, a total of eleven.

And the remaining eighteen? They were enemies — Bukharin, Radek, Krylenko, Unshlikht. Or undependable — Akulov, Bubnov, Sulimov, Chubar, Lubchenko, Chervyakov, Goloded, Ikramov, Khodzhayev, Aitakov, Musabekov, Erbanov, Rakhimbayev, and Petrovsky.

That list revealed a lot. It reflected the situation in the Party, it reflected the situation in the Central Committee, and even the situation in the Politburo. Even the Politburo had undependables — Ordzhonikidze, Rudzutak, Kosior, Chubar, as it was now apparent.

*He* should not have to depend on whether or not *he* had a majority in the Politburo. The party was not the absolute. *He* was the absolute. *He* should not have apparent or potential rivals. Everything potentially dangerous should be exterminated. Not a single man had the right to strive for supreme power. Every inhabitant of the country should understand that, should sense the threat to his existence, his freedom, his safety. He should see his safety only in unquestioning submission; the terror must be constant, it should become the normal and usual method of administration.

*He* had needed the famine of the early thirties to show the countryside who was the boss. The famine took millions of lives, but it brought victory.

*His* rule would also cost millions of lives, but *he* would show the country and the world who was boss.

The first step was taken. *He* had responded to Kirov's death with ruthless blows, creating a climate of fear. The most powerful blow fell on Leningrad. The city would never rise again as the second capital. Throughout the country there was an overt checking of Party documents and a covert checking of every Party member through the NKVD. They were catching, isolating, and when necessary destroying former members of all kinds of opposition, people who had come from other parties or from hostile classes, tsarist clerks and officers, members of religious cults, former kulaks, all people with anti-Soviet sympathies. But all this had happened before, although on a smaller scale. The main event was yet to come.

Zinoviev and Kamenev had admitted their *moral* responsibility for Kirov's murder. How cleverly they had admitted it, putting it in a very ambiguous form — "In view of the objective situation the former activity of former opposition could have led only to the creation of these criminals."

Lousy politicians! They thought they could save themselves with those loopholes. . . . But at that moment nothing more could have been got out of them. And it was impossible to put off the trial; they had to use Kirov's murder immediately. Zinoviev's and Kamenev's confessions made it possible to isolate them. But isolation is a half measure. The Trotskyites had been isolated for five years and they were still awaiting their hour. History shows — it is only one step from prison to throne. To keep that from happening, a scaffold must stand on the path.

The responsibility for Kirov's murder must be criminal, not moral. Zinoviev and Kamenev must be condemned for what they did.

The bourgeois newspapers had not recognized the January trial — it had been closed, you see, and they all quoted the famous line of Mirabeau: "Give me any kind of judge at all — prejudiced, greedy, even my enemy — but let him judge me publicly."

Good! Wonderful! They would have an open trial, they would have a public trial. Zinoviev and Kamenev would confess to their crimes before the whole world. They would confess that they had ordered Kirov killed and that they had been preparing the killings of other leaders of the Party and the government. And therefore they should be destroyed and not isolated.

Would Zinoviev and Kamenev confess? If they were promised their lives, they would. As long as there is life, there is hope for power. Losing life, they would lose that hope forever. And if they resisted, the whole weight of the repressive apparat, the might of the state would attack them. They couldn't withstand it. Never. Their families, their wives and children, would be hostages, they wouldn't be able to stand that either, both being loving husbands and good fathers.

Thus thought Stalin while the other commission members spoke. He had listened only to Bukharin and Radek, who had written the draft. The others were chatterboxes who only needed *him* to hear their voices. They were talking about the role of local Soviets and other nonsense — none of it was interesting and he didn't listen. The main direction of the new constitution had been correctly determined by Bukharin and Radek.

That document would create the face of the Soviet state, a democratic face with great freedoms for its citizens. Against such a constitution all talk of terror and illegality would look like ridiculous lies.

This constitution would provide enormous foreign prestige. Yes, there would be trials, but they would take place against the background of the most democratic constitution, and therefore they would seem absolutely legal and truthful.

Was there any danger in passing that constitution? None, because the power remained in the hands of the Party, and therefore in *his* hands. That was real power. It had to be legalized constitutionally. It had to say right in the constitution that the Communist Party was the leading and directing force of the Soviet state. But candidates could be nominated not only by the Party, but by unions, and the Komsomol, and other social organizations.

No, that wasn't right. There could not be a Communist Party bloc alongside that of other organizations — that would be putting those organizations on the same level, when no equality, no parity was possible. The bloc could only be with the people, not with organizations.

"The bloc of Communists with non-Party members," that would be correct.

Of course, the new constitution would make greater demands on our punitive organs, greater vigilance — the enemies would not dare use the new constitution for their aims, and any such attempts would be nipped in the bud.

And the new electoral system would also demand more of the Party organizations and more vigilance. That was all right — let them work under new conditions, let them hustle. Every election had to turn into a broad political campaign. In the West, voters pick one or the other bourgeois party, but our election campaigns will be mighty political agitation for the Communist Party, for Soviet power, demonstrations of the unity of the Party and the people, a general holiday.

Of course, the new constitution was a good political cover for the coming cadre revolution. But not enough. We must popularize our victories and achievements to show the enthusiasm of the people.

Naturally, that enthusiasm was elicited by the October Revolution. Every revolution gives birth to hopes for a better future, and hopes for a better future elicit enthusiasm. The goal now is to show the people their enthusiasm and show it to the whole world.

To do that, the organs of the press must speak of achievement day in and day out, and not only the press, but literature, art, the theater — they must all serve to show the achievements of the Soviet people, promote the development of their enthusiasm, their faith in the common goal.

Of course, they should write about the flaws, too. But the flaws must be explained by the resistance of hostile elements, and the hostile elements must be destroyed.

Stalin shuddered.

Sulimov, pouring water from a bottle, dropped his glass, which struck a plate.

Clumsy oaf! Can't even hold a glass. Yet he was chairman of the Council of People's Commissars of the RSFSR. A prime minister, so to speak. Was he hung over? He came from the same background, the Fifth Army, a comrade in arms of Ivan Nikitich Smirnov and Tukhachevsky, even though he hadn't belonged to the opposition.

He played at being a simpleton, a democrat. Recently he went to the Central Department Store, walked around like an ordinary customer, then went to see the director, waited his turn to complain like an ordinary customer (few people knew what he looked like), and at the end of the conversation revealed who he was. He terrified the whole store. The newspapers wrote about it with delight.

The Soviet people don't need incognito leaders in order to find out their needs.... A real Soviet leader knows the needs of his people and doesn't wait in lines, imitating the late Kirov who always wanted to show the people his special "democratic" style of leadership.

Stalin stopped listening to Sulimov and other commission members and went back to his own thoughts.

Every revolution has victims. All the history of mankind is the history of victims — victims of wars, or natural catastrophes, epidemics, famines, poverty. Millions die. Humanity quickly forgets its losses, because in the long run every life ends in death, whether natural or unnatural, early or late. Death is inevitable and people come to terms with that inevitability. They remember only those who sent people to die — military leaders, rulers, great leaders of the people. Humanity remembers Alexander the Great, Julius Caesar, Napoleon, Suvorov and Kutuzov, Stepan Razin and Pugachev — no one remembers the people who died under them, because of them, in their name.

But the important thing is never to explain or justify. Napoleon had hundreds of people shot to guarantee his power. Who remembers them now? Millions of people died in the Napoleonic wars, and no one knows them either. But he tried to justify the death of the duc d'Enghien, and history has not forgiven him that one death to this day.

A real ruler must leave behind triumphal anthems and victory marches, not funereal cries and gloomy plaints. The people must sing songs instilling hope and optimism and not sorrow, depression, and lack of faith; they must sing joyously and loudly, at the top of their lungs — this great period must be remembered as a great holiday. The workers in the arts — poets, composers, playwrights, workers in the theater and film — must be oriented this way.

All pessimism, despair, blackening, overt or covert, must be cut down at the roots, ruthlessly. Victorious cries must drown out the moans of conquered enemies.

The debate ended.

"Well," said Stalin, "I think that the comrades have expressed reasonable thoughts and made essential suggestions. I think that we must select an Editorial Commission which will take into account all the opinions and suggestions made here and put them into the final draft of the constitution, which we will then present for discussion to the entire Soviet people. Any objections?"

There were none.

Comrade Stalin was elected chairman of the Editorial Commission.

*Of the thirty members of the Constitutional Commission of the U.S.S.R., the following were shot:*

*In 1937, Goloded, Enukidze, Sulimov.*

*In 1938, Aitakov, Bukharin, Erbanov, Ikramov, Krylenko, Musabekov, Rakhimbayev, Unshlikht, Khodzhayev.*

*In 1939, Akulov, Radek, Chubar.*

*And in 1940, Bubnov.*

*Chervyakov and Lubchenko committed suicide.*

*Panas Lubchenko, before shooting himself, shot his wife, to save her from suffering and torture.*

## 12

Ivan Grigoryevich Budyagin did not talk to Ordzhonikidze about Ryazanov. There was no formal pretext. Ivan Grigoryevich was not in charge of metallurgy. And as for an unofficial talk — for what? Budyagin did not take Ryazanov's problems to heart — he was a capable, knowledgeable engineer, a good organizer, but as a person he wasn't pleasant, he had been a coward about Sasha, he was drunk on Stalin's goodwill, licking his boots, and he didn't know that Stalin's goodwill could turn. Now, apparently, he would find out.

And Budyagin's relationship with Ordzhonikidze wasn't one for frank chats. Their connection had been mutual friendship with Kirov. Now Kirov was gone. But why was Ordzhonikidze permitting the attacks on the economic sector? It hadn't become a mass assault yet, but it was leading up to it: engineers and factory directors were being arrested here and there on the most ridiculous charges. They said that Sergo protested individual cases, but what was needed was to put a firm end to NKVD intervention in the economy.

Yesterday's Plenum. How could Ordzhonikidze have allowed them to destroy Abel Enukidze? His best friend, whom he had known since youth, whom he knew to be a true Communist, a man of crystal honesty and decency. He knew that Stalin was getting revenge for that book in which Enukidze had written the truth.

But Sergo did not lift his voice in Enukidze's defense. He could have stood up and said, "Koba!* You think that Abel did not justify

---

* Stalin's early alias, and now Party nickname, was Koba.

your trust. All right, move him away, send him to Tiflis, let him live out his days — he has served our Party for thirty years with faith and truth." And if you're afraid to defend Abel, then at least defend those innocent and simple people, those wretches who work in the Kremlin — the secretaries, cleaning women, doormen, watchmen, people who are being destroyed simply so that the Enukidze affair will look like a conspiracy. "It's not good, Koba." But Ordzhonikidze didn't say it, he didn't protest, he didn't defend anyone.

Ryazanov was wrong in thinking that Ivan Grigoryevich had lost touch with the country when he was abroad. On the contrary, Ryazanov himself, limited by the interests and cares of his plant, adjusting every day and every hour to the system being created in the country, was the one who was gradually losing his political touch, was no longer thinking independently, refusing to notice what was happening around him.

Fluent in three languages, Budyagin received a lot of information. A technologist, he understood the problems of modern science. Ordzhonikidze valued Budyagin and had put him in charge of scientific works at the Commissariat, including work on the defense industry. Perhaps that did not please Stalin. A month ago, Stalin, Molotov, Voroshilov, and Ordzhonikidze reviewed new models of artillery at the test site. Ivan Grigoryevich was not invited, although he should have been. He hadn't even been informed. Ordzhonikidze's curt "They were pleased" told him nothing.

It had been a slap in the face. That humiliation damaged his prestige in the eyes of the military. What should he do, how should he react? Complain? Resign? It was not done in the Party. That could be viewed as an expression of dissent from the Party line, which would be exactly what Stalin would call it, and he would call Budyagin a saboteur, a deviationist who had at last revealed his true face. Maybe that was what Stalin was trying to provoke him into doing?

Today at ten he was seeing Tukhachevsky and a group of his workers — how would he explain his absence at the test site? "They didn't invite me"? No, that would sound pathetic and unworthy. "I couldn't," that was brief and dry. But Tukhachevsky was unlikely to ask — he was an intelligent and well-bred man.

At exactly ten, the military men arrived. Tukhachevsky was the deputy people's commissar of defense on weapons, Yakir, the commander of the Kiev Military Okrug, and Uborevich, commander of the Byelorussian Military Okrug. Budyagin smiled to himself. Tukhachevsky took advantage of the fact that Yakir and Uborevich had been at the Central Committee Plenum and brought them along for support. They would pressure the Commissariat together, and the first issue on their agenda would be the new tank built last year.

Tukhachevsky's maneuver cheered up Ivan Grigoryevich, and he tried to brush off his thoughts about the test site. Neither Uborevich or Yakir would bring that up, either. They knew how to behave, just like Tukhachevsky.

Ivan Grigoryevich looked at these relatively young men with pleasure, the celebrated commanders of the Civil War, the pride and hope of the army.

Tukhachevsky was a stately and powerfully built man of medium height, handsome, with blue eyes and regular features, whose uniform fit him very well.

Yakir was broad shouldered, with lively brown eyes and a snub nose. He was a man of desperate courage. But there was gray in the black curls, early for a man of thirty-nine.

And last, Ieronim Uborevich, a typical intellectual with fine features, wearing a pince-nez.

And the thought kept nagging at him. Yesterday at the Plenum they had voted to expel Enukidze from the Party. They might have believed Yezhov's lying report, they might not have known about the arrests of the Kremlin personnel, but still. . . . They voted not because they believed Yezhov but because Stalin was behind Yezhov, and they couldn't not believe Stalin. And if there were a war, would they still blindly obey the ignorant orders of Stalin and Voroshilov? That would mean losing the war.

No! They would not yield, just as they had refused to yield during the Civil War. They would use their own ideas, strengthen the army, arm it, and overcome the resistance of the fools in power.

Ivan Grigoryevich had encountered each of them at the front during the Civil War, but especially Tukhachevsky. At twenty-five, Tukhachevsky was commander of the First Army on the Western front. He had not joined Muravyov's anti-Communist rebellion; he had been arrested and almost shot for that. A group of Bolsheviks, Budyagin among them, stormed the prison and released Tukhachevsky. Ever since, Tukhachevsky had called Budyagin his savior.

Commanding the Fifth Army, Tukhachevsky took part in the rout of the White armies. It was then that Ivan Grigoryevich saw the real relationship between Stalin and Tukhachevsky.

Budenny, one of his subordinate commanders, failed to follow Tukhachevsky's orders, allowing Denikin to escape to Novorossisk, then evacuate to the Crimea and create a new front there. Budenny dared to disobey only because Stalin and Voroshilov supported him.

The same thing happened in 1920 near Warsaw. Despite the direct orders of the Supreme Command, Stalin held up Budenny's army outside Lvov and thereby gave Pilsudski the chance to make a decisive attack on Tukhachevsky's army from the flank. It was Stalin's fault. Even Lenin said, "Well, who goes to Warsaw through Lvov?" But after Lenin's death the servile historians blamed the defeat on Tukhachevsky.

The attacks on Tukhachevsky got so bad that in 1930 at a meeting at the Central House of the Red Army one of Stalin's toadies shouted at Tukhachevsky, "You should be hanged for 1920." The culmination of the attack was a discussion of the Polish campaign in 1932 at the Military Academy. Every talk was tendentious, compromising Tukhachevsky and praising Stalin.

Ivan Grigoryevich saw in Tukhachevsky not only a major strategist for the coming war, but a man who, unlike Stalin, understood that there would be war with Germany. And even though the campaign against Tukhachevsky had stopped in 1932, Budyagin thought bitterly that the attitude of Stalin, Voroshilov, and Budenny toward Tukhachevsky held great danger.

Was Tukhachevsky a convinced Communist? He had joined the Party in April 1918, when the Bolshevik victory was not certain. But he understood the significance of the October Revolution for Russia and tied his life to it. He was a born military leader — he considered strengthening Russia's might his life's work. A mighty country meant a mighty army, and the combat readiness of the army worried him. Its firearms were outdated and it was severely lacking planes, tanks, and means of transport and communications. Tukhachevsky, like Budyagin, spoke foreign languages. They knew just how much Russia was behind other countries.

In 1928 Tukhachevsky wrote a report on re-arming the army. Stalin and Voroshilov simply rejected it. He retired as chief of staff and was assigned commander of the Leningrad Military Okrug.

In January 1930 he sent a new report. It was treated like the previous one. Stalin and Voroshilov looked to the past, the experiences of the First World War and the Civil War. Tukhachevsky, a military genius, looked to the future.

However, a year later, Tukhachevsky's reports were taken out of the safe — they understood at last that the army had to be reconstructed and those who had mocked and rejected Tukhachevsky's proposals now had to entrust him with executing the program. Tukhachevsky was named deputy people's commissar of defense on weapons and he took up the task with energy.

Budyagin helped him as best he could. They brought in leading scientists and construction engineers, making up the list together. They spent a lot of time on tank design. What was better, a fast tank, lightly armored, or a slower, well-defended tank with heavy armor? Tukhachevsky wanted a medium tank, well defended but mobile, good both for maneuvering and for breaking through lines. This is what the new model represented.

"This is a marvelous machine," Uborevich said, looking at the blueprint on the table. "It has gone through all the testing; it's time to move on to mass production and training people to use it."

He looked tired, his eyes behind the pince-nez looked sick. Ivan Grigoryevich assumed his unhealthy appearance came from yesterday's Plenum. Apparently, Uborevich was more farsighted than the others.

"We should have it on the production lines in 'thirty-eight," Budyagin said.

"That's a major mistake, a terrible mistake!" Yakir pushed his chair away noisily. "We are used to building light tanks. But now the most important thing is the medium tank with the anti-artillery armor."

"Just don't break my furniture," Ivan Grigoryevich said with a smile.

"We can argue a long time — each model has its good features — but it's time to come to a conclusion," Tukhachevsky said.

Ivan Grigoryevich promised to raise the issue at the very next meeting of the Commissariat's Collegium.

No one mentioned the Party leaders' look at the new artillery, even though Tukhachevsky must have been there. Or perhaps, Tukhachevsky had not been invited, either. Stalin could have settled quite easily for Voroshilov's explanations.

## 13

The officers left and Budyagin plunged back into his unhappy thoughts. Stalin would never forgive their conversation last year. And yet the direction of Stalin's policies, Ivan Grigoryevich was sure, would lead to the most tragic consequences for the Soviet Union and the world Communist movement.

The rise of Fascism in Germany in the 1920s called for a decisive turn in all policies. They should have created a united front of the working class and come closer to the Social Democratic parties. In the face of the Fascist danger, they had taken a hard anti-Fascist position.

But starting in 1929, when Stalin asserted his leadership in the Comintern, the intransigence toward the Social Democrats grew.

The Comintern's Executive Committee in 1929 announced that the main enemy of the revolutionary proletariat was Social Democracy, and that the Communist parties needed a "determined increase in the struggle against Social Democracy, especially against its left wing as the most dangerous enemy." And they had to break off all ties with it, and expose its "Social Fascist" essence.

This irrational extremism made Hitler's rise to power easier.

In 1928, 810,000 people voted for the Nazis in Germany, but on September 14, 1930, when the German Communists fired on the Social Democrats, the Nazis got 6,400,000 votes, an eightfold increase.

Hitler's stunning success should have made Stalin review the Comintern policy, but according to Stalin, the growth of the popularity of Nazism was evidence that the working masses were losing the parliamentary illusions and would inevitably come over to the revolutionary camp. And therefore the destruction of Social Democracy remained the main goal.

The schismatic policy of the Comintern undermined the German labor movement and strengthened Hitler. In January 1933, the Nazis got 11,700,000 votes, the Social Democrats, 7,200,000, and the Communists around 6,000,000. If the Communists and Social Democrats had formed a united anti-Fascist front then, they could have saved the situation. But that wasn't done, and the Fascists took power.

Stalin covered up this terrible debacle with pathetic words. "The establishment of an openly Fascist dictatorship, destroying all democratic illusions in the masses and freeing the masses of the influence of the Social Democrats, will increase the tempo of the development of Germany to the proletarian revolution."

Stalin stubbornly considered the Nazis to be the enemies of England and France and the Social Democrats to be their allies. Consequently, the victory of the Nazis in Germany was a victory of anti-Western forces that benefited the Soviet Union. And the victory of the Social Democrats would have been a victory for the pro-Western forces, to the detriment of the Soviet Union.

What Stalin had said last year to Budyagin — "We are interested in a strong Germany to counterbalance England and France" — was the essence of his political line.

What could Budyagin do? Sit quietly and watch Fascism grow, the most evil enemy of the Soviet Union, the most evil enemy of the civilized world? Or should he raise his voice against this policy?

Ivan Grigoryevich came home late as usual. Lena and Vladlen were already asleep, and Ashkhen Stepanovna was working in her room. A Central Committee lecturer on international affairs, she prepared her lectures carefully, translating — as she put it — official gobbledygook into human language.

Ivan Grigoryevich sat down in the chair next to her small desk.

Ashkhen Stepanovna regarded her desk and the papers and books on it with great hostility and said firmly, "Time to find a new job."

"Specifically?"

"Some museum — historical, archaeological, even the Museum of the Revolution. Or maybe health care ..."

"Dearest," Ivan Grigoryevich laughed, "you've forgotten all your medicine by now."

"Of course. But I meant administrative work. I'm ready to do anything rather than this. . . ."

She looked again at her desk and picked up Stalin's *Questions of Leninism*.

"Here's this year's edition, printed in two million one hundred thousand copies. Soon this will be the only book, like the Bible. While Lenin's works are being published in editions of one hundred thousand. And you can't even quote from him anymore, you can only repeat what Comrade Stalin quoted, and even better is not to mention Lenin at all but to quote Comrade Stalin himself. And not to interpret. He interprets himself. Believe me, Ivan, work has become impossible. My lectures are checked by an ignoramus who cuts out any original thoughts, leaving only what is in the newspapers, and in the same words. And I'm supposed to repeat those words, that nonsense, and read them straight from my paper. What do they need me for? Anyone can read from a piece of paper. And I don't dare even evaluate the facts, and yet my topic, the international situation, changes every day. . . . And I come to the lecture and tell them about events that happened a month ago at best. About the things that happened yesterday or today, I can say only, 'As Comrade Stalin correctly foresaw,' 'As Comrade Stalin so accurately predicted.' And yet he, incidentally, foresaw and predicted exactly the opposite of what happened. I'm lecturing to the Party activists, and people with even the smallest bit of intelligence regard me as an idiot or a cynical liar. And I've been in the Party for twenty-five years, you know."

"Twenty-six," Ivan Grigoryevich corrected her. "It's twenty-five years since we met, so don't try to make yourself younger."

She laughed.

"Yes, you're right," she said and grew sad again. "Ivan, do you remember Pavel Rodionov? He had been in London, too. I didn't even want to tell you this. I arrived in Kazan, gave my lecture, and who do you think is sitting in the first row? Pavel. Smiling at me — think how many years it's been since we saw each other. There I was, reading that nonsense from my piece of paper, and I could see Pavel looking away. He was ashamed of me. And he didn't come over after the lecture; he let me know that he knew all he needed to. I couldn't sleep all night in the hotel. You know, that was the last straw for me."

Ivan Grigoryevich remembered Rodionov very well; he had even been jealous of him. Pavel had also studied medicine, and he walked Ashkhen home after classes. She was so slender, just twenty-one then. Later, when they married, those walks home ended of their own accord.

She came from a wealthy Armenian family in Baku, joined the Revolution, the Bolsheviks, and broke with her parents, and she served the Revolution wildly and fearlessly. Smart, she knew three languages and taught them to Ivan Grigoryevich.

She had worked with Litvinov, bringing illegal literature into Russia, had fought in the Civil War as head of the army's Political Section. They sent Lena to Motovilikha to live with Ivan Grigoryevich's parents because Ashkhen had typhus. He barely saved her then, she almost died. . . . Basically, it was the typical biography of an underground Bolshevik. Now she traveled all over the country giving lectures. But if it was too much for her, then she really should find other work.

"Maybe you should transfer to Litvinov, especially with your languages?"

"No!" She was adamant. "I'm not going to execute those policies. Litvinov is passive, and I can see where Stalin is taking things."

"The Seventh Comintern Congress is opening on July twenty-fifth," Ivan Grigoryevich said. "I think I should send in my resignation."

She turned to him sharply. Her eyes were round.

"That will cost you your head!"

"But if everyone were to think that way, Ashkhen —"

She interrupted. "Everyone does. And they're right. We've lost the opportunity, dear! You were all busy thinking about how to keep people from taking power — Trotsky, Zinoviev, Kamenev, Bukharin. Stalin was the only one thinking about how to take power for himself. And he did. And he'll destroy everyone in his path. The ones who were in his path are doomed, you know that. By the way, yesterday they arrested Ter-Vaganyan."

Ter-Vaganyan came from Baku, she knew his family.

"But he's a Trotskyite," Ivan Grigoryevich said.

"Former! Ivan, don't forget, he's a *former* Trotskyite. He left the opposition back in 1928, and he was reinstated in the Party. He left honestly, I know that. But Stalin doesn't care. If you were in his way even once, you'll be destroyed. He'll destroy them all, you'll see. But you've never been in any oppositions, you have a clean background in that sense. And don't open yourself up for a hit. There's nothing that can be done with him now. We have to wait."

"For what?"

"The failure of his policy."

"It will be too late then."

"No! If the Party cadres protect themselves, it won't be too late. Then they'll be able to knock power out of his hands. You just have to protect yourself. And your children. Yes, yes, the children, and I don't see anything criminal or anti-Party in thinking about the future of your children. And behaving sensibly."

Ivan Grigoryevich stood up. "I confess, Ashkhen, that's not what I expected to hear from you."

She stood up too and said with determination, "Vladlen is nine years old and Lena is pregnant. Think about what I said."

She left the room.

Ivan Grigoryevich could hear her walking around his study and making up the couch.

He chuckled. It was an old habit of hers. If she was unhappy with him or if she didn't want to continue their conversation, she made up his bed in the study.

He went in and embraced her. "Don't be mad!"

"I'm not, but I am reminding you about your children and your future grandchild. You can't sacrifice them so thoughtlessly!"

Ivan Grigoryevich was left alone.

Ashkhen was afraid, the way so many were today. But did he have the right to be afraid? Yes, these were difficult times, hard times. But he had to do his duty, and that would force others to do theirs. Now, when it was so clear, so obvious, that Stalin's strategy had collapsed, that Hitler had come to power as a result of that strategy, this was the time for him to speak up. Otherwise, Hitler would gain so much strength that Stalin would have to yield to him, and who knew the limit of such concessions?

Ivan Grigoryevich hoped that his meeting with Stalin would produce results. He knew that Stalin rejected his position, but that didn't mean that he wouldn't listen. He often took ideas from people he later killed ... more frequently, he killed them first and then appropriated the ideas. On May 2 he signed an agreement of mutual aid with France, and on May 16 a similar agreement was signed with Czechoslovakia. Outwardly, it was done to oppose Hitler. Was it strategy or tactics? In any case, it had to be upheld, that was the path to take.

After his meeting last year with Stalin, Budyagin wrote a memorandum to the Central Committee. He vacillated all year on whether to send it. The conversation with Stalin showed that it would get no results. And Ashkhen felt that he shouldn't send it.

However, since the U.S.S.R. joined the League of Nations after Germany and Japan left and signed treaties with France and Czechoslovakia, he decided to send his report to the Central Committee. The policy of a single, united front had to be developed at the upcoming Eighth Congress of the Comintern.

Ivan Grigoryevich looked through his memorandum again. He had already taken out some of the sharp remarks that would have driven Stalin into a frenzy. Even now it sounded harsh, but the criticism was addressed to the German Communist Party. And he also indicated that the greatest danger to the country came from Germany, even though he knew how Stalin would react to that.

## ❧ 14 ❧

**P**rofessor Marasevich had reacted with the same indifference to his daughter's new marriage as he had to the previous one. His children were adults, contemporary people who understood the times better than he did; let them live as they knew best.

But Vadim was furious. What? Marry a foreigner? Move to Paris? Now on all applications he'd have to write "yes" in answer to the question "Do you have relatives abroad?" And not some old aunt in mothballs, but his own sister, who left on purpose, married a foreigner and an anti-Soviet one at that!

There had already been two articles in *Izvestia* over Charles's slanderous reports in the Paris press. He had not been expelled from Moscow only because the French parliament was going to ratify the Franco-Soviet treaty in February. But he was leaving on his own now, and you could imagine what kind of filth he'd write about the Soviets. Her husband . . . Her husband and his brother-in-law. Yes, yes, the brother-in-law of Vadim Marasevich, the husband of his only sister, would be publishing virulent anti-Soviet articles in the Paris press.

Back when they were in school, Vadim had tried to reform his sister, attacking her for her way of life — clothes crazy, going out all the time, socially passive. Then he accepted it. They were living in new times and his sister blended into the new landscape. His respect for her didn't increase, but they could coexist.

Their family was built on success. Everyone had to make a contribution to the family's success. Problems were not brought home; that wasn't allowed. It was a condition of their life. There was too much hardship behind them. But Vika had violated that rule, she had ruined the family, ruined his future.

It was nothing to their father. His life was settled — nobody would take away his titles, salary, and awards.

But Vadim, what would happen to him? He had started so well. Every magazine was pleased to print his articles. He was recognized as one of the most principled and demanding critics, and he was also considered practically the best orator around. He was invited to every discussion. . . . And now what would Ermilov and Kirpotin, his mentors, say? At the Writers' Congress he had helped both Kirpotin and Vladimir Vladimirovich Ermilov, who was a member of the Editorial Commission. He had even been to see Nikolai Ivanovich Bukharin and Karl Radek, and not as a messenger, but as a worker of the Editorial Commission.

And now all that would collapse. Now he would have to explain that his sister was just a nightclub floozie who had got mixed up with some foreigner and had moved abroad.

He paced the apartment and groaned, as if he had a toothache. He couldn't stand it anymore and burst into Vika's room.

"Cut out the hysterics," Vika said calmly. "What does it have to do with you? You're my brother? So what? What does that mean? Absolutely nothing. I'm not a little girl. I'm not leaving my family. I'm leaving one husband for another. I'm leaving the Architect, do you understand that? Let them ask him why he got on so poorly with his wife that she had to go to another."

"You bear our name, not his," Vadim shouted. "Why didn't you legally marry him? Because he has a *real* wife, and it's not you. You're his mistress, that's what you are! You merely slept with him. You're a Marasevich, understand?"

"What have I done illegal?" Vika asked calmly. "I married Charles legally, I took his name, I got official permission to go abroad. How have I broken the law?"

"You've broken more than the law. You've violated elementary ethics, you've violated the elementary duty of a Soviet citizen. Exile abroad is a punishment, one of the highest forms of punishment. And you're leaving of your own volition. Shame on you!"

"Oh, ho, ho," Vika said and laughed. "You have such social

consciousness, you're so proper — is this something new? You're a coward, and you serve those louts out of cowardice. Everyone despises you. They call you a murderer — I've heard them, a murderer and a flunky.... So don't worry, nothing will happen to you because of me. And stop lecturing me, I'm sick of it! Shut the door on your way out!"

Vadim left her room and slammed the door. Bitch! Whore! If she had been arrested for ties with foreigners, things wouldn't have been easy for him, but better than this. He'd be rid of her after one renunciation — his sister is in prison or exiled for this and that, and that would be it! But now her husband would remind them of himself every week.

After the First Writers' Union Congress put an end to disunity and group interests and consolidated the literary forces, writers turned to the themes of socialist construction, industrialization, collectivization, and the transformation of the country. Literature was developing rapidly.

Of course, most of the new novels had been written before the Writers' Congress, but the congress had been the culmination of a process begun by Comrade Stalin's conversation with writers in 1932. It was Comrade Stalin's conversation and his letters that were the final blow against the anti-Party bourgeois tendencies in literature, to all sorts of literary groups, and the vulgarly sociological and formal schools. It was then, in 1932, that Comrade Stalin gave Soviet literature and theater their direction of socialist realism.

Vadim understood this new direction and "being made wary" was a favorite expression of his. He used it in relation to works he expected to be blasted, and when the blasting came he took part in it. In relation to works he did not expect to be blasted, he caviled, using such expressions as "in a discussion of stylistic and compositional errors." If the work passed muster, then Vadim's voice merely joined the general flow of praise, which naturally did not preclude small and friendly critical notes. And if the work was unexpectedly blasted — and such things did happen to works that had been previously approved at the highest level — then Vadim was saved by his ubiquitous "wariness."

Vadim's main talent was his ability to paraphrase in his own words, quickly, the official point of view, either already expressed or about to be handed down.

As opposed to the hacks, who repeated the edicts phrase by phrase, afraid to miss even a comma, Vadim used refined turns of phrase, unexpected quotes from long-dead (and therefore safe) authors, and even Latin. This created the illusion of a personal position, independent judgment, and erudition. He was considered a loyal but progressive man. The literary bosses appreciated the first, and the literary intelligentsia the second.

And he was also simple, accessible, and sociable. A democrat. Vadim had mastered that style back in school, when he adjusted to the democratic behavior of the Komsomols of the 1920s, when he tried to rid himself of any signs of his profoundly intellectual background and his bourgeois upbringing.

The democratic attitude, the man-in-the-street style, proletarian, came in good stead now when he dealt with the hacks whom he feared but whom he treated as buddies. When they met, he praised their illiterate articles, but he never praised them publicly, nor did he berate them publicly. Thus he preserved his high intellectual standing and the trust of the toadies.

He did not join the Party. He was a non-Party Bolshevik — that was enough. Earlier, belonging to the Party was an advantage, but now it was just the opposite — the purges, the checking of Party documents, put you under a bell jar. Were he a Party member, he would have to inform the Party that his sister had married a foreigner and moved abroad. But as a non-Party man, he didn't have to report to anyone.

Outside the Party, his position was freer. Having friendly chats with the hacks, Vadim had to be careful. But in his own circle, people understood every circumlocution, every reference. They were cynics like him and understood the conditions under which they lived. They accepted the way of thinking, wrote what was necessary, spoke what they had to speak. And among themselves they talked the way they were supposed to talk, delighting in what was decreed delightful, condemning what had to be condemned. Their delight was without enthusiasm, and their condemnation was

without outrage. With jokes and quips they covered and camou-
flaged their next ruthless attack or limitless delight.

With time, Vadim calmed down about Vika. She had been gone
a half year now and no one had asked a thing. The Paris newspapers
weren't sold in the Moscow kiosks, and Vadim did not know
whether her husband was busy writing his lampoons about the
Soviet Union or not.

Vika didn't write home from Paris — she understood that that
was out of the question. Two letters had come, with a Moscow
postmark, which meant she had sent them back with someone. The
letters were brief — I'm alive and well and please write back
through Nelli Vladimirova, here's her phone number.

Vadim forbade his father to write back.

"Who's this Nelli Vladimirova?" he demanded. "How do we
know she won't take your letter to the intelligence center at
Lubyanka Prison first? Don't you know what ties abroad can lead
to? Show me the person who corresponds abroad now. People with
relatives abroad hide it, and you want us to advertise it?"

"But, Vadim," the old man muttered, "can't I correspond with
my own daughter?"

"No. Even she understands that and doesn't write to us at our
address. She knows it's dangerous and what it can lead to."

"But, Vadim!"

"Papa, look at this seriously. She abandoned us, abandoned us
forever. People don't come back from France. The ones who leave,
we don't take back. She wanted that life, she didn't think — rather,
she didn't want to think what our life would be like because of her.
Now you'll have to write in your documents, 'Daughter went
abroad, lives in France.' Of course, you're famous. . . . But there are
no untouchables, remember that. And I do ideological work — they
don't trust people with relatives abroad. I understand that you think
I'm thinking only of myself and my career. No! In this case I'm
interested in the moral, ethical side of the question. She didn't think
about us, why should we think about her? The very fact that she left
has opened us to attack. She's not risking anything; we're risking
everything."

"Well, Vadim, we'll do what you think best," said Andrei Andreyevich.

But Professor Marasevich called Nelli Vladimirova, came to see her and gave her a letter for Vika — he and Vadim were fine, healthy, glad that everything was fine for Vika, too.

"But, please," the old man told Nelli, "don't tell my son that I sent this letter. He and his sister don't get along."

"I don't know your son," Nelli announced.

"But you might bump into him, so please, don't tell."

"All right," Nelli said indifferently.

Professor Marasevich had not expected that Vika would confirm getting his letter. "Papa, dearest, I got your news. . . ." The letter fell into Vadim's hands.

"Can you explain the meaning of this?"

The old man babbled — he had called the lady Vika mentioned, had asked her to pass along his greetings . . . why make such a fuss, it had nothing to do with Vadim, it was just an old man's fancy. . . .

"Do as you like," Vadim replied coldly, "but if you intend to continue this correspondence, we will have to separate."

"What do you mean?"

"Very simple. We will have to give up this apartment. I will live alone."

This threat stunned the old man. He couldn't imagine himself without that apartment, known to all of Moscow. Of course, now, without Vika, the house was not the same, there were fewer guests. And guests from abroad came less frequently. The professor didn't make new acquaintances, but the old friends always showed up if they were in Moscow, and he received them. He just couldn't picture himself without this house, alone, without a wife, without a daughter, and now he would be losing his son. That was what Vadim meant.

"This is very cruel on your part," Andrei Andreyevich muttered bitterly.

"Judge me as you like," Vadim replied, "but may God protect you from learning personally how right I am. You have old-fashioned ideas, which is fine, but it doesn't suit the times, believe me."

"All right," Andrei Andreyevich agreed, confused and frightened by his son's threat. "I won't write to Victoria anymore." That was the end of the conversation and they went to their rooms.

In the morning the telephone woke Vadim. . . . Dammit! Nobody ever called this early. He picked up the phone and heard a businesslike, unfamiliar voice. "Vadim Andreyevich Marasevich? This is the NKVD. Today at twelve you are to appear at Kuznetsky Most, number twenty-four, at the reception, to see Comrade Altman. Did you understand?"

"Yes," Vadim replied, his voice hoarse.

"Bring your passport. Understood?"

"Yes, of course."

The dial tone came on and Vadim hung up.

He knew that it would end this way sooner or later. Bitch! Whore!

Dammit! Why didn't he tell them that he was busy today, that he had a meeting, an appointment, he couldn't come. . . . And why were they calling him by telephone? If he was guilty of anything, let them call him in officially, with a warrant. He was a member of the Writers' Union. They read his articles, they had to have read them if they were planning to talk to him.

Of course, maybe that's why they didn't send a warrant for him. They wanted to warn him that correspondence with Vika would cast a shadow on him and his father, and that they should stop writing her. They were calling him in unofficially. And the call was so rude because it was an ordinary clerk who had called.

And what could they expect from him? He had broken off with his sister long ago, before she left for Paris. He was a Komsomol. They hadn't even talked to each other in the last three years. And his father? What can you expect from the old man, he's got these family superstitions, you know.

Oh, God. . . . What if they kept him in custody? But no, they have a warrant when they arrest you. But still, the NKVD terrified him. The fear with which he grew up, which he thought he had conquered when he joined the Komsomol, had engulfed him again.

Having become one of the most orthodox critics, having become an "intellectual club" in the hands of the lowbrows, he thought he had nothing to fear — his country needed him! Yes, people like him were needed by the government and they should understand that at the NKVD.

He stood before the mirror doing his tie. Damn! His hands were shaking. And it was getting close to noon.

How could his father have been that stupid — to call Nelli Vladimirova. She might be an informer, a decoy. He had warned his father, and now, despite his high position, his father was afraid. His high-placed patients were being arrested, exiled, and all his colleagues, all those professors and celebrities, were trembling with fear. And what about his own colleagues? Pretending they were masters of people's minds, they too were trembling with fear. And if something happened to him, they'd disassociate themselves. They were not friends, they'd be upset only that they had "missed" recognizing him. He knew their smug smiles, the aplomb that cost nothing.

Should he talk to Yuri Sharok?

He hadn't seen him in a long time. But they had been friends, childhood friends. They had shared a desk for almost nine years. And they saw each other after that ... Yuri Sharok had been to their house so many times, and Vadim had got him passes to the theaters. After all, they were the only two left from the old school crowd.

Yuri Sharok had to help him. Let him explain everything to them. Perhaps Altman doesn't know that Vadim is not only the son of the famous Professor Marasevich, consultant at the Kremlin hospital, but is himself a famous critic.

And most important, Yuri Sharok would confirm that Vadim was solid in his convictions for Soviet power.

He had to call Yuri Sharok, get his advice, bring this up casually, maintaining his dignity, not showing his anxiety.

And Yuri Sharok had reason to worry, too. There had once been something between him and Vika. Once when he came home he had gone into Vika's room and Yuri Sharok was there and Vadim understood — just from their faces. And before that — at Nina's New Year's Eve party — he was making out with Vika in the hallway. Nina even made a scene over it. Of course, once Yuri Sharok started working in the NKVD, he stopped coming over, but maybe they met on the side, who the hell knew. Vika was a whore and Yuri was a ladies' man. Basically, Yuri Sharok had to help him, he just had to.

He dialed Yuri Sharok's number, heard a gruff plebeian voice, his father the tailor. Dammit, he didn't even remember his name.

"He's not home," the gray, alien voice said. "I don't know when he'll be in."

He hung up. Vadim didn't know Yuri's work number. Besides, you don't talk about such things over the phone. What was he to do?

What kind of a man was that Altman? Young, old? Intellectual, or a boor? The former would be better — he'd be able to talk to him. And what if he was a boor? Sitting in his office in his boots, smoking shag, smelling up the place on purpose, play-acting the proletariat.

In the last few years Vadim had learned how to talk to boors the way they deserved. He thought he had stopped fearing them a long time ago. No! The voice of old Sharok had driven him crazy; he was still afraid of them.

And Vadim felt even greater horror of the mysterious unknown and powerful boor who was sitting at Lubyanka waiting for him.


He turned out to be a red-haired, stoop-shouldered Jew in a military uniform, with a long nose and sorrowful eyes.

Seeing Altman, Vadim sighed in relief. This skinny red-haired soldier didn't look like a boor. Sunken cheeks, narrow shoulders . . . maybe he had even sawed away on a violin when he was a kid.

"Sit down."

Vadim sat. Altman took out a sheet of paper from the desk, put it before him, and dipped his pen in ink.

"Surname, name, patronymic? Year and place of birth? Work and position?"

Interrogation? Why, what for? Altman's monotonous voice was irritating.

"Member of the Writers' Union U.S.S.R. I would like to know —"

"You'll find out everything," Altman interrupted. "Position?"

"There are no positions in the Writers' Union."

Altman looked at him. "Then what do you do there?"

"I'm a critic, a literary and drama critic."

Altman stared at him again.

"I get fees for my articles," Vadim explained.

Altman was still thoughtful. Then he wrote, "Critic."

This small victory encouraged Vadim, and he added, "The fees, of course, are insignificant — in that sense, a critic's work is unrewarding. But we survive.... I live with my father, he is Professor Marasevich...." Vadim paused, awaiting Altman's reaction to such an important name, but not a muscle moved on his face, and Vadim went on. "He heads a clinic and is a consultant at the Kremlin hospital."

Altman's bored face reflected nothing. He turned the page, ran his finger down the fold. It was a clean sheet, lined.

Without looking up, he asked, "With whom have you had counterrevolutionary conversations?" His voice was even, just as bored as his face.

Vadim had not expected that. He had expected to talk about Vika. He was prepared for that, he had a logical and convincing answer for that. But "With whom have you had counterrevolutionary conversations?" No one. He couldn't. He was a Soviet man, an honest Soviet man. The question was a trap. Let Altman ask about a specific case, he'd be ready to answer, but he had to know what it was. If he began arguing, he'd just get this thug mad, and he was the boss here, within these bare walls, with barred windows painted halfway up with white.

"I don't quite understand your question," Vadim began. "What conversations do you mean? I —"

Altman interrupted. "You understand my question perfectly. You know very well which people I have in mind. I suggest you be honest and frank. Don't forget where you are."

"But, really, I don't know," Vadim babbled. "I couldn't have any counterrevolutionary conversation with anyone. This is some mistake."

Altman looked at the page. "You're a member of the Writers' Union, right? You're surrounded by writers? And none of them ever says anything counterrevolutionary?" He asked question after question, and his voice was monotonous, as if he weren't asking Vadim, but lecturing him. "You want to persuade me, you want to prove to me that all the writers are absolutely loyal to Soviet power? Is that what you want to prove? Are you taking responsibility for all the writers, for all the intelligentsia? Perhaps you're taking on too much?"

Vadim said nothing.

"Well?" Altman repeated. "Playing at silence, are we?"

Vadim shrugged his fat shoulders.

"But no one talked counterrevolutionary with me."

"You don't want to help us," Altman said with a quiet threat in his voice.

"I do!" Vadim said. "Helping the organs of the NKVD is everyone's duty. But there were no conversations. I can't just make them up."

Even though the whole situation — this stark office and the robot Altman with his monotonous voice — intimidated Vadim, he had relaxed. He was vulnerable only through Vika, but Vika had not come up. As for counterrevolutionary conversations, that was a mistake.

Altman said nothing, and his eyes revealed neither thought nor feeling. Then he turned the page, and checked the name.

"Vadim Andreyevich!"

That was insulting. Altman did not disguise that he didn't even remember Vadim's name, didn't make the effort to remember it, he was so insignificant.

He looked into Vadim's eyes for the first time, and Vadim felt cold. There was so much hatred in his gaze, in his implacable executioner's squint.

"But I —"

"I, I," Altman's quiet voice was about to explode, to turn into a scream. "I repeat, you forget where you are. We didn't call you in here to educate us, do you understand that or not?"

"Of course, of course," Vadim said.

Altman quieted down and then asked in the same dreary voice, "With what foreign citizens do you meet?"

At last! They were getting to Vika!

Vadim looked surprised. "I personally do not meet with any foreign citizens."

Altman looked into his eyes again and Vadim felt cold again. "Perhaps you've never even seen a foreigner in your whole life?"

"Of course I have."

"Where?"

"Foreigners come to my father's house. My father is a professor of medicine, a world-famous figure.... And of course, foreign scientists visit him, that's natural, and it is done officially, with the knowledge of the right departments.... I don't know them well, I'm not a doctor, I don't take part in their conversations. By the way, official people are always present at these conversations.... But I do remember a few names. A few years ago Father was visited by Professor Kramer of Berlin University, and another professor, Rossolini, I think. And there was a professor from Columbia University, I don't remember his last name, but he was called Sam Veniamnovich."

Altman wrote something down. Not the names of those professors? How strange. He could have read about them in the newspapers. Vadim mentioned Professor Igumnov and Anatoli Vasilyevich Lunacharsky, who had come to their house with foreigners. He named a Polish professor who had come with Glinsky, a famous Party worker, a friend and comrade in arms of Vladimir Ilyich Lenin; he named a few more people.

And he stopped.

Altman was silent awhile, too, and then asked, "And what did you talk about with these foreigners?"

"Me, nothing. They were Father's acquaintances."

"Did you sit at the table?"

"Sometimes."

"Well then?"

"I don't understand...."

"I asked, 'Well then?' What did you do at the table? Talk?"

"No, there was nothing for me to talk to them about, they were men of science."

"Ah, so you didn't talk. You just ate and drank. And what about your ears? Were they stuffed with cotton? You ate, drank, and listened to their conversations. What did they say?"

"They talked about various things, mostly medicine."

"And the orchestra conductor, too — he talked about medicine?"

And here Vadim said something he thought was clever, and it cheered him. "Yes, about medicine. He asked my father's advice on his illness."

Altman picked up the page and, mispronouncing them, read all the names Vadim had given. "Is that all?"

His monotonous voice made it clear he expected more.

"I think so."

"Think some more."

And once again his voice made it clear that he was waiting for the one name, the reason Vadim had been brought here.

It was clear to Vadim. The investigator wanted Charles, Vika's husband, that damned viscount! He had visited Vika, but Vadim hardly ever saw him, just greeted him coldly when Vika introduced Charles to him and his father, but he hadn't dined with them. He said he had an important meeting, so Vika introduced Charles into their family not only without his knowledge, but without his participation. It all had to do with Charles, and only Charles. He had to name him, name him freely, casually.

"Well," Vadim said, "there's my sister's husband, they live in Paris. . . . But I don't maintain any ties with him at all."

"Is that all?" Altman asked again.

"Yes, all I can remember."

Altman pulled the forms over and started writing in a neat clerical hand, glancing at the paper he had used to write the list of names from Vadim.

Vadim watched him write. Slow, quiet work that no one could stop. That inexorability frightened Vadim.

When he finished, Altman handed him the transcript. "Read it and sign it." And he looked at Vadim with that hatred. As if he were deciding whether it would be better to hang Vadim or chop off his head.

Squirming, cold under his gaze, Vadim read the transcript.

Two pages of text without paragraphs or digressions answered the question "With what foreign citizens do you meet, where, when, who else was there?"

The names Vadim had given were written down correctly. But

there were a lot of them — Russian and foreign. The foreign names belonged to those who came to their house, the Russian names to those who brought them, but the whole thing looked crazy, impossible. It looked as if foreigners came all the time and Vadim did nothing but talk to them. And all of this because of Vika, because she married a Frenchman, and it looked as if the foreigners were at their house because of that.

But formally it corresponded with what Vadim had said. There was nothing to complain about, and it was too scary to complain. He was oppressed, squashed by that executioner's squint, the inexorability, the monotonous voice, the unexpected flare-ups of anger and hatred. Vadim signed both pages of the transcript.

Altman put it in a file.

"No one must know about your visit here or your evidence. Understand?"

"Of course," Vadim hurried to reply. He was ready to agree to anything, just to get out of there.

"You must not tell anyone anything. Otherwise, you will be in a lot of trouble."

"I won't!"

"Consider that an official warning."

"Understood."

Altman looked up and narrowed his eyes meanly.

"We'll return to your counterrevolutionary conversations. We'll talk about it in more detail. I'll call you."

## ❦ 15 ❦

**V**arya saw her friends Lyova and Rina only at work. And they never talked about Varya's ex-husband, Kostya. Lyova once tried, and Varya put him down harshly so that he would learn. Lyova never brought him up again, and Rina didn't care one way or another.

Igor Vladimirovich was still kindly, attentive, and imperturbed. But Varya sensed that after her breakup with Kostya, Igor Vladimirovich was harboring hopes, which he covered with marked propriety. After his subservient behavior at the union meetings he had fallen in her esteem — but he was a good administrator and unarguably a talented architect. Varya was interested in how his mind worked; she liked his resolution, his logic, and his persuasive arguments. He always took Varya with him to meetings where technical questions of construction were discussed and where he demonstrated his projects and proposals. He never took Lyova, or Rina. Igor Vladimirovich did it very tactfully. Lyova was on a rush job, Rina was working on a complex project, and he didn't want to tear them away, so Varya accompanied Igor Vladimirovich to the technical meetings.

She went to the meetings with pleasure. It was a pleasant atmosphere, with intelligent, clever people, outstanding in their field. Gradually she began to understand the complicated issues of building a hotel and had to be impressed by the erudition and brilliant logic of Igor Vladimirovich's talks. He was outstanding, even here among these outstanding men, and that made Varya better disposed toward him.

Of course, fear hung over him as over everyone else. He was no hero, but he tried to the best of his abilities to remain a decent person. He loved his work, was a creative man but a weak one. Creative and talented people apparently were often weak. The newspapers reported famous writers, actors, and artists were signing demands to destroy, liquidate, and shoot people whose guilt was not yet proved. How could writers, actors, and artists believe in mass espionage and mass sabotage? Even she didn't believe it. They didn't believe it either, but they were afraid.

Varya didn't see Igor Vladimirovich's name in the newspapers and, thank God, he hadn't signed such demands. His behavior at the union meetings wasn't important, even though it had bothered her then.

Igor Vladimirovich saw her home from work a few times, saying it was on his way.... They went down Herzen Street for some reason. *For the Sake of the Child* was playing at the movies, and they went to see it.

The next day, they went across Red Square to the Moskva River and sat on the parapet, watching people go by and inventing life stories for them.

Once, walking past the metro on Arbat Square, he bought her three roses. She dropped one, and they both bent down and bumped their heads, which made them laugh.

These walks were becoming dangerous — he was beginning to court her. She made Zoe join them — they lived in the same building, so it was natural to walk home together. Igor Vladimirovich did not show any displeasure, and made the usual jokes, but the next day, when he saw Zoe with Varya, he was disappointed. He said, "I can go only as far as Vozdvizhenka with you today."

At the corner there, he said good-bye.

Another time Varya left at the same time as Igor Vladimirovich. Zoe wasn't around, so Varya said, "I'm in a hurry today, Igor Vladimirovich, so I'm taking the trolley."

"I'll put you on it."

He walked her in silence to the trolley stop, and stood in silence waiting for it. When it arrived, he suddenly asked, "May I call you?"

"Yes," Varya said and got in.

He did not call, but he sent a basket of flowers.

"A new suitor?" Nina asked.

"Perhaps. . . ."

The flowers were lovely, but she did not love Igor Vladimirovich and never would. To love him meant accepting all the existing rules, the way he had.

She was waiting for Sasha. . . . In Sofya Alexandrovna's last letter, she added, "Dear Sasha, we're waiting for you." Then she changed it to "I'm waiting."

Sofya Alexandrovna looked at it, smiled, and said, "Thank you, Sasha will be so happy to read that."

It would be stupid to return the flowers. And it would be stupid to talk about it at work. Varya decided to write to Igor Vladimirovich.

Dear Igor Vladimirovich,

Thank you for your sweet present, the flowers are lovely. But in our poor communal flat that basket created quite a stir and started all kinds of discussion relating to my former husband. To avoid agitating my neighbors in the future and to avoid giving them food for gossip, I ask you not to send any more flowers.

With the fondest greetings,
Varya

She sealed the envelope and the next day she went into Igor Vladimirovich's office, put it on his desk, and smiled at him. "Read it and don't be angry!"

She left his office.

Igor Vladimirovich came into their room and smiled at Varya, to show her that he had read and understood her note.

Varya's days and evenings were busy, but she still made time to visit Sofya Alexandrovna and drop by Mikhail Yurevich. They were the only people she wanted to see.

Sofya Alexandrovna was having heart trouble. She did not complain, but Varya saw how hard it was for her to get up from her chair, how short of breath she was, and how she kept taking medicine.

"How can I help you, Sofya Alexandrovna?"

"It's all right, it'll pass," Sofya Alexandrovna usually said. "I'll make it to Sasha's return."

"Stop that, Sofya Alexandrovna," Varya would say angrily. "I can't stand watching you suffer. Get ready, I'm taking you to the clinic."

"You don't have time, you're working and going to school, and it takes all day to be seen by a doctor."

"I'll take two vacation days."

Varya came by the next evening. "Sofya Alexandrovna, we're going tomorrow, I made arrangements at work."

Sofya Alexandrovna could not walk quickly and it took a long time to get to the clinic. It was crowded and they had a long wait until at last it was Sofya Alexandrovna's turn. She went into the office, and Varya followed.

"Who are you?" the doctor asked.

"Her daughter."

"Wait outside."

Sofya Alexandrovna said, "Please wait for me, Varya."

The visit to the doctor didn't change anything. He prescribed drops and nitroglycerine for acute attacks. He didn't even excuse her from work, and Sofya Alexandrovna went back to Zubov Boulevard, where she worked as a clerk in a laundry.

Varya pictured poor Sofya Alexandrovna being attacked by crazed customers, whose laundry was constantly being lost or switched, Sofya Alexandrovna replying in her sickly, weak voice and putting the nitroglycerine tablet under her tongue. And the administrator had started picking on her. He had learned about Sasha somehow, and even wanted to fire her for not revealing the fact when she applied for the job — but he couldn't, because nobody else was willing to work for that salary. Sofya Alexandrovna replied to his nasty comments in the same weak and sick voice. Horrors! How can you make a person in that condition work? Was the doctor blind?

Varya couldn't help Sofya Alexandrovna at the laundry — she had her own job — but she did try to help her out at home. Sometimes Varya felt that this was her real home, she was so comfortable and at ease. Amazingly, nothing there reminded her of her ex-husband, Kostya, as if he had never lived in that apartment.

This was where Sofya Alexandrovna lived and this was the place where Sasha's spirit was present.

After doing the housework at Sofya Alexandrovna's, Varya visited Mikhail Yurevich next door. The room, stuffed with cupboards, shelves, and cabinets that in turn were packed with books, albums, and files, was always crepuscular. The only illumination was on the table where there were jars, glasses with brushes, pens, pencils, as well as tubes of glue and paints, scissors, and razors — the paraphernalia of Mikhail Yurevich's work. Varya would tuck her feet under her in the old armchair with the broken seat and tall back.

The room smelled of paint and glue. Mikhail Yurevich looked cozy in his plaid jacket, an old-fashioned bachelor wearing a pince-nez, bent over the table, repairing the pages of an ancient book.

On one visit, Varya saw a volume by Stalin on his table. "You're reading that?"

"I have to. For my work."

"Where do you work?"

"At CBEA."

"CBEA? What's that?" Varya laughed. "I've never heard of it."

"The Central Bureau of Economic Accounting. It used to have a more accurate name, the Central Statistical Bureau. I'm a statistician, Varya."

"It must be very boring," Varya noted. "Just numbers and more numbers."

"No, no. Those numbers stand for life."

"When I see figures in the newspapers, I stop reading. It's boring. And it's all lies."

"No, figures don't always lie," Mikhail Yurevich said seriously. "Sometimes they tell the truth. Here, for instance . . ."

Mikhail Yurevich opened the book by Stalin to a marked page. "This is Comrade Stalin's speech at the Seventeenth Congress, comparing 1933 with 1929 — and it turns out that the number of livestock has gone down." He raised his finger and read, "Horses down from thirty-four million to seventeen million, cattle from sixty-eight million to thirty-eight million, sheep and goats, from one hundred forty-seven million to fifty million, and pigs from twenty-one million to twelve million. We lost one hundred forty-three million head of cattle in those years. More than half."

"Hoof and mouth disease?" Varya mocked.

"A complex question. Comrade Stalin explained that the kulaks — the rich peasants — killed the cattle and urged others to do the same."

"The kulaks?" Varya asked, still sarcastic. "And how many kulaks were there?"

"Well, in that same speech, Comrade Stalin says that they composed about five percent of the rural population."

"And that five percent killed half the country's cattle? You believe that?"

"I didn't say that I believed it; I read you the words of Comrade Stalin."

"Your Comrade Stalin is lying!" Varya was incensed. "We have a family in our apartment — village folk — and their old village neighbors come to visit, and I've heard them talk a hundred times — the collectivization was forced, in a few days, in January, without preparing shelter or feed for the cattle. The cattle ended up in the street — and they perished. The kolkhoz workers didn't give a damn. They were forced into the kolkhozes, their livestock taken away — and these animals were no longer theirs, so they didn't care about the cows, sheep, pigs, and horses. Your Comrade Stalin didn't say that! Deceit and lies, everywhere!"

Mikhail Yurevich looked at her, thought, and then said, "Varya, please don't misunderstand me. I share your indignation, but remember the times in which we live. It is not safe to express your indignation. There are many bad people around. You should be more careful."

"But I can be frank with you."

Mikhail Yurevich responded, not right away and not with complete assurance. "With me you can. . . . But I hope that our conversations remain between us."

"Naturally. Do you doubt me, Mikhail Yurevich?"

"I trust you, Varya, you are a wonderful and honest little girl."

" 'Little girl!' " Varya laughed. "I was married."

"That doesn't matter. To me, you're a little girl. . . . And I worry about you, you're very open and defenseless. Danger lurks everywhere. You could suffer for a single careless word, you could ruin your life. Promise me not to discuss these things with anyone but me."

"Promise."

"Really?"

"Absolutely."

"You must know that this is the only way you can count on my trust."

"Of course, Mikhail Yurevich."

"In that case, I will tell you more. The head count of livestock went down by half, and meat production was reduced by a factor of twelve. And it was the same with milk, butter, wool, and eggs. That's why there's nothing in the stores — and that's in Moscow! You should see the provinces. Just imagine, Varya, how much fertilizer agriculture lost when it lost one hundred forty-three million head of livestock. And that's organic fertilizer! That's the cause of the agricultural crisis."

Varya listened. Mikhail Yurevich was a good man, but everyone was the same nowadays. Speaking so carefully.... "Agricultural crisis." She snorted.

"What is it, Varya?" Mikhail Yurevich asked.

"You keep saying 'crisis,' 'fertilizer,' 'productivity.' All these, Mikhail Yurevich, forgive me, are just words. You know entire villages are perishing of famine, our neighbors told me. And I've seen it myself here in Moscow, at the Bryanks Station."

"It's the Kiev Station now."

"Call it what you will, what's the difference? I remember people lying on the ground, peasants, women, children, alive and dead. They had fled the Ukraine and the famine, and the militia wouldn't let them into Moscow, to keep the city looking good, and they brought out the corpses at night, to make room for more starving people, so that they could die under a roof and not in the street, so that their corpses could be collected efficiently from the stations and not from all over the city.... And we walked past them and got on the train and went to visit friends at the dacha, and others walked past and got on the train and went to their dachas. And we all probably thought that we were moral people."

"Varya! Varya! What could we do?"

"What? What a strange question! I read that during the famine before the Revolution — I don't remember the year —"

"In the early 1890s," Mikhail Yurevich said.

"During that famine people contributed money, organized soup kitchens. I saw a photograph of Tolstoy in a canteen for starving children.... And I remember when I was little, my sister, Nina, and Sasha Pankratov and Maxim Kostin and other kids went around collecting money for the starving people of the Volga. Nobody hid the fact that there was famine; they helped them."

"That was in Lenin's day," Mikhail Yurevich said.

"That's my point," Varya said. "But now, 'Thanks to Comrade Stalin for our happy life!' Thanks to him for the right to die at the station and not on the street. Comrade Stalin openly tells us how many sheep and pigs died, but has he told us how many people died?"

"It's not in his speech," Mikhail Yurevich admitted.

"You see," Varya crowed. "He told us about pigs but not about people. You can blame the kulaks for the pigs — they slaughtered them, those contrary kulaks — but you can't blame them for the people, he'd have to take the blame himself. Now you're a statistician, Mikhail Yurevich, how many people died during collectivization?"

"It's hard to say.... There is no official data and there never will be; they didn't count the dead. The starving regions were simply isolated from the rest of the country."

"Can't you statisticians figure it out? Isn't statistics a science?"

"It is. And it helps you find out fairly accurately what official sources are hiding."

"And what do you get?"

"You see ... in early 1933, the population of the country was one hundred sixty-five point seven million. However, at the Seventeenth Congress," Mikhail Yurevich said, patting the book, "in January 1934, Comrade Stalin said that the population at the end of 1933 was one hundred sixty-eight million. We statisticians had not given Comrade Stalin that figure, and it frightened us, because we know that saying the population growth in 1933 was two point three million was a lie. On the contrary, the population of the country had gone down in 1933 — famine, high mortality, especially among children. Even in the cities, where the food situation was much better, the birth rate was lower than the mortality rate."

The neighbor Galya spoke outside the door, "Mikhail Yurevich, your kettle is boiling."

Varya got up. "I'll turn it off. Shall I make you some tea?"

"No, thank you, I don't want any. To tell the truth, I forgot I had put it on. Would you like some, though?"

"I had some at Sofya Alexandrovna's."

Varya went to the kitchen and came back to settle in the armchair again.

"Yes, as I was saying," Mikhail Yurevich went on. "How did Comrade Stalin come up with one hundred sixty-eight million? I'll tell you. You know that in the second half of the twenties, when the New Economic Policy raised the living standard, the population grew at approximately three million a year. And Comrade Stalin used that rate for the early thirties. His math was very simple — the last census was in 1926, and the population then had been one hundred forty-seven million. Seven years had passed. Seven times three is twenty-one million, and one forty-seven plus twenty-one makes one hundred sixty-eight million. In early 1937 there will be a new census, and the statisticians and the government expect a figure of one hundred seventy million. Fine, we'll accept that. But then this is what we get. I repeat — in 1926 the population was one hundred forty-seven million. If the normal growth rate is three million, in 1937 the population should be one hundred seventy-seven million. But our leaders expect a maximum of one hundred seventy million. What happened to seven million people, where did they disappear to? And the 1937 census won't give us one hundred seventy million. According to my figures, the maximum will be one hundred sixty-four million. That means that the direct tangential losses will be thirteen million people at a minimum — people who starved to death, who were killed in the course of the dekulakization, and losses due to a falling birth rate."

"Thirteen million, how horrible!" Varya said thoughtfully. "How many did Russia lose during the World War?"

"One and a half million...."

"One and a half million during the World War and thirteen

million during collectivization. . . . They overthrew the tsar because of that million and a half, and for that thirteen million people shout, 'Thanks to Comrade Stalin for our happy life!' But I still don't understand why they died. All right, the livestock died; but the people sowed wheat, they harvested, there was bread."

"There was no bread," Mikhail Yurevich said firmly. "In that same speech Comrade Stalin maintains that in 1933 we harvested eighty-nine point eight million tons of grain. But that's not true. We harvested twenty-one million tons less than Comrade Stalin says, and much less than in 1927–1929, the pre-kolkhoz years. Besides which, by 1933 the urban population had grown by twelve million. It doesn't produce bread, but it needs to be fed. In 1927–1929 we exported two point five million tons abroad, but in 1930–1932, bad harvest years, we exported twelve million tons. Our country had never exported that much."

"People were starving, and they were taking wheat out of the country?"

"Yes. They needed hard currency to buy Western technology. Industrialization!"

"They simply took wheat away from the peasants," Varya said. "I was told the militia, the army, and the OGPU took it away. Peasants were tried for sabotage if they didn't surrender their grain, and their property was confiscated and they were exiled."

They fell silent.

"Yes," Mikhail Yurevich said after a pause, "they took all the grain away, doomed them to death. . . . You're right about that, Varya. . . . But the dekulakization? They dekulaked not only the kulaks, the rich peasants, but also the middle-income peasants and even the poor ones, for whom they used the ridiculous label 'subkulaks.' According to my calculations, we dekulaked a minimum of ten million people, a minimum. The great majority was exiled to the north and to Siberia. Many of them died, of course."

"It's monstrous," Varya said. "And it's all hidden from the people."

"Well," Mikhail Yurevich said with a smile, "what would you expect!" And he picked up his glue bottle.

"Can't the country be industrialized without these sacrifices?"

"I think it's possible. By 1922, after the World War and the Civil

War, the country was destroyed, bankrupt. The plants were empty, the equipment had been taken apart to make cigarette lighters. And in five years, from 1922 to 1927, everything was reestablished, up from the ruins — industry, and agriculture, and transportation — without human losses, without mass deaths, famine, exile, and executions. It turns out that industry can be developed without excesses. That was the basis of the New Economic Policy. But now, now, apparently, the circumstances have changed. Politics." He looked at Varya. "But, Varya, you should not repeat the figures I gave you."

"Why not? Comrade Stalin gave those figures."

"Comrade Stalin spoke only about the reduction in livestock. He did not mention human losses. Those are simply my calculations. And, please, don't repeat them anywhere; forget them."

"Don't worry, Mikhail Yurevich, I won't tell anyone about your calculations. I've forgotten them. There! I'll talk only about what Comrade Stalin said, about the reduction in livestock."

"Better not talk about that either!"

"Why not? Stalin himself said it."

"Stalin uses these figures to deal with the problems. But coming from you, it will sound as if you're enjoying the problems. And then Stalin also spoke about the great achievements in other areas, which is not a theme you will pursue, as far as I can tell, and you will be accused of being one-sided."

"And Comrade Stalin wasn't one-sided?"

"What do you mean?"

"He talked about cows and horses but not about people! But thirteen million people more or less, who cares! Gone, so what?"

Mikhail Yurevich put away his tools, tied up the file case from which he had gotten newspapers, and gave Varya a serious and concerned look.

"We are living in hard, harsh, and even cruel times. We are caught in a great turning point in Russia's history. What can we do? We do not choose the hour, date, and year of our birth. But we must take the times into account. That does not mean that we must toady, lie, or betray, but it does mean that we must be careful not to say things that could be disastrous for us and our families. Was Sasha a bad person, or, let us be frank, a not-Soviet person? And look what they did to him. For a joke in a wall newspaper, for getting into an argument with a teacher, a teacher of what? Accounting.... Is that newspaper and the teacher worth what was done to Sasha, ruining his life? No, of course not.... He could have published a different newspaper, not argued with the accounting teacher, and still remained an honest and decent man. Just like you. If you talk about these things, your life will be broken like Sasha's, and more than that: Now you won't just get three years of exile. Now there are different punishments. So, Varya, be careful."

Varya said nothing. Mikhail Yurevich was right. He was afraid for himself, for her; fear was overpowering everyone.

She didn't want to argue with Mikhail Yurevich, but she couldn't stop herself.

"Mikhail Yurevich, you said that we must not betray the principle of morality and ethics. But if people are starving to death in front of us, and we don't help them, we keep quiet and pretend that nothing is wrong, is that moral, is that ethical?"

Mikhail Yurevich took off his pince-nez and wiped the lenses with a piece of flannel. His gaze was bewildered and helpless, like that of all nearsighted people when they take off their glasses. Varya felt sorry for him.

"Mikhail Yurevich," she said, "I didn't want to insult you, and if I did, please forgive me, for God's sake. It's important for me to clear this up for myself. The conclusion seems to be — do not do evil but do not do good either. Or, more accurately, you can do good, but carefully, only when it's not dangerous for you."

Mikhail Yurevich looked at her.

"No, you misunderstood me. The need to do good is ineradicable in man, thank God, and it must be done, without looking around. I'm asking you to do something else — not gab. Keep away from politics, Varya, far away. You love your work, your studies, do that. The rest is not for you."

## ❧ 16 ❧

Stalin paced in his study. Yagoda and Yezhov sat opposite each other at the table.

Yezhov, as usual, had a big notebook, while Yagoda did not. He never wrote anything down; he remembered everything.

Stalin paced in silence, casting sidelong glances at Yagoda's grim face. Yagoda was displeased that Yezhov was there. Yezhov was now secretary of the Central Committee, in charge of the administrative organs, including the Commissariat of Internal Affairs. And he was also chairman of the Commission on Party Control — he had to be fully aware of the Party task being assigned to Yagoda. Moreover, Yezhov would be in charge of how it was performed.

Yagoda was accustomed to speaking to *him* one on one. Yagoda wanted to be *his* confederate. But *he* did not need confederates, *he* needed executives. *His* directives were the directives of the Party, and they were given in the presence of Yezhov, secretary of the Party's Central Committee.

"Zinoviev and Kamenev have been repenting their sins for nine years," Stalin said at last. "They have been covering themselves in filth and begging for forgiveness. They have accepted the moral responsibility for the murder of Comrade Kirov and have been condemned for it. Why did they accept it? In order to save their lives. They thought this would save them from the real and true responsibility. They thought of themselves. They did not think of the Party, they never thought about the Party, only of the hour when they could get their revenge. No! Let them disarm themselves completely, let them help the Party at last."

He stopped talking and went on pacing. Then he spoke again.

"Today's international situation demands a joining of all proletarian forces. Who is impeding that? The Socialists, the Social Democrats? They always hindered but the leaders of the Socialists are coming closer to Fascism, turning their parties from Social Democratic ones into Social Fascist ones. Under these conditions, the departure of the more aware workers from socialism is inevitable. They will move toward us. But who is in their way? Trotsky. Trotsky is forming a Fourth International, gathering forces hostile to our Party and our country, slandering us, pushing away the leftist Labor Socialists and the avant-garde intelligentsia, and the national liberation movements in colonial countries. Who benefits from this? The British and French imperialists, the German Fascists, and the Japanese militarists. That's for whom Trotsky is working. He spent his whole life fighting against the Bolshevist Party and he is doing it now. And throughout its history the Party has fought against Trotsky and it will fight against him now. Let Zinoviev and Kamenev help the Party in this struggle, let them at last prove their loyalty to the Party in deed and not just in words, let them show that they have disarmed totally before the Party."

Stalin stopped pacing. Yagoda and Yezhov said nothing.

"Who benefited from Kirov's death? Trotsky and those who support Trotsky. Who needed Kirov's death? Trotsky and those who support Trotsky. First, it shows the world the instability of the Soviet Union, encouraging the Japanese militarists, the German Fascists, and the British and French imperialists. Second, it directs the internal counterrevolution in the U.S.S.R. onto the path of terrorism. With Kirov's murder, Trotsky began individual terror of the U.S.S.R. And so we must expose Trotsky as the organizer of Kirov's murder, as the creator of terrorist groups in the U.S.S.R. preparing terrorist acts against the leaders of the Party and the state, as an ally of fascism, militarism, and imperialism. So let Zinoviev and Kamenev and their allies . . ." Stalin paused here and repeated, ". . . and their allies expose Trotsky as the organizer of the murder of Kirov, as the organizer and inspirer of terror against Soviet power and the leaders of Soviet power. Not much is required of them — to confess that Trotsky gave the order to kill Kirov, gave the order to prepare terrorist acts against the leaders of the Party and the state. To whom did he give the order? To their organization, a united organization of Trotskyites and Zinovievites, let's call it the United Center, say.... That's a good name. There was a Leningrad Center in Leningrad, let this be the United Center."

Yezhov made a note in his notebook. Stalin looked at him with narrowed eyes, looked away, and continued.

"In order to give credibility to the testimony of Zinoviev and Kamenev, we will have to place Trotskyites in the defendants' dock with them. The more Trotskyites, the better. And the bigger and more famous the Trotskyites, the better. I do not think it will be hard to find them. There are many in the prisons and camps. Bringing rank-and-file Trotskyites to trial will make the lot of Zinoviev and Kamenev easier. They are not the sole killers of Kirov, they are merely members of the organizations that acted on the orders of their leader, Trotsky. Let them blame Trotsky for everything, let them damn Trotsky. At their trial they took the moral responsibility for Kirov's murder. But they are Marxists — what is the difference between moral and direct responsibility? I don't see any difference...."

He paced the room in silence once more and then went on.

"Of course, it will be difficult with the Trotskyites. They are tougher. And they don't have years of repenting behind them, they didn't beat their chests and admit their mistakes like Zinoviev and Kamenev. And they've been in prison for a long time, they'll use that for an alibi. It won't work. No prison or camp is an alibi. Revolutionary and counterrevolutionary work shows that you can participate in revolutionary or counterrevolutionary activity even when in prison, you can give directives to your allies, you can correspond with your leaders."

Something crossed Yagoda's face quickly, but Stalin noticed it.... Yagoda didn't like this; there could be no comparison between the old tsarist prisons and today's, where even a fly couldn't get in or out.... Yagoda knew his work, but Comrade Stalin didn't know and he was living with old-fashioned ideas.

Looking at Yagoda, Stalin repeated, "You can correspond. It's possible. And people do, you know. The conspirators are experienced, that Smirnov or Mrachkovsky ... Mrachkovsky must be sick of being in prison, by the way; he's not very educated but he's active and considers himself a military strategist."

Yezhov made a neat note.

"Basically," Stalin concluded, "if you bring several hundred Trotskyites from the prisons and camps, you will find twenty or thirty among them who will understand the dead end of their struggle against the Party, who will understand the swamp Trotsky has led them to, and will want to get out of that swamp with an honest confession. Of course, this is not an easy task. But the NKVD does not have easy tasks. The struggle with the enemy is difficult but honorable work. In doing their work, the Chekists must understand that they are doing a responsible, Party assignment."

He stopped in front of Yagoda and said slowly and convincingly, "The Party has incontrovertible proof that Trotsky is undermining the work of the Soviet Union. The organs need do only one thing — force the members of the United Center to admit their participation in terrorist activity, in particular, the murder of Comrade Kirov." He paused, never taking his eyes from Yagoda. "They cannot fail to admit it, because it corresponds to the facts. Not admitting these facts will lead to the most dire consequences."

Yagoda and Yezhov left the office.

Stalin was alone.

Yagoda's displeasure at Yezhov's presence was more than simple rivalry. Today's demonstration by Yagoda was not the first. He had not hidden his compassion for Medved and Zaporozhets. He had sent them off in a special railroad car instead of a prison train. He reassured them. Just hold on, boys, everything will work out, it just happened this way, it wasn't our fault, *he* had insisted, but we'll take care of our own.

Why was he allowing Medved's wife to see her husband? Why was that done so openly for all to see?

The head of the NKVD's transport section, Shanin, had sent Zaporozhets two records of old Russian songs. Why had he done that? To console a friend in need? Zaporozhets couldn't live without those records?

Even Pauker, head of *his* personal guard, a buffoon and a coward, a barber from Budapest, even he dared to send Zaporozhets a radio. He wasn't afraid to do it. They felt sorry for him, commiserated, "Our poor Vanya got it for no good reason." . . . But there was no room for pity in their work.

It was a demonstration of the fact that the workers of the NKVD knew everything and would not let one of their own get hurt. They wanted to show *him* that they were strong, that they were for one another wherever they may be. Didn't they realize what *he* could do to Medved and Zaporozhets?

*He* could have them shot.

And *he* should have done that.

Instead *he* sent them to do managerial work, in fact, sent them to a sanatorium, one for two years, the other for three. And so the NKVD workers decided that they were *his* confederates, that *he* was afraid of them, that *he* was in their hands. And they were demonstrating their strength, independence, and displeasure. This was an embryonic conspiracy, a new conspiracy, a Cheka conspiracy.

Yagoda and the NKVD executed *his* will. For now. And only for now. And so Yagoda and his apparat had to be changed. Yagoda and his apparat were willing to fight enemies inside the Party. But only with those who had officially participated in the factions — with Trotskyites, Zinovievites, Sapronovites, and perhaps with rightists, although he had his doubts about the rightists. But they would go no farther, they would be no help in the coming cadre revolution; in essence, the basic cadres of the NKVD were the old Chekists, that is, Party cadres, who considered themselves ideological and considered their struggle with enemies an ideological struggle.

In punishing the enemies inside the Party, they imagined themselves politicians and their work as political work; they had forgotten that they were not the GPU, the Main Political Directorate. They were no more than executives and guards.

But it was too soon to change them now. Let them finish off Zinoviev and Kamenev, they would do that, they were already doing it, and they could handle it. They had been working with Trotskyites and Zinovievites for a long time, they knew their cadres, they were preparing the trial.

Vyshinsky would run the trial — he would manage that. And

Yezhov, right after the trial, as secretary of the Central Committee would replace Yagoda and bring in people to replace Yagoda's apparat.

Would they resist? It was doubtful. The blow would be unexpected. And *he* had a counterbalance, the army.

The army was always dependable. But no army was dependable if you drop your vigilance even for a second, if you loosen the reins even for a bit. All the coups d'état were accomplished by the army or, more properly put, by the military leaders. Only the October Revolution did not depend on the military leaders but on the soldiers — they had the weapons.

But the military leaders were always undependable. Today's military cadres were even less dependable than the cadres of the NKVD. There were hidden allies of Trotsky there, many who had worked with him when he was commissar of the army, and for many he was part of their "heroic" past. They considered themselves heroes of the Civil War, and in their hearts they did not recognize the role and significance of Comrade Stalin in the Civil War; they hated *him*.

For now they were keeping quiet, and if they did recognize *his* role in the Civil War, they squeezed it out through clenched teeth. . . . These were the men Tukhachevsky was counting on. He was a potential Bonaparte, a tsarist officer who joined the Revolution out of ambition.

Tukhachevsky and his men would never forget their defeat near Warsaw in 1920, which they tried to blame on Comrade Stalin. Even Lenin supported them obliquely with his sarcastic question, "But who goes to Warsaw through Lvov?"

But Lenin was always too trusting; he saw Tukhachevsky as an honest military specialist loyal to the Revolution. He had been persuaded of that by Valerian Kuibyshev, who in turn had been persuaded by his brother, a fellow student of Tukhachevsky's and now corps commander.

And Trotsky, of course, had supported Tukhachevsky.

No matter what Tukhachevsky said in his little book, *Campaign on the Vistula, he* was right and history would confirm *him*.

Now Tukhachevsky was lying low, supposedly doing military research, writing military works. He had never belonged to any opposition, he had taken his own path, he said, had never bet on anyone, only on himself, an independent professional, far from political intrigues and squabbles, prepared to bring order to the country at any moment. And if necessary, he could also save the ideals of the Revolution from dictatorship, that is, save the Soviet power from *him,* Stalin — that was his ultimate goal, that was his main task! He saw himself as the dictator.

The political organs were also undependable. They had even more Trotskyites than the command staff. And the army was still peasant, and after the collectivization and dekulakization, that contingent was not dependable. Now even three-quarters of the workers were children of former kulaks and subkulaks.

Getting rid of Tukhachevsky wouldn't be enough. He had to destroy all the potentially dangerous forces in the army. The main ones were Tukhachevsky, Yakir, and Uborevich.

Of course, they were famous men. Famous today. But who would remember them tomorrow?

A change in the commanding staff would not damage the army. The younger officers would become senior commanders, the senior ones higher commanders, and they would all be in debt to *him,* only to *him,* it would be *his* army. Along with the destroyed commanders, all the myths of the Civil War would vanish, a new history of the Civil War would be created, the true history of the Civil War, in which *his* role would be correctly and properly reflected.

*He* had to deal with the army with the speed of light.

For now *he* would limit himself to Shmidt, Primakov, and Putna.

Corps commander Putna was an old friend of Tukhachevsky's, they had fought together. In 1923 he had belonged to the Trotsky opposition. Formally, he had left it, but he had been in it. Shmidt, Primakov, and Putna had to be tied in with the coming Zinoviev-Kamenev trial. Let them testify against the officers. That would put Tukhachevsky on the alert, but . . .

Now the army was externally monolithic, headed by Voroshilov, with Tukhachevsky as his deputy. Tukhachevsky was busy with questions of re-arming the army. As the chief military theoretician he was prognosticating about the coming war. In all his lectures and discussions, Tukhachevsky maintained that Germany was the potential enemy. Of course, Tukhachevsky hated Germany. He hated it personally — he had been a military prisoner, had escaped five times, successful only on the fifth attempt. He hated them traditionally as a former tsarist officer, because the Germans had beaten them in the last war. . . . And as an old tsarist officer, he saw France as a natural foe of Germany and a natural ally of Russia. He might not even want to understand that the defeat of Germany in the Great War had changed the situation. Germany's enemies were the ones who joined against it with the Versailles Treaty, France and Britain.

No matter what Hitler said, no matter what he wrote in *Mein Kampf,* it was all a bluff. . . . In threatening the East, Hitler was blunting the vigilance of France and Britain. Germany's potential ally was not France or Britain, but the Soviet Union. The Soviet Union's potential enemies were France and Britain — France, because of its influence in Europe, and Britain because of its Asian and African colonies.

Tukhachevsky was pushing Germany into the arms of France and Britain with his position, helping form a bloc of those three countries against the Soviet Union. Tukhachevsky was provoking a military situation, that was why he was preparing an army that, at the right moment, he would use for a military coup. And after the coup he would maneuver.

Was a military coup possible? Of course. Having the army in his control, demagogically using the unhappiness of the peasants, the unhappiness of the apparat being replaced, demagogically proclaiming that the Revolution needed defending from "Stalinist dictatorship," he could not only pull off a coup but strengthen it, killing all the cadres loyal to *him.*

The monolith had to be destroyed, the army had to be separated from politics, separated from the people, and thereby placed in dependency on the state leadership. The army had to be a weapon of the authorities. The Revolution had created it as a political force and in the Civil War that was necessary in order to hold political power. Now it was not necessary. Now it was harmful and dangerous — if the army is a political force, then it can pretend to political power or to a role in the struggle for political power.

The army had to be broken up, it had to institute ranks again, as it was in the tsarist army, the way it is in every army in the world.

Introducing ranks would separate the commanding staff from the troops and would break up the commanding staff into many categories, and that would focus the officers not on the country and the Party but on their own position inside the army.

They had to develop different pay scales for the different ranks, high salaries and a system of privileges — additional pay for length of service, pensions, housing for the staff, clubs, and so on — that would separate the army even more from the people. The people never liked officers. Introduce a new uniform for the officers, so that they stood out from the population. . . .

Rescind all the limitation on the Cossacks and reintroduce their uniforms. The Cossacks were particularly unhappy with collectivization. They were used to their ways, so restore the traditional uniforms of the Don, Juban, Ter, and other Cossacks, let them wear their outfits — that would satisfy their pride and separate the people even more. *He* had to show the army that *he* loved it, helped it, and trusted it fully. Especially the command staff. The political organs could be reorganized — give the commanders the perception of greater independence.

This would neutralize the army when the changes of the NKVD apparat took place. And then, using the new NKVD, he would deliver the swift, decisive blow to the military cadres, to Tukhachevsky and his company, the so-called heroes of the Civil War who were convinced that their past military service freed them from serving the Party leaders faithfully. No one needed those "heroes" now.

Of course, the romance of the Civil War was necessary. It was needed for the young people. Let us make more films about the heroes of the Civil War, but not the living ones, only the dead ones. Nothing about the living. Who knew what would happen to them?

Now the main task was to use Kirov's murder. For a start, an open Trotskyite-Zinovievite trial, a big trial, lots of people involved. And shoot them all.

That trial would signal the start of the destruction of all enemies, active, hidden, and potential; it would bring on other trials, open and closed; it would start the cadre revolution.

Kirov, Kirov, Kirov! The people must not be allowed to forget that victim, the people must remember that victim and must avenge him. The love of Kirov must be inculcated deep in the hearts and minds of the people, the people must not forget him for a minute.

There must be books about Kirov, films about Kirov. Towns and villages, factories and plants, museums and theaters must be named after Kirov. Everything must remind the people of Kirov — he must become a relic, an eternal ache, an unhealing wound of the people. The wound must be opened over and over, it must be an eternal reminder to the people of the enemies that must be destroyed.

*All of Kirov's comrades in arms in Leningrad were destroyed.*

*Also shot were the majority of the members of the Leningrad Oblast Committee and the City Committee and of the Commission on Party Control.*

*In five years, from 1933 to 1938, the Leningrad Party organization was cut in half.*

*At the Seventeenth Party Congress, Kirov had headed the Leningrad Party delegation of one hundred fifty-four people. Of them, only three were left in 1939 — I. V. Stalin, A. A. Andreyev, and M. F. Shkiryatov.*

## ❦ 17 ❦

The fall of 1935 was approaching, the second autumn of Sasha's exile. The cow shed was finished and Sasha was without work again. Once the ice came to the river, he — lonely already — would be cut off from the world completely. The autumn rains came. The village seemed deserted; even the dogs were quiet. Sasha reread old newspapers, old magazines. He knew them by heart.

In the summer of 1935 Zida had gone to her daughter for the school vacation, but she did not return in September, and another teacher was sent to the school. She was gone for good, vanished from his life as mysteriously as she had entered it. In the winter, Sasha got a letter from her: "Farewell, Sasha, thank you for everything you gave me. I wish you freedom and happiness. Think about me now and then." And she added Yesenin's lines — *"How could I forget you! In my nomadic life, I will speak to friend and stranger about you."*

There was no return address, and the postmark was illegible. She was gone. Why? Because he had read her diary? But he had sincerely repented about it, he had begged her forgiveness, he had explained that he was afraid it might cause trouble for her or for others, and she had not argued, had not taken offense, and their relationship seemed to have improved. And yet, apparently, a scar had remained. And Varya. Sasha thought about her, Zida could sense it, even though she didn't let on or act jealous. Perhaps there was something else, too — she saw that they were taking the exiles away from the Angara, and they would take Sasha, too, and perhaps she didn't want to be around when it happened, so she left. It was probably the right thing.

Sasha didn't send his letter to Stalin.

Of course, there was much that was encouraging in the newspapers. There were new names, new national heroes. The first line of the Moscow Metropolitan subway system was opened, new factories and plants were in production.

Was an oppressed, terrorized nation capable of such deeds? No, the people were not oppressed or terrorized, the people were for the Party, for Stalin, and Stalin was inseparable from them. He met with metal workers, kolkhoz workers, commanders of the Red Army, graduates of the military academy, with women kolkhoz workers, Stakhnovites, tractor drivers, and cotton pickers.

But if the heads of Lenin's comrades in arms were being lopped off, then what was the hope for Sasha's head?

In the past, being a Communist meant belonging to a great brotherhood of like-minded people, and now it was more dangerous than being a White Guard. The White Guard was not hiding behind anything. The Communist hid behind his Party card, and you had to be especially vigilant with him, or so it seemed from the newspapers now.

And he, little fool that he was, had considered himself a clever politician — a Komsomol leader, he had dreamed of going to the Sverdlovsk Communist University and then to the Institute of the Red Professors and had dreamed of becoming a Party worker. But he ended up wanting to become an engineer — the country needed specialists, and in the future he pictured himself being a manager, that is, also a politician. Politics was not what he had imagined in his youth — something simple and direct, honest, idealistic, without intrigues and lies. He had been a naïve fool and that's how he had ended up here.

Contrary to his real interests Sasha had gone to a technical school instead of a history institute. He loved history and knew it well, but could a historian take an active part in socialist construction? What is discovering an ancient document worth, compared to laying a brick in the foundation of a blast furnace? A document is the past, the blast furnace is the future. That's what he had always believed, convinced that material values had a decisive significance for humanity in general and for Russia in particular — it had to be turned from a backward country to a progressive one, from an agrarian state to an industrial state, a mighty proletarian power, the stronghold of the coming world revolution. Who could have time for archives or research?

Of course, humanity could not exist without spiritual values, but these had to serve the education of the people. Sasha loved literature as well as history, and he could read French as easily as Russian. No matter how busy he was, he read a lot, had a good memory for poetry, and though he had never cried, even as a child, he could get misty-eyed over a beautiful line.

His apartment neighbor Mikhail Yurevich had once asked him why he didn't write: "A man who writes becomes accustomed to expressing his thoughts in a literate and literary way. Knowing how to write is the first sign of being an intellectual. In classical schools writing was taught, even though they didn't create writers. If it weren't for the journals, the literary circles, the extemporaneous writing of verse and even of stories, the battles of epigrams, that is everything that we call literary amateurism now, I am not certain that we would have had Pushkin. . . . Writing, if only for yourself, develops observation, imagination, and fantasy and civilizes a man. I think you are making a great mistake."

Sasha often thought of Mikhail Yurevich. He spent hours as a child in Mikhail Yurevich's room near the kitchen. Mikhail Yurevich gave him books to read. And during Sasha's arrest, Mikhail Yurevich came out to the corridor to say good-bye and offered him money. A clean, decent, marvelous man, unyielding in his views and convictions.

Not only didn't Sasha keep a diary here on the Angara, he didn't make notes. He didn't even have a pad. Tomorrow they might come and search, and then you'd have to explain who you'd written about; a mention in his pad might destroy a person.

If he could just survive, if only they let him out when his term was over.

Of course, they could just announce that he had been given a new term, without accusing him of anything, and there would be no discussion! But what if he had great luck and was released?

They wouldn't simply release him, of course. They'd forbid him to live in twenty or thirty cities. There would be a mark in his passport, so that they could pick him up again whenever they wanted to. And every time he tried to get a job, he'd have to indicate his sentence on the application.

He could work as a driver, but every motor pool and every garage had personnel people who checked everyone, and he wouldn't be able to hide his past.

That meant he couldn't apply to any enterprise or institution. He had to find something that would be available without filling out applications so that he could stay out of their way.

But what? Some free profession. He couldn't draw, or sing, he had never tried acting, and you had to fill out applications in theaters too. Too bad he didn't learn to play the bayan from Fedya, he could play at dances and weddings. But it was too late now; Fedya would be leaving soon.

And he needed a pseudonym — that was the main thing. That was the only way to hide from "the all-seeing eyes and the all-hearing ears."

Mikhail Yurevich had suggested he write. They had had a literature club at school, where the kids read their poems and stories, but Sasha hadn't joined. He thought it silly to read hopeless works when Pushkin and Tolstoy, Balzac and Shakespeare were available.

But he went to the history club, run by Alexei Ivanovich Strazhev, a wonderful history teacher and a wonderful storyteller. They worked by subject. Sasha took the French Revolution and Alexei Ivanovich praised his work. Once he even invited Sasha home and had a long talk with him over his essay "Saint-Just: An Attempt at a Political and Psychological Portrait." Alexei Ivanovich said that, with time, if Sasha seriously studied that period, he would help him get some of his work published. Sasha no longer remembered where, either in some historical journal or in the *Proceedings* of the Communist Academy.

But Sasha didn't study history, although he didn't lose his interest. He read what he could get his hands on, and he was glad he had asked his mother to send him his books. . . . There they were on his table. Matthews, Jaurez in translation, Lefevre and Cardel in French, articles by Marx, Engels, and Lenin on the French Revolution, books by Lukin and Tarle.

He had the material. Of course, historical works are not published under pseudonyms, but he could write historical fiction. Stories about Robespierre, Saint-Just, Danton, Marat, Charlotte Corday, or the tragic fate of the Utopian Communist Baboeuf. There were so many names, so many events, so much revolutionary romance!

Sasha kept thinking about Altayev's works, which he had loved as a child, *Under the Sign of the Shoe,* about the peasant wars, or *Liberator of the Slaves,* about Lincoln. The main thing was that Altayev was the pseudonym of the writer Margarita Vladimirovna Yamshchikova. She had spent a life under a pseudonym, reworking historical subjects into interesting children's books.

Perhaps he would be able to do it, too. He knew history and he knew how to use historical sources. Alexei Ivanovich had taught him that. And he had no other way out.

Sasha's first story was about Saint-Just. He couldn't tell if it was any good, but he kept writing. If they arrested him again and went through his papers, he would say, "I'm writing biographies and stories for children and young adults." They would laugh at the new "writer," but there was no crime in what he was doing. His stories weren't anti-Soviet; on the contrary, they were about a revolution that Marx, Engels, and Lenin had valued highly. Vladimir Ilyich Lenin called it a great revolution.

The important thing was to write as much as possible.

His main expense was kerosene. Sasha wrote late into the night and got up early to hurry to his table — his future, his freedom, was in those pages. He wrote and wrote, reworking every page several times, every chapter, and then the whole story. He made two copies of the final draft — one for himself, one for his mother. She'd at least have the stories if anything happened to him. Sasha hurried so that he could send them to his mother with the first post of the winter. But as he copied them down for his mother, he made new changes. He thought he would never finish.

He sent the first stories about the French Revolution to his mother only in the early months of 1936.

"I have free time, so I'm playing with my pen. Just don't show these to anyone."

And in the meantime Sasha was as sad and lonely as before. He dropped in only on Fedya, whose cramped store had a special coziness, with that special hardware-store smell, also cozy and pleasant, probably because it differed so much from the stale village odors. The counter was a wide block, and scales hung from the ceiling. The shelves along the walls held tobacco, matches, bricks of tea, buttons, thread, brass bowls of shot, chunks of pig iron, shells and gunpowder in tins, sugar wrapped in blue paper, as well as lengths of homespun cotton, necklaces of cheap beads hanging on nails, rings, earrings, and chains. . . .

Every needle, every ring cost money — Fedya had to keep track of everything, answer for everything. And he had to sell everything before it spoiled, rotted, or grew rancid, and if the inspector came by, he had to feed him, fill his gullet with alcohol and give him some for the road.

Fedya was always happy to see Sasha. He had time to socialize since they no longer delivered new goods to him. A new storekeeper would arrive in Mozgova when the first sleigh road cleared, and Fedya would start courses in Krasnoyarsk on January 1, 1936, for two years, when he would become chairman of the Regional Merchants Union.

One day, Fedya announced that he and Sasha were going fishing that evening.

"The water grasses are on the bottom now, the water is clearer, the fish haven't gone down to the bottom yet, and tonight should be quiet and dark, unless the stars come out. Take a nap after lunch, so you're not sleepy in the boat, and as soon as the sun starts setting, come over and help me load the boat. Wear your cap."

Sasha came back to Fedya's before dark. They brought the fishing gear down to the boat: nets and harpoons, a brazier, dried chocks made of resinous pine, and a towing line with a float, in case they got a very large and powerful fish, like a sheat-fish that could pull the harpoon out of their hands.

"It pulls so hard," Fedya said, "you can't even stay on your feet, or you'll come flying out of the boat. You'll never hold it."

Fedya set up the brazier on the bow, put in the chocks, and lit them. The reflections of the light danced on the dark water.

"Sit there and row," Fedya said. "I'll work with the harpoon first, then I'll let you. Row quietly, don't scare off the fish, just stay along the shore. When I hit, hold the boat steady...."

Rowing quietly, Sasha moved along the shore. The chocks were burning bright. Fedya sat with the harpoon on the starboard side, looking into the patch of light that moved with the boat. Then he struck hard. The water churned. Sasha stopped rowing and held the oar by the side, to keep the boat from turning or drifting away. Fedya was working hard, it must be a big fish. He pulled it out and tossed it into the bottom of the boat.

Sasha rowed forward again. They had come upon a school, Fedya struck without missing, the bottom of the boat filled with fish — slimy-backed, fat-sided fish, big ones, but not as big as Fedya had promised.

"Stop!" Fedya said.

He handed Sasha the harpoon, added to the fire, and started pulling on the oars.

Sasha took the harpoon, stood in Fedya's place, and felt the excitement of the hunt — he tried to control himself; you don't hit fish with trembling hands.

The boat moved slowly and silently, a beam of light falling on the water, and Sasha could see the bottom clearly — sand, stones, grasses, shells, leaves.... But no fish. With his left hand Sasha pushed his cap down over his forehead. Fedya had been right, you need the visor. And suddenly the beam came upon a long body. The fish stopped as if it couldn't understand what was happening, gently moving its fins. Sasha tensed, and a thought came from nowhere: "If I get it, I'll send the letter to Stalin." And he struck as hard as he could. The spear entered the fish's back with a crunch. The water got murky, the harpoon shook in Sasha's hands, and he leaned in on it, pushing the fish against the bottom.

"Fine, bring it in!" Fedya said softly.

Sasha pulled in the harpoon, a huge fish jerking on the tip. Sasha tossed it in the bottom of the boat, adding to the mound of fish struggling there.

"You'll do fine," Fedya said.

\* \* \*

Sasha didn't believe in omens. And it wasn't the catch that strengthened his decision. The ice would come any day — tomorrow's mail would be the last — and if he didn't send the letter with it, it would have to wait for the winter road. But if he did send it, the letter would soon reach Moscow. And what if! What if it got onto Stalin's desk?

Sasha neatly rewrote the letter, sealed the envelope addressed to "Comrade Stalin, the Kremlin, Moscow," and put on the stamps. The mail boat came the next day. The mailman saw that it was registered and warned "Receipt in the winter" (the receipts were written in Kezhma), tossed the letter into the sack, and started rowing.

And so Sasha's letter went down the Angara to Moscow, to the Kremlin, to Comrade Stalin.

## ❧ 18 ❧

In December 1935 the first winter mail came. And that same day Lidya Grigoryevna Zvyaguro was sent off to Krasnoyarsk. They had sent a sleigh from Kezhma. Sasha put both her old suitcases, tied with cord, into it, came back, and picked up Tarasik bundled up in a warm gray scarf.

Tarasik whispered softly.

"What did you say, Tarasik?"

"Dead people don't get out of the grave. I saw when my parents died. And they don't sail on boats, either. You were lying."

And he gave Sasha a reproachful look.

Larisa was on the porch, wailing.

"Stop it, Larisa," Lidya Grigoryevna said severely. "You're frightening Tarasik."

Larisa stopped wailing, and confined herself to quiet sobs, sniffs, and drying her tears with the edge of her scarf.

Lidya Grigoryevna offered her hand to Sasha. "Good-bye, Sasha, thank you."

"What did I do?" Sasha laughed.

"You did. Thanks."

"Maybe you'll write from your new place?"

She laughed bitterly and the grin on her plain face looked like a grimace.

"I doubt I'll have the opportunity. The show is only beginning."

The driver snapped the reins. The runners creaked in the snow, and the sleigh took off, with the driver walking alongside. He climbed on, shook the reins again, and the horse jogged down the well-worn ruts. Sasha watched them until the sleigh disappeared in the woods. Lidya Grigoryevna did not turn back once. Neither did Tarasik.

Now Sasha was alone in Mozgova.

(Later, in August, during the trial of the so-called United Trotskyite-Zinovievite Center, when they tried people who had already been in prison, Sasha wondered if they had sent Lidya Grigoryevna to Moscow in connection with this trial. But her name did not come up in the newspaper accounts, and Sasha never did learn what had happened to her and her Tarasik.)

After he saw Lidya Grigoryevna off, he went home to go through the mail — letters and newspapers sent from Moscow in the summer and fall. There was a lot.

His mother wrote that she found his school transcript and his driver's license and would hold on to them until he returned. She had sent the books he had requested. It was a good letter. Sasha's reasoning that his request for his papers would reassure his mother was right. Varya wrote that she had started attending the Construction Institute at night.

Despite the meager information, his mother's letters and Varya's additions encouraged him — life went on, his documents were safe, waiting for him, he could get a job as a driver, his transcript showed that he had graduated from the institute. Of course, if he wasn't released, he wouldn't need them. But still, they were official, material, threads into the future. They might even come in handy in the camps — perhaps they wouldn't send him out to the felling site but would let him work at his specialty. There was no answer from Stalin, but Sasha didn't expect one before February or March.

He was letting his beard grow out again — why shave here? Despite the cold, he went cross-country skiing, and tried to hunt — unsuccessfully.

One time, skiing alone, he came across five skiers in army helmets. Sasha got off the path to let them through.

They also stopped. "Hello, old man!"

They were fooled by the beard.

Sasha regarded them with interest. He had never seen soldiers here. Young and healthy boys with red cheeks and frost on their lashes and brows, in woolen sweaters, cotton-padded trousers, fur-trimmed jackets, felt boots with leather soles, fur mittens, and extra-insulated helmets. Each one had a short, hand-pulled sled.

"What village is this?" the first soldier asked.

"Mozgova."

"Right, Mozgova. How far to Kezhma?"

"Twelve kilometers."

"Right, that's what it's supposed to be."

"Where are you from?" Sasha asked.

"From Nizhneangarsk. Have you heard about the ski run from Lake Baikal to the Barents Sea?"

"No."

"You should read the papers, old man. Can you read?"

"Yes," Sasha said with a smile. "What do you have on the sleds?"

"Sleeping bags and food. We're covering four thousand kilometers."

Sasha shook his head.

The skiers leaned on their poles and rested.

"Have you been traveling long?"

"A month. The Baikal Range got us. Do you know the range?"

"Yes."

The skier clicked his tongue. "A tough nut! Steep slopes, thick brush, gale-force winds, and the frosts are horrible, as you can see. We had to climb up the outcroppings with our skis in our hands. And when we got across, there was the taiga, no ski trails, just fresh snow. We had to make the trails. . . ."

"That must have been rough," Sasha said sympathetically.

"You bet! The worst part is that we're behind schedule; we're five days late. They've been waiting for us in Kezhma for five days. Our base is there."

"And where do you go from Kezhma?"

"From Kezhma to Podkamennaya Tunguska," the skier said readily, obviously glad to have a new person to talk to. He straightened. "All right, old man, I've talked too long." He turned to his companions. "Let's go?"

"Let's go."

"Twelve kilometers to go and then we'll steam in the bath, get a rest, get some sleep."

He picked up his pole and pointed at his team. "Remember us, old man! It's an historic moment. You're seeing the great northern marathon with your own eyes. Do you know what a marathon is?"

"I do," Sasha said and smiled again.

"You're an educated man, I see. A hunter, are you?"

"Yes. And how will I remember you, what are your names?"

The senior man poked himself in the chest. "I'm Yevgeny Yegorov, and these are Ivan Popov, Andrei Kulikov, Konstantin Brazhnikov, and Alexander Shevchenko. Will you remember?"

"I will. Definitely."

"Well then, you can tell your children and your grandchildren: I saw the heroes of the great northern marathon. Well, so long!"

And they went on, toward Kezhma, with an unhurried, steady, and confident stride. Sasha watched them with sadness and envy — they were free, going from Baikal to the Barents Sea. When he was younger they did not approve of setting records. Sport was for the masses and it was for physical development. But it was good for people to test their strength, their ability, their will and character. And how lucky those lads were not to know about exile and lack of freedom.

That summer, in the May papers he read that five daring skiers finished in Murmansk on April 30, 1936, at six P.M., after 151 days.

But then, after his meeting with the skiers, Sasha awaited a reply to his letter to Stalin.

However, February, March, and April passed and there was no answer.

It was still cold, there was still snow in the woods, but you could see hare and fox tracks in it, birds were flying from tree to tree, the sun was feeling warm, and the first melting spots were visible on the southern slopes. In a week or two, all the snow would be gone, the mountain streams would be bubbling, still hemmed in by ice along the edges, and the woods would come alive. The blizzards would be replaced by warm, almost summery days, the sun would melt snow before your eyes, revealing yellowed grass and rotten leaves.

And at last the ice moved on the Angara. . . . Broken up, it stuck in the narrow passes between islands, on the sharp turns, on the sloping edges, building up into a huge dam and then collapsing under the weight of the water that had collected upstream, rushing down with the speed and noise of a waterfall. Huge floes struck the shore, rubbing them and tearing them, chopping off small islands, tearing out and carrying away tall trees along with boulders broken off from the banks.

The ice passed and the Angara returned to its bed, and the larches, enveloped in a gentle haze, burst into leaf; wood thrushes burst into song at dawn and flew down to the ground.

Sasha used to love the spring — it excited him, filling the world with joy and hope. Here on the Angara, spring meant loneliness, sadness, and grim foreboding. The mail service — his only tie to the world — was interrupted again until June.

He had read and reread the newspapers, books, and letters, there was no one to talk to. Even Fedya was gone.

On warm sunny days Sasha went down to the Angara. The men were covering their boat bottoms with pitch, the women working on the nets. Sasha would sit on a big chunk of driftwood and watch the river and the far shore beyond which was the mainland, the country.

The hook-nosed peasant Stepan Timofeyevich, with whom Sasha had cut wood for the cow shed, came over. "What are you sitting around for, boy?"

"There's nothing to do."

"Come help us with the pitch."

There were two big covered boats for transporting cargo on the shore.

Sasha helped them turn the boats on their sides. They dried them, painted them with hot pitch, and left them to dry in the sun, so that when the water went down, they could hand them over to Ivan Parfenovich, the chairman of the kolkhoz, ready to go.

Ivan Parfenovich paid Sasha for this work through his landlord again. And in the summer, when Sasha cut hay on the islands, he got paid again through his landlord, who forgave his rent and fed him well in exchange.

But even work didn't save him. Nothing did. Sasha's depression swept over him more and more. There was a little over six months left to the end of his term. Would they add another? Send him to the camps? His letter had never reached Stalin — he had been stupid to have counted on that; it was either added to his file or thrown away. His life was ruined! Even if they left him here to live, what would he do? Become Anagarized, as Lukeshka used to call it? Marry an illiterate girl who chewed resin from larch trees, which was supposed to be good for the teeth? Sasha had tried it to cut down on his smoking, but he couldn't get into the habit. It was sickly sweet and stuck to his teeth. Everything here irritated him — he was sick of it all. Soloveichik had done the right thing, running away. If he survived, then he was free right now. And if they caught him, then he was in the camps. So what? Others didn't run away, and they were in the camps now, too. Soloveichik at least had a chance at freedom.

## ❧ 19 ❧

Sharok was the only operative called in to the meeting at Molchanov's. Around the table sat section and department chiefs, their deputies and assistants, about thirty or forty people. Sharok did not bother counting, but he noticed that he was the only one there with a single stripe; the rest had two or three, and some had commissar stars.

Molchanov, a dark-haired man with a simple and pleasant face, tall, with a sturdy build, had a sense of humor despite his rather severe look, and enjoyed teasing Dyakov and his bureaucratese.

"Well, he's off again," he'd chuckle, listening to Dyakov's report. "Get to the point."

But today Molchanov was strict. In the tense silence, he announced in his steady voice that a Trotskyite-Zinovievite conspiracy had been discovered, headed from abroad by Trotsky and in the U.S.S.R. headed by Zinoviev, Kamenev, Bakayev, Evdokimov, and other Zinovievites, as well as the well-known Trotskyites Smirnov and Mrachkovsky. Smirnov and Mrachkovsky were in prison, of course, but they were working from inside.

Further, Molchanov said that the Zinovievites and the Trotskyites had entered into a United Center that was creating terrorist groups all over the country with the aim of killing Stalin and the other members of the Politburo and taking power. They had already killed Kirov.

The confession of moral responsibility for Kirov's death by Zinoviev and Kamenev at the January trial was nothing more than a trick to avoid criminal responsibility, to hide the existence of the

United Center, to hide their terrorist organization, their terrorist groups, and to win time.

Molchanov paused and added significantly, "The Politburo and Comrade Stalin consider these charges proved. There is no doubt of them, nor can there be. We have only one assignment — to obtain confessions from the accused. Bear in mind that Comrade Stalin and Secretary of the Central Committee Comrade Yezhov are taking this investigation under their personal control. Is that understood?" He paused again and said firmly, "We have been entrusted with an exceptional responsibility. We must execute our assignment to the end. In response to the high trust of the Central Committee and of Comrade Stalin personally, we must prove that Chekists are infinitely loyal to the Party and its highest interests. Any questions?"

Everyone was silent.

"Fine," Molchanov said. "Then listen. . . . On orders of Comrade Yagoda, you are to hand over your cases to other investigators and come under my command."

In conclusion he announced the makeup of the investigative groups.

No one asked any questions at the meeting, but everyone had some. Could it be possible that the NKVD, with its gigantic staff of agents, with its all-encompassing network of informers who kept every former oppositionist, wherever he might be, under constant surveillance, would not know about such a broad and diffuse conspiracy, would not know about the existence of numerous terrorist groups scattered, as Molchanov had said, all across the Soviet Union? Could that be possible? How could the NKVD not have noticed such an organization? Especially since that organization had supposedly existed for several years. And they, the workers of the NKVD, had overlooked it. They should all be court-martialed, and yet there wasn't a single word of rebuke. After all, the section in which Sharok worked under Vutkovsky dealt specifically with Trotskyites, Zinovievites, and right-wingers, and he had never heard anyone breathe a word of a terrorist group.

At the meeting Sharok took quick looks at Vutkovsky, who sat, like everyone, in silence, with a severe, aloof expression, but Sharok sensed that Vutkovsky was as stunned by Molchanov's words as the others, perhaps even more, since this reflected on his section. He was in charge of those people. This made it seem as if he and his men had done a bad job.

But they hadn't; Sharok knew that. Everyone did. There were no terrorist groups, no wide-reaching conspiracy. Every man Molchanov named was in prison, some arrested recently, after Kirov's murder, others a long time ago. This conspiracy had been created in order to execute Zinoviev and Kamenev, Smirnov and Mrachkovsky, and other former foes of Stalin.

And the goal of the investigation, including Sharok's goal, boiled down to beating the necessary confessions out of these people, who wouldn't be making them easily. After all, they were Zinoviev, Kamenev, Krupnyaki. . . . They should be shot to hell. Think of all the people they had killed. And they were Jews, too. But the Trotskyites, even though most of them weren't Jews, were a stubborn lot, strong, and you wouldn't be able to force confessions out of them.

The plan was to deliver to Moscow several hundred former oppositionists from prisons, camps, and from exile. If even one-tenth of them admitted to the existence of a Trotskyite-Zinovievite terrorist organization, that would yield twenty to thirty confessions, under the weight of which the main defendants would break. But for that kind of an explosion, you need a detonator. Three men were marked for that role — Valentin Olberg, Isaak Reinhold, and Richard Pikel.

Sharok did not know Olberg. He had lived in Berlin and later in Turkey and Czechoslovakia. When he came to the U.S.S.R. he had worked in Gorky at the Pedagogical Institute.

Molchanov immediately appreciated Olberg's significance. He had recently returned from abroad; he knew Trotsky's son, Sedov; he would sign a confession that he had been sent to the U.S.S.R. by Sedov on Trotsky's orders to organize the murder of Stalin. And "Lenin's pre-death testament," warning the Party against Stalin, had been circulating around the Gorky Pedagogical Institute, whose students would form the group preparing to murder Stalin.

Olberg was an "easy" suspect, but Sharok didn't get him.

Sharok didn't get Richard Pikel either, former chief of Zinoviev's Secretariat. For a short time Pikel had belonged to the opposition, even though he had broken with it quickly. Sharok read his dossier.

Fought in the Civil War. In the late 1920s he left political life and worked in literature and the theater. There was a personal characterization in the dossier — a genial, sociable man, good at bridge.... Something that didn't get into the dossier but remained in the reports of informers was that Pikel had played cards with important Chekists — Gai and Shanin. Gai was head of the Special Section and Shanin of the Transport Section. Pikel often visited their dachas and traveled abroad with their help. Sharok realized that he would not get Pikel because his old friends would take him. And so it was. Gai's people interrogated Pikel.

The investigation group in which Sharok was a member got Isaak Reinhold, the hardest of the trio.

Reinhold, like Pikel, had been in the opposition for a short time and even though he left quickly, he was on file; he was a well-known manager, former head of the Cotton Industry Ministry. In January of last year his deputy, Faivilovich, had been arrested in the Kirov case. And Reinhold was immediately fired and expelled from the Party. As *Pravda* wrote on January 11, 1935, "during eight years Reinhold maintained the closest ties with the vile scoundrel of the Trotskyite-Zinovievite opposition, L. Ya. Faivilovich."

Reinhold had met with Kirov. Apparently, that was the reason for trying to use him as a detonator — a former oppositionist, a friend of Kirov's, expelled from the Party and arrested for ties with one of Kirov's murderers, Faivilovich. According to the report, he was a hard, willful, and imperious man. Not an easy case.

This supposition was confirmed by Alexander Fyodorovich Vutkovsky, a caustic and calm Pole, whom Sharok considered one of the smartest men in the State Security Division and perhaps in the whole Commissariat.

Vutkovsky closed the dossier, put his elbows on the table, rested his chin on his fists, and looked at Sharok with his animated and wise eyes.

"Not *de jure* and not *de facto*."

Sharok was used to Vutkovsky's manner of speaking and understood without things being spelled out. Reinhold would probably not give formal evidence and would not enter into discussions.

Sharok agreed with respect.

"Well then," Vutkovsky said, "be his guardian angel."

The order was clear. If Reinhold didn't talk, someone else would break him, not Sharok. Sharok would be the "good guy," get Reinhold's trust, and continue in that role if the others didn't manage to break him.

That suited Sharok. Breaking people was dirty work! Let others do it.

Sharok's foreboding and Vutkovsky's prediction were justified.

The guard brought a tall, husky man into his office, a man of forty or so, with a handsome, energetic face, who was wearing a fashionable suit, wrinkled from being in the cell, a typical Moscow intellectual with gentlemanly pretensions. There were many like him on the Arbat, and plenty lived in Sharok's building. He hated them — their intellectual condescension and Party rank were written all over their faces. Vipers like that had to be exterminated, with no kid-glove treatment.

Sharok met Reinhold with the long-established ritual of the first interrogation — he shone a lamp on him, lowered the lamp, ordered him to sit down, began looking into his papers, as if studying Reinhold's case — an old and trusted trick that gave him time to think over his method of interrogation.

There were two, as Sharok joked to himself: the deductive method and the inductive. The first consisted of accusing the suspect with the maximum charge and then moving on to details. The second, the inductive, started with the details: the names, meetings, dates, inaccuracies, corrections, discrepancies, a piling on of inessential things followed by the main charge, and if the accused didn't admit it, the charge could be supported from his various statements. Sharok chose the latter. If he instantly accused Reinhold of terrorism, he wouldn't answer any questions at all.

After reading the papers, Sharok set them aside, picked up the interrogation form, and calmly asked the questions.

Reinhold replied just as calmly, confidently staring at Sharok. He was also prepared for a duel. His look was neither nervous nor beseeching, he was studying his opponent; he had a firm and beautiful voice, the voice of a man used to giving orders, speeches, and lectures.

That confident voice annoyed Sharok. It wouldn't be any trouble to make sure that smug son-of-a-bitch could never utter another word. But it was too soon for that.

Among the other questions on the form, Sharok asked about Reinhold's participation in the opposition. Reinhold replied that during the internal Party discussion before the Fifteenth Congress, he had shared the views of the opposition, but soon after he had reviewed them, broken with the opposition, and never had any further ties with it.

Sharok wrote down only, "Participated in the Trotskyite-Zinovievite opposition."

Sharok put down the pen and said, "Tell me more about your opposition activities."

"What activities? In the discussion I voted for the theses of the opposition and then broke with them and never participated again."

"In voting for the opposition, you met with other oppositionists. Who?"

"Comrade Sharok," Reinhold replied convincingly, "it's been almost ten years. My case was examined in the Party organization, to whom I gave full and exhaustive explanations. You can look at them. I have nothing to add."

"Isaak Isayevich," Sharok said firmly, "you are mistaken if you hope to improve your situation by impeding the investigation. You must cooperate with the investigator in your own interests."

"I know my own interests," Reinhold parried, "and I will defend them myself. And you're not going to catch me with those tricks." He nodded over at the form. "Look for fools somewhere else.... Furthermore, you're not going to get another word out of me until you tell me the charges. Bear in mind, I know the law as well as you do."

He stared at Sharok mockingly; he obviously thought he was a minor investigator who didn't understand with whom he was dealing.

"Isaak Isayevich," Sharok said as gently as possible, "I am simply talking with you. I want to clear up a few things, and you're demanding that I charge you. Do you want to be charged?"

"You could have called me in for a pleasant chat. But I've been arrested. Consequently, you are accusing me of something. What?"

Everything was clear. He'd have to use extreme measures. But he had to make one more try.

Sharok sighed, shuffled the papers on his desk, and gave Reinhold a sympathetic look.

"Well then, Isaak Isayevich, remember this, please — I tried to come to terms with you, I tried to find a common language. One day you will understand and appreciate it." He gave Reinhold a significant look. "Yes, you will appreciate it."

He stopped talking.

Reinhold sat before him in the relaxed pose of a man who is sure of himself.

"When was the last time you saw Kirov?" Sharok asked.

Reinhold laughed. "Comrade investigator, the charges!"

Sharok frowned and said nothing, dragging out the time. No matter how determined Reinhold might be, uncertainty bothers everyone.

Then Sharok said, "Citizen Reinhold, I hope you remember what I told you. And now I will obey your demand. So. We have absolutely reliable information that you have met with Citizen Lev Borisovich Kamenev."

He paused again.

Reinhold was silent.

"Is that or is that not true?"

"Is that the charge?" Reinhold replied with a question.

"Yes."

"I've met with Kamenev," Reinhold said with a shrug. "What's criminal about that?"

"Kamenev is one of the leaders of a terrorist organization and he brought you into that organization."

Reinhold sat up in the chair and looked at Sharok seriously for the first time.

"Is that or is that not true?"

"Are you serious?" Reinhold asked at last.

"Of course. The investigation has absolutely reliable evidence, incontrovertible."

"Well then," Reinhold replied coolly, "then try me on the basis of that evidence."

"If we try you, you'll be executed."

"Go ahead."

"You're not sorry to give up your life?"

"I am. But I will never admit to things I did not do. It is out of the question. Don't even bother!"

"Can you imagine what awaits your family if you are shot as a spy and terrorist?"

"Don't try to scare me." Reinhold laughed. "You can shoot me and my family, but you're not going to get another stripe from handling my case."

Sharok got up and straightened his uniform. "You choose your own fate."

He pushed the bell.

The guard appeared in the doorway.

"Take him away!"

"Wait a minute," Reinhold said, pointing to the transcript. "Why haven't you recorded my statement?"

"You didn't make a statement," Sharok replied.

"But I denied the charges."

"I didn't make any formal, written charges. Consequently, you did not make a formal statement. Our friendly discussions are not transcribed. And remember this, Isaak Isayevich, I spoke with you in a friendly way, but you were hostile to me."

He turned to the guard. "Take him away!"

Molchanov coordinated the work of all the investigative groups. Every other day he had a meeting of the investigators, during which everyone reported on his suspects, and thus Sharok was well informed of the general course of the investigation.

Olberg gave the needed statements immediately. He confessed that he had been sent on Trotsky's orders by his son, Sedov, to Moscow with the mission to kill Stalin. The teachers and students of the Gorky Pedagogical Institute, who were preparing a terrorist act against Stalin on Red Square during the parade, had already been arrested and sent to Moscow.

Pikel had not given the needed statements yet, but Molchanov's chuckle and his brief comment — "Gai and Shanin will deal with it" — told Sharok that everything would be all right with Pikel too. And Sharok later learned Gai and Shanin simply came to Pikel's cell, called him by his first name, and persuaded him to give evidence against Zinoviev in return for his life and freedom.

Pikel agreed, but on the condition that everything Gai and Shanin promised was confirmed by Yagoda, who received them and confirmed it.

After the meetings Molchanov asked Vutkovsky and Sharok to stay and told them he was unhappy. Reinhold was the only detonator that Molchanov's secret Political Section had, and he wasn't talking.

Sharok was wary as he thought about what to do next. If Molchanov expressed his dissatisfaction with the tactics of his interrogation, he would have to refer to Vutkovsky, who had dictated those tactics. He would have to sell out Vutkovsky. But what if Vutkovsky denied giving the instructions, for after all, he had never written them down. Then Sharok would be not only a bad investigator but also a troublemaker.

Sharok's worries were groundless. Vutkovsky replied for him: "At this early stage of the investigation, extreme measures won't help with Reinhold. He is aggressive. We have to gang up on him. Let Mironov's people deal with him. They're interrogating Zinoviev and Kamenev, and we're connecting Reinhold to Kamenev. If it works out for them, fine; if it doesn't, he'll come back to us and we'll decide then."

"Then who's left?" Molchanov asked.

"We have the hardest ones," Vutkovsky said, "we have to go through several hundred Trotskyites from the prisons and camps, and they've never repented once."

He looked at Molchanov significantly.

The meaning of that glance — Zinoviev and Kamenev had been repenting right and left for nine years, every year to bigger sins. They had started down the road and they would go to the end. They had accepted the moral responsibility for Kirov's murder, and they would accept the criminal responsibility, no one had any doubts about it, it was logical. But the cadre Trotskyites were intransigent: every year they got tougher, the years in the prisons and camps made them tougher, you couldn't break them, they were hard.... And out of people like that they had to find at least twenty or thirty to confess to being terrorists and spies, people who officially called themselves Leninist Bolsheviks, people who not only did not repent but who did not hide their views, who openly attacked Stalin and accused him of betraying the Revolution. You couldn't do anything with them, they feared nothing, not even death, they were possessed, fanatics. . . .

"Actually," Vutkovsky concluded, "I see no other way out with Reinhold."

"Get to it!" Molchanov said grimly.

# ⚜ 20 ⚜

Having told Poskrebyshev not to put anyone through on the telephone, Stalin looked down the list, supplied by Yagoda, of Zinovievites and Trotskyites selected as defendants in the coming trial.

The Zinovievites were obvious — Zinoviev, Kamenev, Bakayev, Evdokimov — they were the main ones and they just needed to be squeezed a little more.

It was more complicated with Trotskyites.

Stalin put checks next to two dozen names on the list. They would get special attention. He had marked them because he knew these people, some better than others, but he knew them. They were people, and that meant they were weak — like all people, if you push them, they'll say what you need.

Man is weak and he becomes strong only when facing weak authority. That is the fatal flaw of bourgeois democracy. The principle of changing power at the top dooms democracy.

Lenin had posited that there was an hour when history offered a real leader the opportunity to take power. But he had guessed the hour as a revolutionary of the Western type who had been given the chance by history to appear in the East. He saw and used the weakness of the regime, but he didn't know the causes of that weakness: The Russian people, even though capable of occasional rebellion, were used to being ruled. Kerensky's regime was a weak regime, with pretensions and illusions about a parliamentary republic, and thus it had to fall. A parliamentary republic was unthinkable in Russia; the peasant with his common sense would want the regime to hold him in a yoke.

Lenin said that dictatorship demands absolute rule, but he did not understand that autocratic rule demands conformity of ideas. The Russian people on the whole had a single faith. They hadn't known religious wars or serious religious movements, as the West had. For almost a thousand years they had kept the religion given to them by the authorities. Now they would get a new faith, and it had to be the only one, otherwise the people would not accept it.

The tsarist regime's weakness was its stupidity and self-confidence: bureaucracy turned its ruthlessness to naught; the fear of world public opinion weakened its ferocity; the fiction of legality allowed its enemies to act. The revolutionaries felt strong, and an enemy who feels strong is dangerous to the authorities. Everyone should feel helpless before authority. The coming trial would have to show that; this trial was important as a jumping-off point for the future ones.

Could that be called terror?

Stalin went over to the shelves and took down a volume of Engels, opening it to Engels's letter to Marx of September 4, 1870:

> Terror is to a great part useless cruelties, committed for the sake of their own reassurance by people who are themselves afraid.

Terror most certainly did not consist of useless and meaningless cruelties. Yes, terror was cruel, but it was always premeditated, always followed a determined goal, and was not always committed by frightened men. On the contrary, frightened men did not dare to use terror, they did not assert themselves, they yielded to the enemy. It was terror that realized the goals of the French Revolution and made its historical processes irreversible. And the failure to use terror led to the failure of the Paris Commune. Engels, writing a year before the Paris Commune, did terror a disservice.

From another shelf Stalin took down Plekhanov and turned to a marked page in that volume.

"What is terror?" wrote Plekhanov. "It is a system of actions, the goal of which is to frighten a political enemy, to spread horror in his ranks."

This definition was more correct than Engels's, because it

confirmed the positive role of terror, but even it was insufficient. It limited the object of terror to the enemy, to the opponent.

Terror was not only a means of suppressing other forms of thinking but, more important, the means for establishing unity of thought that stemmed from a single fear. Only in that way could the people be ruled in their own interest. There had never been any power of the people, nor could there be; there could only be power over the people. The greatest fear was inculcated by mass secret repressions, and they were and should be the main method of terror.

But now it was important to have a public, and publicized, preparation, it was important that all the ringleaders — men known throughout the land — confess. And the more famous their names, the more people would be convinced of the righteousness of the cadre revolution, the righteousness of mass replacements of people, the righteousness of what was called terror.

These show trials would be difficult. They would have their negative sides, but their positive result would be more significant. The significance and scope of these show trials had to be increased and expanded — both in the list of names and in the list of crimes. The murder of Kirov had to be used more fully — Kirov had to become the ultimate victim. His death had to become the basis for all the coming trials, which had to be on a grand scale and worldwide. Everything else would take place behind the scenes. And the most important trial was the first — if it was successful, the others would be too.

After that link would come a long chain — Trotskyites, Bukharinites, high-ranking Party officials, and young Party bureaucrats thirsting for power, the two-faced delegates to the Seventeenth Congress, members of the Central Committee and the Politburo who dreamed of trampling *him,* their friends and puppets in the Oblast and regional committees, in the Republics and People's commissariats.

According to the Party census of 1922, there were four hundred thousand Party members, about eleven percent — forty-four thousand — members since before the Revolution or joining in 1917. *He* remembered those numbers well. Almost fifteen years had passed, during which many of the eleven percent had died and many had been expelled for being Trotskyites, Zinovievites, Sapro-novites, or Bukharinites. How many were left? Twenty or thirty thousand, at most. A pathetic handful! And yet they thought they were the masters. Twenty thousand out of the present two-million-strong Party! One percent! The Party could manage without them.

*He* would let loose an avalanche that would replace tens and hundreds of thousands of undependable people and open the way to people who were loyal to *him* and only to *him,* people for whom *he* and only *he* would think.

This cadre revolution would create a new, truly socialist order, guaranteed protection from any attempts to destroy it. This cadre revolution would be uninterrupted. It would keep the apparat in submission and the people in fear.

The cadre revolution had another, equally important, side. Terror not only inculcated unquestioning submission, it taught the people to be indifferent to victims, taught them that human life was not valuable, destroyed bourgeois concepts of morality and ethics in them. And then the people would obey without resistance. Collec-tivization and dekulakization had proved that. They took away land, cattle, and inventory from the peasants, and they submitted. The famine of the early 1930s took millions of lives, and people died docilely.

Now *he* had to conquer the hardest part — the apparat — conquer the old cadres, conquer the Budyagins, and the only way to conquer them was by destroying them. The Zinoviev-Kamenev trial would be the start.

No one could imagine the scale of the coming cadre revolution. *He* alone imagined it. But *his* epoch must not enter history as the epoch of terror. *His* rule must enter history as the epoch of great achievements of the Soviet people, made under his leadership. In the people's memory *he* must remain as a firm, strict, just, and humane ruler. Yes, *he* was ruthless toward the enemies of the people. But *he* was generous to the people themselves. After Nero's death, all his statues were smashed. That would not happen to *his* monuments.

As for the repressive organs, the principle of power had to extend to them, too — they should be feared, but also loved. The word *Chekist* had to be romanticized. It should have the aura of revolutionary ruthlessness, Bolshevik intransigence, Party principle and honesty. And that would make the enemies look even more disgusting, but the embodiment of Chekist valor had to be only one man — Dzerzhinsky. Dzerzhinsky was dead and posed no threat at all.

# ❧ 21 ❧

**S**harok was exhausted. He wasn't getting enough sleep — the interrogations lasted all night, the reports to the bosses all day, meetings with Molchanov every other day, and the suspects, all cadre Trotskyites and Democratic Centrists brought from prisons and camps, would not give evidence. They were not afraid of anything, not torture, not the truncheons, not threats of execution. They hated Stalin, they hated the State Security organs, they didn't fall for any tempting offers, and they didn't believe anything the investigators said. People with years of the camps behind them replied in a way that didn't allow you to catch them, much less would they betray themselves or anyone else. They were loyal to Trotsky, and it was impossible to force them to say that Trotsky was a terrorist, murderer, and spy.

Sharok was losing his hair over this damned job.

His mother stared at him one morning and said, "You seem to be going bald, son. . . ."

He snarled in reply, and his mother compressed her lips. She couldn't even tell the truth to her own son. She felt sorry for him, he worked too hard, he was bound to get sick.

Yuri had changed a lot over those three weeks of nightly interrogations. He had always been rude, obnoxious, and brazen with people who couldn't retaliate, but he had never soiled his hands with the dirty work. He had always left that to others. Even as a teenager he had never got into fights — he was afraid of being hit, and he couldn't get over that fear even now. They would throw a man on the floor in front of him, beat him with rubber truncheons, and Sharok would bend over, shake his head and demand a confession. But he would never be the one to throw him down or beat him.

But now he threw them on the floor, kicked them, and beat them with rubber truncheons.

Lidya Grigoryevna Zvyaguro drove him crazy. She had been brought back from Siberian exile, an old Party member expelled back in 1927, a Democratic Centrist, and they were the wildest, most intransigent fanatics, bastards, and sons-of-bitches!

She refused to talk.

"Where is my son, Taras?"

Who was this Taras? There was no Taras in her file, and the old dossier brought from the archives clearly said "No children" in the "Family Situation" line.

"You have no children."

"How do you know?"

"Here's your file, the interrogation of 1927."

"I didn't have any then, now I do."

"How old is your son?"

"Seven."

Sharok stared at her in amazement. A son ... seven years old. Who would have wanted that ugly old woman with buck teeth? But, she had a baby. Of course, in camps and exile any woman was a woman, even if she was a hundred years old. She'd been in the camps and prisons since 1927, but she got pregnant, and at her age, that was strange.

"You were kind of late for having a child."

"My problem."

"Of course," Sharok said and laughed wearily. "So where is he, your son?"

"I'm asking you where he is! I was brought from the Angara to Krasnoyarsk, taken inside the building, and Taras was left downstairs in the reception area. I never saw him again. I was taken out through the courtyard, put in a car, then a train, and brought here, to you, in the Lubyanka. On the road I went on a hunger strike — I'm still on it, and I demand to be told where and how my son is."

Sharok looked at her with interest. This looked like his chance. Usually, people like her did not worry about the fate of their loved ones. They had given up everyone and everything for politics. But this old woman lived not only for politics, but also for her son.

"You're making a mistake," Sharok said. "Drop your hunger strike; if you die, your son will be an orphan."

He pulled over the inkwell and his pad. "Be precise — surname, name, patronymic of the child?"

"My last name is Zvyaguro. His name is Taras Grigoryevich."

"Where are his documents? His birth certificate?"

"He doesn't have any."

"Why not?"

"What difference does it make?"

"Lidya Grigoryevna," Sharok said gently, "I am prepared to help you. In isolating the parents, the organs are required to care for minor children. They probably took care of your child, too. If that is so, we must do his documents properly so that he can be found. If he left the reception area himself, we'll launch a search. For that, we need a description."

"He's an ordinary boy, seven years old, blond, blue eyes. He lisps, and he was wearing a white shirt and brown pants. His coat is dark blue, padded with cotton, a warm gray scarf, felt boots.... He had no documents on him, he has no documents, I adopted him, I picked him up in Siberia, his parents are dead. He knows his name — Tarasik — and he knows me as his mother, Lidya Grigoryevna."

It was all clear. An old maid, she adored her Taras, she would do anything for him.

"Was the adoption legalized?" Sharok asked.

"You ask strange questions. How could I legalize it? I don't have a passport where he can be added. But Alferov, the authority in our region, knew about it. I wrote an official letter to him."

"Hm, it's very complicated," Sharok said thoughtfully. "You have no formal rights to the child. He's not yours. And we're not obliged to give you information about him."

"He's my son," Zvyaguro said. "I brought him up. He considers me his mother."

"Yes, yes, of course," Sharok agreed. "In human terms, I

understand. You love the child, he loves you. But we do not have the right to ignore the legalities — not me, not anyone else. There are thousands of prisoners in this country, and we can tell them only about their real, legal relatives. Understand! Anyone can call himself somebody's child! The boy is an orphan, and I think he'll end up in an orphanage, that's all."

"Until you tell me what has happened to him, I will not give up my hunger strike."

"Don't be ridiculous. No one will pay any attention to your hunger strike. How can you have a hunger strike in a common cell? You don't take your portion, but the others share with you. This isn't 1927. They paid attention to hunger strikes then, but not now; people don't give a damn about your hunger strike, don't you realize that?"

"As you like," Zvyaguro said. "Until I get precise information on where my son is, I will not eat and I won't talk to you."

"All right, let's say I find out and tell you that he is in a certain orphanage in a certain town. Then what?"

"I'll know where he is. For now that is enough. You can shoot me. But as long as I'm alive, I want to know — and I have the right to know — how my son is."

"You have no right, as I've explained. Wherever you may write to complain, you cannot write 'my son,' because he is not your son, not even an adopted son, simply someone else's child, so no one will pay any attention to your complaint."

He stopped and regarded Lidya Grigoryevna. She was so ugly, dammit! But connected to an important name, Zvyaguro! She had been in the textbook of Party history, which was discarded now, however. If he could break her, it would make up for his failure with Reinhold.

Sharok leaned back in his chair.

"Lidya Grigoryevna! You are smart and an experienced politician. You understand the futility of your demands. I am not obliged to search out an orphan you happened to meet by chance. He won't starve to death, he'll be placed in an orphanage, but of course, not under the Zvyaguro name. He will be placed under a name that you will never learn, nor will you ever know which orphanage. You know all that, but apparently your affection for the boy is beyond such understanding. That is very human, and I sympathize. Our business will pass and be forgotten, so will this office, these papers, and you and I, but the child will remain. And you must live for his sake. I understand that ideas are very important and significant, but a child is more important and significant. I will be direct with you. We will not only learn about your son, we will help you get him back. But you must help us."

She sat, her head still bowed, and looked off to the side.

Sharok went on. "If you remain like this, you are of no use to your adopted son ... excuse me, what was his name?"

She did not reply but continued to sit with her head down, looking to the side, and he could not catch her eye.

Sharok tried to understand her silence — was she trying to guess what was in store for her, was she preparing to rebuff him, or, perhaps, was she going to agree?

"Keep this up and you are doomed to prison, camp, and exile," Sharok went on. "You see what's going on. The Party is increasing the struggle with anti-Party, anti-Soviet elements...."

He stressed *anti-Soviet* on purpose. They always got angry and protested when they were called that. But Zvyaguro was still silent.

"The opposition cause is lost, the people and the Party have rejected it, it doesn't have a chance. Do you pose a threat to the Party or to the people? No! A single wave of the hand and you're gone. Come back to the Party, the people, help us build socialism. After all, that's why you joined the Revolution in the first place."

Sharok paused, waiting for Zvyaguro's reaction. But she was still silent and avoiding his eye; she seemed to be looking all over the prison floor.

"I know what you will say — that you were in the Party before I was born and there's nothing I can tell you. But I'm not the one trying to persuade you, it's the Party, the people who are persuading you. If you will, your son is the one you are abandoning to fate."

He paused again, but Zvyaguro still sat there.

Her silence encouraged Sharok; she was listening instead of arguing.

"Help us defang Trotsky politically. From abroad he is directing terrorist activity in the Soviet Union. He has acted through the

United Center in Moscow, which included on one side Zinoviev, Kamenev, and other Zinovievites, and on the other, the former major Trotskyites, Smirnov and Mrachkovsky. Kirov was murdered on the orders of that center, and they were planning terrorist acts against Comrade Stalin and other Politburo members. Didn't you know about that? Well, you've learned it from me. Help us strike the final blow against Trotsky and Trotskyism. Many former Zinovievites, Trotskyites, and Democratic Centrists are helping us. We want you to give evidence that such a terrorist organization had existed, that there had been directives on terror. Who, what, where, and when — that you can decide for yourself. That's a technical question. The important thing is to confirm that Trotsky managed this conspiracy from abroad through Zinoviev, Kamenev, Smirnov, Mrachkovsky, and a few others. All honest people want to help you, but you must help us. You will not be betraying anyone. Rejecting a mistaken ideological line, rejecting a useless battle is not shameful. However, in saving your life, you will be saving the life of your adopted son. You know, unfortunately, what our orphanages are like."

Her silence was beginning to annoy Sharok, and he raised his voice. "Lidya Grigoryevna! I've explained things to you and rather clearly, I think. You must make a choice. I am not insisting on an answer now. I am not rushing you. Think it over, I'll send for you tomorrow."

Without looking up, she asked, "What will happen to Taras?"

"As soon as I get a positive answer from you, I will take measures immediately. We will bring him to Moscow, show him to you, legalize the adoption, and place him in the best Moscow kindergarten, or, if you prefer, we will send him to your family — you have a nephew, I believe" — he leafed through her file — "in Yaroslavl, and we can send your Taras to him."

"I see," Zvyaguro said softly. "And if I refuse to take part in this comedy, you won't find Taras and you won't do anything for him."

"Absolutely nothing," Sharok agreed. "We can help you only if you help us."

He regarded her calmly, seemingly with sympathy, but in his heart he rejoiced. She was an idealist, before the Revolution she had spent time at hard labor, she had done eight years in our prisons, camps, and in exile, and he was going to break her. He had found her weak spot, her Achilles' heel.

And the local representative from Angara, Alferov, had not written anything about Taras. He said she was a cadre, an implacable Democratic Centrist, but he didn't write that she was bringing up that boy, he knew about him, he knew about him from Zvyaguro herself, but he didn't write about him. He must have realized the significance of this circumstance for their investigation, but he hadn't mentioned him. Why not? We'd find out.

"Are you making similar deals with the others?"

"We are, occasionally. In most cases no deals are necessary."

"You're using children as blackmail."

"Lidya Grigoryevna!" Sharok said severely. "I don't have time for this. I've offered you a simple, direct, painless way out, equally beneficial to you and to us. You know that we will get the evidence we need from you. We're strong enough to do that, but I want to avoid it. All opposition will be destroyed once and for all, and those who understand that and help us will be allowed to live; those who resist, we will kill. I've spent a lot of time on you only because I sympathize. If you like, accept my conditions; if you don't, I can't guarantee your life or the fate of your adopted son."

She looked up at Sharok. He had never seen such hatred, it even scared him, it was so strong. And then — that bitch, that whore, spat at him. Sharok recoiled, and the spittle hit his chest. You bitch!

Sharok got up, wiped his uniform shirt with a handkerchief, strode over to her, and lifted Zvyaguro's head. She looked at him challengingly. He punched her with his right fist, then his left, her head bouncing back and forth between punches. She was so ugly with those buck teeth, not even human — just an ugly monkey! He beat her from the right, from the left, not letting her fall from the chair. And without a sound, or a groan — the bitch didn't even shut her eyes — she stared at him with hatred. . . .

Finally she fell from the chair. Sharok called the guards and they dragged her back to her cell.

Ever since that night, Sharok no longer feared his suspects. He punched them in the face, kicked them, beat them with the rubber truncheons. And as he beat them, he grew more furious. But with time he learned to control himself. As soon as the prisoner gave in, he stopped the beating, returned to his desk, lit a cigarette, and sat for a few minutes in silence, resting. It was hard work. And then he would resume the interrogation. He wrote down the statements with an injured air, as if he had been beaten instead of the suspect, as if it were the prisoner's own fault that he had been forced to do such unpleasant work.

But the people giving the needed evidence were insignificant, not even secondary figures, but third rate. The serious prisoners did not give evidence. From them, Sharok could not get any really substantial results.

And then, at a meeting at Molchanov's, he learned that in addition to Olberg, even Pikel was giving the necessary statements. Only Reinhold was still holding out. He had been in Chertok's hands for three weeks, they had tried every damn thing, but he wouldn't give. Now Vutkovsky and Sharok had to try again.

Reinhold came back to Sharok.

For three weeks Chertok, the most terrible investigator in the apparat, a sadist and butcher, had kept Reinhold on a treadmill, up to forty-eight hours without sleep or food, beating him viciously, signing an order for the arrest of his wife and child in front of him ... but he got nothing.

But Sharok saw a different Reinhold from the one who had sat in front of him at the first questioning. His formerly chic suit, now filthy, torn, and ragged, hung from him. He had lost about thirty-five pounds, had grown a beard, and his eyes had the febrile glimmer of a man who had not slept or eaten in days, who had been subjected to humiliations, beatings, and torture. And still Reinhold looked at him with his hostility and intransigence.

But Sharok knew that the hatred and intransigence were concentrated on Chertok, the man who had tortured him. This was the point of the combination, from hot to cold, from cold to hot; Vutkovsky and Sharok had suggested the combination of good guy and bad guy, and now they were responsible for making it work.

Sharok offered Reinhold a seat. "There was a time, Isaak Isayevich, when I had hoped to be your investigator. I thought we could find a common language, but we didn't, not through any fault of mine, Isaak Isayevich. It was your fault. Was it better with Chertok? I don't think so. We know him well here."

Sharok was telling the truth. Chertok was known as a sadist. It upset Sharok that their names were so similar — they were sometimes confused.

"So, Isaak Isayevich," Sharok continued, "I have been given an unfortunate responsibility."

He looked at Reinhold with sympathy and resignation, the way you look at a doomed man, a dead man. He looked at Reinhold and handed him the Resolution of the Special Session of the Commissariat of Internal Affairs, which sentenced Reinhold, Isaak Isayevich, to be shot for his participation in a Trotskyite-Zinovievite conspiracy, and sentenced the members of his family to exile in Siberia. The resolution was stamped with the big round seal of the NKVD.

Reinhold read the paper, put it on the desk, and asked, "Am I supposed to sign it?"

"Of course."

Reinhold looked around the table for a pen. Sharok was astonished by his firmness. Or was it apathy, the desire to die after everything that Chertok had done to him?

He waited in silence as Reinhold looked for a pen and couldn't find it.

"I can give you some good advice, but you don't listen to me," Sharok said.

Reinhold looked at him interrogatively.

Sharok looked over at the door stealthily — an old trick to make the conversation seem frank.

"Write to Comrade Yezhov, write what you like, insist on having your case reexamined, but most important, ask him to postpone the execution of the sentence. Find excuses for it — you're shocked by the sudden arrest, exhausted by Chertok's interrogation, and so on, but you want to rethink your position and for that you need time. Try it. I promise you that in a day or two your request will be on Comrade Yezhov's desk. And I think that Comrade Yezhov will give the order to reexamine your case. I will give the order to send paper and ink to your cell, and you can write it by morning. Do you agree?"

Reinhold was silent.

"Well, then," Sharok said dryly, "you didn't take my advice last time, either, and look what you got." He pointed to the OSO sentence. "Don't listen now, either, but it will cost you your life."

"All right," Reinhold agreed, "I'll write."

## 22

When he got home from Altman's and thought it over, Vadim was horrified. Having listed about two dozen people who had visited his family on the Arbat, he realized that he couldn't maintain that they had never talked about anything except medicine. That was ridiculous. Altman had stated it directly — counterrevolutionary conversations. That meant, something from their house that reached them. . . . But what? Earlier, two or three years ago, talented young theater people used to gather at their house, and so did famous actors, but there had never been political talk, not even jokes. What did they want from him?

He was terrified of another meeting with Altman. What was that butcher getting ready for him? He started with one thing but was thinking about another, jumping to a third, catching Vadim in something, keeping him in suspense. . . . In order to resist, to get out of this mess, he had to know exactly what was going on, what they wanted from him. He couldn't possibly live in this state of not knowing.

He thought about it ceaselessly, and fear did not leave him day or night. He had to talk with Yuri, a comrade, a childhood friend. Let Yuri find out what they wanted from him. He wouldn't ask him for help or protection. Vadim could defend himself. His whole life was an open book, he was an honest Soviet man, a dependable helper to the Party in his struggle for a true Party art, a man who was endlessly faithful personally to Comrade Stalin.

Of course, he had promised Altman not to tell anyone, but Yuri was all right, he worked there. He had to do it now, before they called him in again.

Yuri was home — he answered the phone himself — and seemed pleasantly surprised. "Vadim? What planet did you fall from?"

"You're the one who's been missing. I'm always home. I called you, you weren't in."

"Lots of work."

"We should get together."

"Sure, I'd like that myself, there's lots to talk about. But when?"

"How about today?"

Yuri laughed. "You can tell who has an easy profession. My dear man, all my evenings are busy, I have only Sundays. But I'm working this Sunday, too. Let's call each other next week."

"Yuri, this is impossible. I have to see you. Soon."

"We haven't seen each other for a year, and suddenly it's urgent."

"Yes, Yuri, yes. It is urgent."

"What's happened?"

"Nothing in particular. But I need your advice."

"I can do that over the phone."

"This is not something for a telephone conversation," Vadim said desperately.

He was losing ground. If he didn't meet with Yuri before Altman called, everything was lost. And Altman could call any day.

"Yuri! This is your old comrade. Please! If this weren't so important for me, I wouldn't bother you. Do you want me to come to your house?"

"I'm leaving soon. Mother is heating up lunch."

"Yuri, come eat at my house! Fenya has breast of veal with mushrooms and pirozhki for the bouillon." He was pleading.

Sharok thought and then said, "I'll call back in ten minutes and tell you if I can make it."

He called in ten minutes. "You've convinced me — I'm coming. But I don't have a lot of time, so let's have a quick lunch."

Sharok was happy to see him, he smiled and patted Vadim on the back. "You keep getting fatter, Vadim, breast of veal, pirozhki, you're not watching your weight."

"No time for that, dear man."

"Of course, you take on everyone with your pencil, killing them off one by one.... Well, what's wrong?"

They went into the dining room. Fenya brought out the soup tureen, served the bouillon, and set the plate of pirozhki on the table.

Vadim waited for her to leave. "Nothing much. I'm probably wrong to be bothering you with it. But you see, I'm not used to this business, I've never been in this situation before. And even though I know it's nothing, that there's no danger for me, it's unpleasant."

Sharok laughed. "We lawyers were taught to drop the first page of a prepared speech and start with the second."

"Yes," said Vadim, "I was called in to the Lubyanka...."

Sharok's face changed instantly. He didn't frown, he didn't look grim, he looked tense. His lips were compressed into a line and his gaze hardened.

"Some fellow named Altman called me in, I didn't get his rank, but he was a horrible guy, formal, dry, soulless. I was knocked for a loop, and I think I did some stupid things. All I wanted to do was to get out of there as fast as I could."

His voice trembled. Didn't Yuri feel sorry for him?

But Yuri's face was still tense, and he was staring off somewhere beyond Vadim.

Fenya looked in. "Shall I serve the veal?"

"Go ahead," Vadim said and waited for her to close the door. "Actually, nothing much happened, he asked me about foreigners I knew. I named everyone I knew, he wrote it down, I signed, and he let me go. But he said he'd call me in again. And I can't understand what for. What does he need from me? I've never dealt with any foreigners, I haven't been in any conspiracies, you know me.... Well, if it's because Vika moved to France, what do I have to do with that?"

Sharok was suddenly interested. "She went to France? What for?"

"She got married and moved away."

"Whom did she marry?"

"Some correspondent."

"Ah," Sharok muttered. "An anti-Soviet."

"He's anti-Soviet? You know that?"

"All correspondents are anti-Soviet, except the ones from Communist newspapers. And you can't trust them much, either."

They concentrated on the veal.

"Then what's the problem?" Sharok asked.

"I don't understand the real reason for dragging me down there. What for? The foreigners who come to see Papa? But they come officially, they are accompanied by official persons. Then what? He asked me, 'With whom have you had counterrevolutionary anti-Soviet conversation?' What conversations? That's nonsense. I couldn't have had any with anyone. I'm an honest Soviet man."

"There is no Soviet man who never, at least once, said something anti-Soviet," Yuri explained.

"In that case, I'm an exception," he replied. "I don't have conversations like that. And the prospects of discussing this with that Altman don't please me. I could talk to the head of the Writers' Union, Alexei Maximovich Gorky, but I stupidly promised Altman not to tell anyone about it."

Sharok bent over the table and brought his face close to Vadim's. "You promised that?"

"Yes."

"Then why did you tell me?"

"But you work there," Vadim replied meekly, realizing that he had made another mistake.

Sharok pushed away his plate. "Do you understand what you've done to me?"

"Yuri —"

" 'Yuri, Yuri!' " Like Altman, he mimicked Vadim in irritation. "What Yuri? You were trusted, you promised to keep silent, and you broke that promise. I work there. . . . Do you know what I do there? Maybe I'm a janitor!" He paused and then said grimly, "I work in that institution, I have been told a work-related secret, I am obliged to report that to my boss."

Vadim looked at him in bewilderment.

"Yes, yes," Sharok went on in irritation. "I have to do that, it's my duty. You told me. Where's the guarantee that you won't tell anyone else? And add, 'I know someone who works there, I told him everything, he'll help me out.' "

"Yuri, how can you say that?"

"Why can't I? Since you've put me in this ambivalent position, I can do anything I want!"

"Yuri, believe me."

"I have my duty," Sharok announced. "Our institution requires that every worker there report to his bosses on everything that has to do with that institution."

He got up from the table and looked at his watch. "Time to go."

"Yuri, are you really going to do that?" Vadim gave him an entreating look.

Without looking at Vadim, Sharok asked huffily, "Do you promise not to tell anyone about our conversation? Why do I even ask, you had promised Altman, too."

Vadim clutched his hands to his chest. "I swear to you ... not a word. I didn't tell anyone besides you, believe me! You're the only one I dared tell. I thought —"

Sharok interrupted. "You've told me what you thought, don't repeat yourself. Here's my advice, as a friend — don't get any more involved, not a word to anyone — not about being interrogated, not about meeting with me. Stop gabbing, go on living as you have, otherwise they'll guess that something has happened and they'll force you to tell."

"Who'll guess, who'll force me?" Vadim was flabbergasted.

"Those who need to," Sharok said persuasively. "You couldn't have been called in by accident. We don't do things by accident, we don't bother people for nothing, we don't shoot sparrows with cannons. You were called in and questioned, a statement was written up, you were warned not to talk about it, and that means that there is a case, and a serious one. The people around you — do you really know who they are? You think something is a trifle. It's not a trifle! I know very well that neither you nor your father had anti-Soviet conversations. But you meet people outside the house. You meet lots of people, Vadim, you have a wide circle of acquaintances, I know that. Dig around in your memory." He looked at Vadim and added meaningfully, "One joke, heard or told, that's a charge."

He put on his military overcoat and buttoned it up. "So long!"

But a ray of hope glimmered. Good old Sharok, a real friend. He didn't abandon him. He hinted, he told him that the case was about a joke. Oh God, to die because of a joke!

He went over all the jokes he had heard recently. All trifles, nothing. Jokes were usually told in passing: "Have you heard . . . ?" "You haven't heard the one about . . . ?" The only one he remembered that could be considered even a tiny bit criminal was the one about Radek and Stalin. Where did he hear it? Elsbein, the critic Elsbein, he was the one who told it. Vadim was having lunch at the Writers' Club with his old friend and mentor, Ershilov. Elsbein appeared in the door, looked around the room and headed for their table, sidling, sidling — he limped, leading with one shoulder as he walked. Ershilov moved back a chair for him, and Vadim frowned: He didn't like the guy. Phony smile, beady eyes.

"Have you heard the latest?" Elsbein asked. "Stalin calls in Radek and says, 'Listen, Radek, you like to make up jokes, and I heard you make them up about me. So don't do it, don't forget, I'm the leader!' And Radek says, 'You're the leader? That's one I haven't told yet!' "

Ershilov smiled, so did Vadim. Elsbein got up and went to another table.

Vadim didn't think much of that. Of course, Comrade Stalin was mentioned in the joke, but Radek was a major Party figure, albeit a former oppositionist, a repentant Trotskyite, but a famous man. He was famous for his jokes, which had sort of a legitimacy because Radek was an official. Formerly one of the leaders of the Comintern, and now a famous journalist, a columnist in *Pravda* and *Izvestia*. Of course, when Elsbein told the joke, Ershilov smiled wanly, but his eyes weren't smiling. And Vadim didn't repeat the joke to anyone, did he?

He did. . . . To the barber, Sergei Alexeyevich, his barber Sergei Alexeyevich, who worked here in the Arbat, on the corner of Kaloshin, and whom Vadim had known since childhood. His father's barber, who had cut his hair before the Revolution and still did. When his father was sick, Sergei Alexeyevich came to the house, to cut his hair and shave him, and Vadim's late mother had taken Vadim to him. He was a respectable and good-looking man with a handsome beard, friendly and kindly.... He put a board across the arms of the barber chair, said, "Well, young man," picked up Vadim and set him on that board, cut his hair, and joked with him.... Later, Vadim went by himself, without his mother, who had died. He went as a young man and as an adult, and now it wasn't Sergei Alexeyevich who treated him with condescension, but Vadim who spoke down to Sergei Alexeyevich. It was unlikely that Sergei Alexeyevich read the newspapers and journals in which Vadim published, but he must have heard about his success at least from Fenya, who had come to work for them ten years ago on Sergei Alexeyevich's recommendation — they were from the same village or maybe she was a relative.

Out of friendship, Vadim told him the latest political news and commentary on newspaper reports. It fed his ego, making him look like a significant person, close to the powers that be.

Sergei Alexeyevich raised his eyebrows and always repeated the same good-natured phrase no matter what he heard — "Lev Davydovich had to be there somehow." He said that about Trotsky the way people quoted popular punch lines.

When he heard the joke about Radek, Sergei Alexeyevich smiled politely and said his usual "Lev Davydovich had to be there somehow," that is to say, Trotsky taught Radek to be so sarcastic with Stalin.

Could Sergei Alexeyevich have denounced him? He was a close friend, practically a member of the family. He had known his father for twenty years now, and his late mother, and he'd known Vadim since he was in diapers, and Fenya was his relative. But what if he was a professional snitch? It was a convenient place — tens, hundreds of people passed through his place — and everybody was happy to chew the fat. He always said his little line about Trotsky with an ambiguous smile, and not only when he talked with Vadim — he said it to everyone, so everyone knew that he meant Trotsky when he said Lev Davydovich. Was he trying to get people to talk about Trotsky?

Vadim remembered Fenya's story about how they protected themselves in the village when they took away all their grain. "Our parents had seven mouths to feed," Fenya said. "What would they give us? They were taking all our grain, they searched everywhere, swept every corner. My late mother came up with the idea — we stuffed our mattresses with grain instead of straw, we slept on it, it was hard and the grains stuck us. But at last we had a little bread; we baked it secretly, so the neighbors wouldn't turn us in."

Fenya was from a kulak family. Once her father came to visit, he sat in the kitchen and looked around beseechingly, cautiously, of course he had been dekulaked. And, after all, Fenya was related to Sergei Alexeyevich. How hadn't he thought about it before, not realized its significance. A friend of the family. Our friend. He was everyone's friend in the Arbat. And he was writing "information" on them all. And he could have written about Vadim.

When he went to the Writers' Club and met Elsbein and Ershilov, Vadim peered into the faces, looking for a giveaway — a flash of embarrassment or something. No, they behaved normally. But someone had denounced him.

Elsbein? Everyone knew that Elsbein had been at Kamenev's house almost every day, had worked in Academia Publishing House. Kamenev was arrested, and Elsbein wasn't. It was strange, of course. But on the other hand, Elsbein was the one who told the joke. He wouldn't denounce himself, would he?

Ershilov? Ershilov was above petty denunciations. His specialty was major denunciation, each of his critical articles was a political denunciation, each of his exposés essentially a sentence. So he wouldn't bother with such trifles.

So, if the problem really was in that joke, then only Sergei Alexeyevich could have denounced him.

Thus, he, Vadim Marasevich, had become known as a spreader of anti-Soviet jokes, spreading them everywhere, even at the barbershop. His sister had moved to Paris, had married an anti-Soviet, and Vadim was busy with anti-Soviet activities here.

But it wasn't true! He wasn't anti-Soviet! Of course, it was stupid to tell that joke to Sergei Alexeyevich, especially since he probably didn't even get it. And the joke wasn't about Stalin, it was about Radek. For the intelligentsia, Radek was a joke.

No matter how Vadim reassured himself, he knew that things were bad, very bad. Altman would interpret that joke differently

— it was a joke about Comrade Stalin. And where? At the barbershop! And whom else did you tell? No one. Right, no one, why should we believe you?

What a terrible fix he was in! He couldn't deny anything. Denial was stupid and it would make it look worse.

But if he confessed that he told the joke to Sergei Alexeyevich, he would have to say where he heard it. He would have to name Elsbein. And who else was there? Ershilov. And he would have to name Ershilov, too. If he tried to weasel out of it, they would put him in jail.

Would they really do that? Then his life was over. Why should he perish? He was only twenty-five! For whose sake? Radek, who made up these jokes, for Elsbein, who spread them? It was easy for Radek, he'd just say, "They attribute them to me, I didn't say it," and there were a lot of jokes attributed to him. And Elsbein, the son-of-a-bitch, the provocateur, tells these jokes in front of a witness, in front of Ershilov. And Ershilov's a fine one, too! A Party member, more than that, a member of the Party Committee, why didn't he reprimand Elsbein? That would have been a signal for Vadim — he would have joined in and he would never have told the joke to Sergei Alexeyevich. They were both awful, Elsbein and Ershilov. And he had no intention of sparing them. Yes! Elsbein told the joke, but in the presence of Party Committee member Ershilov, who laughed approvingly, and Vadim thought therefore that there was nothing criminal in it, and rather carelessly told it to the barber.

But Vadim was nervous, his thoughts were confused. He was afraid of a new meeting with Altman. On the other hand, the uncertainty was killing him. He couldn't wait to be called in, heard out, and recorded; after all, he would have done his duty honestly. Of course, a case might be started up, but Ershilov would get out of it. He was too big and important, they wouldn't raise a hand against him. As for Elsbein, let him get out of it as he could, let him admit that he told that vile story and explain why he was spreading it all over the restaurant.

If only Altman would call him soon. Vadim stayed at home waiting for the call, and if he went out he insisted that Fenya ask who was calling and get the caller's name. Fenya didn't write down the callers' names and Vadim was furious, even though he knew that the NKVD didn't leave messages with the maid.

"I've told you in plain Russian — write down the names. There's paper and pencil by the phone. How hard is it to make your scribble?"

But Fenya didn't wish "to scribble," and the next day she reported that some man called but didn't leave his name.

"Did you ask?"

"I did, and he hung up."

Why wasn't Altman calling, damn him! Maybe he was on vacation, or maybe they closed the case. . . . Perhaps Yuri had said to Altman, "I know Vadim Marasevich. He's one of us!" "One of us!" Good words, dependable words. He had always wanted to be considered one of the guys. In school and at college, not "our comrade," but "one of us." "Comrade" was too transitory, too temporary. "One of us" was forever.

That's what Yuri must have said, "one of us," and Altman had thrown out that silly statement. It would be good to call Yuri and find out, but Vadim didn't want to force it, and Yuri wouldn't tell him anything. It was enough that he had hinted about the joke, he shouldn't have done that, by rights. He had acted nobly — Yuri was a fine guy — and Vadim shouldn't ask him for anything else. It wouldn't be diplomatic.

A month passed, a second, life went back to normal, and Vadim grew calmer. Even if Altman were on vacation, he would have come back a long time ago. Maybe he was fired, well, all the better, that meant he was replaced by someone smarter, who immediately saw that Vadim's case was trumped up and closed it. The important thing was that Yuri must have said something positive about him.

Vadim calmed down. His articles began appearing in newspapers and journals again, and once again he stood on tribunes and thundered and exposed scoundrels.

They were pleased with him. Even Vladimir Vladimirovich Ershilov said, "Good for you, you're thinking the right way!"

## 23

After his conversation with Yezhov, Reinhold was transformed.

He not only signed everything Sharok wanted, he added a lot, giving his statements greater acuity and persuasiveness.

Sharok could only guess what Yezhov had promised him, what they had agreed on. His life was promised him, his innocence confirmed, the Party's will announced — that was clear, but in whose name? Yezhov's name carried authority, but would Reinhold settle for it, or had an even higher will been transmitted to him, which made him feel part of a major Party and state action? Reinhold had retained what Sharok had always hated — intellectual hauteur and willfulness. He changed Sharok's formulations in the statement with more clever and grammatical ones, saying, "Write it this way."

It was good for the case, but it annoyed Sharok, and he didn't let Reinhold get too cocky. He listened to him attentively and with a stony expression, but like a man who decides, while Reinhold merely proposed. Reinhold, a smart man, sensed that distance and accepted it — he didn't want to get into arguments with his investigator, especially since Sharok accepted almost everything, rejecting only what didn't fit the overall scenario, which Reinhold didn't know and Sharok did. He was the suspect, Sharok the investigator; he was incarcerated, Sharok was free. If the case went well, Sharok would get a medal, while no one knew what Reinhold would get, though Sharok thought that Reinhold believed completely in the promises that had been made.

They had achieved a mutual understanding, an alliance. Sharok's reputation went up — his suspect, Isaak Isayevich Reinhold, was giving broad, convincing, and sharp evidence. Olberg could give evidence only about what happened abroad; he signed whatever they wanted but he had no imagination, so the investigators had to do the thinking for him. And since they didn't know how things were abroad, they couldn't come up with anything believable except that Olberg had been sent by Sedov on Trotsky's orders to organize a terrorist act against Stalin. . . .

As for Pikel, after the failure of his confrontation with Zinoviev, he had fallen into such a depression that his friends Shanin and Gai had to be called in again. They moved Pikel to a good cell where Shanin and Gai sat up late with him. They drank wine, dined, played cards, and cheered him up, telling him that Zinoviev had given the necessary evidence earlier, but at their personal meeting had suddenly recanted, but everything would be fine. Under the influence of this information, accompanied by food and drink and cards, Pikel cheered up, thereby reassuring Yezhov and Molchanov, who were afraid that Pikel could not be used in the trial in his depressed state.

Thus, the scenario kept changing. Of course, Olberg and Pikel were useful, and they would play their role — evidence is evidence, collaboration is collaboration. But the main "detonator" was Reinhold, and the most important investigator was now Sharok, who was in charge of Reinhold.

Reinhold was interpreting his accidental meetings with any former oppositionists, whether in a private house or at an official business meeting, conference, and even congress, as meetings where the details of the conspiracy were discussed. All he had to do was remember the date and place, and the person he named would have no alibi.

As a major figure in the state apparat, Reinhold had participated in many meetings with other former oppositionists and also major figures. Thus, his evidence was totally accurate in terms of time and place, and that, in its turn, supported his version of the content of their conversations.

Reinhold said that he was a participant in a Trotskyite-Zinovievite conspiracy and, working under Zinoviev, Kamenev,

and Bakayev, had planned the murder of Kirov and also Voroshilov, Kaganovich, and other state and Party leaders. Kirov's murder
had been committed on Zinoviev's orders.

On Molchanov's orders, the three of them — Reinhold, Pikel,
Olberg — met in the office of the chief of the Economic Section,
Mironov, to coordinate their statements.

The statements of Reinhold, Olberg, and Pikel, fully in accordance with and supporting each other, carefully tested by Molchanov and Yezhov (as Sharok guessed) and reported to Comrade
Stalin, were now the main charge against Zinoviev, Kamenev, and
the others, and would become the basis of the coming trial.

In a conversation with Vutkovsky, Sharok even expressed
surprise at Reinhold's strange fervor.

Vutkovsky, a wise and careful man, reflected and then said,
"Reinhold understands his task to be a Party task. You know, I
think that he believes in it sincerely. He is a powerfully motivated
personality."

Sharok pretended to be satisfied by that explanation. What was
the difference between Vutkovsky and Reinhold? One made up lies,
the other pretended to believe them. And doing it in the interests of
the Party. Liars! Both were saving their skins. And he, Sharok, was
saving his skin, too, but he was executing his duty, obeying the
boss's orders, which accorded with the law and regulations — the
responsibility was on those who made those laws and signed those
regulations.

The highest law was Stalin. And everything that was done in
Stalin's interests was justified. Sharok had hated the Communists all
his life. Except for Stalin. Stalin was killing off the Communists
himself, especially the old Communists. They had destroyed everyone and now their turn had come, now Stalin was breaking them,
God grant him strength. Working in the organs, Sharok tied
himself forever to that system, and his own life depended on its
strength and stability. The guarantee of that stability was Stalin.
And therefore Sharok was faithful to him and only to him. And
everything done in Stalin's interests was justified.

He sensed that Reinhold was working from that same point of
view. Sharok reported his results personally to Yezhov, and once,
looking through Reinhold's statement, Yezhov pointed out that at

one meeting Reinhold had attended, Rykov had been present, and at another, Bukharin and Tomsky, and that back in the 1920s Reinhold had seen Ivan Nikitich Smirnov, Mrachkovsky, Ter-Vaganyan, and Dreitser.

"He's awfully quiet about them," Yezhov noted.

The hint was understood. At the very next interrogation, Reinhold claimed, and signed a statement, that not only were Zinoviev and Kamenev part of the conspiracy, but so were the Trotskyites Smirnov, Mrachkovsky, and Ter-Vaganyan, as well as Rykov, Bukharin, and Tomsky. Sharok, as ordered, put Rykov, Bukharin, and Tomsky in a separate statement.

The evidence of Reinhold, Olberg, and Pikel was the basis for the charges against the main defendants of the coming trial. They also needed evidence from the rank-and-file participants in the terrorist conspiracy. The members of the opposition who were brought in from prison, exile, and the camps had not yet cracked.

Convinced that the case still wasn't moving, Molchanov called a new meeting of the investigative groups, this time with Yezhov himself present.

Sharok wasn't at that meeting. On the orders of his superior, Dyakov, he took a trip to Leningrad, to familiarize himself with the files of several former Zinovievites who could be used in the trial or who could give necessary statements. He selected several teachers of social sciences and gave orders to bring them to Moscow.

When he returned from Leningrad, Sharok went to see Dyakov.

Vladimir Nikolayevich Lunin, who also worked in the section and was in charge of investigating Socialist parties, was in the office. Sharok had noticed before that Lunin had stubbornly avoided working on this trial. And now he was telling Dyakov that he was working on a group of Anarchists and couldn't drop the case.

Dyakov grimaced. "Anarchists! There are no Anarchists now! Do you know what Comrade Yezhov said at the last meeting? If any of us hesitates, has doubts, feels that he can't struggle against the Trotskyite-Zinovievite gangs, let him admit it openly and honestly, and we will free him from work in the investigative group. Do you understand the meaning of those words, Vladimir Nikolaevich? Everyone who admits his inability to lead an investigation will be arrested immediately as someone sympathizing with the suspects."

Sharok listened to Dyakov calmly. In charge of the main witness Reinhold, Sharok was dragging it out, meeting with Reinhold every night, and every day making his statements fit in with the statements of other suspects, thereby avoiding interrogating hopeless Trotskyites, especially after his failure with Zvyaguro. And he knew why Lunin was avoiding them, too.

"I'm not refusing any work," Lunin said calmly. "I am doing the job given to me by my chief. And if my chief orders me to take on another case, I will. Of course, your suspects are terrorists, but it was the Anarchists who were considered the real terrorists. . . . If you can prove to the authorities that we should stop investigating Anarchists, then I'll be happy to do what I'm told."

With those words Lunin stood up, a tall, well-built man, and left the office.

"Saboteur!" Dyakov said with hatred. "Refined intellectual!"

Sharok was surprised. "I thought he had been an assistant to a commander of a cavalry squad."

"Doesn't matter. He's a refined intellectual. And unfortunately, Vutkovsky supports him."

"Well," Sharok said with a smile. "Vutkovsky is an intellectual, too."


Valentin Olberg stated that members of the terrorist group he had created at the Gorky Pedagogical Institute included among other teachers and students a history teacher, the Communist Sokolov, and the physics teacher Nelidov, not a Party member and a nobleman, as well.

Dyakov decided that Nelidov was the easier of the accused, and with his help they would be able to tie the Trotskyites with the tsarist aristocracy. He took Nelidov for himself, leaving Sharok with Sokolov.

But it turned out to be quite different from what Dyakov had supposed.

Sokolov was an experienced propagandist and he understood that the trial would be an action directed against Trotsky, Zinoviev, and Kamenev, that the judges would be executing Stalin's will, and that there was no point in resisting. He told Sharok that he recognized the task of the investigation and that he was obligated to help.

Especially because, for many years, as a teacher of history, he had inculcated a hatred of Trotsky in his students and had come to feel it himself.

Sharok did not specify the means by which the students at Gorky Pedagogical were planning to attack, knowing that any fiction would make the fact of that intention suspect. Sokolov passed through easily, and the following morning Sharok placed his statement on Vutkovsky's table.

The Nelidov case proved to be a very different matter. Contrary to Dyakov's expectations, Nelidov was difficult, perhaps the most difficult of them all. He had almost no living relatives and no piety for the Party, since he had never belonged.

Sharok dropped by Dyakov's office once and saw Nelidov — a young man of thirty-five, with intelligent eyes and a high forehead. He seemed to be afraid of Dyakov, who had lost control and had succumbed to fits of fury and hysterics, screaming at Nelidov. His fear would be replaced by a guilty smile, but he still wouldn't sign anything.

This second investigative failure meant that Dyakov was risking his bosses' displeasure, that he would probably be taken off the investigation and removed from the central apparat of the NKVD. Dyakov was desperate to show that he could work in the new conditions. He grasped at the first opportunity.

In Olberg's version, the students at Gorky Pedagogical were planning to kill Comrade Stalin with a pistol.

Frinovsky, chief of the Border Patrol Department, present at the discussion of this version, burst into laughter. "A person with a pistol, marching in a column on Red Square, is going to hit someone standing on the Mausoleum? Do you know the distance? So, the Gorky Institute has such snipers? Let me have them — I'll replace entire divisions with them."

Frinovsky was right, and even though the investigation was willing to accept a lot of incongruities, this version was simply stupid.

Molchanov turned purple. He also knew that it was a stupid idea, but he thought it important for the students to confess to the fact of preparing a terrorist act, while the actual method would somehow slip by unnoticed in the general flow. Now Frinovsky had deprived him of that possibility.

Dyakov spoke. He stood up and proposed a different variant — a bomb. He was investigating a physics teacher, Nelidov. Why shouldn't he have made a bomb at the physics laboratory at Gorky Pedagogical Institute? Nelidov, of course, was giving him trouble right now, not making a statement, but if he were to be faced with testimony and material evidence, he would confess.

Molchanov liked the idea. First, the bomb sounded more convincing than a pistol, and second, the mention of material evidence was important, because there wasn't going to be any other material evidence — no documents, no letters, no pamphlets, nothing except the confessions of the defendants. But they would surely find explosives of some sort in the institute labs.

And so Dyakov headed for Gorky with a group of workers, and returned quickly to Molchanov's office. Dyakov placed on the table several empty rusty metal balls about six to seven centimeters in diameter, and read an official document cooked up in Gorky to the effect that these shells had been hidden in the courtyard of the institute by the terrorist students so that they could later be filled with explosives. Dyakov also read the deposition of the Gorky City military commandant that these were shells for bombs and that, if filled with explosives, they would have a powerful destructive charge.

This official conclusion had an effect, but not on everyone.

Chief of the Special Section Gai picked one of the balls up and chuckled. "These are about as good for making bombs as for making chicken cutlets. Any artillery man will tell you that, and any chef can confirm it."

There was an awkward pause. But Molchanov apparently wanted to have "bombs" at the trial on which to base the charge of terrorism, or perhaps he had already reported upstairs on it and now there was no backing out.

"Show these balls to Nelidov," he told Dyakov. "If he resists, bring him to me."

He squinted at Sharok. "Help Comrade Dyakov."

This was a warning to Dyakov — his subordinate was trusted more than he was.

Nelidov laughed when he saw the balls and explained why they technically couldn't be used for making bombs.

The intellectual and delicate Nelidov was quite exhausted, but he held fast. In his heart Sharok even sympathized with him. He had read up on the Nelidovs in the encyclopedia — they were an ancient, noble line, going back five hundred years to the days of Ivan III, not like these new-baked rulers who had made a sudden leap from the mud to the throne. Nelidov behaved like a true Russian aristocrat.

Sharok knew that showing Nelidov those balls had been a major tactical mistake. It showed Nelidov that they had no evidence against him, and it merely strengthened his resolve and stubbornness. Nelidov did not make a statement this time, either.

That night he was taken to Molchanov.

Molchanov looked at Nelidov sternly and asked angrily, "Why won't you give evidence?"

"You see," Nelidov said, "I'm not used to lying, especially since I can't allow myself to implicate innocent people — my students and my colleagues."

Molchanov interrupted him, "Whom are you calling innocent people? You must confirm what the other suspects have said, which corresponds to the truth, and which you alone contradict. Or, perhaps, everyone else is lying and you alone are telling the truth?"

"Yes, I am telling the truth. And you won't hear one lie from me."

Molchanov raised his voice, "Nelidov, I'm warning you for the last time. We've dealt with your whole class, your whole state, your armies, and don't worry, we'll deal with you alone very quickly."

Nelidov took a step toward Molchanov's desk. His movement was so unexpected that Molchanov recoiled.

Leaning his hands on the edge of the desk and staring straight into Molchanov's eyes, Nelidov said, "I'm not afraid of you, remember that. You can do what you want with me, but I will never slander myself or innocent people. Remember that: I never will."

# ☙ 24 ☙

In early June at the Plenum of the Central Committee Stalin gave a speech on the draft of the constitution of the U.S.S.R. The Plenum approved the draft and passed a resolution on convening an All-Union Congress of the Soviets to discuss it.

But the main issue at the Plenum was the question of changing Party documents. It appeared to be a purely technical matter but actually the change of Party cards meant a universal, total, and thorough check on every Communist.

The purges weren't achieving the desired goal. A Communist came to the tribune, told about himself, and then others spoke. His pals praised him, his enemies denounced him, but his length of time in the Party was the determining factor. "Member of the Party since April 1917" was sinless, and a "member since 1905" was a saint. Purges like that did not reveal the real face of the Communist.

It would be another matter to check the Party documents, in the course of which the Communist's entire biography would be studied diligently: every day of his life, his ties, relatives, friends, colleagues, his statements, and his dossier at the NKVD.

The change in Party documents was a good basis for the cadre revolution. Each Communist had to feel he was under constant, never-sleeping surveillance.

*He* himself had to remind the Party publicly that the most important quality of every Bolshevik today was the ability to recognize the enemy, no matter how well disguised. *He* reminded them that the Party had the right not to give out Party cards to those who did not live up to the calling of Communist.

June had been a pressured month. *He* met with aviators, chatted with Gubkin about oil in the Urals; with Kaganovich and Ordzhonikidze *he* visited the Moscow-Volga Canal, the construction of which should be completed next year. Moscow would then become a port on five seas — White, Baltic, Caspian, Azov, and Black. The canal would solve the problem of water delivery to Moscow; it was a component of *his* general plan for the reconstruction of Moscow. *His* plan.

Stalin chose sites for the monumental figures of the founders of the Soviet state, Lenin and Stalin, by the sculptor Merkurov.

On June 8, *he* visited the ailing Gorky. Molotov and Voroshilov went with him. And ten days later, on June 18, Gorky died. A national mourning was announced, and on June 20 Gorky was buried in Red Square.

Was *he* sorry about Gorky's death? Everyone dies at his prescribed hour. As an artist Gorky had dried up earlier, but he did his job, he united the intelligentsia. In order to get a nation to submit, you either destroy or buy its intelligentsia. Actually, destroy part of it and buy the other and keep it terrified. Gorky had accomplished that mission, saying, "If the enemy does not give up, it will be destroyed," and in the name of the intelligentsia he made a major contribution to the cadre revolution. But writers do not always fully understand what they say, often just to be witty or for a clever turn of phrase they don't quite say what they mean. Who knew how Gorky would have acted during the trials of Kamenev, Pyatakov, Bukharin, and the other bastards, among whom were many of his personal friends? But he left behind a slogan, a good slogan.

But no matter who dies, life goes on. It must go on. On *his* initiative very important decisions were taken — "On the work of higher educational institutions," "On banning abortions," "On pedological perversions."

The new state had to stand on firm ground. The Revolution broke the back of the old order, but they must create a new order, firm and stable. For that it must use the forms of life and mores developed over the centuries that have stood the test of time.

The family cannot be destroyed by divorce. Children improperly brought up become deformed members of society, people without responsibility or care.

There should not be any pedological experiments with children, studying children with the aid of meaningless, stupid, harmful charts and tests, turning them into guinea pigs for scientific charlatans. A child had to be taught and brought up like children had always been, the way *he* had been taught and brought up. Of course, the content of the education and the aim of bringing up children were different now, but the essence — teaching and bringing up — remained.

That was why *he* found time to chat with the members of chorale ensembles. Choral singing was truly folk singing. *He* had once sung in a choir. It develops the sense of the collective in a man, a noble, aesthetic feeling. That had to be supported and encouraged.

On the evening of July 9, Beria, secretary of the Krai Committee, called from Tbilisi.

"Comrade Stalin! Today the bureau of the Krai Committee heard a report on the discovery of a counterrevolutionary terrorist organization in Georgia, Azerbaijan, and Armenia. Serious accusations in loss of vigilance were made against the secretary of the Central Committee of Armenia, Khandzhyan, who categorically denied the charges. This evening, an hour ago, he came to me and behaved in a challenging manner, accusing me of persecuting old Party cadres, of falsifying Party history. He was in a wild and agitated state, threatened to kill me, and almost did, but I killed him first in self-defense."

Stalin said nothing.

"Do you hear me, Comrade Stalin?"

"I do," Stalin said softly.

And said nothing more.

Beria was also silent.

At last Stalin asked, "What was your story for the apparat?"

"Suicide."

"And the public version?"

"I think it will be the same."

"How old was he?"

"Thirty-five."

Stalin paused and then said, "A supervising worker of the Central Committee will fly out to you tomorrow."

He hung up.

Stood.

Walked around the office.

The secretary of the Krai Committee had shot the secretary of the Central Committee of Armenia.

The first such incident in the Party.

Of course, Beria was not defending himself. Khandzhyan had not tried to kill him — he wasn't like that, he wasn't capable of killing the secretary of the Krai Committee; he knew what that meant.

Beria simply shot him. But he admitted it honestly to *him*. He could have lied, he could have said that Khandzhyan shot himself, he could get witnesses, write up a statement. He could do anything. But he didn't dare lie to *him*. He was a criminal, of course, but a faithful criminal.

Of course, it was hard for Beria. The Transcaucasia did not want to recognize him — in 1931 he had been promoted from representative of OGPU* to First Secretary of the Central Committee of Georgia, and in 1932, First Secretary of the Transcaucasia Krai Committee. He was a rank-and-file Cheka man, not even a member of the Central Committee of the All-Union Communist Party, and this in Georgia, where there are major Party people. They considered themselves founders of the Transcaucasian Party organization, and they didn't want to deal with Beria, an investigator from the Cheka.

*He* came to know Beria closely in 1931, on vacation in Tskhaltubo. Beria, then in the OGPU U.S.S.R. in Transcaucasia, took personal responsibility for *his* safety, creating a triple ring of two hundred fifty Cheka bodyguards and never leaving *his* side for six weeks.

You can study a man in six weeks. *He* studied him well. Beria gave *him* thorough, detailed information on every leader in Transcaucasia. *He* learned who said what about *him*, what they thought of *him*. Beria informed *him* correctly, honestly, confirming what *he*

---

* OGPU was the ancestor of the NKVD.

*himself* had suspected. All of them were against "rewriting history," as they called restoring *his* true role in the history of prerevolutionary Caucasia. They were "witnesses," they claimed, "direct participants," they said. Of all the Old Bolsheviks, they were the most intransigent, considered themselves *his* equals, considered themselves to be "participants in the revolutionary struggle in Transcaucasia" as much as *he*.

Beria talked about himself, too. In detail, but whether in honest detail was another question. He was born in the village of Merkheuli, near Sukhumi, had studied in Baku at a technical school, joined the Party in March 1917, and worked in the underground. On Party orders he got in touch with the Musavatist agents.

Beria stressed this point, named all the members of the Baku Committee who had made this decision, put on the table their written confirmation that they had given him that order.

*He* didn't look at the papers, pushing them aside. *He* knew that the papers were in order or Beria wouldn't be showing them to *him*. But the man was in *his* hands — he had ties to the Musavatists.

Beria knew how to serve and back in Tskhaltubo, *he* decided — Beria is the man who could deal with that haughty caste in Transcaucasia. But he needed power for that. He couldn't deal with them if he worked for OGPU. As leader of OGPU he had liquidated the remains of the Musavatists, Sashnaks, Mensheviks, dealt with the Trotskyites, but he had to be the Party leader of Transcaucasia in order to lead the cadre revolution there.

Right after *his* return to Moscow in the fall of 1931, the leaders of the Transcaucasian Krai Committee of all three Republics — Georgia, Azerbaijan, and Armenia — were called to the Central Committee. The agenda was not announced. *He* spoke for an hour, about the economy, about national affairs. He spoke calmly. And just as *he* was getting up, *he* added, "What if we form the leadership of the Transcaucasian Krai Committee this way — first secretary: Lavrentii Kartvelishvili; second, Lavrentii Beria."

*He* saw their reaction. They were stunned, they didn't even stand up although *he* was already on *his* feet.

And Kartvelishvili said harshly, "I will not work with that crook."

Lavrentii Kartvelishvili dared to speak to *him* that way! Of course, back in 1931 they allowed themselves many things. They allowed themselves to accuse *him* of recommending a crook to head a Party organization.

Everyone chuckled. *He* would never forgive them for that chuckle. Only Khandzhyan did not chuckle. He sat with a stone face; he knew chuckling was inappropriate. Clever. And a clever man was a dangerous man.

And then *he* said, "All right, go on home. We'll settle the question later."

Of course, *he* did what *he* wanted. Lavrentii Kartvelishvili was sent to do Party work in Siberia, Mamii Orakhelashvili was made first secretary and Beria second. And a few months later Orakhelashvili was transferred to Moscow as deputy director of the Institute of Marx, Engels, and Lenin.

Beria became first secretary of the Transcaucasian Krai Committee.

In the years that followed, he had acquitted himself well. He replaced all the secretaries of all the Regional Committees, shook up the apparat, and was accomplishing the cadre revolution in Transcaucasia by himself, without Yagoda or Yezhov. He had direct access to *him*.

But Armenia proved difficult for Beria. Khandzhyan was a bone in his throat. Khandzhyan did not recognize Beria and he protected his Armenians, even defended his commissar of education, Stepanyan, when that son-of-a-bitch criticized Beria's book *On the Question of the History of the Bolshevik Organizations of Transcaucasia*.

Beria had written the book on *his* orders. The book properly illuminated *his* role in the history of the Bolshevik Party in general and in the Caucasus in particular. It was a needed book. Everyone understood that. But Stepanyan mocked it, criticized it for its pseudoscholarship and numerous falsifications. Whom was Stepanyan attacking? Beria? No, he was attacking *him*. Beria demanded Stepanyan be shot as an enemy of the people. Khandzhyan wouldn't allow it. He condemned Stepanyan, but wouldn't allow him to be shot. He wouldn't let anyone be touched. A clever man. A two-faced man.

But still — shooting the secretary of the Central Committee of the Communist Party of the Republic in your office is an extraordinary thing.

When Lenin had heard that Ordzhonikidze had slapped Kobakhidze, he was very upset. He practically demanded that Ordzhonikidze be expelled from the Party. And who was that Kobakhidze? An ordinary member of the Georgian Central Committee. And a deviationist at that.

Of course, Khandzhyan was a bastard. But still, shooting him in an office, without trial or investigation?

On the other hand, losing Beria?

Stalin called for Malenkov.
Malenkov appeared.
Stalin looked at him grimly.
A long look.
And Malenkov understood. Stalin was either displeased with him or planning to give him a serious task.

Without inviting him to sit, Stalin paced the room and said, "Khandzhyan shot himself today in Beria's office. He couldn't stand the charges of losing vigilance. Have a plane ready to take you to Tiflis tomorrow. Make sure that everything goes smoothly."

He paused and then added, "And, most important. Tell Beria that everything he said to me on the telephone today he must write down, sign, put in an envelope, affix his seal, and give to you for me. When you return, you will give it to me personally. The paper Beria writes must not be addressed to anyone, not to me, not to anyone else. A simple statement of the facts and his signature. That's all! Do it!"

Two days later Stalin opened the envelope Malenkov had delivered. Beria had done everything as *he* had ordered: he described in detail the circumstances in which he had shot Khandzhyan. The letter was not addressed to anyone. There was no reference to the telephone conversation, and *his* name was not mentioned.

Stalin put Beria's letter in his personal safe.

\* \* \*

And two days after that Stalin and Yezhov met with the leaders of the NKVD — Yagoda, Agranov, Molchanov, and Mironov.

In making his report, Molchanov spread out a map that showed graphically Trotsky's ties with the leaders of the United Center in the U.S.S.R.

Stalin was not pleased. "It's not convincing. Only talk. We need documents, letters, notes."

"There are no such documents," Molchanov replied.

Stalin noted the firmness of the reply. They didn't want to manufacture those documents, they were afraid, afraid of what? If the defendants have agreed to testify, then why can't they confirm the veracity of the documents?

"There are no documents," Stalin repeated. "What is there? Conversations? With whom? With Sedov? Unconvincing. The orders must come personally from Trotsky. Goltsman maintains that he got orders from Sedov. What if Goltsman is lying? Maybe he met with Trotsky and not Sedov? Trotsky was in Denmark, Goltsman in Germany — it's not far, a few hours' travel, they could have met."

Molchanov did not argue, which meant he accepted it. And Yagoda and Agranov were silent — they accepted it too.

Then Mironov reported on the course of the investigation — who had given what statement, who was still resisting.

Stalin's eyebrows shot up in surprise. "Kamenev is not confessing? Really?"

"No, he's not."

"He's really not?" Stalin asked furiously.

"No."

"He's done so much and he won't confess?"

"No."

"He's not worried about his life?"

Mironov shrugged.

"He has two sons. Isn't he worried about them?"

Mironov did not know what to say.

"I'm asking you a question!"

"I think he is worried."

"Ah, you think!" Stalin was angry. "Then don't tell me that

Kamenev or Zinoviev or anyone else isn't confessing." He looked around the room. "Tell them that no matter what they do, they cannot stop the course of history. Either they save their skins or they die like dogs, tell them that! If they want to save their lives, they have to make confessions! Work on them, work until they crawl on their bellies with their confessions in their teeth!"

Everyone was silent. When Stalin was in a rage, a careless word could end up costing dearly.

After a pause, Stalin said calmly, in a low voice, "Tell Zinoviev that if he voluntarily agrees to appear in court, in open court, and confesses everything, his life will be spared. And if not, he will be tried by a military tribunal. And he will be shot. And all his allies, present and past, will be shot. If he does not need his own life, let him think about the lives of the people he had dragged into the swamp."

Yagoda and his assistants left.

Stalin stood up and walked around his office. Yezhov also stood, but Stalin gestured him to sit down.

"How many people will they actually bring to the trial?"

"Sixteen."

"Of them, eight are worth something," Stalin said with a laugh. "The rest are worthless."

"The rest are executions," Yezhov said cautiously.

As if he had not heard, Stalin went on. "They brought in almost four hundred people and they managed to break only sixteen. Fine work."

Yezhov knew that these rebukes were addressed to Yagoda, and he also knew that Stalin expected a reaction from him, but he hadn't sensed yet what the reaction was supposed to be.

"Mironov and Molchanov are good workers, especially Mironov," Stalin continued. "But they are formalists, they dot 'I's' and cross 'T's,' the transcript is everything as far as they're concerned! Why? They want the insurance of the transcript — in case there's a problem, they've got the transcript and they're off the hook. But what problem are they anticipating, I'd like to know? The fall of the Soviet regime? Well, if Soviet power ends, they'll be the first ones hanged, and no transcript is going to save them, no one's going to look at those transcripts. Then what are they afraid of? A change in the Party leadership? Is that what they're insuring themselves against? Apparently, that is the very thing they are preparing for. Especially since they are Yagoda's people. And Yagoda is sabotaging the preparations for the trial. He is sabotaging. He is not afraid of a change in leadership, he is hoping for a change in leadership, is sure of a change in leadership."

Stalin came to the table and pushed in the chairs on which Yagoda and his assistants had been sitting.

"Let him run this trial. We will not interfere. However, at this trial he must prepare the next. At this trial we finish the Zinovievites; and at the next, the Trotskyites. They must name names ... names, names, and more names. They must understand — the more known Trotskyites they name, the more convincing their version about Trotsky, the more help they give to the court, the more chances for their survival. I repeat — names, names, and more names. . . . The bigger the names, the better. We must demand that from Yagoda, from his assistants, from all the investigative groups. I think that you must take over the work of that apparat and gradually take the investigation into your own hands. Yagoda is not a dependable man. But I repeat, this trial, the trial of Zinoviev and Kamenev, Yagoda must complete himself."

Stalin still paced his office slowly.

Yezhov waited patiently. He understood, sensed, that Stalin was about to say something important, perhaps the most important thing. . . .

"All the Trotskyites had been in the military in the past. Many remain in the army. Division Commander Shmidt, for instance, voted for the opposition in 1923. They say he left, but who believes that. He's a close friend of Primakov, who should choose his friends more carefully. Shmidt and Primakov will be defended of course by Comrade Yakir, but Comrade Yakir should wait for the end of the investigation. Commander Putna also voted for the opposition in 1923. He is not a sincere man and incidentally he is a close friend of Tukhachevsky. Their ties should also be checked. I wonder what Putna will tell about his friend and mentor Comrade Tukhachevsky. I think the ties of Comrade Tukhachevsky with German military circles are of particular interest. Did you bring the material with you?"

"Yes." Yezhov opened the file.

"Tell me, what do you have there?"

Yezhov picked up the first page. "Biographical data. . . ."

"I don't need that. I know his biography. What do you have about Germany?"

Yezhov took out another page. "First of all, German prison camp. The first time he ended up there on February 19, 1915, in the Carpathian Mountains, and was placed in Stralsund Camp for military prisoners. He escaped and was captured three weeks afterward, when he was looking for a boat to get to Sweden. He was placed in Badstuer Camp in Meklenburg, he escaped, and was captured at the Danish border. He was put into a soldiers' camp near Münster, he escaped, and was captured thirty meters from the Dutch border. After that he was imprisoned in Fort Zoridorf, where he tried to escape by tunneling, but he was detained and transferred to Section Nine of the Bavarian fortress of Ingolstadt, for repeat offenders. He escaped from there in the fall of 1917, this fifth attempt being successful."

"What is the distance from this Bavarian fortress to the Russian border?" Stalin asked.

"One thousand, one hundred twenty kilometers."

"And how did he cover that distance? A Russian officer?"

"He speaks German and French fluently."

"That's not enough to cover that distance in hostile territory. Who helped him?"

"There is no information on that. He escaped with Officer Chernovetsky. He was captured in three days, but Tukhachevsky got away."

"One was captured, the other got away. Interesting. They found the trail, got one but not the other, they let him go a thousand kilometers unhampered. Interesting, very interesting. Go on!"

Yezhov picked up another sheet of paper. "Now his official visits. The first time Tukhachevsky went to Germany was in 1923 as a communications officer of the High Command of the Red Army. He participated in the preparations of Soviet-German military negotiations and treaties in accordance with the German-Soviet Rapallo Treaty, and then with the inspection team after the treaty was signed, and then twice between 1926 and 1932 on questions of military cooperation. Since these negotiations and treaties concerned German military objectives on our territory in Leipzig, Kazan, and Kharkov, they naturally left behind documents signed by Tukhachevsky. The last trip was when he passed through Berlin returning from the funeral of King George of England, in February of this year."

"Who else of the High Command has been in Germany?"

"Yakir, Uborevich, Eideman, and Timoshenko had studied in the Academy of the General Staff in Germany." He added guiltily, "And some others have studied there or been there."

Guiltily, because he had not prepared a list. Stalin understood and said severely, "Prepare lists of all military men tied to Germany. Naturally, not all of them are German spies. Comrade Timoshenko, for instance, was sent there to study, and he studied. What he learned there is another question. Of course, he has not distinguished himself in military work. He's a simple man, a man of the people, while Yakir, Uborevich, Eideman, and some others — they have to be checked thoroughly."

Stalin paced the room in silence and stopped at the window. Was it time or too soon? Everything had to be in Yezhov's hands. Yagoda could not be trusted with this. Yagoda could warn them. But it was too soon to replace Yagoda with Yezhov. Yagoda would finish the Zinoviev-Kamenev trial. But it was time to start. Yezhov could keep his tongue.

Stalin left the window, sat down in his chair, and looked at Yezhov.

"Tukhachevsky says that he is a fierce enemy of Germany. But actually, I think that he has many friends among Germany's generals. His biography is clear about that. And the military, both ours and Germany's, wants to get rid of the Party leadership. I don't know if it is in the interests of German intelligence to share this information with us. But we must try to get it. I think that the task is fulfillable. But it must be begun only after the trial of Zinoviev and Kamenev is finished."

And after a pause, he repeated what he had already said, "Yagoda is not a reliable man."

## ❧ 25 ❧

They dropped the story of the bomb allegedly made in the chemistry lab of the Gorky Pedagogical Institute. The documents Dyakov fabricated in Gorky were added to the case as evidence of the terrorist acts the defendants had been planning.

However, this was very weak proof of the existence of a gigantic terrorist conspiracy that involved the whole country. Sharok was not the only one to see that. Everyone saw it.

The attempts to break the former members of the opposition did not yield results. Of the four hundred people brought out of prisons, camps, and exile, only two gave the needed testimony. And these two were not enough, either. To prove that Trotsky was running the terrorist center in the U.S.S.R. from abroad, they had to sacrifice four German Communists who had come to Moscow on the eve of Hitler's rise to power. All four were told that they had to do their Party duty and give the needed evidence. Naturally, they were promised their lives in exchange.

With these forces, the investigative groups led the attack on the seven main defendants — Zinoviev, Kamenev, Bakayev, and Evdokimov, all former Zinovievites, and Smirnov, Mrachkovsky, and Ter-Vaganyan, former Trotskyites.

The difficulty with the former Trotskyites was that they had been in prison for a long time — Smirnov, for instance, since 1933 — and therefore had an alibi. How could they run terrorist activities from inside prison?

But Stalin did not wish to accept that.

"Smirnov must be tried with Mrachkovsky," he ordered.

It was not difficult to guess why Stalin wanted Smirnov shot. Ivan Nikitich Smirnov had defeated the White general Kolchak in the Civil War, and enjoyed great popularity and authority in the Party, even though he had been in the opposition for a short time, breaking with it in 1929. But in time he had insisted on obeying Lenin's demand to remove Stalin as General Secretary. If he got Smirnov's confessions, Stalin would give greater credibility to the trial and satisfy his thirst for revenge.

Stalin's orders that Ivan Nikitich Smirnov be tried with Sergei Mrachkovsky was understood to mean that their personal friendship, which went back to the Civil War and continued despite prison, had to be presented as the friendship of conspirators. And Mrachkovsky was under Smirnov's influence; thus, if Smirnov gave in, so would Mrachkovsky. This was the information that Slutsky used in running the case.

Slutsky was a high-ranking official, head of the Foreign Section, and consequently could speak in the name of the leaders of the NKVD. Harsh measures would never break people like Smirnov and Mrachkovsky. They had to be handled by a lying, clever man capable of making people like and trust him. Slutsky was one, an actor by nature, who knew how to pretend to be kind and sincere.

However, when presented with the charges of terrorist activity, Smirnov replied, "That one won't work. I've been in prison since January 1, 1933, and you can't prove a thing against me."

"We won't be proving anything, Ivan Nikitich," Slutsky said gently. "If you don't confess, you will be shot without trial. At the trial, the other defendants will brand you as a terrorist and murderer, and that's how the Soviet people will remember you. But if you obey the Politburo's suggestion and help the Party expose Trotsky completely, your life will be spared, and in time you will be given work worthy of you."

Smirnov regarded him silently and mockingly.

"You don't believe me?" Slutsky asked.

Without a word, Smirnov kept staring at him with mockery.

"Ivan Nikitich," Slutsky said as gently as possible. "You have been fighting the Party since 1927. And now for the last ten years you have been isolated from society and the people; you, the pride of the Party and of the working class, have been either in prison or in exile. And yet you have the chance to free yourself of that nightmare in just one blow. Think, Ivan Nikitich! You are at the final line, believe me, the last one. Do you really want to end your heroic life so ingloriously? And for whose sake? For Lev Davydovich? That's a lost cause. And you formally broke with the opposition, formally.... Break off in fact! Help the Party destroy Trotsky completely. For that you will have to confess to some unpleasant things, shameful things, moreover things with which you had nothing to do, I know that. But there is no other way out. Think, Ivan Nikitich! I beg of you. You can't even imagine the degree of my respect for you, my awe for you. I fear for you, Ivan Nikitich.... I understand that you are insulted, embittered, you value your honor, but for a Communist the highest honor is to defend the interests of the Party. Bow before the Party, Ivan Nikitich; otherwise you face death, inglorious death." He pointed at the floor. "Down there, in the cellar. Who needs that, Ivan Nikitich?"

Smirnov kept on looking at Slutsky, without a word.

Slutsky's failure upset Yagoda, Agranov, and Molchanov — most of all because Slutsky had disobeyed Comrade Stalin. Comrade Stalin had clearly said, "Connect him with Mrachkovsky." Comrade Stalin had pointed out Mrachkovsky as the weak link in the pair. That meant that they should have started with Mrachkovsky and not Smirnov, as Slutsky had.

Slutsky hurried to correct his mistake, even though in his heart he felt that it would be even harder with Mrachkovsky than with Smirnov.

Smirnov was a talented and well-educated man, albeit self-taught. Mrachkovsky was innately courageous, but explosive and crude. When he was arrested, he fought back, he had to be tied up, put in the cooler, and in general was a difficult prisoner.

Slutsky, a coward, decided to deal officially and properly with Mrachkovsky. He explained the case and said that the Politburo had decided to finish up with Trotsky once and for all. Mrachkovsky was being given a choice — either help the Party and thereby restore himself in its ranks or be destroyed as a proponent of Trotskyism. He added that Kirov had been killed on Trotsky's orders (which was not true), Zinoviev and Kamenev had already confessed (which also was not true), that only Ivan Nikitich Smirnov was resisting (which was true and which gave a semblance of truth to the other statements). Thus Mrachkovsky was given a choice — with the Party against Trotsky, which would give him his life and a future, or with Smirnov for Trotsky and against the Party, which would give him no life or future. He, Slutsky, personally represented only the investigation here and was telling Mrachkovsky what he was supposed to tell him as part of his job. But if Mrachkovsky had no objection, he would dare to express his personal opinion, too.

"Go ahead," Mrachkovsky said.

"Sergei Vitalyevich," Slutsky said in a sincere voice. "You are a hero of the Civil War, and the people, the country, and the Party know you that way. You are a great military leader, and if you had not gone into the opposition, you would certainly be one of the leaders of our army now. Of course, if you accept our demands now, you will have to go through several unpleasant days at the trial. But then ... Then, Sergei Vitalyevich, there will be a war. You know what Hitler is preparing. And when the war starts, you, Sergei Vitalyevich, will take up a worthy place in the defense of the country, a place commensurate with your abilities, knowledge, experience, and talent. And those few days at the trial — who will remember them? And if anyone does, it will be as yet one more proof of your courage, your loyalty to the Party, and your endless fidelity to its ideals. It is hard for me to say the words that I must say, but I must say them — you face a choice between a glorious life or an inglorious death."

"What do I have to sign?" Mrachkovsky asked grimly.

Mrachkovsky not only gave the needed testimony, but he agreed to persuade Ivan Nikitich Smirnov. In this he failed. At their meeting, Smirnov called Mrachkovsky a coward and refused to talk to him.

Infuriated, Mrachkovsky gave additional evidence against Smirnov — allegedly back in 1932 at a secret meeting Smirnov suggested joining the Zinovievites and switching to terror tactics.

Thus to the evidence of Olberg and Reinhold against Smirnov was added the testimony of his best friend, Mrachkovsky. This might have been enough to get Smirnov into the trial, but not enough to force him to confess to anything.

After Slutsky's failure, Smirnov was passed on to Gai, chief of the Special Section on intelligence agents and "operative techniques," who was called "Nadyusha," from his code name "Measure N."

Gai was a cynical and cruel man. Once, when Gai was giving him instructions on interrogating a Trotskyite, Sharok said that he wanted to put together a list of questions, a questionnaire.

Gai looked at him scornfully and said, "Want to see my questionnaire?"

"Yes, of course."

Gai pulled out a rubber billy club, twirled it in the air, and said, "It's all I need. And I suggest you get one."

But this was before Stalin's official instruction on using physical methods of influence, and Sharok was afraid to keep that kind of "questionnaire" under his desk.

Gai simply announced to Smirnov that he had been exposed by the testimony not only of Olberg, Reinhold, Dreitser, Goltsman, and Mrachkovsky, but also of Zinoviev and Kamenev, and all he could do now was confirm their evidence and confess his guilt.

In substantiation of his words, Gai handed Smirnov the transcript of the interrogation of Zinoviev and Kamenev. "Read it."

Smirnov refused. "You can do anything you want," he said, "you can even give me a New Testament According to Matthew in which he says that I am a terrorist. You have all the printing presses you need to do whatever you need."

"You don't believe it?" Gai chuckled. "You will."

He picked up the intercom phone and spoke to someone, and then started writing, paying no attention to Ivan Nikitich.

There was a knock at the door.

"Come in!" shouted Gai.

The door opened. A guard led a man into the room, and Smirnov did not recognize Zinoviev at first. He could barely stay on his feet, he was breathing heavily, and his face was bloated and sick.

Supported by the guard, he sank into a chair.

"Citizen Zinoviev," Gai said, "do you confirm the evidence you gave in the investigation regarding the participation of Ivan Nikitich Smirnov in terrorist activity of the 'United Trotsky-Zinoviev Center'?"

"I do," Zinoviev muttered, barely audibly.

"But Citizen Smirnov denies it," Gai said.

Zinoviev raised his weary, empty eyes and said to Smirnov, "Ivan Nikitich . . . you have to think politically. If we meet Koba halfway, Koba will meet us. This will open the door into the Party for us."

"He'll open the door to the Party for us when hell freezes over," Smirnov replied. "Don't you know Koba? You trust him? He's a liar and a cheat. He started this whole case to destroy us."

"I'm not sure," Zinoviev whispered. "But if you don't meet him halfway, he will destroy you for sure."

"I'd rather die an honest man and not as a liar, coward, and prostituting cur."

Zinoviev was taken away.

Afterward, Gai wrote up a transcript of their meeting, in which Zinoviev reaffirmed his statement about Smirnov's participation in terror, to which Smirnov replied each time, "Deny, deny, deny."

Gai made a neat stack of papers on his desk, then took a few out, and said, as if in passing, "Do you know Safonova?"

Ivan Nikitich looked up for the first time.

"Safonova," Gai repeated. "Do you know that name?"

"Yes. That is my former wife."

"Then read this."

In front of Smirnov Gai placed Safonova's statement, in which she maintained that in late 1932, when Smirnov was not yet in prison, he had received a directive from Trotsky to organize terror against the leaders of the Party and government.

"You could have made this up too," Smirnov said, tossing the paper back onto the desk.

Gai pushed a button and ordered the guard to bring in witness Safonova.

Smirnov watched the door tensely. Safonova came in; Smirnov had not seen her in many years, but the woman had been his wife once. They had parted as, and had remained, good friends.

Gai indicated a chair. She sat down and burst into tears. Smirnov had never seen his ex-wife cry. She had been a strong woman. But now she wept uncontrollably, and Gai did not stop her, let her cry, the longer she cried the better. At last she got hold of herself and wiped away her tears.

Smirnov nodded at the statement. "Yours?"

She sobbed again, wiped her eyes, and said in a choking voice, "Ivan! There's no other way for us. Not for you, not for your wife, not for your daughter. Only you can save our lives — obey the Politburo. It's obvious that the trial is directed against Trotsky. Even Zinoviev and Kamenev understood that. If you appear at the trial, the whole world will see you, and you won't be shot. But if you don't, they'll shoot you and us, and no one will ever know."

Smirnov listened in silence. This was the woman he had once loved, a principled, intransigent, fearless woman, and look how they had bent her.

"Take that fool away!" Smirnov said.

"You don't want to talk to her." Gai chuckled. "Well, it's up to you."

He called in the guard again and said, "Take her away."

"Ivan!" she started to plead.

"Get out!" Ivan Nikitich stopped her.

When Safonova had been led out, Gai said, "You're very rude to people, Smirnov!"

Ivan Nikitich said nothing.

"Don't forget, you have other relatives. Are you going to talk to them like that, too?"

Ivan Nikitich said nothing. He didn't understand what Gai was talking about. Safonova was a former Party member, a political activist, but his present family? His wife, Roza, did not belong to the Party and his daughter, Olga, was a student. What did they have to do with his case?

Ivan Nikitich found out ten minutes later. He was being led down the prison corridor when suddenly he saw Olga at the end of the corridor. She was disheveled, her hair unkempt, her dress torn, and two burly guards were holding her by the arms. Olga apparently did not recognize her father, but Ivan Nikitich tried to rush toward her, only his guard held him tight. Olga was pulled into a cell and the door slammed.

Ivan Nikitich tried to get free, but the guards pushed him into his cell and threw him on the floor.

The lock clicked.

Ivan Nikitich banged on the door.

The peephole opened and the corridor guard's face appeared. "What do you want?"

"Take me back to my investigator!"

"Talk to the warden."

"Bring the warden!"

The window shut.

Ivan Nikitich sat on his cot. So this was that bastard's threat. He was a criminal, just like Stalin. No wonder Stalin befriended the criminals when he was in prison. But they hadn't done anything to his daughter yet, they were just threatening, showing him where his stubbornness could lead, saying: Look what is awaiting your daughter. He had to get hold of himself. Now they were threatening his daughter, then they'd threaten his wife. But the threat could become action. And they would shoot him without a trial or investigation. His life was over, that was clear; whether he signed or not, it was over. Stalin would have him shot, that was obvious. Therefore, he had to save his wife and daughter. He had to give in on something. They would settle for something small. They would. They needed him in the trial. Without him, there was no Trotskyite element to their so-called United Center. Zinoviev and Kamenev were in their pocket — he should have expected that. But he had always known what Stalin was. He had destroyed the opposition politically, had put all the former oppositionists into prison. And now he wanted to destroy them all physically. Smirnov knew he would be destroyed. But he had to save his family. For that, he would have to go to the trial. And he would. But in order to see Smirnov in the defendant's dock, Stalin would have to put up with a change in his scenario.

Smirnov told Gai that he was willing to admit that he had allegedly received instructions on terror from Trotsky in 1932. But that he took no part in the terrorism, because he was in prison, and he did not know if the other defendants participated. In exchange, he demanded that his daughter be returned home immediately and that he be able to verify her safety.

Gai accepted those conditions. An hour later Smirnov was called into Gai's office and Gai told him to call home. His wife answered, and his daughter came to the phone. When they asked how he was, Smirnov replied, "Everything's fine."

Smirnov called home every day from Gai's office, in Gai's presence, to be reassured that his wife and daughter were there.

# ❦ 26 ❦

Three women worked at the receiving desk — one to receive laundry, one to hand it out, and the third to write receipts and take money.

Sofya Alexandrovna was immediately assigned to handing out the laundry. The laundry bundles were heavy, and the conversations with the customers nerve-racking — either something was missing, or the laundry had been torn or stained, or somebody's underpants were there instead of an undershirt. The factory was at fault in many cases, but Lusya, the receptionist, was to blame, too. She looked through the laundry carelessly, and often failed to fill out the receipts properly.

Tamara Fyodorovna, an elderly, severe, and taciturn woman, in charge of writing receipts and accepting money, was the senior worker, and she sometimes reprimanded Lusya.

In response, Lusya, a young woman, would snort, "You think I'm going to sniff around in their shitty underwear?"

But it was Sofya Alexandrovna who paid for everything. She didn't know how to snarl back and she couldn't argue with the obvious, so she immediately signed the complaint forms on missing items or defects. Yakov Grigoryevich, in charge, was very unhappy with this state of affairs. He was a gloomy man, who listened to Tamara Fyodorovna's explanations, dipping his pen in the inkwell nervously, staring at the lists, and then making a squiggle that represented his signature.

Before signing the documents on missing items or defects, he regarded each document with suspicion, and then said to Sofya Alexandrovna, "We never had complaints before you."

"But I'm not the one damaging the laundry," Sofya Alexandrovna would say.

"You're encouraging pickiness," he said holding up a tablecloth. "How can you call this a spot? You can hardly see it, but you don't explain that to the customer. You blame it on me. I have to deal with the factory, I have to do your work."

And so on, every day. And it got worse each day, his attitude ever more rude.

After Yakov Grigoryevich left, Sofya Alexandrovna would take nitroglycerine, sit on a stool, and pant. Tamara Fyodorovna would get up silently and hand out the laundry herself.

"Thank you, Tamara Fyodorovna, I'm better."

Sofya Alexandrovna would get up and go to the counter. She would try to persuade the customers, but they shouted louder, argued, wrote in the complaint book about the quality of the work and the rudeness of the staff.

"They're complaining about you," Yakov Grigoryevich would say gloomily. "I'll have to dock your pay."

"You know that this work is too hard for me," Sofya Alexandrovna said. "I have a weak heart; why don't you let me go?"

"If you're sick, you should get on disability first."

"You can leave of your own volition," Tamara Fyodorovna interrupted.

"And who will we find to replace her?"

"That's your problem, that's why you're the supervisor. You can see she's elderly and sick — why are you mocking her?"

"Watch who you're defending, Tamara Fyodorovna. No one else will hire her, her son is in the camps."

"He's not in the camps," Sofya Alexandrovna began, but Tamara Fyodorovna interrupted.

"Whether they hire her or not is her problem. But you don't have the right to mock a laboring person. We're living in the Soviet Union!"

"Who's mocking her, who?" Yakov Grigoryevich muttered.

"You are! We're witnesses."

"Right," Lusya said unexpectedly. "We are."

Yakov Grigoryevich sat in silence and then said grimly to Sofya Alexandrovna, "You can leave of your own volition."

*       *       *

That was the end of Sofya Alexandrovna's work at the laundry. And the question of a new job came up.

She discussed it with her sisters, Vera and Polina, with her neighbor Margarita Artemovna, and, of course, with Varya.

Varya was glad that Sofya Alexandrovna had left the laundry. "You need a quiet job where you can sit down."

"And where do I find it?"

"We'll look for it."

First of all, Varya thought of Vika Marasevich. She had loads of influential friends who could help. And her father, Professor Marasevich, who consulted at the clinic on Gagarin Alley, maybe he could get Sofya Alexandrovna a job in the office there. That would be perfect, because the clinic was nearby.

Varya called Vika. Vadim picked up the phone, Varya recognized his voice. "Hello, Vadim. . . ."

"Hello, who's this?"

"It's Varya Ivanova, remember me? Nina's sister."

"Oh. Yes."

"I need to speak to Vika."

"She doesn't live in Moscow anymore."

"Oh."

"Yes. Good-bye. Say hello to Nina."

And he hung up.

What a pig. Strange. Had something happened to Vika? Had she been arrested?

Everything seemed to be all right with her husband, the Architect, his name appeared in the newspapers now and then. . . . What was the story with Vika?

Later Varya learned that Vika had got married and moved abroad.

Varya even turned to Zoe, whose mother worked in the ticket office of the Carnival Movie Theater. Did they need another ticket lady?

Zoe jumped at the opportunity to help. She hoped that this would reignite their friendship.

Zoe gave Varya news every day, hopeful news.

There was nothing at the Carnival yet, but there might be a spot at the Art, right in their building. That would be even better.

Then it turned out that there was nothing at the Art but there was a place at the Khudozhestvenny on Arbat Square. Zoe's mother knew all the movie theater administrators.

Then it was a possibility at the Prague Theater, also in Arbat Square ... then the Union by Nikitskie Vorota....

After two weeks, Varya stopped believing Zoe's bulletins. She was just afraid to admit that she was failing.

She'd have to turn to Igor Vladimirovich. And Varya really didn't want to do that. After the incident with the flowers, their relationship had changed somewhat. Igor Vladimirovich still treated her kindly, smiled amiably, and took her along to the technical meetings. He even walked her home sometimes, since they went the same way, but he was reserved, understanding that her letter rejecting him was not caused by her nervousness over what her neighbors might think. It was just that Varya wanted to keep him at a distance. But the appearance of their relationship remained the same and Varya was afraid that Igor Vladimirovich might misunderstand her request.

But she had no choice.

"I have a friend," Varya said, "who lives in our building. I know her very well and love her. She is a lonely, elderly woman, honest, decent, and kind. She divorced her husband a long time ago, and her son was arrested two years ago. She is alone. She has nothing to live on. She had a job in a laundry, but the work was physically tiring and nerve-racking. She had to leave. She is an educated woman, and she could do any sort of clerical work. Couldn't you find a place for her here or in some other planning organization? Could you help her? Of course, somewhere not far from the Arbat, you know how bad the trolleys are."

"Here?" Igor Vladimirovich asked. "But, Varya, we've finished the hotel and our office is going to be planning other sites. We may have a reorganization, there's talk of that. When it's all decided, then we can try to do something. As for someplace else, I ..." He thought. "I'll ask around. What can she do, your protégée? By the way, what's her name?"

"Sofya Alexandrovna Pankratova."

He wrote it down. "Fine! And what can she do?"

"Any office work. Filing, she could be a secretary — she's very neat and organized. Accounting. No, better not. She could register things."

"Does she have a profession?"

"I really don't know. She's been working in the laundry lately, but that was just a job. Close to the house."

"I'll try to find out," Igor Vladimirovich said, "but I think it would be more realistic to wait for our office to be reorganized. I can see that you care about this woman," Igor Vladimirovich added with a smile.

"Yes," Varya said. "She's dear to me. . . . She's in dire straits. She needs help."

Vera, Sofya Alexandrovna's sister, arrived. She was energetic and active. She praised her sister for leaving the laundry. "You did the right thing. It wasn't for you. We'll find you something easier and less hectic. Just bear up for now. And stop being stubborn. At least for Sasha's sake."

Sofya Alexandrovna had refused to accept the money sent by Mark Alexandrovich. He didn't even send it directly to her, because she had returned it the first time he sent it. After that, Mark Alexandrovich gave the money to Vera for Sofya Alexandrovna, and asked Vera to persuade her to accept it. He sent money every month.

Sofya Alexandrovna wouldn't take it, and Vera put it in the bank.

"You have to weigh everything," Vera said reasonably. "Why are you refusing Mark's money? He said the wrong thing about Sasha. But you have to understand his position. He couldn't do anything for Sasha, even though he tried. He told me — he swore that he spoke with the highest authorities, and I have no reason to doubt him."

"I don't need his money."

"Let's say you don't. But what about Sasha? His term is almost up. He won't get residency in Moscow, he'll have to go somewhere, find a job, things won't be easy for him, so be realistic. It won't be Siberia where he can live on twenty rubles a month. It'll be much more expensive. He'll be moving around. He'll need money to survive."

"All right," Sofya Alexandrovna agreed. "Then leave the money in your account. If Sasha needs it, we'll send it to him. After all, they're the ones who put him away, they exiled him, now they're going to chase him all over the country, so let them help him with their money."

"Sofya! Don't be like that! How can you say that Mark put him away?"

"Mark did. Mark, or someone like Mark. They're all the same. My brother? Yes, he's my brother! But I'm not going to forgive him for anything. And not because of Sasha. Look what they're doing to Russia. What they've turned the people into! What Mark himself has turned into! There's nothing human left in him. He's a machine for producing cast iron and steel."

"You're not being fair, Sofya. You're his sister and he loves you. And Sasha, too."

Sofya Alexandrovna interrupted her. "Used to be. Now he loves only one person — Stalin. They're all blinded and stunned by him, he's a god for them — greater than a god, because people who believe in God have a concept of good and evil, charity, redemption, compassion, but they don't. They have only Stalin. He is their god and their conscience."

She took a breath.

"All right, enough about that. Now I have to find a job."

"That's not a problem," Vera said. "I'm looking, and Polina is looking, and her husband, and my husband. We're asking everyone we know; we'll find something."

But the best and most practical advice came from Margarita Artemovna, Sofya Alexandrovna's neighbor, an old and wise Armenian woman.

"You don't need to go work anywhere, Sofya Alexandrovna," she said. "Just take in the children from our building. The Gurovs have a girl of five, Sonya, and she's a very nice girl. The Gurovs are working, both engineers, and they have no one to leave her with. They brought a housekeeper from the country, but they couldn't get permission to register her here, so they had to fire her. The Gurovs are looking for someone to take care of Sonya. Then there are the Fortunatovs, they work, their little Borya is four. Now. Zoya

Vasilyevna Velichkina is in a terrible fix. Do you know her? From the third entrance? Her husband died last year."

"I know her."

"Well, she's a doctor, she works over in Sokolniki, and she drops off her child at the group at the Hammer and Sickle Factory, where her late husband used to work. Completely across town. She has to get up at five. She would be happy to put her girl in your group. Now, there's Lubov Mikhailovna Sapozhnikova, an artist. Her husband goes to work, and she paints at home. She makes copies of portraits of our leaders. The child needs someone to take her outside — that's four children already. I don't know, but I'm sure they could all pay twenty-five rubles, that makes one hundred. You can keep the children playing in the back courtyard, there are lots of trees, it's quiet and nice there. If the weather's bad, you can go to people's apartments, in turn. By the way, the Gurovs have a separate two-room apartment."

"I don't know. The children will have to be fed, won't they?"

"That can be arranged," Margarita Artemovna said confidently. "The parents will handle it. You'll see, others will want to join, too."

"No, no more than four, I won't be able to handle it."

"Fine, four is enough."

Sofya Alexandrovna had the group for a short time, April and May, after which the children went off, some to dachas, others to the country to their grandparents.

One day the building superintendent, Viktor Ivanovich, ran into Sofya Alexandrovna in the courtyard and asked, "Why aren't you with the kids?"

"They're away for the summer."

He thought a bit and said, "Go down to house number five on Levshinsky Alley, to the building inventory office, ask for Afanasy Petrovich, tell him I sent you, take your passport. They need people temporarily; you can work until the fall."

Sofya Alexandrovna went to the inventory office, and they gave her a job. She helped another woman put documents, blueprints, plans, and budgets into order. Nothing had been done with the papers in a long time, and there was a lot of work and it was interesting. Sofya Alexandrovna knew almost all the buildings, they were on the Arbat and side streets.

The documents were collected neatly into binders and put on a shelf in the order of the building numbers. The desk held a list of the documents that had to be in each inventory book, and if any were missing, they had to be found. Sometimes they would be in the book of another building. And all the legal papers had to be checked — were they dated and signed?

Sofya Alexandrovna did her work neatly and her boss was pleased with her. They worked in a cellar, which was dry. Sunlight even came through the barred, sidewalk-level windows.

They had a hot plate, a tea kettle, and they heated up lunch and made tea, and Sofya Alexandrovna was happy and cozy there. She made seventy rubles a month.

But she thought of her play group children often, especially little Sonya Gurov.

"She's so smart, and so quick," she told Varya. "She's heard a lot of fairy tales and she's picked up the language, old-fashioned and quaint. It's so cute! And little Borya Fortunatov, he's wonderful, too — and he keeps pretending he's too sick to do things. I asked him once to pick up his toys and he said he couldn't because he had 'tears in his nose.'"

Varya loved seeing Sofya Alexandrovna so happy, with an opportunity to forget her tormenting thoughts and worries about Sasha, at least for a little while.

"Of course," Sofya Alexandrovna went on, "children are very observant and sensitive. One of them looked at a picture of the forest and asked, 'Are there any wolves?' 'There are.' 'Are you afraid?' 'I am.' 'Aunt Anya isn't, she has metal teeth.' They're so funny."

"They'll be back in the fall and you can start the group again," Varya said.

"I hope so. I enjoy them. Of course, they're a lot of trouble. One has to go to the bathroom, the other has a cold, another needs his shoelaces tied. And they're stubborn, too. I said to Borya, 'Don't walk around without your hat.' And he said, 'I'm not walking, I'm running.' And he wouldn't put it on. Winter will be harder with them, I think. . . . But we'll see. I really like working in the inventory office. I'm learning a new vocabulary, too — 'blueprint,' 'tracing,' 'projection.'"

Varya knew all those words, naturally. "We have the same profession now," she said to Sofya Alexandrovna.

A letter was waiting for Varya at home.

The handwriting was familiar; Varya opened the letter and looked at the signature. Of course, it was from Igor Vladimirovich. "Dear Varya," Igor Vladimirovich wrote.

Your short letter about the flowers gave me a chance to do what I've been wanting to do for a long time — write to you. Now I don't have to feel guilty about forcing a correspondence on you, I'm responding to your letter. I'm writing to you and that brings you closer to me and that makes me happy.

I reread your letter several times. It is the first one in the history of our acquaintanceship, and I'm trying to understand every word, I'm interpreting it this way and that, looking for hidden meanings. Sometimes I find something warm and dear in a phrase, but I recall your usual reserve, and then I think that you're being sarcastic. I don't know what to think without hearing your intonation.

Forgive me, if my modest gift caused problems — I won't do it anymore. I give my solemn oath. I can't forget your permission to telephone, tossed to me from the step of the trolley.

For a stranger, that is permission to continue an acquaintance. For me, who knows you, it was a simple good-bye, and a good-bye, unfortunately, that does not hint of any future.

Do you remember Alexander Park, when it was closed? Puddles. Your shoes. The Kremlin Wall. The Grotto of Venus. A tiny hole in your stocking. The guard's whistle. Our flight. The gates, blocked by a bench. Hurray! We're safe. Now we can tease the guard. That whole walk was made up of endless raindrops.

Tell me something —

You're unique, you're difficult.

I have the feeling that you have problems and I want to

console you so much. When you were married, I knew nothing about your life, but I understood everything. I wanted to help, but I didn't know how.

Yesterday evening I was on the Arbat, and walked past your building, I even took the 31 trolley at your stop, I looked all around, but alas ... you didn't appear.

Could you give me the opportunity to walk you home without Zoe?

It was so hard to create that connection with you, that depends on the same mood, when people are alone together. Just one word from you would be enough to create that tie, and things would be so good.... And then we'd have to start from scratch again the next time.

Once, when you were sick, I decided to visit you, to go without calling ahead (as department head I have a duty toward my subordinates, don't I?). I went up the stairs, stood in front of your door, raised my hand to ring the bell, and frightened, perhaps of your cool reception, I ran back down the stairs and went home. I never told you about this.

I love music, I go to the Conservatory. How I want to listen to music with you next to me.

Forgive me for writing such a boring letter. I need to sit next to you on the parapet of the embankment and look at passersby. Your characterizations of people were so accurate and witty. I need you to drop a flower on the square, it is only details that create a wealth of sensation.

We are together all day at work, but work also separates us. Write me just two words, a telegramlike letter, and then we will be alone again. And I will reply. I want you to like my letters.

When you walked into the National that first time, you were wearing a large-brimmed hat. You took it off and I saw your huge eyes, pure and innocent.

I.V.

P.S. This letter was written almost a year ago, however I didn't dare send it. Now I am sending it without changing a word because nothing has changed in my love for you or in my admiration for you.

I.V.

Varya put the letter on her lap and sat, lost in thought, for a long time.

It was a good letter, a sincere one. He was a fine man, Igor Vladimirovich, and her life with him would probably be easy, carefree, festive, and merry. He belonged to the elite, he was among the "spoiled ones," and all the wealth of the elite was accessible to him, thanks to his talent and hard work and not because he was obedient. It was no small thing, not at all, and that's why she treated Igor Vladimirovich with respect. But the life that had seemed a fairy tale just a year ago, the one she dreamed of in her dreary communal flat, no longer attracted her. Now she knew the reverse side of the coin. She could not and would not live thoughtlessly, when people all around were suffering, when hungry children and old people were dying. She didn't have the strength to fight hunger and injustice, she didn't know how to fight, but she refused to enjoy a feast during this plague.

She was waiting for Sasha. . . . Sasha knew how he had to live, he knew how she must live. Especially now, after all the trials he had gone through. Of course, it would not be easy for him when he returned. Everyone said he would not be allowed to live in Moscow. But wherever he lived, she would help him. Every man needs support. Varya would be Sasha's support.

But Nina's words during their fight over Sasha's photograph worried her; she couldn't forget them. Nina had shouted at her, "If Sasha is your fiancé, why didn't you wait for him, why did you marry that hustler?" Would Sasha see her marriage as a betrayal, too? But it wasn't! She was a girl, she didn't understand, she wanted independence, and she thought that marriage would give it to her. She was mistaken. She had not written to Sasha about Kostya because she didn't want to upset him — it would have hurt him. But when he returned, she would tell him everything, and he would forgive her.

Varya thought about her reply to Igor Vladimirovich. What could she say and how should she say it — in a letter or in person? . . . She decided to talk to him.

Varya went into his office. "Igor Vladimirovich, I've come about your letter."

He grew pale. "Yes?"

"I want to tell you this. I love a man, he is far away and will return in a year. I am waiting for him."

Igor Vladimirovich was silent until he got himself under control and then, with a gentle smile, he said, "Well then, Varya, I'll wait, too. . . ."

# ⚘ 27 ⚘

The work on the main defendants, Zinoviev and Kamenev, had been entrusted to Mironov, head of the Economic Section, the most educated of all the NKVD leaders.

Stalin was pleased with his work. It was at Stalin's suggestion that Mironov became head of the Economic Section, and Stalin often had Mironov join them when he was meeting Yagoda.

This suited Yagoda. Mironov had an extraordinary memory and he made notes of everything Stalin said when they came back. It was not always convenient to write down Stalin's instructions as he gave them, and in connection with the coming Zinoviev-Kamenev trial, it was absolutely forbidden. Stalin's preparation for the trial was secret from everyone, even the members of the Politburo — they learned about the trial only when the preparation was completely finished.

Rumor had it that Mironov was planning to leave his job. Some said that Yagoda was trying to get rid of him, seeing a rival in him, others that he wanted to work in the People's Commissariat of Foreign Trade, since he was an economist. . . . But from the hints dropped by Vutkovsky, who was a friend of Mironov's, Sharok learned that Mironov did not want to participate in the preparation of a trial of Old Bolsheviks. And as Sharok could clearly see, Vutkovsky wasn't very enthusiastic about it either.

As opposed to the perfidious Slutsky and the harsh and crude Gai, Mironov was considered a gentle man in the apparat.

He was convinced that this unpleasant work was dictated by the interests of the Party. He handled the trials of the so-called saboteurs, but he avoided inter-Party affairs, and was not involved in the arrests and exile of former Party members. He did not even know about the Yagoda-Zaporozhets-Nikolaev operation. He did not have the experience of working with Trotskyites, Zinovievites, Bukharinites. And here was Kamenev, former Politburo member, closest friend and comrade in arms of Lenin, Kamenev whom he had once listened to with awe at rallies and had applauded enthusiastically as one of the Party leaders. And it was this Kamenev who was being brought into his office and he, Mironov, had to interrogate him, had to get Kamenev to confess that he was a terrorist and a killer.

He now was an old man, exhausted by prison. But Mironov still saw the young Kamenev in him, the one he had seen and listened to at rallies. He wasn't the Kamenev of those years, not after the horrible years of trials, exiles, and prisons. Short, handsome, with golden but graying hair and a reddish gold beard and mustache and light blue, protruding, and nearsighted eyes, and with the reserved manners of a well-brought-up man, with a professorial bearing and smooth gestures, he seemed, even here, to embody a certain respectability and inspire unwilling sympathy.

Showing Kamenev a chair, Mironov said, "Citizen Kamenev! In your file there are a number of statements by oppositionists claiming that beginning in 1932 they were preparing to murder Comrade Stalin and other members of the Politburo, in particular, the murdered Comrade Kirov, all under your orders."

"You know very well that it's not so," Kamenev replied. "Bolsheviks never resorted to individual terror."

Mironov read him Reinhold's statement.

"There isn't a single word of truth in that."

"Reinhold can confirm all that in a personal meeting."

"Let him."

At the meeting, Reinhold confirmed that he had been at Kamenev's apartment many times when they discussed terrorist acts.

"When were you at my house exactly?"

"You know when! Don't ask provocative questions."

Kamenev looked at Mironov, asking him to act in accordance with the law.

"Citizen Reinhold," Mironov said. "Citizen Kamenev's question is legal."

Reinhold shrugged. "I think I've put it clearly. I was there several times in 1932, 1933, and 1934."

"In that case," Kamenev said, "be so kind as to describe, in as much detail as possible, the layout of the rooms in the apartment."

Reinhold knew he was caught and replied roughly, "I'm not required to answer questions like that. Your apartment isn't a memorial museum yet, and I doubt it will ever be one. I wasn't on an excursion there and I didn't look all around it."

Kamenev appealed to Mironov. "Comrade Mironov, perhaps you will ask Citizen Reinhold about this."

But Mironov also realized that Reinhold was trapped. "Citizen Kamenev, we are not talking about your apartment here, we are talking about your conversations with Citizen Reinhold."

"And yet I ask you to put in the transcript that Citizen Reinhold declined to answer my question," Kamenev insisted.

"But I'm not making up a transcript; this is a preliminary conversation. We will continue it."

The personal meeting ended this way. Kamenev and Reinhold were taken to their cells.

And Mironov called Sharok and asked him to come in.

"Comrade Sharok, you prepared Reinhold. Badly."

Sharok looked at Mironov with unfeigned surprise. His heart contracted — if Reinhold's evidence was disproved, the whole charge would collapse, and the responsibility would of course be Sharok's.

"His evidence repeats often that he had been at Kamenev's apartment. And at the personal meeting, it turned out that he didn't even know its layout. You should have foreseen this and taken Reinhold to Kamenev's apartment at least once."

Sharok relaxed. Of course, Mironov was the big boss. But a big boss and a good investigator were two different things. Breaking a witness is one thing, preparing him for a personal meeting is another. Reinhold gave evidence against many people — it would have been impossible to take him around to all their apartments, and no one would have let Sharok do it. Mironov should have warned Sharok to prepare Reinhold for the personal meeting with

Kamenev. And then Sharok would have checked everything and would have gotten everything ready.

Sharok told all this to Mironov in a polite and restrained manner. Mironov was smart and understood his mistake.

And Sharok was smart, too. At the meeting of investigation groups when Mironov reported to Molchanov that they had failed with Kamenev, that he wasn't giving evidence, and that a personal meeting didn't give results either, Sharok didn't mention the fact that the personal meeting had not been properly prepared. From the look Mironov gave him, Sharok saw that Mironov had appreciated his loyalty. Besides which, Mironov, as Sharok later learned from Vutkovsky, had reported to Yagoda that questioning Kamenev was useless. He should let Yezhov talk to Kamenev as he had to Reinhold, and demand in the name of the Central Committee that he help the Party, and if he refused, to threaten him with execution.

But this time Yagoda declined to use Yezhov's help, and ordered them to bring in the sadist Chertok, a man close to Yagoda, who had often been to his house. Yagoda liked ice-skating and the NKVD people loved watching Chertok, practically lying down on the ice, tying Yagoda's laces. Chertok sucked up to his bosses and was ruthless with his suspects.

Sharok's office was on the same corridor as Chertok's, and as he walked by Sharok heard him interrogating Kamenev.

"You're a coward and a strikebreaker!" Chertok shouted. "That's what Lenin used to say. When Comrade Stalin was fighting in the underground, you were sipping coffee in Paris cafés. You were a burden on the Party, the people, and the working class all your life. Parasite! You killed Kirov, and you'd be happy killing the whole party. If I let you out right now, the first people who saw you would squash you like a bedbug. If I were to bring you and Zinoviev to a factory, the workers would tear you to pieces. You're shit! You're a dead man, dead. I give the order and you'll be shot five minutes later, like a dog, and the firing squad will thank me for it. We're trying to be nice to you, you insignificant louse; we're promising you your stinking life, and you dare hesitate, you shit! Stand at attention, bastard, don't you dare move!"

He kept him on the "conveyor," forcing him to stand without moving until Kamenev fell over, but it didn't work — Kamenev would not give evidence.

The failure with Kamenev and the dubious success with Smirnov allowed Yezhov to take over the investigation. Yagoda's resistance was useless — Stalin was rushing the investigation, and any further delays could have hurt Yagoda badly. And now, the responsibility was Yezhov's.

Taking into account the problems with Kamenev and Smirnov, Yezhov tried a new tactic — he demanded in the name of the Politburo that Zinoviev give the necessary evidence to discredit Trotsky.

Zinoviev, barely able to stand, was brought to Arganov's office at night. Mironov and Molchanov were there and Yezhov ordered Mironov to keep detailed minutes.

Yagoda used some excuse to be absent. Not wanting to play a secondary role, he watched Yezhov jealously, hoping he would make a mistake.

Looking into his large notebook, in which he had written Comrade Stalin's instructions, Yezhov said that they had confirmed information that Japan and Germany were planning to attack the U.S.S.R. in the spring of 1937. The U.S.S.R. therefore especially needed the support of the international proletariat and Trotsky was blocking that support. The Politburo wanted Zinoviev to help the Party expose Trotsky and his bandit organization. If Zinoviev did that, he would prove that he had disarmed himself before the Party completely.

"What specifically do you want?" Zinoviev asked, breathing hard.

"At an open trial you must confirm that — on Trotsky's orders — you and your coconspirators planned the murder of Stalin and other Politburo members. And that you actually executed one such murder — of Comrade Kirov."

"I will never do that, you will never get such lies from me."

"Well then," Yezhov said, peering into his notes, "I will tell you what Comrade Stalin said. 'If Zinoviev confesses, his life will be

spared. If he refuses, he and all the members of the opposition — to
the last one — will be tried by a closed court-martial.' "

"You need my head," Zinoviev said softly. "Fine, give it to Stalin
on a platter."

"But you are betting the lives of thousands of oppositionists, they
are in your hands."

"Whatever I testify, whatever I sign, you will kill me, you will
kill thousands more." Zinoviev gathered his strength and spoke
with firmness. "I repeat, you won't get anything from me."

Yezhov had Zinoviev taken away and Kamenev brought in.
Yezhov hoped that Kamenev, worked over by Chertok, would be
more amenable. But, uncertain of this and not wishing to suffer
another defeat in front of unnecessary witnesses, he dismissed
Arganov and Molchanov, leaving only Mironov, who was in charge
of the Kamenev case.

Yezhov threatened Kamenev as he had Zinoviev. But he added
that they had testimony from Reinhold that Kamenev and his son
had waited in ambush for Stalin's and Voroshilov's cars on
Dorogomilovskaya Street.

"I'd like to know how my son could have been there when he's
been in exile in Alma-Ata?"

"You mean your son Alexander," Yezhov countered. "But
Reinhold is talking about your other son, Yuri. Read it."

He handed him Reinhold's testimony.

Kamenev read it and muttered, "But ... but ... Yuri's just a
Pioneer."

"Do you remember the Resolution of the Central Executive
Committee on April 7, 1935? Perhaps you have forgotten it? Let me
remind you. 'Minors, from the age of twelve, committing theft,
violence, bodily harm, murder, or attempted murder, will be tried
and subjected to all measures of punishment.' It was signed by
Comrades Kalinin, Molotov, and Akulov. So, your son is over
twelve. And for attempting to assassinate Comrades Stalin and
Voroshilov, he will get the appropriate — that is, the highest —
measure of punishment."

"You bastard!"

Yezhov picked up the phone and ordered Molchanov to arrest
Kamenev's son Yuri Kamenev immediately and to prepare him for

the "Trotskyite-Zinovievite Terrorist Center" trial. He then left his office without a glance at Kamenev.

Kamenev was returned to his cell.

He knew what awaited him, and he knew that nothing would help.

At his earlier trial he had persuaded himself that the Party's interests demanded he accept moral responsibility for Kirov's murder. And he got five years of prison for it. In July 1935 he was dragged into a closed court in connection with a mythical Kremlin conspiracy, involving Nina, the wife of his brother, Nikolai, who worked at the state library. Nina and Nikolai were found guilty. And Kamenev himself got another ten years.

His first wife, Olga Davydovna, had been exiled to Tashkent in March 1935. At the same time his older son, Alexander, a graduate of the Zhukovsky Air Force Academy, was arrested and exiled to Alma-Ata.

His second wife, Tatyana Ivanovna Glebova, was exiled to Biisk with her five-year-old son, Vladimir. It had been at her apartment in the Arbat that Kamenev had first been arrested on December 16, 1934.

Only his son Yuri and his five-year-old grandson, Vitaly, remained free. And now they were getting Yuri, a boy whom they wanted to shoot as a terrorist. In seven years, Vitaly would be twelve, and they would get him.

Kamenev unbuttoned his collar. The sun never reached his cell, and it was usually cool there even in July, but today must have been a very hot day.

Kamenev understood that if he did not appear at the trial, he would be shot. If he appeared at the trial, he would also be shot. In both cases the people would be told that he had been a terrorist, spy, and counterrevolutionary. But if he supported false charges with a false confession, they might spare his children. Did he have the right to do that? What was more valuable — his honor or the lives of innocent children? His honor was already gone. It had been battered by the years of constant confessions, admissions of fault, and praise of Stalin. What would another public false confession add to this shameful list? Nothing. And yet . . . and yet . . .

The heat was unbearable. He touched the radiator and pulled his hand away — he had burned it. Those bastards! They had turned on the heat.

He knocked at the door. Again. The peephole opened.

"What do you want?"

"Why is the heat on?"

"We don't know anything about that!"

The window slammed shut.

There was no point in protesting. The more he protested, the more they would turn up the heat.

No, they wouldn't break him. He wouldn't give Koba that final satisfaction. Ten years ago, in 1927, he had yielded to Koba, he had yielded to the Party, he had bowed to the Party to which he had devoted thirty-five of his fifty-three years. Now he, a friend and comrade in arms of Lenin, a member of Lenin's Politburo, the first chairman of the All-Union Central Executive Committee, had to admit to being a spy, terrorist, murderer, and anti-Soviet. The Party didn't need that sacrifice. His confession did not aid the Party, it could only harm it. Stalin was the one who needed it — to discredit the Party, to discredit Lenin, to sully Lenin's circle.

And if he wanted to die like a Communist, if he wanted to end his life in a worthy and dignified way — if only for himself — he must not appear at the trial, he must not make false confessions. Stalin would take revenge, his children would perish. Let them. He was prepared to make that sacrifice for the Party, too. Even if he did confess, even if he complied with all of Stalin's demands, Stalin would kill him anyway, and his children, and his grandchildren. He would wipe out the entire line.

He took off his shirt and trousers and his socks, and in his dirty undershirt and shorts lay down on the cement floor — he could breathe there.

The peephole in the door opened. "Prisoner, stand up!"

Kamenev did not move.

The peephole shut.

Then came the sound of footsteps in the hall. The door opened, three big guards burst into the cell, one with a chair in his hands.

They picked Kamenev up, seated him on the chair, and tied him to it, the rope tight around his stomach.

"Sit still, you son-of-a-bitch!"

A doctor in a white coat came in, took his pulse, checked the tension on the rope, lifted Kamenev's eyelids, looked into his eyes, and left.

The guards followed.

Lev Borisovich couldn't breathe. The chair was right by the radiator, his bound arms and legs were going numb. His head lolled on his chest, but he was still conscious. Pictures floated through his mind. He couldn't tell what he was seeing, he couldn't remember what he had seen a minute earlier. He remembered one thing — Lenin had called him a "horse." When Lenin was sick, Kamenev led the meetings of the Council of Commissars. Then he opened a session one day and said that he had a surprise for the members. And Lenin came in, embraced Kamenev, and said with a laugh, "Well, wasn't I right in my selection of a deputy — aren't you pleased? I knew this horse would never let me down." And everyone laughed and applauded Lenin.

The door opened again, and the doctor accompanied by guards came back in, took his pulse, examined his legs, checked his eyes, and said, "You can continue."

# 28

**H**alf a year had passed without Altman's calling.

Obviously Yuri Sharok had said a few words to him and Altman had decided to lay off. If a comrade asks a favor, you respect it; one day you may have a request of your own. Good for Yuri!

But Vadim had not called Yuri, because it was too delicate a matter. Once, when he ran into him on the Arbat, he shook his hand warmly, walked him to Arbat Square, and said in parting, "Thank you, Yuri!"

Yuri did not reply, smiled, got on the trolley, and waved. Vadim was an idiot, he always had been. Didn't he understand that no one helped anyone in these cases? You could die laughing over these intellectuals. Altman hadn't called him in because he was part of one of the investigative groups preparing the trial. He had no time for Vadim. Sharok didn't even want to think about Vadim's case, even though he could guess — the Foreign Section was interested in Vika's dossier.

But Vadim didn't know any of this. Sharok's friendly gesture reassured him completely.

He was writing a lot now, speaking even more frequently; he was becoming famous. People sought him out. One day Ershilov's nephew from Saratov was visiting Moscow. Just as goggle-eyed as his uncle, just as sharp-nosed, but with a pleasant, shy smile. Ershilov brought him to the Writers' Club, to show him the Muscovite celebrities.

"He works on the railroad," Ershilov said, introducing his nephew to Vadim. "However, he adores the theater. He read your interview with Koonen, and he said, 'Now I don't want to go anywhere else, not the Bolshoi, not Meyerhold, only to the Chamber Theater.' Right?"

The youth confirmed his uncle's statement with a nod.

"*Pas de probleme,*" Vadim replied. "Look at the schedule, pick a performance, and call me."

The bastard Ershilov was using base flattery, of course, but it was still pleasant to hear how far and wide his interview had been read. It had been his first serious work, written a year and a half ago.

In late 1934 the Chamber Theater had its twentieth anniversary and the celebration of it was scheduled for January 1. Vadim thought this would be a perfect occasion to do a lengthy interview, say, with Alisa Koonen, who was about to be named People's Actress of the Republic. Everyone knew that the resolution announcing awards to the Chamber Theater's director, Tairov, and Koonen was ready, perhaps even signed. An interview on the eve of the resolution would be wonderful.

At first Koonen wouldn't grant an interview, but Vadim's father had helped him. "Alisa Georgyevna wouldn't refuse me."

And she didn't. She picked December 26 as the date for the interview, at exactly four-fifteen, at the theater itself.

Vadim started working. He sat in the library, going through reviews, rummaged in books, and found an interesting pamphlet that apparently no one had ever opened, with commentaries from the Western press about the Chamber Theater's tour.

In 1923 the Chamber Theater gave 133 performances in Paris and in Berlin and other German cities. The reviews were outstanding, and Vadim copied them into his notebook — "Russians triumph ..."; "Sound the horns — the Moscow Chamber Theater is the only theater in Europe ..."; "If the Moscow Chamber Theater is the child of Bolshevism, then Bolshevism not only does not destroy, but on the contrary it liberates creative forces."

There was negative reaction, too. Vadim read it and laughed. "These methods are crude. So crude that the audience is ready to send these miserable shoemakers back home."

The background material was growing. At home Vadim went through Tairov's *Notes of a Director* one more time. He had read it in one sitting a long time ago and still remembered it well. His father kept the inscribed copy in his desk. And locked the drawer. Not because he valued the autograph so much but out of caution — the book had been designed by the artist Alexandra Ekster, who later had moved abroad. No need for the many strangers constantly at their house to know that the Maraseviches kept books like that.

Vadim decided to start the interview with an epigraph from Tairov, appropriate for the anniversary — "And still the Chamber Theater appeared. It had to appear — it was so written in the book of theatrical destiny. . . ."

And then, he would build the interview not in the banal, usual way, from the early steps to the heights, but on the contrary, from the pinnacle, from *Optimistic Tragedy,* its present triumph, back to its sources, to *Salome,* the play that marked the theater's rebirth after the October Revolution.

On the twenty-sixth, Vadim, bearing roses, pushed the doorbell at exactly a quarter past four.

Koonen opened the door, smiled, and said, "You're the impatient journalist?"

"I'm terribly embarrassed," Vadim began.

"Don't be, I'm also impatient in my work. Your name is Vadim? Did I remember correctly?"

She left for a minute while Vadim took off his coat — "I'll give the young girl the flowers, she'll put them in a vase."

The "young girl" came in to put the vase in the room. Vadim was surprised, for the "young girl" was pushing thirty. But then he realized that Koonen's use of the word implied that she was taking care of the girl. A real aristocrat, she didn't call her a housemaid or servant, she used the gentle forms.

Koonen was observing him.

"You resemble Yevgenia Fyodorovna. I loved your mother." And without any transition she added, "Do you know that I came up with the title, *Optimistic Tragedy?* The author, Vishnevsky, refused to define his play as a tragedy. Alexander Yakovlevich, our director, tried to explain that he had written a tragedy.

" 'Maybe so,' Vishnevsky said hotly, 'but it is optimistic!'

" 'Then why not call it that?' I said. *'Optimistic Tragedy?'* "

Vadim took notes and then looked up, still shy.

"Well, what else can I tell you?"

"Do you feel free to explore when you undertake a new role or do you hold to the playwright's intentions?"

She laughed. "That's something I never worry about. Freedom is essential. Otherwise, as Alexander Yakovlevich says, the theater ceases to exist as an independent art and turns into a record that merely transmits the author's ideas. Have you seen *Desire under the Elms?*"

"Yes, twice, in fact."

Koonen looked at him in silence.

He did not quite understand her look.

"I liked it very much."

"Thank you. But I wanted to tell you that I played Abby very differently from the way it was interpreted in America. There, Abby was played as a negative heroine. I wanted to raise her image to the heights of great tragedy. Not to accuse Abby, but to justify her, to reveal the roots of what led her to catastrophe. She was not a moral monster, but a person with a horribly tragic fate."

She rose from her chair, went over to the wall, and took down a framed photograph, which she placed on the table in front of Vadim.

"That's O'Neill." She lit the redwood torchiere so that Vadim could see better.

It was a good face, thought Vadim, aloof and severe, unusual.

"You see what he wrote — '*To Mme Alisa Koonen, who made Abby and Ella living images for me....*' Then there are compliments, you don't need to read that. O'Neill had seen our performances in Paris. He was staying outside Paris and came in especially to see us."

She hung the photograph on the wall, returned to her armchair, sat down, and leaned back.

"Do you know what else O'Neill said? 'The theater of creative fantasy had always been my ideal. And the Chamber Theater has realized that dream!'"

Vadim had stopped being nervous at last, and he even managed a smile. "Maybe we could talk about *Phèdre?* Jean Cocteau said, 'Tairov's *Phèdre* is a masterpiece.'"

"There's been so much said and written about *Phèdre* already.... Why don't I tell you something few people know. We brought *Phèdre* to Paris in 1923.... It was our first evening in Paris, we were all excited, we were surrounded by journalists, having interesting conversation, when I suddenly felt my heart stop. I learned that no French actress or any touring ones had dared to play *Phèdre* out of reverence for Sarah Bernhardt. It had been in her repertoire to her very last appearances. Can you imagine my state? Fear, meekness, horror. And just then a friendly elderly journalist took me aside and gave me a small bit of advice — 'I think you, a young Russian actress in Paris to play *Phèdre*, should write a few words to our great French actress and ask for her blessing.' It was marvelous advice. In the morning I sent her a respectful note and a bouquet. I don't think she read it. The next day all the front pages were framed in black. 'Our great Sarah has died.' "

They talked about her tours in Germany.

"But there," Koonen said, "we weren't 'unknown Bolsheviks.' The word of our Paris success had reached them and Germany's theater people did not simply express their delight with our plays, they seriously studied Tairov's work as a director, the actors' work, the principle of set design, the use of light. The synthetic actor, proclaimed by Tairov, the actor who had equal mastery of all theatrical genres, particularly interested the German theater specialists. Especially because Tairov's book, *Notes of a Director,* had just come out in German."

"We have the book with an inscription from Alexander Yakovlevich," Vadim said. "It's dedicated to you." He was feeling very comfortable by then.

The last question was about *Salome*.

Koonen thought.

"We've talked for fifty minutes, I have a perfect sense of time. Why don't you check me?"

"Yes," Vadim said, looking at his watch, "you're absolutely right, it's five after five."

"I can give you a few more minutes. Don't write, listen. Do you remember Wilde's play?"

Of course Vadim did. It was based on the biblical story of the love of Salome, stepdaughter of King Herod, for the prophet John.

"Before the February Revolution, *Salome* was banned by the Church censors. And when the ban was lifted, both we and the Maly Theater put it on. Tairov was attracted by the rebellious air of the play, the powerful, unbridled passions. Alexandra Ekster designed the play fantastically. It was some of her best work in expression, temperament, and sense of form."

"Alexandra Ekster?" Vadim repeated, pretending to write down the name. God, his father was keeping Tairov's book under lock and key because of her name, and here was Koonen raving about her.

"The climax in the play," Koonen continued, "is the dance of the seven veils, in reward for which Salome demands John's head from Herod because he had rejected her. That dance has often been done as an erotic, seductive dance. In our play Salome dances for the terarch not to seduce him but with only one wild thought — to get the prophet's head as a reward...."

Koonen shivered and then laughed. "When I think of *Salome,* I get cold. I don't know why we didn't get sick, didn't get colds! The theater wasn't heated, the audience sat in warm coats while we were onstage half naked, really. But the play was a great success...."

At the door Vadim asked, "Would you like to see the interview?"

She smiled and said, "It's not necessary, I trust you." And then she asked unexpectedly, "Do you like sitting in the fifth row?"

Vadim did not know what to reply.

"It's the best row. I'll have them reserve seat seventeen for you. Come to our plays. It's been interesting talking with you."

On the way home, Vadim walked down Tverskoy Boulevard. No, he didn't walk, he ran, beside himself with joy, understanding that he had a gold mine in his hands.

What regal bearing, what openness, how she raised her interlocutor to her own level, without considering for a moment that her words might be misunderstood. And why should she? Her fame belonged to the people, the country.

And what a storyteller! How generously she shared her thoughts! The true generosity of talent! Incidentally, why not call the interview that — "The Generosity of Talent." Not bad at all.

And what about that fine anecdote about the electric equipment? The lines were writing themselves in his head: "And what did the actors buy with the money they earned in Germany? The latest electric equipment for their theater in Moscow!" A wonderful detail — an example of true service to the arts.

And what about what Litvinov said when the theater came back from its European tour — "It is a great victory to show Soviet theater in countries where they consider us barbarians and then win over the audiences. It is very important that the first tour of a Soviet theater abroad was such a triumph."

That political theme had to be developed in the interview.

At home Vadim threw off his coat, went to his room, and started banging on the typewriter. A few hours later he dropped by the kitchen and said to Fenya, "Let me have a quick snack, tea and sandwiches."

Vika — who was still in Moscow then — looked in and stared at Vadim.

"What was she wearing?"

"Who?" Vadim didn't understand.

" 'Who?' Koonen, of course."

"What was she wearing?" Vadim had to think. Something brown ... or was it green? ... No, blue. He didn't remember. He remembered only his first impression when she opened the door. She was beautiful, slender, and without makeup — just a little lipstick.

"Retard ..."

She was asking for it, but Vadim didn't respond. The main thing was not to lose the feeling of joy in his heart, not to lose it over his stupid sister. He finished his sandwich and rushed back to his typewriter.

Somewhere in the middle of the night he finished, reread it, got up, stretched happily, and looked at his watch. It was four-thirty; he had stayed up all night.

The interview was marvelous, Vadim was congratulated, newspapers asked him to review plays at the Chamber Theater, people asked him for passes.

And they still did.... Ershilov and his nephew for instance.

Then ten days later he ran into Ershilov and they went to the Writers' Club for some cognac, and Ershilov begged again. He had to get tickets for his wife's gynecologist. You can never say no to the gynecologist, you understand.... For *Egyptian Nights*.

"You can get tickets to any theater," Vadim said.

"I don't know anyone at the Chamber, that's why I'm asking."

Then he called once more, asking for an old school friend. A geologist from Khibiny, hadn't been to Moscow in a long time, wanted to go to the Chamber Theater, please help out, Vadim.

Vadim refused, but promised to take Ershilov with him to the premiere of the comic opera *Bogatyry*.

"Is it any good?"

"Are you serious! First of all, they found the lost score of a comic opera by Borodin. That's a sensation in itself! It was performed only once at the Bolshoi, back when Borodin wrote it. Second, the Chamber hasn't done a musical play for about five years — all of Moscow is anticipating this opening. And third, the libretto is by Demyan Bedny, rather crude, but nevertheless . . . And fourth, Tairov's set and costume designer is Bazhenov. Have you ever heard of him?"

"All right," said Ershilov, "let's go see *Bogatyry*. It's a date."

# ⚵ 29 ⚵

**Y**ezhov's failure with Zinoviev and Kamenev afforded Yagoda great satisfaction. While Yezhov pondered a new plan of action, Yagoda had to beat him to the punch. Yagoda was more experienced than Yezhov and sensed that, despite their resistance, Zinoviev and Kamenev were exhausted and the end was near.

Yagoda had the heat turned up unbearably in Zinoviev's cell. Zinoviev, an asthmatic, suffered terribly, and developed liver complications as well. He rolled on the floor in pain and demanded a doctor, who prescribed pills that made his condition worse. The doctor's orders were simply to keep Zinoviev and Kamenev alive, for the trial.

Every hour Yagoda received reports on their condition. He did not leave the NKVD, he slept in his office, knowing that they might break at any second. And the moment came — Zinoviev asked to see Molchanov.

In Molchanov's office, Zinoviev asked for permission to talk with Kamenev. Molchanov realized that Zinoviev was planning to capitulate. He called Yagoda and told him of Zinoviev's request. Yagoda understood, too, and had Zinoviev brought to him.

Yagoda greeted him gently and said, "Dear Grigory Yevseyevich! Free yourself and us from this nightmare. I will let you see Kamenev immediately. You will be alone and will be able to talk as much as you like. But, Grigory Yevseyevich, I beg you — be reasonable!"

Then Zinoviev was taken to a cell and Kamenev was brought

there a few minutes later. They were left alone. The cell had a table, two chairs, and a hidden microphone.

"There's no way out," Zinoviev said, breathing heavily. "We have to attend the trial. I don't have the strength."

"Neither do I," Kamenev said. "But it will be over sooner or later. You have to bear it."

"If we go on trial, we'll save our families and the families of the other defendants. They can't have a trial without us, they need us more than anyone else. If there's no trial, Koba will kill not only us, not only our families, but everyone else and their families too."

He caught his breath and went on. "We must think not only of ourselves and our families, we must think about the thousands of people who have been on our side and of their families. We are responsible for them. I propose setting one condition — Stalin must guarantee our lives, our families', and the lives of our former allies and their families. Why us? In promising our lives, he confirms that the real issue is not punishing us for crimes we committed — because he knows that there were no crimes — but a deal: our lives in exchange for accusing Trotsky of terrorism."

"He'll make all the promises he wants — and then renege. He can't be trusted."

"We won't trust him, we'll trust the guarantees he makes officially."

Zinoviev was broken — that was clear. He would participate in the trial, and he would give the evidence they wanted, including evidence against him, Kamenev.

Of course, Stalin's promises would be kept for a while. For how long was a different question, but they would be kept for a while. And only for those who cooperated. The ones who refused would be handled immediately — they, and their families, their children ... his little Yuri.

"This vileness," Kamenev said, "can be done only if Stalin gives us guarantees in the presence of the entire Politburo. The entire Politburo. Then it won't be his personal guarantee, but the guarantee of the Politburo. And that guarantee can be violated only by a decision of the Politburo."

"Right," Zinoviev agreed.

And this was the condition that Kamenev presented to Yagoda when he and Zinoviev were brought to him.

Yagoda promised to report it to Stalin.

Of course, he had already done so. Yagoda had heard their entire conversation, and he hurriedly called Stalin before Yezhov could appear unexpectedly and report it first.

Yagoda was pleased. The laurels of victory over Zinoviev and Kamenev belonged to him and his apparat. Stalin would be pleased.

But none of it worked out the way Yagoda had expected. Stalin ordered him, Molchanov, and Mironov to appear immediately and demanded they tell him everything in detail.

He listened to their report in silence. He stared at them with his heavy, angry gaze.

These scoundrels were sitting there, pleased with themselves. Triumphant and overjoyed. Why were they happy? Because they prepared the trial? Yes, of course, but the real reason was more complex. They had saved Zinoviev and Kamenev, Smirnov and Mrachkovsky; they had saved all kinds of shit like Olberg, that's why they were happy. In exchange for an honest confession the defendants would preserve their lives — and these Chekists felt that they were the ones who saved them. The blood of Old Bolsheviks would not be on their conscience. They saved "Lenin's comrades in arms." They wanted to stay clean. *He,* Stalin, would have to pardon Zinoviev and Kamenev. *He* would take the responsibility for the consequences of that politically incorrect decision, and these uniformed bastards would feel joy and triumph — they had saved Zinoviev's and Kamenev's lives, they were humanists and humane men, their Cheka conscience was clear. They hadn't managed to break Zinoviev and Kamenev; they were worthless, corrupt spongers who couldn't break two people who had been destroyed politically and morally long ago. And now *he* was supposed to do it for them?

Stalin rose and began pacing.

Yagoda, Molchanov, and Mironov sat silently by the wall, anxiously watching Stalin walk slowly and quietly.

"At first glance this is not bad," Stalin said at last. "But only at first glance. Do they want to save their lives? Of course. Everyone wants to save his life. Life is dear to every person. Of course, there are people who accept death, but those are people with ideals, prepared to die for those ideals. Zinoviev and Kamenev lost their ideals long ago — and therefore they have no reason to die. There is another reason for which people are willing to die — that is honor, the honor of a Communist, the honor of a Bolshevik. Do Zinoviev and Kamenev have that honor? Of course not. They have been deceiving the Party and the working class for so many years that they lost their honor and conscience long ago — and so that's no reason for them to lose their lives. Are they clutching at life like all ordinary mortals? No, they don't consider themselves ordinary mortals. They want to save their cadres. If they are spared their lives after all their crimes, then what can be demanded of their followers? That's their point. By saving themselves, they are saving their cadres. That's the guarantee they are demanding. I ask you — why should the Party give them such a guarantee?"

He stopped talking but went on pacing the room slowly and softly.

Yagoda, Mironov, and Molchanov said nothing, stunned. Stalin had changed his mind, he didn't want to guarantee the defendants' lives. Yet there would be a trial, Stalin would insist on a trial no matter what, and they would have to get evidence from Kamenev and Zinoviev by other means.

Stalin went back to the table and sat down.

"Did you give them any guarantees?"

"Comrade Stalin," Yagoda said at last, "we did not, nor did we have the right to give any. They were the ones to demand a guarantee and they demanded it not from us but the Politburo. We promised to pass that demand to the Politburo."

"You promised," Stalin repeated. "You promised them a deal with the Politburo. But can the Politburo accept such a deal? Have you thought about that?"

He paused and then said, "You promised to pass along their demand to Comrade Stalin. And what is Comrade Stalin supposed to reply? That he does not agree to such a meeting. And how will they interpret that? As a death sentence. Why bother with a trial? Then what happens to your work? You spent a half a year on it — with no result. You have made an error, promising to pass their demand on to the Politburo. You should have heard them out and said that you would discuss their demand yourselves. Then you would have asked for our advice and we would have told you that you could not pass such a demand to the Politburo, that you did not have the right. And so let them decide their own fate. That's what you should have done. That is not what you have done."

He paused and then said, "Now the question arises — how to correct your mistake? I see only one way."

He looked at everyone with his piercing, heavy gaze. "If we decline their demand, passed along by you, then you will be compromised in the eyes of your apparat. We do not want that. We do not want to compromise the leadership of the NKVD apparat. We value and support the leadership of the NKVD. And only because of that, the Politburo is forced to accept the demands of Kamenev and Zinoviev. But this is the first and last time. In the future you may hear out such demands, but you do not have the right to promise to present them. Remember that."

Zinoviev and Kamenev were brought to the Kremlin in a closed limousine by Molchanov and Mironov.

Stalin, Voroshilov, and Yezhov were at the table. Yagoda sat by the wall.

Without greeting Zinoviev and Kamenev, Stalin gestured casually at chairs by the wall.

Zinoviev and Kamenev sat down, and Mironov and Molchanov sat next to them.

Stalin regarded Zinoviev and Kamenev silently and indifferently, the way one might total strangers. The past had vanished, the past did not exist, there was no reason to recall these people. Two crumpled, frightened faces. And these mediocrities had wanted to overthrow *him. Him!* Criminals and bastards! They should have been destroyed long ago.

"We are listening," Stalin said coldly.

"We were promised that the Politburo would listen to us," Kamenev said.

"You expect all the members of the Politburo to drop their work, leave their cities and republics just to listen to you? They've seen and heard enough of you already."

Kamenev glanced at Zinoviev.

Stalin saw the look and understood. He knew Kamenev well enough. With that look Kamenev was calling on Zinoviev to insist on the fulfillment of the promise they had been given — the entire Politburo had to be there. Kamenev had always followed Zinoviev. But today the weaker was Zinoviev.

"If a meeting with this committee of the Politburo does not suit you," Stalin said, "we can end it."

Stalin had figured correctly. Zinoviev rose from his chair.

Zinoviev used to have a high-pitched voice, almost squeaky. Now he spoke softly and slowly, barely able to form the words. An old woman! He had always been a woman. He couldn't even die with dignity. And yet he had sent packs of others to be shot. All those people he had killed in Petrograd. If he had taken power in the Party, he would have had Comrade Stalin shot without entering into these discussions. Did he really expect to get out of this situation?

But Zinoviev was talking, breathing heavily. "Neither I nor Lev Borisovich had anything to do with Kirov's killing. . . . You know that perfectly well."

He looked up into Stalin's eyes. But Stalin did not look away. "However . . ."

Zinoviev lowered his head. "However, it was demanded that we take . . . take the moral responsibility for that death. Your words . . . your words that our confession was necessary for the Party were conveyed to us."

Zinoviev took a breath.

"We sacrificed our honor and accepted it. . . . But we were tricked and put in prison."

He took another breath.

"And what do you want now? Now you want us to be tried again, where we, former members of Lenin's Politburo, former personal friends of Vladimir Ilyich Lenin, will be presented as bandits and murderers. This will shame not only us, but the Party, the Party to which . . . which . . . for good or bad . . . we have devoted our lives. . . ."

He burst into tears. Molchanov gave him a glass of water.

Disregarding Zinoviev's tears, Stalin said, "The Central Com-

mittee warned you more than once that your position with
Kamenev and your behavior would lead to no good. And that's
what happened. . . . We are telling you once more — obey the Party
and your life will be saved. You don't want to? Again you don't
want to. Well then, you have only yourselves to blame."

"We've been tricked many times," Kamenev said. "Where is the
guarantee that we won't be tricked this time?"

"You demand a guarantee?" Stalin feigned surprise and looked
at Voroshilov. "They demand a guarantee! The word of the
Politburo isn't enough for them! They've forgotten that there is no
higher guarantee in our country!" Stalin looked at Voroshilov again
and then at Yezhov. "Your opinions, Comrades? I think that this
conversation is a waste of time."

Yezhov shrugged as if to say: That's clear.

"They think they can dictate conditions to us!" Voroshilov said in
outrage. "They do not understand, or pretend not to understand.
Comrade Stalin wants to save their lives. If they don't value their
lives, fine! The hell with them!"

A pause ensued until Stalin spoke. "It is a great pity that Zinoviev
and Kamenev think in a bourgeois manner. A great pity. They do
not even understand the purpose of the trial. To have them shot?
That's ridiculous, Comrades, we can shoot them without a trial.
Zinoviev knows well how that is done. The trial is directed against
Trotsky. In their time Zinoviev and Kamenev knew that Trotsky
was a sworn enemy of the Party, but later, attacking the Party, they
rehabilitated Trotsky, rehabilitated him out of their factional
considerations, yet Trotsky remains a sworn enemy of the Party.
Zinoviev and Kamenev know that. Here is the question — if we
did not shoot Zinoviev and Kamenev when they fought against the
Party together with Trotsky, then why must we shoot them after
they help the Central Committee in its struggle with Trotsky? And
the last point . . ."

Stalin paused, pondered, something human and confidential
flickering in his eyes. And what he said sounded unexpectedly
touching and heartfelt, "We do not want to shed the blood of our
old comrades in the party, no matter what mistakes they have
made."

Zinoviev sobbed again. And Molchanov rose again to pour him

water. But Stalin noticed that Molchanov's face was different now. It wasn't the same expression as when he'd first come in. Then Molchanov was happy, glad that Zinoviev's and Kamenev's lives had been saved. And Mironov was happy, Mironov, whom *he himself* had advanced as Yagoda's deputy. That humanitarian was especially pleased.

And why shouldn't they be pleased? They would not be held responsible before history for the death of the "innocent."

Kamenev rose. "Comrade Stalin, comrade members of the Politburo. In my name and the name of Comrade Zinoviev I state that we agree to the conditions presented to us and are prepared to stand trial. But we ask you to promise us that none of the former members of the opposition will be shot now and that they will not be shot later for their former opposition activity."

Stalin, pretending to recover from his momentary weakness, said wearily, "That goes without saying."

From the Kremlin, Zinoviev and Kamenev were brought back to the prison in the same limousine, but to different cells — and were given beds with fresh linen. They were allowed to take showers, and they were fed well. The doctor switched Zinoviev to the diet he needed. For the two weeks before the trial began, the people who dealt with them behaved properly.

And yet on August 19, 1935, at ten minutes past noon, when they were brought into the court set up in the October Room of the House of Unions, Zinoviev looked bad — his puffy face with bags beneath the eyes was a gray, clayish color. Gasping with asthma, he opened his mouth wide to breathe in. He unbuttoned and removed his collar and sat through the whole trial dressed like that.

Kamenev's face was also gray and there were circles under his eyes, too, but he looked more robust than Zinoviev. He kept looking about the room, hoping to find acquaintances. He had been chairman of the Moscow City Council for many years, he knew every important Party figure in Moscow, but he didn't see any of them in the courtroom. The only people present were NKVD men dressed in civilian clothes.

Yagoda and other leaders of the NKVD listened to the trial in the next room.

Only Reinhold looked healthy, as if he had come from home instead of prison. He spoke with confidence, and when Vyshinsky got something wrong, he asked for permission to speak and corrected him tactfully.

All the defendants had memorized their scripts and responded exactly as the procurator demanded. In the course of the trial they named as coconspirators Sokolnikov, Smilga, Rykov, Bukharin, Tomsky, Radek, Uglanov, Pyatakov, Serebryakov, Mdivani, Okudzhava, Commander Putna, Commander Primakov, Commander Dmitry Shmidt. In their final statements, each fully admitted his guilt, confessed to being a killer, terrorist, and bandit.

Only Ivan Nikitich Smirnov violated the scenario. As he had promised Molchanov, he confessed that in 1932 he had received instructions from Trotsky on terrorism, but because he had been arrested on January 1, 1933, and had been in prison continually thereafter, he had not participated in any terrorist activity. In the course of the trial Smirnov denied the existence of the "center" and refuted the testimony of Mrachkovsky, Zinoviev, Evdokimov, Dreitser, Ter-Vaganyan, and Kamenev.

Some questions Smirnov refused to answer at all.

Vyshinsky demanded all the defendants be shot.

At two-thirty in the morning of August 24, the court pronounced sentence — death by shooting for all defendants.

By law, the defendants had seventy-two hours to appeal for clemency.

However, on August 24 they were brought out to be shot.

Zinoviev lost all control and hysterically shouted for Stalin to keep his promise. In order to stop the shouting, the lieutenant accompanying Zinoviev pushed him into an empty cell and shot him with his pistol.

Kamenev was stunned, did not say a word, and accepted death in silence.

And only Ivan Nikitich Smirnov walked down the prison corridor calmly and boldly, and he said before being shot, "We deserve this for our unworthy behavior in the court."

*Smirnov's daughter, Olga, and his wife were arrested immediately and shot in 1937.*

In *1937* Zinoviev's son, Stepan Radomyslsky; Bakayev's wife, Anna Petrovna Kostina, a Party member since *1917*; Mrachkovsky's brother and nephew; and Ter-Vaganyan's brother, Endzak, were shot. Ter-Vaganyan's wife, Klavdiya Vasilyevna Generalova, was arrested in *1936* and spent seventeen years in the camps.

Soon after Kamenev's execution, his first and second wives were shot. In *1939* his elder son, Alexander, was shot.

Kamenev's son Yuri was shot on January *30, 1938,* one month before his seventeenth birthday.

Kamenev's grandson, Vitaly, was arrested in *1951,* at the age of nineteen, and sentenced to twenty-five years. He died in *1966.*

Thus did Comrade Stalin keep his promise.

## 30

**V**adim didn't get to the premiere of *Bogatyry*. He had a strep throat, a fever of 103. He gargled with medicine, but nothing helped. Fenya made a broth from dried mushrooms. That was what they had always used in the village, and it did ease the pain, and he at least had good broth. . . . He asked for the newspapers, he hadn't seen one in a long time. Litovsky's review praised *Bogatyry*. Vadim didn't bother with any other reviews; he tossed the newspapers on the floor, he'd have time to read them later, and he'd have time to go to the play. Now he was sleepy.

On November 14, Ershilov called. "Any better? Are you strong enough to read the papers? Read *Pravda,* now."

"What's there?" Vadim asked lazily.

"The resolution of the Committee on the Arts banning *Bogatyry*."

"No!"

"Yes. . . ."

And then, on November 15, *Pravda* published another article, this time by Kerzhentsev, called "Falsification of the National Past." It didn't leave a stone unturned when it came to the librettist Demyan Bedny. At the end of the article, he wrote:

. . . D. Bedny's play is a distortion of history, a model of not only anti-Marxist thought but also of a frivolous attitude toward history, spitting at the national past. . . . All D. Bedny remembered of the bogatyry was their snoring . . . he depicted the Russian people as sleeping on their stoves. A pathetic regurgitation of these old attitudes, alien to Bolsheviks and ordinary Soviet poets, was evident in this play.

Now it was Vadim who called up Ershilov. "What's happening? I'm still in bed...."

"They say Demyan Bedny's been kicked out of his Kremlin apartment," Ershilov reported with a laugh. "They say he's sleeping at friends' houses.... Soon they're going to take on your entire Chamber Theater, you'll see. And you'll have to join in the fun."

"Me join in? I'm sick, and I haven't even seen *Bogatyry,* you know that...."

"Seen it or not, you'll have to join in."

That bastard Ershilov was right, maybe he knew something but didn't say? On November 20, *Pravda* published an article, "A Line of Errors," signed "Viewer." The attack on the theater was a strong one. ... Vadim read it and reread it:

> Everything was done to free this theater from its formalist-aesthetic "legacy," to make it viable, full of content, and truly Soviet. But that did not happen. The theater's director learned his political lessons badly.
>
> Modesty — that's what the Chamber Theater always lacked. Shameless self-promotion — that's what it had too much of.
>
> The Chamber Theater presented politically incorrect plays frequently and public opinion, backed by other theater companies, severely condemned such plays at the Chamber Theater, and they were removed from its stage....
>
> The director of the Chamber Theater, A. Ya. Tairov, stubbornly continued his error-filled ways. In 1931 he staged a thoroughly chauvinist play, *Sonata Pathetique,* by M. Kulish. Then came *Bogatyry,* a play by D. Bedny, thoroughly false in its political tendencies....
>
> Tairov instituted "sovereignty" in the theater, which stifled any creative initiative arising from the collective. Yet no one had given the theater to Tairov.
>
> The Chamber Theater never managed to establish a creative collective, because the best actors were not allowed to work. The Chamber Theater, as a result, lags behind the general

growth of Soviet culture, it is straggling at the tail end of the line. . . .

That same day Vadim was called by the executive secretary of the newspaper where he often published.

"There is a feeling here at the paper, Vadim Andreyevich, that we too should respond to the events at the Chamber Theater. . . . We're asking you to write something."

"But," Vadim said, "I'm sick, I had a rheumatic attack after my strep throat, and I'm supposed to stay in bed. I didn't see *Bogatyry* because of my illness, and the other plays mentioned I never saw or don't remember because I was just a child."

"I'll tell that to the editor," the secretary said sourly. "I didn't think you'd refuse us, Vadim Andreyevich."

On November 23, on page six of *Pravda,* a small article appeared: "The Collective of the Chamber Theater Speaks," subtitled "A. Ya. Tairov Covers Up Errors."

Then a meeting of the theater staff was held for two days. Several dozen people, including the theater's most famous actors, spoke.

L. Genin, an honored artist, said, "The actors were forced to praise any play accepted by the director, even if they thought it bad."

But what astonished Vadim was Tsenin's speech — "Tairov did not wish to discuss the work on a play with the theater workers."

Vadim remembered Tsenin well, he was in *Optimistic Tragedy,* and during her interview Koonen had praised him. And look at Tsenin now!

Vadim had published his interview with Koonen a year and a half ago. Of course, he could say that it had been an assignment, but they would remember at the newspaper that he had offered it to them. The basic text wasn't his, however, it was Koonen speaking. But his remarks and questions revealed his delight with the theater and with Koonen. And that could be used against him. A lot of people envied his success then; they'd get theirs back now.

Ershilov added fat to the fire. He came by to tell Vadim about the expanded meeting of the Committee on the Arts, to which he and Elsbein had been invited.

"If you were well, you'd have been invited, too. You'll read about it in detail either tomorrow or the next day, but you should know this now — Kerzhentsev accused Tairov of political hostility."

"What about *Optimistic Tragedy?*" Vadim asked. There was no "political hostility" there.

"It never came up. Kerzhentsev said, 'The Chamber Theater has become a shamed name.'"

A fine mess. . . . What a fool he'd been for refusing to write that article. Should he tell Ershilov about it?

"The newspaper called, asked me to write for them, but I said I was sick and couldn't do it."

"Big deal. Call up and say that you're better. Call right now."

Vadim called, came back to his room, and said that everything was fine.

"You did the right thing."

Vadim shouted to Fenya to bring him a second pillow, so that he could sit up in bed to write. He picked up a book to prop up his writing pad, but it was too slippery. He looked around his desk and bookshelves and found an old notebook — that was fine. He opened it and found a notation:

*Chicago Tribune,* March 22.
We hope to see them soon. Their departure darkens the Paris stage. We will await impatiently the return of the brilliant actors, and in remembering them, we will often turn to Russia, since now we know that the light on the European stage comes from the East.

It was from the pamphlet "Political Responses in the Western Press to the Tour of the Moscow State Chamber Theater."

*Brilliant actors! . . . the light on the European stage comes from the East* . . . no wonder the bourgeois press praised them — their art suited the bourgeoisie.

He thought of Koonen with hostility. "Young girl" . . . Calling a thirty-year-old woman "young," she was play-acting at being a lady with a servant. She wasn't simple and democratic with her interviewer because she was talented and generous but because she was indifferent. It didn't matter whom she talked to as long as she had an excuse to talk about herself and her success.

"Viewer" was right in that *Pravda* article. The Chamber Theater lacked modesty. Really, it was all shameless self-promotion! "We beat the Maly Theater in that competition." The Maly Theater was here and here it would remain, while your survival was questionable. The people, the country, need the Maly Theater, dear Madame Koonen, but it's not clear whether the country needs you. The West needs you, yes, the West applauds you. . . . But you won't get the applause of our Soviet audiences.

Andrei Andreyevich was shown Vadim's article at the hospital. It wasn't clear whether his colleagues were praising it or mocking it. "Your son writes a tough article."

That evening Andrei Andreyevich, as usual, dropped in on Vadim, pulled a chair up to his bed. "I read your article. . . . As you can understand, that house is now closed to us. And I'm afraid that it's not the only one."

He sat in silence, staring at the floor, and then got up. "Have you taken your temperature?"

"My temperature is normal," Vadim barked. "If that house is closed, we'll find better ones."

And he slept the good, deep sleep of a man who has done his duty.

In the morning the phone rang. Vadim, half asleep, picked it up and heard the familiar, official, crude voice.

"Citizen Marasevich? You are to report today at noon to the NKVD of the U.S.S.R., to Comrade Altman."

The same office, barred windows, the same Altman in military uniform that hung on him as if he were a hanger, the same sunken cheeks and sorrowful eyes.

Altman rummaged in the desk drawer, took out a file, opened it, and removed the statement from the last interrogation. He reread it.

Vadim watched him nervously. He felt animal fear, not knowing what to expect from Altman this time.

Finishing the last page, Altman asked softly, without looking at Vadim, "You do not retract your statement?"

"Of course not, I signed it."

"Do you want to add anything?"

He was getting a chance. He had to take it. "You see," Vadim began, "you asked me last time about anti-Soviet conversations. Your questions made me think deeply. I understood that you weren't asking randomly, there had to be some basis for asking the question. And I assumed that the basis might be a joke that I told an acquaintance, just randomly, but I did tell it."

"What's the joke?" Altman leaned back, preparing to listen and looking at Vadim for the first time.

Vadim told him the joke, who told it to him, and to whom he told it. He added that he hadn't attributed any significance to the joke. It had been told in the presence of a member of the Party Committee, who even laughed at it. And he had told it to his barber, Sergei Alexeyevich. When you're in the chair, you're always chatting, especially when you've known the barber since childhood, a man outside politics, his entire attitude toward politics summed up in the gag, "Lev Davydovich had to be there somewhere."

This was the version Vadim decided on here in that office — a calm, restrained, and, he thought, convincing version.

Altman was silent. The most unnerving part was his silence — he let Vadim know his displeasure and dissatisfaction. He looked like an oaf.

Then Altman picked up a piece of paper and said, "Repeat, who told you the joke?"

Vadim repeated.

"When was it?"

Vadim named the month; he didn't remember the date.

"Whom did you tell it to?"

And he discovered that he didn't know Sergei Alexeyevich's surname. Altman wrote down the name and the address of the barbershop.

"What other jokes have you told and to whom?"

Vadim shrugged. "Me? Jokes? Nobody."

"Are you trying to tell me that you didn't know any other jokes in your whole life except this one? Is that what you're trying to tell me?"

"No, of course, I've heard lots of jokes in my life, but I never told them to anyone."

"Well, what have you heard?"

"I don't remember. At any rate, they weren't political."

"What kind then?"

"Just jokes ..."

"Marasevich! Are you trying to tell me I'm a jerk? I'm not a jerk."

He narrowed his eyes like an executioner and said angrily, in fact he hissed it, "There are no jerks here."

Vadim thought Altman was crazy. And that scared him more — you never know what to expect from a madman.

"But I can't remember," Vadim muttered.

"You can't remember," Altman said, staring at Vadim with hatred. "Who's going to remember for you? Me? Then sit in my chair and I'll take yours." He got up. "Well, sit down, sit down." He stepped aside and pointed at the chair. "Go on, sit down!"

Vadim froze in horror. That madman was going to kill him, shoot him with the gun hanging from his belt.

Altman sat down just as unexpectedly as he had stood up. After silently staring musingly and sadly into the corner, he asked, "Do they tell jokes at the Writers' Union?"

"Probably, they must."

"Be precise. Do they or do they not tell jokes? Not 'probably,' but precisely."

"There are hundreds of people in the Writers' Union."

"I'm not asking how many people are in the Writers' Union, I'm asking — do they tell jokes there?"

"Some people certainly tell jokes."

"Who are these 'some people'?"

"I can't name specific people...."

" 'Can't'?" Altman screwed up his mouth into a vicious grin. "You mean you won't.... You got caught on one joke, and you remembered it, if we catch you in another, you'll remember others, but it will be too late. All right! Do you know Alexander Pavlovich Pankratov?"

"Pankratov? Oh, yes, Sasha Pankratov, of course, I knew him, we were at school together."

"Do you know where he is now?"

"He was arrested, exiled. I think he's somewhere in Siberia."

"Who told you this?"

"What do you mean?" Vadim was bewildered. "We lived on the same street, went to the same school, everybody knew it."

"You really do think I'm stupid," Altman said. "You're trying to tell me that the whole street talks of nothing but the arrest of Pankratov. You're telling me that you're still in school and that's all anyone talks about there, too. . . . Is that it?"

"I ran into old classmates on the Arbat, and they told me that Sasha Pankratov was arrested."

"And that's it?"

"Meaning?"

"Meaning!" Altman exploded again. "I'm asking you in plain Russian, is that all you know about the Pankratov case?"

"I don't know anything about his case. I do know that he was arrested, but not for what. . . ."

"You don't know? You don't know anything! You know one joke, the one joke you told in your entire life!"

Altman stopped, then came another long pause, and then another unexpected question.

"Did you write a letter in defense of Pankratov?"

"A letter," Vadim muttered, "a letter . . ."

"Yes, 'a letter, a letter,' " Altman said, grimacing again. "A letter in defense of Pankratov. Did you write one?"

Vadim remembered Lena Budyagina's dining room, where they sat when Nina suggested writing a letter in Sasha's defense. He remembered Lena, Nina, and Maxim. . . . Sasha had been arrested two years ago; Vadim had forgotten him by now.

"You see," he began uncertainly, "when Sasha Pankratov was arrested, I was visiting my classmate Lena Budyagina. A few other classmates were there too."

"Who?" Altman interrupted. "Who specifically? Be concrete, Marasevich, don't shilly-shally, don't force me to fish a statement out of you. It took you almost a year to remember your barber; do you think we're going to go on this way? No, we're not going to give you a year for each name — we have ways of making you remember faster. We have our ways. And the first is to keep you here. Here, in a cell, you'll remember much faster."

Vadim took a breath. His hands were trembling, his head was in a vise.

"Well," Altman said, suddenly quiet and calm.

"At Lena's there was me, Nina Ivanova, and Maxim Kostin, we were all in the same class. . . ."

Altman wrote down the names on a piece of paper.

"We talked about Sasha Pankratov. Nina Ivanova suggested writing to OGPU to say that we knew Sasha Pankratov as an honest Komsomol. I opposed it, saying that we knew Sasha as a good Komsomol at school, and six years had passed since then, and he could have changed. Lena Budyagina —"

"All right, all right," Altman interrupted, impatiently. "Enough! So you discussed how to defend a convicted counterrevolutionary. Right? If Pankratov was sentenced under Article Fifty-eight, doesn't that mean he's a counterrevolutionary?"

Vadim could have said that Sasha had not been sentenced then, only arrested, and that they didn't know what article he would be charged under, and that he had actually opposed Nina. But he was afraid of contradicting Altman, afraid that he would fly into a fury again, so he agreed docilely.

"Yes, of course, if Pankratov were convicted as a counterrevolutionary, that means he's a counterrevolutionary, there's no question."

"And you wanted to defend a counterrevolutionary."

"But I personally —"

"What does 'personally' mean? I'm not interested in what each of you said. Only the fact is important. You got together, four of you, a group, and discussed how to help an arrested counterrevolutionary. You were planning to send a letter in his defense. Did you send it?"

Vadim could have said that they didn't send it precisely because Vadim had objected. But he was afraid of lying, afraid that Altman would catch him and it would make things worse, much worse. So he said, "I personally was opposed to it, and we asked for the advice of Ivan Grigoryevich Budyagin, Lena's father, you know, Ordzhonikidze's deputy, and he said that we shouldn't send that letter."

"Well, there," Altman said with satisfaction. "Now it's more or less clear, not everything, of course, but something."

He put down the interrogation list, picked up his pen, and started writing down the transcript.

Vadim sat opposite him, afraid to move a muscle.

Altman wrote for a long time, looking at the paper where Elsbein, Ershilov, and Sergei Alexeyevich were written down, then at the paper with Lena, Nina, and Max.

Vadim realized that everyone he had named might be called in. Well, so what? He did not feel any pangs of conscience. He had been called in and interrogated, why not them? He hadn't said a single word that wasn't true. He didn't blame anyone, or betray anyone, he told what had happened. And if they were called in, let them do the same. Why should he sacrifice himself — for what? for whom? No, he wouldn't sacrifice himself, and they didn't have to sacrifice themselves — they would tell the truth and nothing would happen to them.

Altman at last stopped writing and handed his pages to Vadim. "Read it; did I write it down accurately?"

Vadim started reading. Everything was accurate, but the picture it created was awful. Elsbein told the joke in the presence of Ershilov, and Vadim told it to his barber, Sergei Alexeyevich. In every conversation Sergei Alexeyevich mentioned Trotsky with obvious sympathy, his words clearly indicating that all accusations against Trotsky were groundless. Nina Ivanova suggested writing a statement in defense of convicted counterrevolutionary Pankratov. The question was discussed in the apartment of Deputy Commissar I. G. Budyagin, discussed by Vadim, Nina Ivanova, Elena Budyagina, and Maxim Kostin. On orders of Deputy Commissar Budyagin, the letter was not sent.

The further Vadim read, the colder he felt. "Sergei Alexeyevich mentioned Trotsky with obvious sympathy." Most likely, Sergei Alexeyevich was an informer (and Vadim wasn't going to worry about him), but still, Vadim couldn't maintain that the barber had mentioned Trotsky with sympathy — it was more like irony. Then the discussion of the "statement" . . . "on orders of Budyagin." It sounded like an organization. It depended on how you interpreted it.

"Well," he heard Altman's quiet and slow voice. "What doesn't suit you there? Don't bother with stylistic and grammatical nuances. They are insubstantial. The essence is substantial."

Vadim was surprised to hear such words from Altman. He had been convinced that Altman wouldn't even know words like that. How had he failed to notice that Altman was an intelligent man?

In the meantime, Altman continued. "Whom are you planning to save? Don't. Each of them will be capable of saving himself, I assure you. And you can save yourself only one way — by signing the statement. Why? Because the statement is correct."

He should have argued. But arguing was useless. He would merely anger Altman. Even if he got a word changed, so what? The important thing was to get out of there.

Feeling Altman watch his hand move, Vadim signed the transcript.

Altman took back the pages, added them to the transcript signed last time, closed the file, put it in the drawer, leaned back in his chair, and looked at Vadim in a completely different way, a friendly way.

"Vadim Andreyevich, do you understand what you have just signed?"

"I signed it."

"Yes, and I appreciate that."

His executioner's look was gone. His hysteria was gone. A calm, intelligent, and friendly man was speaking with Vadim.

"I repeat, I appreciate, a great deal, what you did, just as I appreciate your literary work. I liked your last article about the Chamber Theater. I was surprised that you managed to write it when you were upset, for you had to be upset after meeting me. For some reason people feel that meeting us is dangerous, and that's wrong — meeting us is useful. Your article was good, although certain aspects elicit — I wouldn't say objections, but — how shall I put it? — minor corrections. Not even in content, but in form. But that's not the main point. That's something else — in your place I would disavow that interview with Koonen."

Vadim was stunned. He had never suspected that Altman knew so much about him.

Pleased with the effect he had made, Altman continued. "You have many people who envy you, and they'll attack you: 'Comrade Marasevich writes one thing, yet eighteen months ago he wrote another.' An attack like that can be avoided. You yourself should have recalled the interview and shown that even then, a year and a half ago, the theater had the flaws of which it is being accused now. But you did not do that."

He looked at Vadim again, but strangely now.

"You should have. Because you were praising the theater's productions when its managing director was that old spy and terrorist Pikel. You read the papers, don't you? You do know why Pikel was shot?"

"I didn't even know him," Vadim babbled.

"That would have to be proved, Vadim Andreyevich, and that is difficult. You're a regular at the Chamber Theater, practically a resident. You have a regular reserved seat in the fifth row. And you didn't know the theater's director?"

"But I really —"

"Fine," Altman interrupted. "We won't talk about Pikel, or the theater, or art, otherwise" — and he laughed, a very pleasant laugh — "the argument will sidetrack us. I want you to be very clear about what you have confessed. First — an anti-Soviet joke was told in your presence. Did you come to us, or at least to the Party Committee, and relate what had happened, denounce the anti-Soviet person? No, on the contrary. You started telling the joke yourself. And to whom? Your barber. Only to him? You maintain that you told it only to him. We have no reason to believe you. If you told it to one, you could tell it to someone else. But, at any rate, you heard the joke and we know from whom and we also know to whom you told it. Is that random? Things do happen by accident, you hear something by accident, tell someone by accident — that happens, even though we don't forgive that either. A person must understand what he is doing. But with you, Vadim Andreyevich, this was not accidental at all."

Altman was squinting again as he looked at Vadim, and Vadim's heart was thumping with fear again. Altman's gaze went back to normal and he said, "Why wasn't it accidental? Because, Vadim Andreyevich, you are a secret Trotskyite."

He raised his hand in response to Vadim's outraged movement. "Easy, easy! You met in a group and discussed a letter in defense of an arrested counterrevolutionary. You maintain that you objected to such a letter. Let's say we believe you. But why did you object? Because you shouldn't defend a counterrevolutionary? No, because too much time had elapsed since school. Is that the Soviet approach? No, the Soviet approach dictates a completely different position: 'I do not want to — and will not — defend an arrested counterrevolutionary. I won't even discuss it.' That's the Soviet approach. You did not show it. On the contrary, you participated in the discussion, and you certainly would have signed the letter except that Budyagin forbade it, and you don't even know why he did. You were acting not out of your civic conscience, but on someone's orders. On what basis was your position formed? It is rooted in the circumstances in which you grew up. You grew up in a home where foreigners were like family. Professor Cramer, Rossolini" — his voice showed disdain — "oh, dear. Are you sure of the loyalty of those foreigners to us; can you swear that they come here only because of scientific interests? Can you?"

Vadim was stunned into silence.

"You can't," Altman replied for him. "And you ate at the same table with them, eating and drinking, listening to their conversations, and you never came to us, not once, to say, 'Foreigners are saying the wrong things.' And your sister married one of them, a well-known anti-Soviet. Her husband is not only anti-Soviet, he is a spy, he left just in time, he managed to escape justice. And he didn't leave alone, he took your sister with him — and that, too, is probably no accident. Are they short of beautiful girls in Paris? No. By the way, his French fiancée was from a rich family, and he threw her over for your sister. I'll tell you why — because he wanted to get her out in time. Yes, yes. Her nose wasn't clean, either; he had orders to bring her out too, to save her, and so he did."

He sat in silence, his hands folded on his skinny belly, looking at Vadim with sorrowful eyes.

"Look at the whole picture, Vadim Andreyevich. It's not a pretty one. It looks very bad for you. Just for that joke against Comrade Stalin you should have been put away a long time ago. . . . And besides the joke you have the foreigners, and the defense of arrested counterrevolutionaries. And yet we haven't put you away, Vadim Andreyevich, we have spared you. . . . Why? I'll tell you straight —

we appreciate you as a critic. In your articles you stand for the right things. But are you sincere or are you pretending? Judging by this" — he nodded at the desk drawer — "we could doubt your sincerity; there is enough here for such doubts. And" — he gave Vadim a significant glance and then went on — "you have to prove your sincerity to us. . . . That's the situation, Vadim Andreyevich. What do you think of it?"

Vadim shrugged. "I don't know. . . . It's all so bizarre. . . ."

"You must think through your behavior very thoroughly, Vadim Andreyevich."

"Of course, of course," Vadim muttered. "I will be more careful in the future."

"Well, caution is a good thing," Altman agreed, "but what do we do about this?" He nodded at the drawer again. "What am I going to report to my chief? As soon as they read this file, I will be asked, 'Which cell is that Marasevich in?' And what do I tell them? 'He promised to be more careful' — is that what I say? Then they'll put me in the cell intended for you. And I don't want that, Vadim Andreyevich, I don't want that at all."

He stopped again.

Vadim was afraid to move. He was suffering from heartburn, he needed to take some bicarbonate of soda, he even had some with him, he always did, but he was afraid to ask for water.

"So, Vadim Andreyevich," Altman said in a merry voice, "we have to finish up. I repeat — you have to prove your sincerity. And if you do, then all this" — and he knocked on the desk drawer — "will look like a bizarre coincidence. Do you understand me, Vadim Andreyevich?"

"Yes, yes, of course."

He understood very well what was being demanded of him. And he understood that he would agree to their demands, but he was afraid to say it himself.

"What does 'yes, yes' mean?" Altman said with a frown. "What do you understand?"

"I understand that I must prove my sincerity."

"And how?"

"I don't know . . . I'm ready. But . . . I don't know."

"Well, then, I'll give you a hint," Altman said firmly. "You must help us in the struggle against the enemies of the Party and the state."

"But my articles, my speeches —"

"Your articles and speeches are known to us. But they deal with literature and art, and we want to know about people who work in literature and art, who they are, what they really think, not just what they say in meetings. We want to know what they say offstage. We need a reviewer."

"Please."

Altman took out a piece of paper and handed Vadim a pen. "Write!"

"What?"

"That you are prepared to help us."

"But I will help; why write it?"

"And I am going to report," Altman said, pointing to the ceiling, "that you gave us a verbal promise to help?"

He opened the drawer, took out the file, and tossed it irritably on the desk.

"These are your affairs, nasty affairs, they're written down, but you don't want to write down the good things. . . ." He looked at his watch. "Well, you decide. Nobody's forcing you to do anything. We've been chatting here for the last two hours. As you can guess, I have other things to do."

Altman leaned back, squinted, and a scornful smile appeared on his lips. "Make up your mind."

Vadim dipped the pen in the ink.

"What should I write?"

He asked calmly, even with dignity — now they were interested in him.

Slowly, with pauses, without hurrying but confidently and harshly Altman dictated, " 'I, the undersigned Citizen Marasevich, Vadim Andreyevich, promise to inform the organs of the NKVD about all actions and statements, both verbal and printed, that endanger Soviet rule. Also, on orders of the organs of the NKVD, I will review works of literature and art for them.' Fine. We don't expect you to give us reports with your own signature. You never know — you might lose one, forget it somewhere, and someone will find it . . . we don't want to complicate your life. So you'd better use a pseudonym for these reports. You can use a man's name or a woman's. Would you be offended by a female pseudonym?"

Dammit, Altman was mocking him.

"Better a man's," Vadim replied.

"Fine. . . . Your name is Vadim. How about Vaclav? Does Vaclav suit you?"

"Yes."

"Add — 'The information will be signed Vaclav.' Got it? Now sign it."

# 31

Before breakfast Stalin went into the garden and walked along the paths. The poppies were in bloom, and the gillyflowers looked good against the grass — white, light blue, and dark purple. But a little farther were flowers he didn't recognize, which you could see from the veranda, wrapped in the middle with black paper, as if bandaged. Why was there paper on the flowers? . . . Why black paper? It wasn't a pleasant sight.

Valechka, the housekeeper, brought in his breakfast.

He beckoned with his finger, brought her out on the terrace, and pointed at the flowers.

"What is that?"

Valechka laughed. "Those are gladioli, Josef Vissarionovich. The lower buds open before the tops. But it's better when they bloom at the same time. So the lower ones are wrapped in black paper, to keep them from blooming until the top ones do. We used to do the same back in Zubalovo —"

She shut up in fright, remembering that Vlasik had forbidden her to mention Zubalovo.

Stalin did not reply and gave Valechka an angry look. He returned to the room, did not touch his breakfast, threw on his topcoat, and went to the gate.

Valechka watched him go with tears in her eyes — she felt sorry for Josef Vissarionovich. She had hurt him — accidentally, but she did. How awful, he left without eating, it was so terrible. . . . The devil had pulled her tongue to mention Zubalovo. . . .

*　　*　　*

The car drove down the narrow road leading to the Mozhaiskoe Chaussee. Stalin paid no attention to the colonel sitting next to the driver, did not notice the cars ahead and behind filled with his guards. He looked at the pines to the right, the birches and larches to the left — the entire forest was combed and checked, guarded invisibly, but it was his bodyguards who might send a bullet into the back of his head or between the eyes. Pauker assured him that every bodyguard watched not only the road but his partner, and therefore any "accidents" were out of the question. Nevertheless those grim pines, those birches and larches losing their foliage autumnally, pressing against the road, were unpleasant and made him anxious.

Stalin felt calmer when the car came out onto Mozhaiskoe Chaussee and raced down it to Dorogomilov Street — there were no pines, no birches and larches, with a hidden sniper behind each one. This was the street, the protection well established, the traffic stopped, here fear did its job. . . .

In ancient times when a ruler traveled down a street, his subjects were required to fall facedown and lie there without lifting their heads, to express their alleged servile submission. Of course, that's not what it was for. People were supposed to lie there with their heads down so that there could be no possibility of an assassination. A raised head was immediately chopped off by a guard's sword. Not a bad system. The ancients knew how to protect themselves from the crowd. But not all of them knew how to protect themselves from a palace coup.

Had *he* been right to break *his* promise to save the lives of Zinoviev and Kamenev?

*He* had.

Why was it right?

Because the trial answered the needs of the Party and state, and the confessions of the defendants answered the needs of the Party and state.

To spare the defendants for the crimes to which they confessed would mean shedding doubt on the credibility of their confessions, the credibility of their monstrous crimes.

To spare them would mean that these monstrous crimes were forgivable.

To spare them would mean permitting others to commit these crimes.

To spare them would mean irreparable harm to the Party and the state.

Victor Hugo said that a criminal remains a criminal whether he wears a convict's suit or a monarch's crown. A beautiful but meaningless, typically French, phrase. A criminal acts out of personal motives, a ruler acts out of the interests of the state and therefore cannot be a criminal, because only the ruler can decide what corresponds to the interests of the state and what does not.

Lenin talked a lot about the truth and demanded the truth. Of course, Lenin was a great revolutionary, but a revolutionary brought up, unfortunately, on Western concepts of ethics and morality and therefore not without certain bourgeois prejudices.

"Conscience" was an abstract concept, an empty one. Conscience was a cover-up for thinking differently. "I'm not a politician, I do not have political views, I have only my conscience." A clever and sneaky formulation.

People with a so-called conscience were dangerous people. They considered it right to decide for themselves what was moral and what was immoral, and they extended that right to everything, including politics. Their so-called conscience allowed them to judge the actions of the Party and the state, that is, *his* actions. Their so-called conscience allowed them to have convictions that did not coincide with *his* convictions. That had to be stopped once and for all.

Marx once wrote that people should not be imprisoned for their political or religious beliefs. It was easy for Marx to write that — he didn't have government power. And Marx was not without bourgeois prejudices. If he had been given state power, he would have seen that political views quickly turn to political actions, and a man who thinks differently is a powerful enemy.

Lenin created a Party capable of taking and holding power. But such parties had already existed in history. They took and held power, but they held it for only a period of time.

*He* had created a Party that would hold power forever.

*He* had created a Party of a completely new type, a Party distinguished from the parties of all time, a Party that was not only a symbol of the state, but the sole social power in the state, a Party that made belonging to it not only the chief merit of its members but the content and meaning of their lives. *He* had created the idea of a Party per se, as an absolute that replaced everything — God, ethics, home, family, morality, and the laws of social development.

There had never been such a Party in the history of mankind. A Party like that was the guarantee of a state's inviolability, *his* state.

But if the Party is an absolute, then its leader is also an absolute — the highest embodiment of its ethics and morality.

And whatever *he* does is ethical and moral. There can be no other ethics or morality. Ethics and morality must serve the state, must correspond with the interests of the state, with *his* goals.

Now the main goal was the cadre revolution. In order to destroy enemies present and future, *he* first had to destroy enemies past.

They came out on Borodino Bridge. Stalin liked it. *He* liked the powerful stone bulls on which it rested. *He* liked the obelisks in honor of the Battle of Borodino with their metal memorial plaques. *He* liked the semicircular colonnades with military designs. Powerful, fundamental, beautiful architecture. This was how things should be built and not the way today's formalist architects built things — clumsy boxes expressing nothing.

They went up onto Smolensk Square and came out onto the Arbat.

So, the first phase was over, the first trial ended, the defendants shot.

What were the results of this trial? It certainly justified itself. They were done forever with Zinoviev and Kamenev, physically and politically. That was the first result.

Second, at the trial Pyatakov, Radek, Sokolnikov, Serebryakov, and other Trotskyites were named. They were already arrested and the investigation of the United Center, to which they belonged, was under way. But charging them with terrorism was not enough. After all, terror is a form of struggle. Marxists officially did not recognize terrorism, not because it was allegedly immoral but because it was not effective. The Socialist Revolutionaries, for instance, considered it effective and used it. And the People's Will used it. Individual terrorism had old and deep roots in the Russian revolutionary movement. If they stressed it too much, it might take root in the consciousness of young people. Imitators would spring up. That could not be allowed. Therefore, the members of the United Center had to be accused of other, no less serious, charges.

Third, Bukharin, Rykov, Tomsky, Uglanov, and other right-wingers were also named, and the basis for a trial was established. And when Tomsky shot himself after the trial, he merely confirmed the seriousness of the charges made against him and, consequently, against all the Bukharinites.

Fourth, military men were named and arrested — Commanders Putna, Primakov, and Shmidt — creating the basis for liquidating the military conspirators headed by Tukhachevsky.

These were the positive results of the trial. But there were negative lessons, too. The most negative was its poor preparation. It had not been well planned or considered. The details were sloppy, allowing that scoundrel Trotsky to organize a rebuttal campaign in the bourgeois press.

Of course, that was to be expected, but the mistake with Goltsman was outrageous. Exactly a week after the defendants were shot, a Danish newspaper published the fact that the Bristol Hotel, where Goltsman stated he had met with Sedov and then gone on to see Lev Davydovich Trotsky, had been torn down back in 1917, and there was no other Bristol Hotel in Copenhagen.

This was a major mistake. It had been created by Yagoda to discredit the trial.

Yes, *he* had given them the idea of a meeting between Goltsman and Trotsky, but why did they choose a nonexistent hotel? Why did they have a hotel at all? Goltsman could have said that they met at the train station.

It was so clear, so simple. No, they had to have a hotel, a nonexistent hotel at that. There would be no more mistakes like that. There would be no more Yagoda.

Yagoda sat before Stalin, trying to explain the mistake with the Bristol — one of the men had mixed up the lists of hotels in Oslo and in Copenhagen; there *was* a Bristol in Oslo. The man had been severely punished.

"How?" Stalin asked.

"Reduced in rank and transferred to work in the camp directorate."

Stalin gave him a heavy look. "It was an act of sabotage, meant to discredit the trial. The guilty man should be court-martialed. And the ones who urged him to do it should also be turned over to the Military Tribunal."

"Yes, sir," Yagoda replied. "But the man — his name is Dyakov —"

"I am not interested in the names of saboteurs ruining the assignments of the Party," Stalin interrupted.

"Yes, sir." Yagoda's lips were twitching nervously. "But this man ... he made the mistake alone."

"Alone." Stalin regarded Yagoda. He was saving his people, sparing them. "All right, let him bear the responsibility for everyone else."

He paused and then asked, "Where are the Trotskyites who did not give evidence?"

"For now, here in Moscow."

"Interrogate them all again and turn over the ones who still refuse to the Military Tribunal as terrorists. The decisions of the tribunal are not to be made public. As for active Trotskyites who did not capitulate at all, they must not take up space in the camps anymore. They do not belong on Soviet soil, not in the camps, not in the prisons, not in exile. The Soviet people must be freed of them."

"Yes, sir." Yagoda's lips were still twitching.

"These people are enemies of the Party, enemies of the Soviet state forever. Smirnov's behavior in court proved beyond any doubt that he came to the trial in order to compromise it. Let his allies pay for it. Enough! We've been fussing with them for ten years. Our state has more important things to do than feed sworn enemies of the Soviet power."

"Yes, sir."

Stalin chuckled. Yagoda was afraid of taking the responsibility, afraid to do it without documents, statements, confessions, without the usual formalities.

"Send them to camps and have the local directors carry out the sentences."

Stalin's stare drilled into Yagoda. Yagoda was hoping that they would prepare documents of justification there. No, that wouldn't happen.

"No interrogations, no charges are to be made," Stalin said. "Let the camp directors make up lists of cadre Trotskyites who are continuing their counterrevolutionary activity, their counterrevolutionary conspiracies, and their anti-Soviet statements. And then carry out the sentence according to those lists. And carry them out immediately."

"Yes, sir," Yagoda repeated obediently.

"And the last thing," Stalin said, never taking his eyes from Yagoda. "The members of the United Center must admit not only their terrorism with the aim of taking over power, but their intention to restore capitalism in the Soviet Union with the aid of Nazi Germany and militarist Japan, of course, in exchange for major territorial concessions. For instance, the Ukraine to Germany, and the Far East to Japan. . . ."

After a pause, he asked, "Have you understood your task?"

"Of course," Yagoda replied hurriedly.

"I hope you will manage with it?"

"Without a doubt," Yagoda said in an unexpectedly firm voice. His lips were no longer twitching. The slightest manifestation of uncertainty would be noticed and Stalin would lose confidence in him.

As soon as Yagoda left, Stalin had Pauker and Vlasik come in. They had been waiting out in the reception room for a long time. Stalin told them that he was leaving for Sochi in two hours from the Kursk Station.

No one, not Pauker, not Vlasik, ever knew when and from what station Stalin planned to leave Moscow. He always announced it at the last moment. That was the way it was done, and that's why *his* train in Moscow and *his* ship in Gorky had been standing ready for the last two weeks.

This time the ship would not be necessary. Stalin said that he would go to Sochi directly from Moscow and not through Gorky and Stalingrad, as he sometimes did.

Most of the Politburo members were on vacation. But Yezhov stayed in Moscow, in charge of the preparations for the trial of the United Center, openly interfering with Yagoda's work.

It was clear that Yezhov was getting involved in his work not simply as Secretary of the Central Committee, but on Stalin's special orders. Yagoda had obviously lost Stalin's trust, and that explained Yezhov's crudeness, haughtiness, and shameless behavior.

Yagoda understood what it meant to lose Stalin's trust in general and for himself in particular. He knew too much. Witnesses who are not trusted do not live.

That was so, but Genrikh Yagoda had learned much at Stalin's side. He knew the distribution of power in the Politburo.

By late August the Politburo members began returning from vacation. Everyone was back except Stalin, Zhdanov, and Mikoyan. And Yagoda immediately posed the question of a trial of Bukharin and Rykov since they were candidate members of the Central Committee.

Yagoda's move was the right one. Only Kaganovich, Voroshilov, and Molotov voted for trying Bukharin and Rykov.

On September 10, *Pravda* published an article saying that the investigation of Rykov and Bukharin had ended because of lack of evidence of criminal activity.

But that move did not save Yagoda. On the contrary, it merely hastened his fall.

On September 25, 1936, a telegram signed by Stalin and Zhdanov came to the Politburo in Moscow from Sochi. "We consider it absolutely necessary and urgent for Comrade Yezhov to be appointed people's commissar of internal affairs. Yagoda has definitely shown himself to be clearly incapable of exposing the Trotskyites-Zinovievite bloc. OGPU is four years behind on this case. This has been noticed by all Party workers and the majority of representatives of the NKVD."

Those last words meant that, except for Yagoda, the leaders of the NKVD were to stay on.

In a few days Yezhov was appointed people's commissar of internal affairs, and Yagoda was appointed people's commissar of communications. Rykov, who had held that post, was relieved without an indication of another position.

There were no other changes in the NKVD except that Yagoda's deputy, Prokofiev, was transferred to the Commissariat of Water

Transport, and Yezhov was given two more deputies, Marvei Berman, former head of the GULAG, and Mikhail Frinovsky, former commander of the border troops. The other workers remained in place, even Yagoda's personal secretary, Bulanov. Yezhov, of course, brought a few people with him from the Central Committee, but they were appointed assistants to the former heads of sections — Molchanov, Mironov, Slutsky, Pauker, and others.

Moreover, Stalin expressed his trust of the old leaders of the NKVD, inviting them on December 20 to a small banquet to celebrate the anniversary of the founding of the Cheka — OGPU — NKVD.

The atmosphere of the banquet was warm, friendly, and trusting. Stalin did not allow any conversation about the preparation for the United Center trial.

"Enjoy yourselves, friends," Stalin said.

And the friends did enjoy themselves. They drank vodka, ate special herring, salted the German way, which was obtained by the tireless Pauker, head of the Operatives Section, head of Stalin's personal bodyguard, even his personal barber. To put your throat under someone's razor — what could show higher trust? Before the war Pauker had been a barber at the Budapest Operetta Theater and bragged that the greatest operetta stars of Budapest found talent in him and had suggested he go on the stage.

He was a first-rate comedian, he could imitate anyone, he told jokes masterfully, especially Jewish jokes and dirty jokes. A jester by nature, he could make even the grim Stalin laugh.

This time Pauker imitated Zinoviev being led away to be shot.

Supported by Frinovsky and Berman, who played the guards, Pauker helplessly hung from their shoulders, whimpering, and rolling his eyes in fear. When they reached the middle of the room, Pauker fell on his knees, grabbed Frinovsky's boot and pressed his face to it, howling, "Comrade.... For God's sake.... Comrade.... Call Josef Vissarionovich.... Comrade...."

Everyone laughed.

Stalin chuckled.

Pauker repeated the performance, but this time he was Kamenev. He did not fall on his knees, but on the contrary, he straightened, stuck out his belly, raised his arms to the ceiling, and, imitating

Kamenev's intelligent voice, piteously said, "Hear me, O Lord!"

Everyone laughed except, as Stalin noted, Mironov and Molchanov. They didn't like it. And they couldn't hide it, just as they couldn't hide their joy when, in *his* office, they heard *his* promise not to shoot the defendants. They pitied them. Ah, that naïve Russian pity.... Give a Russian supreme power, and he'd lose that power with his naïveté.

But Pauker, that vile clown, overdid it. Politics was not a circus; tragedy should not be turned into farce. A lackey should know his place. That pig's real place was on the gallows. Pauker would just as easily depict *him* that way. Cheap sell-out!

Stalin raised his shot glass and said, addressing Mironov and Molchanov, "Your health, Comrade Mironov, your health, Comrade Molchanov. Let's drink to the health of Comrades Molchanov and Mironov and to all real Chekists who understand and perform seriously the tasks set before them."

Without lowering his glass, he looked at everyone sitting at the table. But not at Pauker, Berman, and Frinovsky, who were still standing in the middle of the room.

*Almost all the workers of the NKVD who prepared this and the following trials were destroyed.*

*People's Commissar of Internal Affairs of the U.S.S.R. Yagoda was shot in March 1938.*

*First Deputy Commissar Agranov, in 1937.*

*Deputy Prokofiev in 1937, and Deputies Berman and Frinovsky in 1939.*

*Chiefs of the sections of the Main Directorate of the State Security of the NKVD U.S.S.R. Molchanov, Mironov, Pauker, Shanin, and Gai were shot in 1937. Slutsky committed suicide in 1938. Chertok, when they came for him, threw himself out the window of his office.*

*Many of the investigators were destroyed with their section heads.*

*Between 1937 and 1939, around twenty thousand Chekists were killed or sentenced to long terms at hard labor.*

## ❧ 32 ❧

Sasha waited for the winter post with as much impatience as he had waited for his first mail here over two years ago.

The last newspaper he had read was the issue of *Pravda* with the prosecutor's summary in the Zinoviev-Kamenev trial. He was shocked by it then, unable to believe those terrible accusations.

Now Sasha received the newspapers from late August, September, and October, with all the materials and transcripts of the trial.

The defendants confessed to killing Kirov, that they had also planned to kill Stalin and the more famous leaders of the Party and state, that they were acting under the direct orders of Trotsky. The trial had been open but quick; it took just a few days, and there had been no defense attorneys. The defendants had readily talked about their horrible deeds, and their testimony resembled one another's like drops of water.

Sasha just couldn't accept it. Old Communists, the Bolshevik guard, comrades in arms of Lenin, heroes of October, the legendary commanders of the Civil War, people who had given up their lives to the Party had become killers, saboteurs, and spies. Members of Lenin's Politburo, people who had prepared and won the October Revolution, now threw glass into the workers' food, ruined machines, and were in the employ of foreign spies. If you were to accept this as the truth, then you had to stop believing in the Party. If the Party could have been led for decades by criminals, then what was that Party worth?

They admitted it themselves? Sasha didn't believe that. Monotonous confessions that sounded as if they had been memorized from the same crib sheet could not have been sincere. They were not confessing. Someone was playing their parts. They had made up actors to resemble Zinoviev and Kamenev, Smirnov and Mrachkovsky. Mrachkovsky, who had been born in a tsarist labor camp, a hero of the Civil War, he was supposed to be a Japanese and German spy, a killer and poisoner, and he was supposed to tell about it himself with pleasure? No, Sasha couldn't accept it. Actors! Or hypnosis! Drugs! Perhaps they had been tortured. No, you couldn't torture these people into admitting they were spies and killers. This was the show that Zvyaguro had warned him about.

But Stalin had to know that it was a sham. Without Stalin's approval, they wouldn't have dared put on a show like that. Lidya Grigoryevna Zvyaguro had been right — he would destroy the Party, destroy it morally and physically. That disgusting trial, that illegal trial put an end to Sasha's doubts. Stalin said one thing and did another. He said he was for the people, but actually he had terrified them. Fear and violence were the only weapons of his power. And if Sasha could not stop the violence, he didn't have to give in to the fear. That was the only way to remain a man.

But apparently, Stalin's methods didn't always work. The behavior of Ivan Nikitich Smirnov in court was evidence of that.

On the very first day of the trial, August 19, Ivan Nikitich categorically rejected Mrachkovsky's evidence that Smirnov had passed Trotsky's directive on terrorism to the Moscow center.

On the second day, August 20, according to the papers, "during almost three hours of questioning Smirnov tried to avoid the question posed directly by the procurator of the U.S.S.R., Comrade Vyshinsky, trying to diminish his role, denying his terrorist activity against the leaders of the Party and the state."

Two days after that, on August 22, the newspapers wrote that Smirnov was "trying again to avoid responsibility for the work of the Trotskyite-Zinovievite Center."

VYSHINSKY: When did you leave the center?
SMIRNOV: I didn't plan to leave it, there was nothing to leave.
VYSHINSKY: Did the center exist?

SMIRNOV: What center...?
VYSHINSKY: Mrachkovsky, did the center exist?
MRACHKOVSKY: Yes.
VYSHINSKY: Zinoviev, did the center exist?
ZINOVIEV: Yes.
VYSHINSKY: Evdokimov, did the center exist?
EVDOKIMOV: Yes.
VYSHINSKY: Bakayev, did the center exist?
BAKAYEV: Yes.
VYSHINSKY: Then how can you, Smirnov, maintain that there was no center?

Smirnov was the only one who behaved courageously to the very end and on August 23, in his final words, according to the newspapers, "as he had in the preliminary investigation and the court continued to deny his responsibility for the crimes committed by the Trotskyite-Zinovievite terrorist center after his arrest."

So, they hadn't broken everyone. So, it wasn't a show. Then what was it? How had they broken the others?

But what astonished Sasha even more were the reactions. Collectives of factories and plants, institutes and commissariats — that was to be expected, they were part of the herd. Even three days before the trial, the newspapers were full of resolutions of workers' meetings:

"No mercy for enemies of the people!" "Put an end to sworn enemies!" and other such demands.

But the reactions of famous writers, actors, scholars! That was truly horrifying.

On August 15, four days before the trial, when the procurator's office had announced the discovery of the conspiracy, the famous writer Stavsky wrote: "Villains and monsters, may your names be damned and scorned for the centuries!"

On August 20, the Soviet writers were out in full force.

Anna Karavaeva: "The hearts of millions of people are trembling, making fists with furious hatred for the villains of the Trotskyite-Zinovievite bloc."

Vladimir Bakhmetyev: "Unto generations, the vipers keeping

warm in the back alleys of perishing imperialism will be recalled with uncooling anger and scorn."

Nikolai Ognyov: "The sentence of the Supreme Court will be the sentence of all the Soviet people. This sentence will be harsh and just."

August 21.

Alexei Tolstoy: "The treachery being judged now not only by the Soviet courts but by the entire international proletariat is the most vile and base of all treacheries known to history."

August 25.

Vs. Vishnevsky: "The Presidium of the Union of Soviet Writers hotly welcomes the decision of the proletarian court on the execution of the Trotskyite-Zinovievite agents of Fascism, terrorists and saboteurs. . . .

"The events . . . raise the question of the radical check of the composition of the Union of Soviet Writers. You must know with whom you are dealing. We must know all 3,000 members of our Writers' Union. We will have to study thoroughly all the links of our union and its apparat."

The more Sasha read their demands, the more confused he felt. These were writers! Writers! The conscience of the people! In Russia, writers were always the conscience of the people — Pushkin, Tolstoy, Dostoyevsky, Chekhov. . . .

So the writers believed! So they knew that it was the truth, that the defendants really had been killers and spies. . . .

Perhaps it really was true?

Even their former allies in the opposition were attacking them in the newspapers: Rakovsky, Pyatakov, Radek. After all, they had just recently been leading Trotskyites, his faithful friends and followers. They knew that if innocent people were tried today for having once been in the opposition, then they themselves could be tried tomorrow — they had been in the opposition, too. And if they confirmed fabrications, then tomorrow new fabrications could be directed against them. No! They couldn't support lies. . . . Then, was it all true? Were Zinoviev and Kamenev, Smirnov and Mrachkovsky really killers and spies?

Even the hero of October, Antonov-Ovseyenko, also a former Trotskyite, wrote in *Izvestia,* on August 24: "They are not only double-dealers, craven vipers of treachery, they are the diversionary troops of Fascism."

And what about scholars and scientists?

"Destroy ruthlessly these enemies of the Soviet land!" demanded academicians Bakh and Keller.

"Our love for the Party and Stalin is unbounded," wrote professors Luira, Vishnevsk, Shereshevsk, Gotlieb, Margulis, Gorinevskas, Vovsi, and others.

And what about cultural figures?

The director Ptushko: "We must increase Bolshevik vigilance, protect the achievements of the Revolution from the Trotskyite-Zinovievite traitors of the homeland."

People's Artist of the Republic M. Klimov: "Three days ago *Izvestia* published a poem by tenth-grader Iva Nerubino. It addressed the Trotskyite-Zinovievite terrorists — 'There is only one trial for you — to shoot you like dogs!'

"I am an old man, a People's Artist, and I wholly endorse those words spoken by a teenager."

The poem horrified Sasha — a child was demanding people be shot like dogs. And why should dogs be shot? Children loved animals. Or didn't they anymore?

What was going on? What was happening? Where was the truth?

Usually Sasha would skim all the mail, the newspapers, and then read everything thoroughly. This time he couldn't tear himself away from the newspapers. He reread the accounts of the trial and the reactions several times, trying to understand the words. He knew that his fate was involved, too. Now he understood both Vsevolod Sergeyevich and Lidya Grigoryevna — black times were coming and they would begin with a show.

After the execution of Zinoviev and Kamenev, the newspaper hysteria ended immediately. On September 10, the statement of the procurator's office was published. "Investigation has not substantiated legal data for bringing N. I. Bukharin and A. N. Rykov to criminal responsibility...." The people's commissar of internal affairs was removed from his post and replaced. Stalin had to retreat. The Party turned out to be stronger than Stalin. The Party cadres were still able to withstand Stalin, to limit him, to stop his terrorist policies.

But the most important thing was the draft of the new constitution. It was hard to believe. It introduced equal and direct suffrage with secret ballots. It guaranteed total democratic rights and freedoms for the citizens of the U.S.S.R. — equality regardless of sex, nationality, or property status. They were guaranteeing freedom of speech, press, conscience, gathering and meetings, parades and demonstrations, associating in social organizations.

All that meant a turn toward freedom, democracy, and legality. Trials like the one in August were now impossible and would never be repeated. The end of illegality! Even Stalin said, "We need the stability of laws now more than ever...."

The Soviet Union had become a mighty country if it could pass such a constitution! The Soviet government had announced that it did not consider itself tied by the treaty on nonintervention in Spanish affairs, which meant that we would help Republican Spain, do our international duty, fight Fascism. There was information on volunteers going to Spain to defend the republic. If Sasha were freed — and now, how could they not free him? — he would sign up to fight in Spain, where the Communists were fighting the Fascists, where the Communist Fifth Regiment had held Madrid.

Hope for freedom beat in his chest. If he could only last until January! Now Sasha was protected by the law. The constitution, a new revolutionary upsurge. No one would dare add to his sentence; they were obliged to release him. He would go see Alferov and demand release. A delay of even one day would be a crude violation of the law and the guilty parties would be punished severely. The law was the law. It applied to everyone, and no one had the right to keep a man in exile even one extra day.

And in anticipation of that day, Sasha became anxious, even began bustling preparations. If they released him — and they had to release him — would he have enough money for the trip? They had to get him to Taishet, but then? A ticket to Moscow was fifty rubles, no less, and he had to eat along the way. He had to have enough. Even though he told her not to, his mother sent him twenty rubles every month. He earned his room and board by his labor, and he went fishing, did mowing. He spent money only on smokes and kerosene. Now he would start economizing.

And at last the long-awaited day arrived.

Sasha packed the night before — anything could happen. They could arrest him immediately. They could order him to proceed immediately to Krasnoyarsk. Constitutions and laws were fine, but the NKVD had its own laws.

That night Sasha had trouble falling asleep, planning his conversation with Alferov. Sasha went over it, imagining possible complications, sensing the unexpected.

He had waited three years for the hour of his freedom — would it come? What if Alferov was not in Kezhma, what if he'd gone to Krasnoyarsk? He went there for several weeks at a time. He also traveled around the region. The region was enormous and the only transportation was a sled in winter and a boat in summer. And if Alferov wasn't there, there was no one else to talk to. He'd have to wait for his return, suffering and worrying.

Sasha left home before light, at seven in the morning. Twelve kilometers took three hours of walking. He'd be at Alferov's by ten.

It hadn't snowed for several days and the road was packed hard. The snow lay in heavy pillows on the fir branches. The very air seemed frozen, yet bluetits fluttered from tree to tree, and somewhere far off a woodpecker pounded at a tree trunk, red-breasted bullfinches sang from the treetops, and long-beaked birds fussed in the branches of the cedars. These infrequent sounds of the forest emphasized its silence.

Sometimes on the left Sasha could see the smooth whiteness of the Angara, which would disappear behind the trees. It was about −30 degrees Celsius. Sasha was wearing warm underwear, a sweater, felt boots, a coat, and a fur hat with lowered ear flaps and a piece of cloth that was sewn on the back to keep snow from falling behind the collar. He didn't have a hood. He carried a stout stick, which made it more fun to walk and could come in handy to chase away a wolf.

As Sasha had figured, he arrived in Kezhma at ten and approached Alferov's house. A light flickered behind the frosted window. It came from a lamp or the stove. . . . There were tracks by the porch, someone was home. Sasha used the metal knocker on the gate — no response, not even a barking dog. Alferov must be sleeping. But he couldn't wait. The cold was getting under his coat and his toes were cold. If he stood still, he'd freeze. Sasha knocked on the window where there was a light. He knocked again. He thought he saw a shadow move across the kitchen, float and stop by the window, trying to see who was knocking. The shadow moved away and time passed. The landlady must have been putting on warm clothes. The door on the porch creaked, there were steps in the snow, the latch clicked, and the gate opened. The landlady stood before Sasha in felt boots, fur coat, and scarf.

"Who do you want?"

"Comrade Alferov."

"You're early, he's asleep."

"I came from Mozgova."

"Come in then, you can wait."

Sasha followed her into the entry. Like her, he took off his boots, and she showed him slippers in the corner, which he put on and went to the kitchen.

"Take off your coat and sit down, it's warm in here," she said.

Sasha hung up his coat and looked around.

He liked his own landlady's kitchen in the morning, when the stove was still warm from the night before, and there was a fire on the range, heating up breakfast, and a pile of wood brought in from the shed gave off cold and birchbark smells.

The landlady put a bowl of pickled berries and a piece of fish pie on the table and poured him a glass of tea.

"Eat, have some tea, warm yourself."

"Thank you."

Sasha held the glass in both hands, warming his stiffened fingers, and sipped the tea.

A door slammed in the house and he heard the cough of a smoker.

"Viktor Gerasimovich is up. He has his own sink, where he washes and shaves," the landlady said, as if to reassure Sasha that Alferov wouldn't come out to the kitchen. "He has his own entrance."

The door slammed again. Alferov was back from the yard. He stamped his boots, shaking off the snow. Then the tap was turned on and water splashed into a basin.

This was a signal for the landlady, who brought a samovar, bowls of berries, and the fish pie to the dining room, then came back and put out a frying pan, broke eggs, and started frying them.

They could hear Alferov come into the dining room, push back a chair, sit down, and pour tea. The landlady picked up the frying pan and took the eggs to the dining room.

"Good morning, Viktor Gerasimovich, how did you sleep, nothing bothered you?"

"Thank you, I slept well," Alferov replied.

"Someone waiting for you, Viktor Gerasimovich."

"Who?"

"A man, Viktor Gerasimovich."

"Where is he?"

"In the kitchen. It's so cold outside, I let him in to warm up. He came from Mozgova."

The chair was pushed back. Alferov stood in the doorway, looking at Sasha. "You? Why did you come?"

Sasha stood. "Yesterday my term ended —"

"Oh," Alferov said, not letting him finish. "Come in here."

Sasha followed Alferov into the dining room, sat down at the place indicated, opposite Alferov.

"Will you have tea?" Alferov asked.

His face was puffy — either from sleep or the vodka he'd had the night before. Since the last time Sasha had seen him, he looked tougher and grimmer. He was wearing trousers tucked into his boots and a sheepskin vest over his shirt.

"Thanks, your landlady gave me tea already."

"She's very hospitable. One day they'll come to kill me, and she'll feed them first. 'Took in, fed, and warmed an orphan' — do you remember that Christmas tale?"

"I do."

"Yes. How did it go? 'The stars were sparkling, it was cold, a tiny tot came down the street, blue with cold.' And an old lady took him in, saved him from freezing in the street. Did you walk?"

"Yes."

Alferov dug into his eggs. "That story used to make me cry when my nanny read it to me. I felt so sorry for the orphan. And then I forgot it. Hadn't thought of it until today. And now I did."

"Looking at me?"

"Perhaps."

"So you felt sorry for me," Sasha said with a laugh.

"It's possible. I just went to the outhouse, excuse me, I almost froze my ass, and even though we have a good outhouse, it's in the shed, there's no draft, and you've just walked twelve kilometers. And so I expressed my sympathy to you in verse. You like literature, I believe?"

"Yes, I like to read, when there is something to read."

"It's tough here," Alferov agreed. "The teacher used to give you books, and now she's gone. Why don't you make friends with the new one? She's also young and pretty."

Sasha looked grim — it was a tactless question.

"You don't like her, then." Alferov laughed. "There, you see how free and easy you live, Pankratov? For a prisoner, for thousands of prisoners, for hundreds of thousands of prisoners" — he paused to let this number sink in — "for these prisoners women are completely off limits. And if one of them is lucky enough to find a woman, he isn't picky. Any woman at all. But you, you need one not only with an education, but one who ranks high in every category. That's how free and easy you live."

Sasha was annoyed by Alferov's chattiness. This wasn't the time for it, now, when Sasha's life was being decided. Alferov wasn't gabbing for nothing; there was a reason behind it. And he had brought up the new teacher for a reason. He must know that Sasha had been given a new term, but he wanted to amuse himself, play on Sasha's nerves.

Sasha lowered his head.

Dreariness, gloom. No, he couldn't take any more living in Mozgova, in that horrible loneliness. The hell with that kind of life! His mother? Well, what about her? She'd get used to it eventually. Children die in infancy, too.

"What should a man do with this free-and-easy life," Alferov

went on, "especially a man interested in historical science? Eh??
Especially when there's nothing to read."

Without waiting for Sasha's answer, he said, "Write. Eh? Am I
right?"

Of course. Alferov had read the stories Sasha had sent to his
mother. What a bastard, he didn't have to mention it.

"I write, too," Alferov continued, "not history, of course, but
philosophy. I can show off a bit," he said. He went to his study and
came back with a bundle of printed pages. "See, the galleys of my
new book, which I wrote here in Kezhma. *The Sources of the
Philosophy of Descartes*. Have you read Descartes? No? A curious
philosopher, trying to combine God with the reality of the world.
You're not interested in philosophy? Too bad. An historian has to
be a philosopher and vice versa."

He paused, thought, and then chuckled. "I can guess your
thoughts — That son-of-a-bitch Alferov read my works! He put his
filthy paws into my creative soul! I confess, yes, I read them, yes, I
did. That's my job. Don't worry. Your words went where you sent
them. But I am your first reader and first critic. Would you like to
know my opinion?"

Torture! Discussion instead of learning his fate. But he had to get
hold of himself. If he got nervous now, he'd show Alferov his
uncertainty about being released, and he must not show that. He
was a free man as of today, and that's all! And the rest could go to
hell!

Without great eagerness he replied, "I'd like to hear."

"From the point of view of form, your works are helpless, naïve,
even primitive. All those lofty phrases, all those adjectives and
beauty."

Alferov poured himself more tea. He offered some to Sasha, but
Sasha refused.

"I'll continue. The great French Revolution is one of the most
dramatic and edifying — I stress that, edifying — moments in
human history. And you write about individual people, individual
episodes. For whom? For children, teenagers, adults? It's not clear.
What conclusion are they supposed to draw from what they've
read? And then" — he stared at Sasha — "aren't you afraid that the
editor will look for parallels?"

"What parallels?"

"They had a revolution, we had a revolution. How did their revolution end? With the Thermidor, the single and personal power of Napoleon, the empire . . ."

"But that revolution was a bourgeois one, and ours was a proletarian one."

"Yes, yes, of course." Alferov broke off the conversation. "Well, maybe, you'll be published, if everything's all right with you. As you know, we don't publish prisoners. So I wish you luck, even though I have my doubts."

He stopped, wiped his mouth with a towel, lit a cigarette, and offered Sasha the box.

"I'm used to my own."

Squinting, Alferov watched Sasha light his hand-rolled cigarette, put out the match in the ashtray that Alferov had moved over to him. Was he afraid that Sasha would throw the match on the floor?

"Comrade Alferov," Sasha said. "My term of exile ended yesterday."

Alferov looked surprised. "Really?"

"Yes," Sasha repeated, "and I already told you that. I was sentenced to three years taking into account my preliminary incarceration. Therefore, as of today I am free. I'm asking for my documents."

"What documents do you have in mind?"

"The ones that should be given in these cases. You must know."

"Well, I'll give them to you and then what do you do with them?"

"I'll leave here."

"Where to?"

"Home."

"You're not allowed to go to Moscow."

"Why not?"

"You fall under the resolution of the Council of People's Commissars of the U.S.S.R. on the passport system. There are cities in which you are not allowed to live. Moscow is one of them."

"But that resolution came out before the new constitution."

"The new constitution," Alferov countered, "does not replace the laws and directives of Soviet power. Some laws, rather regulations, will be changed, reexamined, but the laws protecting the dictatorship of the proletariat will remain in force. Have you read Comrade Stalin's speech on the constitution?"

"Yes."

"Comrade Stalin says clearly, 'The draft of the new constitution leaves in force the regime of the dictatorship of the working class.' What more do you want? And by the way, have you noticed, the constitution has no paragraph on freedom of movement, as it is usually formulated in bourgeois constitutions, that is, the freedom to choose where you live, the freedom to settle wherever you want. We will not allow tramps and hoboes. The limitations of the passport system have not been rescinded yet, and I doubt that they will be."

Turning away from Sasha and looking out the window, he added significantly, "On the contrary, I think they will be increased."

"Be that as it may," Sasha said, "there is a law — a man cannot be held in prison even a single day longer than his sentence. No one has done away with that law."

"And where did you see that law?"

"I read it," Sasha lied.

"That's not true, you couldn't have read it, there is no such law. There is logic — if a prisoner's term has ended, and he is not released, then he is being kept in prison without any basis for it, that is, something illegal is being done."

"Well, so let me go."

"I'm not keeping you."

"But I can't leave without documents."

"Your documents are in the Krasnoyarsk Krai Directorate of the NKVD. The distances are vast here, and there are plenty of exiles in this territory. They haven't managed to get your documents here today, they'll come in good time, wait. If you don't want to wait, please, I'll give you permission to travel to Krasnoyarsk. There you'll have to go to the Directorate of the NKVD and demand your documents. What document they'll give you, I don't know."

There was a threat in those words — the document might be a confirmation that he had finished his term, or it might be a new sentence.

Sasha was silent.

"So you choose," Alferov said. "Will you wait here for the documents or go for them in Krasnoyarsk?"

Sasha thought and then said, "I have to get my release today. If I don't get it, I'll send a telegram to Comrade Kalinin."

Alferov laughed. "And they'll put it right on Kalinin's desk?"

"I don't know. But someone will respond to the telegram."

Alferov narrowed his eyes again. "Did you get an answer to your letter to Comrade Stalin?"

So. The letter to Stalin was probably in his desk. That's why he was laughing.

"Did you do the right thing sending a letter to Comrade Stalin?"

"Don't I have the right to appeal to him?"

"Of course you do. Everyone appeals to Comrade Stalin, you read the papers, you know. They report on their achievements, thank him for help in their work, thank him for his leadership. Naturally, prisoners appeal to him, too, quite a few of them. You appealed to him, you sat through half your term without complaint, and suddenly — 'I'm here unfairly, let me out!' Had new circumstances appeared in your case? No, there was nothing new. And you see, you didn't even get an answer. To get an answer you must have a basis for a reexamination of your case, and there isn't any."

"Well, if there isn't, there isn't," Sasha said. "But a man has the right to hope. You can't take that away from him."

Alferov moved aside his tea glass, put his elbows on the table, and looked at Sasha seriously.

"You're right, a man has the right to hope. But a man must think about his actions. That is his responsibility. Did you seriously think that your letter would reach Comrade Stalin? That your case would be reexamined? No, you didn't think that and you didn't hope for that. You are too smart for that. It was an unconsidered action. In writing that letter to Comrade Stalin, you reminded them of yourself, of your existence, reminded whoever at the NKVD received your letter. Moreover, you accused the NKVD of condemning you unjustly. Do you need that?"

Sasha was silent. Who was this man? Friend? Foe? He was saying outright — you shouldn't have written to Stalin, you shouldn't have irritated the organs, you shouldn't have attracted their attention. Yet Sasha had known that all along. And still wrote the letter.

"Maybe I shouldn't have written," Sasha said, "but I wrote it, wrote it a long time ago, and there's no point in discussing it now. But as of today it is illegal to keep me in exile. And surely I have the right to complain about that. I don't know when my documents will reach you; they might never come."

"And you'll be better off out there?"

"Freedom is always better than prison."

"You are right. Freedom is better than prison."

Alferov stood up and walked around the room. Like last time, he went over to the chest, picked up the carafe with liqueur, but this time he didn't pour himself a drink. He picked up two shot glasses and put them all on the table.

"Well then, Alexander Pavlovich, last time you didn't want to drink with me, but this time I hope you won't refuse. Then you were an exile and I was your gendarme. This time, as you maintain, you are a free man, that means you can drink, and moreover, you must mark the occasion."

He poured two glasses, raised his, nodded to Sasha, and drank. Sasha drank his. The liqueur was bitter but tasty.

"So," Sasha said. "I have nowhere to go. Waiting here for my documents is useless. I can't do it and I don't want to do it. Give me a pass to Krasnoyarsk, and I'll seek truth and justice there."

"You didn't find it from me, so you'll seek it there." Alferov chuckled and nodded toward the carafe. "Did you like it?"

"It's tasty."

"Have another?"

"Why not?"

Alferov drank, wiped his lips, and waited for Sasha to finish.

"Have you thought about this? You go to Krasnoyarsk along the winter road, but I don't have horses for such trips, you have to get there on your own, it'll be expensive. Let's say you get there. You show up at the NKVD and they say, 'What are you doing here, your documents have been sent to Kezhma, go back and get them from Comrade Alferov.' Eh? Would you like that turn of events?"

Sasha moved the glass and looked at Alferov angrily. Enough! He was tired of being Alferov's morning game!

"Citizen Alferov!"

But Alferov interrupted. "Why so official? We've drunk together. Call me Viktor Gerasimovich."

But Sasha was angry and he repeated, "Citizen Alferov! Excuse me, Citizen Alferov! This is a useless and humiliating conversation. I am officially asking you to give me a document stating that my term is over or give me a written refusal with an indication of your reasons."

"Yes," Alferov said musingly, "you didn't understand me.... Too bad. . . . Well, one day, you will."

He went to the other room, which served as his study, sat down, and wrote for a long time, then looked into a file and wrote some more. Finally he blotted the paper and came back.

"So, Alexander Pavlovich" — he stressed Sasha's name and patronymic sarcastically. "Here is an attestation that you have served your time. There is a section, see, 'where being sent.' I wrote Kezhma. That means that from me you go straight to the militia, and they will give you a passport in exchange for this, a temporary one, for three or six months. Take whatever they give you. Don't ask any questions. Get a passport today — tomorrow at the latest — and leave! The mail is going to Taishet tomorrow; try to leave with it. You'll manage, the mailman won't charge you too much — just toss your suitcase in the sleigh and walk. Don't visit Moscow. Go to some nonrestricted city, exchange your temporary passport for a permanent one, and then move somewhere far from Moscow. Everyone's trying to live at the one hundred and first kilometer from Moscow — I don't advise it, there are too many others like you, and you shouldn't be in a bunch, you should separate. You don't need extra ties, you shouldn't have any ties. You're young, healthy, and handsome. You've spent three years in one place, now travel around, see Mother Russia, see the world. Understand what I'm saying, my advice is for your benefit. I didn't deceive you. Your documents really haven't come from Krasnoyarsk. And that is why I am letting you go."

After a pause he added significantly, "That is why I am rushing you. Have a safe trip!"

He offered his hand and held Sasha's. "Remember everything that I said to you. . . . By the way, we spoke only about your historical works. Isn't that so?"

"Yes," Sasha replied grimly. "Certainly."

Sasha did not know that the new grandiose trial of Pyatakov, Radek, Sokolnikov, Muralov, and other important figures in the Bolshevik Party had started two days earlier in Moscow.

But Alferov knew.

That trial was the start of 1937.

# Part 2

## ❧ 1 ❧

From Alferov's Sasha went to the militia station and got a temporary passport. A small piece of paper, folded in half — surname, name, patronymic, nationality, year and place of birth — given upon receipt of proof that term of administrative exile was completed, changeable for a permanent passport within six months.

The next day at dawn, Sasha left Kezhma.

The sleigh was filled with mail under a tarp in front, and in the back was a woman with two girls, wrapped in scarves so that you couldn't even see their eyes.

Sasha's bag was stuffed in the back, too. He walked behind the sleigh. The horse moved steadily, running only on downhill slopes. The mailman would get up on the box then, his legs dangling, while Sasha would hold on to the edge of the sleigh and trot behind, like the horse.

However, hills are rare on the bank of the Angara River and so he almost never had to run. On the right was the taiga, on the left, the Angara, and beyond it on the other shore was more taiga, all the way to the horizon. The mailman did not hold the horse back, but he didn't urge it on, either. It was seventy kilometers to Dvorets, where Sasha would have to make other arrangements to get to Taishet. It was a two-day journey, for the days were short and you couldn't travel at night; you also had to stop at noon — to eat something hot, warm up, and feed the horse.

They covered fifteen kilometers and stopped in the village of Nedokura, at the house of one of the mailman's friends. They were expecting him, got the food ready fast, but by the time the woman got out of the sleigh and they carried the sleeping girls, undressed them, put them on the potty, ate, then got the girls bundled up again, put them in the sleigh, surrounded them with hay, and tucked in the fur rug, an hour and a half had gone by.

In the hut Sasha got a look at his traveling companion — a young woman who looked like a white-collar worker or the wife of one, or perhaps the wife of one of the regional bosses. She had a fur collar on her coat and a wool dress. The mailman treated her respectfully.

The older child could feed herself, but the mother had to feed the younger one, and her hand trembled, spilling the cabbage soup. She bit her lip and wiped the table with her hankie, and Sasha looked away so as not to embarrass her. The lady was either melancholic or sickly: pale face, tense, cracked voice. As they left she thanked their hosts politely, her only conversation, but she had paid no attention at all to Sasha. He had tried to help her, picked up the younger girl, but the woman muttered, "No, no," anxiously and took away the child.

This convinced Sasha that she was the wife of one of the Kezhma bosses — she either knew or had guessed that Sasha was an exile and was therefore avoiding him. Something new! The exiles who lived in Kezhma proper worked, talked with their co-workers and supervisors, and did not suffer any ostracism. Vsevolod Sergeyevich had told him so.

But this woman was avoiding him. That meant her husband held a high rank — secretary of the Regional Party Committee or chairman of the Regional Executive Committee.

That made it all the more strange that she would be traveling with the mail, for the regional bosses had their own transportation — a trap, a pair of horses, and a coachman. And with such a long trip and this terrible cold, how could a husband send his wife and small children off alone?

They left Nedokura. It was eighteen kilometers to Okunevka, where they would spend the night, and they had to get there before dark. The mailman made the horse speed up and, afraid of tiring him, no longer got on board. When the horse switched to a canter, he ran alongside. And Sasha ran behind, holding on to the sleigh.

It was getting dark when they got into Okunevka, a small village blanketed in snow, almost deserted looking — no light, no smoke.

A small semidark hut, with people sleeping on a shelf built alongside the oven-fireplace. The woman put the girls there. They tossed a ragged sheepskin coat onto the floor of a cubby behind the stove.

In the dark Sasha took off his felt boots and his socks, put them on the stove to dry, lay down on the sheepskin, covered himself with his coat, and fell asleep instantly.

It had been a hard day. Thirty-three kilometers on foot in the snow churned up by the horse's hooves, in felt boots and heavy clothes. And add to that the twelve kilometers from Mozgova to Kezhma — a total of forty-five. He had gotten up at four, dragging his suitcase and books to Kezhma — he didn't want to abandon his books, and mailed them from Kezhma to Moscow.

It seemed that no sooner had Sasha fallen asleep than they woke him up. A light flickered in the stove's hearth, his companion was packing in the dim light, the girls whining. The mailman went out to harness the horse, came back, tossed off his fur coat, had breakfast, picked up the fur rug for the sleigh, and waited for the others to get up from the table. The woman hurried the children, anxious and oppressed, avoiding not only Sasha's eyes but the landlord's too.

Three years ago, when Sasha was led to the Angara, people were talkative. When he and his fellow exiles went to sleep, the mailman or driver would sit up late talking to the homeowners. But now, both in Nedokura and Okunevka, no one talked. What? Tired? Cold and weary from the road, in a rush to get to sleep? Or had people stopped talking in the last three years?

They left at last. The weather was good. Even though it was cold, there was no wind. They covered twenty kilometers quickly, stopping in Sava, where they had a quick snack and fed the horse. They went on and reached Dvorets by nightfall.

Sasha did not recognize the town in the dark. But he wouldn't have recognized it in broad daylight either. He had spent one night here three years ago, in the summer, and all he remembered was the bank where he said good-bye to his fellow exile Soloveichik.

They dropped off the woman at a dark hut; when the mailman

knocked, the window lit up dimly, the gate opened, and the woman brought the girls in. The mailman carried in her things, and asked Sasha when he returned, "Where are you going?"

"To the post office, I guess. I'll try to arrange passage to Taishet."

"The post office is closed, you know."

The mailman spoke curtly as he fussed with the hay and the fur rug thrown in the sleigh.

"I'll wait."

"It's cold to wait around," the mailman grumbled, without looking at Sasha.

Sasha knew it too. He'd freeze overnight.

"Maybe you should go to the commandant's," the mailman said. "The man on duty is supposed to handle people like you."

"What do you mean, people like me?" Sasha demanded.

"You know, exiles."

"I'm not an exile, I'm free!"

For the first time in three years he could say that. He slept where he wanted, went where he wanted, no one could stop him, no one asked for his papers, no one would check them. He had removed the mark of Cain! If he went to the commandant's office, to sleep there or even sit up all night, it would mean admitting that the establishment had something to say about his fate. All right! He would set his suitcase down near the post office and pace all night until the post office opened. He wouldn't freeze — after all, night watchmen didn't freeze.

The mailman flicked the reins, the sleigh moved, and Sasha followed. And he spent another short night in a cramped, impoverished hut, where the mailman had left him and where, apparently, they gave lodgings to anyone, as long as some money was paid, even a ruble.

Sasha paid the ruble, spent the night on a narrow bench, then jumped up in the morning and ran to the post office to find out that the mail would leave the next day for Taishet.

The mailman from yesterday drove up, turned in the letters and packages, and the new mailman showed up, too, the one who would be going to Taishet. He turned out to be an old acquaintance of Sasha's — Nil Lavrentyevich, the same one who had brought him and Soloveichik from Boguchany to Dvorets. Sasha recognized him immediately — a bustling little man with a mobile, small-featured face. Just as he had eighteen months ago, he was counting and recounting sacks and packages and checking the official seals.

"Hello, Nil Lavrentyevich," Sasha said joyfully.

He really was happy to see him. He was a familiar face, they had gone up the Angara together and Sasha remembered his wife well, a sickly woman, wrapped in a big scarf, silently sitting in the sleigh. He remembered his stories about prospecting for gold, about being a partisan, and his restrained but still horrible stories about the kulaks brought to the Siberian taiga and abandoned in the snow.

But Nil Lavrentyevich pretended not to recognize Sasha, or perhaps he really didn't. They had met in the summer and now it was winter. Sasha was wearing a fur hat and coat, felt boots, and Nil Lavrentyevich had transported lots of people in the last three years, and countless people had given him mail or received mail from him. How could he remember them all, especially since he didn't serve Sasha's area?

In response to the greeting, he didn't even look up, just waved his hand in a way that seemed to say, "Hello, I don't know you, but since you're saying hello, well then, hello."

"Do you remember me, Nil Lavrentyevich? Two summers ago we went up the Angara, remember, we came here from Boguchany, and your wife was with us, remember? We stopped in Goltyavino, where Anatoly Georgyevich and Marya Fedorovna lived, remember?"

Nil Lavrentyevich narrowed his eyes at Sasha and asked sternly, "What do you want, lad?"

"I need to get to Taishet," Sasha said nervously. "I'll just put my suitcase on board and I'll walk."

"Do you have a travel certificate?"

"Why would I need one? I have a passport. See."

Sasha took out his passport and offered it to Nil Lavrentyevich. He squinted at it.

"A passport's no document. Does it show where you're supposed to go? You have to get a travel certificate from the commandant. It'll say that So-and-so is going to Taishet or through Taishet."

"Nil Lavrentyevich, please understand, travel certificates are given to those who are returning from exile."

"And where are you coming from?" Nil Lavrentyevich asked mockingly.

"Yes, but I've already gotten my passport. I had a travel certificate as far as Kezhma, and there I got a passport, and now I can go wherever I want."

This declaration elicited an uncertain look from Nil Lavrentyevich. He hadn't seen people who could go wherever they wanted, only those who were going where they were told.

"Go to the commandant," Nil Lavrentyevich concluded and turned back to his sacks.

"Nil Lavrentyevich, please understand," Sasha begged, "they won't talk to me there. They'll say, 'You have a passport, you're a free man, work out your own problems.'"

Nil Lavrentyevich did not reply. He was busy with his sacks and packages and didn't even turn his head.

Sasha had an awful pain in his chest. For the first time he felt fear, undefined and humiliating. His hands were sweating and his back was soaked. This ridiculous mistake would keep him here. The mail would leave, and he would stay. And who knew for how long? Going to the commandant was not only useless but also dangerous. At best they would say, "You have a passport, go where you want, take care of your own problems." At worst, they'd hold him while they did a check on him, sending to Alferov or even all the way to Krasnoyarsk.

Alferov had wanted to spare him problems and unexpected hassles in getting a passport in an unfamiliar city, but he hadn't taken into account that here in the taiga, from Irkutsk to Krasnoyarsk, from the Angara River to the great Siberian railroad, for people released from exile or moving from one location in exile to another, there was only one document — the travel certificate. Without that document, an exile was a fugitive. And no one wanted to be responsible for a fugitive. Give him a lift, and they'll get you for being an accomplice, helping him flee.

It was a mistake to have reminded Nil Lavrentyevich about himself. If he hadn't, he might have thought that he was an ordinary man, maybe on a business trip.

No, Nil Lavrentyevich wouldn't have thought that, he would have figured out who he was — he had a good eye, and people on business trips don't ask to hitch a ride. He had it figured out, the wise bird, and he just didn't want to get involved.

Ashamed of his begging tone, Sasha said pathetically, "You're not just going to abandon me here? Nil Lavrentyevich!"

His voice shook. He was dying of shame, humiliation, and despair. It was slipping out from under him, his long-anticipated freedom; everything was turning out so differently, so unexpectedly.

"Please, Nil Lavrentyevich!"

Nil Lavrentyevich tied a sack, straightened, looked at Sasha, and turned away. But just then he glanced sidelong at a girl sitting behind the counter.

Sasha took the hint, went over to the counter, and handed her his passport. "Can I get to Taishet with the mail?"

The girl looked at his passport and handed it back.

"You have to talk to Nil Lavrentyevich. Nil Lavrentyevich, can you take a passenger?"

"The sled is full," Nil Lavrentyevich grumbled.

"I'll walk," Sasha said. "Just my suitcase in the sleigh, and it's not heavy."

"Got to follow orders," Nil Lavrentyevich mumbled. "If I gotta take you, I'll take you."

That's all he had wanted. Everyone saw that he hadn't taken the passenger on secretly, but publicly, not of his own volition, but on orders, and the one who should check the documents had done so, publicly, and the passenger's documents were all right — he had a passport and could go where he wanted.

And once everything was solved, Sasha was even more ashamed of his weakness. What had he been afraid of? At worst, he would have left his suitcase and walked behind the mail coach.

At that moment Sasha did not realize that he really would have looked like a fugitive without a suitcase.

They set out in a caravan — three sleighs. In the lead one was Sasha's traveling companion from Kezhma with her children. She did not greet Sasha or look at him, but she didn't look at or talk to anyone.

The Taishet road was rather wide, well traveled and packed down, so it was much easier walking than along the banks of the

Angara. And more fun — it was a large group, even if everyone was traveling separately.

Nil Lavrentyevich often sat on the sleigh — apparently the load wasn't all that heavy — but he never offered Sasha a seat.

Three years ago Sasha had been heading for the Angara. Who was left of their group? Kartsev was dead, Soloveichik probably was lost in the taiga. Volodya Kvachadze was sent to Krasnoyarsk for a new sentence, Ivashkin must have ended up in the meat grinder again or, maybe, was actually released. But they didn't let you out easily under Article 58.

But he had been let out!

Why had he been so lucky? Why was he the one to get out of that hellish, hopeless vicious circle?

Alferov?

But if he shouldn't have been let out, could Alferov have done it independently? Would he have taken the responsibility?

Not likely!

Then what? Accident? No, *they* didn't allow accidents in *their* system.

Did someone intervene? Budyagin? Mark?

No, if they couldn't have helped *then,* they certainly wouldn't have been able to help *now*.

Then it was Alferov? Apparently so. If not for Alferov, Sasha would have been as lost as the others.

He had sensed Alferov's goodwill all these three years. There could be no doubt about it. Even Zida ... Alferov knew about their relationship, so he should have at least transferred Sasha to another village. He didn't.

Alferov had taken risks. And he was at risk now! What made him tick? A good feeling for Sasha? Ridiculous! Alferov was a professional Chekist, with no sentiments at all. To give a certificate that a man's term under Article 58 was up without the sanction of the regional NKVD ... Who would be willing to do that in these times? ... Yesterday Alferov freed him, and tomorrow a decree could come extending his sentence or orders to deliver exile Pankratov to the Regional Division. What would Alferov do? How would he explain it?

What was behind his behavior?

Opposition to what was going on in the country. Then he would want to leave the system. Alferov was a philosopher, he wrote books, he must have asked to go off to do research work, which meant they hadn't let him go and had kept him here, in exile in effect. Vsevolod Sergeyevich had been right when he said, "I'm afraid he's our future colleague, so to speak."

Maybe as a "future colleague" he could behave this way? He knew he was doomed and wanted to live like a human being in his last days. The order on Sasha had been held up. Alferov knew it was an accident and that's why he had hurried Sasha to leave and had arranged for a passport in Kezhma, so that Sasha wouldn't have to deal with the police for at least the first six months of his life in freedom. And let Sasha know that his life would not be easy.

That his life would not be easy Sasha had seen in Dvorets. How did the mailman know he was an exile? It must be written on his face. Maybe people could sense his uncertainty and wariness.

These were Sasha's thoughts as he walked along the Taishet tract. The silent woman with her children was in the first sleigh, and her driver was a silent old man. In the middle of the caravan was a load covered with a tarpaulin, accompanied by two peasants who sometimes rode on the sleigh and sometimes walked alongside.

On the second day, Nil Lavrentyevich tied the reins of his horse to the second sleigh and walked behind with the two peasants. The road was free and wide and they could walk three abreast and talk.

From their conversation Sasha learned that the silent woman was married to the secretary of the Kezhma Regional Party Committee, who had been arrested in Krasnoyarsk. "Took him out of the meeting hall," one of the drivers said. And his wife was headed either for Krasnoyarsk or Moscow to try to help her husband, or to Russia to hide with relatives, so that she wouldn't be arrested and the children taken away. And Sasha understood that this secretary hadn't been the only one arrested. They took secretaries not only in their region but in others, and not only secretaries of regional committees, but also workers from the committees and regional executive committees and various other institutions. A big boss came from Moscow, called a meeting at Krasnoyarsk, and right there publicly called them "enemies." And they took the "enemies" from the meeting straight to jail.

They talked without rancor but also without pity, without gloating but without sympathy. It was the way it had to be, if Comrade Stalin said so; that's the way things were nowadays. It was no secret and no surprise. They wrote in the newspapers about enemies, enemies all around, wherever you looked — enemies, saboteurs, spies who were ruining the Russian people as they had ruined the countryside long before.

Sasha recalled once again how three years ago Nil Lavrentyevich had spoken of the kulaks sent out here. He pretended to understand the interests of the state, but he spoke with compassion for the miserable people torn out of their native places and sent God knows where and for God knows what, doomed to suffering and torment. He had sympathy for the miserable children thrown into the snow. He knew that if the same fate befell him, he wouldn't find protection or help from anyone. He was supposed to be defended by the beloved Soviet power, and it was that power that would be tearing him out of his native place, exiling him, and throwing him into the snow with the children.

Now, three years later, Sasha didn't see any of this in Nil Lavrentyevich — not compassion, not horror, not confusion, not sympathy for the woman traveling with her children in the front sleigh, not for those arrested in Krasnoyarsk, the ones the men were talking about and whom Nil Lavrentyevich knew. Why the change? Because earlier the disaster affected peasants and now it affected those who had destroyed the peasants? They used to arrest others and now they were arrested themselves? They reaped what they sowed?

But Sasha didn't sense any gloating. Then why the indifference?

They traveled a long time, almost a week, stopping in villages to sleep and to eat lunch. There were many more villages along the way than on the road Sasha had taken to the Angara. And so they lingered longer at table for lunch and breakfast, there was no hurry. But they didn't discuss the arrests, the "torn-out" people, even though they knew about them. The closer they got to Taishet, the more arrestees there were. Sasha overheard talk about the camps in Taishet, and the fugitives hiding in the woods. The road became dangerous. He could sense that people were nervous. And their caravan was no longer three sleighs. It was long, and they were passed by carts with frisky, well-fed horses with good harnesses, not from kolkhozes, and in the carts were soldiers, sometimes two to a cart, and a man in civilian clothes — arrested. The soldiers would order the caravan off the road, where the sleighs would stick in the snow, the carts would race past, and then the drivers would have to haul the sleighs back onto the road, cursing at the departed soldiers.

The last night before arriving in Taishet they spent in a village. Not everyone in the caravan stopped. Some drivers headed on to Taishet — they had houses there. But Nil Lavrentyevich and the peasants with the heavy load, and the wife of the former secretary of the Regional Committee with her daughters, and a few other drivers stopped in the village closest to Taishet. Sasha never even learned its name. But from the talk, he learned that Taishet was overcrowded. Every place was full.

They left the village early in the morning, no longer in a caravan. Everyone traveled on his own. It was only twelve kilometers to town.

Approaching the city, at the crossroad where the forest road separated from the main one, two soldiers on horseback, with rifles slung over their backs and whips in their hands, were stopping traffic.

"Go find out what's up," Nil Lavrentyevich said.

Sleighs and carts were spread out all over the road, bunched up and blocking the way. As he passed them, Sasha had to walk in the fields alongside, stepping deep in the snow. Why the roadblock? Were they looking for someone? Checking documents?

As he reached the front sleighs, Sasha understood the cause for the delay — a column of prisoners was heading toward them from Taishet, a long, black, silent column, three abreast. On either side there were guards with rifles and dogs on leashes.

The column reached the intersection and stopped. Now he could see the prisoners — in jackets, torn coats, in rags, some in hats, some in caps, a few in felt boots, most in shoes tied with rope, birch-bark slippers, their faces exhausted, unshaven, emaciated, their eyes hungry. Sasha had never seen anything like it in his life; he could have never imagined it.

The guards ran along the length of the column — "Tighten up! Damn!... Hold on to each other! Damn!... Damn!... Damn!"

The column tightened, huddled closer, grew thicker.

The dogs barked hoarsely, the guards shoved people with rifle butts. The column tightened even more. The forest road was much narrower than the main road — and they were pulling the column into a tighter line.

An order rang out, the column moved into the forest.

Sasha counted fifty-two rows — one hundred fifty-six men.

The column passed. The mounted men followed.

The road cleared up and traffic continued. But Sasha still stood rooted to the spot, his eyes following the prisoners until Nil Lavrentyevich's sleigh drove up.

## ℀ 2 ℀

On January 8, 1937, Stalin received the German writer Lion Feuchtwanger at the Kremlin.

Not the best candidate, he was no Roman Rolland or Bernard Shaw. But specialists maintained that he was popular in the West. An enemy of Nazism. Lived in France, an émigré.

Some of his novels were published in the Soviet Union. Stalin had had time to read *Jew Süss,* he had flipped through *The Oppermanns,* and leafed through *The Ugly Duchess.* He wrote in a lively way. His main theme was the Jews, and so he hated Hitler and sympathized with the Soviet Union, seeing it as the main enemy of Nazi Germany. That meant he could and should present the Pyatakov-Radek trial in the right light. That's why they needed him. They had to influence international public opinion. In the West they had wanted an open trial — and they got it. Zinoviev and Kamenev had been tried openly. The Westerners still didn't believe them. All right, let one of them be present at the next trial. Let him see, let him listen, let him be the witness.

Stalin read the report on Feuchtwanger again. Fifty-two. Born in Munich to a Jewish bourgeois family, university graduate, fought in the World War. A bourgeois intellectual. Appended was a long list of works. If he goes to the trial and if he illuminates it properly, we'll publish all his books. And pay him well. No one refuses money. Especially bourgeois intellectuals.

Poskrebyshev came into the office, shutting the door behind him.

"Tal is here, he brought the German writer Feuchtwanger with him."

"I told you to bring them in without announcing them."

Confusion appeared on Poskrebyshev's face. But he didn't dare say that Stalin hadn't given that order.

"Let them come in."

Poskrebyshev opened the door to let in Feuchtwanger and the head of the Press Section, Tal.

Stalin walked toward Feuchtwanger, shook his hand, cast a quick look at him, invited him to sit down with a gesture, walked around the desk, sat down, looked into Feuchtwanger's eyes once more, and closed his eyes. Everything was severe, strict, controlled. The time for smiles had not come, it would come during the conversation. Make a man wary, scared, and then be nice to him — a tried-and-true method, it was very effective.

A typical Jewish face, rimless glasses, medium height, neat, reddish hair, pouting lower lip.

The aim was to make this man like *him* and send him to the House of Unions to attend the trial. If things went well, he would write well. If he wrote badly, that would mean discrediting *him,* Hitler's main enemy, and that was out of the question for Feuchtwanger. The important thing was to make him do it; it was important that he be a personal witness.

Stalin nodded to Tal to begin the conversation.

"Mister Stalin is listening," Tal said in German and stroked his narrow beard with the thumb and forefinger of his left hand. What do you call those beards?

Turning to Tal, Feuchtwanger spoke. Something long and substantive, with pauses, apparently with repetitions.

Tal translated briefly, "Mister Feuchtwanger asks how you envision the role of the writer in the socialist society."

And he started playing with his beard again.

Dammit, what is it called? And what does a relatively young man need with a beard? A mustache, that's for a man, that's a sign of manliness, but a beard. . . . Everyone else has shaved his beard, but this man wears one. Bukharin, Rykov, Kamenev had beards. They imitated Lenin and Trotsky. Well, Kalinin, too, he was trying to look like a peasant. But Kaganovich was fine, he shaved his beard and left a mustache. Once *he* gave the beard a look, Kaganovich understood and shaved.

"The role of the writer is great in any society," Stalin began in a calm and quiet voice. "We recognize that role and appreciate its significance. The question is on whose side is the writer, what forces he serves — reactionary or progressive."

Feuchtwanger spoke German. Stalin heard the name Gogol and understood what he was saying.

"Take Gogol, for instance. In his essence he was a reactionary writer, but in the Soviet Union he is widely printed and read," Tal translated Feuchtwanger's words. Stalin noted that Tal played with his beard only when he listened or spoke to Feuchtwanger. When he spoke to *him,* he left his beard alone. But, dammit, what was it called?

"The writer's views are one thing, his objective role in society another. Writers are rarely good philosophers," Stalin said.

"Tolstoy," Feuchtwanger said.

Stalin did not reply. The German had to know that *he* could not be interrupted.

"Writers are rarely good philosophers," Stalin repeated, "just as philosophers are rarely good writers. For us it is not Gogol's personal views that are important, but the objective role of his works. Gogol's objective role consisted in ruthless criticism and condemnation of the landowning, serf-owning order of tsarist Russia. Such criticism is progressive criticism. After all, we have destroyed that order and created a new one. And our people, especially young people, must understand why we destroyed that society."

He suddenly recalled what those damned narrow beards were called — Espagnoles. What a ridiculous problem that dandy Tal had given him.

"Gogol did much for the criticism of the old order. And he did it not as a philosopher but as an artist, as a writer. That is why our people love, value, and read Gogol."

Stalin stopped. He sat without raising his eyelids.

Feuchtwanger, intending to say something, turned to Tal. Tal shook his head so that Stalin did not see. Feuchtwanger understood that Stalin's silence was merely a pause.

"As for Tolstoy," Stalin said at last, "his philosophy did not stand up. Can the German anti-Fascists or the Spanish Republicans accept his theory of nonresistance to evil? They cannot. Tolstoy is great as a writer, as an artist describing the life of the people, the patriotic exploits during the Napoleonic invasion. It is on such examples, the examples of the defense of the homeland, that young people should be brought up. We are not interested in Tolstoy's philosophy as he expresses it in his philosophic works. And too often in his novels he lectures and thereby lowers the artistic value of his novels."

He looked up. Tal was translating. Feuchtwanger was listening closely, occasionally nodding to show that he understood. When Tal finished, Feuchtwanger looked at Stalin, mutely asking permission to ask the next question. And he saw permission in *his* face, in *his* gaze. Stalin was convinced that they had made contact. *He* knew how to do it. *He* could let a person know without speaking whether *he* wanted to listen or not, whether *he* gave permission to speak or not.

Tal translated that Feuchtwanger agreed completely with Stalin's words. However, he was interested in the role of Soviet writers — should they belong to the ruling class, should they have a Communist worldview, what was the state of freedom of speech and freedom of literature in the Soviet Union?

"Writers are among the ranks of the intelligentsia," replied Stalin, "and the intelligentsia is not a class but a social layer between the bourgeoisie and the proletariat. Sometimes it serves the bourgeoisie, sometimes the proletariat. But I repeat, the writer's personal views are one thing, the objective role of his works something completely different. We have writers who say they are for the working class, for Soviet power, who are even members of the Party, but in their works they cannot express the interests of the proletariat. On the contrary, their alleged leftist views, their alleged progressiveness reflect the petty bourgeois element. And there are other writers, who came out of the bourgeois class, even the nobility, whose works serve the proletariat. Talent has raised them to the peak of comprehension of the historical process. You don't need to go far for examples. Tolstoy — not the one you mentioned, but the other one, Alexei Tolstoy, a count, an émigré, who did not accept the October Revolution right away. How does he work toward our common goals? He works well, and that's why he is read and revered."

Stalin spoke, as usual, slowly and quietly, with long pauses, during which Tal translated what he had just said. He sat sideways in his chair, leaning forward, so as not to miss a single word of Stalin's.

"May I understand you to say that writers whose work does not serve the proletariat are not allowed to publish their works?"

"No," said Stalin, "you may *not* understand me that way, that is the wrong understanding. We are facing the real threat of a war with Fascism. And naturally, the heroic leitmotif in the writers' works is the most important — it corresponds to the spirit of the nation, its mood, and its needs. But along with that we have authors who never even touch on the heroic theme, who do not think about the reader, do not consider the reader with his needs, tastes, and desires. We have a major lyric poet, whose creativity not only does not serve the interests of the broad masses but is simply incomprehensible to them. And do we ban him? No, we publish him. It's another matter that no one reads him. They don't read him, and that means they don't buy him." Stalin suddenly smiled, revealing small, tobacco-stained teeth. "In the West, do they publish books that are not bought?"

He answered himself. "No, they don't, it's not profitable. But we do, even though our publishers also lose money. But we do. For the book lovers. For those who worship the sky-dwellers."

"But take André Gide," Feuchtwanger said. "He dared to criticize the Soviet Union and he was attacked in your press."

Stalin stood, stepping softly on the carpet, walked around the room, and stopped in front of Feuchtwanger, pointing at him with his index finger. "No one gagged André Gide. But when he was here he praised everything, and when he got back home, he slandered everything. Our people do not like hypocrites. Our people created a great state through impossible sacrifices and dare to hope that foreigners will tell the truth, will affirm the greatness of their achievement. How else can the people treat those who do not notice their success and, on the contrary, deny that success and malign them? Isn't that so?"

Feuchtwanger shrugged and said uncomfortably, "You have presented the psychology of the Soviet man very accurately. But Westerners have a different psychology. They are used to freedom of thought, to the freedom of different thoughts."

Stalin paced the room some more and stopped in front of Feuchtwanger again.

" 'Freedom of different thoughts' ... Then why do you complain about our critics? André Gide expressed one thought, our critics another. That's not attacking him, that's a literary polemic. Doesn't it exist in the West? They all argue! ... But we're talking about something else. ... A month ago we approved a new constitution. It does not speak of what we *want* to do, but what we have *already done*. The most important thing is that we have created a socialist order. We have liquidated class antagonism, exploitation of man by man, the poverty of the majority and the wealth of the minority, unemployment. We have achieved the right of everyone to work, rest, have an education, medical service, and so on, created full racial and national equality, and created and guaranteed true democracy. I repeat — true democracy!"

His finger touched Feuchtwanger's chest, and he looked down at him through half-shut lids.

"In the West they talk of equality of citizens, but I ask you, what kind of equality can there be between master and worker? In the West, many talk about freedom of speech, of meetings, of the press, but they are empty sounds if the workers have no place for their meetings, no typesetting machines or paper. Our constitution guarantees these freedoms with material goods. That is socialist democracy, that is our understanding of freedom. Now, when Fascism is mocking the democratic strivings of the best people of the civilized world, our constitution is an indictment against Fascism. Bourgeois freedom is a fiction. Has your parliamentary system stopped Hitler? No, it hasn't. Instead of combating Fascism, your ministers wasted time answering ridiculous questions of their deputies. Isn't that so?"

"That is definitely so," Feuchtwanger confirmed, "and many people in the West realize it. But will you allow me to be frank?"

Tal translated.

"Tell him to say everything he thinks. Let him ask whatever he wants. Explain that well to him! And gently!"

With a particularly significant look, and stroking his beard, Tal translated Stalin's words.

"I thank you." Feuchtwanger beamed. "In that case, what I

wanted to say, I will say straight. Many of your friends who saw in the Soviet Union's social structure the ideal of socialist humaneness are stunned by the Zinoviev-Kamenev trial. They think that the bullets that struck Zinoviev and Kamenev killed the new world, too. They were men who made the Revolution and asserted the new structures."

Stalin had been expecting that question, but when he heard it he shuddered.

Feuchtwanger watched him, surprised by Stalin's unexpected nervousness.

Stalin turned, paced his office once more, and, without looking at Feuchtwanger, began to speak. "The people who fought well in the Civil War are not always good for the period of construction. However, since they had served the cause, they had pretensions to high posts. They received them. But they turned out to be bad workers. What could be done? They had to be transferred to work they could handle. They were hurt and opposed the Party line and ended up in open struggle with the Party, the state, and the people."

He paused. "That is one category of people. Another is talented people. The greatest among them is Trotsky. He was never a Bolshevik. Lenin wrote and talked a lot about him. He had joined the October Revolution and he was useful during the struggle, no one can deny that. But he was incapable of calm, planned work. History moved him aside. He tried to cross history and ended up outside it. He considered himself a leader and the people chased him from the country. Once abroad, he undertook dubious adventures, which corresponded fully with his nature. His aim was to return to power, at any price, but to have power. And he got quite far along that path."

Stalin stopped in front of Feuchtwanger, lifted his finger, and, looking into his eyes, said, "Far . . ."

Stalin frowned and went on talking. "As for Trotsky's old comrades in arms, they are still on his side. They repented, the Party believed them, gave them high posts in the government, but they deceived the Party, they wanted to bring Trotsky back into power and went as far as their leader."

Still pacing and with bitterness in his voice, he said, "Ten years! Ten years we had to deal with this. We forgave them, returned them, they deceived us again, we forgave them again, gave them high posts again, and once more behind our backs they planned their conspiracies, their intrigues. They killed Kirov and planned to murder other leaders. How much can we stand? The people cannot take it anymore!"

Feuchtwanger looked at Tal silently, asking permission for a question.

"Mister Feuchtwanger wants to ask you something, Comrade Stalin," Tal said meekly.

"Please," Stalin said without turning.

Tal translated Feuchtwanger's question. "The total absence of evidence against Zinoviev and Kamenev made a bad impression on the West."

Stalin laughed, shook his head, and sat down.

"They demand to see written evidence? Naïve people! Experienced conspirators never keep incriminating documents. But they were shown enough clues and testimony. The material was carefully checked by the investigators and supported by their confessions at the trial. We wanted the world to understand what was happening. That's why the trial was presented with maximum simplicity and clarity. Detailed citations from documents, testimony, and different kinds of investigative reports could be of interest to lawyers, criminologists, and historians, but ordinary people would merely be confused by the mass of details, while the total confessions of the accused tell them much more than any papers.

"Let's be frank — those who consider our courts false know very well that false judges can prepare false documents. That's not so hard. But our court is not a false one, rather it's an honest court. They do not need false documents. They need honest investigation that is comprehensible to the people. And the coming trial I hope will also be understood by the broad masses. The people, who are about to embark on a horrible, ruthless war with Fascism, must know about their internal enemies and know how to protect themselves from them. Take Radek, a famous man, brilliant and witty, I had warm feelings for him, trusted him. . . . Well . . ."

Stalin opened a file on his desk and took out a few sheets. "Here is his letter from prison, written December third, see, a long letter, in which he swears he is totally innocent. . . . And here" — Stalin took out other papers — "is his deposition, in which he admits everything, and it is signed December fourth. He sent me a letter filled with lies and the next day under pressure from statements from other witnesses, he confessed."

Stalin thought, glanced at Feuchtwanger, and said, "You Jews created an immortal legend about Judas. And we have to deal with these Judases. Take a look at our life, you'll see much. Will you be here long?"

"My visa is until the middle of February."

"Very good. In the West they are making up fairy tales about torture, hypnosis, actors playing the defendants. Well, I've been told that the investigation on Radek is coming to a close, and perhaps the trial will start this month. I don't know the exact date, that's up to the judges, and our judges are independent and obey only the law. But as far as I know, the trial will be an open one and the accused will have defense attorneys." He nodded at Tal. "We'll ask Comrade Tal to get you a pass. Please go and see with your own eyes, take any translator you want with you. Comrade Tal, will you be able to get a pass for Mister Feuchtwanger?"

"I'll try."

"Tell him about it."

Tal translated.

"Thank you," Feuchtwanger said, bewildered. "I'd —"

"Wonderful, excellent," Stalin interrupted. "Our people have a proverb, 'Better to see once than to hear a hundred times.' So you will see."

"With your permission, I'd like to ask one more question."

"Please," Stalin replied generously. "That's why we met."

"You see, we in the West are used to treating our leaders as ordinary people. But you have a cult of the leader that is almost worship and is often expressed . . ." — here he grew embarrassed, looking for the right word — "forgive me, in very poor taste."

Stalin laughed.

"Poor taste?" He shrugged. "Simple workers and peasants, when could they have developed their taste? They are busy building a new society, heavy construction under difficult circumstances. They don't have time to develop their taste. I can't stand to look at the huge portraits of that man with the mustache, when thousands carry them during demonstrations on Red Square. I can't stand to look, but I look, I must look, I can't turn my back on the people. I am helpless, I am a prisoner of the people."

"However," Feuchtwanger said, "people with good taste do the same. They exhibit your portraits and busts in places that have nothing to do with you. For instance, the first thing one sees at an exhibit of the works of Rembrandt is a bust of you. That's somehow hard to understand.... Rembrandt lived and worked in the seventeenth century."

"These are people who accepted Soviet power very late," Stalin said angrily, "and perhaps still have not accepted it in their hearts. Now they are trying to show their loyalty with all their might. And therefore, they have no sense of proportion.... A toadying fool can do more harm than a hundred enemies."

*He* was displeased by that question. It was tactless. And that German jerk had to feel what *his* displeasure meant. He would attribute *his* anger to the clumsy ass-lickers. But he would see *his* wrath.

*He* did not take *his* heavy gaze from Feuchtwanger, pleased that the man was bewildered and tried to hide it by taking off his glasses and wiping them with a piece of suede.

In a deep, quiet, ruthless voice, Stalin continued. "Let's assume that they are not servile fools but that this is a plot. A plot by people who are trying to discredit the Party leadership." He turned to Tal. "Find out today who did it and punish them. Translate."

Tal translated.

"But I didn't want that at all," Feuchtwanger said in distress. "I don't want people punished because of me."

Stalin thought for a while and then said indifferently to Tal, "All right. Let's respect Mister Feuchtwanger's request. Have the bust of Comrade Stalin removed from the exhibit and give orders for such nonsense not to be repeated."

Tal translated.

Feuchtwanger sighed in relief. "Thank you."

Stalin said confidentially, "All that noise around the 'man with the mustache' is very tiresome and, as you so rightly put it, in poor taste. But you must understand me. I must put up with it because I know what naïve joy this foolishness gives people. Especially since all the praise is not for me personally but for the Party that is leading the construction of socialism in our country. Our people are devoted to the construction of socialism."

He suddenly stopped and lowered his eyes. Then he opened them, looked at Feuchtwanger, and smiled. "We keep talking about our work. But you will see much and learn much. You are a writer, a man of a free profession, you can travel all around the world, while Comrade Tal and I are salaried, we are paid to sit in these chairs. And we learn what's going on in the world from newspapers. And that is not enough. And so we jump on everyone from outside" — he reached out for Feuchtwanger and laughed. "Tell me, dear man, what is happening out in the world."

He lowered his hands gently to the desk, smiled gently, and regarded Feuchtwanger.

Tal translated, also smiling and picking his words to recreate Stalin's gentle, kindly intonation, and from the way Feuchtwanger nodded sympathetically and with understanding, Stalin saw that this man was *his* now; he would go to the trial and write about it correctly.

"The air that people breathe in the West is unhealthy," Feuchtwanger said. "Western civilization has no more clarity or determination. They don't dare defend themselves from the coming barbarism with a fist or even a strong word. They do it meekly, with vague gestures. The speeches of responsible people against Fascism are sugarcoated, with tons of qualifications. It's disgusting to watch the hypocrisy and cowardice of our leaders to the Fascist attack on the Spanish Republic."

"Yes," Stalin agreed, "the attack by Germany and Italy on Spain is blatant aggression. All the progressive forces of the world must resist. The workers of the Soviet Union are helping and will give all possible aid to Spain. The liberation of Spain from the oppression of Fascist reactionaries is not the private problem of the Spaniards but the common work of progressive humanity."

He stopped, and then added with conviction, "Fascism is the most evil enemy of humanity and must be stopped. We will not allow Fascism here. Our agents of Fascism will be rendered harmless. All progressive people of the world must understand and appreciate that."

The conversation had lasted three hours — Stalin had noted the time when Poskrebyshev had brought in Feuchtwanger and Tal. Time to end.

Feuchtwanger said something else. Tal translated, "Mister Feuchtwanger asks permission to be photographed with you."

Stalin called in Poskrebyshev and asked for a photographer.

The photographer came and set up his camera.

Stalin moved to a chair near the wall. He invited Feuchtwanger to sit on his right and Tal on his left. And they were photographed against the oak paneling.

Getting up, Stalin said, "You see, now there will be yet another portrait of the man with the mustache." He smiled and shook his finger. "And it's your fault."

Tal translated.

Feuchtwanger laughed and shrugged. "You are the best and calmest polemicist in the world."

He said it sincerely.

Stalin saw Feuchtwanger to the door, opened it himself, let his guest out and Tal after him. In the reception room Poskrebyshev opened the second door. Feuchtwanger looked back. Stalin had his hand up in greeting. Feuchtwanger replied with a nod and a grateful smile. The door shut behind him.

Going back to his office, Stalin stopped near Poskrebyshev. "I told you in plain Russian to let the writer in without announcing him. Why didn't you obey my order?"

And once again Poskrebyshev was afraid to say that there had been no order to that effect. Comrade Stalin had wanted to show the writer how accessible he was, but he hadn't, in fact, given the order. Apparently, he had forgotten, and Poskrebyshev did not dare let anyone in without first announcing him.

"Forgive me, Comrade Stalin," Poskrebyshev said guiltily. "It just happened, automatically."

"Tell Tal and Stavsky to give the German everything he needs. Print everything he wants before the trial. What he writes about the trial, show to me first."

Stalin shut the door and walked through the office to the window.

Snow lay on the buildings of the Kremlin. It was on the brass cannons near the Arsenal.

*He* had done *his* work with Feuchtwanger. Now let Tal, Stavsky, Vyshinsky, and Radek do theirs. Feuchtwanger would believe Radek — both were Jews, intellectuals, journalists. Everything would sound believable. Radek would try to be witty and erudite during the trial. He'll want to be the center of attention. He considered himself a specialist on Germany, he had negotiated with the Germans back in 1919 and 1921. Of course, he shouldn't mention that because the relations between Germany and Russia were different. Let him talk about his last negotiations with the Germans, with Hitler's diplomats. He wouldn't have to make anything up, he could tell the truth, name names, living names. Only one thing was necessary — that he admit he spoke in the name of Trotsky, at Trotsky's request. And Feuchtwanger would spread that all over the world.... A writer! World famous! An anti-Fascist? Yes, but not a Communist, on the contrary, even an anti-Communist.

*He* would force the world to believe this trial and all the future ones, and that meant all the past ones, too. *He* would allow not only Feuchtwanger to the trial but also foreign diplomats, journalists, any observers at all. Welcome! Of course, they were temporary allies. They were allies as long as he and Hitler were opposed to each other. They were allies until ... until the decisive turn. But then the times would be different, and there would be different songs to sing.

The Pyatakov-Radek trial went well. All seventeen defendants confessed to monstrous crimes. Thirteen people were sentenced to be shot, four to imprisonment, and of them, two — Radek and Sokolnikov — were killed later in their prison cells.

Returning to the West, Feuchtwanger wrote a book, *Moscow 1937,* which he published in Amsterdam.

Feuchtwanger wrote:

Stalin is the Russian type of peasant and worker raised to genius.... Stalin is the flesh of the people, he has preserved the ties with workers and peasants.... He speaks the language of the people. He is extremely sincere and modest, he has not taken any titles, he holds the fate of every single person dear to his heart, he does not allow public celebrations of his birthday, he knows the needs of his peasants and workers, he is one of them.... He gave the Soviet Union a new democratic constitution and has solved the nationalities problem....

Soviet citizens have plenty of food, clothing, movies, and theaters. In ten years they will have apartments in any amount and of any quality.... They head for their demonstrations with childlike joy.... Scientists, writers, artists, and actors live well in the Soviet Union.... The state takes care of them, spoils them with recognition and high salaries.... Writers who deviate from the general line are not oppressed.... Soviet newspapers did not censor my articles.... In the near future the Soviet Union will become the happiest and strongest country in the world.

And more:

I was present at the trial, I heard Pyatakov, Radek, and if it's all made up and fixed, then I do not know what is the truth.... It is enough to read any of Stalin's books, any of his speeches, to look at any of his portraits for it to be immediately clear that this wise and reasonable man could never do something as monstrously foolish as to put on this crude comedy with the help of innumerable people.

The book was instantly translated in the Soviet Union. On November 23, 1937, it was submitted; on November 24, approved; and immediately 200,000 copies were printed. Soon after, in addition to the novels already published in the U.S.S.R., Feuchtwanger's *Success, The False Nero, The Jew of Rome,* and *Prisoners of War* were published. He became a popular and respected writer in the Soviet Union, where much was written about him and he was called a "great humanist."

The tiny wooden train station was stuffed with men, women, and children. Sasha worried he'd never find the end of the line. His suitcase was in the way — it wasn't heavy, but he couldn't push his way through the crowd with it and there was no place to set it down. It was here, at the Taishet station, that he came to appreciate the backpack; you can push and shove as long as your elbows and shoulders work. But here people formed a solid wall, and no amount of strength would have helped.

The door kept swinging open and it didn't shut properly, because the hinge was frozen. Out on the station square the radio was broadcasting full blast — it was a report on the trial of the anti-Soviet Trotskyite Center.

Sasha had no idea of the new trial, but what he heard shocked him. Pyatakov, Radek, Sokolnikov, Serebryakov, Muralov — the greatest leaders of the Party and state — were being called killers, spies, and saboteurs. When had the trial started? While he was traveling to Taishet?

"Performing diversionary acts in collaboration with agents of foreign intelligence services," he heard the announcer say, "organizing train crashes, explosions and fires in mines and industrial enterprises, the defendants in this case did not mind stooping to the most vile methods, consciously embarking on such monstrous crimes as poisoning and killing workers.

"All the defendants have fully confessed their guilt as charged."

Sasha wanted to buy a paper or at least get outside so that he could hear the entire broadcast, but how could he leave without finding the right line?

Gradually Sasha figured it out.... One line, the shorter one, was for ordinary mortals, and he got in it. It was the hopeless line. The other was much longer, for people on official business, who, it turned out, had to cede to those bearing reservations from the Transportation Department of the NKVD. Basically, it was a lost cause; he might never get out of Taishet.

The cashier's window opened fifteen minutes before a train was due, and then the jostling began in the business travelers' line. If there were tickets on sale to Irkutsk, then the ones waiting for the Krasnoyarsk train had to move aside and let the Irkutsk passengers through. But everyone was afraid of losing his place, afraid of being pushed out of line, and people shouted and fought viciously for tickets. Sasha's line was quiet. No one had any rights, no one could raise a fuss or make demands.

The station administrators would come into the cashier's office and get tickets for important officials or perhaps for their friends and relatives. They got them openly, without hiding, and walked out with the tickets in their hands. And everyone kept quiet, no one expressed indignation. The ordinary people, oppressed and obedient, knew that a single word of protest or dissatisfaction and they would be thrown out of the station or into someplace much worse. The official travelers, who were privileged compared to the rest, put up with those who had privileges greater than theirs — a feeling that played an important part, as Sasha learned over the coming years, in strengthening the system of social inequity.

The trains stopped for several minutes, and the lucky ticket-holders rushed to the platform, grabbing their bags and briefcases.

Sasha went out on the platform to see which trains passed through Taishet and to listen to the radio. If not the whole trial, at least excerpts, for he was dying to know what was going on. A loudspeaker hung on a pole on the platform.

Defendant Radek was condemning a letter from Trotsky, sent in December 1935.

"... It would be ridiculous to think that one can come to power without the goodwill of important capitalist governments, especially the aggressive ones like the current governments in Germany and Japan," Trotsky had written. "It is absolutely necessary even now to have contact and agreements with these governments.... We will have to make territorial concessions.... We will have to cede the Primorie and the Amur regions to Japan and the Ukraine to Germany...."

So, last August, when Radek was demanding that Zinoviev and Kamenev "pay with their heads" for their guilt, Trotsky's letter was already in his pocket?

Sasha went back to the station looking for the old man with whom he had left his suitcase. He saw two military police talking to him. Were they asking about Sasha's suitcase? ... No, the old man wouldn't have been showing them his passport and he would have been calmer. They interrupted him curtly and walked down the line and grabbed two men, who showed the military police some papers, which Sasha couldn't make out.

When the MPs were out of view, he pushed his way to the old man and asked cautiously, "Were they checking your documents?"

"The third time they looked at my passport. Now they want a certificate of leave. And where can you get one? Nobody gives them."

The old man was younger than Sasha had thought at first. He was visiting his wife in the camps. He was from Kharkov, where he worked as a chemist, and she was a nurse.

"They didn't check the passports of those men, they looked at some other papers."

"Telegrams, then. Some heading to a funeral, others to a wedding or christening.... You have to show that too."

"Do they check everyone's documents?"

"Documents! They put you through an X-ray machine — who are you and what are you, and where did you come from, and where are you going?"

So ... If Sasha hadn't gone out onto the platform, they would have gotten him. He had to invent something, fast. But when the patrol came over, his heart contracted. The Red Army soldier turned over the paper, read it, and called over the other one. Now they were both examining Sasha's passport; they had obviously never come across a case like this before — a man coming out of exile, without a travel document, but with a passport. How could that be? It shouldn't be! A man out of prison was supposed to have travel papers that showed where he was going, where he was allowed to live. And that's where he would get a passport and where the organs would keep an eye on him. This was improper!

And he wouldn't be able to persuade these blockheads of anything, ever. This was Siberia, with general and total checking. They were on the lookout for fugitives; they arrested even the least suspicious people.

They might not return his passport. They'd take him to the commandant, they would ask Krasnoyarsk — "What do we do with this guy?" And what could they do? "You have a jail, stick him in it, we'll deal with it later." ... And then the Oblast troika would give him a new sentence for the old case. That was the new method — trying people for what they had already been tried.

"Where are you going?"

"To Kansk," Sasha replied trying to sound like a local.

"What for?"

"To my mother-in-law's."

"Where does she live?"

Sasha gave the street and number of the house where Soloveichik had once lived. He remembered it for some reason.

"And who's in this place?"

"What place?"

"Don't understand? In Kezhma."

"My wife, and son ... everybody ..."

The patrolman still played with Sasha's passport and then looked up at him.

Sasha looked at him calmly, even though his heart was in his throat. He had to act steady. He was in the right — he had served his time, he stayed in Kezhma with his wife and child, he wasn't traveling far, just to Kansk to his mother-in-law. It was a foolproof story, he couldn't miss. He practically believed it himself.

"To your mother-in-law's, eh?"

"Yes."

"To visit and have blini?"

"Not to visit, we're bringing her to Kezhma. Getting old."

The man's face got serious again and he regarded Sasha.

Sasha looked back and tried to guess what the man would decide — take him, leave him? Maybe he'd leave him. ... After all, he lived in Kezhma, they had their own organs, Sasha was under their supervision, they were responsible for him. Let them worry!

Whether Sasha had guessed correctly or not, the man folded Sasha's passport and gave it back to him. He and his partner moved on to check the documents of the people leaning against the walls, sitting on sacks and suitcases and on the floor. They handed over their papers meekly and in fright — everyone knew Taishet station and even those traveling legally tried to avoid it — even if you came to Taishet station with your documents in order, you were still afraid.

Sasha stayed in line, unable to move, still staring at the patrol.

The radio was still blaring, but he couldn't hear well, his ears were ringing, he couldn't get over his nervousness, couldn't concentrate. All he heard was the word *war*.

"Defendant Pyatakov gave orders to defendant Norkin to prepare to set fire to the Kemerovo Chemical Plant when the war started.

"Pyatakov confirmed this. 'Yes, I gave Norkin that assignment.'"

Then the announcer mentioned Knyazev. ". . . The Japanese intelligence service wanted to know about using bacteriological weapons during the war in order to infect the trains to be used for transporting soldiers as well as the food and hospitals for the troops. . . ."

The lights were weak; the air smelled of sweat, tobacco, and something sour. Sasha sat down by his suitcase, leaning against the wall.

And when Vyshinsky asked Radek what he wanted, the U.S.S.R.'s defeat or victory, Radek answered without hesitation, "I helped the defeat."

The trial and the self-exposure depressed Sasha. He had nothing to do with the crimes the Trotskyites were confessing to and their confessions sounded wild and absurd. But who would care whether Pankratov had anything to do with them or not? Had he been sentenced under Article 58 or not? Yes. Had he been accused of counterrevolutionary activity? Yes. Then he belonged to that hostile camp, and that was enough to arrest him again. He had to get out of here, hide out in some hole where they didn't check people's passports three times a day.

There were no tickets for the ordinary people, but the line was getting a tiny bit shorter. Why and how, Sasha didn't know. Suddenly the man from Kharkov who had visited his wife was gone. He didn't have a suitcase, just a backpack ... maybe he had jumped onto a moving train?

Everyone else still seemed to be in the line. People came and went, everyone knew his spot in the line. Sasha went to buy milk and bread not far from the station. It was available for a brief time, two or three hours, the line wasn't too bad, but they sold only one chunk of bread per person. He had to buy a mug. They sold milk in frozen circles, and it melted in the warmth of the station. He had it with the bread. It was good, but not enough.

The circles of milk reminded him of Mozgova, where they froze the milk in winter, too. His old landlords must think that he was rolling up to Moscow by now. The old woman had put together food for the road and had sent Lukich to the cellar for bacon and dried fish. Sasha had come into the kitchen and seen everything Lukich had brought and laughed — "That's enough for a whole caravan!" He had tucked some food into his pockets, put the bacon in his suitcase, and left the rest. "Once I get to Taishet, I'll get right on the train."

Now, hungry, unshaven — there was neither a place nor the energy to shave — with inflamed eyes, Sasha slept on the floor, his arms over his suitcase and his head on his arms. His legs got stiff, then his back. It was a rest, but it was torment. The trains passed, passenger trains, freight trains, and rolling stock came on the side tracks and the steam engines made noise.

The mail train from Vladivostok pulled in, new and shiny, white curtains on the windows, with the barred mail car behind the locomotive. They were carrying letters to Moscow — everything was clean and noble and civilized and dignified.

And from Moscow came a freight train with only two passenger cars — first and last — stopping at the end of the station where there was no platform. Guards came out of the passenger cars and stood by the freight cars. . . . Sasha saw for the first time how they unloaded a freight train full of prisoners.

The sliding doors were opened halfway, the guard called out a name, a prisoner appeared in the doorway, loudly calling out his full name, date of birth, and sentence. The guard checked his list, said,

"All right!" and the prisoner jumped down with his bag — the young ones did; the older ones were afraid of heights and tried to slide down on their bellies, falling into the snow and getting on their knees. Then the next one was called, who also jumped or crawled down, and then got on his knees. The whole carload.

The prisoners stood on their knees in the snow, men and women, pathetic figures with pathetic bags.

Then a command — crude, loud, with curses and jabs, with blows from rifle butts — and then they stood up and lined up, in full view of the station and of the people who were on the platform. However, Sasha noticed that no one paid much attention; they must have become used to the sight.

The line of prisoners moved about two hundred meters and then knelt again in the snow, in front of another guard from the camps. Roll call again — name, date of birth, sentence.... One group of guards was turning them over to another. Distant cries, curses, dog barks mixed with the train whistles and the clanging of passing trains.

Sasha raised his collar. He was shivering. This is what awaited him. They had let him out by mistake. The NKVD fixed mistakes like that quickly.

## 4

The sisters almost never saw each other. Nina was in school all day, Varya was at work and then at the institute in the evenings. But it was unbearable living together without talking, seeing mocking scorn on Varya's face over every word on the radio, feeling her disdain because Nina "believed all that." She could expect almost anything from Varya. What would that lead to?

An "enemy of the people" had been arrested on their landing; he had been in the building only three months. His apartment-mate, Dima Polyansky, was expelled from the Party for loss of vigilance. Dima and Nina had been friends since childhood. They met on the stairs, and Dima took her by the elbow and whispered, "I never said two words to him except 'hello' and 'good-bye,' but they wouldn't even listen to me at the Regional Committee. They just expelled me, and that's it."

"The times are serious," Nina said seriously. "They require special vigilance."

Dima recoiled from her and ran up the stairs three steps at a time. Without saying good-bye. She wanted to call up after him, "My dear, I might be expelled any day myself, thanks to my dear sister." Of course, she didn't, but she was upset and her hand trembled as she put the key in the lock.

She shouldn't have been so brusque with Dima. He was a good man, a few years older, an engineer working in aviation. The year before last he had invited Nina to Tushino to celebrate Air Force Day. She had gone with pleasure and didn't regret it. It was a marvelous, breathtaking sight! The day was sunny, there were planes in the sky, snow-white parachutes, joy and triumph everywhere. The pilots were heroic! Nina was proud of them, proud of her country. She still was.

Dima was attentive and polite. He called sometimes, gave her flowers on March 8, International Woman's Day, and a box of candy for the October and May holidays. But Nina didn't take his courting seriously. He was a stranger. Only with Maxim could she talk about her problems, could be frank. Maxim listened closely and his calm soothed her.

The letters he wrote to Nina were reasonable, kind, and circumstantial. Maxim came to Moscow twice on leave, waiting patiently for her to come from school. He stood in line for tickets, and they went to the theater, to exhibits. He got tickets for the Conservatory, even though he didn't understand or like classical music, smiled good-naturedly, and said, "Bach or Mozart, whatever." But Nina loved it and Maxim sat through the entire concert, as long as Nina liked it, as long as Nina was happy. He preferred folk songs, and last year while he was in town they saw *Maxim's Youth,* and on the way home from the movies, he kept singing, *"The blue balloon twirls and spins, twirls and spins overhead, it wants to fall down, the cavalier wants to steal the girl away."* Nina was in a good mood and hummed along, but once a tune stuck in Maxim's head, it stayed there for a long time. By the third day, Nina burst out, "Stop it, aren't you sick of it yourself?"

Maxim retorted, "Maybe I'm planning to steal the lady myself and I'm trying to get her used to the idea."

She smiled and said, "Wait, Max, not now."

Why not now, she didn't know herself. Perhaps part of it was her love for the school, the students. She loved her subject, history, and Moscow had libraries, courses, seminars, museums, everything related to her profession. There was none of that where he lived, in the Far East. Just the monotony of provincial life, children, and then the usual part of army life, moving from town to town. And instead of her beloved work, she'd wash diapers; instead of public work, she'd cook borshch.

Once after Maxim left, Varya had said, "Watch out, you'll lose your little hubby."

Nina was furious. "Don't be so tawdry! 'Hubby,' indeed! You

didn't lose yours" — this being before Varya had left Kostya for good — "and, believe me, no one envies you."

Varya smiled sarcastically and said, "No one envies old maids, either."

They sometimes had exchanges like this, which led to weeks of not speaking.

It was becoming unbearable.

In late November on Nina's birthday, Lena Budyagina called. Nina smiled. She's calling to wish me a happy birthday — what a friend, she never forgets. We could go to the ice cream parlor on Gorky Street for a chat, we haven't seen each other in a long time. But that's not why Lena called.

"Nina," she said. "Papa's gone."

Nina didn't understand at first — had he died? But then she realized that Ivan Grigoryevich had been arrested. She said quickly, "I'll call you back."

And she hung up. Was she frightened? No, why? But you can't talk about it on the phone. She went back to her room, sank into a chair, and thought. Should she go to see Lena or not? Their apartment was being watched. That was clear. There were people taken away from the Fifth House of the Soviets every day — you read that in the newspapers. But how could she not go? Abandon a friend. Alone with a baby. She had to go. But how? The doorman would ask, "Who do you want?" She'd have to say, "The Budyagins." Then he'd call the right people to tell them that a girl had gone to see the Budyagins. And the thread would start that would lead them to the fact that a few years ago Ivan Grigoryevich had recommended her for the Party. One recommendation came from Alevtina Fyodorovna Smirnova, the school's director, and the other from Ivan Grigoryevich, who was now arrested. What should she do? Tell the Party? A fine birthday present.

Nina went to Granovsky Street at six-thirty. People were coming home from work, she could slip in with them. Luckily, the doorman wasn't there.

Lena opened the door, and they kissed. Lena was astonishingly calm and businesslike. And Ashkhen Stepanovna also behaved calmly, even though the apartment was turned upside down. The two rooms were sealed, and things were scattered all over the hallway. It was hard to look at it.

"Don't worry," Lena said. "We're going to move to the Government House on Serafimovich. We've been given a room," she said with a laugh. "A transit point from the Moskva River Embankment to the banks of the Enisei River in Siberia. See, we're packing."

"I see, I see," Nina said sadly.

Ashkhen Stepanovna was putting dishes into a box on the table, while the maid rolled up the carpet on the floor.

"How are you all going to fit all this in one room?" Nina asked.

"That's all taken care of," Lena said with another laugh. "We're moving only the most essential things into the room and the rest we'll give to the building superintendent for storage. They have a special space for just this sort of thing. As you can imagine, it's a big space, since there's a lot of this sort of thing going around. They took Papa away early in the morning; at three they came and told us to move, giving us time to pack. It's very humane. I've been down there, looked it over, it's a perfectly nice room, fourteen square meters on the first floor. The other rooms also have a family each. There are even people we know from this building. And I got the key."

She talked and talked, tossing things into a suitcase, while Nina stood nearby, peering into her face in fright. The mocking smile never left Lena's lips, but her eyes were immobile. And that strange concentration, coupled with the inappropriate merriment and unusual garrulity, created a horrible impression.

The baby cried in the next room. Lena went to him, and Nina followed.

"Come on, little one," Lena said, and picked him up from the cot. "So you've wet yourself, big deal."

She held the baby with one hand and with the other quickly changed the sheet and the oilcloth under it. The tiny boy rubbed his eyes and squinted in the light.

"Our little Vanya will be fine in a minute."

She held the infant so that Nina couldn't see his face.

"Nina, just look how our little Chekist is growing, with blond curls, just like his father, a handsome Chekist. He'll arrest bad men and he'll arrest bad ladies, too, my darling little Chekist."

Nina lowered her eyes. She worried that Lena was losing her mind, didn't know what she was saying, and that she would blurt out something that would put Nina in a funny position and ruin their relationship forever. To stop her talk, she asked, "What happened with Ivan Grigoryevich?"

"Ivan Grigoryevich? . . . Ivan Grigoryevich?" She put the baby back in bed and said, "And this little one is Ivan Ivanovich, his name is Ivan and his patronymic comes from his grandfather, Ivanovich, not from his father."

"I know that, Lena," Nina said gently.

"Right, I forgot. Ivan Grigoryevich was arrested and taken away. Why? Because they're arresting and taking away everyone. Half the building has been taken away." She rocked the bed waiting for the baby to go back to sleep. "Can't you see what's going on? Comrade Ordzhonikidze is the only one left in the Commissariat of Heavy Industry. Everyone else is in prison, waiting trial. They'll be tried, then they'll be shot." She looked into Nina's eyes and smiled again. "How does the song go — *'We'll be in jail, and we'll shoot, the time has come, we'll die.'*"

"Lena," Ashkhen Stepanovna called, "have you packed the baby things?"

"Not yet."

"Hurry up."

"Couldn't they give you a few days to pack?"

Later she berated herself for the stupidity of the question.

"Naïve soul," Lena said. "Don't you understand that someone can't wait to move into our apartment? Serebryakov was arrested, he hasn't even been tried, yet Andrei Yanuaryevich has already moved into his dacha. Nice, isn't it? Fine justice?"

"Who's Andrei Yanuaryevich?" Nina asked, feeling cold and guessing the name Lena was about to say.

"Vyshinsky."

Nina flushed. "Why do you believe gossip? I don't recognize you!"

Lena looked at her. "Of course there's a lot of gossip around, but other than that, everything's fine."

Nina didn't want to part like that. "Where's Vladlen?" she asked.

"With friends. He's getting them to come help us move tomorrow."

Nina almost burst into tears. Their only help was an eleven-year-old, so she sounded sincere when she explained her tight schedule. She was overworked, they wouldn't let her out of school, otherwise she'd definitely help.

"I understand perfectly," Lena said. "Thanks for coming."

"Thank you," Ashkhen Stepanovna said, echoing her daughter.

Nina's relationship with Lena was over, of course, even though she still loved her. But she couldn't go to the house on Serafimovich, to a building inhabited by the families of arrested men. Nina had always idolized Ivan Grigoryevich — a man of the people, a real Communist, a Bolshevik, an old member of the Party. But the ones being exposed in the trials now as criminals and villains, weren't they old Party members? Hadn't the people considered them real Communists and Bolsheviks? They had. So had she. And now her hair stood on end when she read their confessions. Yet imagining Ivan Grigoryevich giving the order to mix ground glass into children's food or poisoning wells was still impossible. But on the other hand, he had lived almost ten years abroad; he could have been obeying orders that even Ashkhen Stepanovna knew nothing about. And if Nina read his confession of treachery and espionage in the newspaper, what would she do then? Certainly they would ask her why she asked Budyagin for a recommendation. Naturally she would tell them how it happened, that Budyagin himself offered to give her a recommendation. It was flattering — Ordzhonikidze's deputy, an Old Bolshevik, had appreciated her political maturity. But what if they said, "But why didn't you come to us when you learned of his arrest? Why did you try to hide it?" That was the question she could prevent. She would go to the Party organization and tell them. They wouldn't blame her for having been in the same class with Lena Budyagina, visiting her home, meeting her father there. Incidentally, Budyagin also spoke at their school when they had Old Bolsheviks come to reminisce. She'd be sure to mention that.

* * *

And still, the fear burned inside her. Should she talk to Alevtina Fyodorovna? She was the only one Nina trusted totally.

After classes, Nina came into her office.

"May I have five minutes?"

"Come in," Alevtina Fyodorovna said, "sit down. What's the problem?"

When Nina told her about the arrest and asked for her advice, Alevtina Fyodorovna asked, "How do you know he was arrested?"

"Lena, his daughter, called me. You must remember her, we were in the same class."

Alevtina Fyodorovna cut off the second sentence, as if she hadn't heard it. "Do you maintain relations with her?"

"Well, we were in school together.... She's a girlfriend...."

"Why did she call you? To warn you?"

Nina got it then. My God, how stupid she had been! Lena had given her a signal, had warned her not to come, not to call, to pretend that she knew nothing and that way stay out of it. But Nina had to push her way into their house.

"It's up to you," Alevtina Fyodorovna said. "If you keep up relations with the Budyagins, then you have to tell your Party organization. But if you don't have a relationship, then I don't think you have to tell them anything. But it's your decision."

# ❧ 5 ❧

Nina considered Alevtina Fyodorovna's advice. Who remembered that Budyagin had recommended her? Who knew that she had visited Lena? No one. When Budyagin's name appeared in the newspaper, then she'd consider her options. But now? Why look for trouble?

She would wait. But she had to cover her rear. To be able to live without nervous tension, at least at home. It was time to take care of that.

However, it turned out to be harder than she had expected to exchange her room. Nina advertised and got phone calls. But the offers were unacceptable — a room next to the kitchen, six square meters, another in a dormitory, the same size, partitioned off by plywood from the next room and sharing a kitchen and toilet with twenty families. Another was a room in a cellar, the window below street level. They were all like that. Nina would have settled for anything, but Varya ... Hearing Nina on the phone and guessing what she was up to, Varya asked, "Are you planning to exchange our room?"

"Yes. I think it would be best for both of us."

"So do I," Varya agreed, "but remember that I'm not moving to a cellar, a communal flat, or a village outside Moscow."

In her ad, Nina had indicated the hours to call. But the phone rang day and night. The neighbors were annoyed, and nothing came of it anyway.

But with time her problems with Varya faded compared to the unexpected events at school — a conflict between Alevtina Fyodor-

ovna and the senior Pioneer leader, Tamara Nasedkina, or simply
Tusya.

Nina couldn't stand that pushy, chatty Komsomol, an uneducated
young woman who had managed to get to Moscow somehow after
graduating from a provincial school. "She used her pretty face and
her reluctance to say no," Alevtina Fyodorovna had commented.
But strangely, Alevtina Fyodorovna had put up with her. Tusya
conducted Pioneer meetings and rallies, bustled about, decorated
the Lenin corner, and was in good standing at the Regional
Committee of the Komsomol. Alevtina Fyodorovna did not demand
anything more from her, and once said to Nina, "They're all
empty-headed."

In the fall of the previous year they had begun preparing for the
hundredth anniversary of Pushkin's death. Tusya got involved. The
Pioneers learned Pushkin's poems, and one little boy began reading,
" 'Winter! The peasant, exulting...,' " but Tusya interrupted, "A
peasant can't be exultant. Under serfdom there was nothing to
celebrate."

And Tusya ordered him to learn another poem.

The story of that incident reached Alevtina Fyodorovna, and at
the Teachers' Council she acidly mocked Tusya and banned her
from the preparations for the anniversary. There were people to do
that without her help.

"The preparation is part of the Komsomol's plan," Tusya said
angrily. "You can't forbid me from doing it."

Alevtina Fyodorovna looked at her in silence, opened her file,
took out a newspaper, found the spot she needed, circled it with a
red pencil, and handed it to Tusya. "Read that. Aloud."

Tusya hesitated.

The elderly teachers seated around the big table waited silently.

"I've read it already," Tusya announced.

"If you don't want to read it," Alevtina Fyodorovna said, "we'll
do so ourselves."

Alevtina Fyodorovna adjusted her glasses and read slowly and
confidently, " 'All Pioneer work in the school must be done with the
approval of the school director. Pioneer work is part of the entire
education and upbringing work of the school. The public and social

work of the Komsomol and the Pioneers must be directed toward the struggle for quality education.' "

She folded the newspaper and put it back. "Do you agree with the resolution?"

"I do," Tusya whispered, eyes down.

"Then obey it. Otherwise you'll have to change your job."

But this wasn't the end of it.

December 1, 1936, was the second anniversary of Kirov's murder.

At the Pioneer meeting Tusya talked about the horrible event. Then she asked Kozlov, from the third grade, to read a page from a book about Kirov's childhood. But no sooner had Kozlov opened the book than his classmate Glazov shouted, "His father killed Kirov!"

Kozlov cried out, "That's not true! My father never killed anyone."

"Then why was he shot? What for? For Kirov, right?"

"Your father was executed?" Tusya asked.

"Yes," Kozlov said, swallowing his tears.

"Then you really shouldn't be reading about Kirov," Tusya said, and took away the book. "Sit down."

There was another discussion over this. Of course, Kozlov's father had been declared an "enemy of the people," his name was even mentioned in some trial, but the boy, a Pioneer, wasn't guilty of anything, was he?

That was the question that Alevtina Fyodorovna asked Tusya at the Teachers' Council. The topic was a tricky one — there were a lot of children from families like that at the school. But Alevtina Fyodorovna knew what could happen when children's cruelty went unchecked.

"Glazov," Tusya replied challengingly, "expressed his feeling toward enemies of the people. He's a child and doesn't know how to make speeches, but he said what he thought. I don't have the right to gag him."

"But why did you have Kozlov, the son of an enemy of the people, read about Kirov?"

"I didn't know his father had been arrested," Tusya explained.

"You're supposed to know these things. If your Pioneer has a father who is an enemy of the people, you must know that. You don't have the right not to know! You must know everything about every Pioneer, and if you don't, then this is not the job for you." Alevtina Fyodorovna looked around the table sternly. "Just think — on the anniversary of Kirov's death to give the floor to a son of an enemy of the people!"

Tusya bit her tongue. She didn't manage to get the better of the old Communist, experienced in Party in-fighting.

But the old Communist had underestimated the young one.

A few days later Tusya had the Pioneers line up. Borya Kaufman, the son of an engineer from the Stalin car factory, was made to face them as they chanted, "Borya's father is an enemy of the people, Borya's father is an enemy of the people." Little Borya stood at attention, biting his lip, trying not to cry. He began to sob and the line chanted more fiercely, "Borya's father is an enemy of the people."

It was a disgusting sight. Nina gasped in indignation, but she couldn't rebuke Tusya in front of the children; it wasn't professional, and she didn't have the right to interfere in Tusya's work. With a stony face, Alevtina Fyodorovna walked past the line to her office.

Nina followed.

Alevtina Fyodorovna took off her coat and hung it up, and then said, without looking at Nina, "What do you want?"

"Alevtina Fyodorovna ... they're children...."

"I know they're children," Alevtina Fyodorovna replied curtly.

As it turned out later, Tusya had told her that what she was doing was on orders from the Regional Committee of the Komsomol and she would do it again in the future. If Alevtina Fyodorovna didn't believe her, she could call and ask the secretary of the committee.

Alevtina Fyodorovna didn't call.

At the next "parade," Tusya had Lilya Evdokimova face the other children. They merrily chanted, "Lilya's father is an enemy of the people, Lilya's father is an enemy of the people." Eleven-year-old Lilya didn't cry, she stood there with her head down, but as soon as it was over, she grabbed her book bag and ran from school.

This spectacle was repeated daily. Schoolwork decreased. Children were skipping school, hoping to avoid the parade, but it didn't help. Tusya had all the information she needed.

Nina learned that it was Alyosha Perevoznikov's "turn" by accident as she was coming to school. Alyosha was her pet, a shy boy with rosy cheeks, who lived with his stepfather. His mother worked abroad. One day Alyosha brought in a photograph taken in Spain — an amazingly beautiful woman, with straight long lashes like Alyosha's, smiling and holding a bouquet to her breast.

The stepfather had been arrested last month, and Alyosha had been taken in by an aunt who lived farther away, and he started coming in late. Nina, the class supervisor, had to put marks in his record against her will. One morning as Nina was walking to school, she saw Alyosha's mother for the first time — in a long fur coat, unusual in Moscow, and bare head, she walked with her arm around Alyosha's shoulders, hugging him close, and asking him not to cry in the parade. Nina fell back. She couldn't look the woman in the eye or meet Alyosha's gaze.

A few days later, Alyosha's mother slit her wrists and jumped from the sixth floor. The school janitor, a Tatar woman, who had seen it, said that a crowd came running and the dead woman was stripped of her foreign watch and all her rings. Alyosha vanished from the school.

They added expulsion of the upperclassmen from the Komsomol to the Pioneer parades. The first to be expelled was Ira Peterson, daughter of the former commandant of the Kremlin. She was sick and not at the meeting. Her friend Valya Shcheslavskaya said that personal matters could be discussed only in the presence of the Komsomol member accused. Shura Maksimov, who was always sticking his nose in, shouted, "Do you want to leave a Komsomol card in the hands of an enemy?"

"She's not an enemy, she's the daughter of an enemy," Valya argued.

Ira was expelled and Valya was reprimanded for appeasement. The next day, the secretary of the Komsomol organization, Tonya Chegodayeva, tendered her resignation as secretary because her father had been arrested the night before. Tonya was expelled, put in front of the meeting, stripped of her Komsomol button, her GTO button (Ready to Work and Defend), her GSO button (Ready for

Sanitary Defense), and her Voroshilov badge. Tonya was an activist and the best student, the prime candidate for a Certificate of Excellence, which she did not get — a week later she and her mother were exiled from Moscow to Astrakhan.

The second candidate for a Certificate of Excellence, Yuri Belenky, was also transferred. He refused to denounce his mother and father at the Komsomol meetings, and when Shura Maksimov leaped up to tear off Yuri's button, Yuri slapped his hand, took off the badge himself, put it on the desk, and left the room, slamming the door. Alevtina Fyodorovna learned that he got a job as a truck driver delivering bread at night — he had his baby sister to take care of.

Alevtina Fyodorovna lost weight. Her English-style suit drooped from her shoulders as if from a hanger, and red blotches spread on her face.

In January, on the anniversary of Lenin's death, tenth-grader Yuri Afanasyev, reciting a report, misspoke — instead of "Lenin died" he said "Stalin died." He corrected himself immediately, and later showed his outline where it was correctly written. Nevertheless, he was expelled from the Komsomol. They wanted to expel him from school, too, but Alevtina Fyodorovna would not allow it — he had only one semester left until graduation. She had him reprimanded "for inattention that grew into a serious political mistake."

And the next day, a new event. Tenth-graders Trishchenko and Svidersky were playing billiards with metal balls in the club room. A ball flew wildly off the table, hit the plaster bust of Stalin, and damaged the nose. Alevtina Fyodorovna was informed of the incident, and the bust was put in a sack and taken to the storeroom.

In the morning, the janitor, Yakov Ivanovich, took two tenth-graders, Paramonov and Kumanin, and went to the factory for a new bust of Comrade Stalin, driving in a pickup truck.

They got the new statue and signed for it. Yakov Ivanovich sat up front in the cab with the driver, while Paramonov and Kumanin rode in the back, to hold the bust. The truck kept swaying on the cobblestone road, so they tied rope to the back of the cab and around the bust's neck.

They reached the school during recess, and as the driver lowered the back of the truck, one of the little kids cried out, "Look, they've hanged Stalin! They hanged Stalin in the truck."

Kids crowded around. Kumanin and Paramonov tried to untie the bust. Tusya arrived and waved her arms at them. "Stop that!"

She climbed up into the truck, pushed aside Paramonov and Kumanin, and ordered the little ones to bring Alevtina Fyodorovna immediately.

The girls ran into the director's office. "Alevtina Fyodorovna! Hurry to the yard. They hanged Comrade Stalin."

Alevtina Fyodorovna did not ask questions but put on her coat and came outside.

Tusya was in the truck bed. "Take a look at this, Alevtina Fyodorovna!" she said triumphantly, pointing to the bust of Stalin tied to the cab.

"Who did this?"

Tusya pointed to Kumanin and Paramonov standing next to her.

"The bust would have broken," Kumanin said, "if we hadn't tied it."

"Why around the neck?" Tusya squealed.

"Stop squealing!" Paramonov hissed. "Show me how else we could have attached it!"

Alevtina Fyodorovna looked at the janitor and driver. "The road was bumpy, it could have broken," Yakov Ivanovich said. "The driver will confirm that."

"Take down the bust and bring it to the Little Red Corner. But carefully," Alevtina Fyodorovna ordered.

"That was political deviation," Tusya said clearly and angrily.

"We'll straighten this out," Alevtina Fyodorovna replied curtly.

It wasn't Alevtina Fyodorovna who straightened it out, but a Special Commission from the Party Regional Committee, checking on the "signals" it had received — a letter from Tusya and a group of upperclassmen in the Komsomol, who charged Alevtina Fyodorovna with stifling all attempts by the Pioneers and Komsomols to express their just indignation and to condemn the enemies of the people; protecting the children of the enemies of the people; not expelling from school Yuri Afanasyev, who had brazenly announced at a meeting that Comrade Stalin had died; and trying to cover up the fact that students Trishchenko and Svidersky expressed their counterrevolutionary essence by breaking a bust of Comrade Stalin and had the bust put in the storeroom, shut the Little Red Corner, and ordered a new bust. No measures had been taken against Trishchenko and Svidersky. Moreover, tenth-graders Kumanin and Paramonov had mocked the new bust of Comrade Stalin. They hanged him by the neck in a truck — the whole school had seen that — and no measures were taken against them.

These and other incidents were results of the opportunistic line the school director was following. For instance, she fired Communist teachers and replaced them with dubious and hostile elements, as for instance the teacher Irina Yulyevna Einwald, the daughter of a bourgeois professor and White émigré and the sister of a recently exposed right oppositionist. Physics teacher Yurenev, a graduate of Munich University with a German diploma, expressed bourgeois views in science. Literature teacher Mezentsev was bringing up decadent feelings in the schoolchildren, praising the symbolist writers Severyanin, Balmont, and Andrei Bely and teaching the children about prostitution, telling them about *The Decameron* and *The Golden Ass*.

And another accusation. The cover of their class notebooks with a picture of "Knowing Oleg" on his horse had a secret code — "Down with Stalin." The hanging stirrup was a "D," the little curlicue next to it was an "O" and so on.... All the students were supposed to tear off that cover and turn it in to their class supervisors, who would turn them in to the assistant principal. However, Tusya's letter maintained, two hundred fifty notebooks had been handed out and only one hundred eighty covers had been returned, which meant that seventy hostile drawings were still in the hands of the students. And the school director, a Communist, had calmly allowed this to happen.

The commission questioned all the teachers, technical staff, and Komsomols, as well as many upperclassmen. They spoke separately with each.

They had a talk with Nina.

She didn't know the chairman of the commission. He must have worked in the Party Regional Committee. But she knew the other two — the deputy chief of the Regional Education Department and a young female teacher of literature from school number 86.

Nina maintained her dignity. She was wholly on the side of Alevtina Fyodorovna, an honest member of the Party. Tusya's accusations were nasty nonsense, revenge against Alevtina Fyodorovna's proper correction about Pushkin. Tusya's interpretation of the poem "Winter! The peasant exulting" was the remnant of the crude sociology of the twenties, condemned by the Party. Mocking ten-year-old children of enemies of the people is poor pedagogy, for "the son is not responsible for the father." So said Comrade Stalin, and Tusya should know that and not set up such charades. The incident with the bust of Comrade Stalin was an accident. Of course, the billiard table should not have been in the Little Red Corner. That was a mistake, but it had been there for many years. As for transporting the bust in the truck, it would have been worse if it had been broken in the back, and the boys found the only solution — to secure it firmly. Well, they tied it improperly, carelessly, they didn't think. A random chain of events. Now as for the teachers. Irina Yulyevna is a highly qualified teacher. Of course, her father, a famous literary critic, did emigrate, but Irina Yulyevna didn't go abroad. Yes, her brother has been accused of right deviation, but Irina Yulyevna herself does not belong to any party. And as for Mezentsev the literature teacher . . .

Nina explained all this calmly and with dignity. Of course there were faults in the school, but what school didn't have any? But the political, pedagogical line was always correct and fully corresponded to the resolutions of the Party and the state on schools.

The commission members listened to Nina attentively, and the lady from the Education Department wrote down her answers. They asked no questions, thanked her, and let her go.

She left feeling calm and certain that everything would be cleared up. Yes, they needed vigilance, but real Party vigilance, not a semblance of it. Yes, they had to seek enemies, but real enemies, not someone like Alevtina Fyodorovna, a most loyal Party member, faithful to the ideas of Lenin and Stalin. And they could not allow a healthy pedagogical and student collective to be disrupted by a troublemaker, an empty-headed and ignorant girl.

However, the collective was disrupted. It was hard to work when you were being watched. But they complained very carefully, just two or three words, and walked away from one another. And even though Nina assumed that everyone had responded as she had, her certainty that everything would be cleared up had vanished. Of course, the times were tense, but the teachers were calm in front of their students, as if to say: Everything is fine. The popular crooner Utesov sang the same old song, *"Everything is fine, lovely marquise, everything is fine, is fine ..."* And that position, in Nina's opinion, was completely natural for people with a clear conscience.

Everyone's conscience was clear, but something was hanging over the school. There had been acute disagreements in years previous, but when they were discussed, the teachers debated, sometimes even argued, but then they reconciled. Now they did not debate or argue. There was a stultifying silence in the teachers' room. The word *commission* was not mentioned. No one told what he had been asked and what he replied.

Alevtina Fyodorovna continued to lead the school with a firm hand, but she was grim and taciturn.

Nina, naturally, repeated her conversation with the commission in great detail to Alevtina Fyodorovna, who listened in silence, staring at her inkwell. And suddenly, for no reason, Nina realized that Alevtina Fyodorovna was completely alone — no husband, no children, no sisters or brothers. She had no one to complain to or to ask for advice. Nina's voice trembled with sympathy, but Alevtina Fyodorovna ignored it.

"Well," Alevtina Fyodorovna said dryly, "you said all the right things."

## 🐱 6 🐱

**B**efore Vika's trip to Paris, Nelli Vladimirova gave her some good advice. "Don't deal with émigrés, they're all poverty-stricken. They'll try to wheedle contributions for the poor, for widows and orphans, for funerals, anniversaries, fund-raising dinners, building churches, children's holidays, they'll put you on their stupid charity and honorary boards," she said, and took a drag of her cigarette. "None of it's worth a damn. They'll embroil you in their fights — they're all at one another's throats, calling one another Soviet spies. Keep away from them from the start, don't get in contact. You're not an émigré, you're the wife of a Frenchman — so be a Frenchwoman. Charles must have a large circle of friends, join their society — after all, he's not a merchant like my Georges, he's a viscount, he's a 'de.' "

That "de" really impressed Nelli.

"And also," Nelli went on, "be moderate, hold out at least a year, the hunger for consumer goods that we all have will pass on its own. Don't go crazy with clothes; show Charles that you don't throw away money. Remember — the French tend to be stingy, so economize. Charles will like that. But they're also proud. A real Frenchman won't let his wife not hold her own with the other wives. The less you spend on yourself, the more he'll spend on you."

Talking and smoking, Nelli paced the room, tall and bony.... A horse! Yet men threw themselves at her.... What was her secret? She was a good woman and a good friend....

"Of course, you don't know how to cook," Nelli said, either asking or stating.

"I don't," Vika confessed.

"Why should you? You have Fenya. Don't worry. No one will put you in front of a stove there. You'll find a new Fenya. And there are restaurants. And men like to cook — they're actually quite good at it. But you still should know how to do a few things."

"For exotica? Borshch, solyanka, shashlik?" Vika grimaced. She hated cooking.

"No, borshch and solyanka are beyond you — it takes great artistry to make them, you need lots of practice. As for shashlik, even here that's a man's job."

"Pelmeni?"

"Complicated and lots of trouble. You have to be able to cook something quickly, when you're back from the theater and need a snack, or on Sunday, when the maid is off, it's nice to feed your husband yourself. An omelette, say, with tomatoes, they have tomatoes year round, not like Moscow. Or maybe grilled cheese — you can manage grilled cheese sandwiches, I hope? The French have only coffee for breakfast, by the way, but you should be able to do these simple dishes."

"All right," Vika said. "I'll keep all that in mind, thank you. But tell me, do you have the phone or address for Cecile Schuster?"

"What do you need with her?"

"We went to the same school, after all."

"Oh, my God," Nelli said, laughing, "sweet childhood memories. Forget it. Cecile forgot a long time ago, believe me, no room for sentiment with her. She's a businesswoman. By the way, she's French on her mother's side. Did you know that?"

"Yes."

"Well, Cecile is working in the fashionable store called Carolina, working with Epstein himself, designing clothes! I called her once, told her who I was, and she hung up. But you know I can handle these things. I went to the store, ordered two of the most expensive dresses, and after that, just imagine, she recognized me. Why is she leery of Soviets? Because they are poor and the émigrés are poor. She needs rich clients, and only rich clients, who can make her famous, so that people will stop saying 'a dress by Epstein' and will start saying 'a dress by Mlle Cecile Schuster.' Get it? And she'll be a success."

"Where is the store?"

"I told you, the Carolina. Ask Charles, he'll take you there. You'll see Cecile Schuster. You'll recognize her, but I'm not sure whether she'll recognize you."

Vika took Nelli Vladimirova's good advice. What did she need Russians for? She wouldn't have any nostalgia for Russia. There was nothing to tie her to Russia. Her mother died a long time ago, her father would die soon, Vadim was an ass, and she couldn't stand him. As for her school friends — where were they? She didn't have any. She forgot everyone. The girls from the Metropole? Whores, snitches, cheap stuff, and the ones who were more expensive would find their own way abroad. What had she seen in Moscow, what was she leaving behind? Pathetic stores, the Architect in his underwear, rudeness, lies in every corner, and fear that Sharok would force her back to Maroseika. . . .

She had escaped! She was gone, gone, gone! Now she was a Frenchwoman. She would become part of Charles's family and they would protect her. But when she got on the train at Byelorussian Station, she worried about stopping at the border the next day at Negoreloe and how the border guards could ruin her life by finding something wrong with her passport. And the customs agents would make her turn out her pockets and find something and force her off the train and send her back to Moscow. She felt panicked. Oh, God, save me from that, help me get through it! But Charles must not see that she was nervous, and certainly not the border guards — her nervousness would attract their attention. She pulled herself together, straightened her shoulders, fluffed up her hair, pulled down her dress to lower the neckline, and put on a haughty expression, the one she used in the Metropole Restaurant to show the lounge lizards that she was unapproachable and could not be asked to dance. Let the bums at the border see that they weren't dealing with a meek, terrified Soviet citizen who trembles at the sight of a policeman, but a foreigner, an untouchable woman.

At Negoreloe the border guards entered the compartment, followed by the customs men. They resembled one another, disgusting mugs, but she didn't even stir. She simply crossed her legs. Charles showed them their documents, gave them their passports, and when they were asked to go out into the hallway, she rose slowly and calmly went out, waiting for them to search the compartment, and then came back in with Charles.

The train moved, picking up speed, and Charles said, looking out the window, "Pologne."

They were in Poland. That was it! She had left Russia, Charles had brought her out of that hell. She leaned into his chest and wept.

He patted her head and said soothing things, touched by the pain with which she was parting from her homeland, which she was leaving for his sake. She had left her family, divorced her husband, and broken off ties with her friends, all for him.

Vika grabbed his hand and brought it to her lips and kissed it. That was her first sincere moment. In Moscow she used to meet Charles at Nelli's apartment. Nelli's husband, Georges, was out all day and Nelli would take off, too, leaving them alone. Charles was very attractive, strong, and experienced. She was no less experienced, but she never showed it, being a decent married woman. But she submitted to him, learning his lessons quickly and well, and did not restrain the passion he aroused in her. She would hold him tight, stunned, spent, submissive. . . . Men liked that, it fed their egos.

But now, in the train, this was sincere. She was filled with tenderness for Charles. He had been so dignified at the border, a man from the free world, and his example gave her strength. Vika opened her purse, took out a handkerchief, and wiped her tears. She would never disappoint Charles, she would be a faithful, loyal wife. She recalled his former fiancée — would there be any unexpected problems from that quarter? Hardly. Of course, Frenchwomen were lively, piquant, and witty, but they didn't have her regal bearing, her majestic modesty, and her silent significance. Anyway, Charles had chosen her. She would always be by his side. She would make their home beautiful and she would show Parisians what Russian hospitality meant.

Vika didn't have to furnish a home because a luxurious apartment on the third floor of an ancient building on rue de Bellechasse, an aristocratic part of Paris, awaited her. It was a cozy street, much narrower than the Arbat, cobblestone and fitted with tall street-lights.

The doors, glass with fanciful wrought-iron guards and a massive brass ring, led into a long lobby with a marble floor. The right wall was mirrored and to the left was the concierge's room and next to it a board listing the tenants' names but not their apartment numbers, so that strangers could not go up without asking the concierge.

Vika took a quick look at herself in the mirror, adjusted her hat, and saw a short plump woman in glasses hurry over to Charles, holding her hands out. *"C'est vous, Monsieur Charles, quelle surprise."*

A maid came down, just as short but skinny, wearing a frilled apron, and she also smiled and said, *"Monsieur Charles, quelle joie, quel bonheur!"*

Charles introduced Vika, *"Madame Victoria, ma femme."*

Both of them babbled joyously, clapping their hands, *"Ah, Monsieur Charles, permettez nous de vous feliciter! C'est un vrai plaisir de voir un tel couple. Vous êtes si beaux!"*

They were happy but not servile.

They know how to share another's joy, not like our envious louts, thought Vika.

The concierge led them to the elevator and said something else to Charles as she looked at Vika. Charles, smiling, translated. "Madame Trubeau informs you that the house has cellars for wine and logs for the fireplace. And she also wanted to warn you that the elevator goes up only to the sixth floor. The seventh is for the maids' rooms."

In the meantime, Mme Trubeau made a gesture, inviting Vika to sit down. There was a red velvet bench next to the elevator, and above it a rectangular mirror, and a red carpet covered the broad staircase.

Suzanne, the maid, went up first, with the luggage that barely fit into the narrow elevator, and opened the apartment. Vika and Charles went up next.

The landing had an oak parquet floor, as did the roomy entry, with oak closets for coats. A long plump stuffed *boudin* lay near the door to keep drafts from coming in the crack between the floor and the door.

Suzanne left one suitcase in the entryway, brought the other to the bedroom, and showed Charles his mail in the wicker basket. Charles excused her, saying that they had eaten on the train.

"I hope that Madame will be satisfied with everything. If you need anything, I will be in my room."

"Thank you, Suzanne," Vika said.

Then she and Charles went through the apartment, looking at everything with great interest. Four rooms. High ceilings with moldings. The biggest room was the living room. Two tables, one by the leather couch and armchairs, the other at the opposite wall, surrounded by armchairs with bent legs and high backs, upholstered in velvet. Vika didn't know what the style was called. There was an upright piano of fine wood made by Baudet, on wheels and with brass handles on the sides, a big old-fashioned globe in two crisscrossed brass hoops, and another two globes on the bookshelves.

Vika twirled one with her finger, the way they had at school in geography class.

"Were there explorers in your family?"

Charles laughed. "No. You'll find globes in many houses. It's a custom. But the Bolsheviks want to conquer the world, while we keep it at home in the form of a globe."

The living room windows opened on the courtyard, planted with chestnut and plane trees. There were flowers in the boxes on the windowsills, the buds about to burst — were they geraniums? The windows were tall, almost from floor to ceiling, rounded at the top. On the secretaire were silver flacons, candlesticks, and a cup with rounded indentations inside. Vika did not know what it was for and thought it was an ashtray. She tossed her match in it and knocked off some ash into it. Charles looked at her with a smile and brought her an ashtray. "If my mother saw that, she would say, 'Russians don't take care of expensive things.'"

He went to the kitchen, washed it out, dried it, and came back with a bottle of wine, splashed some into the cup, which he held by the handle and swished around, while the bubbles settled into the indentations.

"This is an old thing, which belonged to my grandfather — a cup for wine degustation."

Moving from room to room, she thought that she would

definitely have his children, a boy and a girl, and then they'd be a real family. She wanted to tell him right there and then, but she thought she'd wait; after all, she had had two abortions. But the doctors here in Paris were excellent, everything would work out. She pictured herself pregnant, in a full dress, with her hair pulled back modestly. "Victoria is in a delicate condition," the wives of his friends would say. And why not? She was twenty-five, he was thirty-five, the perfect difference, ten years. They would have healthy, good, beautiful children. Charles's parents probably were dreaming of grandchildren, especially since a boy would continue the line and aristocrats took that seriously. Charles was their only son. These were Vika's plans. She knew that Charles was her ultimate dream, a winning ticket. Many girls married anyone at all, just to get abroad, and then looked around for someone better. Vika had heard some things about their lives. None of them made a better marriage — on the contrary, they sank lower. Vika wasn't afraid of sinking to the bottom; she simply didn't want anyone other than Charles.

The study had built-in bookshelves. Vika had never been interested in books, but she knew that it would be a wrong step not to show an interest in the books that Charles loved and used. She ran her hand along the spines, reading the titles aloud. She read French easily, quickly, perhaps not understanding everything, but Charles was next to her, smiling, pleased that she was looking at his books, and he did not correct her mistakes. He was very tactful. He never corrected her in Moscow nor did he do it later, leaving perfection of her accent to her teacher and to Paris. Standing next to her by the shelves, he said that he kept only the books he had to have at hand here. The nineteenth-century Larousse, the four-volume Littre dictionary, the encyclopedia of voyages for 1860 — explorations, discoveries, fifty-four volumes in all . . .

"Oho!" Vika said. "That's a lot!"

"For reference," Charles said with a smile, "although some are out of date."

A short distance away from the encyclopedia lay a volume of Montesquieu. "I forgot to put it back before this trip," Charles explained. "Suzanne knows not to touch anything in my study."

Vika nodded in understanding. The collected works of Montesquieu, Corneille, Flaubert, and Daudet she had seen on the shelves in the living room. She had not read Montesquieu or Corneille, she knew only *Madame Bovary* of Flaubert's, and had only gotten halfway through Daudet's *Tartarin de Tarascon*. She'd have to keep quiet about that or switch the conversation to Maupassant, whose works she began reading when she was ten or so.

Vika was surprised by the dining room. It was the smallest room in the apartment — a long table with chairs crowded around it and a buffet, nothing more. In their apartment on Starokonyushenny, as in all of Moscow, the dining room was the biggest room.

A corridor led to the bedroom, with ceiling-high cupboards and closets on the right and a large bathroom, with a window into the garden, and a toilet on the left.

Vika opened the door, saw the wide wooden bed, and laughed. "Will we be able to find each other in there?"

"We will, we will," Charles promised.

She looked at the three-sided mirror, the chest of redwood with brass handles, no trifles except for a light blue porcelain vase ornamented with bows and garlands of flowers. She would like to put in two more chairs, she'd have to think about it....

*"C'est tout. Ça te plait?"* Charles asked.

He used only those phrases in French that she understood.

Vika wrapped her arms around his neck. "Oh, Charles!"

# ❦ 7 ❦

On the third or fourth day, the woman with her two children showed up, Sasha's fellow traveler from Kezhma. The scarf had slipped from her head, she had a suitcase and bag in one hand, the baby in the other, and the older girl was dragging a bundle, barely keeping up with her mother.

The woman pushed into the station and then looked around in a helpless, harried way. She couldn't deal with the disorder. She didn't know where to go with the children, where to put down her things.

Where had she been all this time? Friends must have sheltered her, trying to get tickets, but unable to manage hadn't wanted to keep her anymore; they were too afraid to keep the children even — otherwise she wouldn't have brought them with her.

Sasha came over to her. "Hello!"

The woman jumped and then nodded; she had recognized him.

"Let me help!" He took the things from her hands, took the girl's bundle, led them into the station, found a spot near the wall, put down the suitcase, sat the girl on it, and put the bundle down next to her.

"Is there anything breakable in the suitcase?"

The woman did not answer, as if she had not heard the question. She stared at Sasha in bewilderment and just as silently followed him to the line, where the last person was a tall red-haired peasant.

"Stand behind him. Even if you go to sit with the girls for a while, you can see him from a distance, so you won't get lost."

She nodded her understanding. And then stared at the floor. She didn't thank Sasha, didn't ask how long she would have to stand in line for tickets. And he didn't ask her any questions — she wasn't capable of a normal conversation.

Then the girls were thirsty and the woman didn't know where to get water, so Sasha took her kettle and went for boiling water. Then she led the children to the toilet, a filthy messy hut not far from the station, while Sasha kept an eye on the suitcase. The next morning he watched the girls when she went to the market for bread and milk.

"Will you eat with us?'"

"I've eaten," Sasha said with a smile, and added jokingly, "I just don't know how to thank you for the invitation. 'Thank you, citizen,' or 'Thank you, comrade.' "

The woman looked at him in fright, expecting a trap in his question, and reluctantly said, "My name is Ksenya."

No patronymic, no last name, just Ksenya.

"My name is Sasha. Now we're acquainted." He wanted to add something light, something to cheer her up, but he couldn't come up with anything.

Ksenya was looking over his shoulder, her eyes turned round in horror. She dropped the bread, and Sasha looked back to see what had frightened her. A patrol was checking documents, just a few feet away.

Ksenya backed against the wall, grabbed her suitcase, looked at the children, the patrol, and the door.

"Don't worry," Sasha said quietly. "Stay calm."

Pushing Sasha aside and not looking at his passport, the patrol leader walked toward Ksenya. He had a practiced eye. She was new.

"Your documents, citizen!"

With trembling hands she got her passport out from beneath her coat.

The man examined it, and nodded at the children. "Whose are they?"

"Mine."

"Why aren't they in your passport?"

"They're in their father's."

"Where are you going?"

"Krasnoyarsk."

The man returned her passport and moved along. Ksenya sank onto the bundle and squeezed her head.

Sasha went out onto the platform to smoke.

The pushy man with the missing teeth was hanging around the loudspeakers again and looked at Sasha but was apparently afraid to speak.

The speech of the prosecutor Vyshinsky was being transmitted. Sasha listened inattentively. He was irritated by the man who kept him from concentrating. He didn't feel like going back inside, the sight of that wretched Ksenya was killing him, and he'd now been at the Taishet station for five days. What if the patrol changed and the new man didn't believe his story about the mother-in-law? They'd take away his passport, drag him down to the commandant, and never let him out.

Sasha kept an eye on the business travelers. Maybe one of them would help him out, even though he knew that they couldn't get two tickets on one business pass. But still, from time to time, he went over to the line and looked. What if?

On the morning of the sixth day, he saw three fellows standing by the cashier. Young, cheerful, pushy, banging their fists on the window, making demands of the cashier. They had to be geologists, miners, though why would there be geologists in Siberia in January? Maybe they were Komsomol workers? Sasha took a better look. They had similar sheepskin coats, felt boots, and fur hats and backpacks. Not Komsomol. Sasha pushed his way to the cashier's window and stood next to them. From their conversation he could tell that they were Muscovites, and that made him happy.

One fellow was very tall, narrow-shouldered, with soft but good features — he reminded Sasha of Father Vasily, which made Sasha like him. His name was Oleg, the guys called him Olazhka, and he was not only the tallest, he seemed to be the senior man and the pushiest.

When the station chief came out, Oleg addressed him. "When are we going to get our tickets? I told you, we're on assignment from the People's Commissariat of Transportation."

"If you're from the commissariat, you should have a letter."

"Our institute is doing surveying work for the commissariat.

There's a branch line being planned for Ust-Kut, or don't you know that?"

"I know it all," the chief interrupted. "But there are no seats! When there are seats, you'll go!"

"We're going to telegraph Moscow," Oleg threatened.

"You can telegraph God, there still are no seats. Irkutsk isn't giving us any seats."

"You're holding up the plans for the railroad!" Oleg said severely.

"Don't try to scare me! I can't carry you on my back. Stop making noise!"

And he left.

"No seats, no tickets, no trains," Sasha said with a laugh, making their acquaintance.

"The bum!" Oleg said. "He's kept us here a second day."

"Second," Sasha said. "I've been here six waiting for a train out."

They started talking. They worked at some planning institute, Sasha never figured out the acronym. Working on the branch line between Taishet and Ust-Kut, they had been on an expedition on the Lena River in the summer. They had visited the settlements Ust-Kut and Osetrovo, they surveyed, and then came back to their base in Taishet, where they did the paperwork, and now they were ready to bring the material back to Moscow. Oleg turned out to be from the Arbat. He lived on Bolshoi Afanasyevsky and had gone to school 9 in Starokonyushenny.

"I know that school," Sasha said. "It used to be Medvenik-ovskaya. We used to go to the gym there. I'm from the Arbat, too, house fifty-one, where the Arbat Art Cinema is. Do you know it?"

Oleg knew the Art and Sasha's building, because he had friends living there, for instance, Melik-Parsadanov.

"Grisha?"

"Yes!"

"We're on the same stairs. And his sister Rita and I ... Do you know Rita?"

"Of course!"

"We were in the same class."

"Well," Oleg said, "it's nice meeting you here."

His friendliness encouraged Sasha. "Listen, guys," he said in a low voice, "help me get out of here. I don't have a business pass."

"How did you end up here?"

"Affairs of the heart," Sasha said quickly.

"Our pass is for three," Oleg said thoughtfully.

"Will the cashier look at it closely?" another of the men said, snub-nosed with light hair and yet with an Armenian surname, Vartanyan.

"She will," Oleg said.

"Then just stick him in. It's handwritten."

They spoke softly so that the other people in the line wouldn't hear.

Oleg took the pass from his pocket. It was written by hand, but on official stationery and stamped with a seal.

"Write it there," Vartanyan said.

"What about Moscow?"

"In Moscow we'll cross it out and say that they were going to send someone else and then changed their minds and crossed it out."

"Where will we find that ink?"

Oh God, would the whole thing be lost because of ink? Ordinary violet ink, but where could you get it here at the station?

"Maybe the cashier has ink," Sasha said, trying not to sound worried. "Should we ask the cashier?"

The station chief appeared. As he walked by, he asked grimly, "Will you detour to Krasnoyarsk? You can get an express to Moscow there."

"Sure."

"Give me your pass."

The chief held the pass against the doorjamb and, looking at the men with an unhappy face, asked, "How many are you?"

"Four," said Oleg.

The station chief wrote in the corner of the pass — *116-4.* The first number was the train, the second, the number of tickets.

This was great luck. The Krasnoyarsk-Moscow train would be easier, and at any rate, they could go to Novosibirsk or even Sverdlovsk, and there were trains to Moscow every day from there.

Sasha offered money for the ticket, but Oleg wouldn't take it. "We'll settle up in the train. The one sixteen isn't due for another two hours."

"Thanks." Sasha looked at Oleg and Vartanyan.

"You can thank us when we get the tickets."

The third fellow did not get involved in the conversation. He had smiled ironically when Sasha mentioned affairs of the heart — he didn't believe him but hadn't protested getting him a ticket. He just stood there with his face toward the door, listening to Vyshinsky's speech. "This is a gang of criminals that doesn't differ from bandits who use brass knuckles and switchblades on a dark night on the highway.... This is a pack of spies, terrorists, and saboteurs. These 'politicians' didn't mind derailing trains, gassing mines and then sending miners down, or attacking engineers from dark alleys. Burn down a factory. Blow children up in a dynamite pit.

"With all our people, I accuse these dastardly criminals who deserve only one punishment — execution, death!"

## 8

After standing near the surveyors for a little longer, Sasha went for his suitcase, which he had left with Ksenya's things.

"I've been waiting for you," Ksenya said. "I wanted to go out; will you please watch the girls?"

"Will you be long?"

"Ten minutes, no more."

"Go ahead."

The girls were quiet, huddled against each other. Sasha felt sorry for them. They didn't know about their father's arrest, of course, but they could see how upset their mother was and knew that something fearful had happened. The other children here looked just as hurt and miserable, the anxieties of the adults were transferred to them, and they sat quietly on bundles and suitcases, without laughing, smiling, or the usual childish playfulness.

Sasha patted the bigger girl's cheek. "What's your name?"

"Lena."

"Lena, Elena. Elena the Beautiful, do you know that fairy tale?"

"My name's not Elena, it's Marlena."

"Ah," Sasha said. "I see, 'Marx-Lenin.' How about you?" he asked the little one.

She whispered something unintelligible.

"What?"

The older girl explained, "Her name is Lina, which is for Stalina."

The girls' names said a lot about their family.

Sasha rubbed Lina's cheek gently. Then there was a stir in the room, the crowd moved, and that told him a patrol was coming.

They approached Sasha. Habitually and calmly he took out his passport — it was the same men.

The senior one took a quick look at the passport and returned it, and then pointed at the children. "Whose children?"

"Some woman, she went out for a minute."

"What woman, what's her name?"

"I don't know, she was here, and she said, 'I'm going out for a minute, watch the children.' "

The senior man crouched in front of Lena. "Little girl, what's your name?"

"Marlena."

"Fine, Marlena! And do you know your last name?"

"I do. Pavlova."

"Pavlova," he said in satisfaction. "Pavlova, you say." He looked at his partner.

So they were looking for Ksenya. And they traced her so easily and quickly. She didn't get away.

"Well, all right," the man asked Lena, "where is your mother?"

"She's here, she just went out."

"And your father?"

"Papa . . ." She looked at Sasha. "Papa . . . went to Krasnoyarsk."

"So you're going to visit him?"

The girl said nothing.

The man stood up and walked away, but never letting the girls and the door out of his sight. And as soon as Ksenya came back, they dove in her direction. They would arrest her and take her with the children to the commandant's office — Sasha had no doubt about it.

He wanted to take his suitcase and go over to his new friends, who were still at the window, but the patrolmen had their eye on him, too, and they might be suspicious if he suddenly ran off with his things. They might think he was a friend of Ksenya's or of her husband's, and it would be better to stay in place, stand there and look indifferent, like the dozens of people all around them. He didn't want to go over to the surveyors because he did not want to arouse any suspicions that he was planning to leave with them.

Yesterday, and the day before yesterday, someone was taken away to check documents. Brazenly, they grabbed people, knowing that no one would protest. And the line moved apart docilely, making way, soothing its conscience with the knowledge that people weren't hauled away for nothing.

"Are these your things?" the patrol would ask the neighbors.

"Not ours, not ours," people would say hurriedly, shrugging, as if to say, We know nothing, saw nothing, and have no idea whose things these are.

No one wanted to get involved. People were shaking with fear. The radio blared throughout the square — "Traitors! . . . Enemies! . . . Spies! . . . Saboteurs!" The defendants were still repenting of their crimes, and the crowd was gradually giving in to panic. That night someone dropped a metal vat from a bench, it struck the floor, and the old women started chattering in fear. If that had happened a month ago, before this trial, someone would have cursed the clumsy oaf, and it would have ended. But now people stayed awake and talked all night, saying that they could throw a bomb in Taishet, too, wherever there were a lot of people.

In the meantime, the patrol had cornered Ksenya. "Your documents!"

She took it more calmly than she had the night before — her documents had been checked twice.

She pulled her passport from under her coat.

The man looked through it, looked up at Ksenya, compared her face with the photograph, and didn't return the passport.

"Come with me, citizen!"

"No, no!" she shouted. "What for? I have the children —"

"The children will wait. You'll be back soon."

The girls cried and held on to their mother.

"Let's go, citizen!" he said even more sternly.

Ksenya was led away. In the doorway, she turned and took a final look at her daughters, her face in tears.

Sasha held the girls and they struggled in his arms, small and wretched.

"Come on, girls, stop it! Mama went for your tickets. She'll get the tickets, she'll come back for you, and off you'll go."

He reassured them this way, even though he was certain that Ksenya would not be released and that someone would come to take away the children and the suitcase.

But no one came.

Sasha was getting nervous. As the radio was giving the defendants' last words, he heard the name Pyatakov, and Pyatakov was connected in his memory with Ivan Grigoryevich and with Mark.

Mark had given up on Sasha, pushed him away. Sasha knew that from his mother's letters. She never mentioned his uncle, even a hint. Of course, it hurt his feelings — he had loved Mark perhaps even more than his father — but what could he do? He got over that too. He just hoped that Pyatakov's arrest would not affect Ivan Grigoryevich and Mark.

Pyatakov admitted that the state accusation was correct.

"I feel my crimes too acutely and I do not dare ask for leniency. I do not dare ask even for mercy. In a few hours, you will deliver your verdict. And I stand before you in filth, crushed by my own crimes, deprived of everything through my own guilt, having lost my Party, having no friends, losing my family, losing myself."

Then Radek spoke. "Citizen judges! After I confessed to treason, I lost all opportunity for defense."

Something crackled in the loudspeaker and only a few words could be made out. Sasha cursed. He had wanted to hear Radek. ". . . received directives and letters from Trotsky, which unfortunately, I burned. . . . We, and I in particular, cannot demand leniency. . . ."

Shestov: "I want one thing . . . to stand before the firing squad and with my blood wash away the stain of traitor."

Horrible to listen to! And how did their relatives feel, their wives and children? Shestov . . . Shestov . . . What had he admitted under questioning? There had been so many names, so many confessions, one more horrible than the other, that things were confused in his head. No, he remembered! Shestov gave orders, in Prokopyovsk, to hide a cache of dynamite. Miners' children, playing not far from the cache, dug in the dirt and the dynamite exploded, killing everyone. That was in 1934. Sasha was stunned.

In 1934 he had been put away for an epigram in his college newspaper, while Shestov got away with it all — the cache and the slaughtered children. Moreover, Shestov confessed that he had been a leading saboteur for five years in the mines of the Kuznetsk Basin, indoctrinating people, organizing murders, robbing banks to subsidize terrorists and saboteurs. And the NKVD was supposed not to have noticed? Go ahead and rob some banks, kill people, and we'll nap.... Who were they kidding?

It was all lies, all made up.

And yet they all confessed. People with legendary backgrounds, whose names thundered fame just a few months ago, who had built this state with their own hands, confirmed the accuracy of the charges, agreed that they were pushing their own country into the abyss.

Radek was the only one to suggest that the trial wasn't all it seemed.

He had unfortunately burned Trotsky's letters. That meant they weren't part of the case. Well then, had they ever existed, and had Trotsky written them?

The letters were a lie. And Shestov said that he got letters from Trotsky through Sedov in Berlin to pass on to Moscow. The letters were hidden in new shoes. One was for Pyatakov, the other for Muralov. Where were those letters?

Last August, when Sasha was still in Mozgova, reading and rereading the material of the United Center trial, he was convinced that they had used actors to play Zinoviev and Kamenev. Or that the defendants were drugged or hypnotized. But Ivan Nikitich Smirnov had disproved that.

Then what was left — torture? Dyakov hadn't used torture on him. And then he imagined torture as something belonging in the Middle Ages and the Inquisition. It was crazy to think that in our day they burned the soles of your feet, drove wedges under your kneecap, or did the "larded rabbit" — cutting strips of skin and flesh from your back. No, you can't light a bonfire in the investigator's office and you can't bring a mutilated man into the courtroom. They must beat them. Beat them so that no one can take it. That's why they confess and bring in others.

Sasha looked at his watch. Dammit! Ksenya had been taken away almost an hour ago and no one was coming for the girls. Maybe that meant she was being released? In the last few days, when they took people away, they came for their things almost at once. Train 116 would be in soon; what should he do if Ksenya wasn't back by then?

Take the girls to the commandant? "You took the mother, here are the kids!" And they'll say, "What's it to you? Why are you interfering? We know that the children have a mother. What's it to you? Show your documents. Aha, exiled in Kezhma, so that's where you met Pavlov. That's why you're worried. A friend of that enemy of the people, Pavlov — an exiled counterrevolutionary, and he's the one who got you out, we see! So that you can sabotage some more! Take him, the son-of-a-bitch!"

Maybe he was exaggerating, frightened by the scream and howl coming from the loudspeaker, frightened by the sight of the prisoners kneeling in the snow. Maybe. But still, it was too risky to go.

Yet what would he do, if his new friends got him a ticket and no one came for the girls? They were sitting on the suitcase, dozing, leaning on each other. Leave them here? They'd come for them, sooner or later! They couldn't arrest the mother and leave little children to their fate! At the station!

Sasha kept looking at the cashier's office. Had they started selling tickets? Dammit, if only the train would be late!

He looked at his watch — fifteen minutes left. The line moved at the window, the clerk was there. The train would be on time. The crowd pushed at the window. Sasha lost sight of the three surveyors.

Now he kept looking in the direction of the station commandant's office, listening to the loudspeaker pronouncing the sentence — "Pyatakov, Yuri Leonidovich; Serebryakov, Leonid Petrovich: the highest measure, execution by firing squad.

"Muralov, Drobnis, Ligshits, Boruslavsky, Knyazev, Rataichak, Norkin, Shestov, Turok, Puhsin, and Frash — execution.

"Sokolnikov and Radek — ten years."

He missed the end of the sentence. Four men left the commandant's office, two turned toward the cashier, two headed in his direction. There. No, they walked past. Had they forgotten about the children?

As usual, when the ticket office opened, Sasha's line moved. It didn't get shorter. It got longer, because everybody who had been sitting or who had walked away got back in. There was talk and argument over whose place was where. And when the ticket office shut five minutes later, the line calmed down and people went back to their places to plunge back into hopeless waiting.

It was the same this time, even though there seemed to be more tickets available. Some people from the general line got tickets. That meant that his new friends got tickets.

And then he saw Vartanyan pushing through to him, waving his ticket. "Hurry up! The guys have run for the train."

"Which car?"

"Five. Hurry!"

The girls opened their eyes. The little one cried again.

"Quiet, Lina, hush!"

"Are those yours?" Vartanyan's eyes bugged out.

"They're not mine, they're not," Sasha said desperately, "but I've got to find someone to watch them."

"Well, do it fast!"

And he hurried off.

What should he do? He'd miss his train. Why was life so unfair! If he didn't take this train, he'd be stuck here forever. But what else could he do? Take the girls with him? That was stupid. They would come for them, for the suitcases. People were being arrested all over the country, fathers and mothers put into prison, and they must be sending their children somewhere. These girls would be sent there, too. He couldn't perish along with them!

He looked around helplessly and his eyes met those of a woman in an unbuttoned, black plush jacket, sitting not far from them. Middle-aged, with a simple, pleasantly open face. She had seen them take away Ksenya and she must feel sorry for the girls. Sasha ran over to her. "Citizen, won't you keep an eye on the girls? I have a ticket for the train, I'm late! Help me out, eh?"

"Oh, I can't, son, I just can't. Don't be mad."

He hadn't really been counting on her.

"Son," the woman said, crooking her finger at him to bend down. Sasha bent down. He could see a small cross on ribbon around her neck.

"Listen, no one will help you. We're all afraid nowadays."

Fine! He was just wasting his time! Fear had devoured kindness, compassion, conscience, everything in people. But he couldn't lose even a minute. What did he need more than anything else, really?

Sasha picked up his suitcase. The girls looked at him.

No, dammit, he couldn't abandon them! He couldn't leave. He'd never forgive himself if he did. He'd torment himself for the rest of his life. He'd take them to the commandant's office.

If he could just pick them up, he'd get there faster. Dammit, why hadn't he traded his suitcase for a backpack? It would have been easier.

"Come on," he said to the girls. "Let's go!" And he stopped.

The two patrolmen came over. One picked up Ksenya's suitcase and bundle, the other said to the girls, "Come on, girls . . . come on, come on . . . let's go to your mama. . . ."

Sasha didn't wait. Pushing people aside, he ran to the door and onto the platform.

Picking up speed, the last car of Train 116 rolled past him.

## 9

It was a troubled night for Vlasik, chief of Comrade Stalin's bodyguards. A difficult and responsible operation was in the offing — changing Comrade Stalin's hat and boots.

Stalin wore what he was used to wearing. He didn't like changing his clothing and no one dared suggest such a thing. Even when he changed winter clothes for summer, or vice versa, he demanded the clothes he had worn the previous winter or summer. He would not allow fittings, would not let himself be measured or try things on, he hated anyone fussing behind his back. If he did agree to change something, it would only be something ready-made. They managed with underwear, socks, shirts, trousers, and jacket. Vlasik knew Comrade Stalin's sizes well. He even found a soldier from the guard who was built exactly like Comrade Stalin. They made a new jacket using the old one as a pattern, and then fitted it on the soldier. Vlasik kept a close watch on Comrade Stalin's belly, to see which hole of the belt he was using.

They also figured out a way to change hats. Comrade Stalin's hats and caps were made to a certain size, model, and shape, and placed next to the old hat or cap. Comrade Stalin put it on and if he left wearing it, everything was fine and he would use it. If he put it on, then took it off, and went back to the old one, that meant he wouldn't wear it and they'd have to have another one made.

But tonight they would have to change not only his hat but his boots — what a problem! The old ones were completely worn out. They made new ones based on the old, taking into account his flat feet and the six toes on his left foot. The boots were taken to the shoemaker, who cut new ones and had them ready in a week's time.

At night they put the new boots by the couch next to the old ones and waited in fear for morning. During a night watch like this, Vlasik drank a whole bottle of cognac. In the morning Comrade Stalin would get up, put on the new boots, walk around the room, look in the mirror at them, and if everything was fine, he would call for breakfast. But if the new boots were uncomfortable or didn't suit Comrade Stalin in some way, he would take them off, put on the old ones, call for Vlasik, and throw the rejects at his feet in silence. Vlasik would pick them up and go away.

In the summer, of course, it was easier. In the summer at the dacha, Comrade Stalin sometimes wore light shoes, and putting new boots next to the old ones posed no difficulties. But it was winter now, and Comrade Stalin took off his boots while sitting on the couch and left his boots right there next to it. Comrade Stalin slept lightly, so you couldn't come in during the night — he'd hear a rustle, wake up, pull the pistol out from under his pillow, and shoot. The only thing to do was to wait for Comrade Stalin to go to the toilet. Everything depended on the night guard's quickness.

They managed it tonight. But still Vlasik worried. Comrade Stalin had been in a bad mood and wouldn't talk to anyone. All he said was that Yezhov was to come at ten the next morning, which was unusually early, since Comrade Stalin went to bed late and got up late.

The next morning, Comrade Stalin rose at nine, went to the toilet, washed, shaved, came back, put on the new boots, walked around the room, went to the mirror, looked at them, and used the call button for breakfast. That meant he liked the boots! That was done. The hat would be nothing compared to the boots. If the hat passed muster, too, Vlasik would have each of his guards issued one hundred grams of vodka.

Yezhov appeared at ten. Stalin was still eating and invited him to join him.

Yezhov thanked him and sat down.

Pouring tea, Stalin moved aside some papers on the table and caught Yezhov looking at them. His manuscript was among them.

In early 1935, after Kirov's murder, Yezhov had started a book,

*From Splinter Groups to Open Counterrevolution.* Everyone was driven to write. It was Gorky's fault — he had announced that literature should be written by working people, "experienced people," and showed with his own example that an ordinary tramp could become a writer. And Yezhov decided he was a writer, and actually showed his drivel to *him,* asking for advice. He had to accept it.

"I've started your manuscript. When I finish, we'll talk. Have you brought the notes for the speech?"

Yezhov opened his briefcase and took out the papers with the main points of his speech about Bukharin and Rykov for the coming Plenum of the Central Committee. Stalin looked through them. Yezhov had pasted together evidence against Bukharin and Rykov. . . . It was all direct. Fine! Mikoyan would fill in the political part and appear as the coreporter.

"Good." Stalin returned the papers to Yezhov. "From whom do you expect objections?"

"Only from Comrade Ordzhonikidze. Back at the December Plenum he tried to obstruct me. And now he's sent people to the factories, gathering material on the prisoners."

Stirring his tea, Stalin watched the sugar melt on the bottom. "Gathering material . . ." The son-of-a-bitch! Lenin had pushed him away in his last years. He had seen that the man wasn't bright, was hotheaded, that he didn't consider his actions and was no politician. *He* had supported Sergo then, kept him on important work in the Transcaucasus, then took him to Moscow, put him in the Politburo, appointed him chairman of the Central Control Commission. Sergo obeyed *him,* fought the opposition well, but starting in 1930 he began to show his real character and began opposing *him* along with Kirov. It was after Kirov's murder that the break came — Sergo sensed something, knew something, but said nothing. Sergo was planning to go to Leningrad, but *he* didn't let him.

"Are you serious? With your heart? Do you want the Party to bury two of its leaders? I forbid it. The Politburo forbids it. If you go, we'll expel you from the Party — I'm warning you!"

Sergo obeyed. He didn't go. But he didn't submit. He didn't

support the trial of Zinoviev and Kamenev, he resisted the arrest of Bukharin and Rykov. Just recently he stopped Bukharin's wife in the yard of the Kremlin and talked to her.... He and Bukharin were friends. Bukharin had run the science and technology sections for him at the People's Commissariat of Heavy Industry for four years. They saw each other every day. What did they talk about?

At the Central Committee Plenum, Ordzhonikidze was supposed to report on the sabotage of the Trotskyites and Bukharinites in industry. What kind of a report would he make? He sent his people to the factories and plants. What for? To gather material on saboteurs? You don't have to send people for that. Yezhov could supply any amount of that kind of material. There was a special Economic Section of the NKVD just for that. But Sergo did not wish to use their materials. On the contrary, Comrade Ordzhonikidze made a point of ignoring the NKVD. Two months ago, at the December Plenum, he kept interrupting Yezhov's report. Everyone else was quiet, the whole Plenum was quiet, but Sergo interrupted with questions, confusing Yezhov, showing that he did not trust him. And he didn't trust him now, demanding the saboteurs' release, demanding personal meetings with them, and he got one with Pyatakov, and that showed him, but he still did not wish to believe. And what was this "believe" or "don't believe"? That concept did not exist for a Party member and could not exist. A Party member has only one concept — "I fulfill the directives of the Party or I do not. I fight against the enemies of the Party or I do not." Comrade Ordzhonikidze knew that very well.

All the conditions had been created for Comrade Ordzhonikidze — authority, popularity, the title of "Chief Army Commander of Industry." But Pyatakov and other economists did the work for him.

He used to be a veterinary paramedic, and never moved beyond it. But he received many honors. Cities, villages, kolkhozes, sovkhozes, railroads were named after him, and last year his fiftieth birthday had been celebrated with great pomp and circumstance. What more could the man want? But he refused to fight the enemies.

Why had he sent people to the factories? He didn't order them to gather material against the saboteurs — on the contrary, he wanted to prove them innocent. He wanted to appear at the Plenum in defense of Bukharin and Rykov. And if he planned to speak out, that meant he hoped to have someone's support. He wouldn't be starting a fight without that. Who was he counting on? Kosior, Psotyshev, Eikhe? But Pyatakov and Radek had planned to murder them, they had confessed in court. *He* had written that into their evidence with *his* own hand. Some of the Oblast committee secretaries? Unlikely. Ordzhonikidze was always battling with them, complaining that the committees were interfering in the work of the enterprises. And they were right to do so. What *he* began in 1934 had already brought fruit — Party organizations had taken over the economic apparat, struck a death blow to the technocracy, but it was still resisting, and using Sergo in that resistance. All resistance had to be stopped at the roots. Bukharin and Rykov had to be condemned unanimously.

"What materials are Comrade Ordzhonikidze's people bringing?" Stalin asked.

"Not all of them are back. But there is reason to think that they will insist that things are going well, that the plans are being fulfilled, that there is no sabotage, just individual problems, the usual technical problems."

"What have we gotten from Papulia Ordzhonikidze?"

"The investigation is taking place in Tiflis."

He was letting Stalin know that Beria, the secretary of the Transcaucasian Regional Committee, was in charge of the investigation and did not report to Yezhov.

Papulia, Sergo's older brother, was deputy chief of the Transcaucasian Railroad. An old member of the Party. Before the Revolution he had worked as a telegraph operator on the railroad and as station chief. Stalin remembered him well. He had been a cheerful but too easygoing man. He didn't let people down, but he was easygoing. Uncultured, didn't want to study. Sergo wasn't too strong in that area, either. He'd open a book once in a while, but Papulia never did. He was sociable, energetic, but there was more steam than effect. He showed off his harshness and directness. He was an epicurean, he liked hunting, he liked dinner parties, he was a good master of toasts, he enjoyed jokes. When he was asked, "Are you Ordzhonikidze's brother?" he replied, "No! Sergo is my brother." He hated Beria. He would come to the committee office and demand loudly, so that all the office staff would hear, "Is that Potian crook receiving today?" No wonder Beria took offense.

Beria was right to arrest Papulia — he had convincing evidence. But that wasn't enough for Sergo, who kept trying to save his brother, and refused to believe in his guilt. "Let the evidence be put on my desk." He demanded a meeting with Papulia, he berated Lavrentii Beria in every which way, berated Yezhov and the organs, and hadn't learned anything from the arrest of his older and beloved brother.

Stalin finished breakfast, pushed aside his glass, and rang for the maid. Yezhov pushed aside his glass, too, using two fingers on the glass holder.

Valechka came in, cleared the table, and asked amiably, "Have you eaten, Josef Vissarionovich?"

"Yes. Thank you."

While Valechka put the dishes on the tray, removed the table cloth, and wiped the table, Stalin paced the room, and stopped by the glass door, locked in winter, that led to the veranda. There was snow on the veranda — Stalin would not permit it to be cleared. Anyone who dared come to the door would leave footprints. The untouched snow outside the house reassured him.

Sergo and his brother were similar in character.

Both were hotheaded, unrestrained. Sergo had some polish, of course, but Papulia ... At first they were afraid to arrest him. He always carried a revolver, never left it at home, and he was an excellent shot. They tricked him, cleverly.... He was called in to the secretary of the City Committee. Papulia showed up, went into his office, and saw a newspaper spread out on the desk and the parts of a Browning on the newspaper, and the secretary bent over them, complaining, "I've taken my gun apart and now I can't put it together again."

"Let me," Papulia offered.

"No, I want to do it myself. Why don't you give me your gun, and I'll use it as a model to put mine back, maybe that will help."

Papulia, the fool, gave him his gun. The secretary put it on the newspaper and started working on his. He still couldn't do it, and angrily he said, "The hell with it! Why are we wasting time? I'll have my adjutant put it together following your gun, while we talk." He wrapped Papulia's gun and his own in the newspaper and went out. Three big fellows from the NKVD burst in and took Papulia. They say he still managed to bruise them and break the desk set. Clever Beria! Yezhov wouldn't have had the brains for that. He was a simple bone-breaker, but a necessary one.

Of course, *he* could start getting rid of Sergo gradually. First send him to some republic as secretary of the Central Committee, and then see.

But time wouldn't wait. *He* had to finish with Bukharin and Rykov.

A red-breasted bullfinch landed on the railing of the veranda and looked in through the glass. "Go feed," Stalin said in Georgian. In Zubalovo his father-in-law hung feeders on the trees and made little houses for lack of anything better to do. But here they simply hung boards with small edges, and that was all right. What do birds need with houses? They need food in the winter, not houses.

Stalin moved away from the door, walked around the room, and turned to Yezhov. "The technocracy still wants independence, it's resisting Party leadership, in the struggle with the Party it has joined the Trotskyite spies. The Party and the people know that, and so does Comrade Ordzhonikidze. He's an able politician. He knows that defending Trotskyite saboteurs means joining a hopeless and losing cause. And no one will support him at the Plenum. I'm afraid that they won't even let him speak, they'll chase him from the tribune, as they've chased better men than him. What will happen to his heart then? Have a heart attack at the Plenum?! Worrying is very harmful to people with heart trouble. Now, Comrade Dzerzhinsky was also worried and he died right at a meeting of the Plenum, but he died exposing Kamenev, Pyatakov, and other degenerates. Comrade Ordzhonikidze will have a stroke while he's defending the degenerates Bukharin and Rykov. What will the people think of that? How will we bury him? As one of the leaders of the Party or as one of its enemies? This is very unexpected for the Party and all the Soviet people."

Not moving an inch, not taking his violet eyes from Stalin, Yezhov listened closely.

"Thus," Stalin continued, "Comrade Ordzhonikidze cannot be allowed to defend saboteurs and spies. But he cannot be silent at the Plenum, either. Why not? Because the Plenum of the Central Committee has the right to ask Comrade Ordzhonikidze why he has surrounded himself with spies, why he has handed our industry over to saboteurs. And Comrade Ordzhonikidze must answer, is obliged to answer such questions. And what can Comrade Ordzhonikidze reply? Nothing! The Plenum will not accept Comrade Ordzhonikidze's justifications. Comrade Ordzhonikidze has found himself in a difficult, complex, and tragic situation. I don't envy him! And whether he defends his saboteurs or not, whether he defends himself or not, the Plenum will not listen to him. And in either case he will have a heart attack. It would be better for Comrade Ordzhonikidze to have a heart attack before the Plenum. A heart attack is a normal thing, the people will understand that. This is the question facing Comrade Ordzhonikidze today — to leave life beloved by the Party and the people or as their enemy. This is the question he is considering and deciding now. That is what he is thinking about today."

He paced the room again and suddenly asked, "You told me that Comrade Ordzhonikidze has four revolvers?"

"Yes."

Stalin shook his head. "It's bad when a man has so many personal weapons. They're always flashing before his eyes. In a moment of spiritual weakness he may shoot himself. It happens. Especially with such hotheaded people as Comrade Sergo. Especially when they find themselves in a situation like Comrade Sergo's. He knows that when Tomsky shot himself, the Party said, 'He was mixed up with the Trotskyite-Zinovievite terrorists.' Ordzhonikidze realizes that the Party would never say anything like that about him or write such a thing, the Party would not shame the name of Comrade Ordzhonikidze with an announcement of his suicide. Of course, it is hard to live with a bad heart, when you can't bring the benefit to the Party that you might have. That happens. For instance, the daughter of Karl Marx, Laura, and her husband, Paul Lafargue.

They saw that they couldn't help the socialist cause and committed suicide. And they weren't so old. And so Comrade Ordzhonikidze can't live with his bad heart anymore."

Stalin stopped in front of Yezhov and added sadly, "I'm afraid Comrade Sergo has no other way out...."

## 10

For the mistake with the Bristol Hotel, Dyakov was fired, and he vanished. Sharok was assigned to his place. Sharok took Dyakov's seat with pleasure, it was a good seat, the position more important and better paying.

Among others, Sharok's duties included arresting people who went through his section. In late 1936 Ivan Grigoryevich Budyagin was one of them.

"Take Budyagin yourself," Molchanov ordered, "and treat him politely."

Sharok was bewildered and almost said that he couldn't take Budyagin, that he knew him and had studied with his daughter in the same class for nine years. But he bit his tongue, because he knew the standard answer: "Enemies of the Party cease being our acquaintances. Dzerzhinsky made arrests himself, he didn't disdain it."

Sharok said nothing, accepted Molchanov's orders, set up a brigade for that night, prepared the necessary documents, but decided to send Nefedov to arrest Budyagin at the Fifth House of Soviets, while he went to arrest an army man, a division commander. He was disobeying a direct order, which could lead to a lot of unpleasantness. But he couldn't go to the Budyagins'.

Sharok wasn't embarrassed by Budyagin himself. Sorry, Citizen Budyagin, I'm doing my job. And the meeting with Lena didn't worry him too much. If they were alone for a minute, he would say, "Lena, you must understand, this is very unpleasant for me, but orders are orders." All that could be handled.

But the problem was that in the Fifth House of Soviets, in the Budyagin apartment, lived his son. His son! Sharok had never seen him nor did he want to see him. But he existed, he lived. For the past month the Budyagin apartment had been under surveillance, and he told the agents to report when the Budyagin grandchild was taken for a walk and who went with him — mother, grandmother, or nanny — who came over to them, whom they talked to. Of course, that information wasn't needed for the case, but *he* needed it. He wanted to know whether the infant was alive or, God grant, was dead, which would have been best for them all — for him, for Lena, who would be put away sooner or later or at best sent to Siberia or Kazakhstan, where life would be much tougher with a baby. If the child were taken into an orphanage, she would lose him anyway, because he would be given another name. And death would be better for the boy than the sufferings of exile or an orphanage.

But his son hadn't died and apparently didn't even get sick. According to the agents, the infant was taken out twice a day, usually by his nanny and on holidays by his mother, Budyagin's daughter. That meant he was there, in the house, in the apartment, and would be there during the arrest of Ivan Grigoryevich and during the search.

And what Lena would do in such a situation was impossible to predict. She could bring out the child and throw him into Sharok's arms, "Then take your son, too! Put him in jail!"

That would start a scene, shouting, the baby crying.

Sharok had supervised many arrests and many searches, and he was used to the noise and the shouts and the babies' crying and the hysterics. But this would turn an official state action into a family squabble, and it would be known that Sharok was related to the family of an enemy of the people, and the word of that would be all over the People's Commissariat the next day. He couldn't possibly go to the Budyagins' himself.

He'd take the risk. He'd manage some excuse for Molchanov. He would take the army man and send Nefedov to Budyagin.

That evening Sharok called in Nefedov and instructed him, told him that the search had to be very thorough, that Budyagin had things worth finding. He might have secret Party documents, which Budyagin as a member of the Central Committee had the right to take home but which, when he was kicked out, he should have returned. But maybe he hadn't. And the documents relating to his former ambassadorial work would be interesting for the case. And Budyagin might have a revolver with an expired license. In that case, Citizen Budyagin shouldn't have a weapon at home, and if he did, for what purpose?

"Don't forget about the license," Sharok reminded him.

Nefedov didn't forget anything. The cases entrusted to Sharok went well. Budyagin and the army officer were delivered to the internal prison by morning. Sharok went home to bed after a sleepless night and returned in the afternoon, sat down at his desk, and opened a file, anxiously waiting to be called in by Molchanov. His excuse was, "There was a possibility that the division commander was armed. I couldn't put my men at risk."

Molchanov appeared in Sharok's office. And not alone. He and Agranov were accompanying People's Commissar Comrade Yezhov.

Sharok jumped up, stood at attention, and reported, "Assistant of Chief of Section Sharok. Hello, Comrade People's Commissar."

Yezhov looked at Sharok without blinking. His violet eyes were cold and ruthless.

And suddenly, for no apparent reason, Sharok remembered a sunny July day in Silver Wood, where Sharok had spent a weekend with Lena. They sat on the ivy-covered terrace with Vadim Marasevich, listening to a pleasant male voice singing at the next dacha, singing a Tchaikovsky romance, *"How I love you, radiant night . . ."*

"He sings well," Sharok said. "Is he a musician?"

"No," Lena laughed. "He works in the Central Committee, Nikolai Ivanovich Yezhov, a very nice man. He often sings."

Only now at that second, standing at attention, did Sharok connect that Yezhov, the Budyagins' neighbor, singing a sentimental romance, with this fearsome commissar who was sending people to their deaths. And something like sadness stirred in Sharok's breast, that that carefree time was gone.

"What are you working on?"

Sharok reported on the case he was handling.

Yezhov was still staring at him. "Do you have enough cigarettes?"

"Yes sir, Comrade Commissar, I do. Thank you for the ones you sent."

"You haven't forgotten," Yezhov said coldly.
And left.
Agranov and Molchanov followed.

The next day Sharok was called in to see Yezhov.
Yezhov's office was now in the building's left wing, and there were complicated passages and crossings from floor to floor. Sharok's documents were checked at every landing.

As he went down the long corridors, upstairs and down, and then up again, showing his pass to the sentries, Sharok thought about why the commissar might want to see him.

Of course, it wasn't about the case he had reported on yesterday. It was a small one, not connected with the coming trial, and didn't interest Yezhov in the least. And it wasn't because Sharok hadn't gone to arrest Budyagin. Molchanov wouldn't report that to Yezhov. You're a bad boss if you have to complain about your subordinates. Handle them yourself. It was something else. If Yezhov remembered sending him cigarettes, then he must remember how Sharok had behaved in that difficult situation. He had dared to approach Yezhov with a suggestion that had been rejected by Yagoda, rejected by his direct supervisors, but at the same time he did not name those supervisors, he did not give them away. Yezhov must have liked that. And there was more. Sharok actually admitted that he had presented a falsified sentence to the defendant. Yezhov could have objected to such lawlessness. He didn't. He approved, he showed his favor by sending Countess Flor cigarettes. At the tobacco counter a pack of Countess Flor was just a pack of cigarettes. But sent by the secretary of the Central Committee to an ordinary investigator, it was something much more — it was a reward. And so Sharok was not expecting problems arising from this meeting. Probably it related to the changes that had begun with the removal of Yagoda. Reshuffling of personnel was inevitable with a new boss.

When he came to the Commissariat, Yezhov brought people with him from the Central Committee and appointed them to responsible but not major positions in all sections. Gradually but inexorably the number of new workers increased. Watching the shifts closely, Sharok saw that Yezhov was promoting not the old Chekists who had worked under Dzerzhinsky, Menzhinsky, and Yagoda, but the new ones, brought in in the 1930s, of which Sharok was one. And even though he was still in awe of Yezhov, deep in his heart he felt a sweet hope that the coming talk would bring a new upward move in his career. It was in this mood that Sharok entered the commissar's reception room.

Yezhov was seated at a very large table, about three meters long, and his office was proportionately large. There were glass-covered bookcases along the walls, drapes on the windows, expensive furniture. Behind Yezhov's back hung a portrait of Comrade Stalin. In the portrait Comrade Stalin was also sitting at a desk and writing.

Yezhov responded to his greeting with a nod and then fixed his strange, immobile gaze on Sharok. "Sit down."

He indicated a chair at the small table perpendicular to him.

Sharok sat.

"I've looked into your file," Yezhov said. "In response to the language question you replied" — he checked the file — "you wrote 'French and German, read and translate with a dictionary.' More precisely?"

"At school we had French," Sharok explained, "I took the whole school course. At the institute, I had German."

"Which do you know better?"

"I knew French rather well, but I've forgotten a lot, it's been a long time and I've had no practice. The German classes were very formal at the institute and I don't know it well at all."

"Could you converse with a Frenchman?"

"I'm afraid not," Sharok admitted. "Understand? Maybe, but I'm not sure. The French speak very quickly."

"You'll have to study languages," Yezhov said. "We're getting new people into the organs, Party and Komsomol youth, mostly laborers. We can't expect them to know a foreign language. But you have higher education, you must know at least one foreign language. Especially since you studied languages at school and at the institute — the state spent money on you. How much time do you need to brush up your French?"

"It all depends on how many hours a day I study and how good my teacher is."

"You'll have enough time and a good teacher. Are there any military men in your family?"

"Military? No."

"Among your relatives?"

"No. Never. My father was a tailor and so was his father."

"Among your friends?"

"No. None."

"Think. Among the parents of school or college comrades?"

Sharok shrugged.

"No, none. At the institute I didn't know the parents of my classmates. Most of them were from out of town and lived in the dorms while I lived at home. At school there were children of some officials, but they weren't military, and I stopped seeing my classmates a long time ago. . . . Actually, one fellow from my class, Maxim Kostin, entered military school, but I don't know where he was assigned. It's been a long time; I finished school ten years ago. Maxim's mother worked as a janitor in the building on the Arbat where my parents live. I think she's still there."

"Fine," Yezhov said. "You're being transferred to the Foreign Section. Today you will hand over your paperwork and appear before the chief of the Foreign Section, Comrade Slutsky. For the time being you will work under the supervision of Comrade Speigelglass."

His gaze was still cold and immobile, but something flashed in the violet eyes at the words *for the time being* and went out instantly.

"You will study language simultaneously with your work. You will be given time for study. Daily. Comrade Speigelglass will explain everything."

Yezhov stood up and tugged at his uniform. He was very short.

"You will keep your old rank and your old salary." His eyes flashed again and he added, "For the time being. And then we'll see. This is new work for you. But you'll manage. Watch how the old cadres work. Keep your eye on them. . . ."

He seemed to stress the last words, or maybe Sharok just imagined it.

\* \* \*

Everything was fine. Language lessons would take at least a half year, maybe a year, and therefore he wouldn't be overloaded with work. Once he transferred to the Foreign Section, that is, the Intelligence Section, he would be freed of the exhausting investigative work, the endless nighttime interrogations, beatings, groans, screams, and blood. And he would be removed from the Budyagin case, which he hadn't wanted to run. Of course, workers from the Foreign Section were used in urgent investigations, but that wasn't often. It rarely happened, and since he was also going to be studying, he could assume that he'd be spared that.

Of course, work abroad was dangerous, but he wouldn't be trained as an intelligence agent. They had enough people of foreign extraction for that, all kinds of Jews, Poles, Latvians, Germans, and even Russians who had lived abroad for a long time and knew the local language, conditions, and customs very well. He would probably be in charge of some country or region, gathering reports and working over the documents. Quiet and respectable work. All the workers of the Foreign Section had higher education and lived abroad, many were members of foreign Communist parties, were former political émigrés, basically were the Party intelligentsia.

When he came back from seeing Yezhov, Sharok reported to Vutkovsky on his conversation with the commissar.

Vutkovsky already knew and ordered Sharok to give his cases to Nefedov. "I wish you success," Vutkovsky said. "I am satisfied with your work in our section and I gave the people's commissar a positive recommendation about you."

He spoke warmly and sincerely. "I'm sorry to see you go. We've grown accustomed to each other in these three years. We've seen our share. . . ." A sad note entered his voice. "What can you do? We serve the Party. I think that's how history will evaluate our lives — they didn't belong to us, they belonged to the Party."

Sharok understood what Vutkovsky was saying and he even pitied him. Sharok was moving on to clean work, catching real spies, while Vutkovsky was staying with the dirty work, inventing spies. He was using the Party as an excuse. . . . But what else could he do? What other excuse did he have?

"You're lucky. You'll be working with Sergei Mikhailovich Speigelglass, a brilliant agent. You can learn a lot from him."

Sharok had also heard that Speigelglass was brilliant. That was his reputation at the Commissariat. His name was surrounded by a certain secrecy; not many had ever seen him — Sharok certainly hadn't. The Foreign Section was on the top floor and it was said that Speigelglass never came downstairs. His talent for disguise was legendary. In the capital of some country, where Speigelglass had lived illegally, he sold crayfish and did so well that the whole city started coming to his shop. He had to sell the business and leave — his popularity was dangerous.

Speigelglass had graduated from Moscow State University, where the then-rector Vyshinsky had protected him. He spoke several languages perfectly, he was highly educated, erudite — a professional, a veteran, and the best man in the Foreign Section. Slutsky, chief of the section, dealt with the leadership, the Central Committee. He was clever, sly, and capable, but all the threads ended up in Speigelglass's hands. He held the whole network.

That's all that Sharok knew about Speigelglass. Sharok didn't like intellectuals, but he'd learned from his experience with Vutkovsky that it was better to work with an intellectual than a boor.

Slutsky greeted Sharok warmly. He was faking it. Sharok's appointment worried him — the man had no ties abroad, not by birth or work, didn't know languages, but Yezhov himself sent him. What was behind it?

Speigelglass must have been wary, too, but he didn't show it — he was restrained, proper, and taciturn. He was diplomatic, "Comrade Yezhov told me that you would like to brush up on your language skills."

" 'Brush up' is too mild," Sharok said with a smile. "I studied at school, but I've forgotten everything, it's been ten years."

"What school?"

"School Seven in Krivoarbatsky Alley, the former Khvostovskaya Gymnasium."

"Who taught French there?"

Sharok was surprised by the question, but he named the teacher.

"Ah, Irina Yulyevna," Speigelglass said, "a wonderful teacher.

What she instills in her students does not get lost. Besides, a language you study as a child comes back quickly."

Astonishing. How did he know Irina Yulyevna, an ordinary schoolteacher?

Sharok couldn't stop from asking, "Are you acquainted with her?"

"She is known to me," Speigelglass replied.

Had Speigelglass prepared for this conversation and was letting him know it? But Sharok's transfer had happened overnight. When did he have time?

"The language groups work every morning. Besides which, you will have special training. What weapons can you handle?"

"I can shoot a revolver."

"The instructor will find out. Your workday will end at eight, so you will have two or three hours for study at home. As for work, you will be part of the group dealing with the White émigrés, in particular the Russian All-Military Union, a group of former officers and soldiers of the White Army. Its headquarters are in Paris, where it is headed by General Miller. You will be given the necessary literature and materials. Try to get on top of the case as quickly as possible."

## 11

The disruption at Nina's school lasted a week. Then all the Party members were called to a meeting of the Regional Commission of Party Control. There were five Communists at the school — Alevtina Fyodorovna; Nina Ivanova; the social studies teacher, Vasily Petrovich Yuferov; the janitor, Yakov Ivanovich; and the teaching assistant, Kostya Shalayev, who was still a candidate member.

The commission was in the Regional Party Committee Building on the corner of Sadovaya and Glazovsky Alley. In the small room the Party members sat around a table with representatives of the commission. In the corner by the window a handsome young man in a brown suit, yellow shirt, and yellow tie sat with his legs crossed.

The chairman of the commission reported the results of the investigation — the commission fully supported the charges made against Alevtina Fyodorovna. Their conclusions — remove her as director and raise the question of expelling her from the Party; the rest of the Party members were voluntarily to give up political work at the school, since they had lost their vigilance.

The words struck like a blow — expulsion from the Party in today's conditions meant arrest. Nina took out a handkerchief, wiped her brow, and looked at Alevtina Fyodorovna.

Alevtina Fyodorovna was courageous. The facts listed in the commission report were correct, but the evaluation incorrect. Alevtina Fyodorovna's arguments were similar to the ones Nina had used but, supported by quotations from the appropriate Party and state resolutions, sounded more weighty. Alevtina Fyodorovna bluntly accused Tusya Nasedkina of instigating squabbles, slander, and ignorance.

Next, Vasily Petrovich Yuferov spoke. He reproached the director of the school for insufficient sensitivity toward the Komsomols who had signed the complaint. The complaint reflected how young people understood their tasks in the present acute political situation, and she should have listened to them, talked to them, prevented a conflict, found a common language with them, and channeled their political activity in the right direction. The impression created was that the director concentrated solely on scholastic achievement. That was fine, but the social and public facets of the Soviet schoolchild should not be forgotten; the goal was to raise not only an educated person but a disciplined fighter for socialism.

Yuferov's steady voice was soporific, and one of the members of the commission stifled a yawn under the guise of smoothing his mustache. And Yuferov, noticing, began to sum up. He did not say whether or not Alevtina Fyodorovna should be fired and expelled from the Party. He switched to himself and asked them to bear in mind that he taught at this school only part-time and that his main work was at a research institute.

Nina announced dryly and briefly that she did not agree with the conclusions of the commission and thought that Alevtina Fyodorovna's arguments were convincing.

Yakov Ivanovich babbled that the driver did not know the way and he had had to sit up front with him, leaving alone the boys in the back who had tied up the bust. He wouldn't have let them, but this is how it happened.

The lab assistant, Kostya Shalayev, had graduated from this school. He was a limited but neat fellow, from a simple family. Alevtina Fyodorovna had been kind to him, arranging for him to stay on in the chemistry lab, with the understanding that in a year or two he would go to a chemistry institute. But Kostya got himself a wife and family, didn't go on to college, and remained a lab assistant. Kostya asked them to bear in mind that he was a young Communist, only a candidate, he didn't have Party firmness yet, he probably should have been more interested in the affairs of the whole school instead of spending all day in his lab, and, of course, it was his own fault, but asked them to take his inexperience, working background, and promise to improve into account.

"Any questions?" the chairman asked, looking at his papers.

"Alevtina Fyodorovna," came a voice from the corner where the handsome young man was still sitting, legs crossed and elbow on the windowsill, "do you know Pavel Pavlovich Ustinov?"

"Yes."

"Tell us in more detail, please."

"What does that have to do with the purpose of this meeting?" Alevtina Fyodorovna asked.

The chairman looked up. "Comrade Smirnova, you are in a meeting of the Commission of Party Control. Please answer all questions."

"From 1921 to 1927 we worked together in the People's Commissariat of Education of the RSFSR."

"And then?"

"Then I was transferred to the school and he remained in the Commissariat, after which he was assigned to some Oblast as head of the Oblast Education Department."

"Did you keep up your acquaintance with him?"

"Yes, while he was in Moscow."

"Do you know that he was arrested as an enemy of the people?"

"Yes."

"From whom?"

"It was in *Pravda*."

"So. And did you know Grigory Semyonovich Ginzburg?"

"Yes. He also worked in the People's Commissariat of Education of the RSFSR, then in the Moscow sector of the Education Department."

"Do you know that he was arrested as an enemy of the people?"

"Yes."

"From whom?"

"He worked in the Moscow Education Department. All Moscow teachers knew about his arrest."

"Did you maintain ties with him?"

"No, not personal ties. We met on business, at seminars and congresses."

He then named about ten education workers who had been arrested, one after another, all of whom Alevtina Fyodorovna had known.

It was clear to Nina that the elegant young man was from the security organs, that he was making a case against Alevtina Fyodorovna, and that she was doomed. They were all doomed, especially Nina. She had defended Alevtina Fyodorovna.

And here, as if he had guessed her thoughts, the young dandy said, "I have a question for Ivanova. Comrade Ivanova, you are a graduate of the Pedagogical Institute. Your whole class was sent out to the periphery to work. How did you manage to remain in Moscow and return to the school from which you graduated?"

The truth! She must tell nothing but the truth! Not a false word, no evasions. But in her nervousness she couldn't control her voice and she stammered.

"You see," Nina said, "I have an apartment in Moscow, and I had to take care of my little sister then. We have neither father nor mother. I explained all this at the institute when they were assigning us. I was told that if I brought a letter from a Moscow school, I could work there. Alevtina Fyodorovna gave me such a letter."

"Then, you were sent to the school at her request?"

"Yes."

"And she gave you a recommendation to the Party too?"

"Yes."

"And your second recommendation?"

"Ivan Grigoryevich Budyagin."

"The former deputy commissar."

"Yes."

"Do you know that he was arrested as an enemy of the people?"

"Yes."

"How did you meet?"

"His daughter was at our school, in our class."

"Do you meet with her?"

"No. As soon as I learned that her father had been arrested, I stopped seeing her and talking to her."

"Did you report to your Party organization that your sponsor had been arrested as an enemy of the people?"

"No."

"Why not?"

"I didn't know we were supposed to report that. His recommendation is in my file."

Not a single muscle twitched on Alevtina Fyodorovna's round Mordovian face. Nina looked at her from the corner of her eye and calmed down.

"Who else of your friends has been arrested?"

Nina shrugged. "I don't know. I don't think anyone...."

"Is that your statement?"

Nina shrugged again.

"Why are you silent?"

"I don't know who you mean."

"I'm talking about your comrade Alexander Pavlovich Pankratov."

"Pankratov? We were also in the same class.... But that was seven years ago."

"And you haven't met since?"

"We have. We lived in the same building. But he was arrested and exiled three years ago."

"How did you react to his arrest?"

"Not at all. I didn't know then and I don't know now what he was arrested for!"

"Did you try to get him released?"

Nina's heart thumped. Which letter was he asking about? The one she wanted to use as a petition at school? Alevtina Fyodorovna had torn it up. Or the letter they were planning at Lena's until Budyagin had told them not to send it? Only Alevtina Fyodorovna knew about the first, and she wouldn't have told anyone. Lena, Max, Vadim, and Ivan Grigoryevich himself knew about the second one, but it hadn't been sent.... However, the stranger wasn't asking out of idle curiosity — he must know something.

In an uncertain voice she replied, "I didn't send an appeal anywhere."

Once again, Alevtina Fyodorovna's face was still.

Nina imagined what the next question would be. If the organs knew so much about her, and even asked what she felt about Sasha's arrest, that meant they had collected information, they had talked to the neighbors, and that bitch Vera Stanislavovna must have reported that Sasha's photo was over Varya's bed. She had always known, she had always felt that she'd end up in trouble because of Varya! What could she say about the photograph? She couldn't tell the truth — then they'd haul in Varya. She'd have to lie, she'd say it was their father in his youth. But what if Vera Stanislavovna had let them in and they'd made a copy of the photograph? And now they would catch her, a Communist, lying to a Party committee, in front of Alevtina Fyodorovna, Yuferov, and Yakov Ivanovich! She'd rather die than suffer that shame!

"I have no more questions," the fop announced.

Nina slumped in the chair and shut her eyes.

"Let's recapitulate," the chairman said. "There is a motion to expel Alevtina Fyodorovna Smirnova from the All-Russian Communist Party and fire her from her work as director of the school for her blatant political mistakes in hiring personnel, perverting Marxist-Leninist education, allowing and hiding counterrevolutionary anti-Soviet actions among the upperclassmen, and also for having ties with enemies of the people. Who is for it?"

The commission members voted in favor.

"Unanimous," said the chairman. "Smirnova, your Party card!"

Alevtina Fyodorovna thought a bit, took the card out of her purse, thought a bit more, kissed it, and put it on the table.

That unexpected gesture confused people, but the chairman regained his composure first and said with a frown, "Citizen Smirnova, you are excused."

Alevtina Fyodorovna left the office.

"I think that Ivanova's file should be passed along to the Party investigator," the young dandy said.

He acted like an outsider, but it was clear that he was in charge.

The chairman nodded. "There is a motion to send the file of Nina Ivanova for preliminary investigation. Who is for it?"

Everyone voted yes.

"Unanimous," the chairman summed up, and looked at the papers on his desk again. He could never remember names. "Now as for Yuferov, Vasily Petrovich, Maslyukov, Yakov Ivanovich, and Shalayev, Konstantin Ilyich . . ."

He paused.

The dandy said nothing.

"Well," the chairman said, "I think we'll stop at a reprimand for insufficient vigilance. Any other motions?"

There were none.

"The meeting is over."

They all left the building together. It was dark, close to five.

"Well!" said Vasily Petrovich, and headed for the Smolensk metro station.

Yakov Ivanovich and Kostya, the lab assistant, turned onto Glazovsky, back to the school.

Nina, waiting until everyone had gone, rushed to Zubovsky Square. Alevtina Fyodorovna lived on Kropotkin Street. Nina had to see her at any cost, say something, console her. It was horrible. She had to get some advice on how to behave, what to do.

She ran as far as Kropotkin Street, turned left, stopped, and leaned back against the wall. There was a car by the curb, the same dandy next to it, as well as Alevtina Fyodorovna, and another man in a leather coat with a fur collar. The elegant young man was telling Alevtina Fyodorovna something, flashing his identification card, and then he and the man in the leather coat pushed Alevtina Fyodorovna into the car, very deftly, neatly, so that passersby didn't notice, got in on either side, and the car made an illegal U-turn and rushed down Kropotkin Street toward the center of town.

## ⚜ 12 ⚜

At home Nina found Varya.

An unpleasant surprise. Nina was hoping to be alone, to think through and to weigh everything. She didn't want Varya to see her confusion, her fear.

Varya was reading, lying on her bed as usual. ("I spend the day on my feet," she would say, "my extremities have to rest sometime.")

"You're home early," Nina said.

"No school. Why?"

"Nothing. Just asking."

"There's warm soup and potatoes," Varya said.

She had even made dinner!

"I'm not hungry," Nina replied.

She sat down at her desk with her back to Varya and covered her face with her hands. If she could only sit this way alone and think. But Varya was there with her feigned friendliness, ready as always to turn spiteful.

"Did something happen?" Varya asked indifferently.

"Why do you ask?"

"You look strange."

"Everything's fine."

"Doesn't seem that way."

Nina turned on her angrily, "Why are you pestering me, what do you want?"

"Can't a person ask?"

"Yes. But without sarcasm."

Varya was quiet for a while; the only sound was the pages

turning. And that bothered Nina too, making it impossible to concentrate.

"What's the story at school?"

Nina turned and stared at Varya. "What do you mean?"

"Well, what happened there?" Varya said without looking up from her book.

"Where did you get that?"

"Someone told me."

"Who told you what?"

"Who told me doesn't matter; but what I was told, you know yourself."

"Still, I'd like to hear it."

Varya shook her head. "What an attitude."

"I'd like to hear from you what they're saying at your school," Nina repeated.

"The regional Party committee sent a commission to your school. Tusya Nasedkina sent a denunciation — she always was a bitch. The facts ... well, there are a lot, I don't remember them all. Your students broke off Stalin's nose, then hanged him by the neck, announced that he was dead at a meeting when — 'thank God' — he was alive. Then, let's see ... yes, Alevtina fired Communist teachers and replaced them with dubious and hostile elements. They read *The Decameron,* Balmont, Igor Severyanin, all those contras."

"Who told you that?"

"I've already said, it doesn't matter."

Varya sat up on the bed.

Now they were looking into each other's eyes. "I'll tell you something else — you were dragged in to see that commission. Yes, and you're just back from the Regional Committee. What happened? Tell me! Have they expelled you from the Party?"

Nina was silent. Varya knew everything.

Still staring at Nina, Varya continued, "I lied to you. There are classes today, but I just didn't go to the institute. I came home to wait for you. I want to know what's going on. You're my sister, you know!"

Nina began to tremble. Whatever else you could say about Varya, she was the only close person in Nina's life. For the first time in many years, Nina realized that Varya — and only Varya — would never reject or denounce her. She wanted to go over to her sister, to sit next to her, put her head on her shoulder, maybe, and cry a little, to tell her that her life was collapsing, ending stupidly, because an arrest was the end of life, the end of everything.

But she didn't. She couldn't overcome the alienation that had built up over the years. She merely said, "Yes, those charges were made against the school. And many others, against me. My Party recommendation was made by Ivan Grigoryevich Budyagin, who's been arrested, and I didn't inform my Party organization. I supported Alevtina Fyodorovna in everything, and she got me the job at the school, and when Sasha was arrested, I wanted to write a letter in his defense." She paused. "Today after the meeting at the Regional Committee, Alevtina Fyodorovna was arrested right on the street and taken away, and tomorrow I have to appear before the Party investigator. Now I'll be blamed because Alevtina Fyodorovna recommended me for Party membership." She wiped her eyes, she couldn't hold back the tears.

"After which you'll be arrested," Varya said.

"Yes," Nina went on softly, "you have to be prepared for that."

Varya stood up, walked around the room, then stopped by Nina and caressed her shoulder.

"Don't cry. We'll think of something. How much money do you have?"

"Why?"

"How much?"

Nina counted the money in the desk drawer and in her wallet. "One hundred ten rubles."

"I have two hundred, so make that three," Varya said. "That's enough. Now listen to me carefully. You are going to pack now, just the most necessary things. I'll take the suitcase and wait for you at the Smolensky metro. We will go to Yaroslavl Station and you will go to Maxim. As soon as you get on a train and it pulls out of the station, I'll send Maxim a telegram to meet you. Understand? Get packing!"

"No, no, you're crazy."

Varya interrupted. "You're the one who's crazy! They could

come for you at any moment, even tonight. Don't you understand that — are you so stupid?"

"But —"

"No buts!" Varya said angrily. "You're going as a *khetagurovka,* get it? Thousands of girls are going to the Far East now, our commanders need wives, and you're going to Max as his bride."

"Wait, stop yelling," Nina begged. "Don't you understand? I have classes tomorrow."

"Idiot! Classes! And if they put you away, you think they'll drive you to school in a Black Maria every day?"

"But I have to be taken off the Party roster at least."

"You think they'll just do that? They won't let you out! Party roster! The hell with it! Nothing will happen to your Party!"

Varya put a chair by the cupboard and reached for the suitcase. "Here! Hold it. If it falls, the noise will be heard all over the building."

Nina caught the suitcase, and stood holding it in the middle of the room.

Varya jumped down from the chair, set the suitcase on the floor, opened it, and threw out its contents.

"Pack your stuff!"

But Nina sat back at the desk. "I have to think."

"Go ahead and think," Varya said as she opened the cupboard and began packing Nina's underwear and dresses. "Think hard, while you can. Open your eyes wide and look at what's going on around you — how many people have been arrested in our building. Vara Mikhailovna Sapozhnikova from the third entrance. She's an artist, and they arrested her. She painted Stalin with pockmarks on his face, she had copied some old portrait. He had smallpox when he was little, and she got eight years for his scars. Some boys in the courtyard were singing, *'Lenin's dead, Hope remains, Stalin lives, Hope is gone.'* They didn't even know who or what Hope was, that it was a pun on Stalin's wife's name, Nadezhda, which means hope. They had heard the song and ran around singing it. They pulled them in. The ones over fourteen were arrested, the others are hassled in school and the parents are hauled in by the NKVD. They're looking for the organizers, the masterminds, who taught

them the song, who sang it first. They've executed your main
Communists. They've arrested your Alevtina Fyodorovna. And
who are you? Nothing. They'll put you away and shoot you. If you
don't feel sorry for yourself, then feel sorry for others. They'll
torture you at the Lubyanka. They'll want evidence against Ivan
Grigoryevich, against Alevtina Fyodorovna, all your friends, the
teachers, poor Irina Yulyevna. If you must know, she's the one who
told me everything and she was right to do so."

Varya straightened and looked at Nina, who was sitting with her
head bowed.

"If they've arrested Alevtina Fyodorovna, they'll brand your
school a 'nest' — it'll be in the papers — 'a nest of scoundrels and
saboteurs.' And you'll be tortured and forced to sign everything, and
many innocent people will be arrested because of you. Where are
your dress shoes? Oh..." Varya pulled a basket with summer
clothes out from under the bed. "There will be parties there, they
must have a Red Army Club."

"And if they come for me tonight, what will you say?"

"I don't think they'll come tonight, since they expect you
somewhere tomorrow. And you won't show up. When they start
looking for you, I'll say, 'I have no idea, we haven't talked for six
months now. I don't know which boyfriend she spent the night
with.' But they won't come. When they see that you're not at school
or at the Regional Committee, they'll think you're sick, and by the
time they figure out you're gone, you'll be with Max and when you
get there, go straight to the registry office and become Mrs. Kostina.
They won't even bother looking for you. Nina Ivanovna Ivanova —
try to find such a person in all of Russia."

Nina still sat with her head down.

"Take off your slippers," Varya said, "I'll put them in a carry-on
bag; you'll need them on the train."

"I'm not going anywhere," Nina whispered. "I can't run away
from my Party. I don't have the right."

Varya bent over and took Nina's slippers off. Nina did not resist,
but she did not move.

"You're not running from the Party, you're running from a bullet
in the head. Does your Party need you dead?"

"I'm not going anywhere, understand, nowhere!"

Varya got up, grabbed Nina by the shoulders, and shook her, so hard that her head flew back.

"Then go to the Lubyanka yourself. Go ahead, repent! Denounce everyone, snitch on them all! Maybe they won't shoot you, maybe you'll just be sent to the camps. And if you become a snitch for them, maybe they won't arrest you at all. Go on, go" — she shook her — "go, do your duty! Go on! I don't want them coming here. Go to them! Go!"

She tore Nina's coat from its hanger and threw it at her.

"Get dressed, go!"

"Wait, calm down," Nina said, her elbows back on the table, "let's think this through."

Varya sat on the bed. "All right, let's."

"Let's say I leave," Nina said. "Let's say I get away. But they'll start in on you. They'll hound you."

Varya laughed and shook her head. "God, forget about that. Who'll ask me anything? I'll tell them the right answers if they do. I'll say, 'I don't live here. Ask the neighbors. I lived with my husband in another place. I sometimes spend the night here. I don't talk to my sister. We argued when I got married. I'm at work all day and at the institute at night.' Don't worry about me! I know nothing about your school affairs. A year ago you went away for a month and I only learned when you got back it was to Leningrad for courses."

"But you knew —" Nina began.

"Who else knows that?" Varya shouted. "Just you and me. As far as they're concerned, I knew nothing about your life and you knew nothing about mine. Maybe you've gone off on some courses now. Enough of that! Stop fooling around! Your life is being decided now. To live or not to live. You have only one chance. To go to Max tonight. Tomorrow you won't have that chance — they'll be watching you or will simply arrest you."

"But they could be watching now," Nina said. "They'll see me leaving and arrest me. That would be the end — if I'm running away, they'll know I'm guilty."

"They're not watching you yet, don't worry! They may have followed you home from the committee, but I doubt it. It's late, and they need their rest. And even if they see us, which I doubt, but say they do, they won't know which of us is leaving. If they come up to us, I'm leaving and you're seeing me off. The ticket doesn't have names. But this is silly — they won't be watching and you'll leave. I'll go out with the suitcase, no one will pay any attention to me, and you go out the back, then straight to the metro. Ninochka, darling, I'm begging you, calm down, think straight, stop being afraid of that lousy Regional Committee. People are being arrested every day there, too; they're all shaking with fear. And because they're afraid for themselves, they'll expel and arrest you."

She shut the suitcase.

"Just have two sips of soup for the road."

"All right," Nina said. She didn't have the strength to do it herself. "Of course, you're right about a lot of things, but I don't want to hide the rest of my life under the name Kostina, afraid that I'll be recognized and exposed, denounced, for running from a Party investigation. . . ."

Varya shook her head. "Who's going to recognize you in the Far East? And if they do, thousands of girls are going there now, and you're one of them. And if you come back in three or four years to Moscow, they'll have forgotten about you by then — the whole Regional Committee will have been arrested. Save yourself, Nina, save yourself! You're lucky you have Max. You love him and he loves you. Do you want to trade Max for a cell in Lubyanka, the camps, and a bullet in the back of your head? You've had enough to eat, let's go!"

Nina looked at her sadly and got up. "You're right, I'll have to leave. Time will pass, this madness will end, and then they can review my case calmly."

"That's right," Varya agreed.

Varya bit her tongue and didn't say that the future held nothing good. She didn't want to upset Nina. Thank God, she had agreed to go.

# 13

As agreed, Ordzhonikidze came to see Stalin at the Kremlin at three o'clock. He gave a brief report on his department, speaking dryly, hostilely, in general terms. Everything was in order, and would be in even better order if not for the unjustified repressions among the commanders of industry.

Stalin handed Ordzhonikidze a telegram from Beria. It said that the leadership of the People's Commissariat of Heavy Industry had covered up an accident at the Balakhninsky oil wells.

Ordzhonikidze looked at Stalin in surprise. "What accident is this? When?"

"It says there." Stalin nodded at the telegram.

Ordzhonikidze read it to the end and looked at Stalin in bewilderment again.

"But that accident took place in June of last year, six months ago. A small accident, which we took care of immediately." He crumpled the telegram in his fist and struck the table with his fist. "Bastard! Provocateur! I do not wish to even talk about him, I want information on my brother, Papulia."

"Put down the telegram."

Ordzhonikidze tossed it on the table.

Stalin picked it up and smoothed it out.

"Why get so excited, especially with your bad heart.... Have you prepared the outline for your report to the Plenum?"

"No!"

Ordzhonikidze put a nitroglycerine tablet under his tongue.

"When will it be ready?"

"I don't know."

"The Plenum opens in two days, you can't put it off. All the speakers have presented abstracts of their speeches."

"I'll present it when it's ready. If I deem it necessary. I am a member of the Politburo and have the right to decide what I'll say. I don't need Yezhov's approval."

Stalin waited and then said, "Yes, you are a member of the Politburo and can express your opinion there. But at the Plenum of the Central Committee you will have to express the point of view of the Politburo, the point of view of the leadership of the Party. Otherwise you put yourself in opposition to the Politburo, in opposition to the leadership of the Party. Otherwise you juxtapose yourself to the Party. Think about the consequences of such a decision. Remember what happened to those who tried to juxtapose themselves to the Party before you. Go home, calm down, and think. When you've calmed down, we'll talk."

Ordzhonikidze got up and pushed back his chair noisily.

"We'll talk at the Plenum."

And he left, slamming the door.

Molotov, Kaganovich, Voroshilov, Mikoyan, and Zhdanov arrived about a half hour later. They discussed current problems and preparations for the Plenum.

Poskrebyshev opened the door.

"Comrade Stalin! Zinaida Gavrilovna Ordzhonikidze is on the telephone for you."

"What does she want?"

"Something's happened to Grigory Konstantinovich."

Stalin shook his head.

"He was here, arguing and taking his pills. I told him, 'Take care of your heart.' He wouldn't. He must have had another attack."

He picked up the phone. "Yes.... What? Stop talking nonsense! You should have kept the gun far away from him. I said, stop talking nonsense! I'll be right there. Call the doctor."

He put down the phone and looked everyone over. "Sergo has shot himself."

Everyone was silent.

Stalin picked up another telephone. "Comrade Yezhov! Comrade Ordzhonikidze has shot himself. Get doctors immediately. If he can't be saved, have Comrade Kaminsky, People's Commissar of Health, come to me."

Without putting the phone down, Stalin said, after a pause, "Well, let's go over and see what's happened."

As they went out an ambulance rushed past them, stopping at the entrance to Ordzhonikidze's apartment. Several people leaped out of the ambulance, open overcoats revealing their white coats, and ran through the building's door.

Stalin slowed down.

"Let's not get in the way of the doctors."

And everyone slowed down. No one said a word.

They slowly went up the stairs. The apartment door was open.

Sergo was in the bedroom on the bed. At the head of the bed, stunned, stood Zinaida Gavrilovna. Stalin had known her for many years and was always astonished by Sergo's choice. He was such a handsome man and he had married a village teacher in Siberia, nothing to look at, quiet, with an unremarkable face. What had Sergo seen in her? She looked at Stalin in fear and bit her lip.

The doctors and orderlies bustled at the bed, wiping the floor, changing the sheets. A small dark man in a white coat silently watched their work, indicating with a nod what needed to be done. He nodded at the chair with the Browning — move it! But Stalin took the gun, checked the safety, and put it in his pocket.

The doctors and orderlies finished their work and stepped away from the bed. Sergo lay there, the covers up to his waist, his hands with entwined fingers over the blanket.

The dark man in the white coat looked at Stalin questioningly.

"Well?" Stalin asked.

"Death came a half hour ago," the man replied precisely, in a military manner.

"This is what happens when a man does not take his bad heart seriously," Stalin said, looking at the assembled company grimly, "and does not follow doctors' orders."

This sentence was intended mostly for the medical team. Everyone was supposed to know that Comrade Ordzhonikidze had died of heart disease. No other version could exist.

"Go!" Stalin said to the dark man, and stared at Zinaida

Gavrilovna, who lowered her eyes. "There will be no autopsy. We will not allow them to cut up our beloved Sergo."

The doctors and the orderlies left.

The members of the Politburo surrounded the bed and looked into Ordzhonikidze's face; only Mikoyan stood apart, leaning against the wall.

"Zina, come into the study," Stalin said.

They went to the study, its window overlooking the Alexander Gardens.

Stalin shut the door tightly.

"What were you babbling on the telephone?"

"I wasn't babbling, Josef," Zinaida Gavrilovna said in a breaking voice. "My word of honor. I was downstairs, and a messenger came with a file, a black one, the usual from the Politburo.... I didn't know him.... I asked, 'Where's Nikolai?' Nikolai, who usually brings the file.... He replied, 'Nikolai didn't come to work today, he has things to do at home.' He went upstairs with the file —"

"I know he had the file," Stalin interrupted. "That's what he was here for, to deliver the papers in the file. Go on!"

"He went upstairs.... Then he came downstairs and said, 'Zinaida Gavrilovna, there was a shot up there....' And left. I went upstairs and saw that Grigory had been killed."

"What do you mean, 'killed'? Are you trying to say that the messenger killed him?"

"No, no ... but still, it's strange ..."

"Did you hear the shot?"

"I didn't."

"If the messenger had killed him, he would have left without a word. Why tell you that he heard a shot? So that you would run upstairs and help, call the doctors, save him, and then have Comrade Ordzhonikidze testify that this was the man who tried to shoot him? Eh? Tell me — why would he tell you that he heard the shot? No explanation. It's silly. Nonsense. I understand your emotional condition, but don't lose your reason."

"But, Josef," Zinaida Gavrilovna began, "I'm not supposing anything, it might not have happened, but yet —"

"Without any 'buts' or 'yets'! Your female stories, your stupid ideas can feed gossip, gossip that is harmful to the Party. Don't you understand that? Pull yourself together! The Party will punish you severely for spreading slanderous rumors. Don't try the Party's patience, Zina. Sergo committed suicide, but the Party does not want to compromise him by revealing that he is a suicide. The Party wants to preserve his good name. And so . . . Sergo died at his post, died from a heart attack. That is the Party and government version. You are a member of the Party and you must support it. And now go to him. And tell Klim to come here."

Zinaida Gavrilovna left, and only when she was outside the door did she bring a handkerchief to her eyes.

Stalin went to the desk. Big note pads with notations in various colored pencils lay open. Stalin leafed through them. There it was — the report to the Plenum. His handwriting.

Voroshilov came in.

Stalin showed him the pads. "Here are the notes for Sergo's report. Have these pads and all the papers in the drawers brought to Poskrebyshev."

# ❧ 14 ❧

I't took two more weeks for Sasha to get a train out of Taishet. People were sitting pressed up against each other on the upper and lower bunks of every car. The ones who had got hold of the luggage racks lay in them — you couldn't sit, there wasn't enough head room. They left their baggage on the floor. The conductor demanded that they move their things, which were blocking the corridor. The passengers put the bags and sacks on their laps, holding them until the conductor went away, and then put them down again.

Children cried, adults scolded, everyone was irritable, rude, and grumpy. Shag tobacco smoke hung thick in the air. The cars weren't heated, the windows iced over, and the passengers kept their fur coats on. The conductor's reply to their complaints was, "When we get to Krasnoyarsk, we'll turn on the heat."

One toilet was locked, the line for the other was impossible, so you had to wait for the station, but at the stations wild hordes attacked the train. It was impossible to push through the crowds, and even if you could, you'd never get back on.

So just sit and hold it until Krasnoyarsk.

Sasha reached Krasnoyarsk by local trains and then from Novosibirsk to Sverdlovsk.

In Krasnoyarsk he had sent his mother a telegram — "TRAVELING, WILL CALL." He had considered the text for a long time and had settled on this. His mother would understand that he was free and that he would call from wherever he settled. She must know that he wouldn't be allowed to live in Moscow. Everybody knew that.

Where should he go? Mark was the closest. The factory he ran was not subject to passport regulations. It wasn't a major center, and they had dekulaked specially resettled people and former criminals. All sorts worked there. Mark had enough power to stick him somewhere and help him get a permanent passport. Especially since their surnames were different.

But Sasha discarded that idea at once. He had seen what was happening throughout the country — at all levels. Everyone was under fire. He didn't want to complicate Mark's situation.

His father? Efremov wasn't a regulated city either; he could spend some time there, get his bearings. But the thought of his father evoked unhappy memories. His pedantic manner, his constant dissatisfaction and irritation — Sasha wouldn't be able to live with his father, who probably had a new family by now. He didn't want to be a burden to anyone.

He couldn't show his face in Moscow. And yet he needed to go there, if only for a day, a few hours, to see his mother, to see Varya. If he didn't go now, then when and where would he ever see them?

He had to take the risk. He could visit Aunt Vera, and his mother and Varya could come there. He would call her from the station. He would be able to tell from her voice if she was willing.

It was risky, dangerous. But there was no other way.

Sasha had a stroke of luck in Sverdlovsk. He was standing near a closed ticket window. There were no tickets, of course. Suddenly the window opened a crack. Sasha was the first to reach it, and he bent over and asked, "You wouldn't happen to have a ticket to Moscow?"

The clerk named a sum. Sasha paid, got the ticket, and rushed to the train. The window shut. That single ticket must have been left by someone who didn't pick up the reservation.

It was a reserved car. Everyone had his own place. Sasha had the upper bunk and could lie down the whole way.

A few people without reservations or maybe even without tickets — who had perhaps bribed the conductor just to get to the next station or the one following — huddled in the vestibule, near the toilet, or sat on the edge of a seat if the "legal" passengers didn't mind.

Searching for his place, Sasha looked into a compartment where three healthy-looking men were sprawled across the bunks. They were wearing NKVD uniforms.

"What do you want, boy?" said the sergeant, looking severe.

"I'm looking for my seat."

"What's your number?"

"Sixteen."

The sergeant looked at the lieutenant. He sat leaning back against the seat, and with a light, almost imperceptible movement of his head, indicated that he approved his sergeant's behavior. The sergeant became even more severe.

"Show your ticket!"

Seeing that the number was sixteen and not knowing what to do next, the sergeant gave Sasha's ticket to the lieutenant.

"Where did you get this?"

"At the ticket office."

"Call the conductor."

The sergeant passed the lieutenant's order to the soldier next to him, maintaining the hierarchy.

The soldier went for the conductor.

So many seats on the train, and he had to have them for neighbors! Obnoxious men with cold, ruthless eyes. The hell with them! Sasha tossed his suitcase up on the bunk.

The conductor came.

The lieutenant showed him Sasha's ticket. "What is this?"

"Can't you see for yourself? A ticket. Car eight, seat sixteen. Everything's in order."

"We're supposed to pick up a man for this seat in Kazan," the lieutenant said significantly, hinting that they were picking up a prisoner to be convoyed further.

"We'll see in Kazan."

"We reserved four places," the lieutenant said.

"Where's the reservation?" the conductor said, returning Sasha's ticket to him. "For me there is only one document, a ticket, and this ticket is correct. Take your seat, citizen."

And he left. He was used to the pretensions of these guards, and it was clear that they were guards. They had taken someone somewhere and now were coming back, and they wanted to travel alone, without strangers.

Sasha pushed the suitcase toward the window, took off his felt boots, put them up against his suitcase instead of a pillow, lay down, covered himself with his coat, and fell asleep.

The train braked sharply, and Sasha woke up. His companions were asleep. The lieutenant was on the top bunk opposite Sasha, the sergeant and soldier on the lower ones. Yet one of them should have been on duty. They must have hidden their pistols under their pillows while they slept.

The train moved smoothly down the tracks. For the first time Sasha was aware of *moving*, leaving exile at last.

Trying not to wake anyone, Sasha put on his boots, got down, went to the toilet, came back, and climbed back up just as quietly and went back to sleep.

When he woke up, the murky, wintry light was coming through the window. He looked at his watch. Nine! The train was at a stop. The window was steamy, and Sasha couldn't read the name. People were up in the car, the door kept opening, letting in bursts of cold air, people were carrying kettles to fill with boiling water at the station, since the train's water boiler wasn't working. Sasha didn't have a kettle, just an aluminum mug he had bought in Taishet. He would have to forgo the boiling water.

Lying on the bunk, Sasha pulled out the newspapers he had got at the station in Sverdlovsk — they had articles on the Pyatakov-Radek trial, articles on the treacherous methods of the Trotskyite spies.

The guards were having breakfast. The sergeant was peeling boiled eggs, banging them on the table and throwing the shells on the floor.

"Let me clear up," the soldier offered.

"No problem — the conductor will sweep up, he's got nothing else to do."

The lieutenant said something to the sergeant that Sasha didn't hear.

"Hey, neighbor, come down for breakfast," the sergeant invited.

"Thanks, I'll wait for the boiler to start working."

"You'll have a long wait," said the lieutenant, without looking. "Climb down. Once we've eaten, we'll go back to sleep. Then where will you sit to eat?"

Sasha took out his mug, bread, an onion, his last two pieces of sugar, and his last slice of bacon. He also put on his boots because the floor was wet and dirty.

The table was set with a tea kettle and a bottle of vodka, and spread on a newspaper was thick sliced bread, boiled sausage, also in thick slices, the peeled eggs, and butter in a mug. The lieutenant and the sergeant sat at the table with their elbows on it. The soldier was sitting next to the sergeant, sitting in silence, a dull-looking lad who at least was conscientious, since he had wanted to clean up. Sasha sat down opposite him and put his stuff on the table. The lieutenant and the sergeant looked at them indifferently.

Then the lieutenant poured out the rest of the vodka for himself and his men.

They drank and followed it with sausage.

Sasha broke off a piece of onion and had it with the bread.

The sergeant poured boiling water and filled Sasha's mug.

The lieutenant held his in both hands, warming them, and then took a sip.

"Where you coming from?" he asked Sasha.

"From Podkammennaya Tunguzka."

"Is it a river?"

"Yes. In Krasnoyarsk Krai, in the Evenki National Okrug."

The lieutenant had never heard of them, but didn't want to show his ignorance, so he showed the usual suspicion of a professional NKVD.

"Working?"

"Yes. In Professor Kulik's expedition. We were looking for the Tunguz meteorite. Have you heard of it?"

"Yes. Fell from the sky."

Sasha sighed in relief. Now they'll find his story believable. The newspaper furor over the Tunguz meteorite had been in the late 1920s and early 1930s, and now they no longer wrote about it. It was fortunate that the semiliterate lieutenant had heard of it. Was Sasha afraid of what he was doing? No. But he was careful. Their behavior was unpredictable — they could pick on any word they didn't understand or interpret their own way. Sasha switched to a safer topic.

"The meteorite," he continued, "fell almost thirty years ago, on

June 30, 1908, at seven in the morning. In general, meteorites are pieces of heavenly bodies that fall to earth from outer space and when they enter the earth's atmosphere, they burn. The big ones burn brightly and are called bolides, and the small ones are what we call falling stars."

"I've seen those," the sergeant said.

"The Tunguz meteorite," Sasha said, looking at him, "was of course a bolide of enormous size and took up about two thousand square kilometers of space."

"Wow!"

"You could see from almost any point in eastern Siberia how the bolide traveled in the sky. When it fell, there was a deafening explosion, which could be heard thousands of kilometers away. In many villages buildings shook, glass broke in the windows, dishes fell from the shelves, and even people and animals fell down. Like an earthquake. The shock registered even in England."

"How do you know about England?" the lieutenant said warily.

"It was in the prerevolutionary papers. The meteorite fell nine years before the Revolution."

This explanation satisfied the lieutenant.

"Where did it go to, the meteorite?"

"Burned. When it entered the earth's atmosphere, it burned, turned to dust."

"Why did it burn?" The lieutenant was suspicious again.

"They fall at enormous speeds — twelve kilometers a second, that's over forty thousand kilometers an hour. Our train, for instance, is going fifty or sixty kilometers an hour, while the bolide was going forty thousand, think of the friction! That makes a very high temperature — ten thousand degrees — and so the bolide burned, leaving only dust. The dust went deep into the earth and on that spot lakes and swamps were formed."

"Then what were you looking for?"

"What do you mean? Remains of the meteorite."

"You're lying, pal! First you say dust, then you say remains of the meteorite. What do you want them for?"

"To determine what meteorites and other heavenly bodies are made of."

"For science, then," the lieutenant mocked.

"That's right, for science."

"Do we need science like that?"

"What do you mean?"

"Just that. We need science for socialist construction, not for seeking out little pebbles."

You jerk, thought Sasha. "The government gave orders to seek these pieces, that means it's necessary," Sasha said persuasively.

Since Sasha had mentioned the government, the lieutenant shaped up. "Well, did you find any?"

"No, everything went underground, mixed with the soil. And the conditions are harsh there — no road, you can't get good equipment, the work is hard, there are midges, people don't want to work there."

"What do you mean, don't want to? If it's a government project, they have to work." The lieutenant did not approve.

"People are hired for the season, for the summer, and then let go for winter. And they don't hire on again the next summer, they don't want to be mosquito and midge food."

"Send prisoners there," the sergeant said. "They won't refuse to work."

"It's not big enough there," the lieutenant reasoned. "How many people?"

"Twenty or thirty."

"Not enough."

"They could set up a special camp," the sergeant proposed. "Just one barracks, they could dig even in winter, they won't die."

"All right, they'll figure it out without us," the lieutenant cut him off. "What's your name?"

"Sasha."

"Don't be mad at me. You see, we're on duty, armed, we're carrying documents, we have to know who we're traveling with. Understand?"

"Of course."

"Vigilance," the sergeant explained.

"You probably read the newspapers," the lieutenant said, "you know about this trial. . . . You see what's going on? Spies all around, saboteurs, they've reached the very top."

"Those vipers have to be destroyed," the sergeant said, frowning, "all of them, those enemies, and their wives, and all their seed."

"Why the children?" Sasha asked with a smile.

The lieutenant looked at him suspiciously. "You pity their children?"

"Children can be reeducated."

"When those children grow up, they won't pity you and me," the lieutenant said. "They'll remember their mamas and papas. Then you'll see the price of your pity."

"Go try to reeducate them," the sergeant said. "I went back to my village, in Vologodskaya Oblast, on leave. At our kolkhoz the chairman turned out to be a saboteur, and the bookkeeper and the foreman were saboteurs, too, Trotskyites. They were put away, of course. They call in the foreman's wife, she's howling and crying, 'Why me, I have little kids . . .' She was young and good-looking. So the investigator says, 'Why did you hide the views of an enemy of the people?' "

" 'What enemy?'

" 'Your husband, Arsentii Nazarov.'

" 'But I didn't know he was an enemy.'

"And the investigator says, 'What's the matter, didn't you see who you were sleeping with?' That's how he put the question. Now she'll know who to sleep with — she got eight years and the kids were sent to an orphanage."

"You see," the lieutenant said to Sasha, "they took care of the kids. . . . They get everything they need at an orphanage. And you felt sorry for them. Do you have children?"

"Yes," Sasha lied.

"That's why you feel sorry for them. Do the enemies feel sorry for us? We arrested one, an important man, chairman of a regional executive committee. We approached him like a human being, with a warrant for a search and an arrest, all legal. And he pulled out his gun and started shooting. He killed one of our men right on the spot, and used the last bullet on himself, the bastard traitor spy. He didn't feel sorry for our two comrades who died in the line of duty. And he didn't feel sorry for his old woman or his daughter. The wife was shot and the girl, who was fifteen, was given eight years. That's what pity can do."

"Yes," Sasha said, shaking his head, "it's terrible."

He finished his tea, thanked them, climbed back up, and fell asleep.

His traveling companions also slept and then lunched, but they didn't invite Sasha. They had lost interest in him. They had found out who he was and they were satisfied. Sasha was pleased; he turned his back on them, pretending to be asleep, and actually did fall asleep.

He woke up late. The train was standing. There was a lot of bustle in the car. They must have come to a big station. Sasha's companions were gone and so were their things.

Two women with a child came in and a man brought in their things.

"Where are we?" Sasha asked.

"Kazan."

So the guards had lied, they just wanted to travel alone as far as Kazan! Well, thank God! The morning's conversation had made Sasha sick, but he hadn't argued with those sons-of-bitches, executioners and killers. It would have been stupid and could have ended badly. But he shouldn't have shared a table with them. He could have said, "You didn't want me in this compartment yesterday and now I don't wish to know you." Or he could have pretended to be sick — "I've got a chill, must be a cold, I guess" — then asked them for boiling water and eaten up on the bunk. But he came down and sat with them. He lied about Professor Kulik's expedition, about the Tunguz meteorite, to make them trust him and he got what he wanted. It hadn't even occurred to them that he was returning from exile.

He would have to live these lies constantly now. He would be making up alibis and telling them to everyone he met, just to avoid questions and interrogations, to cover up his past. It weighed on him. But there was no other way. Any attempt to rehabilitate himself, to get his case reviewed, would be silly and could lead only to a new sentence — not exile this time, but the camps; not for three years, but for five or eight. And if he wasn't careful and didn't hide his past, he'd see the camp gates a lot sooner.

That lieutenant, for instance, and the sergeant would be glad to put him behind bars. Any man who has been in prison had a grudge, and therefore was against Soviet rule. If they were afraid of pathetic children, foreseeing how they would avenge their mothers and fathers, then how could they not stifle people like Sasha? And that created a vicious circle — he was afraid of them, and so had to lie and hide, and they were afraid of people with grudges and shoved them into the camps. And that would not ever change. And his situation would never change. His fear would never end.

Fine! He was hungry. He would get down from the bunk, find the conductor, and demand hot water. Didn't he pay for the ticket? He did. Then be kind enough to give the passengers of your car boiling water! Ah, the hell with it, he was too lazy to get into it. He'd have his bread dry.

He had to rid himself of illusions. Behind him was the exile, ahead were the camps. That was as clear as two times two, and now he was on temporary leave. That was it, temporary leave. And no one could say how many free days he would get. That was a matter of luck.

## 15

In the morning at breakfast, serving tea, Fenya spilled a cup on Vadim's lap.

Vadim jumped up and shook his robe.

"Watch what you're doing, you idiot! Are you blind?"

"I am, Vadim, I'm blinded by my tears." And she started howling, "Oh God! Why such tribulation? He didn't hurt anyone. So quiet, he never hurt a fly. He's an old man, he has grown grandsons, why him? He never bothered anyone, he had no ambition, they asked him to run the barbershop, but he refused, he didn't want to — 'No,' he said, 'I'll stay away from trouble.' Now he's in prison. His wife, Nastya, went to see him, he's in Butyrki —"

"What Nastya, what barbershop, what Butyrki?" Vadim shouted, shuddering and horrified by what he knew Fenya's answer would be.

"You know, Nastya, the wife of Sergei Alexeyevich.... Our Sergei Alexeyevich is in Butyrki now." She howled again. "Nastya went, they won't accept parcels, they won't take money, he's under investigation, they said.... What investigation? What is there to investigate — how he shaved people? how he cut hair? ... Some devil denounced him, may the devils tear him to shreds, may he be covered with a pox, may he dry up and shrivel, may he not be saved, nor his children nor his grandchildren —"

"Enough, enough!" Vadim shook his head; the very unpleasant news had ruined his mood, his workday. "Enough, tears won't help!"

"Then you help, Vadim, you write in the newspapers, you're a famous man, and Andrei Andreyevich treats all the bosses. Try to help! They're bound to listen to you."

The old fool, how could he explain that in these cases no one listens to anyone and no one helps anyone?

"I'll think about what can be done," Vadim said. Fenya's tears were killing him. "Just stop wailing."

Fenya shut up, and went to her room by the kitchen without cleaning the table. And Vadim hurried to his room and threw himself on the bed.

After he had signed the statement for Altman about the joke he had told Sergei Alexeyevich, Vadim stopped going to him for haircuts. He didn't want to see him, he had an unpleasant feeling, something like offense, every time he passed the barbershop in Koloshiny Alley. Why had Sergei Alexeyevich always thrown in his stupid line, "Lev Davydovich had to be there somehow," and chattered stupidly while decent people had to pay for it? And he didn't need the old man anymore. A young and pretty makeup artist had started working at the Vakhtangov Theater, and she also cut hair well. She needed the extra money. Why hadn't that girl come to the theater sooner? Vadim certainly wouldn't have told her the joke about Radek, and Altman would never have tormented him, and he wouldn't have had to sign anything about collaboration, and Sergei Alexeyevich would have worked at his shop until the day he died.

The poor wretch.... Could they have really arrested him over that stupid crack about Lev Davydovich? They could. But what for? They have so much work. There are major trials going on, major actions. Why bother with an insignificant barber?

But the old man had said it mockingly, implying that whatever happened, they'd blame it on Trotsky, that Lev Davydovich had done it. He was telling customers not to believe the NKVD, not to believe that Trotsky was behind all the criminals. That was the way one of the customers must have perceived the old man's joke and reported it to the Lubyanka. Vadim had nothing to do with that. He had talked to Altman about the barber almost a year ago. He had named Elsbein, and Ershilov, too, and both were free, living quietly, no one bothering them, yet they took Sergei Alexeyevich. That meant somebody had denounced him recently — after all, a year ago such talk would not have been considered serious, but now it was a crime. Was that logical? It was.

Vadim asked Fenya if she had done his white shirt and, by the way, when Sergei Alexeyevich had been arrested. Two weeks ago. It all fit! He wanted to hold on to that thought, he wanted to believe it and relax, but he couldn't. That victim was on his conscience, his statement had named Sergei Alexeyevich, Vadim had signed that statement with his own hand. Of course, there was one excuse — back then Vadim thought that the barber was reporting on people and that he was in no danger. But he had been wrong: Sergei Alexeyevich wasn't a snitch, and he had destroyed an innocent man.

It was horrible, horrible.... And he couldn't get any information out of Altman, of course. Every two weeks Vadim met him at the Moskva Hotel to bring him a new denunciation — a short review of a composition that did not conform to socialist realism and therefore was hostile to Soviet power, for example. Altman would read it sitting at a table while Vadim waited on the couch. Of course, Altman had a lot of informers among writers. Vadim didn't doubt that they included Elsbein and plenty of others, but his reports were special, not without literary sparkle, highly professional. And he was a man who was well informed. He was at the Writers' Club every day, he dropped in at the offices of *Literary Gazette* and of the fat journals, he knew all the news. His information was not behind events, but ahead of it, before the newspapers caught up. This is what created a reputation in Altman's eyes.

Altman would light a cigarette, striking matches against his holster, which always annoyed Vadim. That meant he had finished reading. And this was the hardest part. Vadim would look up at him, pale with fear — the lout's behavior was unpredictable. Sometimes Altman pushed aside the pages with a disdainful flick and said, "Not enough." Vadim would excuse himself in a stifled voice — he had no other information. Sometimes Altman gave him a curt "Good-bye," and Vadim beat a hasty retreat, not waiting for the elevator but running down five flights.

Once, having read his review of Afinogenov's *Far Away*, Altman lit up and nodded at the chair, "Sit closer, let's talk."

Vadim sat down.

"But Shchukin played Malko well in *Far Away*. Or do you think he played badly?"

God, did they want him to work on Shchukin? He could say he didn't know him, that such a celebrity didn't let young people near him. But what if Altman knew that his father had been consulted several times by Shchukin, and not at the hospital, but at home?

"Shchukin, of course, is a marvelous actor," Vadim began evasively, "but . . . ."

"I know your 'buts.' I want something else. Take this report home and turn it into an official review. Signed with your name."

"But —"

"What's stopping you? This" — and he pointed to the denunciation — "is one thing and what you will write is another. You'll write an official review, the sort we could commission from any critic, including you. What?" He squinted and continued. "Are you afraid you'll be found out? Who are you afraid of?"

Vadim couldn't take his stare.

"No, no, please . . ."

"Maybe you're afraid Soviet power will be overthrown and you'll be called to account?"

"Of course not! Who could overthrow Soviet power?"

"Exactly. So don't be afraid." Altman squinted again. "And if they do overthrow it, they won't find you. Have we found many of those who collaborated with the tsarist secret police? Just a few individuals, although there were thousands of them. No secret service gives up its people. At the slightest danger, the lists are destroyed first. Any real secret service values and takes care of the people who help it. So you of all people have nothing to worry about."

"I'm not worried," Vadim said. "I was just thinking . . . a review like that might make people think that its author was working for you. . . ."

"And if you had published that article in the newspaper and then we used it in the investigation, wouldn't you be suspected of collaborating too? What's the difference? Or if you had written a bad internal report for the publishing house, and we used it? No review can give rise to suspicions of collaboration. It's just the opposite — the person writes, signs his name, everything out in the open, honest. Why would he need to write open reviews if he were a secret collaborator?"

He stared at Vadim. What was his game?

"Behind our broad back, you have no one to fear," Altman said clearly. "Behind our back — only there are you safe. Without it, you, dear Vadim Andreyevich, would have been lost a long time ago. . . . I'm not reproaching you. We believe in your sincerity, we believe that you want to help the Party in its struggle against its enemies. But we can't help noticing your restraint, your caution. There's no need for it, none at all."

Vadim did not want to find out what Altman meant by excessive caution. He knew that Altman wanted information on conversations, particularly group conversations. But no one had group conversations anymore, and even one on one they were careful not to be too frank — everyone was terrified. Soon he wouldn't be able to bring Altman a single denunciation, and then Altman would force him to make them up. He had found the only solution — he would write reviews, secret ones, or under a pseudonym, but reviews that coincided with the official Party line, which he could have signed with his own name and published anywhere. Ershilov wrote even stronger stuff. And his articles contained charges, too, but Ershilov got paid for his, while Vadim worked for free, out of ideological considerations, you might say. Altman once tried to give him some money, and Vadim put his hands behind his back, "Oh no, no, don't be . . . no. . . ."

"But your time is valuable, you could be writing for the newspapers, you could be getting a fee. Consider this a fee. Don't worry, I don't need a receipt."

But Vadim would not be budged and he did not take the money. And that was probably a good step. It raised him in Altman's eyes. He appeared like a dignified, decent, altruistic man, doing his duty. Altman must have reported to his bosses about Vadim's refusal to take money, and Vadim's stock had gone up with them as well. Of course, who the hell knew — maybe he didn't tell them and kept the money for himself. He had said, "No receipts." That meant no one would ask for the money back, he'd just write, "Given to agent so-and-so." And they'd write it off. . . . Well, the hell with them, his conscience was clear. He wasn't selling himself, he didn't need the pieces of silver, but he'd like to find out why they arrested Sergei Alexeyevich.

Vadim wanted to ask Altman about him. But he was afraid. Afraid to hear the truth, to hear that he was the one whose words had done it. And if his testimony had nothing to do with it, his question would remind Altman of it, and it would be added to the charges against him and would get him involved. It was better to say nothing, to pretend not to know about Sergei Alexeyevich.

But Altman brought him up. At one of their meetings, he took out the notes of Vadim's first interrogation and handed them to him.

"Read that . . . down here." He pointed at the spot Vadim should read. It was his story of the Radek joke, about Elsbein, Ershilov, and the barber Sergei Alexeyevich.

"Your barber is stubborn," Altman said. "He's denying everything, the bastard!" He frowned, probably recalling the interrogations of Sergei Alexeyevich.

Then he looked up at Vadim. "Have you read it?"

Vadim nodded. He couldn't speak.

"Tomorrow at two o'clock you will come to Lubyanka, get a pass, and have a personal confrontation with that barber."

"What?!" Vadim gasped. "Why?"

"For this," Altman said, pointing to the lines of the notes. "You will confirm in his presence what you signed here."

"But, Comrade Altman," Vadim begged, "how can I do that? He's a friend of the family. He cut my hair when I was little, he knew my late mother, he knows my father, how can I testify against him?"

Altman pointed at the notes again. "Did you write the truth here?"

"Of course."

"Then confirm it."

"But it's such a trifle."

"Perhaps," Altman agreed. "Then all the more reason to confirm it. What's there to be afraid of?"

"But he didn't tell the joke, I did!"

"Confirm that, too." Altman chuckled.

"Then my testimony will figure officially in his case?"

"Yes, so what?"

"But how does that fit with what I do for you?"

"Very nicely."

"I told the joke and I'm walking around free. He listened to it and is in prison. Then what does that make me? A provocateur?"

Altman grimaced. "Why such loud words? And such empty ones. We have harsh punishments for provocateurs, remember that! If there had been provocation on your part, we would have punished you. But there wasn't any. You told the joke and admitted it honestly. But he listened to the joke and not only didn't report it, he denies that he heard it from you and denies his own words, 'Lev Davydovich had to be there somehow.' Why is he denying it? He might have said, 'Yes, I heard that joke, but didn't pay any attention to it. . . . Yes, I mentioned Lev Davydovich, the way everyone does now.' And that would have been it! Over! No, he denies it. Is that an accident? Far from it. You are naïve, dear Vadim Andreyevich, you're up there in your literary clouds. . . . But the enemy is treacherous. You have no idea where the ties of your innocent barber lead. This," he said, pointing at the transcript, "does look like a trifle, but behind a trifle there can be much more. So stop thinking and drop the sentimentality — 'He knew me as a child, knew my late mother.' All we want is for the barber to tell the truth and to explain to us why he had been hiding that truth. So you can explain to him that it's for his own good to tell the truth."

# 16

aiting for them to bring in Sergei Alexeyevich, Altman dealt with some paperwork, while Vadim kept his anxious eyes on the door, jumping at the slightest noise in the hall.... Horrible, horrible, horrible... How would he be able to look at the face he'd known since childhood? How would he catch someone who was almost family in a lie?... My God! Why was Sergei Alexeyevich denying such a trifle? Was he protecting Vadim? That's noble, of course, but totally unnecessary, and that's what he would tell him: "Sergei Alexeyevich, I understand you're trying to protect me, that's very noble of you, but totally unnecessary. I accepted my guilt, I confessed that it was I and no one else who told that joke to you."

The door opened and an old man, accompanied by a guard, shuffled into the room. At first Vadim didn't recognize Sergei Alexeyevich. The face was bruised, his head shook. He held up his loose trousers with his left hand and the fingers of the right hand, in which he usually held scissors, kept moving and that hand, strangely moving in the air, devastated Vadim. "God," he thought, "the man is drawing his last breath, but the reflex is still alive."

Altman stared at Sergei Alexeyevich, then nodded at the chairs by the wall, "Sit down, Feoktistov!"

Sergei Alexeyevich sat down without looking at Vadim — either he hadn't noticed him or hadn't recognized him.

"Citizen Feoktistov!" Altman said in a severe voice. "Do you know this citizen?" He pointed at Vadim.

Sergei Alexeyevich raised his head with difficulty and turned to Vadim.

Vadim thought that he saw something sparkle in his eyes and then go out, and Sergei Alexeyevich lowered his head.

"I asked you, do you know this man?"

Sergei Alexeyevich swallowed and said with difficulty, "Yes."

When his lips moved, Vadim saw that he was missing teeth. He used to have all his teeth.

"What's his name?"

"Vadim Andreyevich Marasevich," the old man whispered.

"Then, you confirm that you know him?"

"Yes."

"How did you meet?"

"I cut his hair."

"Do you cut other people's hair? And do you know them all by name?"

"Not all, but I know my steady customers. . . . His father, Sergei Alexeyevich, a professor of medicine, had been coming since before the Revolution —"

"I don't care what happened before the Revolution," Altman interrupted. "Tell me what happened after the Revolution. What conversations have you had with Vadim Andreyevich Marasevich?"

"None," Sergei Alexeyevich said without looking up.

"And he with you?"

"None!"

"Has he told you any political jokes?"

Sergei Alexeyevich lowered his head even more.

"So, you're being stubborn," Altman said viciously. "Let's hear out Citizen Marasevich. Citizen Marasevich, do you know this man?"

Suppressing the shiver in his voice, Vadim said, "Yes."

"His name?"

"Feoktistov, Sergei Alexeyevich."

"How do you know him?"

"He cut my hair, shaved me."

"And how do you know his name?"

"What do you mean? . . . I've been going to him for fifteen years, how could I not know it? And my father goes to him."

The questions were ridiculous, but Vadim understood why. Altman was treating him the same way he did Sergei Alexeyevich, not as an accuser, not even as a witness, but as the accused, to put him on the same footing with Sergei Alexeyevich. And thank God he did, so Vadim would not look like a traitor.

"Citizen Marasevich! Did Citizen Feoktistov have anti-Soviet conversation with you?"

"No, no! He never had anti-Soviet conversation with me."

"And you with him?"

"No."

"Then you didn't tell him anti-Soviet jokes?" Altman feigned surprise.

"I told him a joke about Radek."

"The Radek who was tried and found guilty?"

"Yes."

"And what's the joke?"

Vadim repeated it.

"And how do you see it?"

Vadim said nothing.

"I asked you how you see the joke, Soviet or anti-Soviet?"

"It's just a joke," Vadim said.

"In which the words of the spy and murderer Radek about our leader Comrade Stalin, mocking words, are repeated. Is it Soviet or anti-Soviet?"

"Anti-Soviet," Vadim said.

"And you told it to Citizen Feoktistov?"

"Yes."

"With what aim?"

"Just to tell it."

" 'Just to tell it,' " Altman repeated. "And how did Citizen Feoktistov react to it?"

"He laughed and said, 'Lev Davydovich had to be there somehow.' "

"What Lev Davydovich?"

"Trotsky, apparently."

"How did you find this reply?"

"It was another joke."

"A joke?"

"A joke, current line."

"What does that mean?"

"Well, Trotsky's role is now evident in all kinds of anti-Soviet activity. There is plenty of evidence of that in the trials, and so it's become a current line."

"But you told that joke last year, before Radek's arrest."

"Yes."

"Why do you think Citizen Feoktistov connected Radek with Trotsky back then?"

Vadim shrugged.

"All right." Altman went through the papers on his desk and stared with hatred at Sergei Alexeyevich. "Citizen Feoktistov, did you hear Citizen Marasevich's testimony?"

"Yes," Sergei Alexeyevich whispered.

"Did he tell you that joke about Radek?"

"I don't remember."

"Did you mention Lev Davydovich Trotsky?"

"No, never."

Altman laughed.

"Sergei Alexeyevich," Vadim said suddenly, getting up from his chair, "why are you being stubborn, why are you denying obvious things? I took all the blame for it, I admitted that I was the one who told the joke — me, not you. I'll pay for it, not you. Why be so stubborn? Are you protecting me? But I don't need it, it's totally unnecessary. We don't need it, either of us, believe me."

Altman stared expectantly at Feoktistov. But he did not react to Vadim's words; he didn't even look up.

"Well, we'll write it down," Altman said.

He wrote for a long time and then read the minutes aloud. Vadim confirmed his former statement, and in Sergei Alexeyevich's replies he added "I deny" in every case.

"Is that correct?" Altman asked Vadim.

It was correct, but it looked horrible.

Vadim hesitated. Sergei Alexeyevich was digging his own grave.

"Citizen Marasevich, is it correct?" Altman repeated his question, and he sounded irritated.

"Yes."

"Sign it."

He showed him where to sign, and Vadim did.

"Citizen Feoktistov, is it correct? Reply!"

"I deny it," whispered Sergei Alexeyevich.

"That's what it says here, 'I deny it.' Get up!"

Sergei Alexeyevich barely managed to stand.

"Come here!"

Shuffling, Sergei Alexeyevich came to the desk.

Altman pushed the minutes toward him. "Read it for yourself."

Sergei Alexeyevich read it and nodded his head.

"Sign here."

Sergei Alexeyevich did.

Altman pushed a bell and a guard appeared in the doorway.

"Take him away!"

The guard moved toward Sergei Alexeyevich and took him by the elbow.

At that moment Sergei Alexeyevich looked up at Vadim. Vadim blanched.

"Oh, Vadim Andreyevich, Vadim Andreyevich..."

Altman banged his fist on the desk. "No talking! Take him away!"

The guard pulled Sergei Alexeyevich harshly and pushed him out of the office.

"How do you like him?" Altman asked. "We've bothered with him for three months now. Stubborn bastard."

"All over that joke?"

"The joke is a trifle," Altman said. "There are more serious things involved. By the way, do you know about Feoktistov's friends in the military?"

"The military? No idea."

# ❧ 17 ❧

**O**rdzhonikidze was buried with fanfare on Red Square. Newspapers devoted entire pages to his demise and funeral. The whole country mourned dear Comrade Sergo, Beloved of the Country, Commander of Heavy Industry. Stunned by the loss, scholars, scientists, men of industry, Stakhanovite workers, military men, writers, actors, and artists spoke out in print.

But they couldn't get through it without an enemy attack. A poet published an elegy on the death of Comrade Ordzhonikidze. At a meeting of his fellow writers it was praised. Touched, the poet replied, "When Comrade Stalin dies, I'll write an even better one." The idiot had to be shot.

The funeral delayed the Plenum by a few days and it wasn't convened until February 23. Now things would go normally. Bukharin and Rykov would be arrested right at the Plenum. Let the other members and candidate members of the Central Committee see how it's done. Then, at a show trial, Bukharin and Rykov would admit everything, tell everything that was required of them.

How many times had Bukharin repented? He'd repent this time too. How could Lenin have mentioned in his "testament" a man he himself had described as "soft as wax"? Can a leader be as soft as wax? During the Brest Peace the SRs, the leftists, proposed that Bukharin arrest Lenin and create a new cabinet of ministers. Bukharin refused and relayed the information to Lenin. Lenin made him promise not to tell anyone. But after Lenin's death he talked to everyone, publicly, to show what factional battles can lead to. And now, almost twenty years later, *he*, Stalin, blamed him for it — secretly plotting to arrest Lenin! After all, he had confessed it himself! The Socialist Revolutionaries hadn't come to *him*, but they came to Bukharin; they didn't make that suggestion to *him*, but they did to Bukharin. There was no real evidence that he had refused. Maybe he had agreed but the plot failed. And if he did refuse, maybe it was because he was afraid that the plan wouldn't work. He told Lenin? Where's the proof? Lenin's dead. That's what's wrong with talking too much. And now everyone will know. Bukharin was planning to arrest Lenin.

Was he a lightweight, just a chatterbox? Perhaps. But then, don't aspire to leadership, to the role of the Party's favorite. *He* had been wanting to get rid of Bukharin for a long time. In the middle of the 1920s, after the destruction of the Zinovievite opposition, *he* was hoping to break up the right wing, to separate Rykov from Bukharin by hinting to Rykov, "Alexei, the two of us ought to get together." Alexei didn't want to, and now he would pay for it.

Just two months ago at the December Plenum of the Central Committee, Bukharin was still feeling confident. Yezhov had accused him and Rykov of forming a bloc with the Trotskyites and told him he had known about their terrorist activity. Bukharin shouted at Yezhov — "Silence! Silence! Silence!"

Why the ridiculous shouts? No one supported him. Only Ordzhonikidze asked a few questions, trying to confuse Yezhov. He failed. And then *he* said, "Let's not hurry with a decision, comrades."

And *he* proposed a resolution, "To consider the question of Rykov and Bukharin unfinished. To continue the examination and put off a decision until the next Plenum of the Central Committee."

*He* had outmaneuvered them. Why? First they had to have the Radek-Pyatakov-Sokolnikov trial in January and only then return to Bukharin.

They passed the resolution. At the trial in January everything was proven — the names Bukharin and Rykov sounded throughout the land. In those two months, every single day, Bukharin got mounds of transcripts of the interrogations of his former supporters in the right opposition and his former students at the Institute of the Red Professors. On February 16 alone, he was sent twenty such transcripts, let him read them. And to that were added constant personal confrontations with Sokolnikov, Pyatakov, Radek, and his former students — Astrov, for instance.

As a result, Bukharin was completely demoralized. He announced a hunger strike, saying that he would not come to the Plenum until the charges were dropped. He was still a naïve eccentric. Whom did he think he would frighten with a hunger strike? A while back *he* had given Yagoda instructions that hunger strikes were to be regarded as a violation of prison regulations, as a continuation of counterrevolutionary activity inside prison. But a hunger strike inside your own apartment, with your young wife at your side. Who can prove that he's really fasting?

*He* punished him for that hunger strike. The first point on the agenda for the Plenum was "On the anti-Party behavior of Bukharin in connection with the hunger strike announced to the Plenum." The second point was "On N. Bukharin and A. Rykov."

Bukharin showed up at the Plenum. He didn't stop his hunger strike, but he showed up. The Plenum participants greeted him hostilely. *He* watched closely. Only two were suspicious, Army Commander Uborevich and Akulov. Akulov even said something to him, something supportive, probably.

Then Bukharin fell down in the aisle, a show of weakness from hunger. If he were so weak, then how did he get to the meeting room? Or had he hoped that the question would be postponed "due to illness"? It wasn't.

*He* came over to him. "Against whom are you on a hunger strike, Nikolai? The Central Committee of the Party? Look at yourself, you're skin and bones. Ask the Plenum to forgive you for your hunger strike."

"Why is that necessary," Bukharin replied, "if you're planning to expel me?"

"No one is going to expel you from the Party. Go on, go on, ask the Plenum for forgiveness, you acted badly."

That was *his* answer. *He* said it quietly. And Bukharin believed it, the eccentric, he perked up, got up from the floor and asked forgiveness for the hunger strike. He muttered something about a monstrous accusation, but he did ask forgiveness. He got down from the tribune and sat on the floor in the aisle. What was he trying to say by that?

And so, sitting on the floor in the aisle, he heard Yezhov's report. This time Yezhov added accusations of terror, of preparing a coup d'état, forming a bloc with Trotskyites and Zinovievites, organizing kulak uprisings, selling the U.S.S.R. to the capitalists, and murdering Kirov. Sitting on the floor, Bukharin listened to Yezhov in silence and kept looking at *him,* waiting for *him* to defend him. But instead of *him*, Mikoyan spoke, describing Bukharin and Rykov as enemies of the Party and of the people. The morning session ended with that.

They later checked: Bukharin ate lunch at home, to make the Party happy. He came to the Plenum sated and kept watching *him*, waiting for *him* to come to his defense. No, dear Bukharin, you were the one who called Comrade Stalin "Genghis Khan with a telephone," and as you know, Genghis Khans are in no hurry to pardon.

The next day Molotov and Kaganovich spoke, lambasting Bukharin completely. Even slow-witted Molotov came to a conclusion. "When we arrest you, confess. The Fascist press maintains that our trials are provocative. If you deny your guilt, you will prove that you are a Fascist hireling."

No one supported Bukharin. Everyone was against him, interrupting when Bukharin said, "It's hard for me to live." Even *he* interrupted him with "And is it easy for us?"

*He* did not speak. *He* simply suggested creating a commission to develop a decision on Bukharin and Rykov. They did. Thirty-six people, chaired by Mikoyan.

Twenty people spoke at the commission. Six proposed execution, seven were for turning it over to the courts without execution, and the majority voted for *his* "softest" proposal, to expel them from the Party, not turn them over to the courts, but send the case to the NKVD.

And if the case was going to the NKVD, they should too.

And right there at the Plenum, on February 27, Bukharin and Rykov were arrested.

Then on March 3, Comrade Stalin gave a speech.

"Saboteurs, spies, and agents of foreign powers," Comrade Stalin said, "have penetrated all the country's organizations. The leaders of these organizations were too feckless.

"As long as we are surrounded by capitalists, we will have saboteurs, spies, and killers.

"The strength of today's saboteurs is that they have Party cards in their pockets.

"The weakness of our people is blind faith in people with Party cards.

"Saboteurs can show systematical successes — putting off their destruction until the war."

*And so at the February and March Plenum of 1937, Comrade Stalin officially declared war — which he had begun ten years earlier — against his own people.*

*According to scholars, in early 1937 there were five million people in prisons and camps. Between January 1937 and December 1938, another seven million were arrested. Of them, one million were shot and two million died in the camps.*

# ❧ 18 ❧

Charles's parents lived in Algiers. His father was an important figure in the French colonial administration. They sent letters with warm regards and kisses for their daughter-in-law, and Charles sent them kind words and kisses from Vika.

In the mornings Suzanne brought breakfast — coffee, milk, croissants, butter, and jam. After breakfast, Charles worked in his study, and somewhere around one, Suzanne informed Madame that lunch was ready and the table set. They usually dined in restaurants. Vika adored Parisian restaurants and cafés, where the atmosphere was relaxed and everyone smiled. In Moscow, going to a restaurant was an event; here it was a part of life. There were no doormen or coat checks, you left your coat on a coatrack or tossed it on a chair next to you, the maître d' led you from the door to a table of your choosing without forcing you to sit with others, the waiters were helpful and gave everyone a menu, so you could read and decide. . . . After a few months Vika had already developed favorite spots, like the Rotonde, and walking home along boulevard Raspail made a wonderful stroll before bedtime. But they didn't go there that frequently, and Vika never knew where Charles would take her — to the Rotonde or somewhere on the banks of the Seine or to some unfamiliar neighborhood. It depended on his business.

One time Charles said that they would be going to the Closerie des Lilas. He had an appointment there with a colleague.

"You'll enjoy it, you might meet someone famous. Hemingway used to like it there, he usually sat at the counter, but he's in Spain now."

The café was on the corner of boulevard Montparnasse and avenue de l'Observatoire. Charles wanted to show Vika the observatory that gave the street its name, but it was closed.

They stopped at the intersection. Looking at the passing cars and holding his hand, Vika said, "I still can't believe that I'm in Paris and with you. Sometimes I think it's all a dream."

Vika liked the Closerie des Lilas. It was cozy and animated. Many of the customers knew one another and greeted Charles. His journalist friend waved to them, and they joined him at his table. Vika took part in their conversation, using simple phrases. She was pleased. She liked speaking French.

They had finished dinner and Vika was thinking about dessert when she looked up from the menu and saw the man who had just walked in.

Of medium height, around sixty, with horn-rimmed glasses and deep vertical lines between his eyebrows. Vika may have paid attention to him because the room seemed to hush for an instant, as if to welcome that gentleman. He had an imperious and significant face.

He put his coat on a free chair, looked around, saw Charles, came over to their table, and made a general bow.

Charles rose and they shook hands.

"Please convey to your editor my gratitude for the article on my book."

"It could be no other way, Monsieur Gide, it is a marvelous book."

"Not everyone thinks so."

"They do not know Russia. I lived there for several years and I am amazed by your powers of observation. It is a miserable country. The only good thing there I brought back with me."

He introduced Vika.

Gide shook her hand politely and smiled kindly. "Victoria! It really is your victory. I hope, Madame, that you will be the first Russian to read my book about Russia. Even though I am not sure that you will like everything in it."

"I'm sure I will!" Vika replied, smiling sweetly. "My husband has told me so much about it, he adored it. And I trust his taste."

*   *   *

At home Charles said, "André Gide is my favorite contemporary French writer. He was widely published in Russia. They even issued his collected works. He was once an admirer of the U.S.S.R."

Charles took a book from his shelf and opened it to a marked page. "Here's what he wrote before his trip to the U.S.S.R.: 'Three years ago I spoke of my love and delight in the Soviet Union. An unprecedented experiment was taking place there, which filled our hearts with hope, we expected great progress from there, an impulse is being born that can captivate all of humanity. In our hearts and minds we have tied the fate of culture with the U.S.S.R. We will defend it.' "

Charles put down the book and said, "I'm writing a major study of Gide and I remember his opinions in the early thirties — 'If the U.S.S.R. needed my life, I would give it instantly.' "

He picked up the book again. "And here's what he wrote now. 'It has been decided once and for all in the U.S.S.R. that there can be only one opinion on any question. . . . When you talk to a Russian, it is as if you are talking to all of them at once. This consciousness begins to form in childhood. The general tendency in the U.S.S.R. is the loss of the individual — can it be seen as progress? . . . In no other country except Hitler's Germany is the consciousness so unfree, oppressed, frightened, and enslaved.' "

Charles looked at Vika.

"Of course, no one dares talk," Vika said in Russian.

"His thoughts on power are just as interesting. Listen. 'The dictatorship of one man and not the dictatorship of the proletariat. The destruction of opposition in the state is an invitation to terrorism. Gagged and oppressed from all sides, the people are deprived of the possibility of resistance. In the best situation are the lowest, the groveling, the base. The more insignificant the people, the more Stalin can count on their servile loyalty. The best vanish, the best are killed. Soon Stalin will always be right, because there will be no one around him left able to propose an idea.' "

He put down the book. "You're not bored?"

"No! I've never heard anything like this.... I mean, he formulates it with astonishing accuracy."

Charles was still reading. "Here's another interesting observation. 'The best way to avoid being denounced is to denounce someone first. Denunciation is raised to the rank of civic good deeds.' "

Vika blushed, shuddered, and turned in her chair, trying to hide her reaction.

Charles looked at her inquisitively.

"Go on, please, it's fascinating." Thank God, she got herself under control. Why had that bothered her so much? It was all behind her now. Sharok, and the Maroseika, and that miserable thing she signed, everything was back there, beyond the border. And "the border was locked." And yet, just that phrase made her feel endangered.

"Listen some more then. 'The goods are unacceptable. The windows of Moscow stores bring you to despair....' "

Vika laughed. "That's for sure."

Charles put the book down, smiled gently, bent over, and took her hand. "Have I upset you with the reading?"

"Why, dear?"

"Russians are such patriots."

"Yes, I'm Russian, but I don't have anything in common with the Soviets."

"I told you that I'm writing an article on this book," he said and chuckled. "I'm considered a specialist on Soviet Russia."

"You are a specialist," Vika said.

"Who is disliked by our leftists.... Of course, they don't like Gide either."

"Communists?"

"Communists and those close to them. Roman Rolland, Louis Aragon, André Malraux, and many others. They are talented but not very bright, naïve people. If you have no objections, I'll read a few more lines."

"Of course, of course."

" 'All that is required of an artist or a writer is obedience, everything else will fall into place. There is nothing more dangerous for culture than that kind of mental condition. Art that puts itself in dependence on orthodoxy, even under the most progressive doctrine, is doomed to failure. Revolution must offer the artist freedom above all. Without it, art loses its meaning and significance. A great writer, a great artist is always an anti-conformist. He moves against the current.'

"Marvelously put!" concluded Charles.

"Marvelous!"

"However, Gide ends on an optimistic note. 'By the U.S.S.R. I mean those who are its leaders. Even the mistakes of one country cannot compromise the truth. Let us hope for the best. Otherwise nothing will remain of this wonderful and heroic people, so worthy of love, except speculators, executioners, and victims.'"

Vika reached out. "Let me see."

She read a few paragraphs out loud. She turned the page, read a little more to herself, and announced happily, "You know, I can understand almost everything now. Just a few individual words that I don't know."

"Talk with Mademoiselle Irina, have her include this reading in your homework."

Mlle Irina was Vika's French tutor. She came to Vika twice a week. Vika had broken one of Nelli Vladimirova's rules. Mlle Irina came from an émigré noble family. She had been born in Russia, and then moved from the Crimea, to Turkey, Bulgaria, and at last France. She had graduated from the Sorbonne and according to Charles was considered the best private teacher in Paris. A pretty, polite, and friendly woman, she never involved Vika in any émigré affairs and in general did not talk about them. Gently, with a smile, she made her repeat the same word as many as twenty times. She gave a lot of homework — reading, writing, translations — and praised her. For the first time in her life, Vika was working diligently.

"Wonderful," Mlle Irina said about André Gide's book. "I like him very much myself. For our next lesson, please translate the first five pages."

Twice a week Vika went with Suzanne to the market and came back stunned. After the meager and impoverished fare of

Moscow, she couldn't believe that there was such abundance in the world.

At home she proudly told Charles about the bargains she got on asparagus and mushrooms, and even sole, one of the most expensive fish, was cheaper today. Charles smiled, touched by her naïve conviction that by saving centimes she was guarding their welfare.

After lunch Charles went to the newspaper office. He was the political commentator, with a weekly column, and he worked hard. Sometimes, and usually unexpectedly, he took off for a few days abroad — to London, Berlin, or Rome — often leaving straight from the office, with time only to call Vika and tell her. In all this time he had managed to find only two Sundays for her. Once he took her to the Invalides to show her the church and the sarcophagus of red granite holding Napoleon's remains, and on the other Sunday he took her to Versailles.

On the days that Vika was free of both lessons and marketing, she walked around Paris. Not far from their house, on the boulevard Saint-Germain, was the Solferino metro station, and near the Seine, the quai d'Orsay embankment, called that probably because the gare d'Orsay was so close, or maybe the station was named after the embankment.

At first Vika stopped by every shop window, but invariably somebody would try to pick her up. She'd walk away quickly, and if the man followed, she'd go into the store.

Vika bought trifles — cosmetics, once a pretty nightgown, another time slippers and an apron to work in the kitchen on Sundays. She showed her purchases to Charles and he approved of them all. She related with indignation the stories of different men trying to bother her. Charles laughed and said, "Darling, you shouldn't stand by shop windows, that's for tourists or poor elderly women who worry about the prices."

The conversation ended unexpectedly. Charles begged her forgiveness. "I must not have been paying attention to you. If you're looking at store windows, that means you want to buy something. You need to get ready for spring."

"There's time," Vika said and lowered her gaze. But a minute later she asked, "Where are you planning to take me — the Carolina?"

His eyebrows went up. "Oh, you know the Carolina?"

"I heard about it back in Moscow. If a pretty dress from Paris appeared, people said, 'It's from Carolina.'"

"Then that's where we'll go. I'll call the owner and we'll order a few spring dresses, a suit. You'll see what you need."

# ❧ 19 ❧

The assistant principal called from the school. The Regional Committee asked about Nina. People who did not wish to leave their names asked for Nina Ivanovna Ivanova. They called in the daytime, when Varya was at work, and the neighbors told her about the calls, wondering themselves and asked, "Where is Nina?" Varya would shrug indifferently and say, "How should I know? She doesn't report to me. Must have gone off to a seminar."

Now Varya stopped at the Central Telegraph Office on her way to the institute from work. There was a telegram from Kostroma — "EVERYTHING FINE, KISSES." Then similar ones from Kurgan, Novosibirsk, Krasnoyarsk — all unsigned. And finally from Khabarovsk — "EVERYTHING FINE, MAX AND I KISS YOU." She immediately telegraphed Max — "HEALTHY, WORKING, STUDYING, KISS EVERYONE, VARYA." That was supposed to let them know that she was all right, not being dragged in anywhere, living as she always did.

And after a while, no one called, came to see Nina, or asked for her.

And so, it was done. Nina was with Max in safety. They wouldn't find her there. The army was a pillar of power there. Stalin's support, our glorious fliers, tank drivers, gunners, and who else was there? Yes, our glorious cavalry.

Varya remembered the graduation dance at the House of the Red Army. It all seemed so romantic three years ago. The elegant graduates, agile, handsome, merry, with their wild and enthusiastic dancing. Now it was different. Now the NKVD men walked around the streets in military uniforms. As soon as Varya saw the uniform on Yuri Sharok, she began hearing it: They were arresting some military men. An old tsarist general lived in their building, but one who had fought on the side of the Reds in the Civil War, a professor at the Military Academy, an impressive man with gray sideburns and pince-nez. They arrested him! And Muralov was being tried. And she still remembered the newspaper accounts of him leading parades on holidays. And now, if you believed the papers, he was a spy for the Germans and Japanese. Nonsense!

As for Maxim Kostin, nothing would happen to him. He was a follower. A simple but nice man, he was like a brick wall protecting Nina. How would they ever think to look for her in the Far East?

The only person Varya told was Sofya Alexandrovna. There were no secrets between them.

"You did the right thing. They say that not only the director but some of the teachers and some of the tenth-graders, the Paramonov boy from our building — you know, in the fifth entrance? — have been arrested. Could it have been over that bust of Stalin?"

"They arrest people for less!"

"Of course, it's hard for Nina. She really believed," Sofya Alexandrovna noted.

She said it with sympathy. The time had passed when she had been hurt by the indifference of Sasha's friends to his fate, when she was tormented by the thought that everyone was living well and only Sasha was living badly. Now it was bad for everyone; time had leveled everyone, great and small. Ivan Grigoryevich was in prison, and Nina was fleeing arrest. But Sasha, on the contrary, was coming back. Would he get here? She counted the days. If Sasha had been released exactly on time, if he got his documents on time, he could get to the railroad around February 10 and then send her a telegram. Of course, the documents might come late and it wasn't easy getting through the taiga in winter to the railroad, so you had to add at least two weeks. If she didn't have a telegram by the twenty-fifth, that meant something had happened. But for now, she would wait patiently.

Sofya Alexandrovna shared her calculations with Varya. Varya also counted the days, and she thought it would be sooner, which raised her spirits. Like Sofya Alexandrovna, she knew that Sasha would not be allowed to live in Moscow. Well, she'd go to him. If necessary, she would trade her room for one in the city where he would live, she would find work there and switch to the correspondence division of her institute. They would live in some small town, the smaller the better, less dangerous. It would be great to be in a village, but there were kolkhozes everywhere, so a village was out of the question. Perhaps they could live in Kozlov. It was called Michurinsk now. She and Nina used to visit an aunt there. No one knew her and Sasha there. They would work, walk a lot, there were fields and meadows filled with daisies, cornflowers, and clover. Holding hands, they would wander down village roads. That's how she imagined their future. Varya refused to think about the possibility that Sasha would not be released. As soon as he chose the spot where he would be allowed to live, she would go there.

It had been decided firmly and a long time ago; Varya had no doubts that it was Sasha's decision, too. They did not discuss it in letters — letters were read, especially letters to exiled people. But in every letter of Sasha's, in every line addressed to her, she sensed that he was thinking about the same thing, that both were living for one thing — anticipation of their meeting.

Actually, it had begun that evening in the Arbat Cellar, and then in the line along the prison walls, then the parcels, letters, and talks with Sofya Alexandrovna and Mikhail Yurevich about Sasha. That was her love, which had to culminate in a happy reunion. There had been Kostya, of course. She remembered his hairy back and short crooked legs with disgust, but that was just an accident, a mistake. Life with Kostya had helped in one way — it cured her of an interest in restaurants, dances, young men, and parties. She preferred sitting with Mikhail Yurevich or Sofya Alexandrovna and talking.

They constantly brought up Sasha, but Varya never spoke of her love for him — that was understood. Sofya Alexandrovna, of course, understood everything. But sharing her plans for the future would be rubbing salt into Sofya Alexandrovna's wounds — that Sasha couldn't live in Moscow — hurting her some more. In these unhappy times it was inappropriate to talk of happiness. There was no happiness. There was life and the struggle for life, and ahead there was nothing but that struggle.

# ❧ 20 ❧

**S**ofya Alexandrovna rang Varya at work. Her voice was trembling. "Come over this evening."

Varya rushed over immediately. "Has something happened?"

Sofya Alexandrovna showed her Sasha's telegram from Krasnoyarsk and burst into tears. " 'Traveling, will call.' "

Varya embraced Sofya Alexandrovna, who rested her head on her chest.

"Calm down, Sofya Alexandrovna. This is such great joy, and here you are crying! Sasha's coming, he's coming!"

But Sofya Alexandrovna couldn't utter a word, and her small body was convulsed with sobs. The strain of those years, the strain of the last few weeks, the last few days, was gone and at last she could cry the way she hadn't cried since Sasha was arrested.

Varya sat Sofya Alexandrovna down on the couch, took her hands into her own, and caressed them. She had tears in her own eyes.

"Sofya Alexandrovna, we should be dancing with joy, and we're crying! Let's be honest. Did we actually, totally believe that Sasha would be released? We didn't! And he's in Krasnoyarsk already! You have a map, let me see where Krasnoyarsk is!"

Now the future about which Varya had dreamed was taking on real shape. Sasha was free! He would decide where he would live and she would join him. "Sofya Alexandrovna, please, get the map, let's see how he's traveling, through which cities!"

Sofya Alexandrovna took the map from a shelf and spread it on the table. They found Krasnoyarsk. From Krasnoyarsk, Varya made a line with her finger to Novosibirsk, then to Omsk and Sverdlovsk.

"Stop there," Sofya Alexandrovna said. "If Sasha had taken a direct train in Krasnoyarsk, he'd have told me the number so that we could meet him. That means he has to change trains. From Sverdlovsk he can go either through Kazan — I checked — or through Kirov. So it's not clear at which station we should be meeting him, the Yaroslavl or Kazan."

"He says that he'll call."

"Oh, yes, that's right. That means he doesn't want to tell us the train number." She thought and added, "Don't tell anyone that he's coming."

"Why keep it a secret? He hasn't escaped from exile. He was released."

"Sasha doesn't have the right even to visit Moscow. That's why he put it so vaguely — 'will call.' Everything is checked and controlled. Maybe he'll call from the road, maybe from where he settles. No one can guess. But somehow I think that he'll call from Moscow."

"What if you're not home?" Varya said in fear.

"I will be home. I'll start my vacation tomorrow. I haven't used up last year's. And I'll stay by the telephone."

"If Sasha calls, let me know right away," Varya said. "I'll go to the station with you."

"Of course I will. He can't stay here even for a day. Galya will inform on him immediately."

Varya's heart thumped. "He can stay at my place. I'm alone now since Nina's gone."

"Your neighbors know Sasha. And someone will see him crossing the courtyard. He could stay with Vera, my sister — they have a private apartment. Of course, it's small, just two rooms for the four of them, but there's also the dacha, locked up and cold, but it can be heated. We'll see what Sasha says. It's possible that he'll have to keep moving right away, and he'll need food for the road. Will you buy some, Varya? I don't want to leave the house. I'll give you money."

"I have money," Varya said.

"I have to go to the bank first thing in the morning anyway. I'll get some money and drop by work to arrange my vacation."

Sofya Alexandrovna started rummaging in the chest. "Just in case, I'll get some things ready for Sasha; maybe his socks are worn out, wool doesn't last."

Varya stopped her. "There's plenty of time, Sofya Alexandrovna. This is such an event, Sasha's first telegram in freedom, and you're talking about socks. 'Wool doesn't last.' You haven't even let me hold the telegram."

Sofya Alexandrovna laughed. "You're right, here, read it."

And even though Varya knew it by heart, she was thrilled to see it with her own eyes. "TRAVELING. WILL CALL."

"Make a shopping list for me," Varya said as she left.

The difficult days of waiting started. Sofya Alexandrovna took a two-week vacation, did not leave the house, and was the first to reach the phone when it rang, made easier because the telephone was in the corridor near her room. She did not stay on long, afraid that it would be just then that Sasha would call, and fretted when her neighbor Galya spoke at length on the telephone.

But a day passed, another, a third, and Sasha hadn't called.

Varya dropped by in the evening, bringing food for Sofya Alexandrovna and food for the road. Sofya Alexandrovna put the bacon and smoked sausage between the two window frames to keep fresh and put the sugar away in the cupboard.

## ❧ 21 ❧

The train was approaching Moscow. The passengers packed up their things as the conductor swept the corridors, rudely getting in everyone's way.

Sasha breathed on the window, rubbed it with his hand, saw the bare snowy fields, woods, and empty dacha-area stations — the countryside surrounding Moscow, familiar since childhood and tugging at his heart.

What was awaiting him in Moscow?

His mother wouldn't have the control, she'd burst out crying when he called; she would say something inappropriate, call him by name, and the neighbors would hear her, and there might be strangers there too, or people actually waiting for him. Even if everything was clear and Mama said, "Come," how would he get through the courtyard and up the stairs? If one person saw him, everybody would know.

He would call Varya, and she could call his mother or go to see her. But Nina was there. Nina wouldn't inform on him, but still . . . And what would Varya tell his mother? That he was in Moscow, at the station, and didn't know how to contact her? No, that was no good.

Go to his aunts? But what would their husbands and their children, his cousins, think of that? The times had changed and people had changed, and he couldn't stay with anyone or even drop in on anyone. Not only would he be liable for violating the passport regulations, but so would those where he was staying — why hadn't they reported that Pankratov, Alexander Pavlovich, was in Moscow? He couldn't even call — why hadn't they reported that? They had covered up, helped him break the law!

He wouldn't go see anyone; he wouldn't call anyone. He'd leave Moscow as fast as possible. From one train to the other. Where to? Kalinin — it wasn't under passport regulations, it was near Moscow, and he knew someone there — Olga Stepanovna, the wife of Mikhail Mikhailovich Maslov, she had been to Mozgova. It was a small link, but it was a link. He had her address, he had told her what had happened to Mikhail Mikhailovich — it was a sad letter, but he had sent it, he had done his duty. Now he had a reason to drop by — had she gotten the letter? did she have any news of her husband? Maybe she would help him rent a room or a corner. And tomorrow he'd call his mother from Kalinin.

It was the only way! Legal, safe, there was no risk, he wasn't getting anyone in trouble.

And another consideration worked in favor of Kalinin. Once in Mozgova, back in 1935, Sasha read in the newspaper that the Kalinin Oblast was being separated from the Moscow Oblast and that M. E. Mikhailov had been elected as the first secretary of the Kalinin Oblast Party Committee. Sasha remembered him vaguely — Mikhailov had lived in their building or had visited his parents. He remembered because he had been friends with his younger brother, Motya, and knew from Motya that his brother was a big Party worker.

Sasha often went to Motya's to play chess. Motya would give him a head start and would still win. Sasha saw Motya's brother there once — Mikhail Efimovich Mikhailov — and regarded him with awe. Sasha had great respect for Party workers then. This was twelve or thirteen years ago and it was unlikely that Mikhailov would remember the boy who used to play chess with his brother. It was ridiculous to hope that he would help. He would never be able to reach the first Party secretary. But still it was a familiar name, the leader of the Kalinin Oblast was connected to Sasha's childhood, the brother of Sasha's friend. And what if Motya were in Kalinin?

Fine. Right. Decided! The Leningrad Station was just on the other side of the square; maybe he'd be in luck and get a train to Kalinin.

Sasha pushed his way through the crowd of arrivals and greeters, and came out on Komsomol Square.

Moscow, dammit, it was Moscow! He was in Moscow. A trolley pulled up and his heart leaped — the number four, his own trolley, which he always took to get to the square. An old lady with a small boy — her grandson? — got off. Lucky people, not oppressed, not afraid, not worried, just living their normal lives, taking the trolleys, riding in cars. Yes.... There were more cars, but nothing else had changed — the same stands and kiosks, the damned clock with the signs of the zodiac on the tower of the Kazan Station. How many times had he been on this square? How many times had he taken trains here to Pioneer camp, to the dacha? They usually rented a dacha along the Yaroslavl route — in Lyazma, Tarasovka, or Taininka. He knew the closest stations and platforms on all three lines.

And here, around the corner, there should be a shoeshine stand run by an old mustachioed man. There was the booth, and there was the man, sitting on his low stool, the old man was alive! Sasha smiled, and the old man misunderstood. He looked up and said, "Shine?"

"Next time."

But as soon as he came out in the square, he was overwhelmed with fear again — he was making a mistake, asking for trouble, he didn't have the right to come to Moscow. What if there were patrols at the station, the way there were in Taishet, and they demanded his documents?

Lost in thought, Sasha accidently bumped into an officer, who promptly swore at him; several people stopped, and someone could call a policeman at any second. Apologizing, he hurried off, almost ran across the square and into the Leningrad Station. What a humiliating, disgusting feeling! He caught his breath and found the ticket office. The Kalinin train was leaving in three hours, and there were plenty of tickets. He bought one and sighed in relief. Now he had two tickets, one from Sverdlovsk to Moscow, the other from Moscow to Kalinin. The tickets confirmed that he was in transit and not breaking the law.

And the fact that he had calmed down immediately spoiled his mood even more. He was a coward — he had been afraid approaching Moscow, he had been afraid crossing the square, going up to the ticket office, worried that there wouldn't be any tickets and he'd have to spend time at the station. Was this the way he would live now? Hiding in corners, jumping every time someone looked at him, looking over his shoulder, afraid of everyone?

He had to get hold of himself. They were trying to squash him with fear. It wouldn't work! Why didn't he have the right to call home? Who could forbid it?

Sasha went out on the square, found a telephone booth, and dropped in a coin.

There were two long rings and then he heard his mother's voice. "Hello."

His heart thumped again at the sound of her voice. His mother was here, next to him.

"Mama," Sasha said, "be calm. It's me, Sasha. Everything is fine. I'm at the Leningrad Station, going to Kalinin, I'll call you from there tomorrow."

"How do you feel?" she asked calmly, not at all surprised by his call or by the fact that he wasn't coming to her house.

"Wonderful!"

"When is your train?"

He was astonished by her control.

"In three hours."

"I'll be right there."

"What for? Don't."

"At what ticket window are you?"

"I've gotten my ticket."

"Wait for me by the entrance to the station, I'm leaving."

"Mama!"

He heard the dial tone.

Sasha went back to the station and sat down on his suitcase near the entrance.

It was a direct line, the number four trolley, but still, by the time she walked to the stop, waited for the trolley, and rode here, it would take an hour at least.

He could only wait.

Sometimes he got up and walked out of the station, looking at the people crossing the square. The trolleys that came from the center of town stopped on the other side. There was also a metro exit. There was one on this side too. He would have liked to see the metro, but he couldn't leave, he didn't want to miss his mother.

He thought about how steadfast his mother had been when he couldn't come to the house, how she hadn't discussed it, so as not to upset him. How calmly she spoke, after waiting for his call, waiting since the day she got his telegram from Krasnoyarsk, waiting for two weeks while he made his way to Moscow, perhaps not leaving the house, not sleeping nights, listening for the phone to ring, for he had said, "Will call."

She appeared unexpectedly. Sasha hadn't noticed her come up, he just felt a touch. His mother pressed herself against him and wept silently, trembling. He hugged her, kissed her head. She was wearing a gray scarf. When he had last seen her, she had been wearing a black fur hat, tilted so that her white streak of hair showed. It must have worn out, and this rough wool scarf spoke of her poverty.

Then she looked up, fixed him with a long, deep, suffering gaze, her lips trembled again, and she hugged him again.

Holding her by the shoulders, he led her inside, found a free spot on a bench, seated her, and sat next to her on his suitcase.

She was still staring at him in silence.

Sasha smiled. "Mama, hello! Well, say something!"

She went on staring.

Smiling, he ran his hand over his stubbly cheek. "You can't shave in the train, and the barbershops are awfully dirty in the stations."

He had said something almost like this back in the Butyrki Prison before he was sent off. And with those same words he greeted her now.

"When I get to Kalinin, I'll clean myself up immediately."

She asked, "How long is your passport restricted?"

"No fixed term."

She opened her purse and took out an envelope. "Here's some money for you, five hundred rubles."

"So much? Leave half for yourself, please."

"No, don't even mention it. Mark sent it to you. It was in the bank, there's still fifteen hundred there. I'll get it when you need it."

She looked at Sasha. "Sasha, I have to tell you something." She paused, sighed, and without taking her eyes off him, said, "Mark was shot."

Sasha stared in confusion. Mark shot? Mark dead?

"I didn't want to write to you about it. He was arrested in August. The trial was in Kemerovo...."

Sasha said nothing. And she went on, still looking at him, "Ivan Grigoryevich Budyagin was arrested, Lena and Vladlen and the baby were forced out of the Fifth House of Soviets into a communal flat."

What horrible news! Sasha had thought about Ivan Grigoryevich only a few days ago, and he had been in prison already.... Poor Lena, poor Vladlen!

"Did Lena get married?"

"No, she's not married. The baby's father is Sharok, but they don't live together. I don't think they even see each other."

Sofya Alexandrovna was quiet and then asked, "Who do you have in Kalinin?"

"The wife of a friend lives there."

"I have two addresses for you — one in Ryazan, the brother of Mikhail Yurevich, he works in the Obplan, Yevgeny Yurevich, you must remember him, he's been to Moscow. He'll do what he can for you. The second address is in Ufa, the brother of Vera's husband lives there. She wrote to him, too. Of course, Ryazan is closer, but you see. The important thing is not to despair — the worst is behind you. As soon as you get settled, I'll come to visit you."

They had thought about everything, they had got everything ready — Mama, Mikhail Yurevich, and Varya, of course. Sweet, naïve people. Just one suspicious glance from some creep in a uniform with raspberry-colored tabs, and all their plans would collapse.

But it was wonderful having loyal people backing him.

"Are you still working in the inventory office?"

"Yes. I'm on vacation now."

He understood that she had taken the time off to stay by the telephone and wait for his call.

She took out a package from her bag. "Here's some food for the road. Smoked sausage, bacon, chocolate."

"You shouldn't have."

"You can't buy any of that in Kalinin. And you haven't had lunch today."

"Thanks!"

She had saved these things for his arrival, too.

"The things that are going on, Sasha," said Sofya Alexandrovna. "It's awful! They arrest someone from our building every night."

"What are they saying in Moscow about the trial?"

"Saying?" Sofya Alexandrovna laughed bitterly. "Sasha, dear, no one talks to anyone now, everyone's afraid. At night a husband may whisper into his wife's ear, but even then under the covers. A lot of foreigners were at the trial. Lion Feuchtwanger was there, ambassadors were in the courtroom, defenders, the famous Bradue gave a speech. . . . I don't know what to tell you." She shrugged. "I only talked a little about it with Varya, but Varya is absolutely outspoken, she said, 'Vyshinsky is just a lackey, a sell-out, and the whole thing is a lie.'"

Sasha smiled. He remembered Varya angry about a kid in her class who was an informer and a creep. And he imagined how angry her face had been when she described Vyshinsky.

"But the majority believe it, I think, Sasha. Mass psychology is very unstable. It can be turned this way and that. Do you remember the Travkins — they lived in our building, an old woman and her daughter? The older daughter, a Socialist Revolutionary or a Menshevik, had been put away back in 1922. Well now, fifteen years later, they exiled the old woman and her younger daughter. For what? For ties with an enemy of the people. And that enemy of the people is her own daughter, whom she hasn't seen in fifteen years. And — you should know this — the NKVD people are taking all the apartments. And Yuri Sharok is working for the NKVD, he's a big shot."

"I understood that from your letters. Does he still live in our building?"

"He left. Got a new apartment. His parents and his brother, Volodya, a criminal back from the camps, live in the old one. Criminals like that don't get apartments in Moscow, but he did, and right on the Arbat, which is a carefully regulated street."

"That means they expunged his criminal record," Sasha said.

"A horrible man! Obnoxious, with a criminal face, when you walk past him you worry that he'll stab you any minute. Incidentally, he asked about you."

"Yes?"

"With this nasty smile. 'Waiting for your little Sasha?'"

"What did you say?"

"I said, 'We waited for you to come back and we'll wait for Sasha.' I didn't even stop, I just tossed it back at him. They say he works in the Moscow Criminal Investigation Department. . . . Well, enough about our life. . . . Forgive me! How are you?"

"Fine. As you can see, alive and well."

"I told you those things, so that you know what life here is like."

"I can imagine."

"They persecute people like you, picking on the slightest thing. Be careful, Sasha. Don't get into arguments. How do you plan to work?"

"Whatever I get. As a driver would be best. By the way, did you bring my license?"

"Yes, yes, of course. My God, I almost forgot to give it to you." She rummaged in her bag, took out an envelope. "Here is your license, your school record book, the addresses I told you about, and look, here's your union card, but it's out of date, you haven't paid your dues in three years."

"No problem," Sasha said, taking the envelope. "It might still come in handy."

He looked them over — driver's license in a cardboard case, his photograph, a boyish face in a striped football jersey, his school record book with the familiar teachers' names, all his schoolwork completed except he hadn't defended his senior thesis.

"Here are some more documents of yours," his mother continued, going through papers in another envelope, "birth certificate, grade school certificate, membership in some sports association . . ."

"I don't need any of that," Sasha said, "you keep it. Wait, I'll take the birth certificate." If he had an opportunity to get a new passport, he'd need it then.

"I don't want to upset you, Sasha," his mother said, "but we have a very unpleasant situation in the apartment. Galya wants the little room. She refuses to believe that I'm keeping it for Papa, and she keeps watching me. I'm worried that she intercepts your letters and passes them along to them. I had to get my own mailbox. And now when you call from another city, I don't want her to answer the

phone. You know how the operator says, 'Kalinin calling...
Leningrad calling...' So let's always pick an approximate time for
your call and I'll stay by the telephone."

"All right," Sasha said, "but I don't know what time I can get
Moscow."

"I get home at six from work and I'm home all evening."

"I'll call you after seven tomorrow, and then we'll make
arrangements. And I'll write," he said with a smile. "It's cheaper."

"Of course," she agreed, "don't waste money. Write often, every
day if you can. Call only in emergencies. By the way, you can write
to Varya; she'll pass them along to me."

"Are you afraid they'll be looking for me?"

"Yes, I am. They release people very rarely. And if they do, they
arrest them again. And they'll take not only you, but your friends
and acquaintances, even your co-workers. That's their system. It
will be very hard for you, Sasha."

"I know that. But don't worry. It'll be fine."

"God willing," she said softly and her eyes grew moist again. "My
God, why, why did this have to happen to you?"

"Mama, don't." He took her hands into his and pressed them to
his lips. "You should be happy, I'm alive and well, free, I'm free,
understand? It's my good fortune that they took me then and not
now, that's why I got off so easily. If I were arrested now, I'd get ten
years in the camps, at least. For what? For the same as the rest, for
nothing! So you should be happy. Don't worry, don't worry about
anything. I'll write — not every day, I doubt I can manage
that — but you shouldn't worry no matter what. Everything will be
fine with me."

She listened to him in silence, thought a bit, and then said, "Aunt
Vera has offered their dacha in an emergency. In the winter, you
have to warn me so they can open up the house, they have firewood
there. Let's pick a code phrase so that when you say it, I'll know to
call Vera. How about, 'Send me a sweater, I'm freezing.' What do
you think?"

"Fine," Sasha said with a smile. "I'll remember. 'Send me a
sweater, I'm freezing.'"

They had even thought about that, in case he had to escape

quickly from somewhere. His aunt was terrific! Her brother had been shot, but she wasn't afraid to hide her nephew.

"Wonderful," he said, suddenly thinking that he could meet with Varya there.

"How's Varya?"

"Varya is a sweet girl. A kind soul. I love her truly. My sole support, you could say. She sent all the parcels to you. 'Sofya Alexandrovna, it's too much for you, I'll take it to the post office. . . .' Touching, isn't it?"

Sasha nodded. "Yes, of course."

"She took me to the hospital, she came to my laundry and argued with the difficult customers. The girl's got character. She forced Nina to go to the Far East, or Nina would have been arrested."

"Nina?"

"Just imagine. She was so orthodox in her beliefs. They arrested the school director, who had liked Nina, set her apart among the other teachers, and that started it. . . . Varya packed her bag, practically dragged her to the train, and sent her to Max. Varya is wonderful. But very uncontrolled. She says what she thinks. She isn't afraid of anyone. I worry about her, especially since there is no one to protect her, her personal life didn't work out. . . ."

"What do you mean?"

"She ran off and married a gambler, billiard-player, a hustler who sold her things."

Sasha got up. "My feet are falling asleep, I need to stand up a bit."

He was stunned. "Do you mind if I go out for a minute and have a smoke?"

"Go on, go on, I'll wait."

He left the station and leaned against the wall. A fine welcome to Moscow he had received. Mark shot . . . Budyagin will be shot, too, of course. . . . But he couldn't think about them now. Varya, Varya, the only joy, the only light in his life. The tender girl who danced with him at the Arbat Cellar, invited him to go ice-skating, tender and pure, and she slept with some lowlife hustler. And then she'd sit down and write, "How I'd like to know what you are doing now." "Tender and pure" — that was all his fantasy, he made it up in exile, created an ideal image and worshiped it, what an idiot. And he fell in love with that girl. What girl? Someone's wife, as it turned out, and one who wasn't too particular in her relationships.

He ground the unfinished cigarette in the snow and came back into the station.

"I interrupted you, Mama, you were talking about Varya."

"Maybe it's not interesting for you?"

"On the contrary. I just don't understand why she married that man if he's a hustler."

"She was stupid, seventeen, an orphan, she had pennies and nothing else. And he offered her the high life, restaurants, the best tailors, the best shoes, hairdressers. Thank God that she came to her senses quickly and threw him out. They were living in my apartment, renting the small room."

They had lived in his apartment and slept on his bed! Why had she let them in, how could she have been party to it?

"And then?"

"What happened then? She came to her senses and threw him out. And then the melodrama started — he threatened to shoot her, lured her out of the house at night. He came in disguise — Varya laughed when she told me about it — his cap over his eyes, his coat collar turned up ... and she told him, 'Go ahead and shoot me, they'll shoot you!' She sent him packing and went back to Nina's, but came to see me almost every day. And whenever she saw me writing to you, she'd quickly say, 'Sofya Alexandrovna, let me add a little something to Sasha.' A kind girl, and very special."

She really was kind and probably was special, and, apparently, loved his mother. And he had to be grateful for that. But he had taken her kindness for something more. Where did he get that? From that one sentence, "How I'd like to know what you are doing now," he had decided that she loved him. Fool! Was anybody ever as stupid as that? Building your life on the basis of a single sentence from some girl? Well, life was cruel in everything else, it was cruel in this too.

"How's Father?" Sasha asked.

His mother shrugged.

"The same.... He came to extend his lease on the apartment. I think it expires in March. He'll probably move back to Moscow." After a pause, she added, "He has a wife and daughter."

That's what he had thought. His mother hadn't told him any of this, she didn't write about it, didn't want to upset him. Ah, Mama, Mama, my dear, my only one. How would she live if his father returned? And with a new family? They'd start exchanging rooms, force her to live in some slum in Cherkizovo or Maryina Roshcha, where there was no central heating or kitchens, and she'd have to cook on a kerosene stove. And he'd be scuttling around like a hare, hiding, unable to help her or to protect her.

"I'm asking you for only one thing, Mama: Don't let them take advantage of you. Promise me that!"

"I promise, and don't worry about anything." Her voice was steady and firm. She must have gone over this conversation in her mind many times. "I'll tell you something else. I'm not leaving our apartment. After all, it's your home."

"Fine! That's just what I wanted to hear from you."

He smiled bravely, even though he felt miserable. All he wanted was to get on the train and shut his eyes. But his mother must not see how lost and desperate he felt. It was a new life for them all, and his mother had to accept that.

"If you keep worrying, Mama, it will drive me crazy. My future's not bad at all, I'll find work quickly, I'm sure of it."

Sofya Alexandrovna regarded Sasha in silence, just looking and looking, and he realized that his words weren't getting through, that her thoughts were concentrated on one thing only — that they were about to be separated again.

"You won't miss your train?"

Sasha looked at the clock. "We have a half hour."

"The clock could be wrong, why don't we go to the platform?"

Sasha looked at his own watch. "No, everything's fine. We have time. It's cold there and warm here. I don't want you to get chilled."

He was dragging it out on purpose — no panic, everything under control.

"What clothing do you need?" Sofya Alexandrovna asked.

"Not a thing. I have everything. When I get to Kalinin, I'll settle in and then I'll let you know."

Now he looked at his watch. He got up and said, "Time to go to the train." He hugged her, kissed her, and said, "We'll be back living together, you'll see!"

She nodded, many small, quick nods of her head.

"Go home. I'll call you tomorrow."

"I'll see you to the train."

"Why get into the crowd on the platform?"

"I'll see you off."

The train hadn't arrived yet. The platform was filled with people, it was windy, unpleasant, and everyone was nervous and grumpy — what was going on, the train was supposed to leave in a few minutes and it hadn't even arrived!

At last they saw the train, bending around a curve, approaching the station.

"Let's say good-bye now," Sasha said. "You'll get crushed here. I'll go look for my car."

"No, no, not yet!" She hurried after him, pushing through the crowd.

There was a line at Sasha's car, and the conductor hurried the passengers as she checked their tickets, "Move it, citizens, move it!"

When Sasha handed over his ticket, his mother pressed her face against his coat and put her arms around him. Sasha quickly kissed her cheek — they were holding people up.

His mother moved to the back of the platform, leaning against a lamppost. Sasha got up into the vestibule of the car, at the very end, so that he wouldn't be in the way but could still see her.

The whistle blew, the conductor pushed the last woman in line into the car and shut the door.

The train moved, leaving behind Moscow, the station, and the lamppost where his mother stood alone.

## ❧ 22 ❧

No sooner had Sofya Alexandrovna come home after meeting Sasha than Varya called.

"Sofya Alexandrovna, where have you been? I've been calling and calling...."

"I met him and saw him off," Sofya Alexandrovna replied. "He telephoned this morning, and I called you right away. They said that you'd be back at eleven, and he had a train to catch. So I had to go without you."

"Oh, my God," Varya said. "They sent me over to Moscow Projects, just for an hour. Oh, my God!"

"Don't be sad. He's nearby now."

"I'll come over right after work. You'll tell me everything."

"After your courses?"

"I'll cut. I'll be there right after work."

"All right. I'll be waiting."

Varya arrived breathless and agitated.

"Well, how is he?"

"Everything is fine, he's alive and well and cheerful. Take off your coat — it's hot in here. I'll give you some tea in a second."

"The tea can wait." Varya hung up her coat and threw off her scarf. "First, tell me everything."

"I've told you the most important things — he's alive and well, cheerful and determined. Of course, he has to live with passport limitations, but they all have that, those who have been in exile. He's not the only one. He's going to Kalinin. He knows people there. He hopes to get a job. He'll call. He sent his regards to you."

Varya listened attentively. Alive, well, cheerful, determined, greetings, everything seemed all right. But there was something missing.

If they had met at the station, they would have fallen into each other's arms, right in front of Sofya Alexandrovna, and they would have stood there and the world would have changed. All their cares and worries would have seemed silly, trifles, nonsense. That was how she had pictured their meeting, and it hadn't taken place because of some stupid copy that someone forgot yesterday and she had to go get.

Varya pulled herself together. All right, things happen, it was her bad luck. It's a good thing that Kalinin was close. She'd go there on her first day off.

"Tell me in more detail," she asked Sofya Alexandrovna.

"What's there to tell, Varya? He hasn't changed at all, though he is rather shaggy. He hasn't shaved in a long time. He was on the road for almost a month. I was astonished by his calm and his courage. He listened to the story of Mark Alexandrovich's execution and Budyagin's arrest with a stony face. He didn't want to upset me by showing his pain. He had always loved Mark and Ivan Grigoryevich. He asked about the trial. He hadn't seen the papers in a long time."

"Did he ask about me?"

"Well, of course, Varya, how can you ask?"

"How did he ask, what words did he use?"

"Words? . . . 'How's Varya?' . . . He asked straight out, like that."

"He must have said, 'What's Varya been doing?' "

"No, just those two words, 'How's Varya?' He asked about you right away and just as I told you: 'How's Varya?' "

"Well, and what did you say?"

"I told him everything about you," Sofya Alexandrovna said with a laugh. "What could I say about you? Just one thing — I would have been lost without you, I couldn't have stood it."

"Come on."

"But it's the truth! And he knows that and he understands it and he's grateful to you. By the way, Varya, I told him about Nina — was that all right?"

"Of course."

"Well, then, I told him how attentive you are, how courageous, how you made Nina go to Max, by force, so to speak, how you got rid of Kostya —"

"What?" Varya froze.

"Well, how you made Kostya leave."

Varya kept her eyes on Sofya Alexandrovna's face.

"How did he know about Kostya?"

"I don't understand," Sofya Alexandrovna said, realizing she had done something irreparable.

"How did he know about Kostya?" Varya repeated, breathing heavily.

"Well . . . I told him."

"What, what did you tell him?" Varya shouted, leaning over, bent in half.

"What's the matter with you, Varya!" Sofya Alexandrovna took a deep breath. Her heart was pounding and she reached for her nitroglycerine.

"What, what did you tell him?" Varya repeated, still bent over, not noticing Sofya Alexandrovna's state nor the tablet she had put under her tongue.

Sofya Alexandrovna took another breath. "Varya, I didn't tell him anything special. You were married, you lived in my place, then you threw him out, he wanted to kill you, but he picked the wrong woman. . . . It was all long ago, two years ago."

Varya buried her face in her hands. "My God, my God, why did you tell him that? Why, why?"

"But, Varya," Sofya Alexandrovna said in a barely audible voice. "It's all the truth, and Sasha would have learned it sooner or later. You would have told him yourself."

Varya looked up. "Yes, I would have told him, but I would have done it myself, at the right time. I would have explained and he would have understood." She covered her face again. "Oh my God, what have you done? What have you done?"

Sofya Alexandrovna said nothing. Her chest ached; the nitroglycerine hadn't started working yet, although she was already slightly dizzy. Oh God, if she just didn't fall from the chair. Varya was in shock, but she was making it worse, poor child. Nothing terrible had happened, Sasha hadn't even paid any attention to it.

He went out for a smoke and then came back and asked for more details about Varya's marriage, and his face was very calm, she remembered.

"Varya, child, calm down, I beg you. You know him, Sasha's not a petty bourgeois. It doesn't matter what you did and what he did. Please, calm down, please."

Varya did not reply. She grabbed her coat.

"Varya, where are you going? Wait!"

"No, thank you, I'm late."

Choking back her tears, she ran out of the room.

God, thought Sofya Alexandrovna, how could she not have noticed? Varya was in love ... naturally she didn't want Sasha to know about Kostya and that whole ugly story.

Her heart was better, the dizziness was going away. Sofya Alexandrovna stood up carefully and went to the bed. She shut her eyes and the dizziness came back. No, she shouldn't close her eyes. The fear of death took hold of her. She knew that the dizziness was just a minor symptom, but nevertheless she was afraid she would die without ever getting out of the bed. God, she would just die. Leaving Sasha unsettled. Leaving Sasha alone in the world.

She felt for the glass tube in her pocket and put another tablet under her tongue.

She could understand Varya. Varya loved Sasha and she was ashamed of what had happened with Kostya. But why hadn't she said anything about her love? She had been helping from the first day of Sasha's arrest, and Sofya Alexandrovna had seen that help as the care of a kind and noble girl and not of a girl in love with Sasha. It was after Sasha's arrest that Varya had told her that once she got out of school, she would marry some lieutenant and go live with him in the Far East. Then the lieutenant vanished, and Kostya appeared, but Varya continued taking care of her. Varya had helped at the laundry and she sent the packages to Sasha. When did her love for Sasha happen? Maybe she just didn't want Sasha to think badly of her — she was a proud girl, afraid of losing her dignity. But, oh my God, so many girls made mistakes like that. Varya must have taken offense at the expression "got rid of your husband." A decent man doesn't get thrown out, a decent man gets a divorce. That meant that Varya had not married a decent man. Sofya

Alexandrovna had expressed herself carelessly. That was a mistake. But why react so tragically?

She had to calm down. She had to think of Sasha first, Sasha couldn't manage without her for now. Varya was a good girl, a fine girl, she loved her dearly, like a daughter, but she mustn't get upset over her crazy ideas. Of course, Varya's life was hard. She could understand that. But still, Varya should show more restraint.

With those thoughts Sofya Alexandrovna dozed off.

She did not know how long she slept, but she woke up feeling that someone was in the room. Varya was near the bed. She smiled at Sofya Alexandrovna and took her hand in hers.

"How are you feeling, Sofya Alexandrovna?"

"All right, dearie, all right."

"Thank God. I've been sitting here, watching you sleep. Please forgive me, Sofya Alexandrovna. I was upset, I suppose because I didn't get to the station to see Sasha. I had wanted to see him so much. And then ... That scene with Kostya was so disgusting that I try not to think about it and I don't like others to bring it up. It was unpleasant to learn that Sasha knew about it. I wouldn't like for him to think of me in that way."

"But Varya, I didn't say anything bad. Believe me, Sasha didn't attach any significance to it. He said that he'd call me and you."

"That's what he said?"

"Of course. He'll definitely call. He'll call me and I'll make arrangements for the next time, and I'll warn you, all right?"

"Wonderful," Varya replied, knowing that Sofya Alexandrovna was inventing this conversation to cheer her up. But nothing could cheer her up now. Her life was ruined; Sasha would never forgive her for Kostya. And even though despair was still choking her, she forced a smile, afraid that Sofya Alexandrovna would have another attack.

"So," Sofya Alexandrovna said, sitting up, "I assure you that nothing bad happened, don't worry."

"Yes, yes, I understand," Varya said hurriedly. "I was just upset that they made me go to that stupid place. I'd been sitting in my office for two weeks without stepping out and the one time I left for an hour, Sasha had to call. So I got upset. And I upset you." She patted Sofya Alexandrovna's hand.

"I didn't hear you come in."

"Sofya Alexandrovna, I have the key to your apartment. Have you forgotten?"

"Oh, yes, of course."

"And the door wasn't locked. The light was on, so I came in and I tiptoed to your bed. After I calmed down a bit at home, I realized that I had upset you. I thought I'd come back and see how my Sofya Alexandrovna was."

Tears came to Sofya Alexandrovna's eyes. Without letting go of Varya's hand, she squeezed it as hard as her strength allowed. "You sweet, dear child, how good you are."

# ❧ 23 ❧

**B**ecause he was saying his farewells to his mother, Sasha barely got a seat on the train. He crowded in on the end of a bench. He couldn't get Mark out of his head, nor could he forget Budyagin or the poor Travkins from their building. Something terrible was happening in the country, unimaginable, and if the newspaper hysteria was to be believed, there would be no end to it. And still he had behaved well with his mother; his calm must have cheered her up some. And she was brave, wanting to let him know that he wasn't alone, that his relatives and friends would help if he needed it.

And he had listened stoically to what his mother had told him about Varya — not a muscle had moved on his face. His mother didn't guess a thing.

But now, sitting among strangers in a crowded car that was taking him out of Moscow, out of his Moscow to strange Kalinin, he felt empty, broken, crushed. The meeting with his mother had cost him all his strength. He leaned against the back of the seat and shut his eyes. His neighbors were talking, the men playing cards were laughing, but he didn't hear them as his thoughts leaped from one thing to another.

When his exile ended, he knew what awaited him. As he strode behind the sleigh in the taiga and saw the columns of prisoners, as he listened to the radio in Taishet, he had felt the darkness and was prepared for any eventuality. Even in Moscow, while he was waiting for his mother, he knew they could have searched the station and taken him away for violating his passport restrictions. The only thing he wasn't prepared for was what had happened.

He had no right to condemn Varya. She hadn't promised him anything, she didn't owe him anything. They had never uttered a single word of love. Varya had not betrayed him. It wasn't her fault. He had invented her, imagined her. But still, his heart was bleeding. He couldn't stand that some petty crook had lived in his room, had slept with her on his bed, had run his hand over the wall by the cupboard looking for the light switch, and then in the dark had fallen upon her.... Oh, God, for the first time in his life he was jealous. He had never understood it before.

He had to think about Kalinin, about finding a job. First thing, he would visit Olga Stepanovna. She would give him some advice about finding a place to stay. Yes, he'd go to Olga Stepanovna, that was clear. What wasn't clear was how long they had lived at his mother's. He hadn't asked. Why not? Three months, six, a year? And everything kept coming back to Varya, to her billiard-player. He couldn't get out of that circle. The hell with all those thoughts. It was humiliating, but he couldn't suppress them, he didn't want to go on living. Why? Because of a girl who had helped his mother, had mailed her packages, and sometimes added two or three pleasant lines at the bottom of his mother's letters. Because of a girl he had never even kissed! It was stupid, shameful, but he couldn't do anything about it.

The train jerked, and Sasha grabbed the edge of the bench and held on until his fingers hurt.

He should punch that son-of-a-bitch, smash his face — he had taken Varya away from him, the bastard. He had lured Varya with the high life, he had dragged her to pool halls, he had boasted of his winnings, he had embraced her with his filthy paws.... If only it had been somewhere else and not in his own bed.... Enough! Forget Varya! It was over!

Sasha opened his eyes and looked out the window — snow, snow, and more snow ... how dreary....

In Kalinin, Sasha left his suitcase in the baggage checkroom. If he showed up with a suitcase on Olga Stepanovna's doorstep, it would look as if he was looking for a place to sleep, and the neighbors would see that a stranger was visiting her.

Sasha had lost the key to his suitcase a long time ago. But they wouldn't accept unlocked luggage. He went outside, found a rock, and smashed the locks, making it impossible to open the suitcase. It was too bad, of course, but at least they'd take his suitcase and he could get it fixed later.

The attendant tried one lock, then the other, and the suitcase wouldn't open. Sasha got a receipt and asked for directions to the Stepan Razin Embankment.

Sasha had never been in Kalinin and had expected a dull provincial town. He was pleasantly surprised. It was clean and beautiful. Sasha went down the main thoroughfare, Sovetskaya Street, and crossed several squares — Red Square, with Lenin Park, Sovetskaya Square, and Pushkin Square. The City Council, the City Party Committee, and the theater buildings were on Lenin Square.

The streets were paved, the sidewalks were cleared of snow, there was a trolley and lots of cars, the same ones he had seen in Moscow three years ago — GAZ-AA, ZIS-5, and a small van. The only new cars he saw were the M-I, the "emka," near the City Council and the big black ZIS-101 near the Party Committee. He had read about them in the papers.

It wasn't Moscow, but it wasn't Kansk or Kezhma, and certainly not Taishet. People walked in the streets. He hadn't seen laughing faces in a long time. It was the usual, quiet, normal life.

The barbershop was typically Muscovite, with the same chairs, mirrors, and potted plants in the window. It was warm and cozy. The barber cut Sasha's hair, shaved him, put a hot towel on his face. Dammit — civilization was great. And he looked fully presentable. Of course, it was too bad about the boots, but Comrade Stalin himself wore boots. He didn't have a shirt, just a coarse sweater under his jacket, and the jacket was on the old and dingy side, and the trousers weren't the best. But it would do. He had shaved himself in Mozgova, and Vsevolod Sergeyevich had cut his hair and he was no barber! And after Vsevolod Sergeyevich had been sent to Krasnoyarsk, there had been no one left to cut his hair. Where was Vsevolod Sergeyevich now, in what camp, how many years did he get? He wanted to do something for him, send money or a parcel. But only relatives could get information on prisoners. And then not always and not everybody.

* * *

The houses on Stepan Razin Embankment were old-fashioned, two- and three-story houses with columns, but they hadn't been repaired in a long time. They were dilapidated, with cracked and peeling plaster. And from the number of the apartment, 11a, it was clear that the house had been subdivided into communal apartments.

The courtyard was neglected and littered, filled with snowbanks; the door was loose and the stairway dark. Sasha found apartment 11a and knocked at the door, which was covered with torn oilcloth upholstery. A strangely dressed man appeared. He was wearing an undershirt, boots, and jodhpurs with suspenders.

"Excuse me," Sasha said. "I'm looking for Maslova."

He stared at Sasha. "Where're you from? Who are you to her?"

He had a fat face and piggy eyes that stared hostilely at Sasha. Sasha had seen his share of faces like that over the years.

"Who are you to her?"

"No one. I'm from Penza, I teach at the music school. Piano. My colleague, Raisa Semyonovna Rozmargunova, heard that I was going to Kalinin and asked me to call on her high school friend, Olga — sorry, I've forgotten her patronymic . . ." — he rummaged in his pockets and took out a piece of paper — "Olga Stepanovna Maslova, to give her her love and find out why she isn't writing. To find out how she is."

"Well, then what?"

"Then nothing, that's it."

Sasha looked into his eyes with a simple-minded smile.

"She moved," the man said. "A long time ago. I don't know where to."

And he slammed the door.

Sasha went out into the street. It was clear. After Kirov's killing, they picked up all the suspicious people, and she was the wife of a prisoner from Solovki prison camp, the very first one. They had exiled Olga Stepanovna, of course, or else she had moved to where no one knew her, and the apartment had been taken by the creep from the organs. Not a high rank, but a rank. How he stared at him, that swine! He had been deciding whether to arrest him or not.

He was safe, but he could have been caught.

He had been very careless. He had gone to the apartment of the wife of someone in the camps, someone who might even be an executed counterrevolutionary by now. Alferov had warned him: "You don't need to be in a bunch, you need to separate.... You don't need extra ties, you shouldn't have any ties at all...." Sasha had got out of it this time. And he'd be smarter in the future.

It was getting dark. Sasha went to a lamppost and looked at his watch — almost five. Where should he go? Find a garage and ask if they needed a driver? It was too late to be looking for garages in a strange city. And he'd still have to go to personnel, and you never knew who'd be there.

No, you had to have a friend. He'd have to go to Ryazan, to Mikhail Yurevich's brother, Yevgeny Yurevich. What a fine, intellectual name Yevgeny Yurevich was. Sasha remembered him vaguely — he used to visit his brother, whom he resembled, but Yevgeny Yurevich was younger. At any rate, it was a good lead. They were reliable, decent people, and Yevgeny Yurevich was already warned. If he were lucky and he could leave tonight, he'd be in Ryazan by tomorrow. It was only five or six hours from Moscow by train. He only had to cross the square in Moscow to go from the Leningrad Station to the Kazan Station. When his mother had given him the letter from Mikhail Yurevich, he should have changed his plans immediately and gone to Ryazan. Why hadn't he? Because he had bought a ticket to Kalinin? Afraid that there wouldn't be a ticket to Ryazan and he'd have to hang around Moscow for a few hours? Afraid that the sudden change would worry his mother, who would see that he really had no place to go, that he had no serious plans? Or maybe that he was just in a rush to get out of Moscow, afraid of being even at the station?

He was hungry. He hadn't had a bite since morning. His mother's food package was in the suitcase. He'd have to go to the station and then decide what to do.

There were several trains to Moscow passing through Kalinin, but all the seats were reserved. The only direct train was at eight in the morning, and the tickets went on sale at six. And the station restaurant was closed, so there was no place to eat. If he got his suitcase out of the checkroom for his mother's food package, he'd have to break the locks and then they wouldn't take the suitcase back and he'd have to drag it around until morning.

Sasha came out onto Sovetskaya Street. Even though Kalinin had seemed nice in daylight, he didn't want to go wandering around a strange city at night. It was uncomfortable and lonely. Where was he going to eat?

He saw a sign — Café Canteen. There were a lot of people in the brightly lit room. People were coming in and out, not drunks and whores, but ordinary people.

Sasha went in, took off his coat, and went into the dining room. It was rather big and crowded with tables, each for four people. It looked as though all the seats were taken, but there was one table not far from the door with an empty chair. An elderly, intelligent-looking, poorly dressed couple, apparently man and wife, sat at the table as well as a middle-aged man wearing a tie, with a cold, grim, and tense face. A splenetic creep, who resembled the man in Maslova's apartment. And even though the latter had been fat and pig-eyed and this one was skinny and had glasses, you could tell they were of the same tyrannical breed — bearers of power, though not too much power, they answered to no law.

Sasha touched the back of the chair. "May I?"

The woman smiled shyly and looked at her husband, who said, "Please."

The other man said nothing.

Sasha sat down.

Waitresses carried trays with dirty dishes in the narrow spaces between tables. They were hurrying. It was almost closing time. The coat-check man was locking the door behind departing customers and not letting anyone else in. Sasha was in luck — another ten minutes and he wouldn't have got in.

A waitress came over with a main course.

"I haven't finished the first course yet, take it away!" the little tyrant said in a pushy, crude tone.

"The kitchen is in a rush," the waitress said calmly, not taking the dish back.

She was a well-built, slender brunette with full breasts, a tanned face, and an indifferent cold look in her slightly bulging eyes.

She cast a glance at Sasha. "The café is closing."

"I'll be quick."

She glanced over at Sasha again, and her eyes lingered briefly, probing. She took out her notebook and pencil.

"All we have left for starters is cabbage or chicken noodle soup, and meatballs and macaroni for the main course."

"Cabbage soup and meatballs. If possible, stewed fruit or pudding."

"White or black bread?"

"Black."

"Will you have a drink?"

"Drink? ... Oh ... No, thanks."

"Could we have our check?" the woman asked.

The waitress added up their check and told them the amount. The man took out his wallet and paid. The waitress put the notebook and pencil back in the pocket of her white apron and went to the cash register.

The couple finished their stewed fruit and got up. The woman leaned on a cane and smiled again shyly at Sasha.

"Hearty appetite," her husband said. "Stay well."

They didn't say good-bye to the other man at the table. And Sasha thought that he must have been rude to them earlier. That would explain the tense atmosphere, the woman's frightened eyes, her pathetic smile, and the pleasant talk only with Sasha.

Their dirty dishes were still on the table, which was covered with a stained cloth, on the center of which stood a vase with a paper flower, four wineglasses, and four shot glasses.

The creep finished his soup and pushed aside his plate, knocking over and breaking one of the wineglasses. He made a face and went on to his main course as if nothing had happened.

The waitress came over to clear the table and saw the broken glass.

The man nodded at the chairs where the couple had been and said, "They broke it."

The waitress looked at the checkroom, but the couple had already taken their coats and left.

"Some people," she said and shook her head. "Now I'll have to pay for it."

The creep went on eating his meal.

"Do you consider that fair?" Sasha asked him.

"What, what did you say?"

"I asked if you consider it fair for the waitress to have to pay for the glass you broke?"

"Stop talking nonsense," he replied, eating away.

The waitress looked at them expectantly. Interest flashed in her cold gray eyes.

"You're the one who broke the glass." Sasha regarded the official face opposite him with hatred.

"Stop saying stupid things and looking for a fight."

Sasha didn't need a fight, he knew that. But that smug, official face, that brazen, obnoxious disregard for fairness embodied all the hurts and humiliations he had suffered. That damned bastard was from there, part of the machine that ruthlessly ground up people, tortured them, persecuted and humiliated them, turned white into black and black into white, and got away with it. But this one wouldn't get away with it.

Sasha moved aside his plate, leaned over, and said slowly and clearly, "You bastard, do you think she's going to pay for you? I'll shove the glass down your throat. . . ."

He recoiled in fear but controlled himself immediately. "You're using foul language . . . in a public place." He pointed to the waitress. "You're a witness."

"A witness?" she replied, unruffled. "You're the one, not him. I heard you with my own ears."

The man looked around. The waitresses were taking the cloths from tables and the last customers were putting on their coats.

"How much does the glass cost?" Sasha asked.

"Five rubles," the waitress replied and smiled. And the smile made her face sweet and attractive.

"What's the problem, Lyuda?" A fat waitress, with a pile of tablecloths in her arms, stopped by their table.

"This citizen broke a glass and won't pay for it."

"You call a cop and let him write it all down."

The militia, writing it down, just what Sasha needed. But apparently this minor official didn't want the militia involved, either.

"How much do I owe?"

The waitress totaled it and named the sum.

"Let me see!"

She handed him the bill.

He checked it, threw it down on the table, threw money for the meal on top of it, added a five, got up, and went for his coat.

As the waitress cleared, she smiled again. "We didn't let you eat."

"I won't starve," Sasha replied.

"Don't hurry, eat."

She gave Sasha another look and then asked, "What's your name?"

"Sasha."

"I'm Lyuda. I'll bring your main course."

She returned with two plates and put them on the table.

"May I eat my dinner with you, Sasha? Do you mind?"

"Of course not, glad to have you."

She sat down.

"From out of town?"

"What makes you think so?"

"I've never seen you here before."

"Yes, I'm from Moscow."

"On a business trip?"

"No, I was looking for work, but I didn't find anything, so I'm leaving."

"Isn't there enough work in Moscow?"

"I have no place to live there."

"What about your wife and kids?"

"I'm divorced, no kids."

"What's your profession?"

"Driver."

She gave him another look. "When are you leaving?"

"I wanted to leave today, but the train is in the morning."

"And where are you going, if it's not a secret?"

"To Ryazan, I think."

Sasha finished his stewed fruit. "What do I owe?"

"What did you have? ... Soup, meatballs, stewed fruit ... A ruble thirty."

Sasha took out his wallet and put the money on the table. He had the envelope with his mother's money in another pocket.

"Well, thanks," Sasha said.

"What's your hurry? Your train is in the morning. Where are you spending the night?"

"At the station."

"Then what's the rush?"

"This place is closing."

She laughed.

"So they'll close us in together. They'll let us out in the morning."

She finished her food, pushed aside her plate, and asked in a businesslike way, "Have you told me the truth or did you lie?"

"About what?"

"About you."

"You don't believe me?"

"You look like an intellectual and you talk like a criminal."

"Are you afraid I'm an escaped convict?" He chuckled. "No, I haven't escaped from anywhere." He patted his jacket pocket. "I've got a passport and a driver's license."

"And why did you defend me?"

"I don't like bastards."

"So, a lover of justice?"

"Yes," Sasha said, seriously. "A lover of justice."

She thought awhile and then asked, "Would you like to go to a birthday party with me?"

"Whose?"

"My girlfriend Hannah."

"Hannah ... Is she Polish?"

Lyuda laughed again. "Polish? Her real name is Agafya. But when she moved to the city from the country, she changed her name."

"And what's the celebration?"

"I told you, a birthday. Actually, it's her saint's day, St. Agafya."

"And who'll be there?"

"Guests, girlfriends. What do you care? You'll be with me."

"You see how I'm dressed. My clothes are in the baggage check."

"Don't worry, you look fine. You're handsome. At night they

chase you from the railroad station. At least this way you'll be warm."

He didn't feel like going. But knowing he couldn't stay at the station changed the situation. At least he'd be warm.

"Fine! Let's go."

Without getting up, she nodded toward the door. "Go out, make a right, and at the second corner turn into the alley. Wait for me there."

## ✲ 24 ✲

She led him to the edge of town. A sole streetlight glowed above the pump on the dark street.

"Careful, it's slippery here, give me your hand."

Sasha gave her his hand. She took off her mitten. Her fingers were warm and his were icy.

"Cold?"

"No, I'm fine."

"We're almost there."

They turned down a path in the snow, walking past tall wooden fences, tightly closed gates, one-story houses sunk with age as if they had grown into the ground.

They stopped at one house, went up on the porch, and Lyuda banged her fist on the door.

"They're partying and can't hear."

She knocked again. They could hear a door bang inside and a boy's voice inquired, "Who is it?"

"Kolya, it's me, Lyuda. Open up!"

A boy of fifteen led them into the entry, put back the latch, and returned to the room without even saying hello. The walls were illuminated for a second when the door to the room was open. Sasha saw coats and jackets on the coatrack. Then the darkness was pierced by light again when the door reopened and a tall thin woman came out into the entry.

"Is that you, Lyuda?"

"Yes."

"That little devil, Kolya, left you in the dark."

She opened the door to the well-lit kitchen. There was a large kitchen table in there with kerosene stoves and pots.

"Take off your coats and come in."

"Have you been at it long?"

"We're still dry," the woman said with a laugh. She was tipsy. She looked older than Lyuda, maybe thirty-five or so. Her face showed breeding, but the features were blurred. She must be a heavy drinker.

"Come in!"

They followed her into a low-ceilinged room. Three men and one woman sat around a table holding bottles and plates of food. Kolya, the hostess's son, was off to the side. He resembled his mother — the same green eyes, the same fine nose. But his hair was darker.

"Let me introduce my friend Sasha," Lyuda announced and presented him to the hostess. "This is Angelina Nikolaevna, you've seen her already."

Angelina Nikolaevna offered Sasha her hand.

"And this is Ivan Andreyevich, the host."

A powerfully built man, with streaks of gray in his hair, gave Sasha a brief look, as if marking the fact of the meeting, and went on talking with his companion.

"And here's the birthday girl, Hannah. Wish her a happy day."

"Congratulations." Sasha shook the hand of a red-cheeked girl.

"Gleb! Leonid!"

Sasha nodded at each, but Leonid paid no attention to him and went on talking with Ivan Andreyevich. Gleb, a stocky, broad-chested fellow, smiled in a friendly way and revealed his gleaming white teeth.

"Very pleased."

Lyuda took out a package and handed it to Hannah. "Try them on. They're for you. Happy saint's day."

Hannah moved away from the table, took off her shoes, tried on the new ones, stood in them, and then walked around.

"Well?"

"They seem fine."

"Then wear them in good health."

"All right," Angelina Nikolaevna said. "Lyuda, Sasha, sit down."

They sat at the end of the bench, close to each other, for there wasn't a lot of space. Lyuda pretended to move over. "Get more comfortable."

Sasha moved closer, and now their thighs, hips, and shoulders were touching.

"Please eat, drink," Angelina Nikolaevna said. "Everything's on the table. . . . There are glasses, forks and knives, plates . . . are there any more plates?"

"One's plenty for us," Lyuda said.

The table, by Sasha's lights, was extravagant — vodka, fortified wine, sausage, herring, pickles, pickled cabbage . . .

"Would you like some herring?"

"Herring's fine."

Lyuda put herring, pickles, and cabbage on the plate, poured vodka for herself and Sasha in big green shot glasses, raised hers, and shouted at the men, "Quiet, guys! Have you drunk to the birthday girl?"

"We were waiting for you, darling, no one to show us how, otherwise," Gleb said, and laughed. He had a short upper lip and it looked as if he were always smiling — or maybe he always was smiling.

"Let's do it again!" Lyuda said.

"Fine," Gleb said, picking up his glass and embracing the girl with his other arm. She was half a head taller. "Let's drink to you, dear Hannah."

"Cut it out!"

"Down the hatch." Gleb drank, grimaced, and sniffed a piece of bread.

Ivan Andreyevich and Leonid drank, still discussing their affairs, without even looking at Hannah.

Lyuda clinked glasses with Hannah, then turned to Sasha. Her eyes were very close and she laughed without looking away. "Why aren't you drinking?"

Sasha drank and had a piece of herring. He wasn't hungry after his recent meal, but he hadn't seen food like this in three years. His appetite returned.

Lyuda knocked back her glass, shut her eyes, and shook her head.

She poured again for herself and Sasha and nudged him with her shoulder. Then she moved closer. They drank, not clinking or toasting, just for themselves. Everyone else was drinking and praising the food. Gleb's voice was the loudest. He burst into other conversations, quipped, made jokes, looked at Sasha and tried to show how friendly he was. He was an artist, he had studied with the great stage designer Akimov himself, he said, he had gone to Leningrad to take his course and Akimov had wanted to keep him there. But Gleb had ended up in another theater, where the artistic director didn't know anything about art, didn't even know what the colors were called, he mixed up indigo with ultramarine, ocher with vermilion. A mediocrity, a nothing!

Now Gleb painted buses.

"I'll paint your trucks," he told Leonid. "They'll be so terrific, all of Kalinin will come to see them."

"We'll see," said Leonid curtly. Leonid, a stoop-shouldered man, was the engineer of the motor pool where Gleb was painter.

"You can't make something new out of something old," noted Ivan Andreyevich, who was a metal worker at the same motor pool.

"What am I supposed to do? The City Committee wants buses, and you're holding things up," Leonid said and hunched over his plate.

"Hah," Gleb laughed. "You think it's easy? Just slop on the paint and you're done? Oh, it's not like that at all, dearie."

Sasha liked Gleb. He had a pleasant face, a typical Russian from the middle of the country, with fair hair, blue eyes, and a neat nose.

"Leonid Petrovich," Lyuda asked unexpectedly. "Do you need drivers?"

"Of course."

"Take Sasha, he's a driver from Moscow."

Leonid looked at Sasha. He had prickly eyes. He was grim and taciturn, and the more he drank, the grumpier he got.

"Got a license?"

"Of course."

"With you?"

"Yes."

"Let's see!"

Sasha handed it over. Leonid looked at it and returned it.

"You've been working seven years and you've still got a third-class license?"

"I was working as a mechanic."

"Do you want to work as a mechanic?"

"No, thanks. I don't want to answer for others. I'd rather drive."

"If you had a second-class license, I'd put you at the wheel of a bus."

"I'll settle for a truck."

"Come in, we'll sign you up."

He had another drink silently, turning away from Sasha.

Sasha had to find out when he was supposed to go to the motor pool. If it was tomorrow, then he'd stay on in Kalinin and forget Ryazan. Getting a job right off the bat was a stroke of luck. And Lyuda would probably help him get a room. But Sasha didn't want to overwhelm Leonid with questions — the vodka obviously depressed Leonid and he could turn nasty any minute.

Gleb was just the opposite. As he drank, he grew even friendlier and more easygoing. He was a companionable sort, but his eyes were sneaky. He must like to brag and exaggerate. He said that he had gone to Leningrad to study with Akimov, but Sasha remembered that Akimov had staged a play at the Vakhtangov Theater in the Arbat, which meant that he worked in Moscow. But Gleb said Leningrad, so he must be lying. But he was charming, all right.

Everyone went on drinking. Hannah brought out hot boiled potatoes, which were delicious with the pickles and vodka. Everyone was getting drunk, Sasha along with the others.

"Enough about your cars," Angelina Nikolaevna said drunkenly. "You're engineers, artists, but I'm in love with a smith." She put her arm around her husband's neck. "Smith, do you love me?"

"Come on," Ivan Andreyevich said bashfully.

But she went on. "My darling smith, tell me, do you love me?" Without waiting for an answer, she looked over at her son. "Kolya, you devil, go to bed. I've already told you."

But Kolya stayed at the table, his face inscrutable, silently listening to the adults talk. His face had an adult seriousness. He must have been used to parties like this, to seeing his mother embracing her husband in front of everyone. Sasha had seen that the man wasn't the boy's father the minute he had walked in.

"How many times must I tell you?"

Kolya did not budge.

"Why are you disobeying your mother, Kolya?" Lyuda said in a gently chiding way. Her hand was on Sasha's shoulder.

But Kolya didn't pay any attention to her comment, either.

"Go to bed, Nikolai, or you'll be late for school tomorrow, lad," said Ivan Andreyevich.

And only then did Kolya get up and head for the other side of the house. In the doorway, he said to his mother, "Why don't you cut back on your drinking?"

Angelina Nikolaevna laughed. "He's teaching me!" She shook her head. "All right." She poured a drink for herself and for her husband. "Let's drink, smith, you're the only one I have in this whole world. Let's drink to my smith!"

Everyone drank, and so did Sasha and Lyuda.

Sitting with these people, Sasha found his former, preprison, pre-exile life. Among normal, ordinary, and simple people he felt like a free man. Of course, there were still problems about the job, and finding a place to live, registration, and many other complications lay ahead. But he was free at last, dammit! No one was watching him, demanding his papers, no one was asking who he was and where he came from. He was just Lyuda's friend, and it was nobody's business but Lyuda's. Lyuda had been here before with other men, and now he was her new one. And she'd keep him here for the night. And he'd stay. There was no Varya, that had been a fantasy. He was free in every sense now. Let there be Lyuda. After a month of traveling through the taiga, sleeping in stations, and bouncing in trains, he wanted a warm bed. And a good night's sleep. Just one night that wasn't at a station or in a train.

"Let's sing," Hannah suggested, and started a song.

When she finished, Sasha said, "That's a nice song."

Lyuda took her hand from his shoulder, looked at him, and asked quietly, "What, you don't know it?"

"No."

She looked away and after a pause looked back and said softly but firmly, "If you don't know it, keep quiet about it!"

He realized his mistake. The song must have appeared when he had been in exile. Everyone knew it except him, and he had given himself away. Lyuda tugged at her dress, moving away from him with that motion, and asked Angelina Nikolaevna about some woman who worked with her, and Hannah joined their conversation. Gleb and Leonid were talking about some bookkeeper who wouldn't pay Gleb or wasn't paying him enough. Gleb spoke with a smile, revealing his white teeth, and kept saying "dearie," but he spoke with drunken insistence and Leonid replied with drunken surliness, and it looked as if a fight would break out any minute. But Ivan Andreyevich was nearby and changed the subject. Sasha couldn't hear clearly; he wasn't listening anyway.

He had lost the feeling of being like them, a simple Soviet man. No, he wasn't like them. A single wrong word could give him away. At least he had had the sense not to argue with Gleb about Akimov. He hadn't been to the movies or the theater in three years, he didn't know the new songs, the new books, he didn't even know the new cars. Life had changed and he couldn't reveal how much he was behind. It was better to keep quiet, to mumble, until he made up the lost time.

"I need to go outside," Leonid said and stood up.

"I could go for the road, too," Gleb said and joined him.

They went out.

And Lyuda immediately jumped on Hannah. "Your Tamara really let us down again."

"The boss kept her late — urgent work."

"I know that line," Lyuda said with irritation. "He makes her work on the couch and on the desk."

"Come on, Lyuda, don't get started," Angelina Nikolaevna said to calm her down.

"She was supposed to come," Lyuda kept on about it. "If she couldn't, then she shouldn't promise."

"It wasn't up to her. . . . All the bosses work at night now. They don't sleep in Moscow and they keep ours up."

"She shouldn't have promised."

Leonid and Gleb came back and the argument stopped. Lyuda's anger made Sasha uncomfortable. Tamara was merely an excuse to show Sasha how annoyed she was with him.

Sasha looked at his watch. Half past one. He didn't know how to get to the station, and the trolleys had stopped.

"What are you looking at your watch for, dearie?" Gleb asked.

"I have a train," Sasha said.

"Where are you going?"

"Moscow."

"The train's at eight, you have time. We'll give you a lift. Leonid, when is the car coming for you?"

"I told them two."

"Can we give Sasha a lift?"

Sasha looked at Leonid. Would he remember that he had offered him a job? If he did, he'd say, "Why are you going to the station? You're going to drive a truck for me."

"Sure."

He didn't remember. That meant he didn't need any drivers, he was just making noises, half drunk. Fine! Kalinin was out. Time to go to Ryazan.

Not far from the house a canvas-covered truck was parked. On duty at night. Every motor pool had one.

"Where to first, the station?" Leonid asked.

"Drop me off first," Lyuda said.

"That's out of the way."

"Is it so hard? Or are you short of gas?"

Leonid grumbled and got in the cab.

Gleb pulled himself over the side and then helped Lyuda and Hannah get in. They took the seats on either side. Sasha got in last.

Hannah leaned against Gleb's shoulder and fell asleep, or pretended to, so as not to argue with Lyuda anymore.

Lyuda was angry and silent. Sasha said nothing. He didn't care anymore. He sat in the dark, his eyes shut, thinking about nothing.

They drove around the dark city and finally stopped. Lyuda pushed back the canvas and looked around. "We're here."

She got up. "Sasha, help me."

Sasha didn't move from his seat.

"Get out of the truck and help a woman."

Sasha jumped down and caught Lyuda in his arms.

"Go!" Lyuda shouted.

Leonid opened the door and leaned out of the cab.

"Go! Go on, I said!" Lyuda yelled and waved her arm.

## 25

They were standing near a two-story house with a long row of
dark windows along the front. Lyuda tugged at the door — it
was locked.

"Damn! They shut me out on purpose."

She walked the length of the house and knocked at a window,
waited, and knocked again. A light went on, the curtains parted,
and an old woman's voice came through the little pane that opened
in the window.

"Who is it?"

"Auntie Dasha, it's me, Lyuda. Open up."

The little window shut and Lyuda went back to the door. A sleepy
old woman in a robe, her gray hair disheveled, opened it. She let
Lyuda and Sasha in and shuffled off to her room in slippered feet.

Lyuda latched the door and led Sasha down the long and dimly
lit corridor, with rooms on each side. This had been a hotel once,
but in those days they had not hung sinks by the doors or put stools
holding basins under them.

Lyuda turned her key in the French lock, opened the door,
turned the light switch from the doorway, and said, "Come in!"

The room was tiny — a cupboard, bed, table, cot, two chairs, a
mirror, and a few photographs.

"Take off your coat!"

She hung Sasha's coat on the hook next to hers, tossed her scarf
on the chair, smoothed her hair by the mirror, sat down on the bed,
and looked at Sasha. Her eyes were sunken and unfocused.

"Well, how do you like it here?"

"It's nice, warm and cozy."

"Better than in the camps?"

"Why the camps?"

"You don't know contemporary songs. You should be grateful I was the only one who heard you, otherwise they would have figured it out, too. People understand these things now."

"They don't sing songs in the camps?"

"No, tell me, what movie is that song from?"

"What song?"

"The one Hannah was singing."

"I don't know."

"See, you don't know the movies, either. You've just come out of prison."

"What if I had been working up north?"

"Making money?"

"Let's say."

"And you have lots of money?"

"Whatever I have, I've earned. I can lend you some."

"I don't need your money. Do you think I'm a *'Mädchen für Alles'*?"

"You know German." Sasha chuckled. "Tell me, why are you interrogating me?"

"I have to know who I'm going to bed with."

"Listen! Did I try to pick you up? You took me to the party and you brought me here. I was headed for the station. Why did you take me off the truck?"

She sighed. "We're saying silly things. It's the vodka." She lowered her head.

"So don't drink! Which way to the railroad station from here?"

In answer, without looking up, she asked, "Are you mad at me?"

"What do I have to be mad about? You know, other people don't even ask your last name. And you went through the whole questionnaire."

"I know everything without the questionnaire. When we walked down the hall, did you notice? Three of the rooms are sealed. They've arrested ordinary workers from the Proletarka factory. I knew right away that you'd been in prison, I guessed back in the café, if you must know. And I didn't leave you on the street, and now you're insulting me."

Sasha sat on the edge of the chair. He was tired. He hadn't slept in a day and he had been drinking. If he could only get to the station and nap there, and then sleep some more on the train.

"I didn't want to hurt your feelings, but I'm tired of interrogations. I'm a free man; here's my passport."

He reached into his pocket for his wallet, but she moved away. "Don't! I'm not checking your documents."

"Go ahead, at least you'll learn my last name."

"I don't want to."

"Then don't. Yes, I've been in exile, I served my sentence, I don't have the right to live in Moscow. I came here hoping to find a job, but I didn't, so I'm going somewhere else."

She stared at him. "Why leave? Leonid Petrovich promised to take you on, you have a job."

"I don't like it here. You're all too vigilant."

"Darling, it's like that everywhere now."

She sat on his lap and put her hands on his face, pressing her lips against his. He picked her up and lowered her onto the bed.

She woke him in the morning. She was already dressed and wearing her coat, and she looked at him with a smile.

"I'm off, dear, I'll be back at two, I have a short day today." She bent over and kissed him. "You sleep." She pointed to the table. "There's bread and butter, cheese and sausage, and tea in a Thermos. If you want to go to the toilet, you go out into the hallway, third door on the right. Don't worry, all the bastards are at work. There are slippers under the bed. The key to the door is on the table. Lock up afterward, I have my own key. If anyone knocks, don't open. Well, so long, I'm off."

Sasha got up, pulled on his trousers, put on his jacket, opened the door — the hallway was empty and quiet — and went to the toilet. He came back, locked the door, put the key on the table, rinsed his hands in the sink, and munched on the sausage standing up. Then he undressed and went back to bed. God, it was good! And he fell asleep.

He was awakened by the sensation of someone walking in the room. He sat up in bed, his heart thumping.

Lyuda, in a robe, was setting the table.

"Did I wake you?"

Sasha stretched. "I've had enough sleep. What time is it?"

"Three."

"When did you get back?"

"About forty minutes ago."

She sat down on the bed and kissed him. He unbuttoned her robe and pulled her toward him. He didn't let her go for a long time. . . .

"You're exhausting me. I won't be able to move. . . ."

"You will."

"Get up, dear, let's eat, I brought some hot food. I'll go heat it up."

"Wait. I had a shampoo at the barbershop, but I'd love to go to the steam baths," Sasha said. "Is it far from here?"

"It's ladies' day today."

"What does that mean?"

"We alternate — one day for men, one for women. You can wash here." She pointed to the sink. "I'll fill it with hot water." She pulled a big tub out from under the bed. "That's how I wash; I don't like going to the baths. It's filthy there, they steal your clothes, and there are drafts from all the cracks."

Sasha looked at the sink and at the tub. "I have to change my underwear, my T-shirt, socks, and shorts. But my suitcase is at the station in the baggage check-in."

"That's no problem. Shorts and T-shirt . . . I'll run down to the store on the corner and buy some. There're a lot of them in winter. What size are you? Forty-eight, fifty?"

"I don't know."

"Fifty, probably. I'll buy size fifty."

"All right. Take some money from my wallet." He nodded toward his jacket.

She took his wallet and pulled out a thirty-ruble bill. "That'll be enough."

With her foot she pulled the rug from the door over to the sink, put the tub on the rug and a smaller basin on the stool next to it. She set out a brush and soap and brought a large tea kettle with hot water, which she poured into the sink and basin. She put a pitcher of cold water on the floor.

"You stand in the big tub and rinse from the small one. If you need more, there's water in the kettle. Here's a towel and here's my robe. You can wear it until I bring your shorts and T-shirt. I'll lock you in. There are people walking around the hallway. That's it. I'm off." She dressed quickly.

The lock clicked.

Sasha got out of bed, stood in the tub, and soaped himself.

He hadn't washed in a long time, dammit. Maybe a month. He scrubbed his arms, his shoulders, trying not to splash. He took the small basin from the stool and sat down, the better to soap his feet and legs. It wasn't a steam bath, of course, and it wasn't their bathtub in the Arbat, but it was wonderful!

He dried himself and put on Lyuda's robe. It was tight, but the flannel felt good on his back and chest. He sat down on the cot and tucked his legs under himself.

At last he had some semblance of a normal life. He didn't have to run or hurry or change trains, lie or pretend. He was sitting in a clean, cozy room, in a city instead of some village — how could he not be happy over his luck? Lyuda had not suggested bringing his suitcase from the station, which meant she wasn't planning to keep him long. Well, she was right. And he was grateful for what he had. He had rested a bit, relaxed, he had pushed aside his memories of his arrest, the prison, the exile, the Angara, Kezhma, and Taishet. And he wasn't thinking about Varya. He wasn't suffering anymore, he wasn't jealous. He could even think about Moscow without particular sadness. There was nothing he could do about it. Moscow was closed to him, and the only person left there for him was his mother.

His illusions were over, the struggle for existence was beginning, and whether he stayed on in Kalinin or left for Ryazan or some other place, it wouldn't be easy. Maybe he'd be lucky. He had been lucky in Kalinin. He found a kind and good person.

Lyuda returned and tossed a package at Sasha. "Catch those shorts. I bought navy, they didn't have black."

"Do you prefer black?" he asked with a smile.

"Well . . ."

She took off her coat and removed the basin, pitcher, and kettle, rolled up the rug, and when she bent over to wipe the floor, her skirt rode up and tightened around her hips.

"Come here!"

"No, we're going to eat now."

"That's not what I'm talking about," Sasha said sneakily. "Sit down, I want to tell you something." She sat on the edge of the cot. "Let's eat later. I have to go to the post office and call my mother in Moscow."

Her eyes narrowed in jealousy. "Your mother?"

"Yes, my mother. I promised her yesterday, she's waiting for my call. And I'll go see Leonid first thing in the morning. What do you think — he hasn't forgotten about me, has he?"

"He hasn't forgotten, don't worry."

"Listen," Sasha said and stroked her hand. "Well, when I come back, we'll talk. Will you let me stay another night?"

"You're going to exhaust me."

"I'll sleep on the cot."

She laughed. "You'd still get to me from there."

## 26

Не had to wait at the telephone station — only two booths for calls to Moscow. He was put through after an hour.

His mother picked up the phone; she had been waiting for his call. Sasha said that everything was fine, that he had been promised a job tomorrow, that they had a dormitory and if it didn't suit him, he'd rent a room.

"Thank God," his mother said. "Sasha, call Varya."

"What for?"

"Please, I'm asking you, please call her. She was so kind to me, she took such good care of me."

"But I don't understand —"

"You will, Sasha, I'm begging you, please call her and be nice to her. Do you remember her number?"

"Of course not."

"Write it down."

"I don't have a pencil or paper."

"It's the same as ours, except for the last two digits — four four. You can remember that. Sasha, please call her, she's at home now, promise me."

"All right, I will if I can, but I'll have to put in another order for the call, and there's a long line here."

"When will you call me?"

"In three or four days."

"All right. But call Varya. I kiss you."

"I'll try. Kisses."

He hung up and left the booth. There was a crowd of people by the window where they took phone orders.

The man at the head of the line paid, got a receipt, and asked, "How long is the wait?"

"About two hours. Next!"

"And if there are business calls, you'll have to wait three!" someone added from the line.

He wouldn't wait two or three hours. And what for? What was the rush? His mother owed a lot to Varya and wanted Varya to know that Sasha knew and appreciated it. His mother was very proper in that way.

And yet the reminder of Varya stabbed his heart. "She's at home now." That meant she had talked with his mother, knew he was here, maybe she had asked him to call or maybe his mother had offered it herself. "I'll be talking to Sasha, and I'll have him call you."

He thought about where the phone was in her apartment. And he remembered how they all had gone over to Nina's, to invite her to the Arbat Cellar to celebrate his reinstatement at the institute. Nina hadn't been home, but Varya was on the phone. It was in the hallway, not far from the kitchen. She was leaning against the wall, in a short skirt, scratching her knee with her heel. He had hung up the phone. "Let's go!"

She had stared at him with curiosity. "Where?"

"To party! To celebrate my victory!"

But enough of that. It was in the past. He had come to terms with it. He had slept with another woman, and he desired her.

But his mother had said Varya's name, and it stabbed his heart.

Lyuda was napping under a plaid blanket, but she looked up when Sasha came in. She smiled and said, "Lock the door!"

Sasha dropped the hook into the eye, took off his coat and hat.

"I got a little rest at last. Turn around, I'll get dressed."

He laughed. "Are you embarrassed?"

"The night's ahead for us. But now we'll have a meal. You must be hungry."

"A bit."

"Did anyone see you in the hall?"

"No one."

"Good. Turn around."

"What if I don't?"

"You won't get any anyway." She felt around under the bed and found her slippers. "Here, put these on and turn around."

Sasha went over to the cot. There were photos hanging above it, the kind you see in every home — father, mother, children, father separately, mother separately, Lyuda alone, Lyuda with girlfriends somewhere on the beach, everyone in bathing suits, then a man in a military uniform.

"Done," Lyuda said. "Now wash up for dinner."

She set the table with vodka, sausage, cheese, bread, and butter.

"I brought some liver from the café. I'll cook it with some potatoes."

"This is enough."

"It'll spoil. I'll be fast."

She came back from the kitchen with a frying pan of meat and potatoes, sat down, and poured vodka.

"Success."

They drank.

"How are things at home? How is your mother?"

"Everything's fine, thanks."

"She must be worried about you."

"Of course she is. Listen, Lyuda, here's the thing. I have a temporary passport, which I have to exchange for a permanent one. Do you know how it's done — do I get a residency permit first and then exchange passports, or can I exchange it first and then register?"

Lyuda poured a second glass, drank it, followed it with a piece of liver, and looked at Sasha.

"I can help you with the passport. I have a friend who works there. You go see Leonid tomorrow, sign up, and I'll see her first thing in the morning and find out."

"You see ... I hate to put you in this position ... but ..."

"Am I chasing you out?" Lyuda interrupted. "I can put up with the crowding a bit."

"But I wouldn't like to apply at the garage tomorrow with a temporary passport. If I can exchange it, I'd rather come in with a permanent one."

"Fine, I'll find out."

"Do you know this woman well?"

"She's my pal."

"Can she give me a clean passport?"

"What's that?"

"Without a notation of my restrictions?"

"I don't know. I'll have to talk to her."

They drank again. And she said, "She'll take care of your passport. But you realize, of course, that you'll have to take care of her."

"The law requires that my passport be exchanged."

"The law will make you hassle for two weeks with long lines. Do you know how many people like you there are in Kalinin? You've seen Angelina Nikolaevna?"

"What about her?"

"Never mind. I'm just asking, you've seen her, right? Well then! Everything's fine with her. She's registered her marriage with Ivan Andreyevich, she bears his name. I'm telling you, there's tons and tons of people like you in Kalinin. From Moscow, Leningrad, and of our own. So. If you want to do it by law, you'll have to wait at least two weeks. At least. But you can get it in a day. I don't know about the notation. She's a sharp cookie, she'll do anything that's legal, but I don't know if she'd be willing to take a risk.... I doubt it."

Lyuda kicked off her shoes and put her feet on Sasha's lap. He caressed her leg.

"Watch it, don't get too high up. What were you exiled for?"

"You know for what. For nothing."

"Politics? So young?"

Sasha laughed. "I'm not a minor."

She thought some more, then shook her head. "All right, pour me a drink. And watch your hands, I told you. I spend so much time on my feet at the café that I always put my legs up on a chair when I get home. But now you're on the chair. Right? A drink!"

"Won't that be too much?"

"Pour," she said stubbornly. "And have one yourself. And finish the liver. You need your strength."

Sasha poured, they drank. She made a face but didn't follow the vodka with food.

"Do you have a father?"

"Father and mother."

"How about brothers and sisters?"

"No."

"So you're the one and only?"

"Yes."

"Are they good people, your parents?"

"Yes."

She removed her feet from his lap, put on the slippers, walked unsteadily to the cupboard and took out a shawl.

"It's chilly."

She sat back down, thought a bit, pushed away her glass, and suddenly said, "I had a father. A good father. He was a woodworker and my mother worked in a bread plant, and so did my brother, who was two years older than I. I was born in 1914 and he was born in 1912 — he's in the army now. We had a cousin living with us, his mother — my father's sister — died and we took him in. That made five. We lived in a single room, of course, a big room, thirty square meters. We lived happily and calmly. We loved one another. Mother cooked dinner and waited for Father to come home from work. We would sit down at the table and all the meat would be shared equally. Father would have a shot of vodka before the meal, but not more than that. And neither my brother nor my cousin drank. They weren't drinkers. I'm making up for all of them." She giggled nervously. "I'm fulfilling the quota for them all, all by myself. Pour me a drink. You pour, or I'll spill."

She swallowed. She was very drunk, but she had no trouble speaking, she just repeated herself.

"So Father didn't drink, just after work before dinner. At dinner we talked, we talked happily, but Mama was always telling my father, 'Stop interrupting, be quiet.' He kept talking about his work, about the problems and injustices. He liked that word —*justice* — and see where it got him."

She had another sip.

"Father was tall and handsome, he loved me and my brother. And he treated his nephew like his own. His name was Ivan, my cousin, Father's nephew. On his days off Father took us to the zoo and the circus, or just for a walk in the park or by the river. I remember I was in the hospital with diphtheria, and he brought me a stuffed bunny. I loved it, but they wouldn't let me take it home from the hospital. They kept my colored pencils, too. I cried, but you weren't allowed to bring anything home from the hospital. My father always stood up for the truth, for justice. That was his favorite word, *justice.*

"Workers started coming to us, saying that there had been a meeting, taking on all kinds of goals of socialist competition, you know how we pick shock-workers. But Father spoke out against one candidate, whether he was a bad worker or somebody's relative, I don't remember, but Father thought it was unjust and spoke out, and others joined him. Anyway, they blamed him for breaking up a workers' meeting. And took him away at night. I'll never forget that night. Screams woke me up, my mother's screams. They had gone through everything, torn the room apart, and taken my father. Mother started screaming again and followed them down the hallway, and I followed her, crying, and my brother, Petya, too. The cousin was studying in Leningrad. We followed my father down the hallway crying, and they took him away. And then our horrible life began — where to turn, whom to ask, we didn't have any high-placed acquaintances or relatives, we had no one. And everybody said, 'Keep quiet, or they'll get you, too.' Mother kept wandering around looking for Father. We wrote to Kalinin, and Mother went to the procurator, but they chased her away. Then another woman whose husband had been arrested said there was going to be a trial of the men who had worked together in Father's shop. It was a special trial, a troika, behind closed doors, right in the administration building. We stood in the courtyard, the wives, children, Mother with me and my brother. They were brought out that back way, seven of them, and my father walked calmly. When he saw us he just had time to say, 'Ten years.' He was wearing winter boots, they had taken him away in the winter, and now it was spring, I don't remember, late February or March. Mama had brought rubber boots for him to put over the felt boots so that they wouldn't get wet. She gave them to me to pass to him, but the guard pushed me in the chest, I almost fell down, and they took Father away in his felt boots. And we never saw him again, not a letter or a line, my father vanished, he perished for his justice."

She finished her glass and looked at Sasha. "Why do you think I took you to Hannah's party? I don't pick up people in the café. Out of principle. No one. He could be gorgeous, pockets filled with gold. I never went with anyone from the café. We have floozies who do that. They bring men home after work. But I don't! Men make eyes at me and try to pick me up, but I tell them all to go to hell. I have a reputation to maintain. And I didn't take you home because you were handsome. And not because you defended me, though you did act decently. I liked your looks, of course, and all that, but I never pick up customers from the café, oh no! But when you said, 'Justice,' my heart jumped. It was like being stabbed in the heart, I remembered my father talking about justice. Of course, when you started swearing at the guy, I had my doubts. But I ate with you to see what you were like. I saw you were from the intelligentsia, and it was only ten minutes, but I enjoyed myself with you. People like you, who are for justice, always have a hard time. I believed you about your mother and about your divorce and looking for work. I believed you, I wanted to believe a just man, and so I invited you with me."

"And then you got scared," Sasha said with a laugh.

"When was that?"

"When I said I didn't know the song."

"Oh . . . Yes, because I realized that you had been in prison. That meant you had lied to me. And as we pulled up to my house, I thought, 'So who tells the truth about himself anymore? Nobody does, everyone hides something.' And then I thought, 'He'll go away and I'll never see him again.' I thought that maybe you'd met my father or my cousin."

"What about your cousin?"

"Well . . . What did we become once Father was sentenced? 'Family of an enemy of the people.' My cousin was studying in Leningrad then, at the Naval Academy — I don't know, I think he wanted to be a captain. He had a different surname and maybe he didn't mention in his application that his uncle was an enemy of the people. But maybe he did — he belonged to the Party, he was idealistic, he always said you shouldn't deceive the Party, you had to tell your Party the truth. So Mikhail might have mentioned my father. But they left him alone. He was at the academy. In

Leningrad. And he had a friend who worked in the Party Committee. So when Kirov was killed, that friend told him Stalin's words — 'If you didn't manage to protect Kirov, we won't let you bury him.' And Mikhail told the other students. The next day he came home and told his wife, 'They called me into the Party Bureau, they asked me if I had mentioned Stalin's words. I said, "Yes, I did." "And where did you hear them?" I realized that if I told the truth, it would be the end of my pal. So I said nothing. They insisted — "Who told you?" And there was a man from the NKVD there. And they kept asking — "Did you hear Comrade Stalin himself say it?" No, I never saw Comrade Stalin. "Then who told you the words?" I don't remember, it's just a rumor in the city. I saw the NKVD man give a sign and the Party secretary said, "Expelled for spreading anti-Soviet rumors. Your Party card." I gave it to him. And then he said, "Raise the question of expulsion from the Academy." So,' he told his wife, 'I'll be kicked out of the academy tomorrow, too.' Well, his wife started crying. She was young and about to have a baby. She's the one who told us this. Mikhail didn't see that tomorrow. They came for him that night. And she gave birth a few days later. Then she and the baby were exiled. She's in Kazakhstan now."

"And what about your brother?" Sasha asked.

"He moved to the Far East. He lives there now, occasionally writes. When Mama died, I sent him a telegram. He came long after the funeral, gave me some money, and said, 'Leave here and never mention Father or Mikhail and don't tell anyone.' And I'm such a fool, I'm telling you the whole story. Why? Because you told me about yourself. I had it all hidden in my heart for so many years. Now I've told you and I feel so much better. Then, just like my brother told me, I traded my room for one in Kalinin. Instead of thirty square meters, I got this cell."

"Did this used to be a hotel?"

"Who the hell knows? Some say a hotel, some say a brothel, others a workers' dormitory, for the Proletarka or Vagzhanovka. Those are the factories here. They used to belong to Morozov. He was a revolutionary himself. He built dormitories for the workers.

"He wasn't a revolutionary, but he gave money for the Revolution, that's true."

She narrowed her eyes at him. "You won't tell anyone what I told you?"

"Don't be silly."

"I didn't say anything against Soviet power," she said challengingly.

"Stop being ridiculous!"

"We were just chatting! That's all.... What's your mother's name?"

"Sofya Alexandrovna."

"And your father?"

"Pavel Nikolaevich."

"Are they alive?"

"I told you they are."

"Swear on their lives, swear that you won't sell me out."

Sasha chuckled. "All right. I swear."

She looked him soberly and straight in the eyes. "And I swear that I'll never sell you out. Remember, if anything happens to you, it wasn't me."

"You talk funny, Lyuda."

"I know what I'm saying. You've come here from God knows where, but I live here — have for a long time. I know everything. So that! I should go see Elizaveta, but I'm too drunk."

"Who's Elizaveta?"

"The passport woman, I told you."

She hadn't mentioned her name, but that didn't matter. Sasha said nothing.

"I should go see her at home, but you got me drunk."

"I did? Really?"

"You didn't? Well, then, how about another drink? I'll go see her early in the morning before work. We can't talk at the militia precinct house."

Charles took Vika to Carolina's. Monsieur Epstein himself met them at the door and hurried ahead, pulling up soft armchairs.

"Sit down, please! Cecile will be free in a moment, she's expecting you. Oh, it will be such a pleasure for her to dress such an elegant lady." He bowed to Vika. "Madame, your presence here is a great honor for us, but Madame Plevitskaya decided to come in just now." He lowered his voice, explaining to Charles. He spread his hands helplessly. "Believe me, I warned her that we were expecting you and your wife. But an actress is an actress, a celebrity is a celebrity, what can you do? She just showed up.... I was helpless, Monsieur Charles, believe me."

"Plevitskaya, Plevitskaya," thought Vika. "A familiar name ... the actress Plevitskaya." She remembered. In Moscow they had old, prerevolutionary records — Varya Panina, Nadezhda Plevitskaya. Her father told her that Plevitskaya had visited their house on Starokonyushenny...."

"I'll tell you something else," Epstein began.

But he didn't finish. The dressing room curtain parted and a large woman came out. She was fifty or so, wearing a squirrel jacket. Her round face with high cheekbones — almost a Tatar face — shiny black eyes and large mouth immediately attracted attention.

"Pardon, monsieur, pardon, madame," Epstein said and hurried over to the woman. "Oh, Madame Plevitskaya. For you ..."

Vika didn't listen to his murmuring. Behind Plevitskaya came an elegant redhead — oh God, Cecile Schuster. Vika hadn't seen her in nine years, remembered her as a sixteen-year-old, but recognized her right away. Maybe it was because she was expecting to see her there. Cecile, in the flesh.... She had never been considered beautiful in their crowd. She was very thin, with tight curls. But her figure was fabulous. When they were in ninth grade, the music hall opened. And Cecile, whom they all called Silka, passed the auditions and the enormous competition and got a place in the chorus line. She danced, half naked, with the other girls. There was a scandal, of course — the music hall was closed and the girls scattered. Cecile was almost expelled from school, but they let her finish ninth grade and then Cecile and her mother moved to France.

But Cecile hadn't seen Vika in nine years, either, and she wasn't expecting to find her there. She gave a friendly smile, the kind she gave all her customers. And then Vika leaned forward and said in Russian, "Silka, is that you?"

The Russian speech, the familiar voice, the demanding and barely familiar gaze, that barely familiar face, and her school nickname, Silka, suddenly conjured up Moscow for her. Cecile recognized Vika. And calmly, even indifferently, without any interest, she replied, "Yes, Vika, it's me.... What brings you here?"

"I'm with my husband."

She indicated Charles, who bowed.

Plevitskaya, hearing Russian, turned and looked at Vika.

"Well, Silka," Vika said, "hello."

And they kissed.

"My God," Vika said, "you haven't changed a bit."

"I haven't," Cecile said, "but you used to be a sweet and lazy, chubby little girl. You've grown very attractive since then. I didn't recognize you at first."

"What a touching reunion." Plevitskaya turned to Vika. "Have you come from Moscow recently?"

"Just a few months."

Plevitskaya looked at Charles and switched to French. "You have a charming wife, monsieur."

Charles thanked her reservedly and stood up, letting them know that the visit was dragging on.

To soften his coolness, Vika said, "My father is Professor Marasevich. You've visited us on Starokonyushenny."

Plevitskaya's eyes darted and she said with excessive enthusiasm, "Of course, of course . . . Oh my Lord . . . Starokonyushenny Alley. Why that's on . . . the Arbat."

"Yes."

"Well, of course, of course . . . My God, Arbat, Moscow . . ."

It was clear that she didn't remember Professor Marasevich or their apartment.

The door opened and a tall man of thirty-five or so came into the store. He had a military bearing. Vika saw how Plevitskaya looked at him, and understood that he was her husband. She wondered at the difference in their ages.

"My husband, General Skoblin," Plevitskaya said to Charles and Vika. "Just think, Nikolai, this charming young lady was in Moscow just a few months ago."

Skoblin bowed politely to Charles and Vika, then to Epstein and Cecile, and took his wife's arm.

Plevitskaya turned in the doorway and said to Vika, "You really are very sweet, child. I hope we'll see each other again and have a chat about dear Moscow."

Vika bought two summer frocks, a light suit and a blouse to go with it.

She and Cecile spent a long time picking them out. They called Charles in a few times for his opinion, then let him go, then called him back. Cecile marked with chalk where things had to be let out or taken in, and never once asked Vika about her life and plans, never said anything about herself, and didn't try to be friendly. Of course, Vika was not a poor Russian émigré. Her husband was a famous journalist, but Cecile was seeing her there for the first time. Who knew how long their marriage would last? Maybe Vika would show up in a few months asking for help. There was no reason to renew their old friendship. She was happy to serve her as a customer, but no more.

Vika felt that. Nelli had warned her. But nevertheless, she said, "We might get together sometime to chat."

"I have a lot of work for the spring season, from morning to night. But of course, I'll try to make time, and I'll call you. Give me your number."

Vika left it, knowing that Cecile wouldn't call.

A few days later a messenger from Carolina brought two boxes from the store to Vika's apartment.

Vika tried on her new clothes, which fit perfectly. What else could you expect from Paris? In Moscow if she showed up in a restaurant dressed like this, everyone would die of envy.

Charles came home that evening, and she tried on all the dresses for him, asked his opinion, and twirled and changed in front of the mirror.... It ended with him taking her right there, in front of the mirror.... And he didn't let her get dressed afterward. It was a wonderful evening and a fabulous night.

In the morning at breakfast, she said, "I want to thank Cecile, at least by telephone. What do you think?"

"It's not done. You call when you need something fixed. But you're old friends. You could call her as a friend?"

Vika laughed. "What friends? We weren't friends in school, and we haven't seen each other in a decade."

Cecile called two weeks later. "Vika, hello, how are you?"

"All right, thank you," Vika said coolly.

"Listen, Madame Plevitskaya sent me two tickets to her concert at the Gavot Hall. Would you like to go?"

"The tickets must be for you and Monsieur Epstein."

"No, for you and me. There's a note. Nadezhda Vasilyevna invites me and my lovely Moscow friend."

"All right, all right, skip the compliments."

"Her concerts are always sold out."

"Yes," Vika said sourly. She wasn't interested in émigrés, but she didn't have to meet anyone. She'd ask Cecile not to introduce her to people, but it would be stupid to refuse such a flattering offer.

"Where is the Gavot Hall?"

"On rue de la Boetie."

She explained how to get there. "I'll be waiting for you at exactly six-thirty."

There was a large crowd and some of the ladies wore expensive jewelry.

But Cecile did not greet anyone, which made Vika think that none of her customers — at least the steady ones — was here. That meant it wasn't a very rich crowd, not high society, although there must have been people who had been important in the old Russia. Apparently Cecile did not know them.

"You'll enjoy this," Cecile said. "She has an astonishing voice. And an astonishing background. She came from simple peasant stock, only three grades at the parish school for education, and look — she's world famous, travels all over. All the émigrés adore her. They call her 'la Plevitskaya' here. But to tell the truth, I love her as a singer and not so much as a customer. She's demanding, spoiled, and stubborn. You can't argue with her."

The concert was a triumph. Plevitskaya looked gorgeous onstage in her Russian costume, a Russian national singer. She didn't sing Gypsy songs or art songs, she sang folk songs. Applause thundered after every song. Many people wept. When she sang "You're Covered with Snow, Russia," even Vika got misty.

She sighed deeply and thought bitterly of the other Russia, the real Russia, where she and her whole family would have been happy, which she wouldn't have had to escape, if not for that damned Revolution.

Cecile and Vika were sitting on the end of the row, on seats added in the aisle. Just before the concert ended, a young man came over to them, bent down, and whispered, "Madame Plevitskaya asks you to see her after the concert. I'll take you backstage."

The concert ended. The audience gave her a standing ovation, the men shouting "Bravo!" Plevitskaya bowed low, her hand touching the floor, and the audience wouldn't let her go. People pushed toward the stage and threw flowers.

The young man came over to Vika and Cecile and led them through empty and complicated corridors to Plevitskaya's dressing room.

She was changing behind a screen.

"Cecile, Vika, come in. I'll be ready in a moment."

"She's fifty-three, after all," thought Vika. Cecile had revealed Plevitskaya's age to her. "She has to hide even from women."

Plevitskaya came out in a gorgeous yellow robe. Someone rustled behind the screen, and then a maid came out with a big garment bag. She must have put the costume in there.

Plevitskaya sat before her dressing table and regarded her face carefully in the mirror. She started removing her makeup with a tissue.

"Did you like it?"

"Oh, yes, of course," Vika and Cecile said in unison.

There were voices in the hall.

"The fans," Plevitskaya noted. "Let them wait. I told them not to let anyone else in while you were here. Besides, I'm not dressed yet. And I don't feel like seeing anyone else, anyway. I'm tired. I used to sing day and night, and I never got tired, but now I do." As she spoke, she continued rubbing her face with tissues. "And still, when I sing, I think about Russia, I can't forget my Russia. Vika, dear, may I call you Vika?"

"Of course."

"I wish you'd tell me about Moscow. I want to hear about Moscow. Come see us in the country. It's less than an hour's drive. Vladimir Nikolaevich will come for you with the car and bring you back by evening. We'll talk and have lunch. I'm not inviting Cecile. She's too proud and has no time for us."

"Nadezhda Vasilyevna, you should be ashamed of yourself. You know how hard I work. I don't have a spare moment."

"I know, dear, I do, that's why I don't insist. You are a businesswoman and you're bored by me." Plevitskaya spoke without rancor. She had removed her stage makeup and was now putting on lipstick. "That's why I've stopped inviting you. But Vika must come. I want to talk to a real live person from Moscow. Many of the people here have forgotten Moscow. They're forgetting Russia. . . . Will you come, Vika?"

"With pleasure, but I am free only on Wednesdays and Saturdays."

"I'll bear that in mind. I'll call you the night before." She handed

Vika a pad and pencil. "Write down your number. And tell me, which do you prefer — meat or fish?"

"It really doesn't matter, Nadezhda Vasilyevna. Whatever you have is fine with me."

"I'll try to feed you well." She turned to the door. "Jean!"

The young man who had brought them to the dressing room came in.

"Jean, show these ladies out.... So, until we meet again, Vika. Good-bye, Cecile. ... I won't kiss you, I'll just get you messy. ... Vika, we have a date!"

# ⚜ 28 ⚜

Stalin reread Yezhov's memorandum.

Today we received information from a foreign source, deserving our complete trust, that indicates that during Comrade Tukhachevsky's trip to the coronation in London a terrorist act is planned against him. On orders of the German intelligence services, a group of four people (three Germans and one Pole) are planning the act. The source does not rule out the possibility that the terrorist act is intended to create international complications. In view of the fact that we do not have the capability to guarantee surveillance during the trip, nor full protection of Comrade Tukhachevsky while abroad, I consider it wise to cancel Comrade Tukhachevsky's trip to London. Please discuss.

*He* had dictated this edited version to Yezhov. The Germans knew Tukhachevsky's anti-German position, the Poles remembered his movement against Warsaw. The warning sounded convincing. Of course, not to Tukhachevsky. He had gone to London last year for the funeral of the previous king, had returned through Berlin, and no one had touched him. Tukhachevsky would understand that they were simply not letting him out, to keep him from fleeing. He could see how the circle around him was tightening. He knew that the transfers in the army's command were not random — commanders were being moved from units that were loyal to them to units where they had no support. Tukhachevsky heard Molotov speaking about the military at the February-March Plenum of the Central Committee — "If there are saboteurs in all branches of the economy, then how can we imagine that only the military is free of saboteurs? That would be ridiculous. . . . The military is a very large enterprise. It will be checked, not now but later, and it will be very thoroughly checked." Tukhachevsky was at the Plenum of the Central Committee. He heard it and he fully understood that there would be a purge of the army.

After the Plenum, the arrests of military men began, not in the upper echelons, but in the middle ranks. But everyone who was arrested had served with Tukhachevsky, Yakir, or Uborevich. And that also was a warning to Tukhachevsky. Tukhachevsky was on the alert — that meant we had to act swiftly and decisively. It had to be over in a month. *He* had hoped that Hitler would give *him* the weapon for an unexpected and instantaneous way of dealing with Tukhachevsky. He didn't. Well then, we'd use the usual means. And we'll wait for Hitler's reply.

Hitler was maneuvering. And people were attempting to maneuver him. In our favor for now, but those people could be replaced and nothing would remain of their efforts.

Hitler's maneuvers were understandable. He was threatening Russia but occupying the Rhine zone. And nothing happened: Britain and France swallowed the bitter pill.

But Hitler's maneuvers were forcing *him* to maneuver too. For the first time in the history of the Bolshevik Party, *he* had formed a bloc with the Social Democrats in France and Spain. And *he* was right. *He* supported the socialist governments in these countries. *He* was right to support them. *His* policy was a flexible policy. Now there would no longer be a solid anti-Soviet bloc in Europe, and the contradictions between Germany and France would become more acute. All the more reason to expect Hitler to move closer to the Soviet Union.

But no such movement had taken place yet. Too bad. A union of Germany and Russia would be invincible. Only through a union with *him* would Hitler be able to create a new Germany. And *he* saw a reliable and worthy partner in Hitler. They had a lot in common in their policies, strategies, and tactics.

Like *him*, Hitler had created a mighty power, a single, centralized party. He had created an *absolute* state, he had gathered the people around him, had given the state wings with a single idea based on hatred of the enemy. Hatred of the enemy is the most powerful idea because it creates an atmosphere of general fear. But Hitler's idea was nationalistic and in the long run unstable. It would force Hitler to seek an enemy outside Germany, it would push him toward war. He would have to fight Germany's eternal mortal enemy, haughty Britain, master of the ocean, and its ally France. He did not need Russia. Germany had never lived peacefully next to France, which had encircled it with its satellites. Even if Hitler's long-reaching, ambitious plans included world supremacy, he still had to deal with France before attacking the U.S.S.R. He could not fight on two fronts.

You need a mighty army for global war. But what did Hitler have? The old Prussian officer corps, snobbish barons, limited Prussian generals who had fought with Hindenburg and Ludendorff. As soon as a real war broke out, Hitler would be their hostage. Those people would never follow that parvenu, that "Bohemian private," as they called him. As long as the generals were in staff headquarters working out strategic plans, dealing with maps and papers, they were no threat to Hitler. But once they started commanding corps and divisions, once the army was under their command, the living mass of millions of soldiers, well armed and disciplined in the German way and completely obedient, they would toss Hitler away. His storm troopers wouldn't be enough to save him.

There was only one way out for Hitler. He had to get rid of the old generals and replace them with new, talented, and loyal men. *He* gave him that opportunity. Yezhov's people had handed him material on the secret ties between Soviet military commanders and German ones. Hitler could deal with his generals and give *him* the needed materials on Tukhachevsky in return.

Hitler was silent. Yezhov insisted the work was continuing. He had a good channel to the Germans. Yezhov wouldn't dare deceive *him*. But they were losing time. Any opportunity of a military conspiracy had to be nipped in the bud. The commanders of the Red Army had to be changed, starting at the top. It couldn't be put off. *He* couldn't go to bed worrying that the Kremlin would be taken by troops in the night and that *he* would be arrested and shot on the spot. Voroshilov was no protection. He'd hide under his bed in fear. They had to finish with the army no later than June, while the troops were still training, in camps. They couldn't wait for the fall when they would be back in their barracks. The military men were wary. At the Plenum, General Uborevich made a point of shaking Bukharin's hand, while Yakir demanded that Bukharin be shot. They were trying to show that the top brass were not united. But *he* knew that they were. Tukhachevsky, Yakir, Uborevich were as one. June, June, June, no later than June! What was the problem? They had never confessed or repented — they didn't know how. They had found only three former oppositionists among them — Primakov and Putna and Shmidt, the bastard who had insulted *him* at the Fourteenth Congress twelve years ago. Those three had been arrested last year. They were trying to beat confessions out of them, but the bastards wouldn't give in. They weren't soft intellectuals like Zinoviev. They were strong military men. But they would break. The trials had happened before their eyes. Didn't they know that *he* had the means to make them talk? A confession was inevitable and inexorable. When they started breaking, they'd see that.

And yet, it would be good to have a reliable insurance policy, a dossier that could be published or quoted, a dossier with German names, on German stationery, with German seals — the people would believe that. *He* knew the channels Yezhov was using — White émigrés in Paris, Geidrich, chief of the secret police in Berlin. The German staff headquarters had a contract from the 1920s in which the Soviet Politburo offered Germany military bases in Liepeistk, Dzerzhinsk, and near Moscow. Those documents had Tukhachevsky's signature. What else did they need?

Hitler wasn't giving them anything for now. Geidrich and his SS men might not attach particular significance to this operation, but Hitler — what about Hitler? He knew Tukhachevsky's anti-German position, and, at the same time, *he* was giving Hitler an opportunity to free himself of potential enemies among the German generals.

What was the reason for his hesitation?

Stalin pushed the bell to call Poskrebyshev and had him get Kungurov, an assistant.

"Yes, sir!" Poskrebyshev said and shut the door.

Stalin went to the window and looked at the dreary arsenal building. His thoughts returned to Hitler.

In analyzing his policies, *he* had discovered a similarity in their logic. Many times *he* had anticipated Hitler's moves and had been proven correct. Hitler did just what Stalin had predicted. And when *he* had ordered Yezhov to undertake this operation, *he* was convinced that Hitler would accept it. Yezhov assured him that the plan was being run through the Nazi security organs hostile to the Prussian generals and the Reichswehr. Then why were there no results yet?

Of course, there were many dissimilarities between them, too. Hitler was direct. He lacked flexibility and foresight. But they had much in common. Even in their backgrounds. Just like *him*, Hitler was the son of a cobbler and a peasant woman, and even though Hitler's father did not make shoes for long and became a customs officer, it didn't matter. They were both born into the very depths of the people. *He* wasn't Russian, and Hitler wasn't a native German but an Austrian. Like *him*, Hitler was self-taught, and like *him*, Hitler had been interested in the arts as a youth: Hitler painted; *he* wrote poetry. . . . *His* poems were naïve and direct, but Hitler's canvases were probably far from being Raphaels.

Like *him*, Hitler dressed simply. Both wore military uniforms. They didn't advertise their connections with women, and no woman influenced their politics. Like *him*, Hitler was not interested in money. Power was the true ruler's only property. The people must see that their leader is not interested in wealth. He must be a man who needs nothing for himself personally. Hitler was photographed with ordinary people. There were fairy tales about his kindness and sensitivity and attentiveness to the folk — that came from the arsenal of bourgeois parliamentary demagoguery, but if he liked it, it was up to him.

Like *him*, Hitler had been considered unfit for military service. However, *he* had participated in the Civil War and Hitler in the World War. Like *him*, Hitler hated so-called democracy with its endless parliamentary debates. Most important, they both knew the secret of power, they understood the psychology of the people and role of the leader. The people wanted the ruler to think and make decisions for them. That was the primitive philosophy of the people, and *he* and Hitler used it well.

It had grown dark outside and a few oblique drops struck the glass. Stalin went over to the light switch, turned on the light, and went back to his desk.

A lot was being written about Hitler. *He* gave orders to translate and show *him* everything — both what Hitler himself wrote and what was written about him. It all boiled down to the fact that Hitler was a man of strong will who managed to subordinate even very talented men. That was natural — the talent for power is greater than any other talent. They wrote that Hitler was capricious. And Lenin had said that *he* was capricious. Lenin was wrong, people are often wrong, in mistaking willpower, determination, and persistence for capriciousness. Hitler "lacks ethical norms, is not choosy about his means." And what politician is choosy, what politician is ethical? There is no such politician. They also wrote that Hitler was an unbalanced man. . . . Perhaps, perhaps . . . However, his policies were consistent and goal oriented. Like any politician, he maneuvered, made unexpected moves that were inexplicable to many and therefore seemingly illogical. People took that as a sign of being unbalanced. They wrote that in his speeches he sucked up to the people. A real leader wants to be understood by the people and not just by a bunch of intellectuals, and so he speaks simply, understandably, accessibly. And a person's manner of speaking is an individual matter. *He* spoke calmly; Hitler shouted and his speeches were hysterical. Trotsky's speeches had a hysterical edge, yet he was considered a great orator.

Hitler understood all that. However, he wasn't entering into an exchange of information on the generals. Why not? Because he didn't want to help *him?* Impossible. Getting rid of Tukhachevsky was in the interests of Hitler — Tukhachevsky was an enemy of Germany.

All right, time would tell what Hitler's position was. It would show whether he was clever enough to join with Stalin, reliable enough to be trusted. Actually, you can't trust anyone in politics.

So, in the meantime, they had to prepare a condemnation of

Tukhachevsky with their own tried-and-true methods. Forbidding his trip to London was an open challenge.

With a blue pencil Stalin wrote on the corner of Yezhov's report — "TO THE MEMBERS OF THE POLITBURO. Sad as it may be, I must agree with Comrade Yezhov's suggestion. We must ask Comrade Voroshilov to propose another candidate. J. Stalin."

He rang.

Poskrebyshev appeared in the doorway.

"Give this to the members of the Politburo."

Poskrebyshev came to the desk and took the paper.

"Prepare a resolution of the Politburo. In view of the danger of a terrorist act, rescind the decision on Comrade Tukhachevsky's trip to London. . . . Further, accept the proposal of the people's commissar of defense on sending Comrade Orlov to London. Have Voroshilov show this to Tukhachevsky. . . . There. Is Kungurov here? Fine. Bring him in."

Kungurov, one of the research analysts in the office, entered Stalin's study. He was solidly built, clean shaven, and brown eyed. He was wearing an embroidered Ukrainian shirt under his jacket, his trousers were tucked into his boots, and he was carrying a book.

"Sit down!"

He liked this fellow. He didn't look like a clerk, like a bureaucrat. He had a round and rosy-cheeked face, with a pleasant open expression. He was the only one in the Secretariat who smiled. The others never smiled around *him*, but Kungurov did, he smiled in a nice way. He was pleased to see *him* and he couldn't hide his joy. He was helpful. Prepared to do anything *he* asked. He looked like a young Siberian, the kind *he* used to see in exile when he was young. These fellows were unmarried, free of family ties and worries. They weren't hassled or embittered yet. They were friendly and cheerful, like this Kungurov. And even though he wore a Ukrainian shirt, his name made it clear that he came from Siberia or the Urals. He regarded *him* with adoration and loyalty, he listened for *his* every word, he was delighted by *his* every movement.

And another thing. At thirty, Kungurov knew five foreign languages — English, German, French, Italian, and Spanish. An ordinary fellow from a working-class family, he had served in the

Red Guards, and after the workers' courses he had gone on to the university. And there he had learned five languages. Which proved that language ability was purely biological — some people had it and some didn't.

Kungurov made selections for *him* from foreign newspapers, magazines, and books. The basic information came from TASS, the wire service, but Kungurov did special packages just for *him*, on the questions that interested *him* personally. Information that only *he* needed. Now he was working on Hitler's biography, his work, and he always came up with interesting facts. He always seemed to know what *he* needed. He researched and translated. He worked well.

Kungurov showed Stalin the book he had brought. "Comrade Stalin, I've just come from our printer, but I haven't had time to read it yet. Permit me to report tomorrow."

"What's the book?"

"A collection of Hitler's speeches for this year."

"But you've read it in German. Why put it off for tomorrow?"

"I want to read the Russian version. There might be errors."

"What's interesting there?"

"There are some rather amusing statements, especially on peace." Stalin smiled. "The speech at a demonstration in Cologne, right after they took the Rhine."

"Give it to me!"

Stalin found the speech in the contents and tried to turn to the page, but was unable to.

"I haven't had time to cut the pages yet," Kungurov said. "As soon as I got in, there was a note for me from Comrade Poskrebyshev to see you immediately."

Stalin pressed the book against his desk and tore the pages he needed with his fingers. It made an uneven tear and the jagged ends stuck out along the edge. He started reading. . . .

And suddenly and unexpectedly, *his* "alarm" went off, a feeling that never left *him*, that kept *him* alert, that let *him* react instantly to the slightest danger. This feeling never fooled *him*. It helped *him* strike first and thereby protect *himself*, *his* life, *his* position.

Stalin looked up at Kungurov and saw his stunned gaze directed at the torn pages. A hostile gaze. He was silently criticizing *him* for tearing the pages with *his* finger. He dared to criticize *him!* He was upset over some stupid book and didn't even try to hide it.

But *he* knew how to hide it. *He* always could. *He* suppressed *his* annoyance and went back to the text, reading Hitler's speech in Cologne.

> There is no need to show that we want peace. I do not believe that there is a man on earth who spoke more about peace, who strove more for peace, and struggled more for peace than I did. . . . I served in the infantry and I felt all the horrors of war with my own skin. But I am certain that the majority of people look at war with my eyes. . . . That is why they accept my ideas. I am protecting the rights and freedom of my people. I want peace.

"He's a scoundrel," Stalin said.

"Yes," Kungurov said. "Especially to say that right after taking over the Rhine."

But his eyes were still on the tortured pages. Look how it bothered him!

Stalin tore some more pages with his finger, on purpose this time, slowly and calmly, looked at them, then tore some more, skimmed them, then tore all the pages in the book, without looking up at Kungurov, but sensing his tense gaze on his hand.

He slammed the book shut and handed it to Kungurov. "Mark the most interesting passages and give them to me through Comrade Poskrebyshev."

"Yes, sir."

Kungurov left.

Stalin watched him go. He was going to repair the book now, clipping with his scissors.

Stalin got up and walked in the study.

Why had Kungurov's stare set off *his* alarm? *He* could have understood it from some bookworm or eccentric professor. But a former laborer with whom *he* had worked closely, whom *he* considered absolutely loyal. He had condemned Comrade Stalin in his heart over a torn page. It turned out that Comrade Stalin didn't know how to handle books; he was an ignoramus, that Comrade Stalin. He didn't ask for a paper knife, what a crime!

*He* had been mistaken in Kungurov. He wasn't prissy or a bookworm. He was an insincere person. A false one. The pathetic book was more important to him than Comrade Stalin's wishes. He was always smiling at *him*. But *he* had caught him when he wasn't expecting it, and saw that his face could do more than smile. He was false. He listened to every word, watched every gesture — not out of loyalty but for other reasons. What? Was he studying Comrade Stalin? Why? For history? Was he keeping a diary? Writing things down? Was he going home and writing things down? And he'd write a notation today: *Comrade Stalin treats books barbarically; instead of a knife he uses his finger to cut pages.* He works closely with the country's leader, he sees *him*, talks with *him*, history is made before his very eyes. Why not take notes? Why not save every day of Comrade Stalin for history and thereby enter history himself? People close to the great often do that. *He* once saw a book at Nadya's written by the secretary of the French writer Anatole France. . . . *He* forgot the secretary's name. . . . What was the book called? Oh, yes, *Anatole France in Slippers and Robe.* That was it. A nasty book. Anatole France was revealed, turned inside out.

*He* often thought about it. Especially after *he* had made the mistake with Bazhanov. *He* had trusted him when he was *his* secretary. And in vain. He fled across the border, the bastard, and wrote a lot of lies. It was a base thing to do. A chronicler should not dig around in dirty laundry. The chronicler must describe only deeds for descendants to read. *He* didn't need witnesses to *his* private life.

But who was straining to be a witness? Dull Poskrebyshev? Impossible. Tovstukha? He was too smart and cautious. The same held for Mekhlis, Dvinsky, and all the others in *his* Secretariat. They knew what being close to *him* entailed. They knew what those little diaries could bring. But a man like Kungurov, a small, unnoticed clerk, he could take notes. No one would suspect that he would dare to try it. *He* had noticed Kungurov's too-curious stare before. No one ever watched *his* every move like that. *He* had put it down to loyalty and only today saw something else — Kungurov's satisfaction in finding such coarseness in Comrade Stalin. That was something tasty for his notebook.

Stalin went into the reception room and told Poskrebyshev to send Pauker to him immediately.

A panting Pauker rushed in. He had a new military uniform on again, with blue jodhpurs and patent leather boots. He was in a hurry and didn't have time to change, the fool, the shitty dandy....

"Do you know Kungurov?"

"Yes. He's in the Secretariat."

"Today, search him as he leaves — say it's a general check and that you'll return everything tomorrow. Take everything you find on him — books, documents, notebooks, any papers, his cigarette pack if he smokes, his pen. Bring everything to me. And begin a tight surveillance on Kungurov."

Kungurov was searched, and Pauker put everything they had confiscated onto the desk in Comrade Stalin's study.

Stalin sent Pauker away and went through everything. The documents were clean. The book was the one Kungurov had brought to him. Stalin leafed through it. There was nothing between the pages, but the edges had been trimmed neatly. He shook out the cigarettes to see if there was anything hidden in the pack. No, nothing. He unscrewed the cap of Kungurov's fountain pen and held it up to his eye. There was nothing inside, either. Kungurov didn't have a pad, but he did have a small address book. Stalin leafed through it. A few names of workers of the Central Committee with their home numbers, sometimes addresses ... the rest were unfamiliar. But the inside of the cover was worn and erased; there had been notations made in pencil and then erased, once they had been transferred somewhere else. Where were they copied? In a diary?

"Arrest Kungurov immediately," Stalin ordered Pauker. "And interrogate him today. During the interrogation find out what notes he has taken on the work of the Central Committee and the workers of the Central Committee. Give them to me immediately. Search his desk, search his apartment thoroughly, and bring me everything written in his hand and anything that is suspicious. If you find nothing, learn where Kungurov could have kept his notes, and search there, and arrest those people. He is a spy; he kept a diary on the work of the Central Committee."

They checked Kungurov's desk at the Kremlin, they searched his apartment, but they didn't find any notes or diaries. A search of the apartments of his parents and his wife's parents yielded nothing.

Despite the extremity of the interrogation, Kungurov categorically denied keeping a diary.

However, he did confess that he had worked as a spy for the Japanese and had been planning to kill Comrade Stalin. He was shot a week later. His wife was given eight years in the camps. The children were sent to an orphanage. His relatives and hers were exiled from Moscow.

Sharok's language studies were going well. Speigelglass had been right — what he had learned long ago at school did help. Somehow Yuri's old textbooks and notebooks had survived at his father's house. Those worn and yellowed pages revived his memory, and, in fact, he was an able student.

The teacher was about ten years older than he and maintained a stiff, formal manner. He stressed pronunciation, which was the hardest for Sharok. He had the most trouble with the "R," dammit!

"Softer, softer, roll it gently . . . less than that . . . repeat after me."

Sharok repeated after him, but it was no good.

"You have to get used to that sound. Practice on Russian words. Try it at home. When you talk with your wife, pronounce the 'R' that way."

"I don't have a wife," Sharok said with a smile.

The teacher accepted this information without interest.

"Then read newspapers out loud. That's useful, too."

Sharok did not have a wife. But he had Kalya. He had met her in the trolley. The "Annushka," as the A line was called, came to the stop. He helped a beautiful woman up the step. He pushed her by the hips from behind into the overcrowded car, and then forgot to remove his hands. He was instantly attracted to her.

Kalya was a midwife in the Grauerman Maternity Home. Four or five times a month she'd come to Sharok's place when she got off duty. She'd wake him with three brief rings. That was their signal. He'd start kissing her right on the doorstep. He couldn't tear himself away. After the stresses of the night, the shouting, the smashed, bleeding faces, their hate-filled looks, which absolutely drove Sharok crazy, Kalya's touch was enough to calm him, to restore his equilibrium.

"Give me your coat." Without releasing her hands, he would lead her to his room.

She would put down the little bag of cookies and doughnuts that she made the night before, undress, and dive into the warm bed, under the covers. Later they would drink tea and eat her cookies. Sharok loved looking at her, cheerful and strong, with powerful hands. He asked where she got her unusual name, Kaleria.

"Were your family merchants or priests?"

"No, no," she'd laugh. "We're purely proletarian. You won't catch me that way."

Kalya was a stroke of luck. She really was. Now that he had been transferred to the Foreign Section, he'd have to think about a new schedule. Maybe they'd manage to see each other more frequently.

"Are you reading the newspaper aloud?" the teacher asked.

"Every day."

"Good, keep it up."

On his day off, he was home reading the paper when his mother came over to clean up, do the laundry, and cook for him. She had a spare key to his place. He didn't want to burden Kalya with housework, nor was she eager to do it. His mother was always tactful, silently throwing out the stale cookies without asking who brought them and why there was lipstick on the teacups. But here she froze with the broom in her hand as she listened to Yuri reading *Pravda*.

"At the trrraining aerrodrrrome the young parrrachutist Marrr-farrita Petrrova set a worrrld rrrrecorrd. Without opening herrrr parrrachute —"

"Oh, my God, why do you sound like Abrashka all of a sudden?"

"You're right," he said and laughed. "I'm studying a foreign language."

"Keep studying and they'll say that you're not Russian."

Yuri studied eagerly. Who knew? Perhaps the transfer to the Foreign Section was a step toward the People's Commissariat for Foreign Affairs and diplomatic work? It had happened before.

Sharok attended the special classes with less enthusiasm — handguns, using explosives and knives, radio communications, codes. What did he need all that for? They weren't preparing him to be a commando, were they? He wouldn't do it anyway. But these courses were obligatory for all people in the section. Sharok attended without displaying much diligence or success.

But he was very interested in the materials on the White émigrés, the history and organization of ROVS — the anti-Soviet association of ex-officers and soldiers — and read the reports of agents. He didn't know who was hidden behind the numbers and pseudonyms. And he didn't ask. If he had a need to know, they'd tell him.

What Sharok liked best was reading the émigré newspapers and magazines — *Latest News, Renaissance, Illustrated Russia, Watchman*. . . . He received only these Paris papers, even though Russian newspapers were published wherever there were Russian émigrés — Yugoslavia, Bulgaria, Turkey, Poland, Germany, and Manchuria. But they were training him to be a specialist in ROVS, which had headquarters in Paris. So he got the émigré press printed in Paris.

He had never read anything like it. He relished it. Just having a copy of this newspaper would get its owner ten years, and if you could show that the owner had contacts — the one who lent it to him, and where that person got it, and the people he showed it to, and who else was there and what they said — that is, if you could create a group case, then everyone who ever held that newspaper would get the death sentence.

The headlines alone were something — "Under the Yoke of the Soviets," "Moscow's Eye: Agents and Provocateurs," "What Do the Bolsheviks Fear?" "The Bolshevik Contagion." At first they excited him, but then it got boring. They were monotonous, even though they gave piquant information "about our dear state."

The pleasure of the reading lay elsewhere. Sharok was plunged into the atmosphere of old, prerevolutionary Russia, which rose vaguely in his memory from his distant childhood and was supported by the recollections of his parents and their nonacceptance of present reality. Titles flashed before him, princes and barons, and so did names — Milyukov, Volkonsky, Obolensky,

Guchkov, Ryabushinsky.... Services at the Cathedral of Saint
Alexander Nevsky ... Sainte Genevieve-des-bois Cemetery ... The
Cossack Union, solemn reception in honor of Grand Duke Vladimir
Kirillovich ... Restaurants called Mariyanych, Chez Kornilov, Kiev,
and Djigit.

General Denikin was lecturing at the Chopin Hall on rue Daru.
Sharok imagined that he went all out on the oratory, shouting
slogans.... But what the émigrés wrote and said posed no threat to
the Soviet Union, and the White Guards organizations were fully
penetrated by Soviet secret agents. And all those titles —
excellencies and highnesses — weren't worth a thing, for a captain
behind the wheel of a taxi was merely a chauffeur and a colonel on
the conveyor belt at the Renault plant was only a simple worker.

And still, despite it all, it was the only place where the true
Russian traditions were preserved. They had created their Russia on
foreign soil, an artificial world, and they held tight to it. It was a
pathetic sight, but touching somehow; they were Russians, say what
you will.

But they were doomed. They would die in Paris. They would be
buried at Sainte Genevieve-des-bois, and their children and grandchildren would grow up French or German or Serbian. The old
people, they should have lived out their days in peace, but no, they
had to resist and fight. His parents accepted it, even though they had
suffered from the Revolution, too. And hated Soviet power. But
they didn't rebel, they submitted. And Sharok had submitted. No
one could stand up to the force of the state. And there was no shame
in giving in. If you live with wolves, you have to howl like a wolf.
Nobody was forcing them to howl like a wolf in Paris. So why
didn't they sit quietly? No, they had to mess with politics. In the
1920s there were young and healthy officers among the White
émigrés, and they represented a force. But now ... twenty years
after the Revolution ... Were they sending spies into the U.S.S.R.?
He had worked in the NKVD for three years and had never seen
a spy. It was a ridiculous idea.

After reading a pile of newspapers, Sharok returned them and
got a new set. Speigelglass, running into him at work, would hand
him White émigré books. "Take a look, this is interesting."

One day he realized he hadn't seen Speigelglass for a week and figured out that he had gone abroad. No one knew exactly where — at least, it seemed to Sharok that no one knew where he or the others went off to. People vanished, returned, and left again. Unfamiliar faces appeared, silent decoders went in to see Slutsky or Speigelglass. Everyone worked within the limits of his assignment and took no interest in anything else. You did not ask questions. Secrecy was observed here much more strictly than in Molchanov's section, even though his was called the Political Secrets Section. Yuri did not ask questions.

His first real conversation took place approximately a month after he started there. Speigelglass called him in, asked about his studies, a few questions about ROVS, and then asked, "Do you know people abroad?"

"In what sense?"

"In the most direct one. Do you have relatives, friends, mere acquaintances, or foreigners who can recognize you?"

"I do."

"Who, where?"

"In Paris. A certain Viktoria Andreyevna Marasevich, daughter of the famous Professor Marasevich. I went to School Number Seven with her on Krivoarbatsky Alley. I told you about her last time. I believe you know the school?"

Speigelglass said nothing.

Sharok had asked Speigelglass to reveal something personal with his question. He wanted to know how Speigelglass knew his French teacher, Irina Yulyevna. A big mistake on his part. That kind of curiosity was not encouraged there. You had to settle for what you were told. Your boss knew what information you were supposed to have.

With his silent and inscrutable expression, Speigelglass showed that the question was tactless.

Sharok pretended not to notice his displeasure and continued calmly, "I studied in the same class with Viktoria Marasevich's brother, Vadim. Viktoria Andreyevna worked with us in 1934 and 1935. She hung out at foreign restaurants and was mixed up with foreigners, then she married a famous architect and refused to cooperate. Her signed statement is on file. Later she divorced the architect and married a French newspaperman and moved to Paris with him."

Speigelglass listened to Sharok and made notes on a pad.

"Who ran her?"

"I did."

"Did you part unpleasantly?"

"Of course. She threatened to tell her husband, who would go to Stalin. But we let her go because she had dropped her restaurant ties once she got married."

"If she married a foreigner, she didn't drop them," Speigelglass noted.

A clever devil! But Sharok couldn't tell him the real reason — that Vika had seen Lena at his apartment and had begun blackmailing him.

He shrugged. "Dyakov, my boss then, decided to let her go."

So there! You can't check that, dear Comrade Speigelglass. No one knew where Dyakov was now.

"We'll take a look at the lady's signed statement," Speigelglass said. "Since she's living abroad, it should be in our section. All right!" He looked at Sharok, and Sharok saw hostility in Speigelglass's eyes for the first time. "Tomorrow you will move to a dacha, where you will live, ski, and do the same things you were doing here — study French, train, read émigré newspapers, and study the materials on ROVS. One request — don't shave."

He understood! They were changing his appearance. That meant he was going abroad. They wanted to get rid of him. He'd either be lost or arrested there.

Sharok said nothing.

Speigelglass looked at him interrogatively. "Is something wrong?"

"You see," Sharok began, choosing his words carefully, "Nikolai Ivanovich . . ."

He didn't say "Yezhov" or "comrade people's commissar," he said "Nikolai Ivanovich" intentionally, to stress their closeness.

"Nikolai Ivanovich told me that I was being transferred to the Foreign Section and that Comrade Speigelglass would tell me my future duties. I've been here a month and I still don't know about my duties. You are preparing me for some sort of work and I'd like to know what it is."

Sharok realized the risk of a direct question. But there was no other way. They were preparing him as an agent, and that meant certain death since he wasn't really prepared for it. He didn't speak the language, he was a mediocre shot, and his back trouble could make him bedridden at the most inappropriate moment. He was a lawyer by education. And he was taken as an investigator because he was a lawyer. He didn't want to do any other work. And that's not why Yezhov had him transferred. He was certain of it. But for what? The question must be worrying Slutsky and Speigelglass, too. They didn't need Sharok and they wanted to get rid of him. But it wouldn't work.

He added, "I didn't think it proper to ask Nikolai Ivanovich about my role in the section, but if I had known that I would be kept in the dark this long, I would have certainly asked him."

That was a hint that he would go to Yezhov and find support there.

"I informed you from the very beginning about your work," Speigelglass said in a steady voice. "You will work with the Whites. You will be in the group that is handling ROVS. That's why I asked you to learn about its activity and about the White émigrés in general. ROVS is part of it. You are not being prepared for work as an agent abroad. You do not know the conditions of life in the West, you don't know languages, and you would fail out there. Your work will be here. However, that does not rule out trips to the West and meetings with our people there, getting information at the source. Such a trip is coming up soon. By the way . . ."

He paused and then continued in the same steady voice. "By the way, on Nikolai Ivanovich's orders, you will accompany me to Paris. That's why I wanted you to know a few words in French, so that you can function in a café, a restaurant, a hotel, and the Métro. I will do the talking in more complex situations. Of course, all the business conversations will be in Russian. Viktoria Andreyevna Marasevich lives in Paris, and she knows you to be part of the organs. A meeting is very unlikely, but it doesn't hurt to be careful. That's why I asked you to grow a mustache and beard. You'll also have to wear glasses. As for the physical training, it is required for all workers in our section, no matter what post they hold. You know that. I hope that you will never have to use the skills you learn there. But you must have them. Does my explanation satisfy you? Oh, yes, one more thing. None of your friends or relatives in Moscow must see you before your departure. Is that clear?"

"Yes," Sharok replied. "Everything is clear."

※ **30** ※

Lyuda ate very little at breakfast and drank pickle brine
thirstily to counteract her hangover. She put on her coat and
told Sasha to be ready. She peeked out into the hall,
beckoned to him, and led him to her aunt Dasha's room.

"Come out in a couple of minutes. I'll be waiting for you around
the corner."

She had been right to be careful. A man was washing up in the
hallway, bent over a basin. The door to another room was open and
a woman was sweeping in there.

The man didn't look up, but the woman regarded Sasha with
curiosity.

Lyuda was waiting around the corner. They took the alley to
another street. Lyuda was subdued and there were dark circles
under her eyes. Catching Sasha looking at her, she said, "I have a
headache after last night. How about you?"

"I'm all right."

"This is where Elizaveta lives." She pointed to a new five-story
building. "Give me your passport!"

He gave it to her with some inner qualms.

"Wait over there."

She disappeared in the entryway. Sasha crossed the street and
paced back and forth, never letting the entrance out of his sight.

Lyuda's story last night did not surprise him. It was happening all
over the country. What surprised him was that she had talked about
it, something people weren't doing nowadays. And he had told her
about himself, although there was no risk for him. He couldn't hide
anything with his passport the way it was. But no one knew about

her father and brother and might never find out if she kept her mouth shut. Did she blab because she was drunk? No. Even when drunk, people could keep their tongues.

Lyuda came out.

"She'll do it, today, but she said she won't change the notation about restrictions. Neither she nor her boss would risk it. You'll get your passport for five years, but with the notation. Make up your mind."

Sasha thought. He had several months on this one. Maybe he might find another way to get it done. But if he didn't, then what? Would his relationship with Lyuda last? Would Elizaveta still have her job? And what if he left here sooner? He'd have to change his passport at the new place, where he would have no friends and would have to stand in line at the militia precinct and explain himself to them.

"What are you thinking about?" Lyuda said grumpily. "If you want to do it, give me your picture, I'll bring it to her, and you'll have your passport this evening. Hurry it up, she has to leave for work."

"I don't have a picture."

"That's what I thought. I even told her, 'He'll probably bring it tomorrow.' Go get your picture taken. I'll show you a place where they do passport photos quickly. Maybe they can have it for you tonight. And then go to the garage, talk to Leonid, find out what they have. Well, so long." She paused and then added, "If you don't get a place to live in the dorms, come to the café. I'm on until nine tonight."

The photograph was ready the next morning. Sasha headed straight for the precinct and turned the photo in with his temporary passport. Elizaveta looked at his passport, glanced at his picture in the usual, indifferent way, and said, "Come back tomorrow between ten and twelve."

She gave no indication that she knew about him. When Sasha came back, she handed him a new permanent passport. It had cost him one hundred rubles. Lyuda named the sum and Sasha gave her the money. But the passport did have the notation "Resolution of the Central Executive Committee and the Council of People's Commissars of the U.S.S.R. of December 27, 1932." That was the indication that he was banned from living in certain cities, the restriction in his passport.

Sasha had spent the last two nights at Lyuda's. He left with Aunt Dasha and came home late with Lyuda so that the neighbors wouldn't see him. He wandered around the city in the daytime, had lunch in a workingmen's canteen, visited the reading room. They wouldn't give him books or magazines because he had no documents, but the February newspapers were out on the table. He could read all he wanted. Sasha did ask for the January *Pravda*s and the librarian, a sweet elderly woman, got them for him.

It was all the same. "Double-dealers from the Trotskyite-Zinovievite den in Kiev . . ."; "Trotskyite followers in Khirgizia." There was even this — "Trotsky's son, Sergei Sedov, that worthy scion of his father, tried to poison a group of workers with carbon monoxide. . . . A rally of workers asked the NKVD organs to 'clean' the factory of that Fascist scoundrel. . . ."

Sasha remembered the talk in Moscow in 1929. When Trotsky was being exiled, his younger son, Sergei, refused to accompany his father. He did not share his views and chose to remain in the U.S.S.R. They said that on his mother's side his grandfather was the famous polar explorer Sedov and that Stalin, Ordzhonikidze, and Bukharin had given recommendations for Sergei to join the Party. And now, it turns out, he was poisoning workers.

More . . . Yezhov being hailed by workers, and an enormous portrait of Yezhov, a resolution of the Central Executive Committee of the U.S.S.R. giving Yezhov the title of general commissar on state security, and awards to workers in the NKVD. For their work in the trials. An editorial in *Pravda* entitled "The Lowest of the Low" on the Pyatakov-Radek trial. A rally on Red Square, when it was twenty below, at which Khrushchev, Shvernik, and Komarov, president of the Academy of Sciences, gave wrathful speeches and approved of the sentences.

He wondered what the people at the rally thought. Did they believe it?

When Sasha read the full account of the trial, he also felt disgust for the defendants, but on the other hand, where was the proof besides their confessions? They were involved in vast hostile activity throughout the country, got orders from abroad, and there wasn't a single document, a single letter; they were planning terrorist acts, and there wasn't a single gun, a single bullet.

*Show* — Lidya Grigoryevna Zvyaguro had liked that word. She was a wise woman. She understood everything. And he had argued with her when she said that Stalin was worse than a criminal, that he would kill if he had to. Her predictions were coming true.

Sasha returned the *Pravda*s to the nice librarian and asked for the *Literary Gazette*s for January and February.

And there were more demands for killing from writers.... Babel: "Lies, treachery." Tynyanov: "The sentence of the court is the sentence of the people." National poet Dzhambul: "A Poem about People's Commissar Yezhov." Lugovsky: "The Bloody Dogs of Restoration." Nikolai Tikhonov, Ilyuin, and Marshak: "The Path to the Gestapo." Andrei Platonov: "Overcoming Villainy."

All celebrities. A competition among masters to see who could write faster and tougher. Of course, he was no one to judge them. He had been living in a "sterile environment," as Vsevolod Sergeyevich had called it. And still, he wondered how they could look one another in the eye after articles like that? Did they look embarrassed and docile, or did they look triumphant? Were they thinking about what kind of an example they were setting for the people, or were they pretending that nothing at all had happened, that the weather was fine, their health was excellent, and the work was going well.... Well, and if Sasha had not been arrested and exiled and he were working somewhere in Moscow and he came home and told his mother that he had written an article called "Monsters" or "Bloody Dogs of Restoration" for the newspaper, what would his mother say? She would sit down, hide her face in her hands, and weep. How lucky he was not to be famous, so that if he were to do something ignoble, only a few neighbors and co-workers would know about it, and the rest was up to your conscience, whether you drank yourself to death or just went on living blithely.

All right, let's read on.

The newspapers were filled with attacks on managers who hired enemies — at the Amur Railroad one had hired a certain B., in another place, a certain M., and in a third, some guy named P. "In this regard," the newspaper wrote, "we must note the criminal system of hiring workers. They are taken without selection, without checking their backgrounds properly." That was meant for him, a direct order not to hire people like him. That was bad. He didn't know where it would lead.

In the entryway, a watchman got up from his stool and asked Sasha where he was going.

"To the engineer."

"Look in the shops, pass through the garage, and you'll find him."

In the yard under two long roofs were cars without wheels. Apparently there wasn't enough rubber for tires. Sasha went into the garage through the wide entrance. There was a smell of gasoline, acetylene, and exhaust. Two metalworkers were hard at it. The smell, the cars, and the repairmen in their oil-smeared shirts reminded Sasha of the years he had worked as a driver for the Dorogomilovsky Chemical Plant. His teacher there was Ilyushka, a wonderful guy and a kind soul.

In the mornings, practically at dawn, they left the plant and drove along the deserted embankments of the Moskva River.

"Slow down! Slow down!" Ilyushka would shout, "or I'll take over the wheel!"

As soon as Sasha would slow down, Ilyushka would relax and start talking about his fiancée. One day she had demanded that Ilyushka take her to Gorky Park to dance. Ilyushka had spent most of his life in the country and had never heard of the fox-trot. He didn't know how to dance, but he didn't want to admit it to her.

"Don't worry," Sasha promised. "I'll teach you."

They had come back to the plant's garage, which had only two vehicles, the director's Rolls-Royce and their truck. They pretended they had to repair the truck, locked the gates from inside, and started the dance lesson. Ilyushka was a natural folk dancer. He could kick in a sitting position and do other fine steps, but he couldn't get the plain old fox-trot.

Sasha would take his hands and command, "Step left ... step right ... And a one! And a two!"

Ilyushka stared at his feet and got confused.

"Look up, look at me!" Sasha demanded. "And a one! And a two!"

A few days later they dropped by Nina's house. Sasha borrowed the record player that belonged to Nina and Varya and their only record, which had "Rio Rita," a fox-trot, on one side and "Splashes of Champagne," a tango, on the other. And they locked themselves in again, cranked up the player, and Sasha commanded in time to the music, "And a one! And a two!"

Then Ilyushka showed up at work happy — he had taken his girl to the park, they had danced the fox-trot and the tango, even the rhumba, and his fiancée had praised him at first and then got jealous. "Who taught you?"

"And I told her, 'We have a special instructor at the plant, Pankratov is his name.' I praised you, said you were a good instructor."

After that Ilyushka stopped picking on him during their trips and helped him prepare for the exam and taught him how to clean out a carburetor and adjust the spark plugs.

It was a good time, he had worked with good people, and the memories warmed his heart.

Sasha found Leonid in the body shop. Leaning against a counter, Leonid was talking with Gleb, who was sitting on top of a truck with a brush in his hands, wearing paint-splattered trousers and jacket. Both recognized Sasha immediately. Gleb hailed him with a wide grin, and Leonid nodded and said, "Well, decided yet?"

"Yes."

"Bring an application?"

"Yes."

"Give it to me with your license."

Leonid read the application. He had already seen the driver's license.

"Wait here." He left.

Gleb jumped down from the roof of the truck and sat down next to Sasha on a bench. He took out a pack of cigarettes.

"Have a smoke, dearie, even though it's not allowed in here." They lit up.

"I'm finishing up the last one," Gleb said. "It's lousy work, but you know, dearie, I need the money. How about you, you need money?"

"Of course."

"Everyone does. Great men did dirty work. Renoir — do you know the name?"

"I do," Sasha said with a smile.

"Renoir painted dishes, and Kramsoki worked as a retoucher for a photographer, and Polenov — do you know Polenov?"

"I know Polenov, too."

"Polenov said it straight out — 'I don't see anything vile in painting signs.' He did signs, I do trucks. It's a different time."

Leonid came back, returned Sasha's license and the application with the shop director's decision. "Sign up as a driver in the second column.

"The second column," Leonid explained, "are the three-tonners, the ZIS-5s. When you get your second-class license, we'll put you on the bus. Now go over to the secretary's office. She'll do the paperwork."

The secretary was in the room outside the director's office, beneath the sign that announced his name — "Proshkin, N. P." She was typing.

Sasha put the application on the desk. Without taking her hands off the keys, the secretary looked over at him. "All right. Leave me a reference from your last job."

"I don't have one. I lost it."

She looked up at him.

"I've lost all my papers," Sasha said. "Rather, they were stolen." That sounded more believable.

Three other people in the room, two bearded old men and a girl in a sweater, looked up from the papers at the word *stolen* and turned their heads toward him.

"And your passport, too?"

"And my passport, too. I got a new one." He took it out of his pocket and showed it to her. "Just got it yesterday. You see the date?"

She furrowed her brow, then took Sasha's passport and application and went into the director's office.

Sasha worried about what that Proshkin, N. P., would decide.

He'd see the restriction right away. And refuse him. Why take on a dubious person? He could be accused of "lack of vigilance" later.

Sasha sat down on a free chair. No one paid any attention to him. The girl was clicking the abacus again, one old man was working the adding machine, the other was deep in the files.

The secretary came out and handed Sasha his passport. "The director said that we don't have any free trucks."

Sasha did not leave. He was thinking about what to do next. Go explain to the director? Leonid had told him that they needed drivers. That was pointless. He'd just be humiliated if he tried.

Sasha bumped into Leonid in the hallway.

"All done?"

"No, the director refused me."

"What? Come here, tell me about it!"

They went into Leonid's little office. The shelves held spare parts and instead of an ashtray, a butt-filled piston lay on the desk.

"What did he say?"

"I never saw him. His secretary went in, came out, and announced that they don't need a driver."

"What do you mean?" He gave Sasha a mean look. "I have six trucks sitting around without drivers and another six working only one shift!"

Sasha chuckled. "Don't get mad at me. I didn't turn down the work, I was turned down."

"Where's your application?"

"He has it."

Leonid swore and left the office.

Sasha was left alone. He could see the garage yard through the window, the drivers by their trucks, the puddles in the asphalt. Leonid wouldn't get anywhere. It was a waste of time.

Leonid came back looking grim, sat down, and after a silence, asked, "What were you in for?"

"Nothing, really. A silly story at the institute. They didn't like our newspaper."

"Hm ... But he has his reasons, too."

"No, he doesn't. According to the constitution, do I or don't I have the right to work?"

"You know what?" Leonid suggested. "Write to the head of the

Regional Automobile Directorate. His name is Tabunshchikov. He can settle a question like this."

Sasha looked at him thoughtfully. He had an idea ... should he risk it?

"Will you give me some paper?" He picked up a pen, pulled over the inkwell, and started writing. Leonid didn't bother him. He got up sometimes and went out to talk to the people who came by to see him. Sasha kept writing. He reread it, blotted it, and got up.

"What did you write? Let me see."

"Another time. I have to hurry now. Take it easy. And thanks."

At the trolley stop Sasha unfolded the piece of paper and read his application one more time.

> To the Secretary of the Oblast Committee
> Comrade Mikhailov
> From Pankratov, A. P.

Dear Comrade Mikhailov,

I am twenty-six years old. I lived all my life in Moscow, in House 51 on the Arbat. In January 1934 I was arrested and given three years of exile in Siberia under Article 58. My sentence is over and I was released without the right to live in major cities. I came to Kalinin, where I want to take a job in the city garage as a truck driver, but Proshkin, N. P., the director, refused to hire me, even though trucks are standing idle for lack of drivers. The constitution guarantees my right to work, but I am being deprived of that right. What am I supposed to do now?

> Respectfully yours,
> Pankratov

He should change one sentence. If Mikhailov saw him, he might ask, "Why did you decide to come to Kalinin?" He had to cover himself. He should have written "I came to Kalinin where I have relatives." But he couldn't add it now. It was too late. Let it be.

It was a desperate and probably hopeless step. But there was no other way out. If he left here, he'd have the same problems in the new place. But here he had a small fighting chance — Mikhailov might remember him.

\* \* \*

Downstairs, from the pass desk, Sasha called Mikhailov's office. His assistant answered the phone. Sasha said that he wanted to see Comrade Mikhailov.

"On what business?"

"Personal."

"Make an appointment."

"I'm leaving tomorrow."

"Make an appointment when you get back."

"Then let me give him this letter."

"Give it to the mailroom downstairs."

"Please, allow me to give you this letter personally. Believe me, it's very important."

"Name."

"Pankratov, Alexander Pavlovich."

"Do you have your Party card with you?"

"I'm not a member."

"Passport?"

"Yes."

Mikhailov's assistant was young, of medium height and chubby. He wore a semimilitary uniform and boots.

He stood up, looked through Sasha's application, and then looked at Sasha. Sasha suddenly thought that he had met this man somewhere. In his attentive gaze, Sasha read the same thing — Sasha's face was familiar to him and he was trying to remember where they had met.

"Give me your passport, please."

Sasha gave it to him.

"Have a seat." The assistant indicated the chair in the corner and went into the office, shutting the padded door tightly behind him.

The reception room of the secretary of the Oblast Committee was modest. It was outfitted with official office furniture and an official carpet runner. Between the window on the right was an enlarged photograph of Lenin reading *Pravda*, and on the opposite wall, also enlarged, was a photo of Stalin smoking his pipe.

Where had he seen that assistant? Maybe it was just his imagination. But the man had been helpful. He listened to Sasha, he gave him a pass, he took his application into Mikhailov. Nevertheless, there wasn't much hope of success.

At last, the assistant came out and shut the door carefully behind him. Sasha noticed that there was another door leading to Mikhailov's office beyond that.

Sasha rose to meet him.

Returning his passport, the assistant said, "Go to the city garage tomorrow. He will sign you up."

So, Mikhailov had remembered him.

## 31

Charles was cool when he heard about Plevitskaya's invitation. "Well, Ozoir-la-Ferriere is a pretty place."

"Are you against this friendship?"

He laughed. "I have nothing against Mme Plevitskaya. But her husband is too handsome."

Vika laughed too. She gave him no cause for jealousy and she was not jealous of Charles. She wasn't bourgeois. But there was a warning in Charles's words. Nelli called the émigrés beggars, but Charles was thinking of something else.

"If you don't think I should go, I won't."

"You've accepted the invitation, they're coming to pick you up, it's impolite to refuse. But try to be back by seven. I'll call from Prague."

He was leaving for a three-day trip that evening.

A new Peugeot was waiting outside. Vika could recognize car models by now. Skoblin put her in the backseat, got behind the wheel, and they went off, first on familiar, nearby streets, and then in the suburbs. Skoblin was grumpy and concentrating on his driving. He asked a few polite questions and sometimes named the places they were passing — the small village of Joinville-le-Pont, then Champagny, and in the Bois de Vincennes he showed her the spot where a truck had hit their car. The car was smashed to bits and they survived only because they were thrown clear. Nadezhda Vasilyevna got off with bruises and a slight concussion. She was back onstage in a week. He had a broken collarbone and shoulder blade.

"Everything healed," Skoblin said. "Sometimes I feel them in bad weather, but Nadezhda Vasilyevna is convinced that I am hiding my pain and gives me massages."

That was the longest sentence he had said. Vika could see that he was not interested in her as a woman.

Ozoir-la-Ferriere was another pleasant village, just like the ones they had passed — narrow streets, most of the houses two-storied with an attic, wrought-iron fences on the balconies, with shops or cafes on the ground floor. They passed an airy, tall church as they drove into the town. "St. Peter's," commented Skoblin and announced that they'd be there in about ten minutes.

The Skoblin's two-story house stood on the juncture of two narrow streets that came together at an acute angle. The facade with number 345 faced avenue Marshal Pétain. The walls were of gray stone, and had large windows, a tiled roof with chimneys, a filigreed concrete fence surrounded by shrubbery. There was a red path made of rolled brick dust laid through the green lawn. "Very nice," thought Vika. "And it must have cost a pretty penny."

Skoblin left the car at the gate, let Vika pass, and followed her up to the porch with the concrete overhang. The door was opened by a servant, and two dogs burst out from behind her and rushed at their master.

"This is Yuka," Skoblin said, pointing to the black dog, "and the white one is Pusik."

Plevitskaya, in a long and flowing dress that hid her weight, came into the entry. She kissed her husband, kissed Vika, and led her into the living room. Skoblin went upstairs.

"Nikolai, dear, we'll have coffee now," Plevitskaya warned him.

The living room took up the entire right side of the first floor. There were cats on the couch, and another cat — with black and brown fur — lay on an armchair. There was a large table, a fireplace, and upright piano. The windows had open yellow shutters, there were yellow curtains, and the furniture was upholstered in yellow — apparently, Plevitskaya's favorite color.

"I'll have to bring yellow roses next time," Vika thought. She noted that the house looked richer from the outside.

There were many photographs on the walls. Plevitskaya in a Russian dress, in a traveling suit, in a summer blouse in the garden, among her fans in different parts of the world; a portrait of General

Wrangel in a fur hat, of General Miller and General Kutepov; and in the place of honor, portraits of Chaliapin, Sobinov, Rachmaninoff, Balmont, each with an inscription — "To dear Nadezhda Vasilyevna," or "To the famous Nadezhda Vasilyevna."

"My friends," Plevitskaya said with a smile. "I look at them and they look at me."

Displayed prominently in the corner was the black and red banner, with bullet holes through it, of the Kornilov Regiment.

"Nikolai Vladimirovich is the commander of the Kornilovites," Plevitskaya announced proudly. "Do you know who they are?"

"Vaguely," Vika admitted. "Only from school."

"Nikolai Vladimirovich took over the Kornilov Regiment in November 1919 as a captain. He was twenty-five then, and by May 1920 he commanded the Kornilov Division, with the rank of general. He is the commander and I am the mother-commander. . . . If everyone in the White Army had been like Nikolai, the Bolsheviks would not be ruling Russia now."

Maria, the maid, brought in coffee, milk, and pastry and then returned with a bottle of red wine and wineglasses. Skoblin came downstairs with a briefcase. Everyone sat at the table. The dogs lay down nearby, their muzzles on their paws.

Nikolai Vladimirovich drank his coffee quickly and silently, rose, kissed Plevitskaya's forehead, picked up his briefcase, and bowed to Vika. "Forgive me, I'm late."

"Try to get back quickly, Nikolai," Plevitskaya said as he hurried out and turned to Vika. "Well, now we're alone."

She offered some wine to Vika.

"No, thank you," Vika replied. "I'm not used to drinking in the morning."

"What's the difference? Morning or evening, French wine is as light as water. I enjoy it." She poured wine into her glass and drank half of it. "Well, tell me about Moscow."

"What can I tell you?" Vika smiled and shrugged. "The metro was started up recently."

"The metro," Plevitskaya repeated scornfully. "In Paris the Métro has been running for thirty-seven years."

She called the cat that was in the armchair and put it in her lap.

"I miss Moscow, Vika. . . . In Moscow I used to sing at the Yar.

That was a very fashionable restaurant. Sudakov, the director of the Yar, did not allow actresses to go out onstage with décolletage. He said his customers were merchants and their wives and he didn't want anything indecent. I wasn't indecent, but I was very popular in Moscow. Muscovites loved me. From Moscow I went to the Nizhegorodskaya Fair, where Leonid Vilatyevich Skobinov saw me, presented me with a bouquet of tea roses, and said, 'You are a talent.' He invited me to perform in his concert at the Opera Theater. That was a long time ago, dear, in 1909. That's when it was."

She drained her glass, thought, and poured in some more wine.

"Ah, my dear Muscovites, I love them so much. They are kind and their voices are juicy. They speak real Russian. How can you compare them to Petersburgers, who speak French better than they do Russian? I remember there were two ladies who fastened their lorgnettes on me and examined me as if I were an object. And one asked, 'But what is a *kudelka*, what is a *batozhka*?'

"I was angry and I looked into her eyes angrily. 'A *batozhka* is a piece of kindling a husband uses to teach his wife when she is guilty. And a *kudelka* is a bundle of linen, combed and ready for spinning.'

"She looked at me through her lorgnette again. '*Charmant!* You are very sweet!'

"It's that aristocracy that destroyed Russia. It despised its own people, and that's what they got. Even here, I'll tell you the truth. I keep away from those glorious ladies. All they have left are their lorgnettes. They're as poor as church mice. . . . But let's not talk about them, or I'll get angry."

She splashed more wine in her glass.

"When I became famous I settled in Moscow, I took a good apartment in Degtyarny Alley, and while the apartment was being arranged, I rented furnished rooms on Bolshaya Dmitrovka. Do you know where that is?"

"Of course. I know Bolshaya Dmitrovka and Degtyarny Alley."

"That winter was very snowy. It was still snowing in March, covering the trees so that they wouldn't be cold in that wind, and beautiful Moscow stood like a silver tsaritsa in her snowy gown."

Vika looked down at her coffee and pretended to stir the sugar. The flowery speeches made her uncomfortable.

"I always loved Moscow in the winter. It seemed merrier in the winter. Everyone was in a hurry. The coachmen urged the horses on, the bells jingled.... Our years rush by as swiftly as the sleighs, but Moscow still lives in my heart, a sweet dream, a distant one.... And my heart also lives in Petersburg, in Tsarskoe Selo where I sang for the tsar himself." She paused, smiled, and looked out the window, like a good actor holding the pause and letting Vika appreciate the meaning of what she had said. "I was terribly nervous, I asked for a cup of coffee, a snifter of cognac, and I took twenty Valerian drops to calm me down.... And there I was before the tsar. I bowed as low as I could and looked right in his face and saw light pouring from his radiant eyes. My fear passed and I calmed down immediately. I sang and sang. The tsar even asked if I weren't tired. But I, dear Vika, was so happy that I didn't even think about it. I sang whatever came to mind, about the peasant's lot and even a revolutionary song about Siberia. I sang, 'I Remember, I Was Still Young Then.' And I sang the song about the coachman. Do you know it?"

"The racing troika?"

"No, I sang another song for the tsar.

> Here comes the troika
> Like an arrow from a bow.
> And the song flies in the field,
> Farewell, beloved Moscow!
> I may never see you again,
> My golden-headed one.
> I may never hear
> Your Kremlin bells.
> Nothing is forever in this world,
> And fate is taking me far.
> Farewell, wife, farewell, children,
> God knows if I will return.
> The troika has stopped, steam rising,
> The coachman is wiping his eyes,

> *And a pearly tear rolls*
> *Onto his chest.*

"And the tsar said, 'That song brought a tightness to my throat.' The tsar was very emotional about Russian songs. And when he said good-bye to me, he clasped my hand firmly and said, 'Thank you, Nadezhda Vasilyevna. I listened to you with great pleasure. I am told that you have never studied singing. Don't. Remain the way you are. I've heard many trained nightingales, but they sang for the ear, and you sing for the heart.' There, dear Vika, that was my great fortune in life — to hear such precious words from the tsar himself."

"Yes, yes, of course," Vika agreed, noticing that the wine bottle was half empty.

"I sang for the tsar at Tsarskoe Selo many times. I loved singing for him, and he loved listening to me. And he liked to talk to me, so much that the courtiers were offended and criticized me for gesticulating wildly while talking to the tsar. But the tsar didn't criticize me; he knew that I hadn't been taught high-society manners. And they killed a tsar like that! I'll never forgive them!" she said with hatred. "Never! If the tsar had lived in Moscow among the real Russian people, there wouldn't have been a Revolution, the Russian people would never let the Father Tsar be hurt. . . .

"I remember the festivities in Moscow for the anniversary of the Battle of Borodino. People filled the streets. They sang and danced and the sun glistened on the crosses and domes of golden-headed Moscow. And when Great Ivan tolled all the other churches, the forty times forty church bells, followed its lead, the earth trembled and tears came to everyone's eyes. Could a holiday like that be possible in Petersburg? Of course not. The city is filled with aristocrats, Germans, and other foreigners, and they're the ones who came up with this damned Revolution. Chaliapin, now that was a real Russian. Mamontov introduced us. Well, Fyodor Ivanovich Chaliapin said to me, 'May God help you, dear Nadezhda, sing your songs, the ones you brought from the soil. I don't have songs like that, but you, you come from the villages.' Yes, God sent many wise and kind people to cross my path."

A rooster crowed loudly under the window. Vika jumped.

Plevitskaya laughed. "We have more than cats and dogs. We have chickens, too. Nikolai feeds them himself." She rose. "You must be tired of listening to me. I must have bored you."

"Oh no," Vika protested, also getting up. "You tell such interesting stories."

She wasn't lying. It was interesting. This peasant woman with a third-grade education in a parish school, who had shaken the tsar's hand, had been reduced to a refugee by the Revolution, and had risen to fame once more....

"Thank you, then.... Come, I will show you our house, and then we can sit in the garden."

The winding wooden staircase led from the living room to the second floor. At the landing, over the wide, rounded step was a small window. Plevitskaya took Vika's hand. "See, right behind you is the forest, and here," she brought her face up to the glass, "Nikolai built a garage. When you have a car, you need a garage. There's a separate entrance to the kitchen. We don't even hear Maria when she comes in the morning. I usually get up early, but sometimes I have insomnia. All these thoughts keep me awake and I don't fall asleep until morning."

Skoblin's study had bookcases, with French books on some shelves and Russian on others — Turgenev, Dostoyevsky, Tolstoy...

"I used to love Tolstoy, but ever since I read *Destruction of Hell and Its Restoration*, I won't pick him up anymore. He's a nasty old man, covering everything with his spittle, attacking everyone. What do I need with that?"

The walls of the study were also covered with photographs — Kupirn, Bunin, Kerensky, and many generals and officers.

"Those are all our Kornilovites.... Nikolai was in five battles, and he was wounded many times. The Kornilovites did not spare their own lives. If everyone fought like the Kornilovites..."

Tears glittered in her eyes.

"The poor men. They are real heroes. I sang in the trenches for them. The Bolshevik cannons thundered, and I sang. But we didn't win.... I want to show you something."

She took a book from the bottom shelf, not thick but oversized, and opened it to the title page. "Sit on the floor, don't worry, it's clean. See — 'Dezhkin Karagod.' Do you understand the title? It's in our Kursk dialect. It means Nadezhda's Round Dance. And the introduction is by Remizov. An important honor! But you don't even know the name in Moscow. He's banned. He left Russia in 1921. . . . And here, that's my beloved mama, may she rest in peace." She kissed the photograph. "And that's me when I was young. A pug-nosed peasant girl. I'm still that same girl. And there's me again. Performing in a costume. And here's the second part, 'My Road with a Song.' That came out later, in 1930. Rachmaninoff published it. He had his own publishing house, TAIR — TA is for Tatyana, his wife, and IR is for Irina, his daughter. That's me in the country. There's my mother again. My whole life is described in that book. I'll lend it to you. Not this one. This one is mine. I don't give it to anyone. You see where I hide it?" She laughed. "As if it were diamonds. . . . I have two other copies, and I lend them to friends. As soon as I get one back, I'll give it to you."

Plevitskaya opened the door to the next room, which was modestly furnished. "Guest room."

In their bedroom there was a photograph of Skoblin, in his Kornilov Regiment uniform — a handsome, courageous officer, the St. George Cross on his chest, and the skull and crossbones embroidered on his shoulder.

"That's what Nikolai looked like in 1920 when we met. They were still battling against the Reds. We got married in Gallipoli in Turkey. It was a modest wedding, a few fellow officers and the best man, General Kutepov. Poor Alexander Pavlovich. He was kidnapped by the Bolsheviks, they tortured him to death. . . ."

She shed a tear. Opening a small cupboard, she got out a bottle of cognac, poured herself a thimbleful, drank it, and put the cognac away.

Beyond the bedroom, separated by an archway, was a small room, with a low table, a pouf to sit at the table, a bookshelf, a wide wardrobe, and a large mirror.

"My rooms," Plevitskaya joked. "I love this house, right from the minute I first saw it. It pokes out into the street like a flatiron. It's cozy here with a lot of light. The windows open on the north and east and west. We can see the sun rise and we can watch it set. I can't stand darkness. Or loneliness. Would you like to wash your hands? Here's the bathroom."

They put on coats and went out into the garden. The dogs followed, and the cats followed the dogs. Chickens were scratching around outside.

Vika and Plevitskaya sat down in wicker chairs under three birch trees. Even though it was February, it was almost warm in the sun.

"These birches," Plevitskaya said. "I planted them."

Maria came out of the kitchen, and Plevitskaya looked over at the table. Maria went back into the house and returned with the red wine, two glasses, and a plate of nuts.

"She understands me. Her name is Maria Cheka. She's Polish but grew up in France. We speak French. I can't stand Polish. All those hissing noises. And the entire GPU is Polish, Dzerzhinsky and Menzhinsky."

She poured wine for both of them. "Well, I hope you'll drink under Russian birches."

"Of course," Vika said with a smile.

"To Russia!"

They touched glasses.

"Yes," Plevitskaya went on, "we bought this house in 1930. A lot of Russians live here. This used to be forest land, and they cut down trees to build here, but I planted the birches." She touched one and caressed the bark. "You dear trees, whenever I see birches I think of our village Vinnikovo in Kursk Province, we had lovely birch groves.... Do you know," she said, her voice breaking, "I remembered your apartment in Starokonyushenny."

"Yes, that's what you said."

"In Carolina's I wasn't certain. I had just a vague recollection, but later I remembered exactly. Your father and your mother. Tell me," and she looked tense, "I want to check my memory. Was there a brass plate on your door with Professor Murasevich written in script letter?"

"Marasevich," Vika corrected. "Yes, there was a plaque."

"Are your parents alive?"

"Mother died twenty-two years ago, and Father is almost sixty. I worry about him."

"Sixty isn't old," Plevitskaya said coldly. "And worry will just jinx him. God grant he lives a long life. Well, Vika, it was Stanislavski who brought me to your house.... I sang there.... It was very pleasant, a house with real Russian hospitality.... Stanislavski brought me, and I took Klyuev with me. Do you know the poet Klyuev?"

Vika didn't answer.

"He was a quiet man," Plevitskaya continued, "and he often wept. He had only one shirt, a navy blue one, and he wore old, worn boots. I gave him a new pair, and he took them, but he never asked for things. He would sit quietly, tucking his hands into his sleeves. If he did speak, it would be something wise and full of pity.... Where is he now? I read that he had been arrested and sent to Siberia. Then he must be dead. Maybe that's why he wept so often, because he sensed his bitter end was near? You're not too cold?"

"No, I'm fine."

"Let's walk a bit."

They went down the street and the few passersby greeted Plevitskaya.

"There are almost two hundred Russian families here. Our church is named the Holy Life-Giving Trinity. We built it a few years ago. Nikolai and I donated a good deal of money to it, so I am considered a benefactress."

They came up to a one-story house that had a cross on the roof and an icon on the facade. That was the church. Inside it was dark and quiet, with burning candles and icons on the walls.

Plevitskaya bowed low, went over to the cross, kissed it, crossed herself several times, and whispered something. Vika followed suit. She did not feel anything, but it would be impolite to just stand there. This was her first time in a church, though she may have been taken as a child, but she didn't remember.

Plevitskaya prayed fervently and after they left the church, she said, "My late mother told me, when I was very little, 'In church you should have no other thoughts except prayers. You should stand like a candle before God in church.' She was an illiterate woman, a simple peasant, but what significant words she said — like a candle before God!"

Silently they walked. Then Plevitskaya returned to their conversation. "I love the church and the services. You've forgotten God in Russia now, and you yourself must have, too. Isn't that so?"

She looked at Vika severely.

"Yes," Vika said. "We were brought up without faith."

"That's not good. You cannot live without God in your heart."

## ❧ 32 ❧

The secretary at the motor pool was prepared. She demanded Sasha's passport and copied the information from it into a thick notebook, "Driving Personnel." Surname, name, patronymic, year of birth, education — Sasha replied "high school." She asked for a report from his last job.

"I already told you. All my documents were stolen."

"Then indicate your last place of work."

"I'll write to them, and they'll send you the report."

The secretary thought about it. She didn't want an empty space in the form. All the lines in the book had to be filled in.

"When they send it, bring it to me."

"Of course."

She looked at the last question. "Address?" She opened his passport again. "You're not registered anywhere. I can't do that."

"I thought I'd be offered the dormitory.".

The secretary got up and went to see the director. She came back. "There is no space in the dormitory."

Naturally. If they couldn't get him one way, they'd try another.

"I'll rent a room today," Sasha said. "I'll turn in my passport for my registration and then I'll let you know the address."

The secretary hesitated again. Sasha saw her quandary. She had a reason for not signing him up. But they had been given the order to sign him up. She didn't know what to do.

"Trust me," Sasha said. "I won't let you down. I'd leave my passport with you as proof, but I can't get registered without it."

"All right, all right. Give me your military card."

"I haven't served in the army yet."

She looked up at him and then went to see the director again.

This time she was in there longer than the first time. There was a telephone on her desk, an extension of the director's, and from the way it jingled, Sasha could tell that the director was calling someone.

She came out at last, sat down grumpily, moved Sasha's passport over, and stamped it with a rectangle, inside of which it said, "Working at Autobase No. 1."

"As soon as you get registered, go over to the military command, get on the draft list, and then come back to me. But now go over to the engineer and tell him that your work orders will be in today."

This time Sasha found Leonid in the shop. He was in the same position, leaning against the wall. And Gleb was still crouching on the roof of a bus, a brush in his hand.

"Hi!" shouted Gleb.

Leonid nodded silently and looked at Sasha.

Sasha took out his passport and showed him the stamp.

"I gave you the right guy to write to. I'll put you on a good truck. Look it over today. You start tomorrow at seven."

Gleb jumped down, wiped his hands, and said, "Dearie, this calls for a drink. You have to buy a bottle, Alexander."

"Fine."

"Let's go to Lyuda's or Hannah's," Gleb said. "Better at Lyuda's, we can have a good time."

"Fine."

Leonid took Sasha to meet the mechanic. He introduced himself formally — Khomutov.

"Give him vehicle 49-80," Leonid ordered.

The truck was parked under an awning.

"Look it over, then we'll sign the papers. You have no relief man. You'll be working alone. If you're missing any tools, tell me. I'll get them for you." With those words Khomutov left.

The tool kit was in place, but it was empty. The only thing left was the crank. There wasn't a spare tire. And the battery was dead.

Sasha told Khomutov.

"They cannibalized it, the bastards," Khomutov said. "Nobody's keeping an eye on it, so they stole everything."

He sat down at the small table in the corner of the garage, wrote out the request for tools, gloves, spare tire, and a new battery. Sasha got everything without trouble, but the engineer had to sign off for the spare, and he had to exchange the old battery for a new one.

As Leonid signed for the tire, he looked Sasha over from head to toe. "You'll get filthy."

"I'm not supposed to get a uniform?"

Leonid wrote on a piece of paper. "Warehouse. Release a jacket and trousers to Driver Pankratov temporarily."

"Thanks."

At the warehouse Sasha grabbed the old, greasy jacket and trousers. Cotton batting stuck out through the holes, but he was still grateful to Leonid. This way he could protect his only coat, sweater, and trousers.

Sasha changed in the cab, put the battery and spare tire in their place, started the motor, which worked well, and drove around the yard. The gearshift worked well too. The brakes worked, both the regular and the parking brake. There was a lot to do — wash the truck, degrease the engine and everything under the hood, add oil, lubricate the grease points. It was an old truck and had been neglected. He worked all day. He wanted to paint the hubcaps, but that would have to wait until next time.

Sasha worked with pleasure. His documents were taken care of. He was legitimate. All he had to worry about was housing and registration. That wasn't a problem. But he was worried about the military. He wasn't eligible for the draft — they had had military training at the institute, they studied "higher military training," and everyone who graduated was made a junior commander, now called a lieutenant. He had done the military training, but, of course, was never given the rank. He didn't know what would happen at the military registration office, so he wasn't anxious to go there.

The important thing was his documentation. If he had to get out of here, he wouldn't have to worry about getting a passport in the new place. He had one, and it was marked with a place of work.

If he hadn't gone to Mikhailov, he wouldn't have gotten it. Could Mikhailov really remember him? He had put his Moscow address in his letter to him — Arbat, 51. Or did he simply see the logic of the situation? The constitution guarantees the right to work. But he was a brave man! Sasha suddenly remembered his name — Mikhail Efimovich.

His assistant, that chubby fellow in the semimilitary uniform, had been to their building in the Arbat. Mikhailov's parents lived there and he had watched Sasha play chess with Motya, Mikhailov's younger brother. He made comments. Motya didn't like it, and once, when the assistant told him what move to make, Motya scrambled the pieces on the board — "I won't play with prompting."

Their father had a photo studio in their building. He closed it in the mid-1920s. Sasha recalled thinking about the reasons for closing the shop at the time. Mikhail Efimovich was a Party worker and he must not have liked having a father who was a craftsman. Craftsmen were considered petty bourgeois. Sasha's memories of that family ended there because they moved from the Arbat. Oh, yes — Mikhailov wasn't their surname. It was a Party pseudonym based on his name, Mikhail.

Gleb came out, dressed in a suit and a fur-lined leather jacket, a pilot's jacket, and was carrying an old shabby briefcase.

"Finish up, dearie."

Sasha packed the tools in the canvas case, changed, turned in the jacket, trousers, and tool kit to the storeroom.

"Afraid they'll steal it?" the clerk asked.

"The truck's been cannibalized. They're used to stealing from it," Sasha explained.

Then he and the mechanic signed papers stating that Pankratov, A. P., had received the ZIS truck number 49-80 in perfect condition and fully equipped. Khomutov signed the paper without looking at the car. If the driver had no objections, there was no reason for him to look.

Sasha found Gleb in Leonid's office.

"Go on ahead. I'll catch up," Leonid said.

Gleb talked all the way, and Sasha listened.

"You'll like Kalinin, dearie. Have you ever been on the Volga?"

"Never."

"I have a fisherman friend. We'll go visit him in the summer, spend the night, get up before dawn, when the fog is on the water, and you'll die, it's so beautiful."

"Isn't it a bit early to die?"

"All right, we can wait. Where are you living?"

"Nowhere. I need to rent a room."

"You'll find one."

"Do you know anyone renting one?"

"Damned if I do. I haven't heard of any, but I'll ask around."

"Be a pal, do that."

"I will, dearie, I will." Gleb looked around to see if Leonid was catching up. "Why don't we cross over to the store? They won't give us vodka at the café, only red wine. You have to bring your own. Lyuda will put some juice or something on the table and give us glasses. You know. There's the store!"

"How much should I get?"

"Four men, we'll put away two bottles."

"Who's the fourth?"

"Your mechanic, Khomutov. He's your main man now, dearie. And the first thing you do around here is provide a bottle."

Sasha went to the store and came back with two half-liters.

"Give them to me!"

Gleb put them in his briefcase.

Leonid caught up to them.

"Everything taken care of?"

"Fine," Gleb said. "Where's the mechanic?"

"Coming."

They went into the café and checked their coats. The man, who had shaky hands and a wino's face, knew them, but paid attention only to Leonid and hung his coat without a check number. As if to say, I know your coat, Leonid Petrovich. He gave Sasha and Gleb numbers.

Gleb went off to find Lyuda and then came back.

"Let's go."

Lyuda was setting a table for them in the corner. She smiled at Sasha. "I know, congratulations." She bent over and said, "I have good news for you, too; I'll tell you later."

She straightened and picked up her pencil and pad.

"Bring us a couple of bottles of mineral water, glasses, you understand, and we'll think." Gleb read the menu. "Well, dearies, do you think herring will do? And then cornichon pickles, am I doing the right thing or what? Chops. . . . We know those chops. They chopped it off the pig and gave it to us. Schnitzel? That would be better. Sasha take a look, you're the host."

Sasha took the menu typed on a piece of thin paper.

"How about some sausage too?"

"That's fine."

Lyuda came over with the glasses, plates, knives and forks, and two bottles of Narzan mineral water. She cautioned them, "Just be careful."

Sasha ordered herring and potatoes, boiled sausage, and schnitzel.

"Your treat?"

"Who else?" Gleb replied for him. "He's started his job and now he's looking for an apartment."

"He'll have an apartment," Lyuda said with a mysterious smile.

"Then we'll celebrate the apartment too," Gleb decided. "All right, Lyuda, come on, give us the herring at least, we're dying for a drink."

"Here comes Khomutov," Leonid said.

The mechanic Khomutov sat down at the table and started talking about trucks with Leonid.

"We have to separate them," Gleb said, "or they'll start a production meeting here."

Leonid and Khomutov paid no attention to him.

Gleb winked at Sasha and moved closer to him. "Russians don't know how to have fun. They spend all day at work on their problems, they get together over a drink and all they can talk about is work. It makes my ears droop. And yet this Khomutov, I have to tell you, just had a son, and before that they'd been waiting ten years for a baby. Khomutov didn't dry out for a week, he was celebrating so hard. So why can't he talk about the baby, how he suckles his mother's breast, how Khomutov is trying to get his wife pregnant again, with a girl this time. Citizens!" Gleb struck his glass with a fork. "Attention, let's drink with the Narzan at least!"

They drank.

Gleb moved over toward Sasha again. "Dearie, I'll bet you a bottle — no, two bottles, if you like, or more. I can tell you exactly what they are going to talk about. First, they'll complain about Proshkin, then, they'll complain about Proshkin, and third, they'll complain about Proshkin, our director. Did you ever see his mug? You will. He and Leonid are like cats and dogs. He doesn't know a thing about cars. He used to run the bakeries. The pirozhki, the little pies, were being stolen. He'd have people baking all night and only empty pie pans to show in the morning. They took him off that job and sent him to the motor pool. You can't steal a whole truck. It's too big. The pirozhki were little, two bites and it's gone. Am I right, Leonid?"

Leonid mumbled something in response.

"And of course, this makes Leonid mad. He's an engineer and a Party member, he knows the job, and his boss is a jerk. I was in his office once and he was sitting there howling like a dog at the moon. I swear! That's what Proshkin is doing to him."

Sasha laughed.

Lyuda brought the herring and potatoes and set down a platter of sliced sausage.

"Tell me when you are ready for the hot food." She bent over toward Sasha. "Sasha, there's a room right near here, our coat check has one."

"At Egorych's," Leonid said. "That would be good."

"It's a semibasement, but dry. You have to pass through their room to get to yours. The owners are Egorych and his wife, an old woman. They want thirty a month, pay two weeks in advance. Laundry's extra, of course. They give you boiling water. And if you need something cooked, she'll do it."

"It's a good apartment," Leonid said again. "And the owners are good people. They drink, of course, but who doesn't nowadays. And when they get drunk, they don't make noise. They're peaceful people."

*"We're peaceful people, but our armored train is standing ready...,"* Gleb sang.

Sasha hadn't heard that song, either, but he kept quiet about it. He kept quiet a lot now.

"Sasha, how about it, should I tell them yes? If you think too long, someone else will get it."

"I'm not thinking at all. I'll take it."

"Agree to having your laundry done, but you don't need the cooking. You can go to the canteen," Leonid said.

"Well, enjoy dinner." Lyuda patted Sasha on the back.

The mechanic saw her hand and shook his head. Then he went on talking. "They're using me," he complained, looking at Sasha, trying to draw him into the conversation. "He keeps giving me trip vouchers to sign, even though I can see that they're phony. You can't make that many trips. But I sign. If they ever catch on, who's going to be in trouble? Me. 'Why'd you sign?' they'll say."

"There they go, off on their favorite hobby horse," Gleb said with a sigh. "No, these Russians just don't know how to have fun. Why is that, dearie?"

It was obvious. When a man is being squeezed from all sides, trapped by circumstances, he's not very playful. Sasha would have discussed that with Vsevolod Sergeyevich, but it was better to keep quiet about it here with Gleb. Maybe he had posed the question for a reason, and was waiting for some revelations.

"I don't know," Sasha said with a smile, "I never thought about it."

Lyuda came over and called Sasha to the coatroom.

"Egorych," Lyuda said, "here's your new roomer."

The man gave Sasha his hand. "Alexei Egorych."

"Lyuda told me the terms. Here," he said, handing Egorych fifteen rubles. "May I move in today?"

"We should clean up first," Egorych said, pocketing the money.

"He'll go to the train station for his things while your wife cleans up."

Sasha went back to the table.

"We've killed them." Gleb opened his briefcase and showed the two empty bottles. "Let's get another, dearie. There's still time, the store is open."

"The store may be open, but we're closing," Lyuda countered. "You drank two bottles, that's plenty — you'll be in fine shape." She put the bill on the table.

Sasha paid.

Everyone got up.

"Leonid," Lyuda said, "take Sasha to the apartment."

They went outside. Khomutov went home, and Leonid and Gleb

took Sasha to the house where he would be living. They went down five steps to the semibasement. The old lady opened the door. Sasha couldn't see her face well in the dull light.

"Here's your roomer, Matveyevna," Leonid said.

"Ah, Leonid Petrovich, welcome."

They were in a big room divided in half by a plywood partition, and an old curtain hung in place of a door. Low, dirty ceilings, decrepit furniture, filth and neglect, kitchen smells — the stove was in the front part of the room. It wasn't very attractive, but it was a place to live.

"Yes," Gleb said. "The Hotel Luxe."

The landlady showed him the cot in the back room.

"You'll sleep here, and you have a table and there are stools. I can bring you more from the shed if you need them. And this I'll clear away." She nodded at some rubbish. "I'll sweep up and it will be clean and nice."

"Fine," Sasha said. "I'll go to the train station for my suitcase, and you clean up."

"An advance would be nice," the old woman muttered without looking at Sasha.

"I gave the advance to Alexei Egorych."

The old woman was unhappy. "Why did you give it to him? He'll just get drunk. He's fed at the café, so what does he need money for? Give it to me, the way Leonid Petrovich used to."

"I'll pay you in the future," Sasha said.

Sasha said good-bye to Gleb and Leonid and went to the station to get his suitcase.

When he returned, Egorych was home.

"Good night," Sasha said, going to his half of the room.

"Sleep well," they replied.

The cot now had a pillow and a coarse soldier's blanket. No sheet or pillowcase. He'd have to buy them himself.

Sasha undressed, put out the light, and lay down. He pulled the blanket over him. It was scratchy, but he fell asleep almost instantly.

His mother would be waiting for his call on Sunday, so he should really call Varya before then.

"Hello."

He recognized her voice right away.

"Hello, Varya, it's me, Sasha. Can you hear me?"

"Yes, yes, very well," she replied in a hurry, as if she were afraid they would be disconnected. "How are things with you?"

Her voice was tearing his heart apart.

"Everything's fine. I'm working as a driver."

"I'm so sorry that I didn't see you when you were in Moscow."

"It is too bad. But you must know, Mother must have told you what my situation is with Moscow."

"Of course, I know everything. But Kalinin isn't far. I could come to see you."

Sasha hadn't expected that at all, and he didn't know what to say. But he had to say something.

"You see . . . I don't have a place yet."

"But we could sit at the railroad station. I checked. There's a morning train out of Moscow and an evening one back."

"That's impossible," Sasha said. "I work all day and sometimes I have long hauls. By the way, I will be going to Moscow, too. I'll let Mother know, and you give her your office phone number, and then we'll see each other."

She was silent.

"Hello, hello? Varya, you've disappeared."

He could barely hear her voice and he thought it was because of the line.

"Yes," she said at last.

"That's better. When I get to Moscow, I'll call, and then we'll meet. All right? You and Mother will come to wherever I'm unloading the truck."

The operator's voice came on the line, "Your time is almost up."

"Just a minute more! Varya, did you understand?"

In a depressed voice, she asked, "Is there anything else you want to tell me, Sasha?"

He didn't have time to reply.

The operator came on again. "Your time is up."

# ☙ 33 ❧

Sasha had not answered her question. He had nothing to say. He was avoiding any meeting. He couldn't forgive her for Kostya. He didn't know a thing about him and it was like a bolt out of the blue. She hadn't written about Kostya, that's true, but what did she write to him? Nothing special. And he didn't write anything special to her. It had all been between the lines, comprehensible only to the two of them. Sasha loved her. She had felt it, she hadn't been fooling herself. She remembered New Year's Eve, the Arbat Cellar, and the way he had looked at her. You don't forget that. And you don't forget the prison lines. She had written in every letter, "We're waiting for you." Waiting.

Despair hit her. Why had Sofya Alexandrovna told him about Kostya? Didn't she understand that Varya loved Sasha? Now it was over. And because of what? Kostya . . . Oh my God! Such nonsense! She was a girl then, and confused. She had been stunned by the way Sasha walked to his doom between the guards. He looked so pathetic and meek. It was all so terrible, so grim, and she sought a way out of that grimness. She dreamed of independence. She thought that Kostya could give it to her and she went with him. The fool. It was her protest against everything that was happening around them, against what happened to Sasha.

Then she saw that Kostya's independence was a myth. He was a gambler and a scoundrel to boot. And Lyova and Rina were dubious characters, sponging off Kostya. Igor Vladimirovich wasn't like them, of course. He was a talented man, but he had seemed too insignificant at the meeting where he was being inducted into the union, a sheep, and everybody else looked like frightened sheep there too, all those famous engineers and technicians. Only Sasha was a real man, and that's why she respected and loved him.

And it was over. Before the telephone conversation she had hoped, she thought she'd go to Kalinin, at least talk to him at the station, tell him that she loved him, honestly and openly tell him about Kostya. Sasha would have understood and forgiven her. But he put off their meeting, he had made up his mind and rejected her. It was over. All over. My God! How could she go on living? What for?

Mechanically she went to work, mechanically she went into the metro, went to the institute, and came home. Sometimes without taking off her coat she would sit down and look at photos of her parents. She didn't know much about them. Her father had died of tuberculosis at the age of thirty-two, and her mother died a year later, even though she hadn't been sick. "She died of a broken heart," her mother's sister said. "He took pity on her and took her to be with him." Varya was very little and didn't understand what her aunt meant. "Where did he take her?" "Up there," the aunt would say, looking at the sky. Varya wanted to be in the sky, too. "Why won't Papa take us there?" "Because you're happy here, you'll live for a long time. They take people up there who are unhappy here." And now Varya would die of a broken heart like her mother.

Sofya Alexandrovna called. "Varya, I've been worried. Where have you been?"

"Sofya Alexandrovna, I have urgent work that I had to bring home. As soon as I finish it, I'll drop by."

"Did Sasha call you?"

"Yes, he did. Everything is fine."

"There, I told you," Sofya Alexandrovna said happily. "Come over soon. We'll talk all about it."

But there was nothing to talk about. Sasha would not be calling her, either from Kalinin or Moscow. She did not hear joy, or anxiety, or excitement in his voice. Friendliness, artificial heartiness. A formal call. Sofya Alexandrovna must have asked him to do it, to cover up her guilt.

And still, a very distant little voice told Varya that if Sasha took the news of Kostya so badly, then he must love her. And if he loved her, then not everything was lost. She just had to see him, talk to him. But how?

Only Igor Vladimirovich noticed her depression. He kept circling around it and finally came straight out. "Are you upset about something, Varya? You look tired. Why don't you take a week off?"

"A week?" Varya was thrilled. That's what she needed right now. She'd be able to go to Kalinin, to see Sasha. But where would she find him? He hadn't given his address even to Sofya Alexandrovna, asked her to write to general delivery. She grew glum again. "No, it's not worth it, Igor Vladimirovich, but thank you. I just have a headache. I must be coming down with a cold."

"Varya's got a cold, she's not feeling bold," Lyova put in childishly. He was even more talkative than usual of late because Igor Vladimirovich had got him and Varya the title of senior technical constructors. But Rina was still a technical draftsman.

"Why don't we go to the Metropole Sunday night?" Lyova suggested. "Revive the past?"

Varya hadn't been in a restaurant in two years.

She had assumed that in such horrible times, when people nightly waited for that knock at the door, when every family had members who had been arrested, exiled, or shot, it would never occur to anyone to have a good time in a nightclub, to dance and flirt and show off their clothes. They must have all been closed.

"The Metropole? It's still functioning?"

"Why not?" Lyova smiled sweetly. "It's all the same, the bar, and the jazz. There's music, singing, and dancing."

"And what's the occasion?"

"Miron's party. Remember Miron? That nice guy with curly hair."

"Kostya's friend?"

"Well, like all of us."

"What's the party for?"

"He's turning thirty and he wants to have a party with the old crowd."

"Have you kept up with him?"

"Of course. We're friends."

"Who else will be there?"

"Who else ... Me, you, Rina ... Vika's abroad. She left a long time ago, about two years." He switched to a whisper. "You must have read in the papers, Willie Long's father, the one who worked in the Comintern, turned out to be a German spy, and the whole family was exiled."

"Why are you whispering? You just told me that it was in the papers," Varya said and laughed at him.

"Yes, but we shouldn't mention that we were friends."

"What about Big Volya and Little Volya?"

"They've disappeared. I haven't seen them in a long time."

"I won't run into Kostya, will I?"

"Kostya? Don't you know?"

"What?"

"He's in the Taganka Prison."

She should have known.

"For what?"

"Varya, you know what he was up to."

"No I don't, and I don't want to know."

"Right. I don't know, either. His commercial stuff, the lamps and patents, and taxes. And the billiards, probably."

"By the way, you and Rina lived very well off that commercial stuff. You might have taken an interest in the fate of your comrade."

"A good lawyer is going to defend him, but he wants a lot of money, more than I have. Kostya's promises to pay are worthless."

"Do you bring him parcels?"

"When? You have to spend the day in line, and Rina and I are at work."

"You're his friends. How can you abandon him?"

"There's nothing we can do. We're helpless, you know that." He smiled placatingly. "What are you so upset about? Kostya will get out of it."

Varya didn't care about Kostya's fate. She never doubted that he'd end up in jail. But you don't abandon a friend in need.

"So will you come?" Lyova asked. "Miron really wants you to. And you decide about your friend Zoe."

"I'll come alone," Varya said.

"We're meeting exactly at seven in the park across from the Bolshoi Theater. We'll go to the Metropole together. Miron's already made a reservation."

It wasn't the old Metropole. The crystal chandelier still sparkled, and the starched napkins still stood at each setting, and they still dimmed the lights when the orchestra began, and they still illuminated the fountain and the dancing couples with colored lights, and the same majestic maître d'hôtel presided, and the same courteous waiters seated them. But the crowd was different. There were respectable-looking men, bosses, some in uniform, some in suits. There were doubled and tripled tables, banquets for a group of Georgians or Armenians. There weren't many foreigners, and the few present were surrounded by officials. Apparently they had come there after business meetings. No glamorous women in expensive gowns, no beauties like Vika, Noemi, or Sheremetyeva. But there were prostitutes, dressed like ordinary Soviet working girls, and a few real working girls with their dates, out-of-towners in embroidered shirts and boots. They were letting people wearing boots into the restaurant now, and they even danced in boots.

Their table was set with wine and vodka. Miron had ordered an assortment of smoked fish, inexpensive main dishes, and ice cream. The way they used to do it — young people here for the dancing. They wouldn't order much, but they'd leave good tips. It was what they'd done in the past. But Varya could tell that Lyova and Rina were still steady customers. And Miron even more so — a curly-haired, friendly businessman — and he was still disappearing and returning, keeping things vague. That was from the past, too.

When they sat down, a small group of four, Varya realized that she had been invited in order to talk about Kostya. They were all his friends, and Miron was his partner to some degree. He had often called him and in the restaurant he used to come over and whisper about things.

"Well, shall we have a drink?" Miron proposed.

They drank. And the meaningless chatter began, just like the chatter of two years ago. Rina, with her red hair and freckles, grew animated and pretty. Her eyes were sparkling. She wasn't made for the drafting shop. And Lyova was in his element, enjoying life. He drank with pleasure, ate with pleasure, and he'd dance with pleasure as soon as the music started. And Varya thought that people needed so little to be happy. Why couldn't she be as happy as they?

Miron smiled at Varya as if they were old friends, when actually they had never spoken more than two words to each other. And they had nothing to say now, but obviously, he wanted to talk to her.

The music started. Lyova and Rina went off to dance.

"Well, what's up, Varya?" Miron began with a friendly smile.

"Up? The sky is up."

He scratched his nose and moved the glasses on the table. "Listen, Varya, we need to help Kostya."

"Specifically?"

"He needs a lawyer."

Varya did not reply and waited for Miron to speak.

"Did you understand me?" Miron asked. "He needs a lawyer."

"So what?"

"Lawyers cost money."

"How much should I make out the check for?" Varya joked.

"Don't you feel sorry for Kostya?"

"Not in the least. What do you want from me? Tell me!"

"I told you, Varya. He needs a lawyer. He needs money."

"Am I supposed to find a lawyer or give money?"

"I have a lawyer. I need money."

"But you know perfectly well that I have no money."

"You have things that can be turned into money."

"Who told you that?"

"Kostya."

"What did he tell you?"

"I didn't see him, but he got a note out. Here it is."

He pulled a scrap of newspaper from his wallet. On the border, written in Kostya's hand, was *"Varya, sell everything of mine for the lawyer. K."*

Varya put the note on the table.

Miron reached out for it. "Give it to me!"

"Why? It's for me."

The orchestra stopped playing and Lyova and Rina came back to the table.

"Let's drink to Miron," Lyova said. "Miron, are you really thirty years old?"

"Just imagine it, pal. And you'll be thirty soon, too."

Lyova raised his glass. "To you, Miron."

"Wait a minute," Varya said, setting down her glass. "Wait! Miron gave me a note from Kostya." She took it out from beneath the plate. "It says, 'Varya, sell everything of mine for the lawyer.' What's that supposed to mean?"

No one said a word.

At last Rina shook her head and said, "I don't know anything about it."

"Neither do I," Lyova added quickly.

"Aha, you don't know why I was invited here. For Miron's birthday, allegedly. Fine. But you've seen that it was Miron who gave me this note."

"I didn't see who gave it to you," Rina said with a shrug.

"Really, Varya," Lyova said gently, "Rina and I were dancing and we don't know what you were talking about here."

Varya turned to Miron. "Do you admit giving me this note?"

Miron replied after a hesitation, "No, I didn't give you anything."

Varya put the note in her purse. "Then everything's fine. The issue is resolved. We can drink now."

Miron took a sip, put down his shot glass, drummed his fingers on the table, and looked up at Varya. "You have to understand that Kostya needs help."

"So help him."

"Cut the crap!" Miron was unexpectedly harsh. "If you think you can blackmail us with the note, it won't work. We don't know anything — you got the note, you found a way to correspond with Kostya. So you can tear it up or flush it down the toilet. You're the only one who will get into trouble with it. Yes, I gave you the note. Yes, Lyova and Rina know about it. But if you turn us in, we'll deny it, we'll deny everything. They'll believe us. It's three against one. We were just pals with Kostya, you were his wife. The note is addressed to you, not us."

Rina sat with her head down, Lyova was looking around insouciantly, the way he did when he was looking for a dance partner.

"Now I get it," Varya said. "Of course, it's what I thought. I was mad, I thought you were *fine friends* leaving your benefactor in trouble. I see that you're not abandoning him. But you want someone else to pay. Me. What things am I supposed to have, I wonder. His suits, shoes, rifles, maybe?"

"He's talking about the things he gave you," Miron said. "Lavrov made your coats, and your dresses were made by Lamanov, and your shoes by Barkovsky. Those were the best tailors and best shoemakers. You could sell them."

Varya started to unbutton her blouse. "Shall I undress here, or tomorrow at work?"

"Varya, don't be like that," Lyova said placatingly.

"You're right," Varya said and adjusted her blouse. "Especially since this blouse is mine. Now remember, Miron, and remember well. And you, too. You remember it, too — when Kostya and I divorced, I left everything I had, absolutely everything, except my bras. I still have one and I'll give it to you if you want. Not right now, of course."

"Why lie to him?" Miron asked. "He needs a lawyer. Kostya is looking for money and he thinks that you can sell some things. If you really had left everything, he wouldn't be wasting time on you. He's a businessman. He wouldn't look for money where there's no money to be found. He doesn't have time for games. The trial could be any day."

"I can't help him."

"Fine," Miron said in a menacing way. "That's just what I'll tell him."

"Just skip the threats. I'm not afraid of them. Kostya must be confusing me with one of his fancy ladies. He'd better get it right. There'll be plenty of time in prison to remember."

A young woman with a painted doll's face and long bleached hair rolled up a cart of candies, oranges, cigarettes, and flowers, and said in a childlike voice, "Would you like anything, young men?"

Varya saw the woman look scared when she realized that Miron was at the table. Miron gave her a stern look and said, "We don't need anything."

"Excuse me." She moved away.

Varya watched her go.

"Why are you looking at her like that?" Lyova asked.

"I was wondering what made her take this job."

"What's bad about it?" Rina asked sincerely.

"Pushing a cart over to bunches of drunks and humiliating herself. Couldn't she find anything else?"

"She could," Rina said, "for a hundred fifty rubles a month. She makes thirty a night here. How old do you think she is?"

"Twenty-five, twenty-six . . ."

"How about forty?"

"Forty?"

"Yes," Rina said. In a lower voice she continued, "Her name is Anya, she's been working here ten years with that little cart. She graduated from the conservatory or the Genssin School of Music and ended up in the restaurant orchestra. She quickly figured out that she would make ten times the money she was getting plinking the violin."

"Her job in the restaurant costs a colossal amount of money," Lyova said.

"What do you mean it costs money?"

Lyova and Rina laughed at her naïveté. Only Miron was silent. The music started again.

"Varya, let's dance."

Varya hesitated. Did Lyova want to talk to her?

Varya got up and preceded Lyova to the dance floor. They were playing her favorite tango. She had danced with Sasha at the Arbat Cellar to that tango three years ago. My God! Three years! No matter what Sasha said, he was always in her thoughts. And this was Kostya's gang. They obeyed him even if he was in prison. They were doing what they were told. What did he want from her? Did he think she would get money for the lawyer? Nonsense, he knew that she had no money. Or did he really think that there were clothes left to be sold? It was his criminal background. Every woman who had been with him before had to take care of him now that he was in prison. He thought his reach could extend that far. Well it couldn't! Miron was Kostya's pal. Rina had been Kostya's mistress. But Lyova? Sweet, helpful Lyova? Not him, too? He was dancing with her, leading her around the fountain, a handsome young man with the face of an angel, Lyova, with whom she had been working for the last two years. She thought she knew him through and through. Could he have been involved in dirty dealings too?

And she asked, "What do you have to say about this?"

"Don't give me away." Lyova was smiling sweetly and it looked as if they were exchanging pleasantries. "You won't? Promise?"

"I promise. Word of honor."

"Miron has to get Kostya out of prison, otherwise the trial will reveal things that will put Miron behind bars, too. He needs a lawyer. He doesn't have enough money and he's approached all of Kostya's friends, his billiard companions, all his girls. He even demanded money from Rina and me. Do you know how much he got from that poor Anya?"

"Which Anya?"

"The one with the cart."

"Kostya had her, too?"

"That was after you. So Miron is looking for money everywhere."

"Doesn't he have any himself?"

"No. They tried to buy their way out. They put up a lot, but it wasn't enough."

"What is Kostya charged with?"

"Some kind of work at some institute, a big contract. They split it with someone, and someone else denounced them. A filthy deal, basically. That's why Miron is trying so hard. He could end up in prison himself."

"Well, you tell Miron that he should try elsewhere. And he should leave me alone. And you shouldn't have brought me here."

# ✥ 34 ✥

Sergei Alexeyevich was given ten years without the right to correspondence. Fenya told them about the sentence. She wailed and screamed in the kitchen. Her ranting was unbearable. Vadim would have been able to take it, if not for the thought that it was all too close to home. Sergei Alexeyevich — Fenya — their house. People might find out about his role; Sergei Alexeyevich might tell his wife and children through someone who got out of the camps.

Vadim walked on the Arbat in fear now, and approached his entrance with even greater fear. He expected one of Sergei Alexeyevich's sons to be lurking there, ready to hit him. He feared Sergei Alexeyevich's sons most of all. Two big men, the older one a plumber. Fenya always called for him, even though the building had its own plumber. The other son was an elevator repairman, also a big fellow, and he had been a hoodlum as a teenager and was no better now. His name was either Kolka or Vitka. If they heard anything from their father, they would kill Vadim for sure!

The best thing would be to fire Fenya, so that there was no reminder of Sergei Alexeyevich. And it was no longer safe to keep her, anyway. But how? His father was attached to her. She knew his tastes, fed him well, took care of the laundry, and was basically a member of the family. His father would never agree, even though finding a replacement would be easy — after the mass arrests of the Party and government elite there were lots of unemployed people, including well-trained servants, wandering around Moscow.

But his father wouldn't hear of firing Fenya.

"Understand me," Vadim said. "That barber is a relative of hers, so they could come for her, too. And who knows what she might say about us out of fright? Vika is in Paris, we have foreign visitors, many of your patients have been arrested and even shot. So why take the risk? We're not going to toss her out onto the street. She's an experienced servant, she'll find a job instantly. And we'll find a new one, just as qualified."

"I'm used to Fenya, I trust her, and I do not wish to have a new person in the house."

"In these times a new person is a thousand times better than an old one," Vadim insisted. "She could always say, 'I've just started working for them and don't know anything.'"

"No, no, no," Andrei Andreyevich said stubbornly. "I will not give in to panic. I want to have peace in my own house at least. Half the doctors who had treated Lenin and Stalin at the Kremlin hospital have been arrested — Levin, Abrikosov, Pltenev. These are honest decent men, wonderful specialists. Tomorrow they could fabricate a case against me. You go to work with only one thought — that they will announce who was arrested last night. And you learn the most incredible things. I repeat, I want peace and quiet. I am used to Fenya, she is loyal to us, and I do not wish to have a new person."

"As you please," Vadim said with a shrug. "If you have made that decision, then fine. It's easy for you, Father, you leave early in the morning and come home late at night. You're at work all day. But I work here in the house, and having to listen to Fenya's keening or her stupid conversations on the phone with Sergei Alexeyevich's wife, the tears and mourning, interferes with my work."

Andrei Andreyevich looked at him angrily and then said, slowly and clearly, "You above all should at least leave people the right to their own suffering."

What was he trying to say? Aligning Vadim with those in power and expressing his dissatisfaction with the authorities that way? In essence, the alienation between them had happened a long time ago, either when Vika got married and Vadim threatened to change apartments or when Vadim wrote the article about the Chamber Theater.

Of course, he knew that the article was not pleasant for his father.

But you have to be fair — if you don't like that your son's pen serves the regime, then break off relations with Nemirovich-Danchenko, too. Don't Nemirovich-Danchenko and Stanislavski serve the regime, or weren't they the ones who showed the death of the old class and the triumph of the new in *Days of the Turbines*? And why did his father go to the rehearsals of *Man with a Gun* with Pogodin? He hadn't been to the theater in several years, but he didn't refuse Pogodin. And he gabs on the phone with Mikhail Romm, and Vadim had seen parts of Romm's film *Lenin in October* at Mosfilm and was amazed. How can you falsify history like that? Of course, no one had any shame anymore. Everyone was praising Stalin. Among the simple folk it had become fashionable to drink the first toast to Stalin and only then to the birthday boy. And that was right and reasonable. And in that sense he was no different from the rest.

Had his father heard something? Impossible! Yet, he did act as a consultant at the NKVD clinic, and perhaps one of the bosses hinted something to the effect that your son is a fine man, we're pleased with your son ... Expressed thanks. Treated him as one of them — since the son was, the father had to be, too. ... We trust you. We've arrested all your colleagues at the Kremlin hospital, but we left you alone. ...

Or did his father run into one of the boors, who, infuriated by his father's old-fashioned politeness, said something like — don't act so stuck up, old man, your son helps us, and you do your work and treat us, too. And his father would have realized that Vadim was on good terms with the NKVD. And that would not have pleased him. As for every decent man of the old style, the NKVD meant the police, the gendarmes, the Third Division. Any ties with that organization were unacceptable, indecent.

Of course, the news must have upset him. He brought him up, and a good boy had been turned into an informer. Then he should feel sorry for his son, who was in a mess, in a catastrophe. It was the good and kind ones they were breaking now. His father had been living in this state for some time. He should know that no one cooperates of his own free will with the organs. So feel some pity! His father had become cold and cruel. It was a bitter thing to do, but nevertheless, he had to make one last attempt to make him agree.

"Father," Vadim said. "Let's not argue, let's discuss it calmly.

You know that I'm not a coward, but you can see what's going on. It's like a sandstorm blowing across the land. If you're slow today, it may be too late tomorrow. Would I have even brought up Fenya six months ago? But now, after those trials, I'm afraid, afraid for you, and afraid for me."

Andrei Andreyevich said nothing. That was a good sign. He must be vacillating.

"I have no one in the world closer than you." Vadim's voice shook. "You know, I never told you this, but I barely remember Mother. All my memories are of you. I do remember Mother making jam at the dacha; I was sitting near her, and a wasp stung me. . . . I remember her rocking me in a hammock. . . . I thought she was taller than you, was she?"

"No, we were the same height."

"I remember when Mother was in her coffin and the mirror in the hallway was covered with a black scarf and I was afraid to go in there. . . . And then that horror Vladislava Leopoldovna came to live with us. It was so hard to say her name. I preferred not to call her anything."

When their mother died, Vladislava Leopoldovna, a distant relative of their father's, was brought in to bring them up. Her bed was placed in his room and that immediately set Vadim against her. Exactly at eight, not a minute later, she put out the light. She forced Vadim to sleep on his back with his hands outside the blanket.

"Why do I have to sleep like this?" he asked. He liked sleeping with his hands under his cheek and curled up.

"So that you don't develop nasty habits," Vladislava Leopoldovna explained.

He didn't understand.

In the morning she watched him brush his teeth. "You're the oldest. You have to set the example for your sister." Then they went for a walk and she made them walk next to her. Then they had lessons, Vika drew and he had to make words with blocks. If he was lazy or made mistakes, she punished him.

Fenya saved him. Bringing carrot juice for the children, she came in the room once during their studies. She saw Vladislava Leopoldovna twisting his ear. She shouted, "Why are you deforming our child? He's not used to that!"

Sustained by Fenya's support, Vadim burst into tears, fell to the floor, stamped his feet, and threw up. Fenya must have told his father, because when they got back from their evening walk, the bed was gone from his room, and Vladislava Leopoldovna went back home forever.

"By the way, how was she related to you?"

"Third cousin," his father said with a smile.

His smile encouraged Vadim.

"You think I'm less attached to Fenya than you," he began again. "But it's not true, I'm very attached to her. But there come times when reason must prevail over feelings. We are living in complex and difficult times. We cannot deny the successes of socialist construction. They are visible to all. But we must not deny the imperialist threat. It is natural — the first socialist state in history, the only one in the world, is surrounded by enemies. . . . That is the cause of all our excesses. . . . 'You have to break eggs to make an omelette —' "

"No, no, no!" Andrei Andreyevich exploded. " 'Imperialist threat,' 'break eggs to make an omelette.' . . . I do not want to hear ever again that Fenya has to look for another job!"

Vadim had not seen his father that angry in many years. He rose to go to his room.

"Sit down, I'm not through." Andrei Andreyevich got his breath back and looked directly at his son. "Naturally, I thought about what would happen to you if I were arrested. And I came to the conclusion that I didn't have to worry. In that sense you are standing rather firmly, and so, I hope that cup will pass you by."

# ❧ 35 ❧

In December Sharok moved to a dacha outside Moscow, where he studied French with the same teacher and the special training with another instructor. Every two or three days he received fresh newspapers from Paris and books selected by Speigelglass, as well as materials on ROVS.

Not too far away was the ski club of the Locomotive Society, and they had set up cross-country paths. Yuri spent two hours skiing right after lunch. There were two Chinese men, a Vietnamese, and a European, maybe a Swede or Norwegian, living at the dacha. The Chinese and the European spoke English, Yuri practiced his French on the Vietnamese; all four spoke Russian poorly. They met only at meals. Arvid, the Scandinavian, not his real name of course, went skiing with him. He was very good at it, while Yuri hadn't been on skis in over ten years and couldn't keep up with Arvid. He'd wave him on — don't wait for me, go ahead. Arvid would rush off and soon disappear into the trees.

The ski path led to a meadow out of the woods and then followed along the railroad. The dull winter sun shone above. You could hear the trains pass, and then it would grow quiet again. Yuri enjoyed skiing and often stopped to breathe the fresh, cold air. He'd stand there, leaning on his poles, thinking. . . .

The last conversation with Speigelglass seemed to clarify the situation. But Sharok couldn't decide if he was happy with his transfer to the Foreign Section or not. Of course, Yezhov had sent him there for a reason. He wanted to replace someone. But they needed an agent for every position in the section. Even if it was a desk job in Moscow, it still needed a professional. Compared to them, he was a pawn, with zero qualifications. He could make mistakes easily, and real agents would use his mistakes, and a mistake could mean his head in this business.

The clouds parted, the snow sparkled, and Sharok turned to face the sun, pushing his hat back from his forehead and squinting. . . .

Life was good. . . . But it was also filthy and distorted, and covered with shit. . . . The sense of danger suddenly filled his heart.

His other job was harder, but there he was destroying the people he had hated since childhood, the people who had destroyed Russia — the Old Bolsheviks, the so-called Leninist Guard — and at the same time all the Jews, Latvians, and Poles who had made the October Revolution. He was destroying them in the name of the Revolution and the Communist Party, but that wasn't the point. The point was that he was destroying them. Of course, there were almost no Russians in the Foreign Section. Jews, Latvians, Poles, Germans, Romanians, and, among the agents, Spaniards, Scandinavians, Frenchmen, and Englishmen. And now he would be fighting with those Jews, Germans, and Poles against real Russians. Because ROVS was made up of Russians. They were naïve and stubborn, but they were Russian. And he would have to fight them, there was no way around it. They were stupidly picking a fight. And with whom? With the state! Let them die!

Before Sharok left for the dacha, workers in Molchanov's and other sections were being arrested. They weren't mass arrests. For the time being, they were arresting individuals, but it had begun. This made Sharok anxious. He had not forgotten how the Kirov affair ended. Everyone was swept away — the guilty and the innocent, and not only witnesses who knew or had heard about the affair, but even those who might have guessed. There were no witnesses left. But they weren't bothering the Foreign Section. The work here was subtle and special. They weren't involved in actions like the Kirov affair. They had other interests. The Kutepov case? That was an exception. So if he made no mistakes, he was safer here. Is that why Yezhov had him transferred there?

And suddenly Sharok had a flash of insight.

"Look around." That was what Yezhov had told him. "Watch how the old cadres work. Keep your eye on them." Not the "senior

comrades," not the "experienced agents," but the "old cadres." He
was supposed to replace someone in the Foreign Section, but before
that happened Yezhov would demand a report on the work of the
"old cadres." That's why Slutsky and Speigelglass were so wary of
him. Naturally, they were planning protective measures. Before
they allowed themselves to be destroyed, they would try to destroy
Sharok. So that's the crossfire he was in!

All right, we'll see! Sharok pushed his hat back on and went
forward on his skis.

And so he lived at the dacha. . . . He called home rarely, saying he
was in Kaluga on business, to ask about his folks. He called Kalya,
whom he truly missed — that was the hardest part — and promised
to be back soon.

One day a tailor from the NKVD came to measure him. He spent
a long time fussing.

"We're going to make you a suit."

The only unpleasant part was not shaving. He looked slovenly in
the mirror and felt itchy. But that would disappear with time and
in another week or so he'd have a real beard. His mustache had
grown in quickly. It was thick and soft. He liked it.

In the middle of March a car came to the dacha and the driver
found Sharok. "You have orders to pack your things and come to
the office. I will drive you."

Speigelglass was waiting for him in his office. Sharok didn't
notice if Speigelglass had pushed a button or not, but a man in
civilian clothes came in — a barber. He cast an appraising eye on
Sharok, then gave a number to Speigelglass, which Sharok didn't
hear, took a pack of cards from his pocket, spread them out before
Speigelglass, and pointed to one of them.

Speigelglass bent over to look at it and then looked at Sharok.
"Fine!"

The barber swept the cards from the desk and put them back in
his pocket.

"Go with the comrade," Speigelglass said. "He will take care of
your beard."

When he got out of the barber's chair in the small shop, Sharok
looked at himself in the mirror — a handsome blond in his thirties,

with blue eyes, his hair parted on the side, a reddish mustache not stained by tobacco, and a small, neat beard. Young liberal industrialists, lawyers, and fashionable physicians looked like that in the old, prerevolutionary magazines. Sharok chuckled with pleasure. He looked older, but he liked the way he looked.

The barber was also pleased with his work and walked him over to the tailor — the fat, vile Pole who had come to the dacha. The suit was ready for a fitting. The tailor made chalk marks and pinned things. As he took off Sharok's jacket, he said, "It will be ready the day after tomorrow."

Sharok's look satisfied Speigelglass. "When you get your outfit, including the shoes and glasses, you will be photographed. Now, look at this."

He opened the desk drawer, took out a file, and handed it to Sharok.

"This is the file on our agents in ROVS. I'm leaving now. You will remain in my office and read these materials. Do not answer the telephone. So no one disturbs you, I will lock you in. If you need the toilet, here it is."

Speigelglass turned the knob on what seemed to be a bookshelf and it turned out to be the door to the toilet.

He looked at his watch. "I'll be back at five. Of course, you realize that you must not make any notes. Try to remember the basic points."

The lock clicked.

Sharok sat down and opened the file.

It was the file on agent YEZH-13, code name "Farmer," General Nikolai Vladimirovich Skoblin, deputy chairman of ROVS in Paris, and his wife, the famous Russian folksinger Nadezhda Vasilyevna Plevitskaya, code name "Farmer's Wife."

## ❧ 36 ❧

Sasha didn't get to meet with his mother and Varya in Moscow. Several of their trucks were sent to Opochka in connection with the hundredth anniversary of Pushkin's death. They held the drivers' passports in exchange for passes, but Sasha's passport was returned. He was not allowed to go into what was an official border zone. That meant he wouldn't be allowed into Moscow, either, as the dispatcher explained to him. And then he gave Sasha a sympathetic look, as he tried to cheer him up. "Don't be sad. It'll work out."

"Who says I'm sad?" Sasha said.

They were rubbing it in. But in nothing else did Sasha suffer discrimination. He worked without a relief man, which was better, because he could repair things himself. Waiting for the motor pool mechanics was impossible, and even if you bribed them with a small bottle of vodka, they'd do such a lousy job that you had to redo it yourself anyway.

Sasha at first did turn for help to the electrician Artyomkin. His name was Volodya, he was a skinny, stoop-shouldered guy in glasses. He did good work, read a lot, and was collecting a library. But he spoke too frankly about things, and so Sasha avoided talking to him. He would say with a chuckle, "Come on, Volodya, more work, less talk."

The work varied. It depended where they sent you. Most often it was from the brickyard to the river port. Now that the Volga-Moskva Canal was opened, ships could go to the capital.

Sometimes he went out of town. Highway work was better — you could rack up more mileage. But Sasha was rarely sent onto the highway. The "in" group went, the ones who were friends of the dispatcher and the mechanic. They went to the best places — the warehouse, the meat-processing plant, the bread factory, the bakery, the liquor-bottling plant. They came back with little packages for themselves — there was always a little something. They were also transferred to the new trucks, given new tires, days off, tours to vacation spots, and titles as shock-workers and Stakhanovites.

The same thing held waiting on line. If you didn't complain about the delays, they would credit you with all the trips you were supposed to have made and didn't, even add an extra one, though you may have hung around half the day waiting or driven around with an empty truck.

Sasha kept away from all that. He didn't get involved, he kept quiet at the mandatory meetings, and he didn't add trips he didn't make. That's why they kept sending him to deliver bricks and cement. It was dirty work, but his conscience was clean.

Where did all the featherbedding come from? It hadn't been like that before. People knew their work. Now the managers were incompetent, and their subordinates began cheating, losing self-discipline, losing their conscience.

Even good people did it, not openly of course.

One morning before his shift, the blacksmith Pchelintsev came up to Sasha. It was at his house that Sasha had spent his first evening in Kalinin.

"Pankratov, why are you letting me down this way?"

"What?"

"You've been working here for three months, and you haven't joined the union. You're not paying your dues. They checked my list. All I have is people in arrears, and you're not even on there at all."

"I lost my union card, I told them that when I was hired. I have all new documents, including my passport."

"Why didn't you inform the local committee? They would have given you a new card."

"Didn't have the time."

"You don't have the time, and I get the heat."

"I'm sorry."

"You need to be readmitted to the union. You've dropped out.

And then I'll get into more trouble." He thought a bit and then said quietly, "You write a declaration that you've lost your documents, that you informed the director, and got a new passport. And you lost your union card. What union were you in?"

"Communal workers."

"Since what year?"

"Since 1929."

"Well . . . that's what you should write. You lost everything. And date it from when you started work. Hear me?"

"I heard you. I'll do it."

"Do it now and give it to me. And I'll put you in from that date and stamp your book. Write down how much you earned each month, February, March, and April. You'll get your ticket tomorrow. But not a word to anyone. Hear me?"

"I hear you."

The next day Pchelintsev handed Sasha a union card with stamps glued in for three months. And he was credited with membership since 1929, just as Sasha had said.

Of course, he had to give him a bottle for the favor.

Sasha called his mother once a week. He didn't call Varya. After their one conversation, after her words, "Isn't there something else you want to tell me, Sasha?" he was confused. She expected him to say, "I love you." But he couldn't say it. It had all died out after his talk with his mother. He remembered with shame his wild jealousy, the despair that he couldn't handle. He hadn't been interested in the past of other girls he had been involved with. Katya had told him that she was going to marry some mechanic — fine, go ahead. But this girl, the kid sister of one of his classmates, whom he had seen only because they lived in the same building, made him jealous. He thought he had dealt with it. He thought it was over and he had freed himself of his love for her. But he hadn't, and his pain and suffering burst forth during that conversation. Otherwise he wouldn't have been so taken aback by her offer to come to Kalinin and sit with him at the train station. "That's impossible!" He had betrayed himself with his stupid excuse — "I work during the day." As if she didn't? She fell silent after his "impossible." She understood. And then at the end, she asked, "Is there anything else you want to tell me, Sasha?" This was strange, beyond comprehension. She had gotten married, had lived in his room with her husband, had slept in his bed with another man. She had loved her husband. Let's say she fell out of love, let's say.... And she instantly fell in love with Sasha, who was off doing time. Fell in love with him without seeing him. That just didn't happen. And if it did, then it wasn't love, but fantasy, the same thing that had happened to him. But his love had been nourished by her additions to his mother's letters — "How I'd like to know what you are doing now"; "I'm alive, working, and missing you"; "We're waiting for you." Plain words, you didn't have to look for hidden meanings in them. But when he wrote to her, he weighed every word. He was afraid that his feelings would bind her or be misunderstood. She couldn't have found anything at all in his letters except for "dear Varya." That meant she was spinning fantasies. How old was she? Sasha calculated. Twenty. Of course, twenty is a romantic age. You can imagine a love for an exile, wait for him, and then rush to him. Just fantasies, nonsense.

Still, he couldn't forget Varya's voice, but he'd get over it. He would and she would. And with time the phone conversation receded from his mind, and he was less and less upset that he had not spoken the right words to Varya.

But one night, in June, he had a strange dream.

The militia were banging on the basement door and demanding that the old couple tell them who their roomer was.

"Hide in the trunk," Matveyevna said.

"How can I hide in the trunk?" Sasha laughed. "I'll never fit." He laughed and laughed, and they kept banging on the door. But now it wasn't the militia, it was a woman asking to be let in. Varya.

In the morning, as he poured boiling water into his mug, Sasha asked, "Matveyevna, I dreamed about you last night."

"Oh, dear, what was it?"

Sasha told her his dream.

"The girl who was knocking wants to be with you. She's trying hard. Did you get into the trunk or not?"

"No, of course not."

"That's good. But the laughing is not good. It's an omen, be careful."

The old woman jinxed him. That morning Sasha was sent on a long haul, to Ostashkov. He was driving fast when the steering wheel tore out of his hands, and the car went off the road. He was lucky that it didn't end up in the ditch. He had had a blowout.

He got out of the cab, wiped his forehead, and took out the jack. He wanted to change the tire right away, but his hands wouldn't obey him. He sat down on the grass and chewed a blade. He sat a long time, unable to concentrate. Trucks passed and stopped. Drivers jumped down and offered to help. He waved them off. "I'll manage."

He had never believed in omens, and certainly not in dreams, but the old woman had warned him to be careful. Maybe she was right about Varya, too.

Sasha changed the tire and drove on. "She wants to be with you." The old woman's words agitated him, and his thoughts went racing off again. He was building castles in the air again. He had forgotten how he had suffered in the train thinking about Varya. Enough. He couldn't pay that much attention to her words, or her voice, and it was certainly ridiculous to believe dreams.

Sometimes after work Sasha dropped by the café. Sometimes Lyuda was on duty. She smiled at him and waved, but she didn't put him at her table. Sasha would eat and leave. If she was nearby, he'd say good-bye. If she wasn't, he'd leave anyway. Once he came in with Gleb, and Lyuda put them at her table, fed them, and they paid and left. Lyuda had been friendly, but she made no effort to stop Sasha.

Maybe she had someone visiting her, relatives perhaps. Or they had noticed Sasha at the apartment and she was afraid to bring him over. Later he figured it out — she didn't want to continue their relationship.

There was nothing surprising in that. Even back at the smith's house, when she moved away from him upon guessing that he had been in prison, Sasha saw that she was cautious. The story of her family didn't fit in with her caution. But maybe that's why she was being extra careful now.

Fine! She was nice and their relationship had been good, and she had helped him out in a hard moment in his life. The passion had come and gone. It was just an affair for both of them, and both had known it from the beginning.

And he didn't have time to think about Lyuda. He was driving all day. He usually did at least a shift and a half. He overfulfilled the plan. And then between shifts there were rallies and meetings and political hours. Sasha tried to avoid them, made extra trips, came back late. After a haul he had to fill out paperwork, wash the truck, and make minor repairs — it wasn't a new machine — and then shower and change. There was the whole evening. The café would be closing.

Sasha didn't make friends with anyone at work, and he maintained a connection only with Gleb. Gleb had finished painting the buses and had gotten paid. He paid off Leonid, who had gotten him the job. "Don't worry, we'll find more," Gleb said. "Work isn't a wolf, it won't run off into the woods." He was a fine fellow. He was upset that the winter had passed without Sasha seeing him ice-skate. He claimed to have won the region's first prize two years ago, but he didn't show his prize to Sasha. He played the piano and the bayan and adored the singer Vadim Kozin.

He would play a few chords and imitate Kozin, singing and drawing out words. Without taking his fingers from the keys, he would look over at Sasha. "Do you feel where that's coming from, dearie? How could anyone resist that? Not any single woman, I assure you."

Sasha would laugh.

Gleb would play on the old upright piano, which had little white elephants along the embroidered runner on top and a loose pedal attesting to the instrument's age. His landlady was just as aged, his own aunt, a precise, clean little old lady with frightened eyes. Gleb was very formal with her and took her by the elbow when she peeked into his room and seated her in the armchair. She liked listening to her nephew sing.

The house was old, but neat. Everything was locked. The front door had a huge hook and the gate was latched. She was afraid of thieves and hooligans. In the yard, surrounded by a tall and ancient fence, were neat rows of vegetables.

Gleb had many friends, but he didn't invite anyone home, except Sasha. He could drink anywhere — a coffee shop where you

couldn't have liquor, or with his feet dangling from the embankment parapet, in a store with a stranger taking turns with the
bottle — but he didn't drink at home. When Sasha brought a bottle
over one night, Gleb shook his head.

"No, dearie, I have a rule. Not a drop around auntie. Why don't
I sing for you instead? Something *à la* Vertinsky?"

He had perfect pitch and could imitate very well.

"Listen, Gleb," Sasha would say. "You could perform in public."

"I can do everything," Gleb replied seriously. "Watch."

He showed Sasha his sketches for the sets for *Hamlet, Beautiful
Helen,* and *Krechinsky's Wedding,* which according to Gleb had been
praised by Akimov. He rested the pages against the back of a chair,
stepped back, cocked his head, and looked at them.

Sasha liked them. They were beautiful.

"Right," Gleb agreed without false modesty. "I was in love with
a woman then, and you know, dearie, all talent, inspiration,
mastery, it all comes from that. . . . Creative energy is the rechan-
neling of sexual energy. There you are, dearie! Love is the source of
inspiration."

"Especially in Repin's *Barge Haulers,*" joked Sasha.

"Dearie," Gleb cried, "don't be like that. You have to understand
my thought. Potency is the basis of everything, that's what I'm
saying. When the potency ends, so does the artist."

"Titian lived to be a hundred and worked until he died."

"So?"

"He was potent until the age of a hundred?"

"Dearie! My grandfather married at eighty-two and had three
sons from that marriage. Titian, my dear boy, died of the plague.
And if it weren't for the plague, he would have gone on for years.
And what about Raphael? Yes, Raphael! Who is a greater painter
than Raphael? No one! And he died at thirty-seven. Of what?
Overwork? No! All the great artists worked like oxen. Even though
they say that Raphael died of a cold, don't believe it, dearie, they're
lying! Raphael died of sexual exhaustion in the arms of his
Fornarina. He was a wild and temperamental man, and he overdid
it. And Korovin would throw down his brushes and jump on his
models. And what about Brullov? Or Delacroix, the aristocrat, who
had stomach trouble all his life and was always groaning and

moaning, but he didn't let a single model pass, not his own, not anyone else's."

Gleb knew dozens of similar stories, and he liked to tell them and he liked to drink when other people were paying. He was stingy, but he hid it with smiles, jokes, and raptures. An easy guy! He didn't ask questions and never had bad things to say about people. He apparently knew something about Lyuda, but he said nothing. But he gabbed and lied and laughed, and embraced Sasha. Yet as soon as the conversation turned to a subject he didn't want to discuss — politics, for instance — he immediately shut up and then changed the subject to something else. And began laughing, joking, and lying.

One time, rummaging through his papers, he showed Sasha posters from the Leningrad Drama Theater, with Akimov as the designer of *The End of Krivorilsk, Armored Train 69*, and *Tartuffe*.

"I thought he staged plays in Moscow," Sasha admitted.

"There was a time when he did in the late twenties and early thirties. But do you know what he's doing now? He's artistic director of the Leningrad Comedy Theater. So there!"

So, Gleb didn't lie about everything.

Once he brought Sasha to visit his friends, in a decent home. On the way he sang the praises of the daughters of the house. "Madonnas! Notice their bearing! You won't be able to stay on your feet! They're colossal!"

Sasha, however, easily stayed on his feet.

Two anemic maidens with braids to the waist, with round brows and intelligent eyes were happy to see Gleb and were polite to Sasha. They dragged them to their room to show off their latest acquisition. It was a copy of *Rossia* magazine with Bulgakov's *White Guards*.

"Dearies!" Gleb was truly astonished. "To be able to find that nowadays — amazing!"

"Have you seen *Days of the Turbines* at the Moscow Art Theater?" the younger one asked Sasha.

"I did, but I was only fifteen. I remember that Yanshin played Lariosik."

"Is it true that Yanshin is married to a Gypsy?"

"I don't know."

They were called to tea in the dining room.

Two elderly ladies were at the table, and on the table was sugared jam and homemade shortbread baked for the occasion.

Then they made music. The maidens played "Autumn" from Tchaikovsky's *Seasons* in four hands, and at Gleb's request they also played Schubert and Chopin. Gleb did not approach the piano, but he smiled and made sweet jokes.

Coming home, he was in raptures. "What wonderful people! The highest class of intelligentsia! Where can you find people like that anymore? Only in the city of Kalinin. They live modestly, but did you notice the tea service? From the Imperial Porcelain Factory."

Sasha didn't know anything about porcelain, but he said something nice about the family, even though the girls had left him indifferent.

"Why don't you get married?" he asked Gleb.

"Married?" Gleb was truly surprised. "Are you crazy, dearie? An artist marry?"

Another evening they bought some vodka and went to visit some other friends of Gleb's. Two women in their thirties, salespeople at the stationery store, hospitable and merry, who put out lots of zakuski to go with the drink. They drank. Gleb took a guitar, tied with a red ribbon, from the wall, strummed and sang a bawdy song.

He sang it well. But the saleswomen protested. "None of that."

"All right," Gleb said, and sang a love song.

Sasha listened and watched. Gleb was singing about Varya and him. Oh, God, he had never felt heartache so badly before. He wanted to go home to Moscow, to the Arbat. He wanted to see Varya and hold her. Damn it all! He couldn't live without her, and the hell with the gambler. What did the ex-husband have to do with him? He had hurt Varya, he had. That's why her voice was so sad at the end of their conversation.

Sasha got up and said his good-byes. Gleb went out with him. He said grumpily, "Well, we're not going to make hay with you around." Then he smiled. He couldn't stay angry long. "Do you want to be an anchorite all your life? 'What the fuck is that?' you're supposed to say. Do you know?"

"I do."

"But I'll tell you, dearie, you missed it today. Those women are willing. It doesn't matter that they're saleswomen. They're not picky in bed. You can do what you like and they'll even thank you for it afterward."

Sometimes they went to the city park. Music was playing and the girls who worked at the local factories stood around the dance floor. The new Western dances had only reached the provinces, and Sasha, who knew them from years ago, danced them well.

He saw a young woman who moved well and he asked her to dance. She was slim and flexible, and it was a pleasure to dance with her. People watched them. The jazz reminded Sasha of the Moscow of the Arbat Cellar and New Year's Eve, and he thought of Varya, who was as slim and light as this unfamiliar blonde. He asked her a few more times to do the fox-trot, the tango, the Boston waltz, and the rhumba. She didn't know all of them, but she was quick and responsive.

"Dearie," Gleb said. "You're a terrific dancer. Colossal!"

Gleb nodded at Sasha's partner, who was standing with a girlfriend and looking expectantly at Sasha. "Shall we see them home?"

"I'm not in the mood."

"You're being picky, my dear. All right. Then let's go, I'll introduce you to Semyon Grigoryevich."

"Who's that?"

"Our chief choreographer."

"What do I need with him?"

"He wants to meet you."

"What does he want with me?"

"Dearie, this is getting tiresome. He likes the way you dance."

"What the hell do I care?"

"Dearie, he's my boss."

"How so?"

"He teaches Western European dances, and I am the accompanist."

"Then let's go."

They crossed the dance floor and went over to the bench on which sat a large man of fifty, with carefully tended black hair, wearing a dark suit, white shirt, and bow tie. His hands were resting on the head of a cane. He rose slightly to greet Sasha, an elegant and stylish, sophisticated maestro.

"I want to compliment you. You dance wonderfully. Did you study somewhere?"

"No, nowhere."

"You have a natural ability and you lead confidently."

Sasha smiled. "I do my best."

"Come to our classes," Semyon Grigoryevich invited. "Gleb, bring your friend."

"I will," Gleb promised.

## ✂ 37 ✂

So, Agent YEZH-13, code name Farmer, was General Nikolai Vladimirovich Skoblin, one of the leaders of ROVS in Paris. The agent with the code name Farmer's Wife was General Skoblin's wife, the famous singer Nadezhda Vasilyevna Plevitskaya.

Sharok read the file several times.

Nikolai Vladimirovich Skoblin was born on June 9, 1893, in the city of Nezhin to the family of a retired colonel. In 1914 he graduated from the Chuguev Military School and joined the army with the 126th Pulsky Regiment. He distinguished himself in battle against the Germans and Austrians. After the October Revolution the young captain, then commander of the Kornilov Regiment, fought against the Reds in the northern Caucasus, and in May 1919, was appointed commander of the Kornilov Division, joined up with the volunteer army of Mai-Mayevsky, and attacked Moscow.

Nadezhda Vasilyevna Plevitskaya was born January 17, 1884, in the village of Vinnikovo, Kursk Province, into the family of the peasant Vasil Abramovich Binnikov. His eleventh child. Her devout mother gave the child to the Trinity Convent in Kursk. She ran off from the convent with a traveling circus, sang in a café chorus, moved to a ballet company, where she married the dancer Edmund Vyacheslavovich Plevitsky. With time she became one of the most popular performers of Russian folk songs and traveled all over Russia. She sang for the tsar. After the Revolution, in the summer of 1918, she sang for Red Army troops, and the newspapers hailed her as the "worker and peasant singer." She ended up in Odessa.

When the Reds retreated from Odessa, she was captured by the Kornilovites on September 4, in the village of Sofronovka.

Sharok noted that throughout the World War and the Civil War, details of Plevitskaya's life were not clear. There were many men — a new fiancé, Captain Shangin, then the Bolshevik Shulga, then her second husband, Captain Yuri Levitsky, then commander of the Second Kornilov Regiment Colonel Pashkevich.... There was only one precise date — September 1921, Gallipoli, Turkey — her marriage to twenty-eight-year-old General Skoblin.

Skoblin and Plevitskaya left Gallipoli for Bulgaria, where on September 1, 1924, General Wrangel announced that the White Army was being transformed into ROVS. Skoblin retained his rank of general and commander of the Kornilovites. Then, there was a vague period again — Bulgaria, tours for Plevitskaya in the Baltics, Poland, and Czechoslovakia — and then Berlin. After Berlin, all the information was exact and clear. In Berlin Skoblin befriended the wealthy businessman Mark Yakovlevich Eitingon, the brother of NKVD General Naum Eitingon. Plevitskaya's career was flying high abroad. She and Skoblin traveled all over the world — Brussels, Belgrade, America, and then France, where they settled. In 1926 there was another triumphant trip to America, and in May 1927, their return to Paris. In 1928 the commander in chief of ROVS, General Kutepov, brought Skoblin onto active duty with ROVS.

The file had Skoblin's letter of 1930 to the Central Executive Committee of the U.S.S.R. for personal amnesty and Soviet citizenship. On the next page was the resolution of the CEC of the U.S.S.R. concerning personal amnesty for Skoblin and Plevitskaya. And instructions to pay agent YEZH-13 two hundred dollars a month. This was right after General Kutepov's kidnapping; however, Sharok did not find any evidence of Skoblin's direct involvement in that.

Besides his regular reports on the actions of the White émigrés (movement of saboteurs, recruitment of agents, and so on) there was a lot of information on the infighting for leadership of ROVS, which led to Skoblin being named chief of the "inner line" of ROVS, that is, its secret police, its OGPU, in 1935. Their aim was the struggle against infiltration of ROVS and the White émigré community in general by agents of the NKVD. After his appointment, it became much easier for the NKVD to do its work.

How did they get Skoblin and Plevitskaya to work for them? wondered Sharok. Not the two hundred dollars a month. It couldn't be. Plevitskaya made a lot of money. Had they become disillusioned with the White idea and come to believe the Red? The young general, experienced and high-ranking by the age of twenty-six, commanding a division without higher military training, what did he need with the Red idea? He knew that he would never have a military career in Moscow, yet he was talented and ambitious. Plevitskaya's motive was more obvious. She was older than her handsome husband and in love with him. She followed wherever he went. And she was convinced that she would be even more successful at home than abroad.

But Skoblin, Skoblin? He couldn't understand it. He had received amnesty and been given citizenship seven years ago, but they weren't letting him or Plevitskaya into the country. They kept them abroad and obviously intended to keep them there a long time. They needed him in Paris. There was nothing for him to do in the Soviet Union. So, he was doomed to this role for the rest of his life. And if he failed, he would end up in prison for many years. Incidentally, the émigré press had hinted recently about the traitorous role of the couple. Even the famous Burtsev, who had exposed many provocateurs in the tsarist secret police in his time, was among the accusers. Incidentally, Burtsev felt that Plevitskaya was the main spy, tied to the NKVD through Mark Eitingon. However, Skoblin managed to evade all the accusations so far, proving that all the accusations were the results of inner ROVS intrigues. Besides which, the accusers and the accused were united by their hostility toward the head of ROVS, General Miller. But how long could Skoblin and Plevitskaya last now that they were the object of suspicions?

And why were Slutsky and Speigelglass interested in them just now? They had agents in ROVS who were not as high up but who had just as much information. Why was Yezhov so interested in Skoblin, when all the efforts of the NKVD were concentrated on the Radek-Pyatakov trial and preparation for the Bukharin-Rykov trial?

In February the NKVD apparat was stunned by the news — Molchanov, the head of the Secret Political Section, the man in charge of preparing the Zinoviev-Kamenev and the Pyatakov-Radek trials, had been arrested. In early March they arrested the chief of the Special Section, Gai, his deputy, Volovik, the chief of the Transport Section, Shanin, and a few other workers of the apparat.

On March 21–23 at the NKVD club, Yezhov led a meeting of the core of the Main Directorate of Security. His speech was terrifying. He attacked not only the Trotskyite-Zinovievite-Bukharinite monsters, but he also attacked Yagoda, Molchanov, and other scoundrels who had taught their subordinates to interrogate in kid gloves. He claimed that Yagoda had written on the transcripts of interrogations "nonsense," "rubbish," "impossible," "incorrect" in an attempt to protect the people being interrogated.

After Yezhov, his first deputy, Agranov, addressed Yagoda and Molchanov with the same harshness. "Yagoda and Molchanov took the wrong line, the anti-Party line.... Molchanov was trying to smear and hold up the investigation.... The liquidation of the Trotsky band would have not happened if not for the intervention of Comrade Stalin ... who pointed out the mistakes of the investigation, and gave orders to expose the Trotskyite Center and Trotsky's personal role.... It was on the basis of these orders of Stalin.... This work created the opportunity to include new workers in the investigation...."

There was metal in Agranov's voice, but everyone knew that his wife had been in the cellars of the Lubyanka for several months now. Denying Yagoda and praising Stalin, Agranov hoped to keep his luxurious office on the second floor.

But he was arrested after the meeting.

They arrested Yagoda's secretary, Bulanov, and the head of the Ukrainian NKVD, Katsnelson. The head of the Gorky NKVD, Pogrebinsky, shot himself on April 3. They arrested Yagoda and then his former deputy Prokofiev, and Artuzov, Balitsky, Deribas, Firin, and many other important workers of the NKVD, who knew too much. They were replaced by completely new people or comparatively young ones from the provinces or from within the apparat, which was how Sharok regarded himself. Yezhov suddenly discovered a "Chekist conspiracy" in the NKVD and liquidated it with determination.

The Secret Political Section headed by Molchanov suffered the greatest losses, especially the First Section where Sharok used to work. They arrested Vytkovsky, and his deputy, Shtein, shot himself. Lieutenant Viktor Semyonovich Abakumov was promoted. That same Abakumov had been brought with other clerical workers last year from the GULAG system to do filing. He filed and did other paperwork. But now he was interrogating former workers of the Secret Political Section. He was a crude and barely educated man. Sharok shuddered at the thought that he might have been interrogated by him. Abakumov would not have worried about the fact that Sharok had been the one person who had been good to him there. Abakumov was dumb and illiterate, and Vutkovsky had wanted to send him back, but Sharok had stepped in. He felt sorry for the man and showed him how to do the work. They became friends in those two weeks that they worked together. Abakumov was grateful. He understood that Sharok had helped him stay on in Moscow, and he looked at him with faithful, doglike adoration. But if Sharok were in his hands in interrogation, all the gratitude would vanish and he'd break every bone in his body.

Thank God he had been transferred to the Foreign Section. Yezhov didn't touch the Foreign Section. There was no one who could replace their specialists, and he couldn't destroy their work abroad. But sooner or later Yezhov would get to the Foreign Section, because there were too many people there who knew.

Speigelglass understood that too. The total destruction of "witnesses," which included him, of course, was under way. And that's why he thought it was no accident that Yezhov had introduced Sharok to him personally. He thought it possible that Speigelglass's fate might depend on Sharok, even a casual word of his. And in their business, fate meant life or death.

Nevertheless, their relationship did not change on the surface. He made no attempt to befriend Sharok nor did he show hostility.

Just before their trip in late April, they talked about Sharok's wardrobe.

"I have a few nice ties," Speigelglass said. "I'll bring them for you. They'll go well with your suit. And I have a half-dozen new handkerchiefs. We'll get you slippers as soon as we arrive."

Their trip to Paris brought them together. Sharok was traveling under the name Sharovsky, a worker at Exportles, a timber concern. Speigelglass was also traveling under an assumed name.

They rode in a two-seat compartment in the international car. Austere and taciturn at work, Speigelglass turned out to be a pleasant companion.

When they had settled opposite each other in the compartment and the train started, Speigelglass smiled for the first time. "Do you like trains?"

Sharok shrugged. "It's nice in a train like this, of course.... But I haven't traveled much. Mostly just outside Moscow."

"I like it, I like looking out the window" — he opened the curtains — "I like the expanses of our land, the forests, the groves, the fields. I find our Russian monotony very soothing. I continue thinking about my work, about what lies ahead, but I do so calmly, even aloofly. I recommend you try it. When we get to Europe, you won't have that opportunity — everything is compressed. There's so much flashing by, your eye won't get any rest."

There was a knock at the door.

Speigelglass got up and answered.

The conductor brought them tea in glasses and cookies and asked them to pay for their bedding.

Speigelglass paid and then took out a bottle of liqueur from his bag. He opened it and offered it to Sharok. "How do you like it, in your tea or on the side?"

"On the side."

Speigelglass took out a set of small metal cups, which fit inside one another, and gave one to Sharok, but he poured his liqueur into his tea.

"I don't use sugar, I'm afraid of hereditary diabetes, so I have tea and coffee with liqueur or cognac. Well, bon voyage!"

Sipping tea and chewing the cookies, Speigelglass said, "Yuri Denisovich, we are going on serious business. We will be in difficult situations, you understand that.... We will have to depend on each other, perhaps even save each other. Therefore we must trust each other absolutely. Agreed?"

"Absolutely."

"There should be no misunderstandings between us. You and I have two foreign passports, but essentially, you and I are one person, one man doing the Party's bidding. And without full mutual trust, we cannot fulfill our assignment."

"Of course," Sharok said with that special reserve and respectful intonation he used whenever he spoke of the Party.

"There. You, of course, were surprised that I knew your French teacher at school, weren't you?"

"I hadn't thought about it."

Speigelglass looked at him. "Hadn't thought about it?"

"I mean," Sharok said, trying to squirm out of it, "that I allowed for the possibility of a thorough check on me before being transferred to the Foreign Section, and you might have checked where I studied a foreign language."

Speigelglass looked at him inquisitively. He didn't believe him. "That's not so," Speigelglass said. "In the West there is an important professor, a famous literary critic. The Soviets sent him abroad. He is an émigré, an active anti-Soviet, and a Constitutional Democrat. His son and daughter remained in Russia. His son is a Communist — rather, was a Communist — but he joined a right-Bukharinite group. Now he is under arrest. The daughter teaches French in the school where you studied. That's why I know about her. As you see, everything is very simple. But my knowing about her upset you, didn't it?"

"Yes, it did," Sharok admitted. "I thought that three years of irreproachable work in the organs was recommendation enough."

"You're right," Speigelglass agreed. "No one was checking up on you. I'm glad we've cleared this up. Do you have any other things you'd like clarified?"

"No," replied Sharok. "I have no questions for you."

He said it sincerely, but he thought that Speigelglass could have explained all this when they first met, or at least on their second meeting, when Sharok brought up the school and Irina Yulyevna. He didn't tell him then, but he told him now when he considered it useful. He was sneaky.

"Then to business," Spiegelglass said. "What questions do you have after reading the Farmer file?"

Sharok had two questions. How did they recruit the Farmers and what made them work for us? And for what concrete aim did we need them now?

The first question was improper, because in answering it Speigelglass would have to name the agents who had recruited them. And he didn't need to ask the second question, because Speigelglass would explain that himself. So Sharok asked a third question. "I read their dossier carefully several times. The file is missing one thing. What kind of people are they? Their weaknesses ... what buttons can we push in various circumstances?"

Speigelglass did not reply immediately. "Naturally, the psychology of the agent and the motives that make him work are very important. They allow you to predict his actions and estimate his abilities. But that evaluation is usually subjective. I could share my ideas with you, but I don't think it would be of much use. They are profoundly personal. And you'll have the opportunity to form your own opinions. The main question is the degree of their reliability. The Farmer is a reliable agent. Can we consider the possibility that he is working with us on orders from ROVS? I don't think so. With all the émigré squabbles, that is too dangerous. He could ruin his reputation forever. And in any case, there isn't a single fact that would support such suspicions. But his ties with the Germans are firmly proven. He did not deny them nor does he deny them now. And we are using his ties with the Germans. He had explained it by saying that the majority of ROVS, especially the young people, look to Germany as the U.S.S.R.'s main foe. And he is betting on the young people and not on Miller and the other old men, who in the traditional Russian monarchist policy see Germany as Russia's historical enemy and consider France an ally. Undoubtedly, the Farmer tells the Germans about the situation in ROVS. He tells us about our enemies in ROVS, and the Germans about their friends. In brief, he has his own agenda. He's trying to take over ROVS and is using us to get rid of his rivals. The Germans know about his ties with us, but they consider them useful for Germany."

Speigelglass stopped, finished his tea, and looked out the window. "You know," he said at last, "when I go abroad, especially when I am going for a long time, what I really miss are these vast spaces. I wait for the hour when I'll be back in the train and will be looking out the window just like this." He turned to Sharok. "Help yourself. The liqueur is tasty."

"Thank you."

"Who's the boss in this couple?" Speigelglass went on. "There are varying opinions. Some say she is. She's a masterful woman, and the émigrés even call the Farmer 'General Plevitsky.' But for us and for our immediate goal, only he's important to us — only the Farmer."

Sharok listened attentively. Speigelglass was telling the truth, but not the whole truth. He didn't mention Eitingon once, yet his friendship with Skoblin and Plevitskaya was not accidental. But Speigelglass was quiet about it. He didn't want to mention that connection. Actually, he hadn't told Sharok anything new. In case their relations deteriorated, he couldn't bring up anything compromising. He was careful, very careful. But Speigelglass was about to reveal the most important thing — why they needed Skoblin right now.

"Our goal." Speigelglass's voice was firm again. "I believe you know about the arrests of Shmidt, Putna, and Primakov?"

"Yes, of course."

"And you must remember Radek's vague replies to questions about his ties with Marshal Tukhachevsky?"

"Yes, I noticed. He did it too heatedly and insistently, and therefore unconvincingly." Sharok had already guessed where this was leading.

"The Party's Central Committee and Comrade Stalin have incontrovertible evidence that Marshal Tukhachevsky, Army Commissar Gamarik, Army Commanders Yakir and Uborevich, Commander Kork, and Commanders Primakov, Putna, Eideman, and Feldman have ties with the command of the German Reichswehr. They are spies for the Germans, preparing a military coup, determined to kill Comrade Stalin and other leaders of the Party and the state."

Sharok was not surprised. Having worked for three years in the NKVD, he had learned not to be surprised by anything. In preparing for one trial, they had even collected material against Molotov. It was Comrade Stalin who named the enemies of the people, the spies, and murderers, and it was up to the workers of the

NKVD to prove their guilt. This time the enemies of the people were military leaders.

"The Farmer must get material in Berlin pointing to these people. He will give us those materials." After a silence, he added, "For this we promised the Farmer help in gaining further advancement in his work."

"In his work" meant in ROVS.

"I understand the assignment," Sharok said with a nod.

## ❧ 38 ❧

She had to get hold of herself. She shouldn't have gone this long without visiting Sofya Alexandrovna. Abandoning her was inhuman, undignified, and cruel. And there was no point in blaming her, either. She must be suffering herself for telling Sasha about Kostya. If Varya had learned that Sasha had been married, she would have got over it. But Sasha's attitude was different. If he loved her, then he couldn't forgive the betrayal. And if he didn't love her, then listening about some hustler husband and his crooked deals was disgusting, compared to what he had been through, and that's why he turned down her offer to visit him. Varya didn't exclude that possibility.

"Here I am," she began right in the doorway. "I finished my work and came to see you."

"Varya, dearest!" Sofya Alexandrovna bustled about. There was so much joy in her voice that Varya's heart contracted.

"Tell me, how is everything?"

"I'm getting along, Varya. Are you straight from work?"

"Yes, why?"

"A bowl of mushroom soup?"

"I wouldn't refuse it."

Their first meeting after a ten-day hiatus passed normally. Sofya Alexandrovna didn't mention Sasha, she didn't want to open the wound.

"Will you come tomorrow?"

"Of course."

Varya hadn't seen Mikhail Yurevich in a long time. He was never at home. She had even made a joke about it: "Do you think our Mikhail Yurevich is having an affair?"

"Especially since he gets home around dawn," Sofya Alexandrovna replied with a smile. "I hate to disillusion you — but it's been his work, the population census."

Right. She had forgotten that there had been a census in January.

At last Varya ran into him in the corridor, told him how much she had missed him, and asked, "Well, Mikhail Yurevich, have you counted everyone? You didn't leave anyone out?"

"Everyone, Varya, everyone." He looked exhausted and worried. "Everyone who exists. But the ones who don't, well, of course, we didn't count them."

A strange phrase.

"Come to my place, we'll have some tea," Mikhail Yurevich suggested.

"With pleasure."

As usual, she sat with her feet tucked under her in her favorite, sagging armchair.

"They came to see me, too," Varya said. "It was a joke. They asked if I believed in God. 'Yes, I do,' I replied. The census taker, a young man, just stared at me. 'Are you serious?' 'Yes, absolutely serious. Don't you believe in God?' 'No, I don't.' 'What about your mother?' He didn't say anything, looked huffy, and put down 'Yes.' Apparently, I spoiled his results. They want everyone to be atheists, so that they can tear down the last of the churches."

"It's a stupid question," Mikhail Yurevich said. "They never used to have it in the census."

"People are afraid to tell the truth," Varya went on. "So they claim that they are atheists. To say, 'Yes, I believe in God' for an ordinary person is a major exploit. For me, I was just fooling around. But if there are believers in the family of a Party member or a Komsomol, it's a problem. He'll be asked why he's bringing up his family members so badly. And the believer, if he works somewhere, won't be happy, either. They'll throw him out of the shock-workers and Stakhanovites, and he'll lose his bonuses; they'll call him a 'churchy' or 'supporter of churches and obscurantists.'"

"Yes," Mikhail Yurevich repeated, "that question shouldn't be in there. The first census after the revolution was in 1920. And when Lenin saw the question on faith, he had them take it out. He understood the inequity of that question. There are many silly things in the present census. It was planned for the end of 1936 — they wanted to do it calmly over five to seven days — but suddenly everything changed. It was moved to January 1937 and it had to be done in one day. Can you imagine how many census-takers were needed? Over a million. Do you think it's possible to cover the whole country in one day? It's impossible to do it in the cities, much less the countryside. But that's the order and you have to do it."

"But why, Mikhail Yurevich, why?"

He moved the inkwells on his desk.

"I told you the last time. The census has to give a figure of about one hundred seventy million people. The government is certain of that. But I expect a maximum of one hundred sixty-four million — at best. And the question arises — what happened to six million people? And the government's answer will be — the census was taken by saboteurs."

His voice trembled.

Varya finally understood. In order to hide the truth, they had the census taken in one day, and then they could blame everything on the statisticians. What bastards! That's why Mikhail Yurevich was so upset.

"Mikhail Yurevich, calm down, don't worry! Please."

"I'm not worried. But I don't want to hide anything. Six million people, just think! Who are those people? Simple peasants. And what were they guilty of? What did they die for? For nothing. And there are so many of them. Hiding that is unacceptable, immoral. So I'm not worried, Varya. I just feel sorry for people. All of them, the ones who died and the ones who counted them. And we will be responsible for it. And you and me, Varya, I feel sorry for us, too." He smiled wearily. "But we shouldn't be talking about all this. You're too serious for your age. Why don't you go to the theater, the museums? There are so many interesting exhibits now."

"Do you go?" Varya asked.

"Well, I'm an old man. . . . Have you been to the Pushkin show?"

"Of course."

"Well?"

"I didn't like it. At the entrance there's a painting.... Natalya Nikolaevna, you know, tall and with a bare back, majestic. You can't see her face, only her back, and next to her is Pushkin, half a head shorter, looking back. An ugly man with thick lips and a face contorted with rage and jealousy. She is so victorious and he is small and unpleasant, getting underfoot. The feeling is that everyone is laughing at him, mocking him, and he's ready to attack them all, to kill them. A nasty monkey, not Pushkin. How can they depict him like that?"

"You're a very opinionated young woman," Mikhail Yurevich said. "I know that painting. And I hold Nikolai Pavlovich Ulyanov in high regard. He's a witty artist. Incidentally, he was one of the youngest and last members of the *World of Art* group, a master of the psychological portrait. He did a lot of work on Pushkin. And I don't think you're right about the painting, Varya. By the way, you can see Natalya Nikolaevna's face. It's reflected in the mirror."

"Oh, yes, you're right. I forgot," Varya said in embarrassment. "But you see her majestic back, indifferent to everyone."

"I saw the early sketches, Pushkin was simpler, not in court uniform, and he made a different impression. There wasn't that entourage, that magnificent imperial court. You would have liked the other version better, I think. Besides which, there were many other interesting things at that exhibit. But, as I've said, you're too serious. Varya, how old are you?"

She laughed. "Don't you know not to ask ladies their age?" Then she sighed. "When I was little, I fantasized a lot. Everything seemed extraordinary and mysterious to me. Lights in windows, moonlight, lamp light.... Restaurants? Yes, they were a kind of magic to me, too, especially at first, with the music, people all dressed up. For some reason, I thought I was wonderful. It was a beautiful life. Everything was wonderful, especially compared to our pathetic communal flats, our dull lives, all the rudeness around us. And then, when I took a closer look, I realized it was just a mirage. Of course, if you must turn yourself into a mistress, a plaything in bed, then it's fine. Those girls are just amoebas, without thoughts or souls. And I learned that life wasn't in the restaurants and resorts, but in care and worry, in work and school, in prison lines. Life was lousy and full of lies, injustice, and horror, but you still had to find your own place in it. What do you think, am I right?"

Varya didn't say anything about Sasha to Mikhail Yurevich. She once thought that Mikhail Yurevich must have guessed. Now she knew that it wasn't so. In this apartment, in the next room, she had lived with Kostya, and Mikhail Yurevich thought that she loved her husband.

And still this sweet old bachelor in the worn checked jacket with neat patches on the elbows, leaning over the illuminated table with his glue pots and paints, was a part of the world that spun around Sasha. Sasha had sat in this armchair talking with Mikhail Yurevich. He had borrowed books from him, and he had watched him work.

But today Mikhail Yurevich pushed aside the glue and scissors, as if they were in his way. Something wrong was going on inside him.

"Aren't you feeling well?" Varya asked. "Lie down, I'll go."

"No, Varya, everything's fine." He paused. "Varya, remember how you used to look at my journals?" He pointed at the baskets under the table and the bed. "*The World of Art, Apollo, The Golden Fleece.* They interested you then?"

"Of course. They're marvelous journals."

"You see.... They've been lying around in baskets for years, getting dusty and ruined. And there are such good reproductions in them, of Benois, Somov, Dobuzhinsky.... I don't even have the time to flip through them. Take the journals!"

Varya was confused. "What? Mikhail Yurevich...I can't! They're a treasure, they're worth tons of money. You've been collecting them all your life, and now you're going to start giving them away?"

"I'm not giving them away," Mikhail Yurevich said with a sad smile. "It's a present, just to you."

"But it's not my birthday."

"Birthdays aren't the only reason for a present. Please, Varya, I'm asking you. Take them. It would give me great pleasure. I'm an old, lonely man. When I die, this will all vanish."

"Don't talk about death!" Varya shouted. "You shouldn't talk about that!"

"You don't have to talk about it, but you must think about it. It would give you pleasure to look at the journals, to have them handy."

"Aha," Varya said with a laugh. "You want to expand my aesthetic education."

"Varya, works of art should not be hidden under a table or bed. That's not why they were created. Take them, please, Varya?"

Varya shook her head. "No, Mikhail Yurevich, it's impossible."

He thought. "All right, if you don't want a present, just let me keep these things at your place. Read them, look at them, have the pleasure. Hm? How about that? And I'll take them back later."

"But where will I keep them?" Varya wondered. "They'll end up under a table or the bed, too."

"Don't you have a bookcase?"

"I do, but it's full."

"One will be delivered to you! Yes, yes. I'll buy a simple bookcase. It'll be brought to you. I don't have anywhere to put it. You can see that."

"Well, then," Varya said uncertainly. "If you insist . . ."

"Yes, I do insist, Varya," Mikhail Yurevich said with animation. "I'm suffocating from my books and journals. You'll be helping me out."

# ⚔ 39 ⚔

hey met Skoblin at the Traveler's Hotel in the small town of
Aigreville, seventy kilometers outside Paris. Skoblin was late;
his car had broken down, and he had had to stop in Greutz.
    They sat in the corner of the veranda, empty in the
afternoon, protected from the sun by a canvas awning. Speigelglass
introduced Sharok, calling him Sharovsky. Skoblin shook his hand
indifferently. He was cool and aloof, and without waiting for
Speigelglass's questions, began his report.

The operation was run by the head of the political police,
Geidrich, and Berens was in direct command. Berens needed actual
documents signed by Tukhachevsky, which were in the archives of
the Abwehr, the German military intelligence. The head of
Abwehr, Vice-Admiral Canaris, refused to turn them over.

"Why?" Speigelglass frowned.

"The Abwehr is independent of the political police, and Canaris
is not subordinate to Geidrich. Canaris suspects that he is just being
used in some important affair. He has the right, and more than that,
he must know for what purpose the documents are requested, even
if the documents are fifteen years old."

Sharok understood that they were talking about documents of
the early and mid-1920s, when the U.S.S.R. and Germany collaborated closely. Tukhachevsky had led the Soviet negotiating team
and had signed treaties. Now the old documents were needed in
order to make new ones.

"It's possible. Canaris is afraid this may be an attempt to make
the senior officers of the Reichswehr look bad," Skoblin continued.
"Their signatures are on those documents too. Canaris is afraid that

the Sicherheitsdienst will try to get the army leadership. After all he wasn't informed that the operation was aimed at Tukhachevsky. Back in January Canaris got a confidential letter from Rudolf Hess with an order to give Geidrich all the archival documents on past German-Soviet collaboration. But Canaris became stubborn and sabotaged Hess's orders with various excuses."

Speigelglass's face was stony. He spoke in his steady and calm voice, "Last time you informed me that Hitler had approved the operation. He had joked, 'This will be our Christmas present to Stalin.' "

"My report was based on absolutely reliable sources," Skoblin countered. "Even if Hitler were to order Canaris to turn over the documents, he would have to explain why. If he doesn't, it would mean that he doesn't trust Canaris, who could resign. That's why Hess and Geidrich didn't bring Hitler in on the details. He doesn't even know which archive the documents are in."

"What's the way out?" Speigelglass asked.

"Bormann, the Führer's political adviser, has found it."

"You don't need to explain to me who Bormann is."

For the first time that Sharok knew him, Speigelglass lost his restraint.

"You interrupted me," Skoblin parried coolly. "On Bormann's advice, Geidrich sent two units of policemen to the archives at night. With the help of break-in specialists, they found the material and started a fire to cover their tracks. The material is now in the hands of experienced engravers. In a week's time the documents will be ready, but only concerning Tukhachevsky."

"And the rest?"

"Yakir, Uborevich, and Kork were in Germany less frequently than Tukhachevsky and did not sign documents in the twenties. There is little to go on. Therefore, preparation of those documents will take more time."

"I need documents on all of them," Speigelglass said harshly. "I'm prepared to wait no longer."

"You're acting as if I'm the one who's preparing them."

"I know who's preparing them," Speigelglass said. "But I also know who promised to give them to me in February, then in March, and now, as the poets say, April is outside our window."

"I explained the reasons for the delay."

"I'm asking you to explain to the Germans that in case of further delays the documents will no longer be necessary."

"I can't explain anything to the Germans! You know their neatness and punctuality. They will release only foolproof documents, whose quality they can attest to. You have to choose between rushing and reliability."

"Reliability is important, but so are the deadlines," Speigelglass lectured. "I gave my bosses deadlines based on your calculations. I had to change those deadlines twice, and I won't be able to do it a third time. I'm prepared to wait another week, but that's it. Next week at the same time, we will be on this veranda. If for some reason Aigreville is not suitable, let us know the new place through the usual channels. I hope that you will leave for Berlin no later than tomorrow."

Sharok and Speigelglass spent the next week not far from the embassy in a hotel where Soviet businessmen usually stayed. It was small, with tiny rooms, and was comparatively cheap.

Speigelglass didn't let Sharok out of his sight, not for security, not to keep an eye on him, but so that Sharok would constantly see him and so that back in Moscow he could say, "We weren't separated for a minute." Even when they were checking into the hotel, Speigelglass said after some thought, that they wanted one room. The concierge was surprised. "A double bed?"

"No, two singles."

Speigelglass laughed afterward. "He thought we were homosexuals!"

Day and night they were together. Even though Speigelglass must have had other business in Paris besides Skoblin, he didn't meet with anyone else. Did he want to keep Sharok out of other operations?

He was hoping that with time Sharok would be removed from the Foreign Section.

Speigelglass, perspicacious, relieved him of his doubts. "This trip could let us introduce you to a few other agents in Paris. But this assignment is too important. We can't take any risks. The police might catch on to us and keep us from meeting Skoblin at the appointed time. Always limit your trips to meeting one agent at a time."

During the day they went to the trade mission and chatted with one of the ordinary employees. Speigelglass let Moscow know that they'd be held up for a week.

The essence of the operation was no longer a secret for Sharok. But he had learned it not from Speigelglass, but from Speigelglass's conversation with Skoblin. If he were later asked, "What did Speigelglass tell you about this case?" he would have to say, "Nothing." They talked with Skoblin, agent YEZH-13, code name Farmer, about getting documents from the Gestapo incriminating Tukhachevsky, Yakir, Uborevich, and Kork for treason. The authenticity of the documents was not their business. Their business was getting the documents. Other people would make decisions about the documents.

They spoke frankly with each other only about Skoblin.

Sharok didn't like him. He was snotty, hostile, and impolite. In Moscow his informers wouldn't dare meet him without a denunciation of someone.

"You see," Speigelglass said in response, "our domestic informer and the foreign agent are not comparable in any way. Ours has our protection, the foreign one is in mortal danger. Ours is prompted by ideological considerations, loyalty to the Party, or fear, you and I understand that. Sometimes it is pure greed — money, career, the good life. But a foreign agent has other motives, more important than the three I listed — political accounts, a double game, a tendency to like adventure, and much else. In that sense, the Farmer is a typical example. He is interested in the operation personally. He hates the former tsarist officers who served Soviet power and helped the Soviets beat them in the Civil War. Tukhachevsky is a former White lieutenant, Kork a lieutenant colonel, and Uborevich a lieutenant. Skoblin considers them traitors and wants to punish them. Envy plays a role in it too. He and Tukhachevsky were born in 1893 and Tukhachevsky is a world-known military leader, while Skoblin — who, by the way, is undoubtedly talented — is an unknown émigré sponging off his wife. In general, every agent is an individual who must be studied carefully. So be prepared for new conditions every time."

Speigelglass showed Paris to Sharok. They strolled down the Champs Elysees. Imitating Speigelglass, Sharok tried to behave like an ordinary Parisian, but he couldn't keep his eyes off the shop windows. They really knew how to live! They had loads of everything.

They climbed the Eiffel Tower and looked at Paris from above. They went to Montmartre, to the Palais Royale, to Versailles. They spoke French to blend in. Speigelglass talked, and Sharok nodded, adding a word here and there, or a well-practiced phrase. Speigelglass acted like a guide, which seemed natural. He knew Paris well. He was educated, and he knew French literature and art. But he wasn't showing off for Sharok. He talked about Paris in normal tour-guide terms, without getting into subtleties that would be difficult for Sharok.

But the traditional tourist spots didn't interest Sharok. The Louvre! He almost died of boredom when his school class went on a field trip to the Tretyakovsky Gallery in Moscow. Of course, he liked Versailles and the Palais Royale. Those kings knew how to live. Speigelglass was right — Paris was a royal city. It was extravagant and beautiful, but so what? Back home, Peterhof was beautiful, too.

Now the Folies Bergères and Pigalle were another thing, with the half-naked prostitutes, and the stores with pornographic cards and magazines. Yuri had never suspected there were positions and methods like that. He was going to try them out on Kalya back home. . . . Sharok could spend hours there. He was excited by the perfume and powder, the crowd, the frank and enticing looks from the prostitutes, but Speigelglass interfered in his enjoyment. Sharok had to pretend he was bored, too.

But one day he did ask, "Can we go to Montmartre again?"

"Of course."

Sharok was attracted by Montmartre. It was alive, and merry, guitars strumming, hurdy-gurdys playing, artists in blouses painting — and all the canvases were of naked women, with such breasts, such hips, such legs!

But Speigelglass was indifferent to it all. He wasn't interested in women. A dried-up stick! When he noticed that Sharok wasn't interested in museums, he strolled down the boulevards or sat outside a small cozy café watching people go by or sat with his eyes shut, enjoying the spring sunshine. Relaxing. Sharok, sitting under an umbrella at an outdoor table, also relaxed.

"Paris is the liveliest city in the world, but it is the one that most makes you relax," Speigelglass said. And he was right. You order a cup of coffee and sit for two hours, going through the newspapers.

And people did sit in cafés, drinking coffee, reading newspapers, and no one made them leave. They spent the entire day that way. Speigelglass scorned them. "*Rentiers* — coupon clippers." The most disgusting and parasitic variety of the bourgeoisie, according to him. He apparently despised the West sincerely. He pointed out the *clochards* to Sharok and said that the homeless, the prostitutes, and pornography were the ulcers of capitalist society. He was upset that people weren't ashamed to show off their wealth against the background of poverty.

Sharok agreed silently. There was no point in arguing, and it was dangerous, too. Even though he considered that Speigelglass might be complaining about the West just for him. Or maybe, he was simply nervous. Sharok awoke at night and saw that Speigelglass wasn't sleeping. He was hunched by the window and looking outside. And sometimes in the daytime he noticed Speigelglass suddenly lose control. His face would narrow and he would bite his lips. He was probably thinking that they were wasting their time here and there was no certainty that the operation would succeed. At times like that Sharok wanted to get back to Moscow quickly, just to get out of Paris safe and sound.

. . . A week later they were waiting for Skoblin on the same veranda at the Traveler's Hotel.

He wasn't late this time.

The veranda was empty again, and they sat at the same table.

Skoblin took out a red file from his briefcase and placed it in front of Speigelglass.

Speigelglass moved it toward Sharok so that he could see it too and opened it. But the documents were in German, and Sharok couldn't understand anything. Only one paper was in Russian — Tukhachevsky's letter stating that they had to get rid of politicians and take power. Then came documents with columns of figures, and Tukhachevsky's signature on each. Receipts for payments for spying. Sharok saw a photograph of Trotsky with German military men.

Without shutting the file, Speigelglass asked, "Is that all?"

"That's all," Skoblin replied.

"These are only for Tukhachevsky. What about the rest?"

"I told you. They'll need at least two months. They confirmed the deadline. Nothing can be done about it."

After a pause, Speigelglass said, "Good. Actually, it's very bad. And the situation is apparently hopeless. Am I correct?"

"Why hopeless?" Skoblin argued. "You'll have all the materials on the rest in exactly two months."

"Let them do it," Speigelglass said grimly. "You'll let us know, through the usual channels, the exact date and place of our meeting. In two months, no later. Sooner would be better. Either Mr. Sharovsky or I will come. Perhaps both of us."

The bill was on the table. Speigelglass looked at it, took out his wallet, put money on the table, thought about it, and added a few more coins.

# ❦ 40 ❦

On May 1, 1937, Stalin stood on the Mausoleum in Red Square, receiving the military parade.

The sun had already risen above St. Basil's Cathedral, and illuminated the GUM department store with *his* portrait on the facade. It was warm, everything glistened, sparkled, and shone. The bands played. The first ones to march past, in long even rows, were the students of military academies, then came the infantry with bayonets over their shoulders, then came the cavalry on horseback clip-clopping over the cobblestones, and behind them, coming from the Historical Museum, crawled the tanks. *His* army, powerful and invincible, put together by *him*, armed by *him*. *He* had industrialized the country, *he* had reconstructed it, building the world's biggest factories and plants. *He* had turned backward Russia into a world power.

Tukhachevsky stood apart from the other officers, his thumbs inside his belt. He kept to himself. And no one talked to him. They sensed that he was doomed. He accepted his canceled trip to London. He didn't protest or demand explanations. Had he believed Yezhov? Doubtful. He sensed his impotence. The arrests of military personnel were going full swing. Besides Shmidt, Putna, and Primakov, Kuzmichev, Yakir's friend from the Civil War, Golubenko, the former commissar of the 45th Infantry Division, which had been commanded by Yakir, Sablin, commandant of Kiev, who had served under Uborevich and Kork, and Commanders Turovsky, Gekker, and Karkavy. And they had material against Tukhachevsky. Along with Yagoda, his closest assistants were arrested, Prokofiev, Gai, and Volovich, and they gave the needed evidence against Tukhachevsky immediately. They knew what to say. They had spent many years beating all kinds of lies out of people. Only Yagoda was putting up a fight.

The arrests of the military didn't seem to worry Tukhachevsky too much. He was used to it. In the late 1920s and early 1930s, the army was purged of former tsarist officers, and over three thousand of them were sent to the camps and exile. Did Tukhachevsky defend his comrades? Did he say, "I'm also a former tsarist officer, so arrest me, too"? Why not? Where was his honor as an officer and a gentleman? Where was his sense of military camaraderie, his solidarity? He thought he was special. They were ordinary soldiers, he was the highest commander, the pillar of the army. Even the arrest of Putna didn't seem to scare him. He thought that the army could manage without Putna but not without him. He was wrong. Very wrong. No one is irreplaceable.

Stalin loved military parades. He liked watching *his* army, no one else's was as precise and fast. The very nature of *his* army made it obey and not discuss orders. The oath freed the soldier of doubts and hesitation, made him obey the will of his commander. The lower commanders obeyed their superiors. Nowhere else was the apparat so well trained. That was its strength and that was its weakness. As soon as you do away with the top, the army would become incapable of action.

Stalin looked at the commanders again. Tukhachevsky was still in his place, with his fingers hooked in his belt. You're not supposed to hold your hands like that at a parade. He didn't care about anything. Even now, when the warning blow had been struck, he didn't care. They had arrested Yulya Ivanovna Kuzmina, a woman close to him, the wife of Nikolai Nikolaevich Kuzmin, his former comrade in arms, his best friend. . . . *He* had noticed her at a reception. She was attractive, with captivating eyes. She was intelligent. She was studying sculpture with Motvilov. What kind of a sculptor was he? *He* had never heard of him. The husband, Kuzmin, was twenty years her senior, while Tukhachevsky was only ten years older. And he was handsome. Women fell in love with him, hanged themselves, shot themselves over him. And yet he had a family, a wife and daughter, he was in his fifties. . . . But he was upset by Kuzmina's arrest. And his special messenger was arrested, too. . . . It was clear to Tukhachevsky now. So there could be no delay. Whether the materials came from Berlin or not, there could be no delay. *He* would not delay. Let Hitler see that *he* could handle *his* problems without Hitler.

Tukhachevsky did not stay for the parade of the workers. He left. *He* saw him. He didn't look back once. He didn't look at *him* at all. *He* watched those things carefully.

The parade ended. Voroshilov gave a dinner at his apartment for the senior brass in the parade. Comrade Stalin was also present. There were toasts. Comrade Stalin also raised his glass. He briefly sketched the situation in the country, mentioned mass sabotage and espionage in all areas, including the army.

"The enemies will be exposed," Stalin said. "The Party will grind them to a powder. . . . I raise this glass to those who will remain loyal to the people and the Party and will take their place at this glorious table at the anniversary of the October Revolution."

Comrade Stalin's toast was heard in total silence. Not everyone was certain that he would be at the table six months hence.

After the May 1 holidays, Stalin personally took control of the army case. He went through the pages of his big desk calendar. A month. It had to be done in a month. By June first it had to be finished. Now Yezhov brought him daily transcripts of the interrogations. Stalin edited them, Yezhov went back to prison, and the prisoners signed the corrected versions. Then Yezhov came back to Stalin.

Commander Primakov had not given evidence for nine months. On May 8 they dressed him in an army uniform without insignias or medals, returned his glasses, brought him to the Kremlin, and led him into Stalin's study. Molotov, Voroshilov, and Yezhov were already there.

Primakov's letters, sent from prison, lay on Stalin's desk. Stalin pointed to them and said, "I've read your letters. You maintain that you broke with the Trotskyite opposition in 1928 and never had any ties with the Trotskyites after that."

"Yes, that is so," Primakov replied.

"Even here at the Politburo, you continue to deceive the Party," Stalin said. "We have incontrovertible evidence about your ties with the Trotskyites Dreitser, Shmidt, Putna, and others. The Party also has incontrovertible proof about a conspiracy in the army, a conspiracy against Comrade Voroshilov. You discussed the question of replacing Voroshilov with Yakir. We know that too." He turned to the others. "Primakov is a coward. To be stubborn in a case like this is cowardice. We were mistaken. Primakov does not merit the leadership of the Party entering into negotiations with him. He does not understand the Party language. Well then, let the investigators talk to him in their language. Take him away."

Primakov was returned to his cell. They took away his glasses, ordered him to take off his uniform and put on his smelly prison rags again.

"Leave my glasses," Primakov said. "Give me paper and ink. I want to write to Comrade Yezhov."

Primakov was given his glasses, paper, ink, and a pen.

> For the last nine months I have resisted the investigators in the case of the Trotskyite counterrevolutionary organization. At the Politburo, I brazenly refused to tell Comrade Stalin in an effort to reduce my guilt. Comrade Stalin told me directly that "to be stubborn in a case like this is cowardice." And truly, I was being a coward and false modesty kept me from telling the truth. I hereby state that when I returned from Japan in 1930, I contacted Dreitser and Shmidt, and through Dreitser and Putna, Mrachkovsky, and began Trotskyite work, about which I will give full evidence to the investigation.

He turned in the statement, sank onto the bunk, and lay down. There! Today they wouldn't beat him.

Yezhov called Stalin and read Primakov's letter.
"Let him disarm fully," Stalin said.

On May tenth Tukhachevsky was removed as deputy people's commissar of defense and assigned to Kuibyshev as chief of the Military Okrug. Yakir was transferred from Kiev to Leningrad.

On May 12, Yezhov came to Stalin and put the red file with the documents from Berlin on his desk.

"Good," Stalin said. "Go, and I'll look at them."

Left alone, Stalin did not open the file right away. *He* had waited a long time. It could wait a few more minutes. The file, dark red and impressive looking, was before *him* on the table. Yes, *he* had waited a long time, but *he* was calm, even indifferent. It was too late. *He* had solved the problem himself, without Hitler. But *he* should take a look anyway.

Stalin opened the file — just a few documents, about thirty pages. Beneath them was a cardboard file with the Russian translation of the German texts. And a photograph of Trotsky with important Germans.

Tukhachevsky's letter took up half the dossier. It was the main document. The Abwehr stamp was on it — Top Secret. And Hitler's signature on an order to establish surveillance of the generals who had corresponded with Tukhachevsky. Whether it was Hitler's real handwriting or not, *he* didn't know. But Tukhachevsky's letter ... Stalin read it closely. The handwriting was Tukhachevsky's, and the signature was his, and the style was his. It boiled down to the Russian and German generals coming to an agreement to take over the government and get rid of the political leaders.

It was a forgery, of course, but apparently a good one. They had specialists in Germany. And they had the materials to work with. The Germans had enough real letters from Tukhachevsky, written in the 1920s during the Russo-German cooperation.

*He* read closely the secret correspondence with the Germans. The letters had been written by Tukhachevsky and confirmed by the Politburo. One letter, written along the same lines, with the same ambiguity, dealt with secret collaboration, which a third party would hardly guess if he came upon the letter. Say, an agreement on exchanging information could be presented as an agreement on giving espionage information or it could be interpreted as a normal exchange of military and industrial information. Those Germans! They perfected every letter, every comma, but they had overdone the text. Any expert could prove easily that this was a copy of the agreements of the 1920s. And these were the 1930s!

Only Tukhachevsky's name was in the documents. And where were Yakir, Uborevich, and Kork? They stuck in our ambassador

Surits. And what for? Did they decide to get rid of a Jew at the same time? The photo of Trotsky? Of course, they could throw it in, but what was the level of these German agents?

And another thing. Hitler wasn't endangering his generals. That ruined von Sekt, but who needed him? Hitler didn't want to argue with his real generals.

By publishing this one-sided document, *he* would be dependent on Hitler. Hitler could announce that this was a forgery and that his own signature had been faked. He could announce to the world that Comrade Stalin had exposed a conspiracy that did not exist in order to destroy his innocent army brass. That would be credible, since Hitler would not have touched his own generals, which meant that there had been no contact, no whiff of treachery. Hitler had the proof that this was fabricated, and if he blackmailed *him*, he would have a leg up in future negotiations. No, Hitler wouldn't catch *him* that easily. *He* would show Hitler that *he* couldn't be tricked. *He*'d manage without this forgery. *He* had done without before and *he* would manage now. Showing documents was a dangerous precedent anyway. The question arises — why weren't there any documents at the previous trials? Through Feucht-wanger he had explained to the world that the Soviet people don't need papers. They need confessions. So why start using papers now? Because they existed now and there weren't any before. That would cast a shadow not only on the past trials but on the future ones, too, where they wouldn't use documents as evidence. They had developed their own method for the trials — the confessions of the defendants. The method had justified itself. What was the point in rejecting it?

The experience of the past trials had showed that any concrete mention of ties abroad was dangerous. They mentioned the Bristol Hotel in Copenhagen, and it turned out that there was no such hotel in Copenhagen. They said that Pyatakov had flown to Oslo, and it turned out that no planes had landed there then.

Let this dossier lie. If Hitler decided to try his generals, then he'd publish these documents himself. And then we'd print them in our newspapers as yet more proof of the guilt of Tukhachevsky and his group.

\* \* \*

On May 13, the dossier was shown to the members of the Politburo who were in Moscow, except for Rudzutak. *He* didn't trust Rudzutak. *He* warned them that no one else must know about the existence of the file. The documents would not be revealed either at the Military Council or at the trial. Revealing the documents would weaken the negotiating position with France and Britain. They would lose faith in the unity and power of the Red Army.

The members of the Politburo fully agreed with Comrade Stalin's position. Just as unanimously they decided that Tukhachevsky and his conspirators had to be turned over to a military tribunal and shot. Perhaps, some of them had doubts. Why would publishing the documents exposing Tukhachevsky undermine the faith of France and Britain in the power of the Red Army, while the execution of Tukhachevsky would not? But no one expressed that doubt. Of course, perhaps it never occurred to anyone.

Ending the session of the Politburo, Stalin locked the red file in his personal safe and ordered Poskrebyshev to have Tukhachevsky brought to him.

## ❧ 41 ❧

**A** bookcase was delivered to Varya, old but with the glass panes intact, along with four large baskets of journals from Mikhail Yurevich. There were the ones he had mentioned — *World of Art, Apollo, Scales, The Golden Fleece* — and albums of engravings by Benois, Somov, Dobuzhinsky, Bakst, Serov, Lancere, Ostroumova-Lebedeva, and Vrubel. And anthologies of the Acmeist poets — Akhmatova, Gumilev, Gorodetsky, Kuzmin, and Mandelstam — and of the Symbolist poets — Blok, Bely, Vyacheslav Ivanov, Fyodor Sologub — and a few French Symbolists — Rimbaud, Mallarmé, and Verlaine.

After putting them all away in the bookcase and cleaning up the room, Varya went to see Sofya Alexandrovna. She collapsed on the couch, her arms widespread, and said, "I'm tired."

"Why, Varya, it's not a workday."

"I was going through the journals and books that Mikhail Yurevich sent me along with a bookcase."

Sofya Alexandrovna looked at her anxiously.

"What's the matter, Sofya Alexandrovna?"

"Mikhail Yurevich gave you his books? He gave Sasha some of his books, too."

"What do you mean?"

"He said, 'When Sasha comes back, these will come in handy.'"

"Did he give him many books?"

"Look in the bookcase."

Varya opened the case. It held all the books published by Academia, starting with the 1920s. There was the *Questions of Poetics* series — Zhirmunsky, Tomashevsky, Eikhenbaum, Tynyanov, Gukovsky, Vinogradov. Varya hadn't heard of or read any of them except Tynyanov and Vinogradov. There were literary and theatrical memoirs, the collected works of Henri de Renier, Jules Romain, Marcel Proust, E. T. A. Hoffman. A series called *Treasury of World Literature.* Varya had seen them in Mikhail Yurevich's room. The history books took up two shelves.... Why was he giving them all away? What did it mean? Was Mikhail Yurevich afraid of a search and arrest? But there was nothing criminal in the books. Especially since in some of them, introductions by "enemies of the people" had been torn out. It was strange and upsetting.

"Is Mikhail Yurevich home now?"

"His coat is on the hanger in the hall. That means he's home."

Varya knocked on his door.

"Yes, yes, come in!"

Mikhail Yurevich rose from the cot on which he had been lying fully dressed. He found his pince-nez on the night table and felt for his slippers with his feet.

"Are you ill?"

"No, no. Just lying down." He got up and smoothed the blanket. And he put on his jacket clumsily, missing the sleeve at first.

And while he dressed and put on his pince-nez, Varya looked around the room. The empty shelves that had once held his books gave it an unlived-in air.

Mikhail Yurevich sat at the table and invited Varya to sit down. Settled in her armchair, she asked, "Has something happened?"

"What makes you ask that?" he replied without looking up.

"Mikhail Yurevich, something has happened," Varya persisted.

"Dear Varya, what could happen to me? Don't worry yourself."

"Why are you giving away your library? You gave Sasha some books, too."

"Sasha is interested in the history of the French Revolution. He even wrote a few things in exile. Sofya Alexandrovna told me about it. He's a very talented boy, and so I gave him the history books. Let him read them, and you read, too. Someday you'll remember me — 'There was an old eccentric, Mikhail Yurevich, who never wrote his own books, but collected others', and left them to us.'"

Varya walked around the room and stopped in front of Mikhail Yurevich. "Tell me the truth. Do you have a serious disease?"

He shook his head. "Nothing, absolutely nothing."

"Are you having trouble at work? Is it related to the census?"

He shrugged his left shoulder. He only raised his left shoulder. "Who doesn't have troubles, Varya?"

"Everyone has troubles," Varya said. "Everyone is irritated, embittered, picking on one another. They're indifferent to others' misfortunes, some even gloat. 'Ah, they put you away, serves you right. Don't be an enemy, don't be a saboteur! Let them arrest you, I hope they shoot you.' It's horrible!"

"Unfortunately," Mikhail Yurevich said very calmly and aloofly, without looking at Varya. "Unfortunately, the goals of the Revolution are forgotten, but the violence remains and turns into terror, demanding more and more new victims."

He looked at Varya. "Our dialogue is turning into my monologue. Old people are talkative, you know."

"Mikhail Yurevich! I don't want you calling yourself an old man."

"I lost my train of thought. I'm getting distracted and forgetful."

"You said that terror demands new victims."

"Yes. That's right. Idealists believe that you can create with terror. Scoundrels and villains use that. They use terror against the idealists, destroying them while taking over their slogans. You can't build a happy and just society on blood. That's all, Varya. These are the times in which we live, unfortunately. And this leads to troubles, some bigger, some smaller."

"Was the Revolution necessary?"

"Well." Mikhail Yurevich lifted his left shoulder again. "You can't put the question that way. Revolution is an elemental force that brings up new leaders. It is their responsibility to move the Revolution onto the path of peaceful reforms and do away with Stalin's excesses. I hold Lenin to blame for many things — from the moment of the Revolution to the beginning of 1923, the country lost at least eight million people. But by 1921 Lenin had seen that you can't build a new state on the foundation of violence. And he started a new path of development. But Lenin died. And Stalin came."

He stopped. Mikhail Yurevich had never been so frank with her. He had always been cautious. But now, such daring, and without the usual warnings that this was strictly between them and should go no farther. What was the matter with him?

Varya had a sudden thought. "Mikhail Yurevich, I think I know what's happened to you. You're planning to leave Moscow?"

He hedged. "In a way."

"I will tell you a secret that only Sofya Alexandrovna knows. At the school where my sister, Nina, taught, they started our usual story. Commission, Regional Committee, the principal arrested. That same evening I sent my sister to the Far East to save her. So you are doing the right thing. But I'm asking you not out of idle curiosity. I know it's not something you talk about. I thought that I could help you. It will be hard for you to pack alone, and I'm very good at it. I can also get your train ticket, and bring out your suitcases, and then we'll meet at the metro station. That's what Nina and I did."

"Thank you, Varya, thank you, dear sweet girl. I'm very touched by your offer. Have you looked at the journals I sent you?" Mikhail Yurevich asked, changing the subject.

"Yes, at some of them. Not everything, of course."

"Enjoy them, read them. You have lots of time."

## ❧ **42** ❧

If, on May 1, Tukhachevsky had looked back at the tribune on top of the Mausoleum, if *he* could have seen Tukhachevsky's face, then perhaps *he* would not have called for him now. But Tukhachevsky did not look back and *he* had not seen his face. Tukhachevsky had left, showing *him* the back of his head. And *he* was not an executioner. *He* didn't look at the back of the head, *he* looked them in the face. And *he* would look at Tukhachevsky's face one last time. Was he expecting his end? Did he understand that he was doomed, or hadn't he guessed yet? And that man will cease to exist for *him*. It didn't matter whether there was an hour, a day, a week, or a month left before his death.

*He* never pronounced sentence himself. On the contrary. *He* hid the sentence that *he* carried out *himself*. *He* calmed them down. Sometimes it was to lower their vigilance, but that wasn't the case with Tukhachevsky. He was no longer dangerous. He was at the Commissariat doing his work. In a week's time he would leave for Kuibyshev, where he would be arrested. There was no information on Tukhachevsky's contacts with troop commanders. Escape abroad was out of the question. His every step was known, and all the military airfields were under control. He wouldn't get in touch with anyone, nor would he run away.

But still *he* had to see him, look into his eyes, and thereby give him hope for life. Perhaps the priest was still sitting in *him* somewhere? Why not — giving a man hope for life on earth was more charitable than giving him hope for heavenly life.

No, *he* wasn't a priest, and it wasn't charity that was prompting *him*. Charity was not a political category. Charity belonged in the vocabulary of ladies from the aid societies. *He* wanted to see his vanquished enemy while he was still alive with *his* own eyes. And *he* was not giving him hope out of charity, but so that he would remain unknowing until the end, so that he would cling to the hope of life. A man who has accepted inevitable death is far from earthly cares and you cannot any longer affect him. A man who still has a glimmer of hope can be affected. Let Tukhachevsky worry. Let him worry to his final minute.

Tukhachevsky entered the room. He behaved as usual, with dignity. He bowed slightly and sat down in the chair Stalin had indicated, but he made it seem that that was the very chair he was planning to sit in anyway. A sleek and haughty gentleman, a gentleman with an aristocratic face, a gentleman in his every movement.

"You're not taking offense over your transfer to Kuibyshev?" Stalin asked.

"I am prepared to serve wherever I am sent, but the reason for the transfer is not known to me."

"Comrade Voroshilov did not tell you?"

"No."

"Why didn't you demand an explanation from him?"

Tukhachevsky looked at him. It was a calm, clear gaze, but in its depths Stalin sensed mockery.

"My job is to obey orders. I was ordered to turn in my files, and I am doing that."

Stalin sat with his eyes shut.

Then he looked up at Tukhachevsky.

"The Party always trusted you, and it trusts you now. However, you see the state of the country. This is tied to a sharpening of the domestic political situation. The resistance of hostile elements has increased, and the vigilance of Soviet people has increased, too. It happens that Soviet people can be excessively vigilant, overly vigilant, and an unhealthy suspiciousness develops. And we have such phenomena, unfortunately, in the army. It is not good, of course, even though it is understandable. The trials of Zinoviev-Kamenev and Pyatakov-Radek have intensified the atmosphere. It was in this atmosphere that your close friend Yulya Ivanovna Kuzmina was arrested. . . ."

He stopped.

"Yulya Ivanovna," Tukhachevsky said, "is the wife of Nikolai Nikolaevich Kuzmin. You must know him. He has been a Party member since 1903, the former commissar of the Southwestern front, a delegate to the Tenth Party Congress, and a participant in the quelling of the Kronstadt Uprising. He was never in any opposition. . . ."

"We know Comrade Kuzmin," Stalin interrupted. "The Central Committee of the Party is familiar with his contributions. But it is Yulya Ivanovna Kuzmina who has been arrested. I repeat, your good friend. There has been a lot of talk in that regard — bourgeois talk, women's gossip. This talk and this gossip must be stopped. We wanted to protect the authority and respect due our military leaders. The authority of our military leaders is the authority of the army. That's why the Politburo thought it is proper to transfer you to Kuibyshev. Let the talk die down, let the NKVD deal with Kuzmina — and, incidentally, with your special messenger. He was also arrested."

Tukhachevsky said nothing.

Not getting an answer, Stalin continued, "Commanders Putna and Primakov, arrested in connection with the Zinoviev and Pyatakov trials, are giving strange testimony."

Tukhachevsky was still silent.

"I mentioned Putna and Primakov in connection with their old Trotskyite ties, which they did not sever, as it turns out. This has nothing to do with you personally. However, it does complicate the general political situation in the army. Therefore, I repeat, the Politburo deemed it necessary to make certain transfers in the army, in order to put an end to the spread of all sorts of rumors. As soon as the situation is normalized, and the gossip ceases, you will return to Moscow. Besides, I believe that even though it is temporary, work with the troops will be useful for checking on the training that is going on under your plan. What do you think, Comrade Tukhachevsky?"

"I will work where the Party orders."

He avoided a direct answer.

"Fine."

Stalin rose, moved away from his desk, and offered Tukhachevsky his hand. "I wish you success."

Tukhachevsky clicked his heels. "Thank you, Comrade Stalin." And he added, stretching out the words, "Until we meet again."

He made it clear that he had no hopes of ever meeting again. And he was right.

Stalin called Yezhov and ordered him to bring the complete confessions of Primakov and Putna no later than the fifteenth.

That same night, Primakov gave evidence that the Trotskyites wanted to replace Voroshilov with Yakir and it was possible that Yakir was obeying secret orders from Trotsky that Primakov did not know about.

Having read the statement, Yezhov fell into a fury. That bastard Primakov was tricking him. He was trying to confuse the issue. What did orders unknown to him mean?

Yezhov called in the investigator Avseyevich and shook the transcript under his nose in the presence of Leplevsky, chief of the Special Section. He shouted that he could flush these papers down the toilet.

"I'm asking you in plain Russian. What does 'unknown orders' mean? Bring Primakov here. I'll talk to him myself!"

"That's impossible right now," Avseyevich replied. "Primakov is 'resting' in his cell."

"Where's Putna?" Yezhov asked Leplevsky.

"Putna was brought back an hour ago from the Butyrki Prison hospital. Putna is here."

"Bring Putna here!"

He looked terrible. His face was white, his diplomatic bearing was gone, his mustache was askew. He would die the peasant he had been born.

"Well," Yezhov said in a soft voice, imitating Stalin. "Are we going to be stubborn?"

Putna was silent.

"He doesn't want to talk," Yezhov stated, and Avseyevich grabbed Putna by the shoulders. He knew how to beat people, the best places to hit them.

But they had to work Putna over until six that morning.

Nikolai Ivanovich Yezhov stood up from his chair and started in himself. He lit a cigarette and put it out immediately against Putna's bare body. He used up almost an entire pack, until Putna, almost unconscious, signed a statement that Tukhachevsky, Yakir, and Feldman were part of a "military anti-Soviet Trotskyite organization."

Yezhov returned to his office after six and sat down on the couch in the small room beyond his office. Stalin had started coming to the Kremlin early, around noon, sometimes even at eleven. Nikolai Ivanovich had to be in his office then.

The table was set with bottles of wine, cognac, and vodka and fresh zakuski. Nikolai Ivanovich drank a shot of vodka and ate a pickle; they were good pickles, from Nezhinsk. Then he had a second glass and another pickle. He tore off a chunk of French bread, buttered it, and put a spoonful of black caviar on the butter. He didn't allow them to prepare sandwiches for him. That was unappetizing, like a business canteen.

Nikolai Ivanovich had not been home for several days. The interrogations were going on round the clock, as they had a very short deadline. They had two or three weeks to prepare for the trial, and even though it was to be a closed one, they still needed confessions. These short deadlines didn't leave time for the usual methods — the conveyor, the isolation well with water and rats, hunger, thirst, lack of sleep, psychological pressure, threats to harm loved ones — all that took time. And they had no time. So he had to use special methods. They had permission to do so. When Nikolai Ivanovich hinted to Comrade Stalin about it delicately and cautiously, Stalin looked at him heavily and said, "If you do it, don't be afraid. If you're afraid, don't do it!"

"Yes, of course," Yezhov replied. "But I'm taking into account that they'll have to appear before a military tribunal ... in decent condition. As they say, measure seven times, cut once."

"But you do have to cut," Stalin interrupted. "The important word in that proverb is *cut*. You measure in order to cut, and not the other way around."

That was clear permission to use extraordinary methods of physical pressure.

"Yes, yes," Nikolai Ivanovich sighed in relief.

He had no doubts that Tukhachevsky, Yakir, and the others would also be stubborn and deny their participation in the conspiracy. That meant he'd have to use the strongest methods. The "lark," for instance — you put the son-of-a-bitch on his stomach, tie his hands and feet, stuff the middle of a long towel in his mouth, like a bit in a horse's mouth, then tie the ends across his back to his feet and pull the towel so tight that his heels touch his head. And you keep him like that, and pull even tighter, until his back breaks. Or "Frinovsky's saddle," named after Yezhov's deputy. He invented it, although it didn't take particular inventiveness — you put the suspect naked on two electric coils and hold him there until you smell burnt meat. And, if they're very stubborn, you can do the "ball crusher." You throw the naked man on his back on the floor and spread his legs. Two men hold his legs, two hold his arms, and a fifth gradually squeezes his testicles with the heel of his boot. No one could stand that! But it was dangerous — a little too hard, and you couldn't drag the man into a courtroom.

And you had to be careful with burning the hair in the ear, otherwise the ears would be covered with blisters, and you had to bandage the head. That wouldn't work for the courtroom, either. Nikolai Ivanovich had to keep an eye on everything, make sure they didn't overdo it. And he had to sleep in his office.

Nikolai Ivanovich was in no rush to go home. His family life was over. And he had worked so hard to create it, to protect it. . . . They had no children, so they adopted one, Natasha, a fine little girl. She was blond and gentle. She'd climb into bed with them in the morning, hugging and kissing, pressing her little body close to them. Let her be cozy while she was little. And the ones whom he was depriving of parents, let them be happy in orphanages. They'd grow up under new names, they would live like ordinary Soviet citizens. The others would be branded for life — "child of an enemy of the people," and their path was to follow their parents. Let them thank their stupid relatives for "saving" them from the orphanages. Actually, it depended. Natasha was lucky, they took her from an orphanage. But now that their family was destroyed, who knew what would happen to her. . . .

He was adopted, too, brought up in a simple worker's family. He

went to work early, and in 1917, when he was twenty, he joined the
Party. The workers' kids almost all followed the Bolsheviks. The
Mensheviks and Social Revolutionaries attracted the wastrels, the
home-grown philosophers, the rotten intellectuals. The Bolsheviks
saw it clean and simple. They divided the world into ours and not
ours. The strangers had to be destroyed, our own people had to be
helped. There was discipline — you get an order, do it, don't think
about it. The thinking was done for you.

A short man, Nikolai Ivanovich looked like a dwarf on the
tribune, in a parade, and in a crowd. Everyone who stood next to
him looked down on him. He was a good singer, a fine tenor, so his
friends said. He once even auditioned for a lady professor from
Petrograd. Haughty bitch! She heard him out and said, "You have
a voice, but no schooling. That can be overcome. What can't be
overcome is your height. In an opera every leading lady will be a
head taller than you. Sing as an amateur, sing in a choir — that's the
place for you."

He found his own place, not on the stage, not in a choir, not on
the tribune, but in the Party apparat, behind a desk, in a big chair.
This was his real place, he found it, and most important, he found
it in time. The Civil War had ended, and it was the big chairs who
were running things. They had the power.

He was hardworking, quiet, and unnoticeable. He suited everyone. He never associated too closely with anyone, but every boss
considered him his man. By the mid-1920s he was already secretary
of one of the Party Oblast committees in Kazakhstan. Stalin's
inflexible clerical system impressed Nikolai Ivanovich. He had
captured the essence of that system, its heart — the correct selection
and placement of cadres, necessary cadres, your own cadres. And
when the intra-Party struggle for leadership began, Nikolai Ivanovich bet on Stalin ridding himself of his opponents and promoting
his allies.

In 1929 at the height of collectivization and dekulakization, he
was transferred to Moscow as deputy people's commissar of
agriculture. Here he prepared instructions resettling hundreds of
thousands of peasants and transferring millions of homesteaders to
collective farms.

"I feel sorry for the people," his wife once said.

"Don't you feel sorry for me? I don't get out of the office for days at a time."

And he did work day and night. But he prepared neat charts and graphs for the Central Committee with figures on every Oblast and even subdivided them into separate regions. Comrade Stalin noticed him and in 1930 transferred him to the apparat of the Central Committee as chief of Personnel. Working under Comrade Stalin, his career skyrocketed — candidate member of the Politburo, people's commissar of internal affairs, he handled the Pyatakov-Radek trial and was preparing the army trial. In fact, he was the number-two man in the Party. Everyone could see his position now. Members of the Politburo courted him. They had forebodings about their future.

It was nervous-making work. It was usually done by others, but sometimes he had to help out, the way he did today with Putna. During the Civil War the enemy was obvious — the bourgeoisie and the White Guard. In collectivization the enemy was clear, too — the kulaks. They didn't have to confess to anything. They were simply put up against the wall. But now it was different. Everything had to be done with paperwork. Everyone's guilt had to be proved. How it was proved didn't matter. The important thing was that each one signed a statement, and the NKVD had methods to make them do that. You get vicious doing work like that. The only place where he could relax and rest, play with Natasha, was home. And now he had no home.

He had lived with his wife, Yevgenia, for fifteen years! And she had married him for love. What had he been then? An ordinary Party worker. And he had got himself such a beauty, with dark eyes and dark hair. Now, of course, her legs were becoming swollen, and her heart was acting up. She was modest. Educated. In 1929, right after their move to Moscow, she went to work for the Agricultural State Publishing House as an ordinary proofreader. She explained that the work required great literacy. Alone, without his help, she moved up, and became deputy editor in chief of the magazine *The U.S.S.R. Under Construction*, and from what he heard, was a very good worker.

But she had become a bad wife. Last September, as soon as he was named people's commissar of internal affairs, their relations were ruined. She boycotted him. Before, whenever he got home, whether it was five or six in the morning — you couldn't leave the Central Committee before Comrade Stalin — she was always waiting with dinner for him. Even if she had fallen asleep, she would get up and eat with him. Now his dinner was served by the maid. His wife was asleep because she had to get up early. She once even said sarcastically, "I'm not a people's commissar. I have to be at the office at ten."

Last year they started a women's magazine, *Public Activist*. Yevgenia was made part of the editorial board. Her friend Asya Sergeyevna Popova, wife of Sergei Syrtsov, leader of the Syrtsov-Lominadze bloc, was the editor in chief. He once tried to warn Yevgenia about Popova but she replied sharply, "I work with her." All right, he let it go. The Trotskyite husband of one of the magazine employees was arrested. And in front of everyone at the magazine, Yevgenia demonstratively put the wife in her own car. This was a car for which all stoplights turned green and all the traffic police saluted. He didn't say anything about that either. He knew she would say, "I used the car for an important magazine errand." Stupid woman, didn't she suspect that her every step was reported to him? He had given the orders himself. All information about the magazines *The U.S.S.R. Under Construction* and *Public Activist* concerning Yevgenia Yezhova was to be put on his desk. And he learned that Yevgenia had given his car to the wife of an enemy of the people in front of everybody. Think of the gossip that would cause. How his enemies in the Central Committee would use it! She wanted to be known for her kindness. Her husband was a villain, a master of torture and execution, and she was an angel.

And then, the latest information. On her affair with the editor in chief, Uritsky. A stab in the back! Good for the informant — he wasn't afraid to report this. Nikolai Ivanovich had never even thought about the possibility of lovers, because they would know with whom they were dealing. But that bastard Uritsky. Wasn't he afraid of dealing with him, with Yezhov! It looked as if Yezhov weren't so scary. It looked as if you didn't have to be afraid of Yezhov. We'd see, we'd see! Uritsky was related to the writer Leopold Averbakh, which meant he was related to Yagoda.... Revenge? Was it a setup? Where did they meet? They were seen together only at the magazine office. So what? He was the editor, she was his deputy. Why shouldn't they sit and talk? But Uritsky had the same kind of room behind his office as this one. That's where they frolicked. . . . There was incontrovertible proof from the Uritsky family. They begged him to break off with Yezhova. The conversation had been recorded. Betrayal, betrayal, betrayal!

Nikolai Ivanovich poured himself a third vodka. Yevgenia had been loyal, calm, considerate, and pure. He had been proud that in this lousy country there was at least one honest person and that was his wife. No, even in his own family there wasn't an honest person. They were all bastards, the whole country! Take anyone at all — a bastard. Shoot anyone at all — they were all bastards!

Fine, they'd get to them all, they'd shoot them all! As for Uritsky and Yevgenia Yezhova — Uritsky would be arrested tomorrow, as a relative and collaborator of the arrested Yagoda. Yevgenia Yezhova, having worked under Uritsky's direction, would be placed under house arrest until the investigation in his case was complete. And then he'd see.

Having made the decision, Yezhov drank another glass of vodka, had more caviar, drank some tea from the Thermos bottle, undressed, and went to sleep.

## 43

S ofya Alexandrovna called her at work. Varya froze. Sasha
was in Moscow! Sofya Alexandrovna never called unless it
was important.

However, Sofya Alexandrovna's voice was dead, lifeless,
and boded ill.

"Varya," she said. "It's me. Get off from work and go home. To
your house. I'll go there."

And she hung up.

Had something happened to Sasha?

Igor Vladimirovich let her go without a word. Varya put away
her blueprints and her instruments and hurried home. About ten
minutes later Sofya Alexandrovna arrived, sank onto the couch, and
tried to catch her breath.

"What happened, Sofya Alexandrovna?"

With trembling fingers, Sofya Alexandrovna got a tube of
nitroglycerine from her sweater pocket and put a tablet under her
tongue.

Varya waited in silence, knowing that when Sofya Alexandrovna
hurried she lost her breath and needed to take her medicine. The
attack would pass.

"I was watching for you out the window, and when I saw you
come home, I hurried."

She paused and then looked up.

"Mikhail Yurevich committed suicide."

"What? What do you mean? Sofya Alexandrovna, what are you
saying?"

She had considered the possibility that Mikhail Yurevich would be arrested. It had seemed to her that he was expecting to be arrested, and that's why he was giving away his books, and why he had listened so attentively when she told him how she had got Nina out of Moscow in a hurry. He had even nodded, as if agreeing to her plan — she would bring his suitcases out the back way and wait for him at the metro. They had discussed it just a few days ago. And now he had committed suicide!

"When did it happen? How? Why?"

Sofya Alexandrovna did not respond. She shut her eyes.

Varya brought a pillow from the bed over to the couch. "Lie down, Sofya Alexandrovna."

"Oh ... yes ... all right. Let me take off my shoes.... My feet swell up."

"Don't bend over!"

Varya kneeled and untied her shoes.

Sofya Alexandrovna shifted and moved higher up on the couch.

"Varya, you can't imagine how horrible it was." She sighed deeply. "I've been feeling sick all day. Spring, when the weather changes, my heart reacts.... So please forgive me."

"Don't be silly, Sofya Alexandrovna. Lie there, and if it's hard for you to talk, don't say anything. I'll go over to your apartment and find out everything."

"No, no." Sofya Alexandrovna was agitated. "Don't go there, no, not under any circumstances."

"All right, I won't go, I'll do whatever you say, just calm down."

Sofya Alexandrovna lay back on the pillow and shut her eyes.

"Shall I call an ambulance?"

Sofya Alexandrovna took a breath. "No, it's not necessary. I'm better.... I want to sit up."

"Stay put."

"It's hard to talk."

Varya helped her sit up and put a pillow behind her back.

"It was so horrible, Varya, so horrible." She took another deep breath. "I was sick all day, I told you, my heart was bothering me.... My supervisor said, 'Why don't you go home, Sofya Alexandrovna?' I came home and saw Mikhail Yurevich's coat on the rack. That seemed strange. He should have been at work. I thought maybe he was sick. I went to his door and listened. It was quiet. I knocked, softly, no one answered, so I knocked harder. No answer again. I opened the door. And, oh my God, Varya, my God. He was hanging there.... Hanging. And his head to one side, like this."

She bent her head and her eyes rounded with horror. "I was so frightened, Varya, so frightened. I shut the door and leaned against the wall. I thought I was going to fall down.... What should I do? Maybe he was still alive, but I couldn't take him down, I wasn't strong enough.... No one was in the apartment.... I ran out into the hall, began knocking on the neighboring apartments. I roused the whole staircase.... They took him down. Mikhail Yurevich was dead. The ambulance, the militia came. They questioned me. When did I come in, what did I see, whom did I call, who took him down. They wrote up the statement.... And then, Varya, other men came."

She switched to a whisper. "People from the NKVD, yes, yes, they showed me their identification, which wasn't necessary. I recognized them immediately. They ordered me to tell the truth. They asked who came to visit Mikhail Yurevich. No one, I said, he lived a lonely life. How about relatives? A brother in Ryazan, he had visited last summer. Address? I have his address, I had taken it for Sasha, but I said that I don't know it. And now the most important thing, Varya." She raised her voice again. "Did he give me or other neighbors any papers? Do you understand? That's why I called you so urgently — he gave you and Sasha his books."

"So what?"

"Varya, think! You can't tell anyone! They'll go through the whole bookcase, go through every book, looking for something, a piece of paper. And they'll ask, 'Why you?' and 'Who else?' and 'What for?' ... That's why I called you so urgently, to warn you. Keep quiet about the books, or they'll call you in and question you."

"What are they looking for?"

"I don't know, but I think it's something to do with the census. That's what he was doing at the Statistics Office, and he was having problems there lately."

"He wasn't the only one. They were all having problems there. Mikhail Yurevich told me. They came up with six million people fewer in the census than they were supposed to. I remember that precisely. And Mikhail Yurevich could have been doing his own calculations, and that's what they were looking for."

"The room was sealed," Sofya Alexandrovna said. "They took Mikhail Yurevich to the morgue. We have to let his brother in Ryazan know."

"Of course. Give me the address, I'll send him a telegram."

"You have to think it through, Varya. 'They' might be interested in who sent him the telegram."

"I won't sign it. 'Come instantly, Mikhail Yurevich is dead.' Or 'Mikhail Yurevich is very sick.' I won't sign it."

"Wait, Varya. You can't write that he's dead. They wouldn't accept a telegram like that. They'll want to see the death certificate, to make sure it isn't a prank. At any rate, they'll want to see your passport and they'll write down all the information. And who knows if it will reach him in Ryazan. They might confiscate it. Here's another plan. You go to the long-distance phone service at the Central Telegraph office and call Ryazan. I have his telephone numbers, both home and office. Tell him that you're calling from Mikhail Yurevich's office. Mikhail Yurevich is dead, yes, just say it, he's dead and come urgently. And hang up. . . . That's the safest way. . . . Tomorrow morning Yevgeny Yurevich will arrive, the room is sealed, he'll go 'there,' and they'll ask him, 'How do you know about your brother's death?' He'll tell them, 'They called me from his office.' And at the office they'll be able to prove that no one called Ryazan. So we won't be getting anyone into trouble."

"I'm not sure we need all these precautions," Varya said with a frown.

"We do, Varya, we do."

"You mean I don't have the right to inform a man that his brother has died? Relatives aren't allowed to bury their own?"

"They are, Varya, and you have the right. It's so. But when a man dies, they don't usually seal his room and question his neighbors. . . . But you see, they did. We must take that into account. I won't allow you to take any risks."

"Fine," Varya said.

She put on her raincoat and tucked the slip of paper with the phone numbers into her purse. She sat down again.

"It's so awful — poor Mikhail Yurevich. I can't imagine that I'll never see him again!"

"Neither can I." Sofya Alexandrovna wiped away a tear.

"Maybe you shouldn't go home today. Why don't you stay here?"

"Maybe I will, Varya. I just can't walk. . . ."

The coffin with Mikhail Yurevich's body was in a small room at the morgue. They had put flowers around his face to cover up the neck and the rope burns. Varya held Sofya Alexandrovna's arm and led her over to the coffin. Yevgeny Yurevich, who looked just like his late brother but didn't have a pince-nez, gazed at them in bewilderment. Galya, a neighbor, was there, and kept sobbing and wailing, "He was a good man, a quiet man." Three co-workers from the Statistical Bureau came, comparatively young people, with sad faces. They must have liked Mikhail Yurevich. It was impossible not to like him. He must have had many more friends in Moscow, but his address books were taken away with his other documents.

Something should have been said, some words spoken. But no one said anything, no words were uttered. Official phrases didn't belong, and no one dared say real words. They stood in silence, each one bidding Mikhail Yurevich farewell in his heart, and the co-workers and Yevgeny Yurevich carried the coffin out to the bus, and went off to the Vagankovo Cemetery. The coffin lid was hammered on, and the coffin lowered. Everyone tossed a handful of yellowish brown clay, and the grave diggers picked up their shovels. A board with a grave number and Mikhail Yurevich's last name was stuck into the fresh mound. In a year, when the earth settled, they would put up a monument.

Sofya Alexandrovna and Galya went back to the Arbat, Yevgeny Yurevich to the train station. He had to be back in Ryazan today. He would return in three days for Mikhail Yurevich's things. Sofya Alexandrovna suggested he take the books he had left to Sasha and Varya, but he refused. You can't violate a man's last wishes.

Varya was left alone. She went to the graves of her mother and father. She hadn't been there all winter. The cemetery was empty. Last year's leaves were raked into piles and the first green grass was showing through. Flowers were planted here and there.

She walked down the path. The old prerevolutionary monuments were crosses or had crosses on the headstones. Next to them were the new graves — of the atheists. Why did it happen so fast, why did people give up religion so quickly? She had been brought up an atheist. That was understandable, but millions of people had believed for centuries. And they tossed it aside. Easily. They believe in Communism right away. Maybe the day would come and they would toss aside that belief too. No, they wouldn't. It was etched deep into them, pounded into them. It would hold people for eternity.

Varya went outside the cemetery gates and bought some seedlings. She returned to her parents' graves. There was a stone with their names cut into it — Sergei Ivanovich Ivanov and Marya Petrovna Ivanova. . . . How had Nina and Varya survived after their death? Their aunt came, she took them away for the summers to her place in Kozlov. She still had a house there. There were some other distant relatives who helped out. They must have chipped in for the headstone and railing. And at fourteen Nina was earning money. Sasha had gotten the Komsomol Committee to give her a paying job. Sasha, Sasha . . .

Varya kept a glass jar, a broom, and a little shovel wrapped in a rag behind the headstone. She cleaned up the grave, planted purple pansies and white daisies, went to the water tap several times to fill the jar and water the flowers. She washed the stone and wiped the railing with the wet rag. It was getting rusty in spots and would have to be repainted. She would have to replace the bench because it was rotting.

Varya sat on it anyway and turned her face to the sun. She didn't want to leave. There was no place to go, nothing to do. Who needed her? Mikhail Yurevich had needed her. He was happy when she visited. But Mikhail Yurevich was gone. Sofya Alexandrovna needed her. Sasha didn't need her now. What was she going to do, how was she going to go on living? Did she need to live? In fear, lies, and deceit? To repeat the meaningless words, to get up obediently and sit down obediently. Should she go on living like that or should she follow Mikhail Yurevich's example? She would never forgive "them" for his death. She knew why he had committed suicide. She remembered his words, "I won't hide anything. . . . Six million . . . what did they die for? . . . Hiding that is unacceptable, immoral. . . ." Mikhail Yurevich preferred the rope. They had forced him to kill himself. They didn't need honest people, people like Mikhail Yurevich, Sasha.

But it was so frightening to die. To hang in a noose, to lie in a coffin and then in a grave, where worms would eat you. No! Horrible. Scary! Varya looked around. There was no one, no living creature in sight.

But a monotonous male voice disturbed the silence. Esenin's grave was nearby, and someone was reading his poetry by it. Whenever Varya came to Vagankovo — winter, summer, spring, or fall — there were always people there reading his poetry. His books were banned, he was called a kulak poet, he was accused of having morbid moods, but they couldn't extinguish people's love for him.

That thought cheered her up. She didn't want to die, she wanted to live. She had to go see Sasha. Sofya Alexandrovna would eventually find out his address. She would go to Sasha, overcome her shame, her false pride, and explain to him. She would tell him that she loved him.

She heard Esenin's poetry but she couldn't make out the words. She stood up and started walking toward it. She could hear better now.

> And once more I will return to my father's house,
> Take solace in other people's happiness,
> And on a green evening by the window,
> I'll hang myself on my sleeve.

A stoop-shouldered elderly man was reading the poetry. Two old women and a man in a thick sweater were listening.

Varya turned and headed for the gates.

She could still hear.

> The moon will float and float,
> Sipping its oars in the lakes.
> And Russia will go on living
> Dancing and weeping by the fence.

## 44

**P**utna's statement was put on Stalin's desk exactly at eleven hundred hours.

"Is that all?" Stalin asked.

"I understand, Comrade Stalin. We'll hurry. Excuse us."

During the night of May 13, Army Commander Second Rank and Chief of the Frunze Military Academy August Kork was arrested. The fifty-year-old commander, a former lieutenant colonel in the tsarist army, should have broken quickly, according to Yezhov, but Leplevsky reported that two days had yielded no results. Kork was being stubborn and denied everything.

"He still thinks he's the hero of Perekop," Yezhov said. "Give him the worst!"

After the torture, Kork wrote two statements to Yezhov, which the people's commissar felt should satisfy Stalin. They contained a confession that Enukidze had brought Kork into the Trotskyite military group. The group's goal was a military overthrow in the Kremlin, and they set up a cabal composed of Tukhachevsky, Kork, and Putna.

On May 15, Corps Commander Feldman was arrested. With the same methods they beat out evidence against over forty people.

In presenting this statement to Stalin, Molotov, Voroshilov, and Kaganovich, Yezhov asked for and received permission to arrest all the men named.

On the evening of May 20, he ordered Leplevsky to interrogate Primakov once again, since Leplevsky confirmed that Primakov was now especially ready for it. Every night for a week an NKVD agent was in the cell, making sure that Primakov didn't get a minute's sleep. The supervisors kept him awake during the day.

Yezhov personally went to the Lefortovo Prison by ten that evening. Primakov's statements were too important to be left to Leplevsky. Avseyevich dragged Primakov, exhausted, into the room where Yezhov and Leplevsky were waiting for him. Nevertheless, almost five hours later, the back of Avseyevich's jacket was soaked with sweat, and that bastard Primakov was still holding out.

Then Yezhov said, "He's a cavalry officer, commander of the Chervonny Cossacks.... A big man. That means use the toughest methods...."

And Yezhov went out to the toilet.

He came back just when Primakov gasped that Tukhachevsky was head of the conspiracy and was connected to Trotsky. Besides Tukhachevsky, Primakov named another forty officers, and he added that the common talk among the military was that Voroshilov wasn't fit to be people's commissar of defense. This new statement became a part of the interrogation on an assassination attempt against Voroshilov.

When Stalin got Primakov's statement, he saw Yezhov and his deputy Frinovsky on May 21.

"Is Tukhachevsky still in Moscow?" Stalin asked.

"He'll be in Kuibyshev tomorrow," Yezhov replied briefly.

"Arrest him there," Stalin ordered.

Tukhachevsky arrived at his new post on May 22, and immediately went to a Party conference of the Volga Regional Military Okrug. After the meeting he was asked to go to the Party Oblast Committee office to see the secretary, Comrade Postyshev. He was arrested there and shipped to Moscow.


When the most popular methods failed, Yezhov took on Tukhachevsky himself, leaving Leplevsky and replacing Avseyevich with Ushakov. He had a stronger arm and was tougher. He also had a higher rank.

Tukhachevsky was brought in by four burly men. Yezhov ordered them to stay.

Tukhachevsky's face did not show any bruises. On Yezhov's orders he was beaten with rubber clubs and kicked with boots, so that there would be no marks. They spat in his eyes and urinated in his face. But now the spittle and urine had been wiped away.

"Well then, Citizen Tukhachevsky, do you admit your participation in the rightist-Trotskyite military terrorist organization?"

Tukhachevsky regarded him with hatred.

And then Yezhov ordered them to use the extreme measures that he had considered in his back room.

Let's see how the pretty boy cringes. . . .

"Stop," groaned Tukhachevsky. "I'll sign."

The statement signed by Tukhachevsky was brought by Yezhov to Stalin the next day.

However, that day Stalin could not read it. He was talking with the pilots Chkalov, Baidukov, and Belyakov about their coming direct flight from Moscow to the U.S.A. over the North Pole. Comrade Stalin was planning it for after the twentieth of June. According to *his* calculations, Tukhachevsky and the others would be shot between the tenth and the fifteenth, followed by rallies of approval, and right after that would come an upsurge of excitement and triumph over this unprecedented flight. And that would be right. The people would see that destroying their enemies only strengthens the power of the Soviet Union and its international prestige. The flight in a Soviet-constructed plane, the ANT-25, was of great importance. The glorious Soviet pilots would set a world record of long-distance nonstop flight, covering over twelve thousand kilometers. Stalin, listening to Chkalov's explanations, assiduously delved into all the details.

On May 28, Stalin called Yezhov and Frinovsky to the Kremlin and explained that Tukhachevsky's statement wasn't adequate and the following had to be added — "Back in 1928 Enukidze involved me in a right-wing organization. In 1934 I personally got in touch with Bukharin. I started my espionage connections with Germans in 1935, when I went to Germany for training and maneuvers. . . . On my trip to London in 1936 Putna set up a meeting for me with Sedov. . . . I had ties through the conspiracy with Feldman, S. S. Kamenev, Yakir, Eideman, Enukidze, Bukharin, Karakhan, Pyatakov, I. N. Smirnov, Yagoda, Osipyan, and many others."

On May 29, Yezhov called in Tukhachevsky for another interrogation. Frinovsky, Leplevsky, Ushakov, and those four men were also present. Tukhachevsky was worked over again. Beaten and bloodied, he was pushed against the table and forced to sign the statement dictated by Stalin.

Yezhov brought the transcript of that interrogation to Stalin in the Kremlin.

Stalin read it carefully, and as he read, he marked two pages, and then returned to them, looked at them again, and handed them to Yezhov across his desk. "What is this?"

Both pages had dark brown spots, some in the form of an exclamation point.

Yezhov was stunned. It was blood. Leplevsky hadn't noticed, and neither had Ushakov.

"It's blood, Comrade Stalin. The suspect got a nosebleed while he was signing. The investigator didn't rewrite it, I'm sorry."

"What were you looking at?"

"I somehow missed it, Comrade Stalin, forgive me. It happens. But it will be difficult to rewrite it now. We'll eradicate the spots chemically."

"Dirty work," Stalin said with a frown. "Dirty work. Be neater in the future."

On May 22, at the same time as Tukhachevsky, Corps Commander Eideman was arrested. The next day he was brought to Lefortovo Prison, where Leplevsky entrusted his interrogation to Karpeisky and Dergachev. Eideman categorically denied being part of the conspiracy, but Deputy Chief of Section Agas, who had entered the room, suggested he "clean out his ears." There were interrogations going on in the neighboring rooms, and they could hear noise, screams, and groans. "See," Agas said. "We'll be able to make you talk, too." After a few sessions, during which Agas showed him "how it was done," Eideman fell into clinical depression, answered in non sequiturs, and kept muttering "airplanes, airplanes." On May 25, under more pressure, he wrote to Yezhov, in an uneven hand, skipping letters and words, that he was ready "to help the investigation."

On May 28, Yezhov gave Voroshilov a list of twenty-eight workers of the Artillery Directorate of the Red Army. Voroshilov wrote on the list — "Comrade Yezhov. Take all the bastards. 28/5/1937. Voroshilov."

On that same day, Voroshilov called Army Commander Yakir and ordered him to appear immediately in Moscow at a special session of the Military Council. Yakir replied that he could fly out. Voroshilov ordered him to take the train. At the station, four NKVD men entered his car and arrested Yakir.

On May 29, Army Commander First Rank Uborevich was arrested. Just like Yakir, he had been ordered to Moscow and taken at the train station.

On the next day, May 30, he was put face to face with Kork, who maintained that Uborevich was part of the rightist-Trotskyite organization.

"I deny it categorically," Uborevich replied. "It's a lie from beginning to end. I never had any conversations with Kork about counterrevolutionary organizations."

Leplevsky ordered Ushakov to take Uborevich to Lefortovo and get the needed statement. After a few nights of torture, Uborevich confessed to his participation in the military conspiracy.

That way they had statements from all the men who were going to go on trial — Marshal Tukhachevsky, Army Commanders First Rank Yakir and Uborevich, Army Commander Second Rank Kork, Corps Commanders Primakov, Putna, Eideman, and Feldman.

The same day, May 30, the Politburo passed a decision "relieving Comrade Gamarnik from his position as Deputy People's Commissar of Defense because of his ties to Yakir, who has been expelled from the Party for his participation in a military Fascist conspiracy."

Gamarnik was sick in bed.

On May 31, his deputy Bulin and Smorodinov, chief of the department, came to his apartment and told Gamarnik that he was being fired from the army. Before they reached the car, Gamarnik shot himself.

*Pravda* and other newspapers reported that the next day. "Former member of the Central Committee Ya. B. Gamarnik, caught in his ties with anti-Soviet elements, and apparently afraid of exposure, committed suicide on May 31."

Stalin tore off the last page of May from his calendar. It was over. The top army brass was gone; the rest was just a technical question.

Vyshinsky and Ulrikh would manage. But Tukhachevsky and company had to be judged by military men, marshals, army and corps commanders. The people had to see that *he* was not judging the military. It was the army itself that was destroying traitors in its midst.

Stalin called Voroshilov. Tomorrow, on June 1, he had to organize an expanded Military Council under the People's Commissariat of Defense with the participation of Politburo members, and report to them on the counterrevolutionary conspiracy in their workers and peasants Red Army. All the top workers of the People's Commissariat of Defense, all the commanders of military Okrugs and their deputies, and all commanders had to be invited to the council.

"Talk to Yezhov," Stalin added. "Let him give you the basics of your report. Before your report, Yezhov will familiarize the members of the Military Council with the statements of the accused."

*He* put down the phone and leaned back in his chair. It had to be completed in the first ten days of June. May had passed successfully, the program was fulfilled; today *he* could rest.

On the evening of May 31, Comrade Stalin and other members of the Politburo attended the Bolshoi Theater for the opening of the ten-day festival of Uzbek art in Moscow. He sat in the government box and smiled and applauded without looking at the stage. His comrades in arms had not seen their leader in such good spirits in a long time.

# ♯ 45 ♯

On June 1, 116 people from the military Okrugs and the central apparat were present at the Kremlin at the expanded meeting of the Military Council, twenty members of which had already been arrested. The atmosphere was oppressive. At the start of the meeting, the testimony of the members of the "military Fascist conspiracy" was made public. The reading was long and detailed and tiring, and the confessions were incredible and unbelievable.

The "members of the conspiracy" were well known to everyone — their comrades in arms in the Civil War, close friends of many, highly respected, authoritative and talented leaders. However, everyone kept silent. One word of doubt was enough to be taken straight to Lubyanka to share the fate of those who were already there.

Voroshilov gave a speech. He repeated the charges already known to the members of the Military Council and said, "That Tukhachevsky, Yakir, Uborevich, and a number of others were close, we knew. It was not a secret. But it is very far from that closeness, even that kind of group closeness, to counterrevolution...."

Stalin sat with his eyes shut. Klim was babbling, chewing gum.... Just three months ago at the Plenum of the Central Committee, he had boasted that everything was fine in the army, that there were no saboteurs. He was so happy, our dear Comrade Voroshilov, and now it turns out that there was a gang of spies right under his nose.

"Last year," Voroshilov continued, "in May, in my apartment, Tukhachevsky accused Budyonny and myself in the presence of Comrade Stalin, Molotov, and others of forming a small clique to run army policies. The next day Tukhachevsky denied what he had said. . . . Comrade Stalin then said that we had to stop squabbling privately, that we needed a meeting of the Politburo to examine what was going on. And at that meeting we looked into all the questions and came to the same conclusion. . . ."

"He renounced his accusations," Stalin interrupted impatiently. He was sick of listening to the chatter of Voroshilov, who was obviously terrified and wanted to stress that he and Tukhachevsky had been at odds for a long time. He wanted to separate himself from the conspirators. Well, no one was accusing him of anything.

Voroshilov may have caught the dissatisfaction in Stalin's voice and understood that he should be talking about Tukhachevsky's crimes and not his relations with Tukhachevsky. But he couldn't get off the subject. He was so dull-witted.

"Yes, he did," Voroshilov confirmed. "Even though Yakir's and Uborevich's group behaved aggressively toward me at the meeting. Uborevich kept quiet, but Gamarnik and Yakir behaved very badly toward me. . . ."

Stalin moved his chair noisily, stood up, and walked around the long table at which the top brass was seated. The rest were in chairs along the walls. Stalin walked in the passageway and returned to his seat.

Despite that clear signal of dissatisfaction, Voroshilov went on. "I as a people's commissar must say frankly that not only had I not noticed the vile traitors, but even when some of them were being exposed, I did not want to believe that these people, who seemed to have worked faultlessly, were capable of such monstrous crimes. My fault in that is enormous. But I cannot think of any warning signals from any of you, either, Comrades. . . ."

Many lowered their heads and looked down.

Voroshilov raised his voice. "We must check and purge the army literally to the last traitor! We need the most ruthless purge. Even though in quantity we will suffer great losses . . ." He thought a bit, looked at Budyonny (who moved his lips but said nothing) and then finished his speech with the usual words on the invincible might of the Red Army. The meeting ended late and resumed the next day, June 2.

The first to speak was Stalin. Despite Voroshilov's garbled

speech, yesterday had been useful. The members of the Military Council and the invitees were stunned and confused by the charges and testimony read to them. Now he had to give the people gathered here the proper direction.

In his usual manner, briefly and concisely, Stalin reached his first and main conclusion. "There was a military-political conspiracy against Soviet power, stimulated and financed by German Fascists. This is an incontrovertible fact, confirmed not only by the testimony of the accused, but by authentic documents we have showing their treachery and espionage, documents that for obvious political and intelligence reasons I will not quote here."

Stalin paused, letting this sink in among his audience.

Then he went on. "Who were the leaders of this conspiracy? On the civilian side, Trotsky, Rykov, Bukharin, Rudzutak, Karakhan, Enukidze, and Yagoda. On the army side, Tukhachevsky, Yakir, Uborevich, Kork, and Gamarnik. This is the nucleus of the military-political conspiracy, the nucleus which had systematic ties with the German Reichswehr and which suited its work to the tastes and actions of the German Fascists...."

As before, Stalin walked around the table in the narrow passage between the table and the wall, looking into the faces of those seated against the wall. He could see the faces of the men at the table as he talked.

"Were all the named leaders of the conspiracy German spies, and some Japanese spies? No, not all. We do not have such proof for Rykov, Bukharin, and Gamarnik. As for the rest, the proof of espionage is incontrovertible. Take Tukhachevsky. He gave our operative plan — the holy of holies — to the German Reichswehr. A spy?" He looked at all of them in turn. "A spy!... Yakir systematically informed the German staff headquarters ever since he had served as a military attaché in Germany. And how cheaply these scoundrels sell out! Who recruited Rudzutak, Karakhan, and Enukidze? Josephine Ensen — a Danish spy working for the Germans. She could have recruited Tukhachevsky, too. That's what political and moral uncleanliness leads to!"

His heavy gaze went around the room again. The smug military bureaucrats, a caste, were now trembling with fear. Everyone had something to hide.

"Do not think that only those twenty men named here were involved in the conspiracy. It is an important mistake to think so. The conspiracy sent down huge roots. We have traced it. Four hundred people have been arrested in the army."

He made a small pause. "I think that is only the beginning. This is a military-political conspiracy of large scope. It is the creation of the German Reichswehr. These people are puppets in the hands of the Reichswehr. The Reichswehr wanted us to have a conspiracy, and these gentlemen took care of it."

He pronounced the word *gentlemen* with scorn and with a Georgian accent.

"The Reichswehr wanted these gentlemen systematically to supply them with military secrets, and these gentlemen supplied them with military secrets. The Reichswehr wants the present government to be overthrown, and they took up that business. But they failed. The Reichswehr wanted everything to be ready in case of war, for the army to be sabotaged, so that the army would not be prepared for defense. The Reichswehr wanted that and they were doing it."

He pushed back his chair again and started pacing again, faster this time. He would reach the end of the table, turn sharply, and head back. He continued speaking, his Georgian accent getting heavier.

"These agents are the leading nucleus of the military-political conspiracy in the U.S.S.R., consisting of ten patent plainclothesmen and three instigators. They are agents of the Reichswehr. That is the main thing. This conspiracy, therefore, has external connections and not just domestic roots. It is based on the policies of the German Reichswehr more than on the domestic politics of our country. They wanted to turn the U.S.S.R. into another Spain."

He sat down and banged his fist on the table. "You missed it. We had to find the spies in the army ourselves. Our intelligence in the army is weak, it's bad, it is cluttered with spies. Even inside our Cheka intelligence we found a whole group working for Germany, Japan, and Poland. . . . Why were there no signals from local areas?"

Narrowing his eyes, he looked at Voroshilov and Budyonny. "I asked, why did no one signal, why did no one show vigilance? If there is even five percent truth in a denunciation, that's important."

✳    ✳    ✳

The Military Council continued its work on June 3 and 4 Forty-two people spoke. They all wrathfully condemned the conspirators, repented in the lack of vigilance and shameful complacency. Stalin listened closely and calculated which of them should be put onto the special military court as judges. He had a large piece of paper before him, and he wrote down the names of marshals and commanders who had spoken most harshly. He'd write down the names, cross them out, write them again.

He finally had a list of the military court — Marshals Budyonny, Blukher, and Shaposhnikov, Army Commanders Alksnis, Belov, Dybenko, and Kashirin.

The Military Council tired Stalin and he left for Blizhnyanya dacha, leaving orders that Mikhail Ivanovich Kalinin was to appear for breakfast the next day.

Mikhail Ivanovich arrived, a cozy old man who put up meekly with Stalin's jokes. Of course, Stalin treated him gently — why hurt his feelings? What Stalin really liked about him was that Kalinin was a bad billiard-player, but he loved to play, and Stalin usually beat him. He beat others, too, but the others tried to lose to him. They blew their shots on purpose, they were afraid to beat him. But Kalinin played honestly. He tried hard, his little beard shaking — and he missed!

They played three rounds, all of which Stalin won. He was pleased, the balls went right into the pockets. He slapped Mikhail Ivanovich on the back and said, "Don't be sad, billiards is like that — I win today, you win tomorrow." He knew that Kalinin would never win. He was a lousy player.

After that, Stalin went to the Kremlin, where Molotov, Kaganovich, and Yezhov were waiting for him. They went over the lists of men arrested and selected eight to be tried — Tukhachevsky, Yakir, Uborevich, Kork, Eideman, Primakov, Putna, and Feldman. Their individual cases were combined into a group case.

On June 7, Stalin, Molotov, Kaganovich, and Voroshilov saw Yezhov and Vyshinsky and confirmed the final text of the charges — treason against the homeland, espionage, and terror.

On June 8, they were read to the accused.

On June 9, Vyshinsky and Subotsky, assistant to the chief military procurator, interrogated the men briefly and signed off on the authenticity of their statements. The NKVD investigators who had done the interrogations were present.

That same day Stalin saw Vyshinsky twice, the second time at 10:45 P.M., after which Vyshinsky signed the charges.

After Vyshinsky, at 11:30 P.M. Stalin, Molotov, and Yezhov saw Mekhlis, the editor in chief of *Pravda*.

On June 10, on the basis of Vyshinsky's report, the Extraordinary Plenum approved the composition of the special court, with Ulrikh presiding, as determined by Stalin.

On June 11, Stalin saw Ulrikh. Molotov, Kaganovich, and Yezhov were present.

That day, *Pravda* published the news of the coming trial.

Also on the same day, Stalin sent the following decree to the Republics, Krais, and Oblasts:

> In connection with the coming trial of spies and saboteurs Tukhachevsky, Yakir, Uborevich, and others, the Central Committee suggests you organize workers' rallies, and wherever possible, of peasants, as well as rallies of Red Army units, and vote on the resolution to use the highest measure of repression. The trial should be finished tonight. The sentence will be published tomorrow, that is, June 12.
>
> Secretary of the Central Committee Stalin
> 11/6/37

The men were shot at dawn, while Stalin was still sleeping at his dacha.

He awoke at ten, got up from the couch, slid his feet into his slippers, went to the veranda, opened the drapes, and looked at the thermometer hanging on the outside of the door. It was 72° Fahrenheit.

Stalin put on his jacket anyway, opened the door and went out on the veranda, walked down the asphalt path bordered by lilac and jasmine bushes, stopped, and coughed. Like every smoker, he coughed in the morning, bringing up sputum. Maybe his cough was exacerbated by the poplar pollen floating in the air.

Then Stalin went to the bathroom and shaved. When he returned, the bedding had been cleared from his couch and the latest newspapers were on his table.

Valechka brought breakfast on a tray and smiled. "How did you sleep, Josef Vissarionovich?"

"I slept well, thank you."

"That's fine. Have a good breakfast."

Valechka adjusted the blinds so that the sun wouldn't disturb Josef Vissarionovich and announced that there would be no rain today.

"How do you know that there won't be rain?"

"The dew was thick. I went early to cut some flowers, and my ankles got wet."

Sipping his tea, Stalin looked at the papers. The news of the execution of Tukhachevsky and the other bastards was accompanied by approvals of the execution by workers, kolkhoz workers, labor collectives, military units, scholars, writers, actors, and artists. The whole country furiously and wrathfully condemned the traitors. The newspapers had been filled with similar articles the day after Kirov's murder, and during the first Zinoviev-Kamenev trial, and during the second, and during the Pyatakov-Radek trial, and even earlier, during the trials of the Promparty and the Mensheviks.... The people always showed their support of *him*. But this time there was special support. The other trials had been open, the confessions had been printed in the newspapers, the defendants had been shown in the newsreels. Everybody read the confessions then — Mensheviks, Trotskyites, Zinovievites, bourgeois specialists. Now they had tried glorious and famous officers, heroes of the Civil War, people who had not besmirched themselves in any way. They had been tried in secret court. The people hadn't heard a single word of their confessions. They had tried the cream of the army, which the people loved, of which they were proud, about which they sang songs, and in which almost every young man in the country served. They had all heard these names and had come to respect them.

And still, the people believed *him*, not them. The people followed *him*, not them. Without any doubts or hesitation, the people helped *him* cut off the head of the greatest and most experienced enemy — the military caste.

The last potential enemy inside the country was vanquished. *He* had destroyed the slightest threat to *his* unlimited and personal power in this country. Now the battle for Europe was beginning. Now the battle for world domination was starting.

The first version. France and Britain pit Germany against the U.S.S.R. Impossible. Hitler would never attack the U.S.S.R., because *he* had France and Britain, armed to the teeth, behind *him*.

Second version. War with Germany, Italy, and Japan on one side and France, Britain, and perhaps the U.S.A. on the other. Both sides would seek *his* help. It was a question of terms. What could France and Britain offer *him?* Nothing. But Hitler, keeping Western Europe for himself, could give *him* the Slavic countries and the Balkans. In Asia the U.S.S.R. could get China and India, Japan would get Southeast Asia, where it would get mired in a struggle with America. That's how *he* pictured dividing up the world in the near future. And then they'd see.

For now, the best version was neutrality. Let them wear one another out in a war of many years, during which time *he* would gather his strength, restore the army's military might, strengthen the power of the U.S.S.R., and dictate *his* terms to a weakened Europe. Then *he* would become boss of Europe. Then *he* would create the United States of socialist Europe, which would counterbalance the United States of capitalist America.

Naturally, history and the course of events would make alterations in any plans and prognoses. But world revolution was a myth. Capitalism was strong and organized, the bourgeoisie had managed to create consolidated states. Radical changes in the political system could come about only through war. The victory of the U.S.S.R. in the new war would change the state system of the world to the socialist model, that is, the model *he* had created in the U.S.S.R. The idea of the state that *he* created would be the strongest and most eternal in the history of mankind. Religious ideas lasted for millennia, but they were no more than state policies.

There was a knock at the door. Stalin recognized the knock. It was Vlasik.

"Come in!" Stalin shouted angrily.

Vlasik came in and stood by the door.

"What do you want?"

"Comrade Stalin, I want to remind you about your medicine. You ordered me to tell you at twelve —"

"I know. Go!"

Vlasik left.

Stalin went over to the cupboard, took out the bottle, measured twenty drops into a glass with water, drank it, and frowned. Disgusting stuff. No medicine helped, anyway. As the folk saying went, "Take medicine, and you'll be sick for seven days. Don't, and you'll be sick for a week."

What had he been thinking about? Religious ideas.

The state was stronger than both religion and the nation. There were a hundred nations living on the territory of the U.S.S.R., but their national interests were only part of the state interests. The idea of statehood was not new. *He* didn't invent it, but the state as an absolute was *his* idea, and a world state would be *his* creation. *He* was fifty-eight now; *he* had a lot of time ahead of *him*. *He* did not imagine death, *he* didn't think about it, *he* didn't want to think about it. *He* didn't like that kind of talk. History had selected *him* and would not let *him* die like an ordinary mortal. *His* mission was only just beginning. The truly great was the one whose mission and ideas extend to the whole world. Had there been world empires in history? There had. Did they fall apart? They did. But those empires had been conglomerates of various economic, social, and political systems, and they had existed in a hostile environment. That's why they fell apart.

Hitler also wanted to create a world empire. But a German empire, where the bosses would be German and the rest would be slaves. That empire would not last long — it would be destroyed by the injustice of it.

The world empire *he* would create would be united by a single state idea, a single socialist system, a single government, harsh centralization, and total thought control. Where people thought the same, there was obedience.

These were the tasks *he* was facing. Another year or so, and the total consolidation within the country would be complete. Now everything would be simpler. The army was out of the political game forever. The NKVD was in *his* hands. With its help *he* would bring the cadre revolution in the Party and the state to an end.

These were the first results of the liquidation of the military conspirators. They opened a new stage in *his* life and *his* fate.

＊　　＊　　＊

Nine days after Tukhachevsky's execution, 980 top and middle commanders were arrested as members of the conspiracy. Stalin permitted the wide use of physical measures to get new names.

Fulfilling Comrade Stalin's orders, long lists of arrested army men arrived at the Kremlin every evening. *He* wrote in blue pencil, "For execution. J. St." Only once did *he* replace "execution" with "the camps."

When Comrade Stalin was too busy, the lists were handed to one of *his* comrades in arms — Molotov, Kaganovich, Voroshilov, Shchadenko, or Mekhlis. They, like Comrade Stalin, wrote "For execution" on the lists. But unlike Stalin, they did not change execution for the camps for anyone. They were afraid.

*Of the seven commanders who had tried Tukhachevsky, five were soon shot — Blukher, Belov, Dybenko, Kashirin, and Alksnis. Only Shaposhnikov and Budyonny survived.*

*Of the one hundred and eight members of the Military Council, only ten remained among the living. They included Voroshilov, Shaposhnikov, and Budyonny.*

*Of the forty-two men who spoke in favor of execution at the Military Council, thirty-four were shot. Eight survived. Among them were Voroshilov, Shaposhnikov, and Budyonny.*

*A year and a half later, on November 29, 1938, the people's commissar of defense, Comrade Voroshilov, announced with pride, "During all of 1937 and 1938 we had to clean our ranks ruthlessly.... The purge was radical and all-encompassing.... From the very top to the very bottom.... We cleaned out over forty thousand people...."*

*That is over forty thousand people with the most education, experience, and talent, who made up over half of the senior command of the Red Army.*

*That is how Comrade Stalin prepared the Soviet Union for the coming war.*

# ❧ 46 ❧

ow Vadim had an idea concerning the military people Altman had asked him about after the confrontation with Sergei Alexeyevich.

Near the Arbat, in Bolshoi Rzhevsky Alley, lived many of the important military commanders — Gamarnik, Uborevich, Muklevich, and some others. Vadim had seen Muklevich, Romuald Adamovich, commander of the Soviet Navy, several times. He walked down the street on foot — not on the sidewalk, but in the road. A handsome admiral in his naval cap and dark uniform and armed with a dirk. Why he walked and why in the middle of the road, Vadim didn't know. But he bowed to people on the street and smiled at the children.

Vadim learned that Muklevich knew Sergei Alexeyevich. Sergei Alexeyevich would go to the house on Bolshoi Rzhevsky once or twice a month and see his important customers. He had great respect for Muklevich — "a big boss."

So it was over that "big boss" that they were torturing Sergei Alexeyevich, otherwise Altman wouldn't have asked about military men. Sergei Alexeyevich led them to Muklevich. They didn't need Sergei Alexeyevich himself, but they needed Muklevich and maybe they needed some other officers Sergei Alexeyevich serviced. That's why Sergei Alexeyevich didn't confess to anything. He knew that his every word, even the most harmless one, meant death for innocent people. But what they wanted from him was more than harmless words. They wanted him to state that Muklevich had spoken against Stalin and that he had laughed at the attempts to blame Trotsky for everything, that he had laughed with approval over the joke about Radek and had added something unflattering about Stalin. His teeth might have been knocked when he refused to confirm that army men met at Muklevich's house and discussed Stalin and other such nonsense. They beat him until he bled, and poor Sergei Alexeyevich must have repeated what he said at their confrontation — "I deny it, I deny it" — without understanding the main thing. His steadfastness would change nothing. Whether he gave false evidence or not, Muklevich would still be shot, and they would kill Sergei Alexeyevich just like that, for being stubborn. And say what you will, justify it as you might, it was Vadim who had pushed Sergei Alexeyevich into that pit, who had killed a good man by saving his own skin.

He used to hope that his pseudonym would never be decoded. But now he knew that he couldn't believe a single word that Altman spoke. Today Altman forced him to be a witness at the personal confrontation, and tomorrow he might drag him into court as a witness. Why had he demanded an official review of Afinogenov's *The Distant* from him? And why had he agreed to sign it with his own name, idiot that he was? If they had a show trial for Afinogenov, they would introduce that document over Vadim's real name, and his role would be obvious to everyone. And then good-bye to all his plans and dreams. He would never write anything real. He would lose all his mentors. Who would want to support the secret collaborator "Karamora"?

"Karamora" — what a coincidence that on the very day of the confrontation with Sergei Alexeyevich he recalled Gorky's short story about an informer, an agent of the tsarist secret police. In the toilet he saw a month-old newspaper with Gorky's picture marking the first anniversary of his death. And the name flashed in his mind — Karamora! And what about Gorky? He wrote piously about the construction of the White Sea Canal. He exalted Chekists, he praised Stalin, and he handed him the terrible slogan "If the enemy doesn't give up, he must be destroyed." It was easy for him to write "Karamora." It was easy for him to look down from the height of his special position and slander those who, just like that, at twenty-six had to give up their lives over some stupid joke that the provocateur Elsbein told and then immediately denounced him for hearing.

"Vadim Andreyevich, Vadim Andreyevich..." He couldn't forget that voice, and the face of the beaten, exhausted, suffering Sergei Alexeyevich remained before his eyes. Why didn't Sergei Alexeyevich confess? They probably didn't arrest him right away. They must have called him in for "a chat," as they called it. He didn't confess, he didn't turn anyone in! Or was it that old men weren't afraid to die? Even like that, in prison, under torture? And then Sergei Alexeyevich was probably devout and he couldn't break the commandment "Thou shalt not bear false witness." But he could have said that he heard the joke from Vadim. Why didn't he just tell the truth?

But in the NKVD, jokes and anecdotes counted as anti-Soviet agitation and propaganda, a crime. And Sergei Alexeyevich did not want to testify that Vadim had committed a crime, even though he should have guessed at the very first session of interrogation that it was Vadim who had doomed him.

Horror. . . . When had he become such a shit? He had believed in all of it. He had joined the Komsomol sincerely. Back then someone said that he had joined to further his career, to make it easier to get into college. It wasn't true! He saw that new people were building a new world, and he was attracted to them — strong, decisive, confident of their righteousness. He wanted to be next to them, with them. And he wasn't the only one who believed in their ideas. His father's friends — the brightest minds, the greatest talents — weren't they enthralled by the sweep of construction in the 1930s? Didn't they maintain that there was no other path for Russia? But they weren't the point, now. They weren't the ones who were involved with Sergei Alexeyevich. It was Vadim. He was so ashamed. And he was hot. He couldn't breathe. Should he take a cold shower? He didn't have the strength to walk to the bathroom.

Oh God, why did his great-grandfather come to Russia from Poland? He ruined the lives of his descendants. If Vadim had been born in Warsaw, if he had graduated from the Sorbonne or Oxford, with his pen and his ability to work hard and his memory he would have a name by now. Instead, he was writing hack articles. They didn't stifle people there. They didn't grab them by the throat. They didn't know about the Lubyanka, and they didn't ruin people's lives. What enemies of the state was he fighting? The barber Sergei

Alexeyevich? And yet it was Yuri Sharok who had suggested the business of the joke to him. Then Yuri hadn't done anything for him at all. On the contrary, he had told Altman about Sasha Pankratov and Vika. And as for the joke, it was probably Ershilov, or more likely Elsbein — perhaps both — who had informed them that Vadim had heard it.

All right, he had to go take that shower.

Near the bathroom Vadim stopped as he heard the elevator stop on their floor. The doorbell rang immediately. Vadim shuddered and rushed to Fenya. "I'm in my underwear. Get the door yourself."

It was Ershilov. Speak of the devil.

"Where's the young master?"

He had told him a hundred times, "Call first." And he had asked him a hundred times not to call him the "young master."

"I'm here," Vadim said. "Come on in."

Ershilov arrived in a cross-stitched shirt and bragged that he had bought it at Mostorg.

"Why aren't you dressed? The car will be waiting for us by the Writers' Union at six."

He had forgotten that they were supposed to appear at the Zhukovsky Military Academy.

"I just need an instant," Vadim said. "Sit down. Fenya will give you some berries we picked this weekend at the dacha."

It was good that Ershilov had come over. His mood brightened right away. Vadim never refused a chance to meet with his readers. In Russia people would rather see writers and actors in the flesh than eat bread.

A young blue-eyed pilot, who said his name was Khokhlov, pestered Vadim in the lobby. He wanted to talk about literature. He said he liked Alexei Tolstoy and Leonov and when he wanted a laugh he read Zoshchenko.

"What do you write about?" Khokhlov asked.

"Various things," Vadim replied curtly and turned away. If you go to a literary evening, you should be knowledgeable about the speakers.

They had agreed in the car that Ershilov would begin, then would come Anna Karavayeva, then Semyon Krisanov, who would read love poems. Vadim said that he wouldn't overburden the program and would be happy simply to listen to his colleagues.

Sitting up on the stage and not paying attention to Ershilov's revelations about the ties between the intelligentsia and the people, Vadim looked at the audience. There were a lot of people. Blue-eyed Khokhlov was in a chair added in the third row. Some idols he found for himself — Alexei Tolstoy, Leonov, and Zoshchenko had demanded that Tukhachevsky be shot. Pasternak ought to be added to them. Yes, even Pasternak couldn't stand the pressure. Vadim had trembled with joy when he saw his name among the rest. "Tell me, dear, what millennium is it outside?" This one! Everyone signed — Vsevolod Vishnevsky, Vassily Grossman, Tynyanov, Paustovsky, Konstantin Simonov, Antokolsky, Fedin, Sholokhov, Fadeyev, Tikhonov, all of them.... Is that considered the normal order of things? Then he had nothing for which to blame himself. Of course, what happened to Sergei Alexeyevich was horrible, but that would never happen again. It was only because he was inexperienced that Vadim had fallen for Altman's tricks. And wasn't the rest of what he did more humane? He didn't send anyone to prison, he didn't demand anyone's execution. He simply expressed his point of view on different literary works. Moreover, what he wrote had significance only for Altman, while the words spoken publicly by Alexei Tolstoy or Leonov justified the arrests, the trials, and the executions for tens of millions of people. They were destroying the souls of these young Khokhlovs.

Of course, his dear colleagues reassured themselves that they were in a herd, that there were dozens of signatures. As if that justified them! It didn't. It was each one for himself. If you speak out against, it's death. If you refuse to vote, it's death. If you don't sign a group letter, it's death. But then don't throw stones at him! Altman told him clearly, "If you hadn't hidden behind our broad back, Vadim Andreyevich, you would have landed in prison a long time ago." And prison and death in the long run were synonyms. So let's not be pharisees. Let's admit the obvious. We're all guilty, and Themis has no scales that can tell who is better and who is worse.

And still, they'll try to whitewash themselves before their children and grandchildren. They'll say, "The times were like that." They'll say, "We were wrong, we truly believed it all." Maybe they'll be understood and forgiven. But you can't wash off the label "informer" no matter how hard you try.

Ershilov finished his talk. He got a friendly round of applause, bowed, and sat down next to Vadim.

"Well, how was I?"

"Terrific!"

"I saw that you were looking huffy. I wondered, maybe you didn't like what I was blathering about?"

"It was your imagination. I told you, you were great!"

That damned Ershilov, you couldn't hide anything from him. He noticed that Vadim was in a bad mood, and now he'd pester him with questions.

A slight noise rippled through the audience, and the academy's activist ran up to Karavayeva on the stage with a bouquet of red roses.

"Thank you, Stalin's eagles!"

The audience responded with wild applause.

Taking advantage of the pause, Vadim moved over to Ershilov. "I've developed a headache.... I'm going to slip off. Cover for me, please. Tell them I had to go meet my aunt at the train station."

Vadim went home then. There was a light in his father's room and a light in Fenya's room, but no one came out to meet him. It was a family tomb and not an apartment. He went to the kitchen, took out raspberry compote from the icebox, and poured himself a big mug.

What should he do? Where could he go?

Nowhere. The only way out was to stick to his line. He was a literary reviewer, and nothing more. He would go on writing reviews, just like the ones he would write for newspapers and magazines.

And as for Sergei Alexeyevich, well, of course it was terrible and sad and disgusting, but what could you do? There was nothing he could do to help. He couldn't fix it now! But he had behaved honestly at the confrontation. He had taken all the blame. He didn't make up a word. He didn't lie about anyone. He didn't slander anyone. He was prepared to show the transcript to anyone, and no one would judge him harshly. Sergei Alexeyevich kept denying everything, but it was absolutely clear that he wasn't denying it because it hadn't happened, but out of some principle of his. And he had paid for it.

# ❧ 47 ❧

asha didn't go to Semyon Grigoryevich's dance classes. Why waste time? He'd rather spend time at the library or the movies. He had missed a lot of films in those three years. And then Semyon Grigoryevich's classes were way the hell out in the sticks, in factory clubs and even in offices right after work. They pushed aside the desks and danced to Gleb's bayan. Hack work. And Semyon Grigoryevich, though he called himself a choreographer, had no talent. Sasha wasn't interested.

Nothing interested him. He had nothing to live for, nothing to breathe. The noose was tightening around him, and he felt it. Everything seemed to be fine. He went to work in the morning, filled out his trip log, delivered bricks to a construction site, came back, exceeded his allotted workload, but his name never appeared on the Honor Board. He didn't care about the Honor Board, but his workload was no less than those who were considered shock-workers. But they were afraid. If he were arrested again, anyone who had hung his picture on the board would really pay for it. The director and the Party organizer and the chairman of the union — the whole triangle. And they'd write about them in the newspaper — "Enemies and their protectors." They'd all end up in prison.

Sasha was in no rush to show up at the draft board, but he was summoned.

The military clerk, a captain, flipped through Sasha's passport and asked, "Prison term?"

"Yes."

"Article?"

"Fifty-eight, paragraph ten."

"When were you arrested?"

"January 1934."

"Did you do military service?"

"No."

"Why not? You were twenty-three in 1934."

"I was a student at the Transport Institute. We had higher military training."

Sasha handed the captain his grades and showed him military training and the grade "Good."

"Were you given a rank?"

"No, I didn't graduate. I was arrested."

"Sit here for a bit."

The captain took Sasha's passport and record and went to the next room.... He came back with a form on which he wrote Sasha's name.

"Go to the clinic, the address is there, have a checkup, and return here on Friday. Show this summons at work."

Sasha went to the clinic where they checked his heart, lungs, blood pressure, vision, and hearing, and measured his height and weight. By the end of the day they hadn't found any diseases or defects. He was healthy and on Friday he returned to the draft board.

The same captain took Sasha's documents, went into the next room, and then called Sasha in. Three men sat at a table, their hair combed back in the same way, their expressions serious, their eyes stern. The chairman had everyone sign the form attached to the medical report and announced indifferently, "Fit for noncombat duty in wartime."

And that was Sasha's draft status. With his good health and with his higher military training — "fit for noncombat duty." That meant a construction battalion or the kitchen patrol. An enemy of the people couldn't be trusted with weapons.

Several times a tall, flat-chested woman, Kirpicheva, the Party head of personnel, came to the motor pool. She stood at the dispatcher's office and never took her mean eyes off Sasha while he filled out his trip logs. A bad sign.

Especially, since something incredible was going on. The secretaries of the Oblast and Regional Committees, chairmen of Executive Committees, people's commissars and their deputies were vanishing. Even people from the NKVD were being jailed. Sasha accidently heard Leonid telling someone that Bukharin and Rykov had been arrested right at the Plenum of the Central Committee.

Two of the drivers who had gone to Opochka were arrested and the others were interrogated. No one said what he had been asked as they had to sign a promise not to reveal anything. Tabunshchikov, chief of the whole department, was arrested. Sasha didn't know him, had never seen him, but everyone had said good things about him before his arrest.

Just recently at their political session, Chekin, secretary of the Party organization at the motor pool, read to them about the landing on the North Pole of the polar expedition of Papanin, Fyodorov, Shirshov, and Krenkel, the first men to reach the pole. The electrician Volodya Artyomkin got up and said, "The first man to reach the North Pole was the American Robert Peary, back in 1919, on dog sleds." He said it and sat down. Chekin stared at Artyomkin. How could some American have beaten the glorious sons of the Soviet people? Artyomkin should have kept quiet, but he got up again and offered to bring in his book about Peary. Chekin shouted that he wouldn't read any bourgeois lies, and that Artyomkin was trying to belittle the achievements of our Soviet polar explorers. And he shouldn't be undermining our workers with his saboteur agitation.

Sasha was at the political meeting. Everyone was required to be present. You couldn't get out of it. He knew that Artyomkin was right, but he said nothing. That's how he always behaved at work — he kept quiet. And he kept quiet this time. The next day Volodya Artyomkin didn't come to work. He had been arrested during the night. They searched his room, turned everything upside down, and took away some books. He had lots of them. And Volodya Artyomkin vanished.

That day Sasha got into an argument with the foreman at the construction site. "You bastard, how long am I supposed to wait to unload? Move your ass instead of sleeping on the job!" he shouted. He couldn't stop himself.

He had to vent his anger and frustration with himself.

Had he been right to keep quiet? Who had behaved more honestly — Sasha or Artyomkin?

Volodya Artyomkin had been more honest, Sasha more wise.

Would it have helped Artyomkin if he had confirmed that the first man to reach the North Pole had been that damned Peary? They would have taken him along with Artyomkin, and charged them with creating a counterrevolutionary organization at the motor pool. They would have each gotten ten years. But he still felt lousy. He had done time. He knew what it would be like for half-blind Artyomkin. But what else could he do? Falsehood had become the morality of the society. People lied at every turn. And no one objected. They were all tricked and deceived. Fear had been beaten into them all. Fear had been beaten into him, and he was beginning to sink into the quagmire. God, give me the strength to resist, to keep from sinking in the filth up to my neck.

The next morning Sasha drove out from the motor pool. As usual, he parked his truck on Sovetskaya Street, and ran to the newspaper stand to pick up his papers. He opened *Pravda* and gasped as he read the announcement of the arrest of Tukhachevsky and other high commanders, accused of treason, espionage, and sabotage. The trial would take place today, in accordance with the Law of December 1.

Sasha quickly scanned the headlines — an editorial on metallurgy; an article defending Academician Tarle's book *Napoleon;* a report of more successes on the labor front; an account of the visit of the Basque soccer team. And next to them — that article on the celebrated and honored military leaders. And then the rallies with demands for their executions.

Sasha went back to the newsstand. "Please, could I also have *Izvestia* and *Komsomolskaya Pravda?*"

"You're going for broke today," the seller said with a smile. She liked Sasha, as she did all her steady customers.

Writers, actors, directors, academicians, artists, workers, kolkhoz workers — all demanding the execution of Tukhachevsky and the others. The previous trials had been open. Journalists were present, even foreigners. But this was a closed trial. How could anyone demand their execution then? Had executions ever been approved in Russia before this? Had they ever trampled people when they were down? Had they shouted triumphant slogans over executed corpses, mocking them and slandering them? Tolstoy had written "I Cannot Be Still" protesting the death penalty. And Pushkin had not been afraid to tell Nicholas I that he would have been with the rebels on Senate Square on December 14.

If there were rallies all over the country, they would reach Kalinin today, and that meant one at their motor pool. What would he do? Vote with the rest? They were all demanding execution. Did they believe? Why shouldn't he believe? Were they afraid? Why couldn't he be afraid? They were saving their lives. Why couldn't he save his?

No, he wouldn't raise his hand. He'd get out of the meeting. Skip work? They put you in jail for that now. He'd have to be sneaky. He'd leave early and come back late, around eight.

He got to the motor pool an hour before his shift. The gates were still shut. And they never opened. The whole morning shift, drivers, mechanics, and office personnel, were sent to the yard for the rally.

Chekin, the Party organization secretary, and Kirpicheva, head of personnel, stood on the back of a truck. Kirpicheva watched the crowd with her angry eyes.

Stumbling and accenting words strangely, Chekin read yesterday's announcement and a new one — the sentence: all were to be shot. Then he started reading the *Pravda* editorial — "A fatal blow against the Fascist intelligence."

While Chekin read, stumbling and mispronouncing, Sasha thought with horror that the minute was approaching when Chekin or Kirpicheva or someone else who was assigned to do it would make a motion endorsing the execution of Tukhachevsky and the other officers. And if he raised his hand against it, they would pass another resolution — "Condemn Pankratov, ally of the enemies" — and twenty minutes later he would be taken to the NKVD. Tomorrow it would be in the papers and they would start finding out how he had gotten the job. They'd get to the Oblast Committee, to Mikhailov and his assistant. He would take a lot of people with him. No, he couldn't vote against. But he couldn't vote for it either. He would never forgive himself for that. How could he go on living after that?

Sasha pulled out a pack of cigarettes and matches from his breast pocket. As soon as they started voting, he would light up, cupping the flame in his hands, thereby covering his face.

Chekin finished reading and said, "Comrade Baryshnikov has the floor to make a motion."

Baryshnikov, chairman of the union, read a brief resolution calling for execution. "We, the workers of Autobase Number One..." and so on.

"Who's for?" Chekin asked.

Everyone raised his hand.

Sasha stuck the cigarette in his teeth, lit the match, and covering his face, started to inhale.

Leonid, standing next to him, elbowed him in the ribs. "What's the matter with you?"

Sasha pulled his hands away from his face and looked around. Everyone had his hand up. He looked at the speakers.

Chekin, Kirpicheva, and Baryshnikov were staring right at him.

Sasha raised his hand.

## 48

The rally ended. The mechanics went off to their stations, the clerks went to the office, and the trucks moved out. Sasha got his assignment and left.

He was working at a furniture factory today, bringing tables and chairs to the warehouse. They were in big crates, and large shavings poked through the slats. They loaded them by hand and worked without rushing. And Sasha didn't hurry them. He didn't even leave his cab. He sat with his head resting on his arms on the wheel.

Last night he hadn't supported the electrician Volodya Artyomkin. Today he had voted for the death of men he had respected all his life and who had not had a real trial. Tomorrow ... What would happen tomorrow? Apparently, the same thing as today. Vsevolod Sergeyevich turned out to be right — Sasha had raised his hand.

"You're not going to point your finger at someone, calling him an enemy," Vsevolod Sergeyevich said. "But you will have to stay in step with everyone, whether you want to or not." And that's what had happened. He had been forced to march to the same drummer. He used to do it voluntarily. He had believed that "if you're not with us, you're against us." Today he no longer thought so, but he marched along, voting out of fear, out of cowardice. What was happening today was the inevitable consequence of what had happened then. Back then he had demanded victorious anthems from others. Now they were demanding the same thing from him. He should be a ferryman on some river, where he could live without listening to the radio or reading the papers. And he would telephone no one but his mother. Ferrymen probably didn't have to

"It's interesting. I'd never thought about that."

"Think about it!"

"But he probably needs a female assistant."

"He's got one. But we'll go officially, on a trip organized by the Concert Bureau. He has a friend there. It will all be properly done, with dues and taxes. And our passports will be marked — member of the Concert and Stage Bureau. Do you appreciate what that means, dearie?"

Sasha thought. He had been just dreaming of becoming a ferryman, and here was even more freedom. But ballroom dancing was a con. People like Semyon Grigoryevich fleeced dumb sheep to make money. Of course, he was in a bell jar at the garage. But they must make personnel checks among dancers, too. They must force them to attend rallies and meetings. Of course, it was dangerous for him to stay too long in one place, but no one was bothering him here. And if he had to leave Kalinin and start over in a new city, it would look natural. He had been a driver and he was looking for a driving job. But applying to a garage when he was a former assistant to a ballroom dancing teacher? Ridiculous!

This morning, when he raised his hand at the rally, he gave in to fate. The day had come. Resistance was useless. If they gave him work, fine. If they put him away, fine, he'd do his term. He was broken! There was no point in trying to run. They'd catch him and press his face into the dirt.

"No, Gleb," Sasha said. "It's not for me. I have a profession, a job. Why should I run off to the boondocks?"

"You like Kalinin?" Gleb asked with a grin.

"Yes. What's wrong with it? It's a good city."

"Cut it out, Sasha. Not with me. . . . 'A good city.' Better than Moscow?"

Sasha stared at him. "What are you trying to say?"

"All right, are we friends or not? You've got a restriction in your passport."

"Who says?"

"What's the difference? Leonid told me."

Sasha poked around in his plate and speared a fried potato with his fork. "So what?"

He was no longer apathetic. It was obvious that Gleb was offering

vote. Or maybe they were forced to vote at the river administration. They were all tied to the same rope. A country of many millions, singing, shouting, damning invented enemies, and glorifying their own executioners. The herd was rushing at wild speeds and whoever slowed would be trampled, whoever stopped would be crushed. You had to keep running and shouting at the top of your lungs, because the whip would hit whoever was silent. You couldn't stand out in any way. You had to trample the fallen ruthlessly and recoil from those who were hit with the guard's whip. And shout and shout to quell the fear within you. Victory marches and military songs were that shouting.

The loader banged on the cab. "Hey, are you asleep? You're loaded. Head for the warehouse."

That night, the dispatcher said, shaking his head, "Just four hauls?"

"They were slow loading."

"You should have written a complaint."

"You think they'd sign it?"

Gleb was in the garage yard and waved to Sasha. When Sasha put the truck in the car wash, he came over to him. "Greetings, dearie!"

"Hello!"

Sasha came out of the cab, turned on the water, picked up the hose, and washed the truck.

"What are you doing today?" Gleb asked.

"Nothing."

"Want to go out?"

"I'm tired, I'm going to bed."

"I'll buy."

Gleb sometimes paid for himself, but for him to treat was unheard of.

"Where do you want to go?"

"The Seliger, I guess."

Sasha looked at Gleb in amazement. The Seliger was the only real restaurant in the city. And it was expensive.

"Will they let me in wearing boots?"

"They'll let you in barefoot with me."

"What's the occasion?"

"You'll see."

He was serious today. He had said "dearie" only once. But Sasha could see in his eyes that he needed a drink badly.

They ordered a bottle of vodka.

"Let's have the cutlets," Gleb suggested. "Let's vary our menu. They have great cutlets here."

"Whatever you say."

They really did know Gleb here. "I used to work here," he explained to Sasha. "In the band. I played piano. But I got sick of it. Every night busy."

They drank and followed it with a bite of food.

"Do you see Lyuda?"

"Haven't seen her in a long time."

"Why not?"

Sasha shrugged. "It just happens. I go to the café for dinner, I see her. If I don't go, I don't see her."

"She's a good woman, trustworthy and loyal, and she really fell for you, but ..." Gleb looked at Sasha. "She has a guy, you see ... in Moscow. An important man. He got a divorce, and he and his ex-wife are exchanging their apartment for two smaller ones. As soon as that's done, he'll bring Lyuda to Moscow. She has prospects, see?"

"Well, that's wonderful," Sasha said sincerely. "I'm glad for her." And he really was.

It would be easier for her to get lost in the crowd in Moscow. She could have told him herself, of course.

"Don't let on I told you," Gleb warned him.

"All right. But I'll tell you honestly, I really am happy for her."

"She really likes you," Gleb said and poured more for himself and Sasha. "Not just as a man, but as a friend."

"Why do you think so?"

"I've noticed."

"Yes," Sasha said. "We have a good relationship."

"Do you know her friend Elizaveta?"

"Who's that?"

"She works at the militia."

"Have no idea."

Why had he brought up the woman at the passport office? What was he leading up to? Was it just a random question or not?

Gleb looked away and turned his head to the side door, through which entered three musicians in white shirts and black bow ties, dark trousers, and black patent leather shoes. Seeing Gleb, they nodded.

"My former colleagues," Gleb said with a chuckle. "They're good musicians, but this isn't what they should be doing." He pointed at the bottle. "It's part of the job. The clients call the tune, they pay a five or even a ten, they like to live high. One orders a waltz, the other a jig, the third the *lezghinka*. He might even dance it himself, and then he treats the musicians. How can you refuse? 'What's the matter? You don't like me, or my booze?' So you have to drink. And so it goes. Whether you want to or not, you end up crawling home. Oh, there's our diva."

A large woman came through the side door. She was a bleached blonde in a long dress, and she smiled as she went up the steps to the stage. People clapped. Still smiling, she bowed and blew kisses into the audience.

"She used to have a good voice, once.... She doesn't touch liquor, but she snorts. She's managed to hold on to her job here, but soon she'll have to move to some choir or other."

The band played a song from a movie. Sasha knew it now, the way he knew all the other pop tunes. He listened to the radio and he had caught up on all the films. And all the songs came from the movies. They wouldn't catch him that way again.

The restaurant was noisy. People were dancing, dancing badly, but the band played without breaks.

"Bring us a couple of pickles," Gleb told the waiter.

He did.

"Well, down the hatch. You seem grumpy today."

"Me? No, I thought you seemed preoccupied."

Anxiety flashed in Gleb's eyes and then faded. Why was treating? Sasha wondered.

For the first time that evening Gleb laughed. "All right, Sas I'll come out with it. I have a proposal for you. Semyon Gri ryevich, my dance teacher friend, is off to the sticks, somewher Central Asia, to enlighten the aborigines. He's invited me to him as pianist and bayan player. He needs an assistant. Do you the job?"

him a chance to get out. Why now, all of a sudden? Was he doing it for Leonid? If Sasha was arrested, Leonid would get into trouble. He's the one who had brought Sasha to the garage and insisted he be hired. Now did he want Sasha to vanish?

"Well?" Sasha asked. "So what if I have a restriction? I'm not the only one. Kalinin is full of people like that."

"Dearie," Gleb smiled. "Why are you getting upset? You've done a prison term. Today they keep you on the job, tomorrow they fire you. You have a restriction. Today Kalinin is not a restricted city, tomorrow it is. I'm offering you a freer life."

"Like yours?"

"Sort of. You don't paint. . . . You don't play the piano. . . . Yes, like mine. People are making lots of money dancing now!"

"And when are you planning to leave?"

"In three days or so."

"Where exactly?"

"We haven't decided yet," Gleb said evasively.

Sasha suddenly understood. "You have a restriction, too?" he asked directly.

"What makes you think that?"

"What do you have a restriction for?"

"Do you think that Semyon Grigoryevich has a restriction, and Nonna his assistant has a restriction, too?" Gleb snapped. "If we're off to make money, we all have restrictions?" He smiled again. "You're really something, Sasha."

"Well, if you don't, you don't," Sasha said. "But I'm not going anywhere. Let's finish the bottle!"

They drank. Got the bill. Sasha paid half. Gleb did not argue.

## 49

Gleb said silly things, but still, Sasha felt he should check what Leonid had told him.

He found an excuse.

The Honor Board listed the shock-workers for May and June. Sasha didn't find his name there yet again. He asked Leonid, "Why isn't my name up there?"

"You don't understand?"

"Listen, Leonid, maybe it would be better if I left here?"

He looked closely at Leonid's face. It was always grim and grumpy, but you could still sometimes read things in it.

"Leave?" Leonid's brows shot up. "Because of that?" He nodded at the Honor Board. "You need that?"

"It's discrimination, understand? They're keeping me on the bricks and won't give me the good jobs."

Leonid shrugged. "Well, that's up to you to figure out whom you talk to. Discrimination?" He laughed. "Drop it! It'll work out. But leaving? . . . You think it'll be different at a new place? It'll be the same."

He spoke sincerely. That meant he hadn't asked Gleb to do anything. Gleb had brought up the conversation on his own initiative. He wanted to lure him over to Semyon Grigoryevich. What a pig! He could have been honest about it, just asked him, instead of all that talk about passport restrictions. Some friend! Or, maybe he had learned something elsewhere? He had asked about Lyuda and Elizaveta, the woman at the passport office. But if there was a threat to Sasha, Lyuda would have been the first to warn him. It was Gleb's initiative. He and Semyon Grigoryevich were planning to tour around doing hackwork, and they needed another person, an assistant, as they called him.

Sasha was back working on the bricks. They didn't send him to the furniture factory. He hadn't met the quota there, so let him breathe brick dust.

The dispatcher counted up his hauls, signed the sheet, and handed Sasha a sheet of blue paper. "For you."

It was a summons from the Housing Division of the militia to come at nine in the morning, with his passport. He hadn't been in any road accidents, and there were no violations on his record. And anyway, you go to the highway police for traffic violations.

"What is it? What's up?"

"How should I know?" the dispatcher said. "They came from the militia and made me sign for it."

"But I'll miss my run."

"What can you do? Maybe they're mobilizing people. But for what? The sowing has been done. And it's too early for harvesting."

At home another summons was waiting for Sasha. The old woman said, "The precinct man came and left this summons. He had me sign for it. I said, 'What did he do? He's a quiet kid, he doesn't drink.' And he said, 'Sure, none of you drink, I know that. Make sure he's there at nine o'clock sharp with his passport.' "

Should he pack his things? Just in case. What case? If they had wanted to arrest him, they would have come for him. Had they learned that he had gotten his passport done quickly? Were they building a case against Elizaveta? Not likely . . . Lyuda would have known.

Should he leave now, right away? But he'd have new problems in the new place — where was his discharge from his past place of work? Why wasn't there any notation in his passport about moving from his last room? Suspicious documents! You can't be registered in a new house or a new job with documents like that.

The Soviet citizen was bound hand and foot with all those papers, references, and documents! There was no place to hide!

All right, he'd go to the militia.

*　　*　　*

A lot of people had gotten there before him. There were crowds in the hallway on the porch. They were introducing a passport regime into Kalinin and everyone with passport limitations had to leave town within twenty-four hours. Sasha was surprised to see so many people with former sentences in one area. The line was divided into three parts — A–G, H–O, P–Z. He got in his line. It took over an hour for him to reach the barrier behind which sat the clerk.

The lieutenant looked at Sasha's passport. Under the "Registered" stamp he put another one that said "Unregistered." He found Sasha's name on the list and checked it off. "Sign here."

The crowd was pushing from behind. Sasha barely had time to read what he was signing — "Warning to move out of Kalinin." He signed opposite his name.

"You will be paid at work," the lieutenant said. "Leaving work because you are leaving the city. The administration there knows. If you do not leave within twenty-four hours, you are liable to arrest. Next!"

Sasha went to the garage. They had been warned. They gave him his paperwork at the office. He went to the garage and turned over his truck to the mechanic Khomutov. Khomutov didn't examine the truck. He signed off on it, and said, "Too bad you were here such a short time."

"That's how it worked out."

The storekeeper also signed off, and the dispatcher signed off, and so did the union man. Leonid signed below all the others and then asked gruffly, "Where to now?"

"I don't know yet."

Sasha took the paperwork to the cashier's, where they had already added up what was owed him — 78 rubles 24 kopecks, plus 29 rubles 23 kopecks in vacation time. The secretary stamped his passport — "Let go on such-and-such date" — and then typed a reference saying that he had worked as a driver, there had been no problems, and he had been let go because he was leaving Kalinin.

When she gave him the reference, the secretary did not look at him. No one looked him in the eye all day. Only Khomutov and Leonid had said something human and caring. And no one else.

From work Sasha headed straight for Gleb's. He knocked at the door a long time, but no one answered. He pulled himself up to peer over the fence. He saw Gleb's aunt digging in the garden.

Sasha hailed her and asked about Gleb.

She squinted at him and said, "Gleb's gone. He left."

"Where to?"

"I don't know. Maybe Leningrad, maybe not. I don't know. He said he'd write."

"Did he take his bayan?"

"The bayan..." The old woman hesitated. "Yes, he did, I think...."

So Gleb had gone off with Semyon Grigoryevich.

Only now did Sasha realize why Gleb had proposed that he leave with them. "Today Kalinin is not a restricted city, tomorrow it is." That meant he had learned somehow that the passport regime was going to be introduced. Why didn't he just say so? Because you don't say things like that. If they found out that Gleb knew, they wouldn't let him go until he admitted where he got the information. They were preparing this in secret, to get all the restricted passports in one go, catch them unawares, and clean up the city. Someone had warned Gleb, and he must have sworn that it wouldn't go any farther. And that's why he didn't tell Sasha. But he had hinted. And he hurried off so that he wouldn't be sent away. That meant he had a restriction, which meant that he had served time. He hadn't admitted it. Even when he was drinking hard, he kept his mouth shut.

Now Sasha was sorry he hadn't accepted Gleb's offer. He wouldn't have had time to do the paperwork at the garage. But he could have followed, if he knew their address, and he would have had work right away, even if it was only ballroom dancing.

And now where could he go? More nomadic travels.

With those thoughts weighing on his mind, Sasha came home. He hadn't seen particular joy in this city, but he had a corner and work. He had been lucky here — Lyuda, Leonid, Mikhailov. He had gotten his passport, registration, a union card — all the external attributes of a free man.

And now he had to start all over again. They let him rest for a few months. He should be grateful for that. And now he had to wander on, dammit! Where to go? Ryazan, probably. Mikhail Yurevich's brother was there. Maybe he would help. He'd take the morning train to Moscow and then move to the Kazan Station and head out for Ryazan.

He wouldn't even call his mother yet. Not from here, not from Moscow. Why worry her? He'll call from Ryazan and say that he had transferred. That it was better, and that he was fine.

When he got home, Sasha told the landlady that he would be leaving for good in the morning.

"Why's that?" she asked.

"Moving to another job. Do I owe you anything?"

The old woman's lips moved. "Well, you've paid up to the first, I think."

"Then we're even."

Sasha packed his suitcase and backpack. He had more things now. He hadn't bought anything special, but the suitcase was filled with his winter clothes. He got everything in there — fur coat, felt boots, sweater, boots, scarf, warm underwear, and mittens. It's a good thing he had gotten the backpack at the flea market. He stuffed in the sheets and pillowcases and a bundle of dirty laundry. He had got too settled. He had thought he'd live there for a while. It hadn't worked out. And it wouldn't work out in Ryazan; they'd chase him from city to city. He left his glass, plate, and a few other trifles behind. He checked the desk drawers and looked under the bed. He had packed everything. All that was left out was his soap, toothbrush, and shaving kit. He had to wash and shave in the morning.

It was getting on toward eight. It was still light outside, but the semibasement was dark. The light was on already.

Egorych would come home from work, and they would have a farewell drink. He'd ask to borrow their alarm clock. He'd set it for five so that he could be at the station by six.

The steps creaked and the front door opened. He heard quick steps, not the landlord's, but a stranger's. The curtain that served as a door to his part of the room moved and there was Lyuda.

She stood in silence, filling the entire entry, in the light cotton dress she wore to work in the café in summer. She must have come straight from there.

"Hello," Sasha said amiably. "Don't just stand there. Come in, sit down."

She came in and sat down next to Sasha on the edge of the metal cot. She turned to him and regarded him in silence.

"What are you looking at?" Sasha asked just as pleasantly. "Haven't seen me in a long time?"

"When are you leaving?"

"Tomorrow at eight on the Moscow train."

"Where to?"

Sasha shrugged. "Moscow for now; I'll decide on the train. Maybe Ryazan."

"Elizaveta is a louse for not tipping me off."

"What if she had? What would have changed? If I had left sooner, I wouldn't have my paperwork done. It would have made it harder for me at the new place."

"You're right," Lyuda agreed.

She moved closer to him. Her familiar scent enveloped him in the dark, and she caressed his head. "You poor thing." She pulled her hand away. "This morning Egorych said, 'They called my roomer into the militia.' At first I thought it was something to do with your driving. But then one of the kitchen help, who has the same thing in his passport, didn't come into work. He arrived at noon and said, 'I'm leaving.' And everyone learned what's going on. I rushed to see you, but you weren't home. I ran to see Elizaveta at work, but I couldn't push through the crowd. They've moved out a lot of people."

"I'm in big company," Sasha said with a laugh.

"Mikhailov's gone," Lyuda suddenly said.

"Which one? The secretary of the Oblast Committee?"

"Yes. They're arresting everyone, so maybe it's better that you're leaving."

"Maybe. . . . They haven't touched anyone else you know, have they?"

"No . . . no. . . . Are you thinking of Angelina? Her passport is clean. The ones who were refused passports in Moscow and Leningrad in 1933 got passports here. Clean ones without any notations." She sighed.

"Yes, I know that."

"There are lots of people like that," Lyuda said. "Take Gleb Dubinin. He was sent out of Leningrad in 1933."

"Gleb? What for?"

"His mother was either from a priest's family or the nobility. He got his passport here, too."

"Then why did he leave?"

"To make money. I saw Hannah, and she said, 'Gleb and Semyon Grigoryevich went off to Ufa. When they make lots of money, they'll come back.'"

Ufa! Aunt Vera had a relative there. And Vera had already written to him.

"Are you sure they went to Ufa?"

"Yes. He told Hannah to write to him at the Central Post Office in Ufa, to be picked up. He's worried about his aunt. He's afraid she's going to die. He asked Hannah to look in on her. And if anything happens to send him a telegram."

They sat in silence. Lyuda touched his hand and then held it. "You're not mad at me?"

"For what? How could I be mad at you?"

She listened, gazing at the floor. Then she looked up. "I have . . . I don't even know how to tell you this . . . I have a man, a good man, and he loves me. He trusts me and I respect him, and I don't want to cheat on him. With you . . . With you, it was something different. You got me right in the heart at the café, that first evening, remember? And then when I realized at Angelina's that you had been in prison, I changed my mind. I knew that in my position I didn't have the right to be with someone like you. But in Leonid's truck when I thought how you didn't know where to go, that you didn't have a home or a job, I couldn't stand it. I thought, God would never forgive me if I didn't help. I wanted to use you to justify myself before God, Sasha. I hadn't abandoned a homeless man in his misfortune, didn't leave him on the street. And God would forgive me for stealing a father away from his children. I grew up without a father myself, and I know how bad it is, Sasha, to grow up without one. But I was stealing him away."

She dropped Sasha's hand and pulled a hankie from her pocket to wipe her tears.

"Don't pay any attention to me, I'm upset. I felt so sorry for you.... But once you got a job and a room, I decided, enough. I don't have the right. And I really liked you and all that.... Still, I couldn't deceive the man who trusted me and was leaving his children for me.... But today when I heard, I dropped everything and hurried here to see how I could help you."

Now Sasha took her hands in his. "I'm glad that you came. I would have regretted not seeing you, not thanking you for all the things you've done for me. I would have perished without you." He looked at her. "And you know, what I want more than anything else is for you to be happy, to get back from life everything you deserve. I'm saying this from the bottom of my heart."

Lyuda listened tensely, and the tears started to flow again. She wiped them with her hankie.

"Thank you, Sasha, thank you for your kind words. And may you have good luck...." She put the hankie back in her pocket. "Well, let's kiss good-bye."

She got up and kissed him on the mouth. She kissed him hard and held his head between her hands a long time, looking into his eyes.

Then she let go.

"That's it! Good-bye. Sasha, don't think badly of me. Good luck!"

And she vanished as unexpectedly as she had appeared.

The train pulled into the Leningrad Station.

Five months ago his mother had seen him off to Kalinin from here. Now he was here again, and he was through with Kalinin. What was waiting for him in Ufa? And what would happen after Ufa?

Sasha crossed the square. The smell of the asphalt, hot in the sun, filled the air. The familiar childhood smell of Moscow streets. He suddenly thought that he'd see Varya. Maybe life would perform a miracle! He looked into the crowd and the women's faces. No one even resembled her. Then he thought she was walking ahead of him. It was Varya, her figure, her hair, her walk.... With his heart in his throat, he ran to pass her. No, it wasn't Varya!

At the Kazan Station Sasha got his ticket and now he had to send a telegram. The table was covered with ink spills, the inkwells were almost empty, and the pen tied by a string to the table was scratchy. There were no chairs. He had to write standing up.

Someone touched his shoulder lightly.

Sasha jumped. Varya!

He turned.

There was no miracle.

A young Gypsy woman in a shawl tied crisscross over her chest said, "Let me tell your fortune. I'll tell you the whole truth."

"No, thank you, don't."

He bent over the table and finished his telegram.

UFA CENTRAL POST OFFICE FOR PICKUP.

TO GLEB DUBININ

LEAVING ON TWENTY-FIFTH TRAIN FORTY CAR SEVEN. MEET ME. SASHA.

1984–1990
Peredelkino

vote. Or maybe they were forced to vote at the river administration. They were all tied to the same rope. A country of many millions, singing, shouting, damning invented enemies, and glorifying their own executioners. The herd was rushing at wild speeds and whoever slowed would be trampled, whoever stopped would be crushed. You had to keep running and shouting at the top of your lungs, because the whip would hit whoever was silent. You couldn't stand out in any way. You had to trample the fallen ruthlessly and recoil from those who were hit with the guard's whip. And shout and shout to quell the fear within you. Victory marches and military songs were that shouting.

The loader banged on the cab. "Hey, are you asleep? You're loaded. Head for the warehouse."

That night, the dispatcher said, shaking his head, "Just four hauls?"

"They were slow loading."

"You should have written a complaint."

"You think they'd sign it?"

Gleb was in the garage yard and waved to Sasha. When Sasha put the truck in the car wash, he came over to him. "Greetings, dearie!"

"Hello!"

Sasha came out of the cab, turned on the water, picked up the hose, and washed the truck.

"What are you doing today?" Gleb asked.

"Nothing."

"Want to go out?"

"I'm tired, I'm going to bed."

"I'll buy."

Gleb sometimes paid for himself, but for him to treat was unheard of.

"Where do you want to go?"

"The Seliger, I guess."

Sasha looked at Gleb in amazement. The Seliger was the only real restaurant in the city. And it was expensive.

"Will they let me in wearing boots?"

"They'll let you in barefoot with me."

"What's the occasion?"

"You'll see."

He was serious today. He had said "dearie" only once. But Sasha could see in his eyes that he needed a drink badly.

They ordered a bottle of vodka.

"Let's have the cutlets," Gleb suggested. "Let's vary our menu. They have great cutlets here."

"Whatever you say."

They really did know Gleb here. "I used to work here," he explained to Sasha. "In the band. I played piano. But I got sick of it. Every night busy."

They drank and followed it with a bite of food.

"Do you see Lyuda?"

"Haven't seen her in a long time."

"Why not?"

Sasha shrugged. "It just happens. I go to the café for dinner, I see her. If I don't go, I don't see her."

"She's a good woman, trustworthy and loyal, and she really fell for you, but ..." Gleb looked at Sasha. "She has a guy, you see ... in Moscow. An important man. He got a divorce, and he and his ex-wife are exchanging their apartment for two smaller ones. As soon as that's done, he'll bring Lyuda to Moscow. She has prospects, see?"

"Well, that's wonderful," Sasha said sincerely. "I'm glad for her." And he really was.

It would be easier for her to get lost in the crowd in Moscow. She could have told him herself, of course.

"Don't let on I told you," Gleb warned him.

"All right. But I'll tell you honestly, I really am happy for her."

"She really likes you," Gleb said and poured more for himself and Sasha. "Not just as a man, but as a friend."

"Why do you think so?"

"I've noticed."

"Yes," Sasha said. "We have a good relationship."

"Do you know her friend Elizaveta?"

"Who's that?"

"She works at the militia."

"Have no idea."

Why had he brought up the woman at the passport office? What was he leading up to? Was it just a random question or not?

Gleb looked away and turned his head to the side door, through which entered three musicians in white shirts and black bow ties, dark trousers, and black patent leather shoes. Seeing Gleb, they nodded.

"My former colleagues," Gleb said with a chuckle. "They're good musicians, but this isn't what they should be doing." He pointed at the bottle. "It's part of the job. The clients call the tune, they pay a five or even a ten, they like to live high. One orders a waltz, the other a jig, the third the *lezghinka*. He might even dance it himself, and then he treats the musicians. How can you refuse? 'What's the matter? You don't like me, or my booze?' So you have to drink. And so it goes. Whether you want to or not, you end up crawling home. Oh, there's our diva."

A large woman came through the side door. She was a bleached blonde in a long dress, and she smiled as she went up the steps to the stage. People clapped. Still smiling, she bowed and blew kisses into the audience.

"She used to have a good voice, once.... She doesn't touch liquor, but she snorts. She's managed to hold on to her job here, but soon she'll have to move to some choir or other."

The band played a song from a movie. Sasha knew it now, the way he knew all the other pop tunes. He listened to the radio and he had caught up on all the films. And all the songs came from the movies. They wouldn't catch him that way again.

The restaurant was noisy. People were dancing, dancing badly, but the band played without breaks.

"Bring us a couple of pickles," Gleb told the waiter.

He did.

"Well, down the hatch. You seem grumpy today."

"Me? No, I thought you seemed preoccupied."

Anxiety flashed in Gleb's eyes and then faded. Why was he treating? Sasha wondered.

For the first time that evening Gleb laughed. "All right, Sasha, I'll come out with it. I have a proposal for you. Semyon Grigoryevich, my dance teacher friend, is off to the sticks, somewhere in Central Asia, to enlighten the aborigines. He's invited me to join him as pianist and bayan player. He needs an assistant. Do you want the job?"

"It's interesting. I'd never thought about that."

"Think about it!"

"But he probably needs a female assistant."

"He's got one. But we'll go officially, on a trip organized by the Concert Bureau. He has a friend there. It will all be properly done, with dues and taxes. And our passports will be marked — member of the Concert and Stage Bureau. Do you appreciate what that means, dearie?"

Sasha thought. He had been just dreaming of becoming a ferryman, and here was even more freedom. But ballroom dancing was a con. People like Semyon Grigoryevich fleeced dumb sheep to make money. Of course, he was in a bell jar at the garage. But they must make personnel checks among dancers, too. They must force them to attend rallies and meetings. Of course, it was dangerous for him to stay too long in one place, but no one was bothering him here. And if he had to leave Kalinin and start over in a new city, it would look natural. He had been a driver and he was looking for a driving job. But applying to a garage when he was a former assistant to a ballroom dancing teacher? Ridiculous!

This morning, when he raised his hand at the rally, he gave in to fate. The day had come. Resistance was useless. If they gave him work, fine. If they put him away, fine, he'd do his term. He was broken! There was no point in trying to run. They'd catch him and press his face into the dirt.

"No, Gleb," Sasha said. "It's not for me. I have a profession, a job. Why should I run off to the boondocks?"

"You like Kalinin?" Gleb asked with a grin.

"Yes. What's wrong with it? It's a good city."

"Cut it out, Sasha. Not with me. . . . 'A good city.' Better than Moscow?"

Sasha stared at him. "What are you trying to say?"

"All right, are we friends or not? You've got a restriction in your passport."

"Who says?"

"What's the difference? Leonid told me."

Sasha poked around in his plate and speared a fried potato with his fork. "So what?"

He was no longer apathetic. It was obvious that Gleb was offering

him a chance to get out. Why now, all of a sudden? Was he doing it for Leonid? If Sasha was arrested, Leonid would get into trouble. He's the one who had brought Sasha to the garage and insisted he be hired. Now did he want Sasha to vanish?

"Well?" Sasha asked. "So what if I have a restriction? I'm not the only one. Kalinin is full of people like that."

"Dearie," Gleb smiled. "Why are you getting upset? You've done a prison term. Today they keep you on the job, tomorrow they fire you. You have a restriction. Today Kalinin is not a restricted city, tomorrow it is. I'm offering you a freer life."

"Like yours?"

"Sort of. You don't paint. . . . You don't play the piano. . . . Yes, like mine. People are making lots of money dancing now!"

"And when are you planning to leave?"

"In three days or so."

"Where exactly?"

"We haven't decided yet," Gleb said evasively.

Sasha suddenly understood. "You have a restriction, too?" he asked directly.

"What makes you think that?"

"What do you have a restriction for?"

"Do you think that Semyon Grigoryevich has a restriction, and Nonna his assistant has a restriction, too?" Gleb snapped. "If we're off to make money, we all have restrictions?" He smiled again. "You're really something, Sasha."

"Well, if you don't, you don't," Sasha said. "But I'm not going anywhere. Let's finish the bottle!"

They drank. Got the bill. Sasha paid half. Gleb did not argue.

# ꙭ 49 ꙭ

**G**leb said silly things, but still, Sasha felt he should check what Leonid had told him.

He found an excuse.

The Honor Board listed the shock-workers for May and June. Sasha didn't find his name there yet again. He asked Leonid, "Why isn't my name up there?"

"You don't understand?"

"Listen, Leonid, maybe it would be better if I left here?"

He looked closely at Leonid's face. It was always grim and grumpy, but you could still sometimes read things in it.

"Leave?" Leonid's brows shot up. "Because of that?" He nodded at the Honor Board. "You need that?"

"It's discrimination, understand? They're keeping me on the bricks and won't give me the good jobs."

Leonid shrugged. "Well, that's up to you to figure out whom you talk to. Discrimination?" He laughed. "Drop it! It'll work out. But leaving? . . . You think it'll be different at a new place? It'll be the same."

He spoke sincerely. That meant he hadn't asked Gleb to do anything. Gleb had brought up the conversation on his own initiative. He wanted to lure him over to Semyon Grigoryevich. What a pig! He could have been honest about it, just asked him, instead of all that talk about passport restrictions. Some friend! Or, maybe he had learned something elsewhere? He had asked about Lyuda and Elizaveta, the woman at the passport office. But if there was a threat to Sasha, Lyuda would have been the first to warn him. It was Gleb's initiative. He and Semyon Grigoryevich were planning

to tour around doing hackwork, and they needed another person, an assistant, as they called him.

Sasha was back working on the bricks. They didn't send him to the furniture factory. He hadn't met the quota there, so let him breathe brick dust.

The dispatcher counted up his hauls, signed the sheet, and handed Sasha a sheet of blue paper. "For you."

It was a summons from the Housing Division of the militia to come at nine in the morning, with his passport. He hadn't been in any road accidents, and there were no violations on his record. And anyway, you go to the highway police for traffic violations.

"What is it? What's up?"

"How should I know?" the dispatcher said. "They came from the militia and made me sign for it."

"But I'll miss my run."

"What can you do? Maybe they're mobilizing people. But for what? The sowing has been done. And it's too early for harvesting."

At home another summons was waiting for Sasha. The old woman said, "The precinct man came and left this summons. He had me sign for it. I said, 'What did he do? He's a quiet kid, he doesn't drink.' And he said, 'Sure, none of you drink, I know that. Make sure he's there at nine o'clock sharp with his passport.'"

Should he pack his things? Just in case. What case? If they had wanted to arrest him, they would have come for him. Had they learned that he had gotten his passport done quickly? Were they building a case against Elizaveta? Not likely ... Lyuda would have known.

Should he leave now, right away? But he'd have new problems in the new place — where was his discharge from his past place of work? Why wasn't there any notation in his passport about moving from his last room? Suspicious documents! You can't be registered in a new house or a new job with documents like that.

The Soviet citizen was bound hand and foot with all those papers, references, and documents! There was no place to hide!

All right, he'd go to the militia.

✳     ✳     ✳

A lot of people had gotten there before him. There were crowds in the hallway on the porch. They were introducing a passport regime into Kalinin and everyone with passport limitations had to leave town within twenty-four hours. Sasha was surprised to see so many people with former sentences in one area. The line was divided into three parts — A–G, H–O, P–Z. He got in his line. It took over an hour for him to reach the barrier behind which sat the clerk.

The lieutenant looked at Sasha's passport. Under the "Registered" stamp he put another one that said "Unregistered." He found Sasha's name on the list and checked it off. "Sign here."

The crowd was pushing from behind. Sasha barely had time to read what he was signing — "Warning to move out of Kalinin." He signed opposite his name.

"You will be paid at work," the lieutenant said. "Leaving work because you are leaving the city. The administration there knows. If you do not leave within twenty-four hours, you are liable to arrest. Next!"

Sasha went to the garage. They had been warned. They gave him his paperwork at the office. He went to the garage and turned over his truck to the mechanic Khomutov. Khomutov didn't examine the truck. He signed off on it, and said, "Too bad you were here such a short time."

"That's how it worked out."

The storekeeper also signed off, and the dispatcher signed off, and so did the union man. Leonid signed below all the others and then asked gruffly, "Where to now?"

"I don't know yet."

Sasha took the paperwork to the cashier's, where they had already added up what was owed him — 78 rubles 24 kopecks, plus 29 rubles 23 kopecks in vacation time. The secretary stamped his passport — "Let go on such-and-such date" — and then typed a reference saying that he had worked as a driver, there had been no problems, and he had been let go because he was leaving Kalinin.

When she gave him the reference, the secretary did not look at him. No one looked him in the eye all day. Only Khomutov and Leonid had said something human and caring. And no one else.

From work Sasha headed straight for Gleb's. He knocked at the door a long time, but no one answered. He pulled himself up to peer over the fence. He saw Gleb's aunt digging in the garden.

Sasha hailed her and asked about Gleb.

She squinted at him and said, "Gleb's gone. He left."

"Where to?"

"I don't know. Maybe Leningrad, maybe not. I don't know. He said he'd write."

"Did he take his bayan?"

"The bayan..." The old woman hesitated. "Yes, he did, I think...."

So Gleb had gone off with Semyon Grigoryevich.

Only now did Sasha realize why Gleb had proposed that he leave with them. "Today Kalinin is not a restricted city, tomorrow it is." That meant he had learned somehow that the passport regime was going to be introduced. Why didn't he just say so? Because you don't say things like that. If they found out that Gleb knew, they wouldn't let him go until he admitted where he got the information. They were preparing this in secret, to get all the restricted passports in one go, catch them unawares, and clean up the city. Someone had warned Gleb, and he must have sworn that it wouldn't go any farther. And that's why he didn't tell Sasha. But he had hinted. And he hurried off so that he wouldn't be sent away. That meant he had a restriction, which meant that he had served time. He hadn't admitted it. Even when he was drinking hard, he kept his mouth shut.

Now Sasha was sorry he hadn't accepted Gleb's offer. He wouldn't have had time to do the paperwork at the garage. But he could have followed, if he knew their address, and he would have had work right away, even if it was only ballroom dancing.

And now where could he go? More nomadic travels.

With those thoughts weighing on his mind, Sasha came home. He hadn't seen particular joy in this city, but he had a corner and work. He had been lucky here — Lyuda, Leonid, Mikhailov. He had gotten his passport, registration, a union card — all the external attributes of a free man.

And now he had to start all over again. They let him rest for a few months. He should be grateful for that. And now he had to

wander on, dammit! Where to go? Ryazan, probably. Mikhail Yurevich's brother was there. Maybe he would help. He'd take the morning train to Moscow and then move to the Kazan Station and head out for Ryazan.

He wouldn't even call his mother yet. Not from here, not from Moscow. Why worry her? He'll call from Ryazan and say that he had transferred. That it was better, and that he was fine.

When he got home, Sasha told the landlady that he would be leaving for good in the morning.

"Why's that?" she asked.

"Moving to another job. Do I owe you anything?"

The old woman's lips moved. "Well, you've paid up to the first, I think."

"Then we're even."

Sasha packed his suitcase and backpack. He had more things now. He hadn't bought anything special, but the suitcase was filled with his winter clothes. He got everything in there — fur coat, felt boots, sweater, boots, scarf, warm underwear, and mittens. It's a good thing he had gotten the backpack at the flea market. He stuffed in the sheets and pillowcases and a bundle of dirty laundry. He had got too settled. He had thought he'd live there for a while. It hadn't worked out. And it wouldn't work out in Ryazan; they'd chase him from city to city. He left his glass, plate, and a few other trifles behind. He checked the desk drawers and looked under the bed. He had packed everything. All that was left out was his soap, toothbrush, and shaving kit. He had to wash and shave in the morning.

It was getting on toward eight. It was still light outside, but the semibasement was dark. The light was on already.

Egorych would come home from work, and they would have a farewell drink. He'd ask to borrow their alarm clock. He'd set it for five so that he could be at the station by six.

The steps creaked and the front door opened. He heard quick steps, not the landlord's, but a stranger's. The curtain that served as a door to his part of the room moved and there was Lyuda.

She stood in silence, filling the entire entry, in the light cotton dress she wore to work in the café in summer. She must have come straight from there.

"Hello," Sasha said amiably. "Don't just stand there. Come in, sit down."

She came in and sat down next to Sasha on the edge of the metal cot. She turned to him and regarded him in silence.

"What are you looking at?" Sasha asked just as pleasantly. "Haven't seen me in a long time?"

"When are you leaving?"

"Tomorrow at eight on the Moscow train."

"Where to?"

Sasha shrugged. "Moscow for now; I'll decide on the train. Maybe Ryazan."

"Elizaveta is a louse for not tipping me off."

"What if she had? What would have changed? If I had left sooner, I wouldn't have my paperwork done. It would have made it harder for me at the new place."

"You're right," Lyuda agreed.

She moved closer to him. Her familiar scent enveloped him in the dark, and she caressed his head. "You poor thing." She pulled her hand away. "This morning Egorych said, 'They called my roomer into the militia.' At first I thought it was something to do with your driving. But then one of the kitchen help, who has the same thing in his passport, didn't come into work. He arrived at noon and said, 'I'm leaving.' And everyone learned what's going on. I rushed to see you, but you weren't home. I ran to see Elizaveta at work, but I couldn't push through the crowd. They've moved out a lot of people."

"I'm in big company," Sasha said with a laugh.

"Mikhailov's gone," Lyuda suddenly said.

"Which one? The secretary of the Oblast Committee?"

"Yes. They're arresting everyone, so maybe it's better that you're leaving."

"Maybe.... They haven't touched anyone else you know, have they?"

"No ... no.... Are you thinking of Angelina? Her passport is clean. The ones who were refused passports in Moscow and Leningrad in 1933 got passports here. Clean ones without any notations." She sighed.

"Yes, I know that."

"There are lots of people like that," Lyuda said. "Take Gleb Dubinin. He was sent out of Leningrad in 1933."

"Gleb? What for?"

"His mother was either from a priest's family or the nobility. He got his passport here, too."

"Then why did he leave?"

"To make money. I saw Hannah, and she said, 'Gleb and Semyon Grigoryevich went off to Ufa. When they make lots of money, they'll come back.'"

Ufa! Aunt Vera had a relative there. And Vera had already written to him.

"Are you sure they went to Ufa?"

"Yes. He told Hannah to write to him at the Central Post Office in Ufa, to be picked up. He's worried about his aunt. He's afraid she's going to die. He asked Hannah to look in on her. And if anything happens to send him a telegram."

They sat in silence. Lyuda touched his hand and then held it.

"You're not mad at me?"

"For what? How could I be mad at you?"

She listened, gazing at the floor. Then she looked up. "I have ... I don't even know how to tell you this ... I have a man, a good man, and he loves me. He trusts me and I respect him, and I don't want to cheat on him. With you ... With you, it was something different. You got me right in the heart at the café, that first evening, remember? And then when I realized at Angelina's that you had been in prison, I changed my mind. I knew that in my position I didn't have the right to be with someone like you. But in Leonid's truck when I thought how you didn't know where to go, that you didn't have a home or a job, I couldn't stand it. I thought, God would never forgive me if I didn't help. I wanted to use you to justify myself before God, Sasha. I hadn't abandoned a homeless man in his misfortune, didn't leave him on the street. And God would forgive me for stealing a father away from his children. I grew up without a father myself, and I know how bad it is, Sasha, to grow up without one. But I was stealing him away."

She dropped Sasha's hand and pulled a hankie from her pocket to wipe her tears.

"Don't pay any attention to me, I'm upset. I felt so sorry for

you.... But once you got a job and a room, I decided, enough. I don't have the right. And I really liked you and all that.... Still, I couldn't deceive the man who trusted me and was leaving his children for me.... But today when I heard, I dropped everything and hurried here to see how I could help you."

Now Sasha took her hands in his. "I'm glad that you came. I would have regretted not seeing you, not thanking you for all the things you've done for me. I would have perished without you." He looked at her. "And you know, what I want more than anything else is for you to be happy, to get back from life everything you deserve. I'm saying this from the bottom of my heart."

Lyuda listened tensely, and the tears started to flow again. She wiped them with her hankie.

"Thank you, Sasha, thank you for your kind words. And may you have good luck...." She put the hankie back in her pocket. "Well, let's kiss good-bye."

She got up and kissed him on the mouth. She kissed him hard and held his head between her hands a long time, looking into his eyes.

Then she let go.

"That's it! Good-bye. Sasha, don't think badly of me. Good luck!"

And she vanished as unexpectedly as she had appeared.

The train pulled into the Leningrad Station.

Five months ago his mother had seen him off to Kalinin from here. Now he was here again, and he was through with Kalinin. What was waiting for him in Ufa? And what would happen after Ufa?

Sasha crossed the square. The smell of the asphalt, hot in the sun, filled the air. The familiar childhood smell of Moscow streets. He suddenly thought that he'd see Varya. Maybe life would perform a miracle! He looked into the crowd and the women's faces. No one even resembled her. Then he thought she was walking ahead of him. It was Varya, her figure, her hair, her walk.... With his heart in his throat, he ran to pass her. No, it wasn't Varya!

At the Kazan Station Sasha got his ticket and now he had to send a telegram. The table was covered with ink spills, the inkwells were almost empty, and the pen tied by a string to the table was scratchy. There were no chairs. He had to write standing up.

Someone touched his shoulder lightly.

Sasha jumped. Varya!

He turned.

There was no miracle.

A young Gypsy woman in a shawl tied crisscross over her chest said, "Let me tell your fortune. I'll tell you the whole truth."

"No, thank you, don't."

He bent over the table and finished his telegram.

UFA CENTRAL POST OFFICE FOR PICKUP.

TO GLEB DUBININ

LEAVING ON TWENTY-FIFTH TRAIN FORTY CAR SEVEN. MEET ME. SASHA.

1984–1990
Peredelkino

# SKYDANCER

## Geoffrey Archer

### PROJECT SKYDANCER

The brainchild of the Ministry of Defence – terrifying in its simplicity. New warheads had been designed that could evade the batteries of anti-ballistic missiles the Russians had set up in Moscow. For Aldermaston scientist Peter Joyce, it was the pinnacle of his career.

Until documents from the project turned up on Parliament Hill and he is left with two alternatives: write off a billion-pound project, or approve tests which could give Russia the power to wipe out the West at the touch of a button . . .

# SHADOWHUNTER

## Geoffrey Archer

*HMS Truculent* is a nuclear-powered, hunter-killer submarine, and one of the most deadly weapon systems in the world.

Phil Hitchens is its distinguished British commander – who has broken away from a NATO exercise and embarked on his own darkly vengeful and deadly mission.

SHADOWHUNT is the codename of the desperate sonar search for *HMS Truculent*, last seen heading for the Kola Inlet where the cream of Soviet sea power lies unsuspecting at anchor.

*Shadowhunter* is Geoffrey Archer's nail-biting, authentic thriller of undersea battle and international tension – a chillingly credible account of the world brought to the brink of catastrophe.

# THE DOUBLE TENTH

## George Brown

Malaya, 1952 – The War of the Running Dogs.

They shot the Chinese courier and took the documents he was carrying. Then they cut off his hands and rolled him into a shallow grave.

Another act of barbarity in a savage jungle war, another dead Communist and another successful mission for the police and the SAS.

Thirty-five years later – members of the ambush party start dying unpleasantly. One of them has had his hands cut off. The past is catching up with the men who stood in that jungle clearing – the past in the form of a man with artificial hands and an insane rage to reclaim what was taken from him – at any cost . . .

# RINGMAIN

## George Brown

A US state visit in the diplomatic diaries, a Labour MP freelancing as an IRA fixer; and a mole at the top of British Intelligence worth lorry-loads of Armalites to the dangerous men in Dublin ... the high-explosive ringmain circuit is falling into place.

Its last connection is the world's most expensive death dealer who kills the highest placed for the highest price. Code-named Siegfried, he's in London to earn three-quarters of a million pounds with a job on the side.

Between the steel toe-cap going in and the ringmain triggering to detonate, the kill-master will find out which side ...

# INSHALLAH

## Oriana Fallaci

'An immense work, an opus which should earn its creator a slice of immortality . . . Read *Inshallah* and you will roll in the sands of the Middle East, feel your skin crawl with the gore of war and hear your heart quicken with hope. This is fine literature' – *Irish Independent*

This moving, magnificent epic opens on the terrifying night of an assault on the American marine barracks in Beirut, and unfolds to reveal a vast array of characters whose lives and fates are caught up in this war-torn city, the tragedy of the Middle East.

'Make room for Fallaci next to Hemingway and Malraux. *For Whom the Bell Tolls* and *Man's Hope* are to the Spanish Civil War what *Inshallah* is to the dirty genocide of Lebanon' – *Il Giorno*

For the French, American and Italian soldiers in the international peace-keeping force, for the Arabs whose home is besieged by senseless destruction, for the women in their lives, *Inshallah* is a giant canvas on which the author ingeniously blends the daily atrocities with moments of unexpected humour and wisdom. It will take you heartbreakingly close to reality.

'Extraordinary, huge, dense, teeming, devastating' – Zoë Fairbairns, *Everywoman*

Above all, *Inshallah*, with its emotional impact and profound insight, is an unsurpassed portrayal of the horrifying devastation of war.

'An epic war story in the classic tradition . . . the sheer awesomeness of its firepower proves irresistible' – *The Tablet*

# THE FIRM

## John Grisham

**The law student:** He was young and had his dreams. He'd qualified third in his class at Harvard, now offers poured in from every law firm in America.

**The firm:** They were small, but well-respected. They were prepared to match, and then exceed Mitch's wildest dreams – eighty thousand a year, a BMW and a low interest mortgage.

Soon the house, the car and the job are his. Then the nightmares begin; the secret files, the bugs in the new bedroom, the mysterious deaths of colleagues, and the millions of dollars of mob money pouring through the office into the Cayman Islands, dollars that the FBI will do anything to trace.

Now Mitch stands alone in the place where dreams end and nightmares begin . . .

# A TIME TO KILL

## John Grisham

There are crimes of blood, and there are crimes which are
. . . just crimes. The people of Clanton, Mississippi, have no
doubt as to which is which when Carl Lee Hailey guns down
the hoodlums who have raped his ten-year-old child.

There are crimes of race and creed and colour. And so when
people outside of Clanton hear that a black man has killed
two whites, the town is filled with an angry mob determined
to tear down, burn and destroy anything and everyone that
opposes them.

And there are cases which can make or break the career of a
young lawyer and such a case is the defence of Carl Lee
Hailey to Jake Brigance. In the maelstrom that has become
Clanton he'll do anything to defend his client, his case and,
ultimately, his life and the lives of his family.

# THE PELICAN BRIEF

## John Grisham

**The unputdownable courtroom drama from the best-selling author of *The Firm***

**Two Supreme Court Justices are dead. Their murders are connected only in one mind, and in one legal brief conceived by that mind.**

Brilliant, beautiful and ambitious, New Orleans legal student Darby Shaw little realises that her speculative brief will penetrate to the highest levels of power in Washington and cause shockwaves there.

Shockwaves that will see her boyfriend atomised in a bomb blast, that will send hired killers chasing after her, that will propel her across the country to meet the one man, investigative reporter Gray Grantham, who is as near the truth as she is.

Together can they stay alive long enough to expose the startling truth behind The Pelican Brief?

'Grisham is a natural storyteller' – *Daily Telegraph*

'A giant of the thriller genre' – *Time Out*

# FATHERLAND

## Robert Harris

April 1964. The naked body of an old man floats in a lake on the outskirts of Berlin. In one week it will be Adolf Hitler's 75th birthday. A terrible conspiracy is starting to unravel . . .

*Fatherland* is set in a world that almost existed but never was, the Berlin that Hitler's architect, Albert Speer, planned to build – the hub of a victorious Third Reich extending from the Rhine to the Urals.

Among its 10 million citizens is Xavier March, investigator with Berlin's criminal police, the Kripo. A brilliant loner, March is assigned to the case of the old man in the lake. His trail leads him to discoveries of wartime corruption, Swiss bank vaults, love, danger and – most terrifying of all – to the deadly black heart of the Nazi state . . .

# ACTS OF FAITH

## Erich Segal

**Timothy**, abandoned at birth, is headed for a life of delinquency until a chance confrontation triggers his spectacular rise in the Roman Catholic hierarchy. But ahead lies one soul-inflaming passion which will test the strength of his vows.

**Daniel** is the only son of Rabbi Moses Luria. His destiny is to 'inherit' the leadership of the community of orthodox Jews . . . and to break his father's heart.

**Deborah**, Daniel's sister, is raised to be docile and dutiful, the perfect rabbi's wife . . . until love takes her into worlds she never dared to imagine.

*Acts of Faith* is a towering novel spanning more than a quarter of a century, taking us from the tough streets of Brooklyn, to ultra-modern Brasilia, Montreal and the holy splendour of Rome and Jerusalem. It is the spellbinding story of three extraordinary people who will painfully discover that the mysteries of religion are set against those of the human heart.

'Master storyteller Erich Segal has done it again – a real page turner' – *Daily Express*

'A hot blend of power politics, illicit love affairs and paternity scandals' – *Options*

'Undoubtedly another bestseller' – *Times Literary Supplement*

# THE PEACEBROKERS

## Frederick Taylor

*February 1989* – the Iron Curtain is Falling, and in a frozen border post a group of men meet secretly to divide up the spoils which the reunified Germany will offer them.

The men have one thing in common: they are the war orphans of Hitler's Germany, known as 'the Kinder'. Their secret fraternity has built the most powerful mafia in Eastern Germany. Now they have to retrench, adjust to the new order and forge new criminal links with the West.

They choose an unlikely instrument to achieve their ends: British journalist Michael Blessed.

Only when Blessed starts witnessing the first beatings up and killings does he realise that the Kinder mean business; no longer for them the games children play, but the game of ultimate power where no mercy is asked for, or given.

Like Frederick Taylor's exciting prequel, *The Kinder Garden*, this is a gripping, edge-of-the-seat thriller. *The Peacebrokers* strips bare the corrupt heart of the new Europe, uncovering the bloody trail from postwar desolation to today's ruthless politics of greed.

'Excellent . . . original and interesting . . . the writing is high class' – Martha Gellhorn, *Daily Telegraph*

# BESTSELLING FICTION
## AVAILABLE IN ARROW

| | | |
|---|---|---|
| ☐ Skydancer | Geoffrey Archer | £3.99 |
| ☐ Shadowhunter | Geoffrey Archer | £4.99 |
| ☐ Ringmain | George Brown | £4.99 |
| ☐ The Double Tenth | George Brown | £4.99 |
| ☐ Inshallah | Oriana Fallaci | £5.99 |
| ☐ A Time To Kill | John Grisham | £4.99 |
| ☐ The Firm | John Grisham | £4.99 |
| ☐ The Pelican Brief | John Grisham | £4.99 |
| ☐ Fatherland | Robert Harris | £4.99 |
| ☐ The Peacebrokers | Frederick Taylor | £4.99 |
| ☐ Acts of Faith | Erich Segal | £4.99 |

Prices and other details are liable to change

---

ARROW BOOKS, BOOKSERVICE BY POST, PO BOX 29, DOUGLAS, ISLE OF MAN, BRITISH ISLES

NAME _____

ADDRESS _____

_____

_____

Please enclose a cheque or postal order made out to Arrow Books Ltd, for the amount due and allow for the following for postage and packing.

U.K. CUSTOMERS: Please allow 75p per book to a maximum of £7.50

B.F.P.O. & EIRE: Please allow 75p per book to a maximum of £7.50

OVERSEAS CUSTOMERS: Please allow £1.00 per book.

Whilst every effort is made to keep prices low it is sometimes necessary to increase cover prices at short notice. Arrow Books reserve the right to show new retail prices on covers which may differ from those previously advertised in the text or elsewhere.